Praise for *October the First is T...*

'This is 'respectable' sc...
Hoyle speculating abou...
people'

'You can rely on Fred H...
straight science, with no t...

'The John Buchan of Scien... ...antasies are not only
firmly rooted in scientific possibilities but are told at a galloping
pace and with an appealing no-nonsense authority'

Sunday Times

Praise for *Fifth Planet*:

'Very readable and ironically humorous story for the s-f addict'
Evening Standard

'A tense adventure sandwiched between two slivers of higher
maths . . . A very well told story this, with some nice touches of
political prediction' *Daily Telegraph*

'Highly exciting . . . the best so far from the Hoyle stable'
Sunday Times

Also by Fred Hoyle:

ASTRONOMY

The Nature of the Universe
Frontiers of Astronomy
Men and Galaxies
Galaxies, Nuclei and Quasars

CURRENT AFFAIRS

A Decade of Decision

FICTION

The Black Cloud
Ossian's Ride
October the First is Too Late

BY FRED HOYLE AND GEOFFREY HOYLE

Fifth Planet
The Molecule Men
Rockets in Ursa Major
Seven Steps to the Sun
The Inferno

THREE CLASSIC NOVELS:

Ossian's Ride
October the First is Too Late

By Fred Hoyle

Fifth Planet

By Fred and Geoffrey Hoyle

Ossian's Ride copyright © Fred Hoyle 1959
October the First is Too Late © Fred Hoyle 1966
Fifth Planet © Fred and Geoffrey Hoyle 1963
All rights reserved

The right of Fred Hoyle and Geoffrey Hoyle to be
identified as the authors of these works has been
asserted by them in accordance with the
Copyright, Designs and Patents Act 1988.

This edition published in Great Britain in 2016
by Gollancz
An imprint of the Orion Publishing Group
Carmelite House, 50 Victoria Embankment, London EC4Y 0DZ
An Hachette UK Company

3 5 7 9 10 8 6 4 2

A CIP catalogue record for this book is available
from the British Library

ISBN 978 1 473 21095 0

Printed in Great Britain by
Clays Ltd, St Ives plc

The Orion Publishing Group's policy is to use papers that
are natural, renewable and recyclable products and made
from wood grown in sustainable forests. The logging and
manufacturing processes are expected to conform to the
environmental regulations of the country of origin.

www.gollancz.co.uk
www.orionbooks.co.uk
www.sfgateway.co.uk

Contents

Contents

Ossian's Ride

Ossian's Ride

Contents

Preface

I regret that the story set out in the following pages obliged me to do violence to geography at one point: the harbour of Killybege had to be transferred south to the coast of Clare.

My grateful thanks are due to Monsignor Padraig de Brún for showing me the beauty of the West of Ireland in the first place, for putting me to rights on questions of Irish usage, and for conjuring up at a moment's notice an otherwise unobtainable map of the island of Inishvickillane, which he and Professor John Busteed drew up many years ago.

Cambridge: March 1959   F. H.

Prologue

Arthur Grafton Mitchell, aged thirty-one, youngest Fellow of the Royal Society, was dining alone at the George and Vulture in Lombard Street. He had just received an invitation to deliver the Ellerman Lectures for the year 1959 at Princeton University, on a subject related to the chemistry of living material. The honour of the invitation, the remuneration, the dinner he had just eaten, all combined to give Mitchell a sense of great well-being as he lingered over his coffee.

His attention was caught by a strikingly handsome trio at a table immediately close by, two girls and a man. Almost without intent, he began to pick up the threads of a bubbling conversation. Witty scatterbrains, Irish apparently. Then for a moment the swirling torrent of words subsided to an interchange between one of the girls and the man on a problem in the theory of protein structure. This was a problem that Mitchell knew more than a little about. Thunderstruck at the strangers' extreme depth of perception, Mitchell walked the short distance to their table.

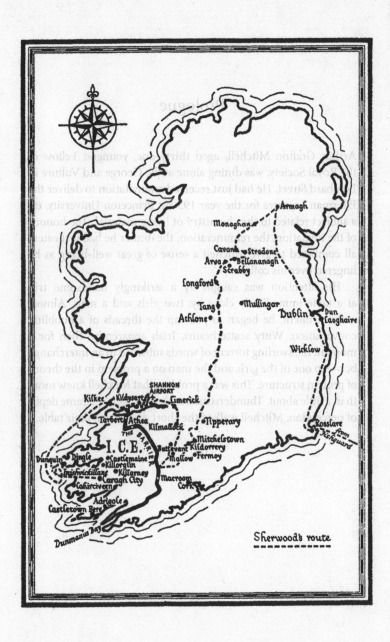

Sherwood's route

CHAPTER ONE

Twelve Years Later

The Old Man was in a regular stew. So much had been clear to Geoffrey Holtum, his private secretary, from a short conversation over the telephone. It was a fair inference that the appalling Irish problem must have something to do with the P.M.'s state of mind. But why should the crisis be any worse in that particular direction than it had been yesterday, or last week, or last year for that matter?

Holtum knocked lightly on the sanctum door. "Come in," boomed the Prime Minister. "Thank heaven you're back, Geoffrey," he went on, "just in time to keep me out of the clutches of the psychiatrists."

"What's happened, sir?"

"What's happened! This!" The Prime Minister brought his fist down with a thump on a large typescript that lay in front of him. Then he picked it up and brandished the pages in Holtum's face.

"This damned stuff. It may be the most significant document that has ever come into my hands, or it may be just a tissue of rubbish. I simply don't know which."

"But what——?"

"What is it? Nothing short of a complete explanation of the whole I.C.E. mystery. That's what it claims to be!"

"Whew! But how——?"

"How did it come into my hands? Listen!"

Holtum wondered when he had ever done anything else but listen to the P.M.

"About a year ago, one of our Intelligence people had a brain-storm, not a bad idea really. Instead of continuing to send our normal agents into Ireland, he got hold of a young chap from Cambridge, a clever fellow, science and mathematics and all that sort of stuff, name of Thomas Sherwood, from a Devon farming family, good solid yeoman stock. I've had a very complete investigation of him carried out by Intelligence." The Prime Minister lifted a large file, and then dropped it back again on the desk top.

"Judging from what Intelligence say, I'd swear that Sherwood is absolutely one hundred per cent reliable. Yet on his own admission he's now completely gone over to I.C.E.! Then, having sold out on us, he proceeds to send me this report, which is absolutely tremendous in its implications, if it happens to be true."

"Does he give any reasons, sir?"

"In heaven's name, yes! I wouldn't blame him for selling his soul to the devil, if what he says in here is true."

"But is there any conceivable motive for sending the report?"

"You know perfectly well that together with the Americans and the Russians we're now working up quite a pressure on I.C.E. If I believed in the veracity of Sherwood's report, I'd instantly recommend that this policy be scrapped forthwith."

Holtum whistled. "And so it might be a colossal bluff."

"Or it might be a warning. I don't know which."

"But surely in the course of such an extensive document it must become clear whether this man Sherwood is on the level or not?"

"That's exactly what I'm going to ask you to judge for yourself, Geoffrey my boy. I've already arrived at an opinion myself. So I'm not going to say anything more that might prejudice you on the main issue.

"I've got an additional copy of the report. I want you to take it away. Go where you can read it quietly without interruption. And take this Intelligence stuff as well." The Prime Minister handed over a couple of fat folders.

"Don't waste any time checking on the facts. I've done that already. Everything is impeccably correct. We even know that some rather peculiar people who appear in the story really do exist. We have this on the testimony of a certain internationally famous pianist, whose name I won't mention. He was invited to give a series of concerts at I.C.E., in the course of which he met, albeit rather briefly, some of the high-ups in the organisation. Strange that we should have to rely on a musician for our best information. Shows what a beating our Intelligence Service has taken from these I.C.E. people.

"Remember, above all, that you're dealing with a very astute young man. Remember that he may even be adept at telling the truth in a way that gives a wholly false impression."

"You mean, sir, that it's more a question of character than of logic?"

"Exactly so. Try to get yourself into this fellow's mind. You're fairly well of an age together. You should be able to judge him better than I can."

Holtum dined at a quiet restaurant, a well-filled brief-case at his side. He took a taxi to his apartment. With a large pot of fresh coffee, he pulled out the P.M.'s bundle of papers. A sip of Cointreau first, and he took up the first page.

CHAPTER TWO

Preliminaries in London

From my school in Ashburton, Devon, I won a Major Scholarship in Mathematics at Trinity College, Cambridge. I took my B.A. degree in June 1969, specialising in my final Tripos in Algebra, Functional Analysis, and Topology. This is relevant to what is to follow.

By the early summer of 1970 I was well started in research, on a problem in the theory of infinite groups. I was just turning over in my mind what I would like to do during the summer vacation, when I received a curious letter from an address in Whitehall. The letter offered interesting employment for the months of July and August. The writer was wholly inexplicit, however, about the nature of the employment. No doubt I would have ignored this communication altogether had it not been for one slightly singular feature. I was informed that, if I were so minded as to accept the invitation, an appointment would be available at 1.15 p.m. sharp on 27th June. The signature was entirely illegible.

There were several things that I wanted to do in London, so I decided that nothing would be lost by finding out what manner of civil servant would fix an appointment during the lunch hour. Was a fat man on a slimming diet? So I wrote in return that I would present myself at the agreed time. I received a second letter describing the particular office I was to ask for, the signature being quite as illegible as before.

I was welcomed by a very nice-looking brunette.

"Ah, Mr. Sherwood," she said with a smile. "You are to come this way."

We walked possibly three hundred yards along a multitude of corridors, and we climbed possibly two hundred feet up and down staircases before we reached a place that looked more like a private den than a public office. A very sunburned, rubbery, bald little man of about sixty motioned me to a chair. His face was weatherbeaten, his temples were creased by a multitude of wrinkles, and his teeth were tightly clamped on a huge meerschaum.

He puffed away for a minute, staring hard at me the while. Then he broke into a chuckle:

"Well, well, Mr. Sherwood, so you fell for the old 1.15 trick after all!"

"I'm only too glad to hear that the trick wasn't just a trivial oversight, Mr.——?"

"Parsonage, Percy Parsonage at your service."

There was a knock, and the brunette came in with a tray.

"Lunch for Mr. Sherwood," she explained.

"That's right, feed him," nodded Parsonage. "I won't eat, myself—didn't breakfast until eleven-thirty."

I had just taken my first mouthful, when he asked: "And how would you like to make a trip to Ireland?"

I swallowed carefully. "From all I hear of Ireland, a man might get himself killed a score of times a week—in your line of business, Mr. Parsonage!"

6

"And what would you know of my business?"

"Nothing at all. That's why it would be foolish of me to agree to go to Ireland on your behalf."

Papa Percy (as I soon learned him to be called) picked up his great pipe, and said:

"I wouldn't have put you down as the sort of young man to turn aside at a suggestion of danger."

"That would depend on whether the danger were of my own making or not."

Thoughtfully Parsonage moved to a wall on which a large map of Ireland was hung. Prodding it, he said:

"Let me show you the cordon beyond which no ordinary visitor to Ireland may penetrate, beyond which even no Irishman may pass unless he has satisfied the most rigorous security check. See how it runs, from Tarbert, in the north, to Athea, south to Kanturk, and beyond directly over the Boggerath Mountains to Macroom and Dunmanway. See how it bends here to the sea in Dunmanus Bay."

For a moment he puffed furiously, and then went on:

"Within this tight wall incredible things are happening. The main activity seems to be confined in the central peninsula of Kerry immediately to the south of Caragh Lake—where Ossian is said to have once ridden over the western mountains to the Land of Youth.

"Now, Mr. Sherwood, I would like to send you on an absolutely individual mission. The last thing I want you to do is to get mixed up with the usual espionage work, ours or anyone else's. Every nation on earth is directing ninety-five per cent of its under-cover activity to Ireland. The place is simply crawling with agents.

7

And the Irish themselves have naturally started an intense counter-espionage drive."

"I don't see any niche in all this that seems specially designed for me," I said between mouthfuls.

"I sincerely hope not. Ireland is a fantastic maelstrom of intelligently organised thuggery. If you're unfortunate enough to get mixed up in it you'll be lucky to stay alive even for a couple of days."

A chicken bone seemed to get stuck in my throat.

"Don't get impatient," said Papa Percy. "In my roundabout way I'm gradually coming to the point. Here, take a look at these."

He took three documents from a small safe and flung them down on the table at my side. The first was concerned with a bacteriological topic, the second was a plan of something that looked superficially like a furnace. The third was mathematical in form, more in my line. When I began reading it in detail, Parsonage roared:

"Don't bother. It's arrant nonsense. Let me tell you something about this one." He picked up the first document. "It was obtained in a most desperate operation. Two of my best men were killed. Yet it contains nothing but rubbish." He strode about the room munching mightily on the meerschaum.

"You see, all our ideas of Intelligence work simply go by the board when we have to deal with this scientific stuff." He flourished the papers. "Our men can't tell whether this is genuine or not. All they can do is fight to get hold of it, and fight they do, often dying in the process."

"So you want me to vet things? I'm not really enough of a scientist, you know."

"I want much more than that! Suppose this junk was genuine. How much would it tell us? Just a little about what was going on in there." He pointed to the wall map with his pipe. "No, I want more than that, very much more. I'm going to give you a lecture. Don't interrupt! How much do you know about I.C.E.? Only a little, I'll warrant. None of us knows very much, for that matter. I'll tell you what *I* know." The little man made an odd sight as he marched around, belching clouds of smoke, his hands behind his back.

"Pour me some coffee," he bellowed.

"I.C.E., the Industrial Corporation of Eire, came into being some twelve years ago. A small group of very able scientists approached the Government of Eire with what seemed an entirely straightforward proposition. Their proposal was to establish an industry for the extraction of a range of chemicals from the organic material in peat—turf, as the Irish call it. Since their initial capital was rather small it was requested that they be allowed to plough back all profit for a period of ten years, after which normal taxes would be paid, subject to a maximum payment of five million pounds in any one year. This seemed tolerably reasonable to the Irish Government, and it was accordingly agreed to.

"Within a short time, I.C.E. was producing an amazing range of valuable chemicals, ostensibly from turf as raw material, although whether this was really so is open to doubt. At British chemical concerns there were many red faces, I understand, during this phase in the history of I.C.E. Still, no one thought anything really remarkable was happening. All was to be explained in terms of the ingenuity of a few really clever fellows, fellows who intended to acquire for themselves a large slice of cake, and who were very sensibly cutting it outside the taxation laws of the United Kingdom.

"Profits increased rapidly. The Irish were regretting the terms of their agreement, when I.C.E. acquired enormous local goodwill by voluntarily paying to the Government the sum of two million pounds. This was in their fourth year, just before the *coup* on which the real basis of their expansion was founded."

"You mean the contraceptive pill," I remarked.

"Yes, the contraceptive pill. Just what the world's population problem needed. Sales were vast beyond precedent. By the end of the eighth year the capital resources of I.C.E. exceeded the thousand million mark."

"I've never understood how it came about that the Church didn't stop it. The contraceptive business, I mean."

"Ridicule, my boy. If I may parody the poet Schiller: 'Against laughter even the Hierarchy fights in vain.' Think of it, contraceptives from turf! For decades the Church had fulminated against their use, while, all the time, outside every cottage there'd been piled a whole mountain of the stuff!

"As a matter of some interest, and as an indication of the perversity of mankind, the birth-rate in Ireland has actually risen since the use of contraceptives became widespread there. Pour me another cup."

Parsonage swallowed the coffee at a gulp, and went on with his lecture.

"Where were we? Still six years in the past. From

every point of view this was the critical stage in the development of I.C.E. The emphasis began to change from chemistry to physics. Unobtrusively, physicists and mathematicians were offered attractive positions and the number who accepted the flattering offers was not insubstantial. The volume of scientific immigrants has steadily increased and is still increasing."

"Doesn't this immigration give an ideal opportunity for finding out what's going on? By sending in a few of your own fellows, I mean."

"You might well think so. Most of what little we know has come that way, but our efforts seem to disappear like rain in a desert. These people are devilishly clever. They've made very few mistakes. They seem to know just who they can trust and who they can't.

"Six years ago I.C.E. began importing metals. As I was saying, this coincided with a marked shift from the chemical to the physical side, all of which culminated a little more than a year ago in a chain of commercially working thermo-nuclear reactors."

I whistled in astonishment. Research in the thermo-nuclear field is of course a large classified subject, so I had no precise knowledge of how things were going here in Britain, or in the U.S., or elsewhere. But it was an open secret that the whole business was turning out to be a pretty sticky proposition.

"How should this be possible?"

Parsonage put down his pipe with a flourish. There was a shower of sparks, which I made haste to quench.

"Now we come to the kernel of the whole infernal business. How was it possible? That's just what I want you to find out!" He glared at me with a fierce in-

11

tensity. "Mark my words carefully. It isn't at all that I want you to find out the technical solution of the thermo-nuclear business. If you do find out, well and good, but on no account must that be your main aim."

"I see through a glass darkly," I managed to interject. Parsonage fairly danced as he stood in front of me.

"See here—a man has £1,000. By playing the stock markets he becomes a millionaire within five years. Don't laugh, it can be done, if you can forecast correctly just what is going to happen. That is what I.C.E. has done! See how they built this reactor! No extensive preliminary research, just a systematic manufacture of all the relevant components. Sherwood my boy, this is the crux of the affair. How did they know beforehand so unerringly just what they were going to do? That's what I want you to find out. Don't worry your head about technical details, about secret agents, about anything other than the principle of the thing. How do they *know*?"

At last I had a glimpse of what Papa Percy was driving at.

"But why me?"

"Why not?"

As I pondered this impossible reply, he went on: "What qualifications are needed, you've got." (Something was wrong with the grammar.) "Just as a baby picks up his mother tongue, so a young man of your age picks up information. You are highly trained in the right sort of thinking. This is a logical problem, not one of scientific or engineering detail."

He tapped the map.

"The scene is set in wild country. You're a country

12

lad; a townsman might find himself in trouble over there. What else?" As I pondered things, he stuffed great fingerfuls of tobacco into his pipe. In spite of a riotous confusion of expression, Parsonage had driven home his point.

"So what you want is the logical tap root . . . ." I got no further.

"Right-right-right-*ad infinitum*! The tap root is what I want, the power source, the driving force. Now you have it, my boy.

"Don't imagine this to be one of your academic exercises. Five years ago it was an academic exercise. We could have moved our troops into Ireland then. We could have taken I.C.E. slowly apart, piece by piece. But we can't do that today, nor can the Americans or the Russians."

"I can't see why not, if you really don't mind being drastic."

"Think, young feller. Use your sconce-piece. When you find someone far ahead of you in one line of business, you can bet a king's ransom to a tin of fishing bait that he will also be ahead of you in other lines, avenues, by-ways, conduits, or what you will. If I.C.E. can make a thermo-nuclear reactor they can make an I.C.B.M. If they can make a contraceptive pill, they can make a pill that would make us all die of laughter."

Parsonage stood before the map, legs apart, defying all laws relating to the smokeless zone.

"We can smuggle you into Ireland through the usual pipe-line, or you may prefer to travel more openly. That's for you to decide. Go away for a couple of days, think about it. Need any money?"

I nodded, and he offered me a bundle of notes. I said: "Not so much, about fifteen pounds only. I'm not going to make myself conspicuous. I might as well begin straight away."

There was one question I would have liked to ask, but my nerve failed. I have always understood that the main danger to an agent comes from his own people. I feared that Parsonage and his pipe might explode if I were to ask him if this were really so.

Nor did I tell him that it had been my dearest wish to get a chance to visit Ireland. I had been pondering precisely the question whether my funds would run to such a trip when his first letter had arrived.

Nor did I tell him later that besides buying a few necessary articles I contrived with his fifteen pounds to take out twice the brunette from his office.

CHAPTER THREE

Into Enemy Territory

I caught the 3 p.m. express from Paddington to Fish-guard deliberately with only a minute or two to spare, as a precipitate young student might be expected to do. There was a vacant centre seat in one of the compart-ments, so I heaved my rucksack on to the rack and settled down, ostensibly to read *The Times*. Behind its welcome shield I reflected on the situation.

It had been an obvious decision to try to enter Ireland in the most open possible manner. If I failed I could always fall back on Parsonage's 'pipe-line'. If I suc-ceeded I could go about my business with less possibility of interference from Irish counter-espionage. This sug-gested the reflection that although I was still in England, the affair had already begun. For the Irish must certainly have men on the train, men who would watch and talk with the passengers, men who were trained to separate sheep from goats, which isn't after all a difficult matter. The slightest false move now could lead to disaster a few hours later, when I should have to run the gauntlet of Irish immigration.

The visa was my chief worry. It took three months to get a genuine visa, always supposing that one were granted at all. I had been in favour of waiting, but

Parsonage would have none of it, insisting that within an hour he could supply a forgery that was entirely indistinguishable from the genuine article. No doubt this was true, but I was less sanguine about Papa Percy's ability to conjure my name at a few days' notice into the lists possessed by the immigration officials. Unless this documentary sleight of hand had been well and truly executed I was going to be in the soup. The argument that had appeared so convincing in the shelter of Parsonage's room now seemed rather threadbare.

"Even if you were to wait, there is no guarantee that you would get a visa, and even if you got a visa there is still no guarantee that you would ever get into Ireland," he had argued. "Very wisely, the Irish are managing the whole visa business with an assumed air of incredible inefficiency. This allows them to turn down, and turn out, anyone they please. It dissuades the genuine traveller, and above all makes difficult any diplomatic protest from our side."

This was the first of my two worries. Money was the second. Since Irish currency is now as 'hard' as it is possible for any currency to be, I was obliged to ration myself to the very moderate official allowance. I might of course have risked carrying more, but if I were searched the game would instantly have reached an ignominious end, for any British traveller with more than the allowance of his own Government in his pocket would instantly come under the gravest suspicion.

Parsonage had brushed the matter aside by insisting that, once in Ireland, I could pick up as much money as I wanted from an agent in Dublin, to wit a Mr. Seamus Colquhoun, who lived at an address in Marrowbone

Lane. This arrangement was probably perfectly in order, but I had a strong feeling that the more I could keep away from official espionage the better I would be pleased.

These reflections seemed to exhaust the potentialities of *The Times*, so I started a paper-back written by an angry young author who had gone down from Cambridge a few years earlier, I am sorry to say from my own College. It was tough going, but I stuck determinedly at the task until the train reached Cardiff.

After Cardiff, I made my way to the lavatory at the near end of the compartment. It was locked. A voice in my ear remarked:

"Funny, it's been locked every time I've come past, ever since we left Reading."

It was a ticket-collector, or rather (for precision's sake) it was an individual in ticket-collector's uniform. He banged hard on the lavatory door and shouted "Hi, inside!" When, after a couple of minutes of shouting and banging, there was no reply, he remarked in what I took to be a commendably casual tone:

"I think we'd better have that there door open."

With a tool from his pocket, the like of which I hadn't seen before, he shot back the bolt, opened the door, glanced inside, and said in a slightly puzzled manner:

"Bloody silly trick. There's nobody in there. Can't say I see how the door got fastened. Ah well, sir, it's free now," he added.

He was right, there was nobody inside. But it needed only the briefest scrutiny to see that something was very wrong, or more accurately that something had been very wrong. For here and there dark blotches were spattered over the interior of the place. I touched one. My hand came away sticky and red.

"There's been some serious trouble," I said as I stepped back into the corridor. The ticket-collector had evidently gone into the next compartment, so I crossed quickly through the connecting door. A glance down the corridor showed that in the odd second or two the fellow had vanished. My instinct was to follow quickly, but reason insisted that it was best to think first. There must be an explanation of why the ticket-collector had opened the lavatory door, of why he had disappeared. I glanced down at my trousers and cursed aloud as I saw I must have touched one of the dark patches. Damn it, must I go bloodstained through the trickiest part of the whole business?

My first thought was to change into walking shorts. I had deliberately not dressed in outdoor clothes and boots, because I felt that it would be wrong to over-emphasise the student-hiker attitude. Now I would have no choice, it seemed. In a few strides I was back at my compartment. There were still three men in it (two people had left the train at Cardiff), but my ruck-sack was gone.

It is said that a dying man can review his past life in a second or two. Balderdash of course, but it is surprising how fast one can think when the occasion warrants. The thought exploded in my head that at all costs I must behave as an innocent young student would behave. In short I must raise the devil of a shindy. Scarcely checking my speed I opened the compartment door, looked up at the rack, and said in the most surprised tone I could muster:

18

"What's happened to my rucksack?"

Two of the men, ages perhaps thirty to thirty-five, were drowsing or pretending to drowse. The third fellow was much older, maybe fifty-five. At my question he put down a book, looked me over with questioning blue eyes, and said in pronouncedly Irish speech:

"But you fetched it yourself, not a moment ago."

"I did no such thing! Surely you must have seen someone come in and take it?"

"Certainly someone came in. My attention was on my book here, so I naturally took the person to be yourself. He was of about your height and colouring."

"You'd better find the guard," remarked one of the younger men.

"I'll find the guard and the police at the next stop." The fellow was of course right, I should go at once and find the guard. But at all costs I must first have time to think.

It seemed inconceivable that my rucksack could have been stolen by anyone who knew the real purpose of my journey. Or was it inconceivable? Could my connection with Parsonage already be known to the Irish? Was there a spy in his office? Even so, the Irish would scarcely take action here on the train. Assuredly they would wait until I reached Rosslare. No, the business could have nothing personal to do with me, it must be the rucksack. Yet the rucksack contained nothing but a couple of books and my walking outfit—a good disguise for a man who had urgent need of a quick change of clothes, perhaps for a man whose present suit was liberally dappled with blood? The disguise would be useless, however, if I were to let out an enormous roar at the first glimpse of my own shirt, pants, and boots. Therefore it followed that I must be hit over the head, or worse, on my way to find the guard.

It was natural that this process of reasoning should cause me to direct an over-piercing stare at the man who had suggested seeking out the guard. It was equally natural that he, being taken unawares, should have betrayed his complicity. There was no 'sudden start', so beloved by the writers of fiction, no 'sudden pallor', no 'beads of perspiration'. All that could be seen was a ripple of emotion that crossed the fellow's face, as fleeting as a puff of wind on a grassy meadow. Yet if a confession had been sealed, signed, and delivered, the situation couldn't have been clearer.

Three of us leaped upwards. Strong hands gripped my waist and shoulders, heaving hard to throw me to the floor. But my right hand had reached the communication cord in time, and the weight and pull of their bodies only whipped the cord down the more fiercely. Already the train brakes were on.

Quite incredibly, one of the fellows seemed to think he could bluff the matter out:

"There, look what you've done! It'll cost you five pounds."

His companion had other ideas, however. "Don't be a fool, Karl. Let's get out of here."

I was too shaken to do much to stop them, but I managed to stick out a foot in time to trip Karl as he moved quickly to the door. He fell across the corridor, striking his head a resounding blow on the brass hand-rail that ran along the outer window. His companion gave me a furious glance, grasped Karl firmly by the shoulder, and humped him along the corridor. I decided to let them go. They were probably armed, and shortly I would be having other troubles.

The outer door was flung open and a voice shouted:

"Now then, what's going on in here?" (Do the more robust elements of officialdom have no other way of approaching a crisis?)

"That is very much what I would like to know," I replied.

A large guard hauled himself into the compartment. Outside there seemed to be the driver, fireman, and perhaps three or four other officials. Everywhere along the train heads were sticking out of windows, male and female, hatted and bare, blonde, white, brown and black.

"One of you must have pulled the chain," observed the guard to the Irishman and me.

"I did."

"Why? What's the matter? Everything looks in order."

"I pulled it on impulse."

The guard leaned out, and remarked to the driver: "He says he did it on impulse."

"Impulse be b——. We're late," was the driver's view of the matter. The guard turned heavily on me:

"Now, young man, this is a serious matter. It's going to cost you five pounds."

The thought struck me that a hundred years ago five pounds must have been quite a substantial sum. Stopping a train without good reason must then indeed have been a serious matter. But now, after a century's inflation, of what significance was a fiver to a man with a taste for entertainment?

"I did not say that my impulse was unfounded."

The Irishman decided to rescue us from further misunderstanding:

"This young gentleman has just had his rucksack stolen."

"That's no reason for pulling the chain. He could have come along and found me without stopping the train."

"There you reveal your ignorance of the matter—if I may say so. Had I tried to find you, I should unquestionably have been hit over the head, coshed, if you prefer the word, and possibly obliterated without trace."

The guard again addressed his colleagues:

"Better come inside, Alf. We've got a bloody lunatic to deal with."

Alf the fireman climbed in with considerable agility. Evidently my trump card had better be played without delay.

"Mention of blood reminds me that the lavatory near-by, the one immediately to the left down the corridor, happens to be liberally spattered with the stuff."

"Didn't I say he was daft?" breathed the guard in stertorous fashion.

"Wouldn't it be worth while stepping along to the lavatory, just to verify my story? It will consume only a few seconds of your valuable time, and it will save Alf and me from doing serious damage to each other."

The guard responded in commendably scientific

spirit. "Oh-ho," said he, "we'll soon see about that."

As he forged into the corridor, by the way that Karl and his companion had departed so hurriedly only a few moments before, it occurred to me to wonder if the stuff in the lavatory really was blood after all. Suppose it turned out to be catsup? The nearest pair of doctors would undoubtedly be only too ready to subscribe to the guard's rough and ready analysis of the affair. But did catsup become tacky as it dried?

A worse thought: if events were to follow the accepted pattern of the thriller or detective story, assuredly the lavatory would turn out to have been cleaned of every telltale speck. What would I do then but point out the unnatural cleanliness of the place?

My fears were groundless, however. In a trice the man was back.

"This is a serious matter," he announced. "What's been going on here?"

I decided that the fooling had lasted long enough. "Could I see your credentials, please?"

This caused him to blink rapidly for about ten seconds. Then, "My what?" he boomed.

"Your credentials, your *bona fides* as a member of the police force."

"I'm not in the police, you bloody lunatic."

"That's exactly the point I am delicately hinting at. Don't you think this is a job for the police? By now, every criminal who was on the train must be at least a couple of counties away. Alf, you got any steam left in this old tub?" The latter remark brought out the raw primitive in Alf. "I'll put some steam in your bloody kisser if you don't shut up," he growled as he

23

dropped to the ground outside. The guard banged the door shut and crossed into the corridor, where he stood truculently until we reached Swansea.

I suppose the guard could hardly be blamed too much for questioning my sanity, for my story sounded quite fantastic, even to my own ears, as I described it to Inspector Harwood of the Swansea Police. Naturally I said nothing of the real reason for my journey to Ireland, but everything else I described as accurately as I could, exactly as it had occurred. I soon came to think highly of Inspector Harwood, for he contrived to maintain a commendably straight face throughout the whole of my outrageous narrative. At the end he said:

"Well, Mr. Sherwood, I'm afraid we shall have to ask you to remain in Swansea for a day or two until we have had the opportunity to check up on this odd business. I'm sorry to have to delay your holiday. I know how I'd feel about it myself if I was in your position. But I'm sure you'll realise that it's really absolutely necessary."

Should I ring Parsonage and ask him to get me out of this ridiculous situation? An idea occurred to me, and I decided not to be such a fool.

"Naturally, Inspector, I'm not pleased about being held up, but if that's the way it is, there's really nothing to be gained by arguing. Might I ask you to fix me a rather inexpensive place to stay at? You see, I didn't bring much cash with me, as I didn't expect to be here in Wales for more than an hour or two."

"There's no difficulty about that, sir. We can advance you a reasonable amount for living expenses. There's quite a tolerable bed-and-breakfast establishment in Cromwell Road. I'd be glad to make arrangements for you to stay there."

"Is there anywhere that I could buy a razor and a toothbrush?"

"That won't be so easy at this hour, but no doubt we can fix you up."

It was after 10 p.m. when I reached the bed-and-breakfast establishment of Mrs. William Williams. With great kindness my landlady offered to fry eggs and bacon when she learned that I hadn't eaten since lunchtime. I went through to the dining-room, where I found my Irish travelling companion finishing up what had evidently been a hearty meal.

"So they sent you too," he remarked. "Now they can keep an eye on the pair of us."

He indicated that I should sit at his table.

"Me name's George Rafferty. Not very Irish, but it's the best I can offer."

"Mine's Thomas Sherwood. How do you do? Did the police persuade you to come here?"

"Persuade, you say! That's good! I was *told* to come here. Young feller, that policeman is going to have something to answer for when he stands in the Judgment Box. Sending an Irishman to Cromwell Road."

Rafferty seemed to have no wish to leave, for he stayed talking as I ate.

"And did you lose much in that rucksack of yours?"

"Nothing of real value. A few personal things and a couple of books. The nuisance is that I'll hardly be able to replace the books."

"I cannot conceive that you will not, unless you are

25

an antiquarian, which I hardly imagine is the case?"

I laughed at the implied question. "No, no, I'm a mathematician, or rather, an embryo one. Is there a bookshop in Dublin where I can buy technical mathematical books?"

"That I do not know for sure. But anything you can buy in London you can buy in Dublin, which probably answers your question."

Mr. Rafferty was evidently not as accustomed to hogging ninety-nine per cent of the conversation as Papa Parsonage had been. At the moment his apparent desire to chat was something of a nuisance, for my immediate concern was with Mrs. Williams's handsome plate of bacon and eggs.

"And why would you be wanting to visit Ireland, if it's not impolite of me to ask?"

In view of the hour, place, and situation it *was* somewhat impolite, but I resolved to practise on Mr. Rafferty. Soon I would be telling the same story to the immigration authorities. In many particulars it was substantially correct. I knew that as a liar I was not very convincing, so I had resolved to keep always within a fine margin of the truth.

"Oh, for two reasons, of which frank curiosity is probably the more important. Considering the remarkable changes that are going on in Ireland, this is natural enough, I suppose."

"I would say entirely so. Yes, it's great changes that are going on in Ireland. And isn't it a shame to see how backward England is becoming?"

I decided to pass lightly over the last remark. "My grandfather's name was Emmet. We have a tradition that he was a descendant of Robert Emmet's family. I cannot say whether this was really so or not, but certainly I have many relatives in Yorkshire, which I believe is where Robert Emmet came from."

"Ah, there is a fine passport to have in Ireland!" Mr. Rafferty beamed genially. "So you will be wanting to visit the Wicklow Mountains, and the scenes of the last of the Rising?"

"Yes, I'm going to do a little walking in the mountains. But most of my time will be in Dublin."

"So it should be," exclaimed Mr. Rafferty with some warmth, "for Dublin is the fountain-head of all that is happening in Ireland. Soon it will be the greatest city in the wide world."

Next morning, Mrs. Williams brought the message that I was to call at the police station. My rucksack had been found.

I unpacked it under the watchful eyes of Inspector Harwood. Everything was there, including the two books. It bore but one sign of misadventure, a large dark stain across the outside, just where it could not fail to be seen.

"Well, that's certainly satisfactory from your point of view, sir. I wish all the news was as good."

"I am sorry to hear that things are not going well, Inspector."

"I expect you are, for it means more delay, I fear."

"What's the trouble?"

"Well, sir, strictly I ought not to say, but I expect you'll already have guessed that a body was thrown from the train. We found it in the Severn Tunnel."

"That's certainly very bad—for the body, I mean."

Inspector Harwood frowned slightly at this under-graduate sentiment.

"I won't keep you much longer this morning, Mr. Sherwood, but I shall want you to call in here again tomorrow. By then we ought to be in a better position to get to the rights of the matter. In the meantime there is just one further question that I'd like to ask."

"Yes?"

"Can you be perfectly sure that you did not see the ticket-collector a second time, the one who opened the lavatory door? When you stopped the train, did he turn up outside your compartment?"

"I can be absolutely certain that he did not. I naturally kept a close look-out for the fellow, but I didn't see him again."

"Thank you. I just wanted to be quite clear on the point."

I lunched on Welsh mussels and brown bread at a café hard by the docks. In the afternoon I discovered a bus that ran into the Gower peninsula. The sea at Oxwich beach was calm and I had a fine swim, and a fine appetite to boot when I returned to my abode in Cromwell Road. Mr. Rafferty was not to be seen that evening, nor next morning at breakfast. Apparently Inspector Harwood had given him his release.

Whether it was the excitement of the last two days, or the mussels, or the swim, I awoke sharply during the night with the absolute conviction that someone was prowling about the room. I lay for a moment, im-mobile with fear, half expecting to be seized by the throat, or to hear the ticket-collector breathing sundry gory details in my ear. Then with an enormous effort of will I flung back the bed covers, rushed to where I thought the light switch must be, fumbled, and found it at last. There was of course no one. I tossed fitfully for a good hour before I was able to win my way to sleep again.

In the morning, in friendly sunshine, I found Inspector Harwood with a large pile of photographs.

"Now, young man," said he, "I want you to see if you can identify this man Karl or his companion, or the ticket-collector, anywhere in this set of faces."

I looked carefully through the pile, but there was no photograph of Karl, or of his companion, or of the ticket-collector. But there, sure enough, was a picture of Mr. George Rafferty. I flicked it on to the table in front of Inspector Harwood.

"This is the only face I've seen before."

"Ah yes, Mr. George Rafferty," remarked Harwood in a dry voice. "It may interest you to hear that Mr. Rafferty has skipped away. The little Irish bird has flown."

The last of the day was falling as the boat steamed out from Fishguard Harbour. I watched the land receding, the bright land of Wales, until at last it became obscured by advancing night. Perhaps in a few hours I should be back among those green fields, back among those wind-swept uplands, back with the shame of an instant defeat. Worse still, perhaps I should never come back. With these thoughts in mind I turned to the golden glow that still lingered deep in the western sky. Then at last I made my way below to the second-class dining-room.

Over a meal of bacon, sausage and tomato, bread and butter, jam, and a flagon of tea, I reflected on the four days I had spent in Swansea. Curiously, instead of being annoyed at the delay I was rather pleased that I had stuck it out, that I had not been tempted to get in touch with Parsonage.

This report would make a better story if I could recount events on the ship of a similar bizarre quality to those that overwhelmed me during the journey from Cardiff to Swansea. Honesty compels me, however, to say that, so far as I am aware, there were no singular occurrences during the night. There must certainly have been agents aboard in plenty. No doubt there was a current of intense drama running at a lower level, but it never broke through to the visible surface. In short, I spent an uncomfortable night dozing fitfully in the saloon.

Still more of an anticlimax, I must frankly admit that my passage through Irish immigration turned out to be absurdly easy. It is worth recounting, nevertheless, for my first encounter with the Irish authorities was not without its interest. My interrogator was a large, jolly-looking man, of just the right type to ensnare an un-wary victim, especially after a sleepless night.

"Name?"

"Thomas Sherwood."

"Date of birth?"

"29th August 1948."

"Occupation?"

"Student."

"Where?"

"Cambridge."

"Father's name and place of origin?"

"Robert Sherwood. Halberton, Devon."

"Object of visit."

"Curiosity."

"Where do you propose to exercise your curiosity, Mr. Sherwood?"

"Three weeks in Dublin and its environs. One week in the Wicklow Mountains."

"Why are you curious?"

"No explanation is needed. Everybody is curious about the developments that are taking place in Dublin."

"Why the Wicklow Mountains?"

I told him the story of my grandfather.

"H'm, a Mr. John Emmet, your grandfather?" He rummaged among a pile of papers, and glanced at one particular sheet. Then, apparently satisfied: "Let me see the contents of your rucksack."

I unpacked slowly and carefully, laying my two books on the table in front of him.

"And how, might I ask, did you come to acquire that great stain across the front of the rucksack?"

I began to tell the story of the lurid events on the train, but I hadn't gone far before he seemed to swell and to become as red as a turkey cock. Then he broke into peal after peal of laughter.

"No more, Mr. Sherwood, no more. Yes, we know all about what happened on the train. We've got our eyes and ears open, you know."

He wiped his face and became more serious as he stamped my passport.

"There. And now away you go. See to it that you

keep to your programme. You know the rules. Report each week at any Guard Station. Don't think we like all these restrictions on genuine visitors, but they've been forced on us by the very dubious segment of humanity that has lately been invading our shores. Stick to Dublin and the Wicklow Mountains, Mr. Sherwood, and you'll have a very pleasant holiday."

As I stepped out into the railway yard I could still hear his rumbling chuckle. He was of course quite right. No agent in his senses would behave in the way I had behaved. An agent's deepest instinct is to avoid all conspicuous action. None would have squawked as I had squawked.

It was a clear, fine morning when I reached Dublin, with promise of a glorious day. As I strolled the short stretch of the Liffey to O'Connell Street, three huge Guinness lorries raced past me. In truth, these people must be heroic drinkers.

I paused for a moment at the Bridge, then quickly walked to College Green. A porter was on duty at Trinity.

"I believe you have a room booked for me. I'm from the other Trinity, Cambridge. Sherwood is the name."

He looked over a list in just the manner that porters have the world over.

"Yes sir, you're on Staircase 24, second floor. Keep on the right side. You'll find it close by the Library."

My room contained a wash-basin and jug of water. I splashed my face liberally, then stripped and climbed into bed. My last thought, before the mists of sleep overcame me, was to wonder whether Papa Percy had used real blood. He'd certainly taken no risk of my failing to get into Ireland. Plainly the outrageous comedy on the train had completely deceived Mr. George Rafferty, the little Irish bird—the little Irish agent more like! But it was depressing that Papa Percy hadn't seen fit to tell me just what was afoot; he evidently took me to be very dumb. Perhaps he was right, at that, for until my second interview with Inspector Harwood I hadn't really understood what was going on. The crowning insult was the showing of the picture of poor Mr. Rafferty. Maybe I am dumb, let me admit it, but not quite to that degree.

One last disturbing thought: how was it known that an Irish agent would just happen to be in my compartment? Was every train to Fishguard packed solid with them?

CHAPTER FOUR

The House in Marrowbone Lane

My first day in Dublin passed with little event. I slept until mid-afternoon, had a snack at a rather palatial 'self-help' restaurant in Grafton Street, and then spent the hour or two before Hall learning the detailed geography of the College.

I was welcomed at dinner by a lively group of students, for the most part medicals and scientists up for the Long Vacation. We went along later to the rooms of one of them, and talked away twenty to the dozen until about 1 a.m.

Apart from this congenially familiar situation, there was a good reason for satisfaction; a product of the suspicious mind with which for good or ill I happen to be possessed. Was it possible that Parsonage had overbid his hand? Had not my passage through immigration been just a little too easy? Suppose the Irish were wise to me, as the Americans say. Would they send me home, jail me, or just watch me? Obviously they'd follow me around and see whom I contacted. Bad for Mr. Colquhoun! In any case, after the preposterous events on the train, it would manifestly be prudent for them to keep an eye on me, at least for a day or two. Here my association with the Trinity undergraduates would be immensely valuable. No one, not even the most skilful actor, could masquerade successfully as a student in their company. No pretence could possibly survive for more than a minute or two. It would be clear to the authorities that at least in this respect I was exactly what I claimed to be.

At this stage I might add a word or two about my plans, rudimentary as they undoubtedly were. Ostensibly I was to spend roughly a month in Ireland, of which the main portion would be passed in Dublin and its environs. The balance of my visit was to be in the Wicklow Mountains. And I was to report to the police at the end of each week. This, then, was the official position.

I had decided that I would not break loose from this schedule until the end of a fortnight. I would spend the first week in Dublin. The time would not be wasted, for Dublin was a useful barometer. It is true that the real power of the Irish economy lay to the west, but some measure of it must show itself in the capital city. I would take long walks, checking up on the tremendous building development that seemed to be going on. The speed of this development would give some idea of the strength of the underlying driving force.

After reporting dutifully to the police at the end of the first week, I would go down to the Wicklow Mountains. The whole point of this was to provide a good excuse for my outdoor clothes and mountaineering boots. I would have real need of these over in the west. This was of course the reason behind my Emmet story. Also it shouldn't be too difficult to find out if I were being followed—once I got into the hills, that is to say. Assuming that I was not, I intended to return to

Dublin, check again with the police, and then at long last head towards Kerry. In this way I hoped to have a whole week in which to cover my trail before there should be any real foundation for official suspicion, which would of course be roused when I failed to show up at the end of the third week.

The fly in the ointment was Seamus Colquhoun. A visit to Marrowbone Lane was not to be avoided, for I simply did not have anything like an adequate amount of money. But whichever way I tackled this hurdle there was an awkward stride to be made. Perhaps the best plan would be to put off seeing Colquhoun until the end of the second week. There would then be less chance of my being followed. But would I necessarily find Seamus at home? It would be infuriating to be delayed and to lose part of my solitary week of grace. But if I hied *chez* Colquhoun more or less straight away I should be maximising other risks. Suppose Seamus were being watched? The more I thought about the business, the less I liked it. With this reflection I fell at last asleep.

In spite of all I had heard, I was quite unprepared for the tremendous changes that were sweeping through Dublin. The city was being systematically demolished and rebuilt. For some reason, perhaps one of sentiment, the architectural tidal wave had not yet reached the area of College Green. This was of course why I had not seen it on the first day.

The new lay-out was of a kind that must surely be unique, for, by and large, the place was being converted into a vast area of smooth lawns, flower-beds, and clumps of trees. Dotted here and there were medium-tall buildings about twenty storeys high, some apartments, others offices and shops. The materials were very largely glass and metal, the metal very beautifully coloured—bronze, sea-blue, and delicate yellows shaded like spring flowers.

The geometry of the matter was of course perfectly clear. By the use of tall, but not too tall, buildings, space was being employed far more efficiently than it is in broad flat cities like London. But instead of using the gain to crowd more and more people into the same area, as Americans have done in all their big towns, Dubliners were wisely laying down floral parks and handsome tree-lined avenues.

All this was surprising enough, but what astonished me more than I cared to admit was the news that it was still less than a year since the whole rebuilding plan had first been put into operation. In about ten months almost the whole of the city north of the river had been reconstructed. I resolved to discover something of the methods that were being used, which plainly must be of a novel kind.

This little project proved maddeningly difficult. It was tolerably easy to get into buildings that were nearing completion, and very interesting they proved to be. I spent many hours engrossed in the details of internal lay-out, lighting, sound-proofing of apartments, and so forth. But try as I would I couldn't get anywhere near the early stages of any construction. Every new structure was invariably cordoned off, not just in the immediate vicinity of the building itself, but over an extensive area around it.

It would have been easy of course to have broken

through one of these cordons and to have got past the guards. Such irresponsibility was not to be thought of, however. Already I was attracting some degree of attention. A fellow whom I took to be a detective or security officer seemed to have a knack of turning up wherever I happened to be. In itself this appeared to be a good sign rather than a bad one. For the man was not at all skilful. He was all right for keeping an eye on an inquisitive student, but no counter-espionage service would have employed him on a mission of importance. Even so, I refused to take any unnecessary risk, since it would be absurd to run foul of the authorities over some comparatively trifling incident.

In any case it needed very little to give one the key to the problem. I think it was on the third morning, in the neighbourhood of what had once been Winetavern Street, that I caught a glimpse in the distance of a huge mountainous object that seemed to move. At first I thought that my eyes must be at fault, but thinking over the matter afterwards I saw the sense of it. I was to see many such moving mountains later on, so I will say no more at present about this particular oddity, except to add that it convinced me of the stupidity of trying to keep the whole business secret. If a casual visitor could ferret the matter out in three or four days, what was the sense of it? The Irish were now making the same silly mistake that the rest of the world had been making for fifty years past. It is notorious how the Governments of Britain, U.S.S.R., the U.S.A., and France have sat on scientific secrets, the same so-called secrets of course, each under the impression that they were unknown to the others. A lot of broody old hens.

One particular building occupied my attention very closely, the new Central Rail Station. By all normal standards this edifice was a sheer impossibility. It was built according to an elegant, bold plan with immensely long horizontal arms of unsupported metal. Even to the most casual eye these arms should have broken instantly under the weight they were required to bear.

I made the best estimates I could of lengths, widths, and so on. Then in the evening I looked up the elementary theory of stress and strain—I am ashamed to say I had forgotten it—in Trinity Library. It took an hour or two to clarify my ideas and to seek out the appropriate physical constants—I believe I used the old Smithsonian Tables. But the result was worth the trouble, for the eye had not been deceived. The metal arms in the Central Station were carrying a transverse stress roughly a hundred times greater than they should have done.

More accurately, they were bearing a transverse stress roughly a hundred times greater than a similar piece of metal would have carried anywhere outside Ireland. There seemed but one possible solution to the riddle. I.C.E. must be able to cast metal almost wholly free of the multitude of tiny flaws that greatly weaken the strength of ordinary metals.

I mention this technicality because it greatly fortified my resolve to dig through to the bottom of the I.C.E. business. At about the same time my morale received a fillip in a rather strange way. My rooms were searched.

There was nothing very obvious about it. Probably

under normal conditions I wouldn't have noticed the very slight changes in the disposition of my clothes. Over a before-bed cup of tea, I pondered on the situation. Surely it would be incredibly stupid to search my things if I were under any really serious suspicion. All such a search would be likely to achieve would be to put me sharply on my guard. But suppose I was being taken for a slightly over-zealous student. Then it might be quite sensible to look me over rather closely, even at the risk of my spotting what was happening. The most sensible conclusion was that Irish Security had some interest in me, but only mildly, at a low level.

Enormously encouraged by these arguments, I resolved there and then to give them a devil of a time. Starting the following morning I tramped assiduously from museum to picture gallery, to museum again. Memory is a little dim, but I recollect places in Kildare Street and Merrion Street. Then I thought up a most satisfactory form of torture for anyone who might be deputed to follow me around. I visited the homes and haunts of old Dublin characters. There were the obvious literary men—Shaw, Joyce, Wilde, Le Fanu, Synge. But I cut a far wider swathe than this. My inquiries enfolded such diverse individuals as Sam Lover and the famous Buck Whaley. My high spot was William Conyngham Plunket at No. 18, St. Stephen's Green. This crazy business gave me much quiet satisfaction.

By now the first week was over, and I duly reported without incident to the police. My departure for the mountains to the south was delayed, however, by the Trinity lads, who press-ganged me into a game of cricket played against a team that fared quite happily under the name of the Dun Laoghaire Wanderers. We won our game with quite a flourish, not, let it be said, through my efforts. I had scored a confident 5 when my wicket was disintegrated by a beefy individual. The same fellow cracked a tremendous drive at me later in the afternoon to which I was ill-advised enough to put a hand.

In spite of this inauspicious preparation, the evening turned out exceedingly well. We dined with our opponents, then drank beer, and sang such songs as cricketers will. Our team returned by car to Dublin at close on midnight—the match had been 'away'. The car in which I happened to be travelling stopped at the northern corner of Merrion Square. Two of our chaps got out, and so on impulse did I, assuring the driver that it was no distance at all to Trinity.

I don't know whether it was the beer, or the fluke catch I had held—my hand still seemed red-hot—but suddenly it appeared obvious that the time and hour for Marrowbone Lane had arrived at last. When would I be more likely to catch Seamus Colquhoun at home than at midnight on the Sabbath?

The wave of new building had advanced only as far as the area around St. Patrick's. So perforce I had to quit the broad bright avenues when I reached the old High Street. From now on I walked through the rabbit warren of the Old City.

'Very soon,' I thought, 'all this will be gone. Soon Marrowbone Lane will be gone. And what will Seamus Colquhoun do then, poor thing? Soon he and all his kind will be smoked out into the open. Will they run their affairs from an office in one of the bright new buildings? Will they cease selling bird-seed or whatever it is they pretend to do at present?'

I had already reconnoitred Marrowbone Lane during my tours of the town, so I knew exactly where to find my man, in a little alleyway set discreetly back from the lane itself. It may be imagined how I made the best reasonable pace I could, first along Thomas Street, then through the court of the same name, past a block of flats, and so to my destination.

Now what? Here was a slight problem. Should I knock discreetly on the door? I might not be heard, and then I should be obliged to knock discreetly again, and perhaps again and again. Would this be more likely to attract attention in the lane than one single furious cannonade?

I was silently debating this difficult point, when a voice from behind said quietly in a Cork accent:

"Not a sound, mister, if you value your life!" Something was pressed into my kidneys.

"Won't that gun make quite a noise if it goes off?"

"Close yer flaming beak!" remarked a second voice.

Someone moved in front of me to unlock the door. The gun prodded in my back.

"Quick, inside with you."

"But that's exactly why I came here, because I want to go inside!"

Violent hands seized me from the front and heaved me across the threshold, with far more noise than was really necessary. Three of us were crammed into a narrow entrance hall. A door opened and a faint light showed up a staircase immediately to the right.

"What is it, boys?" asked a third voice from above.

"We found a feller on the doorstep."

"Bring him up."

The room into which I was forced seemed somewhat less depressing than might have been expected in the circumstances. Quite incongruously, it was decorated with rather well-done sporting prints. A grandfather clock ticked away in a corner, a fire burned brightly in the grate, and a half-filled glass of whiskey stood on a small table.

"Stand over there," said the third voice.

I turned to face them. My captors were both young. The one with the gun was well-dressed, almost dapper, like a civil servant; the other, the muscle-man who had dragged me inside, looked like a character in an Irish play of fifty years ago: cloth cap, heavy rough trousers, and shirt without collar. The third man, whom I took to be Colquhoun himself, was middle-aged, dark, bright-eyed, rather full in build, of medium height.

"Mr. Seamus Colquhoun?"

"What's that to you?"

"During winter storms the waves beat heavily on the western strands."

"This is the right moment to buy vegetables on the London market."

"Or fish, for that matter, if you have a taste for it."

Colquhoun showed obvious relief.

"You can put it away, Liam," said he, indicating the gun. "This is one of the fellers we've been waiting for."

For the first time since Parsonage had given me the passwords I really appreciated their effect. No

43

impostor could have chanced on so improbable a sequence.

"You'd best take a look outside, lads."

When the two rough customers had gone down the stairs again Colquhoun turned on me in a rage:

"What a divil of a time to come here. Are you out of your wits?"

"You didn't expect me?"

"No, nor I didn't anticipate a visit from the *Folies Bergère* either. Were you trying to bring the Guards down on us? Or have you been at the Brewery, drinking the Guinness family into bankruptcy?"

"If you weren't expecting me to come, this is obviously the best possible time; the police won't be expecting you to have visitors either."

"That wouldn't stop you from being seen. You must have been as conspicuous walking the streets as the Nelson Column itself."

"Of course I was conspicuous. I'm not silly enough to slouch about the place. If I'm stopped for any reason, then I'm an innocent who happens to have lost his way. What of it?"

Colquhoun was obviously badly frightened. I realised that he would go on and on unless I took a brusque line. Every minute lost on this rubbish was increasing the danger of the return to Trinity.

"This is a well-nigh perfect illustration of what Shakespeare meant by the term 'unprofitable chat'. I came here to get money from you. I'd like it now, with as little delay as possible."

Colquhoun allowed his anger to settle a little.

"How much do you want?"

44

"Seven hundred."

"That's a powerful lot."

"Which is my business, not yours. Let me have it without any more foolishness, please."

Will ill grace Colquhoun left the room. A few minutes later he came back with a bundle of notes. I counted them, and then stowed the roll away carefully in a specially made inner trouser pocket.

"One thing more. I'd like a list of our agents on the Clare and Galway coasts."

"Oh, you would, would you? Isn't that a fine thing to ask?"

"It's a very practical thing to ask, and I'll trouble you for the information. You needn't fear that I'm going to carry a lot of names on a piece of paper around with me, but I want to carry them in my head. I have a pretty good memory, Mr. Colquhoun."

"I'll bet you have, Mr. Sure-sure. Maybe you'd learn a great lesson if I gave you that list. Maybe you'd soon be cooling your heels in jail, or maybe pushing up the green grass of Ireland if you weren't so lucky."

"Is it possible for you to tell me in a simple way what you're driving at?"

There was a glint in Colquhoun's eye as he stared into my face.

"This is the way of it, me fine cock-sparrer. There's no list of agents any more, not to mean anything. We've been cleaned out, broken apart. That's what I mean."

"How did it happen?"

"P.S.D.," was Colquhoun's cryptic reply. The anger had now subsided. He drank the remaining whiskey at a gulp and slumped down in a chair before the fire. Although I was curious to hear more, it would be wise to move before the fellow launched himself into some new rambling exposition.

"No, you shall not go until you hear the rest of it," he exclaimed when I sought to leave. "Besides, there is something you must do."

"Who or what is P.S.D.?"

"The divil pour me another glass!" exclaimed Colquhoun in some surprise. "For a feller who fancies himself as much as you do, you're shockingly ignorant. Or maybe it's a bad joke you're trying to make?"

"Look, Mr. Colquhoun, I'm here on a solitary mission. You are my only contact. When I leave this house I shall have absolutely nothing to do with any of this business you're talking about."

"And that's where you're in for a great surprise, me lad."

"Every minute we spend talking this nonsense increases the risk of my being picked up. So if you have anything really important to say, please stick to the point."

Very deliberately he got up from the chair, fetched an extra glass, and poured two over-generous drinks.

"There's no question of your leaving here tonight. By a miracle you managed to avoid the Guards on your way in, but you wouldn't be so lucky the second time."

In this he was probably right. Once morning came and people were in the streets it would be easier to slip away from Marrowbone Lane. My absence from Trinity would cause no comment either, since I had been intending to leave for the mountains anyway.

"We should have been warned by the experience of the French. They were smashed last year, and P.S.D. were certainly at the back of that. P.S.D. is an organisation that started under the cover of a solicitor's business right here in Dublin. Porson, Shilleto and Dobree were the names. Purveyors of Sudden Death, that's what they're known as nowadays."

"Is it some form of Irish counter-espionage?"

Colquhoun's laughter was a little hysterical. "Counter-espionage eh? It's a great pity the lads aren't around to hear that. Counter-espionage!" He sipped his whisky. "No, me young friend, P.S.D. is espionage pure and clear. The only countering that's done is the counting of profit. What's going on in the west there is worth thousands of millions to the industries of the world."

"You mean that P.S.D. steals and sells trade secrets?"

"That's exactly what I was after telling you, if only you wouldn't always be taking the words out of me mouth."

It crossed my mind that I had yet to meet anyone in Parsonage's outfit who could tell a straight tale.

"The rest of us—British, Americans, Russians, Germans—work maybe a little for the excitement, and maybe a little for patriotism, but P.S.D. works only for money. It's business, big business.

"I can see you're wondering where I come into the picture. Don't make any mistake about me; I'm English, born within the sound of Bow Bells. I've been an operative over here for well-nigh thirty years now."

So this was the explanation of the slight aroma of

47

leprechaun that enveloped all the man's remarks. He was a synthetic Irishman. My determination not to get caught up in Colquhoun's affairs was somewhat weakened by this revelation.

"So I suppose P.S.D. decided to eliminate all potential rivals. How did they go about it?"

"By offering big money to our operatives. When P.S.D. had pieced together sufficient information against us, all they had to do was turn it over to the Guards. They bought out three key men that we thought we could trust."

"How very typical of what happens in all secret organisations. Your so-called friends sell you down the river," I remarked.

Colquhoun looked me over unsympathetically.

"See here, mister, sooner or later the Irish are going to close in on this house, maybe tomorrow, or maybe next week, or next month. It'd be easy for me to get to hell out of here, but I don't, because I've got a job to do, five jobs in fact. Yours was one of 'em. Where would you have been if you'd found the Guards sitting here instead of me? I'll tell you. You'd have been due for a ten-year stretch of hard labour, mister."

He took a smallish notebook from his pocket.

"This book has to be got into the hands of the best man left. We're nearly wiped out, but a few pockets are still intact here and there, particularly to the west. These must be reorganised immediately. Information —names, codes—are needed. They must reach the right man without delay."

He tossed the notebook at me.

"I can't move, meself, and I can't send any of the

boys, because the Guards are certainly on the look-out for 'em. That leaves you, Mister Cock-Sure. You are to deliver that little book to Shaun Houseman, who keeps the Unicorn Hotel at Longford. I want it there within twenty-four hours. I can have a car ready for you at ten o'clock tomorrow morning. You say you have a good memory—Houseman, the Unicorn Hotel, Longford."

I put the notebook on the table.

"See here, Colquhoun, we'd better understand each other a little more clearly. In the first place I have explicit instructions from London not to get embroiled in your affairs."

"That may be, but this is the gravest possible crisis, and the unwritten law is that we must all do what we can to safeguard the others, just as I stayed here at my post to safeguard you."

There was now very little trace of the Irish in Colquhoun's manner or speech. This was not his real name, I had no doubt. Morally he seemed three times the man he had before. Whether this was really so or the effect of a liberal dosing with Power's whiskey I cannot say.

"And although I might be able to deliver the note-book, I certainly couldn't guarantee to do so within twenty-four hours. Your idea of a car is ridiculous anyway. I'm here in this country ostensibly as an impoverished student, and I've no business to be found driving a car. If I were stopped by the police I should be under immediate suspicion. And if I were not stopped—well then, you might just as well have sent Liam instead."

49

I never learned Colquhoun's reply to this argument. We were interrupted by a furious pounding of feet on the stairs. The Irish stage character erupted into the room.

"They've taken Liam," he gasped.

"Where?" demanded Colquhoun.

"Coming down Thomas's."

The only thing to do, and that quickly, was to get into the area of the docks. I grabbed the whiskey bottle and emptied half its contents down the side of my coat. Then I took a small device from my pocket, one that I had made up earlier in the week at the Trinity Chemy Lab. It was a long time since I had played with such a thing, not since my schooldays in fact. I cursed myself for studying mathematics; if I'd done experimental science instead I'd have felt more confidence in the damned thing working properly. It was bound to be a dud, I thought gloomily as I primed it.

Seamus Colquhoun had drunk too much to be capable of swift action, so I left him to fare as best he could. In a few seconds I was in the street again, trotting as fast as I dared (for the night was dark) in the direction of Cork Street. Soon there was a narrow opening to my right. If I could get through to the docks without meeting a patrol, there was still a chance.

I suppose the distance was only about a hundred yards, but it seemed much more before a wide space opened up in front of me. There were moving lights to the right and on an impulse I walked towards them, instead of away.

Evidently a posse was searching along the canal-side. It would be better to take the initiative by walking right into them, rather than be trapped by a couple of patrols in the streets. Obviously all the approaches to Marrowbone Lane would be blocked.

I lurched forward with unsteady gait, singing but not too raucously.

"Hi there!"

I went on without pause. The challenge was repeated in a louder voice. I stopped uncertainly and glanced around in a vague way. A bright light flashed in my eyes.

"Hey, whashamatter?"

Hands patted my hips and then moved swiftly under my armpits. Who would be fool enough to carry a gun? Liam, I suppose.

"It's all right. The feller's stinking." Which was perfectly true. The smell of the whiskey was strong, too strong really if they had had the wit to notice.

"Better be on the safe side and take him in. Kevin and Paddy, you go, and get back again as quickly as you can."

We stumbled along to the end of the dock, each man gripping me tightly by an arm. There were three powerful cars. I was pushed into the back of one and one of the men got in beside me. We had gone maybe a couple of hundred yards in the direction of the Castle when I remarked:

"Shtop. Want to be sick."

The driver slammed on the brakes—no one likes a vomiting passenger. In a trice he was out and had the door open. His companion forced me on to the pavement.

"Now bring yer insides up, damn you."

I had managed to pull the little package from my pocket, so even though they held me by the arms I managed to flick it down on the ground as I staggered to the front of the car. Although my eyes were tightly shut the sudden flash almost blinded me. It took but a few seconds to dive into the driving seat, start the engine again, and pull away from the dazed guards. I had about five minutes' grace, two or three minutes while Kevin and Paddy recovered their sight, and another couple before they got back to the cars.

I parked in St. Stephen's Green, wiping the steering-wheel carefully, and the door handles inside and out, the gear shift and the ignition key—there seemed nothing else that I had touched with my hands. By now the pursuit would be on, but it would be well-nigh hopeless.

I had only a hundred yards to go when there was the rattle of an automatic rifle. It seemed to come from the west, very likely from the area of Marrowbone Lane. Poor old Colquhoun! Arms were nasty things. Much better to rely on a bit of magnesium flash powder. Lucky the thing had gone off.

There was one more obstacle. I still had to climb into College. One of the lads had shown me the way, and I hated it. First an easy gate, then a stretch along a moderately difficult roof, and lastly a beastly medieval sort of railing with revolving spikes at the top, where the only safe thing to do was to take the whole weight on one's hands. By a kind dispensation I got over it without endangering the next generation of Sherwoods.

To calm my nerves I brewed a pot of tea and consumed a few slices of bread and marmalade. The situation needed close review. I had washed my embarrassingly alcoholic jacket. In an hour or so all excessive traces of whiskey would be gone. It was true that I had been seen, but only in a very poor light. Assuming that the police found no mention of me at Marrowbone Lane, it was highly unlikely that I could be traced. If Colquhoun were taken alive it was doubtful whether he would shop on me, and even if he did it was doubtful whether his information would add up to very much. My impression was that he knew nothing of my mission, nothing of where I was staying, not even my name.

I had the money. I had something else besides. In the moment of crisis I had foolishly snapped up the notebook. Now I was morally committed to visit Shaun Houseman.

CHAPTER FIVE

The Minstrel Boy

It was perhaps a little odd that I should have slept well. By the time I had shaved, the following morning, it was fully eleven o'clock, too late for breakfast in College. So I revisited the cafeteria in Grafton Street, stopping to buy a morning paper on the way. There was small comfort to be gained from the account of the 'Death of a Guard', as the *Irish Times* described it:

> This paper has had occasion to emphasise only too often in recent months that the ordinary law-abiding citizen of this country is now surrounded by a rising tide of violence. Scarcely a week passes by without some new outbreak manifesting itself, much as an ugly rash may presage the onset of some dangerous disease.
>
> In the early hours of the morning a desperate action took place between the Guards and a gang whose headquarters were discovered near-by the docks in the Old City. It is with great regret that we announce the death in this action of Guard Paddy Kilpatrick. Although the desperadoes immediately responsible for his death have themselves paid the ultimate price for this appalling crime, it is under-

stood that one member of the gang managed to escape during the confusion. It is confidently stated, however, that his capture can be at most a matter of hours.

Poor old Colquhoun! Was he really a desperado, or was he a patriot living dangerously for his country, dying fighting for his life? Not for the first time I realised that there are questions with no real answer. I couldn't help wondering how logicians ever came to believe in the principle of the excluded middle. There are so many common examples to refute it.

The bit in the paper about myself was plainly absurd. Such statements are made only if the police do *not* expect to make an arrest. I suppose in the hope of scaring their man into making some false move.

I was more worried by the death of the guard. Had he recovered his sight properly after the magnesium flash? Of course Paddy is a common name, and it might not have been the same fellow.

I intended to travel from Dublin to Longford by a tolerably complicated route. I had no intention of rushing the journey, as I had told Colquhoun in the plainest terms. The wisest plan was to stick to my student pose as long as I reasonably could. My behaviour during the past week suggested that I had become greatly interested in the history of Ireland. Very properly this interest could take me to Armagh, where St. Patrick built his cathedral—or, to be less ecclesiastic, where Deirdre of the Sorrows is said to have spent her youth. True, a journey to Armagh would carry me away from Longford, but this was scarcely important compared with quitting Dublin safely and with gaining some knowledge of travel in the interior of Ireland.

My first experience came as a surprise. I had decided to use buses, since they gave the most frequent and varied transportation, especially in remote districts. I dropped into a bookshop to buy a time-table, only to be asked for my permit.

I looked blankly at the girl. "I'm sorry, but do I really need a permit in order to buy a bus time-table?"

"Oh yes, sir! We should be having all the ragtag and bobtail coming in to buy time-tables if it weren't for the permits."

"Then I must acquire a permit, I suppose. Where can I get one?"

"At any guard station, sir."

My first impulse was to go to a guard station, but on second thoughts I decided that the slight risk was not worth the gain. I had no wish to meet Kevin again, remote as the chance of recognition might be.

Besides, I had a better idea. I am ashamed to say that I simply purloined the Trinity Library copy, along with some half a dozen maps of the West. Surely if one needed a permit to buy a time-table, nothing less than special dispensation by the Government would suffice for the purchase of a map.

Actually these restrictions were well conceived by the authorities. I found later that there was no hindrance to local traffic. At whatever place one happened to be, information was always available about the local bus service. The genuine resident was therefore put to no inconvenience. It was ragtag and bobtail like myself who were embarrassed by the restrictions, which I suppose was only right and proper.

After lunch, dressed in cap and tweed jacket, I set off to the bus station; rucksack on back again, I must have seemed a fair approximation to the typical Irish student.

When the bus pulled out of the city into open country I had a severe shock, for the road became truly enormous, a dual carriageway stretching far into the distance, fully a hundred yards wide. It was enormous, judged even by American standards, and it brought home more forcibly to me than anything I had yet seen how great must be the power that was driving this Irish economy.

It struck me that the roads a nation builds provide a fair estimate of that nation's faith in the future. The appalling road system in Britain makes no sense at all, either in terms of economics or convenience, except on the supposition that civilisation itself is on the brink of collapse. The bus too was huge by any standard I had seen before. It managed the journey to Armagh comfortably within the hour.

I was lucky to get a room in a small hotel. Before starting on my tour of the town I dropped into a café for a pot of tea, it being then about 4 p.m. I mention this detail because a curious incident occurred, one that had a considerable bearing on later events. At a table two places removed there was a group of three: two hard-faced cases, maybe forty years old or thereabouts, and a pleasant-looking lad whom I took to be about three years younger than myself. The oddity of their association struck the eye immediately. They finished before me. The boy moved first, going over to the pay desk. Really I am exaggerating when I describe the incident as curious. All that happened was a flicker of expression that crossed the faces of the older men, once the younger one had left them together. I couldn't put a name to that expression, but it was an expression that emphatically I didn't like. I watched the three climb into a Chevrolet car parked immediately in front of the café.

Alas, there is no sign any more in Armagh of Deirdre, or of the Knights of the Red Branch. Yesterday they proudly walked the earth, alive to the warmth of the summer sun, to the scent of new-mown grass. But they are gone now with all their troubles, gone with their loves and their hates and fears. Soon Time's mad head-long rush will stream past us too, and in our turn we shall be enshrouded in the black obscurity of the past. Soon you business men who walk the pavement beside me, soon you will have wasted the brief flash of life, wasted it in your frenzied concern for pounds, shillings, and pence. Soon, you girls, it will be of no concern to anyone whether it is Dick you marry, or Harry, or Tom. Soon, Thomas Sherwood, you too will be like a castle in the sand, obliterated by the onrushing tide of life. Soon our whole generation and age will be gone without trace—no, not without trace, for here and there an idea will be preserved and will become a part of the human heritage down the millennia.

And this of course was the centre-point of the story of Deirdre herself. It mattered little whether she lived with Naisi or Conchobar. What did matter was the idea that not even the King himself is above his own laws. Was this true of the Universe itself?

But this is an intelligence report, not a treatise on philosophy. So I need say no more of my evening in Armagh. I caught an early morning bus to Cavan. Just outside Monaghan two police cars closed in on us. This was obviously one of the lightning searches I had heard of, and it gave me the shock of my young life. What a fool to be caught with a bus time-table and a packet of maps! My impulse was to try to jettison the darned things. They were in one of the front pockets of my rucksack, and I thought that maybe I could get rid of them when I lifted the rucksack down from the luggage carrier. Then it crossed my mind that this would be just what the police were looking for. In any case if they searched me thoroughly they would find the money.

"Everybody remain seated, please," shouted the conductor. Two guards got into the bus and two stayed outside. Systematically they went through the papers of the passengers. For the most part they passed on quickly, but sometimes questions were asked and luggage had to be brought down from the carrier. It was rather like going through Customs. Were the Irish really any better with their present prosperity and restrictions than they used to be in the old days of poverty and freedom? Were restrictions an essential concomitant of prosperity?

My turn was coming up when I had the one great stroke of luck I needed. I suppose that every bus-load of passengers must have contained one or two dubious characters. At all events the police found one. In a trice they bundled him out of the bus into one of the waiting cars. When the two guards climbed back to complete their examination, they were already psychologically satisfied men. They had got a case, fulfilled their quota, ready to be half generous.

I handed over my passport and visa.

"Hey, young feller, your visa is stamped for Wicklow and Dublin. You've no right to be in this part of the country. What's the idea?"

"I wanted to see Armagh. Is there anything very wrong in that?"

"Not if you'd had your visa stamped properly."

"But I didn't know that I would want to go to Armagh when I came through immigration. With the best will in the world you can't always foretell what you will want to be doing three weeks ahead."

"You should have checked with the immigration authorities before you left Dublin."

"I can see that now, but I'm afraid it just didn't occur to me at the time."

"And where would you be going on this bus?"

"I'm on my way back to Dublin."

"This isn't the way to Dublin at all."

"It is, if you don't have to look at everything with a professionally suspicious mind."

He didn't like this, but I knew it was the sort of remark that a real bad hat simply wouldn't make. I hurried on:

"I came up from Dublin yesterday by the direct route, so obviously I don't want to go back the same way. By going via Cavan I can see more of the country."

"How am I to know you left Dublin yesterday?"

"Well, it could easily be checked that I left Trinity yesterday."

"You're at Trinity, are you?"

"Yes, that's my base."

I rummaged in my pocket and produced a bus-ticket stub. "Probably you can verify my statement from this."

He first looked carefully at the stub and then went off for a word with the conductor. When he came back I saw that I had escaped.

"Now look here, Mr. Sherwood, I'm going to give you a chance. It would have served you right if I'd taken you along with that other feller, and left you to cool your heels in jail for a couple of days. Remember that as a visitor it's up to you to respect our laws. If you want to go off to any place again, see to it that you check with the proper authorities before you start."

It flashed through me that I must avoid showing any sign of relief. When the man had gone my neighbour remarked:

"Well, he certainly gave you a grilling."

"Yes, it's a bit awkward when you're not used to all these rules and regulations."

This conversation, continuing intermittently right through to Cavan, was a nuisance. Still I managed to make reasonable remarks of some sort and to think over the situation at the same time.

Manifestly I must reorganise my ideas about travel. There must be no more buses, except in emergency. The solution was plain. I must walk, and why not? In a week I could walk across the whole of Ireland. And I must keep well away from these great main roads. I

61

must journey by paths and by-ways as bards and tinkers have always travelled from time immemorial. I would not be safe in these tremendous buses, these high-speed modern contraptions, even if I threw away my maps, which was not to be thought of. Besides, I was sure that neither Seamus Colquhoun (God rest his soul, as the Irish would say), nor P.S.D., nor I.C.E. ever travelled in any way except by super-streamlined automobile. Yes, undoubtedly the quiet way was the right way.

But there was one particular bus that I must still catch, the one from Cavan to Dublin. It was more than likely the police would take the trouble to verify that I really left Cavan for Dublin, which I did shortly after 11 a.m., as if I were racing for home like a scalded cat.

The bus stopped to take on passengers in the neighbourhood of Stradone. This was what I had been waiting for. I managed to slip away without attracting much attention. It was unlikely that the conductor was in the confidence of the police, but there was no sense in advertising myself by openly asking for the bus to be stopped.

I was now about forty miles from Longford. By nightfall I reckoned on making fifteen miles or more, leaving an easy twenty-five for the following day. I would still be delivering Colquhoun's notebook within three days, just as I had promised. My route lay over the hills to Ballinagh. There I would go quickly across the main road to the south, then to Arvagh, and round the west side of Lough Gowna along the higher ground into Longford.

As soon as I started along a leafy country lane I knew that my new plan was correct; an indescribable relief from the tension of the past fortnight swept through me. Of course I could not easily have got out of Dublin on foot. I had been right to start with a bus, and I had been lucky to learn my lesson so soon.

I bought provisions in a village along my road and ate lunch in a grassy meadow. I wished I knew the names of the summer flowers. Curious how much better one knows the spring flowers.

By early evening I was well across the main road. My way led along an apparently endless twisting road that lifted itself over hill and down dale, and I began to wonder where in all this confusion I could find a place for the night. Not that I had the slightest personal objection to sleeping out of doors, but then one soon acquires an unkempt look. This I wished to avoid, at least until I had fulfilled my commission in Longford.

Sundown was approaching when I reached a small farmstead set in an oasis of pasturage, maybe fifty or sixty acres in area. With the confidence of youth I knocked firmly on the half-opened door. A weather-beaten old farmer appeared.

"I am a traveller, and I wonder if you have a corner where I might lay my head for the night?"

"Will you enter the house?" was the reply, with the courtesy of two thousand years of Celtic culture behind it. "It is a stranger wishing to pass the night," he added to his wife, who was standing back in the shadow so that I didn't see her at first.

"Then he may sleep by the fire. Would he be wanting a bite to eat?"

I wasn't sure of the correct etiquette here, but since it

seemed as if the two had already eaten supper, I answered that I had food in my sack, although a drop of tea would be a great thing to a man who had walked such a long dry way over the hills. This seemed the proper thing, for it soon appeared that neither the farmer nor his wife were anything but loath to drink another cup themselves.

I almost choked over my simple meal when in the middle of it the woman switched on a television set. The thing had scarcely been visible before in the gloom, nor had I noticed the aerial as I approached the house. It seemed as if two different worlds had come into sharp conflict, and yet why not? This is exactly why television has stopped the drain of population from country to town. Here were two people, apparently isolated in a remote spot, who by the flick of a knob could now find themselves immersed in the maelstrom of human affairs.

How wrong it is to imagine that economics represent the prime moving factor in historical change. Give every man £50 and let him spend it on beer, cigarettes, and horse-racing, and there will be no historical change to speak of. But give every man a television set costing £50 and there will be a change of significance, a change that may even turn out to be profound. It is not money that is important in itself, but the things that one can buy with money. So much is a mere truism. But it is not a truism to say that what one can buy depends on technology, not on economics. Technology is the key to social change.

I was now getting pretty fit, and I had little difficulty in sleeping through the night in my impromptu bed.

The farmer was up by daybreak, which suited me well, for in travelling on foot it is best to reckon time by the sun. I washed and shaved under a pump in the yard, and breakfasted on porridge, bacon and eggs, and of course the inevitable mug of tea. For their kindness the old couple would take little by way of recompense, which was to prove typical of all my experience in Ireland while I was living close to the earth.

Shortly after leaving the farm the pathway turned into a covered lane. At this early hour dew was on the grass and the birds were still singing loudly. When an hour or two later I restocked with provisions in Arvagh, I found to my delight that there was no danger of a repetition of yesterday's experience on the bus. No one seemed to notice as I walked through the sleepy little town. Of course the police could not watch every man, woman, and child in Ireland, however much they might have liked to have done so. With the force at their disposal, all they could do was to watch and raid the places where the chance of discovering nefarious activities was at its highest. Arvagh was not such a place.

I should like to be able to record that this little pastoral idyll continued through as far as Longford. But it did not. It was shattered by precisely the sort of event that Percy Parsonage had warned me against. The direction of the wind made it difficult to hear the approach of a car. It came furiously towards me as I reached the corner of a narrow twisting road. Barely in time, I leaped into the near-side ditch. It was the same Chevrolet I had remarked outside the café in Armagh, and it now contained but two passengers.

About a mile farther on I noticed that a big car had been driven off the road into a fair-sized copse. There were tyre marks in the grass, and I followed them for maybe a hundred yards to a spot where the car had been parked. Thick undergrowth had made further progress impossible except on foot, and indeed it was clear from the bushes that were broken and pushed aside that someone had forced their way through not long before. I pushed along the line of the broken foliage for about five minutes before I came out into an open clearing. There, on ground that no doubt had carried a carpet of bluebells only a month before, was the body of the fresh-faced boy who had kept company with the two thugs in Armagh.

They hadn't even troubled to make sure that he was dead; he had simply been left to die. I gave the poor devil what crude first-aid I could, but it was hopeless from the start. I had sat with him for about ten minutes, when amazingly he opened his eyes.

"Don't leave me—alone," was the faint whisper.

I gripped his hand tightly. "No, of course I won't, old fellow."

He tried to speak once again but the best I could catch was the name 'Cathleen', and something that sounded like 'the cannon with the crown . . .' Then it was all over.

I closed his eyes and covered him with my sheet sleeping bag. If I had been a real one hundred per cent agent, I suppose I would have searched through his pockets, but I had no impulse to do so. I was overwhelmed by a sense of tragedy and could do no more than turn sadly away and retrace my steps to the road.

The immediate problem was how to inform the police. To make a personal statement to them was obviously out of the question, an anonymous note was better, but best of all this was something I could leave to Shaun Houseman. It was little enough for him to do in return for my delivery of the notebook. I had intended to slip the notebook into an envelope addressed 'For the attention of Mr. Shaun Houseman', and simply drop it in at the Unicorn Hotel as I passed by. I had no wish to become embroiled any more deeply in the affairs of British Security, or of P.S.D., or of any of the other Intelligences, or with the sort of goons who had disposed of the young lad. My real business was with I.C.E., and the sooner I got down to it the better I would be pleased.

It was now about 4 p.m. and I was barely seven miles to the north of Longford. I should be at the Unicorn Hotel comfortably before six o'clock. Three or four miles farther on I was temporarily forced to a halt by a wave of nausea—delayed reaction I suppose. But the lost time was soon made up, for the nausea was followed by an emotion whose very existence in myself I had never suspected before. I was impelled forward by a wave of a cold fury.

The approach into Longford produced a calming influence, however, so that I was able to hunt down the Unicorn with a more balanced mind. A Chevrolet saloon was parked outside. It looked very much like the Chevrolet I had seen three hours before, but if it was, the number plates had been changed.

I have said already that I am the possessor of a suspicious mind. There seemed now to be no point in declaring my hand, at any rate just for the present. It was obviously a good idea to take a rather close look at the Unicorn Hotel and at its inhabitants, to take a close look at Mr. Shaun Houseman in particular.

I asked for a single room for one night and was told that luckily there had been a cancellation. The register signed, I was shown to a second-floor room by the receptionist. Even while she was showing me the facilities I heard a car start up outside. By the time I reached the window, the Chevrolet was pulling away down the street.

Before dinner I visited the bar. Although it was pretty crowded I saw nobody that I recognised, which in the circumstances was perhaps as well. A man with an air of proprietorship was busy behind the counter. I took this to be Houseman, but I could read nothing from his manner. He looked around fifty, tall, heavily built, putting on weight, hair greying, normal.

I was more fortunate at dinner. I have said that Deirdre and her intimates have vanished without trace. But this I saw must be wrong as soon as I entered the dining-room. For she herself was here, alive in all her original loveliness, no longer a queen, it is true, but a waitress. Surely this must be some descendent of those bygone days. Perhaps the intervening generations had wrought some slight change, for her face was warm and friendly, incapable of the disdain that her ancestor had shown on that last unlucky day.

I was still thirsty from the long walk when she passed. "Deirdre, could I have a glass of water please?" She stopped and stared at me in some surprise:

"Me name's not Deirdre, it's Cathleen."

Of course it was, for her face had reminded me of something far less pleasant than the story of Deirdre. This must be the sister of the dead boy in the wood.

Of course it was, for her face had reminded me of
something far less pleasant than the story of Deirdre.
This must be the sister of the dead boy in the wood.

CHAPTER SIX

The Chase Across the Common

The position was both delicate and exasperating.
Cathleen must be told about the shocking demise of
her brother, and that very soon. But when I suggested
that we have a word together she took me for a fast
stranger with doubtful intentions, which I suppose must
have seemed not at all an unusual event. She trotted
off in a huff, whether simulated or not I don't know. It
took the best part of a couple of hours before I was able
to waylay her alone.

I caught her as she came out of the kitchen.

"Look, mister, if you don't go away from me, it's for
help I'll be shouting."

Plainly I was not of the stuff that the heroes of
American aphrodisiacal literature are made, the sort of
man the girls chase from cover to cover.

"I want to speak to you about your brother. You
have a brother, haven't you?"

This checked her instantly.

"What is it?" she whispered.

"We must go where we can talk without being overheard. Come up to my room in about five minutes. It's
number 17."

There was no point in having our conversation overheard, and no point in our being seen too obviously together. Metaphorically speaking, I could smell rats all over this hotel.

Announcing herself with a light tap on the door, Cathleen slipped inside. I told her as briefly and quietly as I could all I had seen during the afternoon. She made me repeat my description of the lad's appearance several times, until there could be no doubt that he really was her brother. Then she collapsed in a chair and sobbed quietly and uncontrollably.

I stood around, unable to do anything but offer my handkerchief. Then quickly, so quickly that I was taken by surprise, she jumped up. "Come back, you little fool . . ." but she was gone.

I began to curse silently to myself. In my schooldays, in the era of scholarships, I used to be afflicted by a recurrent nightmare. I would dream that I was given an examination paper, all the questions of which I could do with reasonable facility. Then just as I started to write out the first of them, there would come an interruption, the invigilator would cry out: "Excuse me a moment, I have an announcement to make . . ." The announcement would take a quarter of an hour, and would be followed immediately by a second interruption and then by a third, and so forth until the whole three hours was over, when once again the booming voice of the invigilator would ring out: "Gentlemen, time is up." Just as I was handing in my blank paper I would waken, sweating with aghast apprehension.

From the moment I had started on this mission I had suffered one interruption after another. First Parsonage, who couldn't allow me to get into Ireland in my own way. Then the ill-fated Colquhoun, who hadn't the elementary common sense to see that since his organisation had spawned three traitors there wasn't the slightest reason why it shouldn't spawn four, or five, or six . . . And now Cathleen, who must whip away on a desperate course without giving me the slightest chance to help her. I had a shrewd idea of what she might be doing, but I couldn't go padding about a strange hotel in the hope that I'd just chance on the right move to make. Better to stay put. At least she'd be able to find me if she wanted me.

I anticipated her return by packing my rucksack. The sooner I could get away from the Unicorn Hotel and from Mr. Houseman the better. Three times I had been asked by the hotel staff for my passport. Each time I had stalled—I hadn't the smallest intention of handing it over. I knew Houseman, with his own background to consider, would never bring in the police, but he must already be aware that I was someone to be watched.

By a miracle Cathleen had managed to find what she wanted. She came in, breathing fast, with a file of papers clutched in her arms.

"Let me put them in the rucksack."

She handed them over more trustingly than she should have done.

"Come along quickly now. We can creep out by the back way."

Maybe we could and maybe we couldn't. As it turned out, we could. The point, of course, was that at this hour, 10 p.m., Houseman was heavily engaged in the bar. It would be at least an hour before business became lighter and another hour or two before he discovered the loss of the papers. Perhaps he wouldn't even find out until morning.

Cathleen had a couple of bikes ready in the lane outside. "Give over the rucksack to me, and you take this," she said, handing me a spade. I noticed she had a blanket in the carrier on the front of her machine. The next part of our joint enterprise was grimly obvious.

We cycled silently out of the town. I led the way back without difficulty, for it is curious how easily one remembers every detail of a road along which one has walked, in pitiful contrast to the hurrying motorist who sees little and remembers nothing.

We found the wood again, left our bicycles where the car had been parked, forced our way through the undergrowth. He was still lying exactly as I had left him. I held one of the cycle lamps for Cathleen to lift my sleeping bag. She made no cry, but looked for perhaps half a minute.

"Poor Mickey boy," she whispered, and then added in a small voice choked with passion, "I'll get them for this."

In turn she held the light for me while I dug his grave. Once the spade had cut through the surface turf the ground was rich and soft. I guess it must have taken about an hour before I had excavated a trench about three feet deep. We wrapped him in the blanket and lowered him gently. She wept as I filled in the soil again and replaced the grassy turf.

I put my arm around her shoulders and led her back to the bicycles. We started off along the road, but we hadn't gone far before I saw that the girl was exhausted and on the verge of collapse. Clearly we couldn't ride all through the night. Equally we couldn't go back to the Unicorn Hotel. It would be best to get a few miles away from the wood, and then lie up until morning.

We rode along rather shakily for the first mile or two. I had of course discarded the spade and was able to give Cathleen a bit of a push, but it wasn't at all easy in the blackness. Then surprisingly she began to go along on her own steam, and after a while she took the lead.

"Have you any idea where you're going?"

"I want to go to Morag's cottage," was the reply.

Since I had no idea of the whereabouts of Morag's cottage I had no choice but to follow along. We rode back almost into Longford, but cut away on the east side, crossed the wide main road to Mullingar, and a mile or two farther on started down an unsurfaced lane. There was a solitary cottage rather more than half a mile along.

An old woman answered our knock. When she saw Cathleen she exclaimed, "By the saints, what an hour to be on the road!" While Cathleen went inside and told the old woman whatever she wished to tell her, I stood outside examining the approaches to the cottage. I put the bikes where we could readily get them on to the road again if we should be in a hurry, for, truth to tell, I didn't like this cottage business. When he found his papers to be missing, Houseman was certain to begin a frenzied search. I didn't know of course what sort of an organisation he had at his disposal, but it was safest to assume that the organisation would be formidable. He would obviously look for Cathleen at every place he could think of, and Morag's cottage might well be one of these. It would have been wiser to have slept in the woods, but Cathleen was so tired that I couldn't find it in my heart to insist. The one comfort was that the lights of any car could be seen approaching the cottage from afar off. I thought it most unlikely that anyone would on that particular night drive without at least some degree of lighting.

Morag had brewed up a pot of tea. She offered me a cup when I came in from the lane.

"And now be off to bed with you," she said to Cathleen.

"Try to get some sleep," I added, "but don't take your clothes off. We might have to make a quick getaway. I'll keep watch, don't worry."

She nodded, evidently seeing the point.

"Morag, can you tell if a car turns into the lane?"

The old woman answered that she could.

"Then would you be willing to keep a watch, in case I fall asleep?"

"You may be assured that I will."

But I had no intention of sleeping. I took out the file of papers and began to look systematically through them. The first part was scientific, the latter part and the appendices were mathematical. One needed little knowledge of science to appreciate the importance of the first part; it was no less than a description and blue-print of a thermo-nuclear reactor, the disposition of magnets, currents, and voltages, etc. I remembered Parsonage's statement that I.C.E. had produced a working thermo-nuclear reactor, and a piece of the puzzle became complete in my mind.

Not to make a mystery of the matter, I might remark

that one of the entries in Colquhoun's notebook read as follows:

Michael O'Rourke (I), sister Cathleen.

The *I* was probably short for I.C.E. Presumably the situation was that Michael had a job at I.C.E., or at least had had the entrée into I.C.E. territory. It must have been Michael who got hold of the manuscript. In the ordinary course of his business he had brought the manuscript to Shaun Houseman, who must instantly have perceived its fantastic value on the open market. When Michael got wind of Houseman's intentions, he, Michael, had simply been brutally snuffed out. This seemed to make sense, at any rate the sort of sense that one expects to meet in this brand of business.

As I read on, I became more and more uneasy. By now I had reached the mathematical parts. Either my memory was slipping, or there were steps in the various proofs that simply did not seem to follow. At first I thought the stress and strain of the last month, and of the last day in particular, had softened my wits, but bit by bit I found things that were certainly wrong. I even found an elementary blunder: the statement that apart from an additive constant every monotonic continuous function is equal to the integral of its derivative. On a grand scale, this was another nonsensical document of the sort that I had already seen in Parsonage's office.

But it gave me some idea of the subtlety of the people I would soon be dealing with. Evidently I.C.E. had a deliberate policy of turning out spoof documents, which they fed to the foreign agents, much as one might fling hunks of poisoned meat to a pack of snarling wolves. Poor Michael! This was something that I must be careful to keep from Cathleen.

I must have dozed off round about dawn, for I was roughly wakened by Morag.

"Away with you. They're coming up the boreen."

The lane was a little more than half a mile long. Assuming the car came quickly along the very rough surface, it would take the best part of a minute, sixty precious seconds, of which Morag must have consumed ten. I took five more to get upstairs to Cathleen's bedroom, another five to drag her out of bed, ten to get her downstairs, and a final ten to grab my rucksack and the file of papers and to race out after her to the bikes. This left twenty seconds to reach the turn of the lane beyond the cottage before the car appeared. We managed it with nothing to spare.

The car would stop at the cottage, but not for long. However skilfully Morag prevaricated we had left obvious signs of our flight. It occurred to me that I ought to have left the papers behind too. This would have delayed them longer, and might even have caused them to call off the pursuit altogether.

We came out of a thin wood into open fields, and my heart fell, for there were gates across the path. I fretted at the precious seconds that were lost in opening the first of them—the car had started again. But it was the gates that saved us. It takes longer to open a gate from a car than from a bicycle, and what we gained in this way made up for the extra speed of the car on the stretches between.

It must have looked a preposterous race to an

onlooker. I would forge ahead, slide off on to one of the pedals, jump down, and half open the gate. Cathleen following behind would ride through and head for the next gate at full speed. Meanwhile I would slam the gate, making sure it was firmly shut. By the time I reached the next one, Cathleen would have it open and I would ride through and then head for the third, and so on. By this technique we kept the car at bay, a couple of fields behind, and certainly out of shooting range.

At length we came to what I had been hoping for, a stout gate that simply couldn't be opened. I lifted the cycles over. This cost some time—I could now see Houseman in the front seat by the driver. But the great thing was that they could not lift the car over, and to attempt to batter a way through would be to risk damage and delay.

Looking back I saw that we had won. The big car was being slowly turned. Another couple of hundred yards along I saw why. The path—it was now no more than a farm track—ran between stone walls which narrowed here and there enough to prevent the transit of any but the smallest vehicle.

We came out on to what in England would have been described as a common. I knew it stretched away to the south-east as far as the huge trunk road from Cavan to Athlone. My plan was to ride as far as we could in this direction—but more of this later.

The immediate danger was that Houseman would get his car on to the common by some other route. We therefore pushed ahead as hard as we could go. After a mile or two, patches of bog appeared. This was good, because it would make the use of a car extremely hazardous. And indeed there was no sign of any car, presumably because Houseman knew the difficulties— it really takes very little in the way of an obstacle to turn this particular form of transportation into a mockery, just a very short stretch of soft ground. Twice we had to lift the bicycles over belts of bog and peat hags that I thought would be sufficient to stop even a jeep.

I learned from Cathleen that there was ample cover within a mile of the main road—trees and bushes, in contrast to the open ground we were now crossing. This seemed to solve the whole problem. It would be useless for Houseman to try to intercept us at the road. All we had to do was to lie in cover until a bus was due—I had my precious time-table. At the right moment we would mount on to the road, flag the bus to a standstill, and then away! (This was an occasion when the risk of public transportation must be taken). Everything was easy. I discounted an attempt to follow us on bicycles, they were much too far behind for that. Horseback might be a good idea, but I doubted if horses would be ready saddled.

And on this basis I allowed the pace to slacken, not to a dawdle by any means, but to a pace more congenial to a tired girl. In this I grievously underestimated my opponent. I want to emphasise this point because a great deal followed from my mistake. Just as two streams a couple of hundred yards apart on opposite sides of a watershed separate implacably to their respective oceans, so this was the point of divergence of my story. If I had hurried Cathleen along I think I would have married her. I think in the long run I would have taken a comparatively lucrative job with I.C.E., and I think we would have settled down to raise a family in peace and quiet on the coast of Kerry. But because I allowed her a breathing space, scenes of horror were to follow in the short run, and in the long run I was to discover the secret of I.C.E.

I was extraordinarily slow in spotting the form of Houseman's attack. At first I thought that some enterprising farmer must be early at work. We had ridden for ten minutes before I realised that the noise was too loud for one tractor. Surely every farmer in the district couldn't have employment for such an instrument at six o'clock in the morning?

Not until we mounted a low hill could I convey a real sense of urgency to Cathleen. Some two miles back, perhaps a little more, four caterpillar tractors were heading in our direction.

Even now I was not seriously alarmed, for at our accelerated pace I thought we must be moving quite as fast as the tractors. We couldn't be much more than six miles from the road, and after five of these we would be in cover.

But I was not reckoning on a sudden change of the ground. Quite suddenly it altered from the smoothness of the common to coarse tussocky grass. We began to bounce and to lose speed. The tractors would hardly be affected. The position was plainly desperate.

There was nothing for it but to abandon the bikes. We could make better time now on foot. At this stage we were about four miles from the cover by the road, the tractors were two miles farther back still, six miles from cover. On this extremely rough terrain they would probably take about forty minutes to do the six miles. Could we run four miles in the time? Without my rucksack and alone I believe I could have done it. But Cathleen was no faster than I could manage with the rucksack, so there was no point in discarding it.

I will not dwell unduly on the painful slowness of the following half-hour. Nor was it only time that seemed to go 'on leaden feet'. We ran until I thought my lungs would burst, and yet at every stride the tractors closed the precious distance.

Next there came a long stretch of rough uphill ground which had to be taken in the face of quite a fresh breeze. Everything depended on the other side of the hill. With a great effort we should reach the top two or three hundred yards in the lead. If there was reasonable cover on the other side we should be safe.

With every muscle screaming for rest we arrived at the top. Ahead was a mile of open ground, and then, only then, a plethora of trees and bushes. The tractors would run us down before we could cover a half of this distance.

If only we had hurried, back there on the common. If only we had gained ten minutes. If only—but this was the lesson of life compressed into a single hour.

Then I had an idea. I shouted to Cathleen to run on. With fumbling fingers I tore open the rucksack and pulled out the papers. I could see the drivers clearly now, grim-faced men in cloth caps. Houseman was a passenger in one of the machines, a great slug clinging to the rolling monster. But this would give him a problem to think about. In a gust of wind I released

the pages of the manuscript. As if to show its contempt
for this appalling rubbish, this desecration of Lesbesgue,
the breeze lifted the sheets. Within a minute they were
scattered over a couple of acres or more. If they were
to be retrieved, Houseman would have to act instantly,
for even on the ground the sheets chased along at a
merry pace in the direction from which we had
come.

There was never any question as to what would
happen. Houseman jumped down to retrieve one of
the pages, took a quick look at it, and began shouting
orders to his band of hoodlums. Even at the risk, I
paused to watch them. The scene became ludicrous
beyond my fondest hopes. In a sort of fantastic polo
game the tractors wheeled hither and thither. Every so
often a man would leap down from his seat, and another
piece of nonsense had been gathered to the fold.
Chuckling mightily, I trotted after Cathleen, a modern
Meilanion anxious to claim my Atalanta.

I saw already that something was wrong, even when I
was fifty yards from Cathleen. Her eyes blazed with
furious anger.

"You ——" she flared.

I suppress the word not because it was a particularly
bad one. I had heard worse often enough before, but
because this was the only time I ever heard her make
such a remark.

"And me poor brother not dead in his grave these
twelve hours," she added.

Now I saw the appalling thing I had done. I had
casually tossed away the manuscript that Michael had
given his life for. I had thrown it to his murderers, and

I had done so with a laugh. I started to explain, but then I saw the hopelessness of the real explanation. It's perfectly true that in the best society one does not integrate the derivative of a function and expect always to arrive back at the original function. But can one expect such a remark to appeal to a pretty girl in an extremity of anger? Of a surety one cannot.

So I tried an appeal to common sense.

"Look, Cathleen, if I hadn't scattered your brother's manuscript to the winds we'd have been caught by the tractors. And if we'd been caught, Houseman would have got the manuscript anyway. In fact he'll find it harder to get the papers out from the bog than if he'd only had to take them from my rucksack."

This cold logic calmed her a little. But she hammered a fist into the palm of her hand.

"At least you might have fought for it."

No remark could have been better calculated to destroy me. Once again I spluttered with laughter. The trouble went back to my nursery days. I had puzzled for the best part of a couple of years over a little piece that went something as follows:

A asked for it,
B bit it,
C cut it,
D dug for it . . .

I remember that S sought for it, M mourned for it, and that T, most sensibly, simply took it. The problem that had worried my childish mind was the nature of 'it'. It was of course F who fought for it.

"Oh well, if that's what you're thinking of me, I'll be going my way," said Cathleen.

The humour was gone. "That you will not. There's still danger from the road." This was perfectly true. It was by no means impossible that Houseman had sent a car-load of thugs round by the road with the idea of heading us off. If so they were too late, so long as we didn't stand around arguing futile nonsense. I seized Cathleen by the arm.

"Come on, girl, you can say all you want to say once we're safely away from here."

It would make a nice ending to this episode if I could claim a final encounter with the Houseman gang, there among the trees and bushes. But a hundred men might have searched all day in that wonderful cover and never had sight or sound of us. We reached the road and lay down to wait for the next bus towards Athlone. I judged from my time-table that one would go by somewhere between 8.20 and 8.30 a.m. We had only half an hour to pass.

It seemed that the best place would be to leave the bus near a small place called Tang. Cathleen was of a different mind.

"It's to Athlone I'm going."

"But that's exactly where Houseman will be looking for you, if he wants to look for you."

"Maybe it's me that'll be looking for him."

I passed this by. "The towns are a bad idea, Cathleen. I doubt if I could stand up even to a routine police inspection."

"Then it is right for you to stop at Tang, and I will go to Athlone."

"But it's only sensible that we should stick together."

"After what happened back there on the bog, do not think that I will go with you."

A vision came to me of the pages of the manuscript fluttering in the breeze, Michael's life-blood.

"Tell me what better I could have done?"

She refused to meet my eyes. "When I go with a man, it will be with a man who knows how to behave in trouble."

I heard a fast-moving heavy vehicle away in the distance, which was perhaps as well because I don't think I could have found an answer to this last remark.

"Stay here until you see that I've managed to stop the bus."

I climbed down a bank and up on to the road. There was no point in exposing us both to the risk of a chance shot.

I booked two single tickets, one to Athlone and one to Tang. As the bus raced along, I made one last attempt to persuade Cathleen not to continue to Athlone. The fleeting moments soon passed. We drew up to my destination, and I remembered to give Cathleen a note, for she was without money.

"But how will I repay you?"

"Don't bother, it's little enough," and I added unkindly as I pulled my inevitable rucksack down from the carrier, "When you meet up with someone who behaves well in time of trouble, give it to him with my compliments."

I dropped off the bus, and turned into a country road. So it came about that Cathleen and I parted for the first time.

CHAPTER SEVEN

The Journey to the South

The hardest decision of my life was to leave the bus at Tang. The temptation to head a campaign against Houseman seemed almost irresistible. Cathleen would have joined me because of her consuming desire to avenge Michael's death. I had Colquhoun's notebook. With its help it might have been possible to organise some reliable nucleus, after which I didn't think the outwitting of Houseman would have presented an excessively awkward job.

It is difficult to analyse the reasons why I didn't do so. Certainly they had no connection at all with Parsonage's warnings and wishes. His organisation creaked and groaned so badly that my awe of him, if it ever existed at all, had blown away with the west wind. At the time I believed it was I.C.E. that swayed the balance. I was beginning to realise that I.C.E. must simply be toying with its opponents; and must be having a good laugh at them into the bargain. So it seemed quite futile to build up an organisation that in its very nature was defeated from the start. Why not attack the problem right at its source? This, I say, was the reason I gave to myself. Looking back, I realise now that pique may have had something to do with it.

My plan was very simple, which seemed a good recommendation at the time. But I was soon to learn that it is possible to be too simple, both in plan and in mind. My route lay pretty well along two sides of a right-angled triangle, first a walk of about 120 miles to the south beyond Tipperary, then a drive to the west along much higher ground. There would be no stopping at farms and cottages during this last push, which would carry through from the region between Mallow and Cork, over the highest mountains of Ireland, right into the central peninsula of Kerry. I aimed to make the last eighty miles in two or three forced marches, if necessary during night hours.

One of my first acts, a rite, was to burn the notebook. I had a fair portion of it stored away in my head, so there seemed to be no point in continuing to carry around such a dangerous document. Perhaps I should have handed it to Cathleen, but I thought probably not. As I watched the pages turn to ashes, I felt that at long last I was freed from my embarrassing connections. Once again, an error.

During the week that followed I had a greater ease of mind than at any later time, right up to the end of the whole business. I moved with the sun, lying out in grassy meadows reading my books, sheltering from the rain. I slept well at night on hard beds, and sometimes on the harder ground. This was a gentle country I was walking in, without any suggestion of the wider horizons of moor and mountain, of sea and storm, that lay no great distance away on my right hand.

As I tramped along I would sometimes think over what I had learned of I.C.E. Of the technological achievements of this organisation I had now built quite a catalogue. It ran like this:

Item. Masters of metallurgy. To wit the horizontal metal girders of the Dublin Rail Station.

Item. Builders of tremendous earth-moving equipment used to construct enormous roads, among other things. Example, the 'moving mountains' I had seen in Dublin. Probably powered by nuclear engines.

Item. Producing a very large electrical output. In addition to own uses, was now supplying power to even the most remote country cottages. Power must come from nuclear origin, since no appreciable imports into Ireland of coal and oil. Possibly derived from water by thermo-nuclear process.

Item. Vast output of fertiliser. Much of the farmland around me had been reclaimed from bog.

All this added up not just to a great industrial organisation, but to a new world, a new civilisation. It may sound a little odd, but I was even more impressed by the things that I.C.E. was not doing. They were not making cars—or tractors, for that matter. All these were imported from abroad. Why? I believed I knew the answer. Because these were products that could adequately be manufactured elsewhere. I.C.E. was so incredibly confident in itself that it was only doing what others could not do. It scorned to engage in any well understood industrial process.

But of *how* all this was being done I hadn't learned enough to spread on a farthing. I knew of course that many clever scientists had joined I.C.E. I knew the names of a fair number of them. But clever as they were, there were men just as clever outside Ireland, at my own University for instance. So this could scarcely be the whole answer. I thought over every possibility that even the most rigorous racking of brains would produce, but nothing that came to mind seemed remotely plausible.

I passed Tipperary on its western side with the intention of skirting the Galty Mountains. My idea was to keep to the south until I reached a point a little beyond Fermoy, and then at last to swing sharply to the west. By taking this route (which was not the nearest) I would avoid getting close in to I.C.E. territory at too early a moment. It was likely that the border would be protected in depth. This being so, I wanted to tackle it as a rugby player makes straight for a touchdown. I had no wish to be flanked out to the wings.

As I say, I was to the west of Tipperary, I suppose near on ten miles. It was now coming up to six in the evening, so I set about finding a resting place for the night. I discovered a farm under the slopes of Slievenamuck. It was rather larger than I would have wished, but there seemed to be no reasonable alternative. My request for a bed was met with a refusal. "It is unlucky for you that we have visitors already," explained the woman of the house.

"There is no problem in that," remarked a rich voice behind me. I turned to find a clergyman smiling at us.

"There is no reason why he shouldn't share the loft with Tiny."

"That would be very fine if your Reverence has no objection."

"I am only too glad to be of help to a passing traveller. Mrs. O'Reilly will get her young lad to show you the way. After you have washed, perhaps you would care to eat supper with me?"

I thanked him warmly, and departed for the loft, following behind Mrs. O'Reilly's lad. There were two beds, and Tiny was sitting on one of them. He was a gigantic fellow, the sort who plays centre-position in American football, fully 250 lb. He responded to my look of astonishment with a lazy smile, a cigarette between his lips.

There was a pot bowl and an urn with water, so I stripped to the waist and began washing. During this operation, while I was soaping my face and my eyes were shut, a vice seemed to close on the biceps of each of my arms. I struggled violently to free myself but without the slightest success. Suddenly I was released. I opened my eyes, but soap got in them, smarting furiously. Somehow I got hold of my towel.

"You bloody great ape!" I yelled. For it was Tiny. He had sneaked up absolutely silently behind me and had gripped me with his huge hands. Now he burst into bellows of laughter.

I did the best I could to seem unconcerned. I finished washing, put on a clean shirt, and wished heartily that I had never come near the place—I had no taste for spending the night with a gorilla, one that apparently possessed the sense of humour of an eight-year-old child. I considered whether or not I should pack up and leave there and then, but decided that to do so would be abominably discourteous to my clerical friend. I had better stick it out.

At supper the cleric seemed to detect some reserve in my manner.

"Has Tiny been upsetting you?" he asked.

"No, no, nothing of any importance."

"He is apt to be a bit playful. But I'll have a word with him. You will have no further worry, I can assure you. He's really a very good fellow, you know, extremely faithful."

"Do you spend much time in these parts, sir?" I said, thinking it best to change the subject.

"Often, when I am free from my charge in the City of Cork. But from your speech I would say that you yourself are from England, from the west?"

"Yes. I'm a Devon man by origin. I'm enjoying a few weeks rambling here after finishing my finals at Cambridge."

"Ah ha, from Cambridge, a great place, I've heard. You are a fortunate young fellow. By a sad dispensation we have far too few visitors from abroad nowadays."

"Can you explain why that should be, sir?" said I, steering the conversation away from myself and my affairs.

"There is no mystery about it, I fear. The mammon of unrighteousness is upon us."

This sort of remark I can make no sense of, so I left the man to extricate himself, which he did without difficulty.

"Aye, it is a great sin that hangs on us, better it were a millstone."

91

"I cannot say that I've seen very much to support your point of view, sir."

"Believe me, Mr. Sherwood, the young look only to outward symbols. They do not see the maggot busily at work rotting the core of our national life."

"I take it, sir, that you are referring to I.C.E."

"I am indeed," he boomed; "the monstrous iniquity that is fast robbing us of our ancient way of life."

"The ending of poverty is all I have seen on my travels."

"Man does not live by bread alone. That is as true today as it ever was. With increasing prosperity the old virtues, the old sense of values, are all fast being lost, irretrievably lost."

"Do you think prosperity and virtue are mutual enemies, then?"

"Remember the words of Our Lord, Mr. Sherwood: 'It were easier for a camel to pass through the eye of a needle . . .' Better to be poor, and sound in moral wind and limb, than to live in the finest earthly mansion."

"I simply can't agree that poverty is a desirable end in itself, sir. Poverty may often seem virtuous just because it's given no opportunity to be anything else. I'd rather say that only in wealth and prosperity can true morality be judged."

He laughed with a rich chuckle.

"How delightfully argumentative you modern young people can be!"

"I take it that there is a very general agreement in the Church on this subject of I.C.E.?"

"One good thing, and one good thing only, has come from the growth of the hosts of the ungodly. My Church and the Church of Rome now stand nearer together than I would have thought possible."

This explained something that had puzzled me. His dress had seemed different from that of the priests I had seen in Dublin. It was of course the dress of the Church of Ireland. Both my powers of reason and observation were being dulled by so much country air.

I will not attempt to describe the rest of what (to be frank) I found a somewhat tedious conversation. I was a little surprised to find myself rallying staunchly to the defence of I.C.E., but I had yet to see anything of this organisation that offended my sense of morality—such as it is.

The time came when I could decently suggest retiring for the night. I had no particular wish to renew the unpromising acquaintance of the gorilla, but this had to be done sooner or later. It was a relief that my clerical friend had not forgotten his promise to speak a word of caution to 'Tiny'. He came across to the loft with me, took the gorilla aside for a few moments while I made up my bed, and then remarked:

"I think that all will now be well, Mr. Sherwood. What time would you care to breakfast in the morning?"

"Would seven-thirty be too early?"

"By no means. What is the time now, I wonder?"

He pulled out a watch attached to a chain. It was of the kind that one must snap open before the dial can be seen.

"Ah, nine-thirty. Early to bed, eh, Mr. Sherwood?"

I was hard put to it to make any suitable reply, for on the inner cover of the watch I caught a glimpse of a most disturbing design. Stamped in the metal was the imprint of a crown.

I knew now the meaning, or at any rate a part of the meaning, of the words of the dying Michael—the cannon with the crown. I had had the word 'cannon' all wrong. It should of course have been 'the canon with the crown'.

My strong impulse once the Canon had gone was to pack my things and to be away with all haste. Whether I had betrayed my surprise at the sight of the watch I cannot say—I may well have done so. At all events I couldn't avoid the suspicion that the gorilla had been detailed to watch me closely. He stood by the door, a cigarette on his lips, smiling his lazy smile. Regretfully I decided it would be wiser to stay than to try to go.

I lay in bed thinking distasteful thoughts and keeping a wary eye on the gorilla. My after-dinner conversation with the Canon just didn't ring true. All those phrases 'mammon of unrighteousness', 'earthly mansions', are the sort of thing a cleric will say from the pulpit, but not, these days, in ordinary social talk. The man was an impostor, grossly so.

The night was at best unpleasant and at worst terrifying. Eventually the gorilla decided to turn in— his bed came between mine and the door, I noticed. The light went out. I lay listening to his breathing, to make sure that he didn't get out of bed. Nothing happened for maybe an hour. Then very stealthily he did get out. I heard him prowling almost silently about the room, and I had the horrible certainty that he was going to seize me again. It needs not the slightest imagination to realise the impelling desire I had to reach the door, or the lights at least, but I knew as if by divine revelation that the one thing I must never do in front of this creature was to show fear. He came quite close, and then of a sudden let out in the dark his ear-splitting bellow of laughter. Drawing on every particle of my will power I roared: "Get into your bed. If I have any more trouble I'll go straight and fetch your master."

He went back. I decided that since he hadn't attacked me the safest thing would be to seem unconcerned, really to try to sleep. I think that I managed to do so in a nightmarish fashion.

When morning came at last I was up betimes. I noticed that no sooner did I jump out of bed than the gorilla did too. I shaved, washed, and packed my rucksack, all quite deliberately. Then I went down into the farmyard. Although it was still only seven o'clock, I eventually decided to go into the house and to wait there for breakfast. By so doing I hoped to escape from the ever-watchful eye of the gorilla.

In my story thus far there have been occasions when luck has rather decisively taken my side. Indeed I realised once or twice that I had rather been overdrawing my account in this respect. Now, in an instant, I was called on to repay my borrowings, at a usurer's rate of interest. The Canon was already abroad. He was seated at the dining-table. When I came in he looked up with a placid smile. By his side was Shaun Houseman. Then I saw the enormity of what I had done. I had walked unawares into the headquarters of P.S.D.

I remember once playing in a game of cricket in which my side was called on to face up to a couple of ferociously skilful bowlers. Before we started our innings one member of the team marched around the pavilion advising us all that the one hope was 'to take up a hostile attitude'. We duly took up a hostile attitude and were dismissed for a total of less than thirty.

In a rather similar way I now felt that my one hope was to seize the initiative.

"Well, well, Mr. Houseman! And did you manage to recover all those papers from the bog?"

Houseman scowled at this mock-cheerful greeting, but the Canon looked carefully at his manicured nails and said:

"As a matter of fact one or two pages *are* missing, Mr. Sherwood. I am hoping for your own sake that you will be able to tell me what was in those pages."

"What particular piece of nonsense have you in mind?"

The Canon was still looking at his hands. "I would advise you to explain very clearly what you mean by that remark, Mr. Sherwood, or you may find that I am a less patient man than I seem."

"There isn't the least uncertainty about my remark," I said with a bold show of confidence. "The manuscript was an obvious tissue of rubbish from beginning to end."

I suppose he stood to lose several millions on the matter, so it was scarcely surprising that this last statement brought the examination of his finger-nails to an end.

"Houseman, get me the case."

Houseman fetched a brief-case to the table and took out a file, which he handed to the Canon.

"Now show me exactly what you mean."

I opened up the file. These were the papers all right, considerably stained from their windswept flight across the bog. I started reading quite slowly from the beginning.

"I am not prepared to sit waiting for very long, Mr. Sherwood. If I lose my patience with you I shall call for Tiny," announced the Canon. This was the psychological crisis. I had but a single card in my hand, my technical competence. I must seek to get this one card rated at its highest possible value.

"Look, sir, I've already given you a quick assessment of this document. Now I'm going to give you a detailed assessment. But you'll have to wait my time for it, not your own."

He gave in, as of course he had to if he wanted to get any decent information. Once he had the information, it would be soon enough to send for Tiny.

I set to work neither too hastily nor too slowly. Breakfast was brought for Houseman and the Canon.

"I'll have mine too, Mrs. O'Reilly," I said, without looking up. My breakfast was brought. By playing my one good card at least I had won the first round. But would I win any more than the first?

Someone brought in my rucksack. The Canon went through its contents. He was interested in the books, which he examined rather closely. I have the habit of annotating my books with marginal comments.

When at length I had finished, I pushed the file across the table.

"Well, there it is. I won't guarantee that I've found all the mistakes, but you can see for yourself that the ones I have found show up the whole thing for a piece of complete nonsense."

Instead of attempting to understand anything of what I had written, the Canon simply compared my handwriting with the annotations. The two being the same, the evidence against Houseman's document must now have looked very strong, particularly since spoof documents were presumably fairly common anyway.

Something else in the rucksuck interested the Canon: my only weapon—a packet of magnesium flash powder. He opened it up, lit a match, and set the stuff off in one big puff.

"Very pretty indeed. By the use of some such material a person unknown (as the police say) made quite an ingenious escape from the Dublin police a week or two ago. On the sixteenth of July, if I remember correctly. Where would you have been on that day, Mr. Sherwood?"

"In Dublin, as a matter of fact."

"A strange coincidence, I must say! And now would you be so good as to tell me why you happen to be in Ireland at all?"

"Oh, there's no mystery about that. Our people in London are very worried by the high percentage of dud stuff that's been coming through. I was simply sent over to help separate the wheat from the tares."

He was now very calm again, his voice purring like a huge cat.

"Our meeting is indeed a fortunate one from your

98

point of view, Mr. Sherwood, for I fear you would have found little employment for your talents if a kindly providence had not brought you to my door yesterday evening."

"I was beginning to realise that, sir. I'd be glad to hear what terms you have to offer."

He laughed in a melodious, insincere fashion.

"My dear young fellow, need I remind you that a guard was killed during that little operation of yours last month? And you ask me for terms—terms!"

"I cannot imagine there is anything very unusual in that, nor can I imagine that the rest of your men are content to work for nothing."

"What a very mercenary young man it is. Ah well, we shall see what we shall see. There is quite a number of documents to be looked over. When they are finished and I have studied your reports, then perhaps we can re-open this conversation."

Houseman had said nothing throughout this interchange. From his sour expression I could see he had no liking for me as an ally. He started to protest, but the Canon silenced him with a gesture.

There were many features of the situation that were far from being reassuring. But at least the scoundrels had some need of me. And I had a promising idea stirring in the back of my mind. Even so, I was not prepared for the cunning of the Canon.

After breakfast they bundled me into a car, not a Chevrolet. Houseman drove, with the Canon beside him. I sat in the back with Tiny. No attempt was made to conceal the route from me. Near Galbally we turned off on a mountain road, unpaved and of a width not much greater than the car itself. The road wound upwards in an easterly direction, the higher slopes of Galtymore lying two miles or so to the south.

We had climbed maybe a thousand feet by the time we reached our destination, which I had better describe in a little detail. There was a cluster of buildings, the main one a rough-hewn single-storey stone cottage, well built to resist the challenge of any storm. I soon discovered it to have three small box-like bedrooms together with two rooms each about fifteen feet square. One served as a parlour, the other as a kitchen. The parlour faced to the north, away from the high mountain. One could look down a long stretch of bog towards the head-streams of the river Aherlow. At the present season of the year this northern aspect was tolerable, but in winter it must have been an appallingly gloomy spot.

There were two main outbuildings, one a garage, the other a square concrete affair with a small, high window —the only guess I could make as to its function was most unpleasant, to say the least. It was a guess that subsequently turned out to be correct. The conveniences of the establishment were situated to one side of the garage, about thirty yards from the cottage.

The Canon led the way into the cottage and to the sitting-room. Houseman followed, carrying two large brief-cases, which he proceeded to unpack. A very considerable pile of papers was disgorged. The Canon indicated them with a gesture:

"This, you will agree, Mr. Sherwood, is a place where you can have absolute quiet, where you will be free from all unpleasant disturbance. Tiny will see that everything is in order and will prepare your meals."

"We still have not settled the terms of my employment, sir. This is an awful lot of work to undertake."

"No doubt, Mr. Sherwood, no doubt. And yet I think you will readily undertake it, for, you see, I am accustomed to get a little annoyed with clever young men. Tiny is quite extraordinary in his devotion to me, Mr. Sherwood. As you might guess, he simply detests people who give me cause for worry."

"I think you are going the wrong way about it, sir. Good scientific and mathematical work cannot be done under duress."

"An interesting proposition, but one that I have no doubt is quite false. I shall return here in about two weeks, at which time I shall expect to find that you have completed a set of coherent, accurate reports on the whole of this material."

Not to be done out of the last word, I remarked that I would do the best I could, but that it was asking a great deal. Throughout this conversation Houseman had fidgeted about in an uncomfortable way. Quite evidently he was worried by the Canon's glib smoothness. Equally evident, if Houseman had cause to be worried I had a double cause for anxiety.

Indeed I was beginning to feel that Tiny was to be preferred to the Canon, which was just as well, for shortly after midday Houseman and the Canon drove away. I was now left in a remote desolate spot, a wilderness of bog to the west, north, and east, a wilderness of rock and mountain to the south, alone with a monster strong enough to cripple me with utmost ease should he feel so disposed.

CHAPTER EIGHT

The End of P.S.D.

The idea that had occurred to me back at the farm-house was probably a good one: to play along with the Canon and his band of zanies until they acquired confidence in me. Then it would be natural for them to send me into I.C.E. territory, for I could ostensibly be of far greater use to them there. In this way I would fall back on P.S.D. organisation to get me to exactly where I really wanted to be.

But for a variety of reasons I now rejected this notion. It was partly Tiny, whom I detested, partly the desolate surroundings of the cottage, and more particularly the Canon himself. The word 'evil' I have never used before, because I never knew its meaning until now. The Canon was an evil man, no other word will describe him. Even Houseman, traitor and murderer as he undoubtedly was, seemed to feel a deep uneasiness in this sinister presence.

The monster had plainly been detailed to see that I applied myself assiduously to the task in hand. I saw that unless I took immediate steps he would have me at work from morning till night. Like a batsman facing a spin bowler I set about enlarging my territory. I divided the pile of papers into twelve separate groups, labelling them 'First Day', 'Second Day', 'Third Day', etc., all for the gorilla's benefit. When I had finished the work for the day I wrote a tolerable report and placed it on top of the appropriate heap. Then I resolutely refused to undertake any further work, preferring to spend the late afternoon and evening at my own books and reading the few magazines that had somehow found their way to the cottage.

Of course I could have written any sort of nonsense as far as the Canon himself was concerned, but I had a shrewd suspicion that he already might have independent reports on some of the documents. In fact he was probably testing me out. It could well prove suicidal to make a bad assessment of the stuff.

My notion was to lull the gorilla into a false security. I spent the first four days at the cottage. Then on the fifth afternoon I put on my boots and wind-jacket, openly declaring my intention of going off for a walk. I never expected that Tiny would allow this, and was amazed that he took no steps to stop me. Always with a cigarette hanging from his lips, he followed on behind.

I made no attempt to hurry, since it was all to my advantage to conceal my true pace. I move fairly quickly on a mountain, especially downhill. It seemed that a very simple plan would suffice to deal with the gorilla. All I had to do was to arrive at the summit of Galtymore some fifty yards in the lead, and then to set off like the wind down the southern slopes of the mountain.

Things turned out even better than I had hoped for. I reached the top almost 250 yards ahead of the monster. But was the business quite as easy as it seemed? I could have believed that Tiny was simpleton enough to allow me to escape were it not that the Canon plainly regarded him as a trustworthy jailer. And the Canon knew I had outwitted the Dublin police, he knew of the encounter with Houseman. I decided there must surely be a catch somewhere. Manifestly, I would be well advised to proceed cautiously. The upshot was that I decided to return to the cottage, on the argument that if Tiny were really stupid enough to give me a genuine chance of escape, then he would certainly be stupid enough to give me a second chance.

This was probably the best decision I have ever taken in my life. On the descent back to the cottage I was leading the way by as much as a mile, when from far above there came a shout. Tiny had been unable to restrain himself any longer. He came down the steepest part of the slope at a pace that I would not have believed possible. Leaping, zigzagging, and running, he was down on me in an incredibly short time. He stopped short and then slouched towards me lazily. He hit me a buffet rather than a blow, but it was enough to knock me down. With a singing head I raged at him, but all he did was to laugh in his maniacal, un-natural fashion. No word was spoken, but I knew it was a bitter disappointment to him that I had not tried to escape.

From now on I strained every wit and nerve to the problem of getting away from Tiny and the cottage. I was hopelessly outclassed in strength and in speed. It was futile to seek a solution along those lines. Two things had to be done: a close scrutiny of the cottage and of the ground outside, and a psychological study of

Tiny himself. It had to be a battle between brain and brawn, with the scales heavily weighted in favour of crude muscular power.

Gradually I came to realise that Tiny was possessed of a sly cunning, but of a cunning with definite limitations. There was a car in the garage, as I found in the course of my exploration (which I saw no point in attempting to hide, for the more complex my behaviour the harder it would be to distinguish my plan once I had arrived at it). During the evening meal Tiny produced a bunch of keys and a distributor cap. He showed them to me again with his appalling laugh, and then returned them to an inner pocket. So he knew of my discovery of the car, but he could not conceive that I would have any use for it other than its normal function.

At first I thought that only two considerations had any meaning for him; to prevent my escape and to show off his gigantic strength. But there was a third and darker thread to the pattern. Just as I hated his unreasoning power, so he hated me for the things that I was and that he was not. He was hoping that I would try to escape, for then he would have the excuse to pound me to a jelly. He was mortally afraid of the Canon, and so did not dare to assault me seriously without reason. Exactly like a cat with a mouse he continued to give me an apparent chance of escape, just as he had done on the mountain. Like a cat he moved swiftly and astonishingly silently.

I wove my plan from a few gossamer-thin fragments: a length of rubber tubing, a pile of stones where a small object could be concealed, an uncurtained window of the parlour, and a couple of empty whiskey bottles. I made my preparations without haste. Everything was ready by the evening of the tenth day, and it seemed that I had still plenty of time to settle my account with the gorilla before the Canon should arrive.

But events were to fall out in a vastly more shocking way than anything I could possibly have guessed. By what seemed a pernicious ill-fortune the monster managed to avoid the one small error that would have finally settled the whole business. Then in the late afternoon of the twelfth day I heard a car coming up the road from the valley. By an equal misfortune the Canon was returning two days before time.

Both the monster and I turned out to await the car. This time it was indeed the Chevrolet, now with its original number plates back again. There were four occupants: the Canon, Houseman, a man I had not seen before, and—Cathleen. They dragged her from the car. As she passed me, on the way to the square concrete building, our eyes met. No word was needed to convey the imploring message of those eyes. This was the 'trouble' that Cathleen had spoken of in the bus on the road to Athlone.

The Canon was in a false good-humour. He seated himself in the cottage parlour with a tumbler of whiskey and proceeded to examine his finger-nails while he asked me a series of questions about his precious papers. Tiny lounged against the door. Houseman and the other fellow were preparing supper in the kitchen.

"And now, Mr. Sherwood, to raise a rather different matter: I would be glad to hear the terms of your association with the girl out there."

I told him that I knew very little of Cathleen. I told him about our meeting in Longford, about our flight across the bog. There was no harm in this, since it was known to Houseman. I left out all mention of Michael. The Canon still studied his fingers.

"For a young man of your undoubted intelligence, you must realise that this is very unsatisfactory."

"The truth is not always sensational, sir."

Now he looked up with his placid smile. "You know, I think I will go over and ask the girl a few questions. She may be able to tell a straighter story."

"She can tell you nothing different, because I have told you the truth."

"Well, well, I shall soon find out. It will do no harm to put a few questions." He smiled. "In fact I shall quite enjoy an interview with such a very charming young lady."

I would readily have made a cheaper bargain with the Devil than that of Faustus. I would have asked nothing more than to drive my fists repeatedly into that insincere, smiling face. But Tiny was lounging there within a yard of me.

It was maybe three minutes after the Canon had left the room when I heard the first of Cathleen's screams. Tiny lounged against the door, a cigarette still lightly held between his lips. Every muscle of my body screamed to attack him, but I knew it to be worse than useless. He was simply waiting. His chance had come, and now he would break me. Desperately I looked for some weapon. There was an iron poker in the grate. As if he read my thoughts, Tiny moved away from, not towards, the poker. He wanted me to go for it.

It lasted for perhaps half an hour, perhaps only twenty minutes. The Canon returned, his face flushed. The 'trouble' had come and gone and I had failed miserably. True, it would have been futile. True, all our chances of escape would have gone. True, I had behaved for the best in the long run. But I had been afraid.

They brought in the supper, and forced me to sit down and eat it with them. I was nauseated as I somehow swallowed the stuff. But I had no alternative, for it was still a little too light outside to suit my purpose.

"I can see you do me a grievous wrong, Mr. Sherwood," said the Canon in a rich winy voice. "You imagine me to be a man who gives way to cheap, vulgar passions."

I made no reply, so he went on:

"I do not like my guests to be impolite, Mr. Sherwood." He nodded, and the gorilla came forward to fetch me a vicious slap across the face. "I fear that is scarcely as refined a gesture as I would have wished," the voice went on. "Not so refined as my own methods, Mr. Sherwood, but no doubt effective for all that."

This was the beginning of the fury that swept through me. The sickness was gone now, replaced by the same cold, shaking fury that had overwhelmed me on the road to Longford. I shivered in spite of the fire behind my back.

"Come, Mr. Sherwood, let me hear you say that you are indeed glad to hear of my restraint. Let me hear you say it!"

Again there came a stinging blow. I must have been

very white, and was now trembling quite openly. These symptoms were misinterpreted.

"Tiny! Take the lily-livered poltroon outside before he pukes all over the table."

The monster seized me by the coat, and hauled me violently and roughly from the room.

"Must get to the lavatory," I moaned, twisting somehow free from his grasp.

Once in the open air I made off along the stone pathway that led to the lavatory, the monster padding softly behind. I must explain that twenty yards or so from the cottage there were three upward concrete steps. I took these very quickly, knowing that Tiny would also accelerate his pace. It was now tolerably dark and I had to judge the position of his head by the light from the inevitable cigarette.

As he came up to the last step I unwound my body rather in the style of discus-thrower. My right arm was rigid and horizontal, palm downwards. With all the weight of my eleven stone behind it, and with a madman's added strength, the bony edge of my hand hit him right across the wind-pipe, a tremendous judo chop. He went down without a sound, for the throat muscles were untensed. Overbalancing, he struck his head a deep, dull blow on the rocky ground. He was quite silent when I reached him. In this he was lucky, for there is not the slightest doubt in my mind that had the wretch been conscious I would have battered him to death on the sharp edge of the steps.

Even as it was, I could only restrain with the greatest difficulty the mad rage that consumed me. My hands trembled violently as I sought and found the bunch of keys. Now all I had to do was to create a serious diversion. Then I could release Cathleen, and we could sneak away together in the Chevrolet. And I had just the right means for creating a diversion.

I found my pile of stones and uncovered the two whiskey bottles. They were just as they should be. Then I moved stealthily towards the uncurtained parlour window. When I was some fifteen feet away I flung the first missile with every ounce of strength I could muster. The effect was incredible. The bottle went through the upper left corner, carried clear across the room, bursting on the opposite wall. Petrol was sprayed over the room, some into the fire, and in no more than a second the whole inside was a holocaust. Realising that this was far more than a diversion, I threw the second. It went clean through the middle of the window. That would be the last cocktail that the Canon would ever drink.

One of the keys fitted the square concrete building, "Hello, Deirdre, are you all right in there?"

"Me hands are fastened," she whispered.

The fiend had left her tied across a sort of truckle bed, and it was some minutes before I could free the ropes in the black darkness. From her sobs I realised it would be easier for the girl to recover in body than in mind. She cried out as I rubbed her wrists to bring back the circulation. Then I put my coat around her shoulders and helped her out into the open air.

"Where are they?" she asked.

The cottage was now burning fiercely.

"That's their funeral pyre, my dear."

"You mean he's dead?"

I squeezed her arm. "He won't bother you again for sure."

"Thank God!"

I realised with a shock that she meant exactly what she said.

I was anxious to be gone, for there was no sense in delay. The fire might be seen from the valley, with possible complications—I had no wish to meet a car ascending the mountain road. It was improbable that the gorilla would recover his senses for many an hour to come, but there was no telling with such a creature.

The electrical circuits on the Chevrolet were new to me and it wasn't easy to join the right wires—I had no torch. While I fiddled with the thing, Cathleen sat huddled on the front seat. After what seemed an æon I got the engine started.

I found the mountain road very trying. The automatic transmission seemed to be pulling the car the whole time, instead of serving as a brake down the steep slopes. But like a man restored to prosperity, luck was again on my side. At all events I reached the main road safely.

The next priority was to get away from the immediate neighbourhood, and then to get some food for Cathleen. The best thing would be to strike the Cork-Dublin road at Mitchelstown. I hated to do this, because of the obvious risk, but there was no alternative, for only on the main road was I likely to find a café or restaurant.

I stopped just outside the small township of Kildorrery. But then I saw by the lights of the large transport café that it would be impossible to take Cathleen inside.

111

Her face was puffed with the ill-treatment she had received and her eyes were red. So I bought a substantial pile of sandwiches and took a couple of cups of strong coffee out to the car. Cathleen drank the coffee, and ate a sandwich under protest.

Luck was again on my side, for we managed another ten miles or so along the main road without being stopped by a patrol car. Then I made a complicated zigzag to the south, through Killawillin and thence on to a smaller road to the west of the Nagles Mountains.

Soon I found a place where the car could be driven off the road into a small wood. This was the right place to stop. We transferred to the spacious back seat and settled down for the night. By a kindly providence, both being dog-tired, we managed to get a fair amount of sleep. Towards morning it grew rather cold, so the engine had to be started and the heater switched on. I didn't mind using up the last of the petrol, since I had no thought of taking the car any farther.

We ate sandwiches for breakfast by the light of a greying dawn. Cathleen's appetite had improved so markedly that her physical recovery clearly would not be long delayed.

Our destinies were now closely interlinked. So there seemed no point in continuing to hide my real objective. When I had finished my tale she said very simply:

"If it is beyond the Barrier that you are going, then I will come with you. I am very tired of the life on this side."

We were now perhaps twenty miles from the Boggerath Mountains, a mere twenty miles from I.C.E. territory. Before we set out I searched through the car and made one important find, a pair of binoculars, which I stuffed into my pocket. Alas, my rucksack was now no more.

So it came about that we set out together over the low hills to the west.

CHAPTER NINE

First Encounter with I.C.E.

We took the first five miles quite slowly. The ground sloped gently downwards towards the Mallow-Cork road. Luckily we struck the road near a point where it was possible to buy simple provisions—bread, cheese, butter, matches, and apples. With a bit of string and a modicum of topological ingenuity it was possible to convert my long-sleeved sweater into an impromptu rucksack for carrying the food. It is strange how helpless one feels in wild country without some means of carrying provisions in a more or less effortless way—to attempt carrying in the hands is of course useless, and even the capacious pockets of an Irish jacket eventually reach saturation.

By now Cathleen was walking much more strongly. Even so, it was clear that the journey to the Barrier must take two days, fifteen miles the first day leaving the last five for the second day. In the mid-afternoon we chanced on a grassy hollow, and stopped there for a rest. I was in need of rest, for a reaction from the previous evening was now strongly upon me. Probably for this reason I suddenly had a compelling desire for Cathleen. When I took hold of her she made no protest. But this is a personal matter, out of place in an intelligence report, so I will say no more of it.

There were two smaller roads, both running roughly north and south, to be negotiated. A couple of miles farther on we found a tumbledown shepherd's hut. It was not an ideal place to spend the night, but at least it did not possess the squalor that a more complete building might have had. The walls were complete up to a height of three feet or so and there was grass on the floor.

While Cathleen collected a pile of heather to lie on, I set about sealing the walls against the wind by plastering the space between the stones with soft turf from the bog. Then we had a great stroke of luck. With the coming of darkness a mist enshrouded the moor. It would now be safe to light a fire. Not too far away was a considerable pile of dry cut turf, of the sort that can be seen everywhere throughout the west of Ireland. Very soon we had a large warming blaze, and we ate a simple, pleasant supper beside it.

The mist stayed down, which was good. It enabled the fire to be kept going throughout the night, for one thing. For another, it would now be vastly easier to sneak across into I.C.E. territory. I had abandoned my first idea of crossing during the night with Cathleen. This would be too strenuous. The mist gave us all the advantages of a night crossing anyway.

We pushed along steadily throughout the morning, choosing our route by compass the whole time. The ground rose steadily to a height approaching 2,000 feet, which was a sure indication that we were on the crest of the Boggerath Mountains. By lunch-time I was convinced that we must be across the Barrier already.

While we were eating, ragged patches appeared in the mist. At first I didn't realise our incredibly good fortune. It was only when the mist cleared for the second time that I noticed the huge turning aerials. They were about six miles away to the west, mounted on a tongue of high ground to the south of the town of Millstreet. The binoculars taken from the Chevrolet revealed their nature and purpose.

I cursed myself for a fool not to have guessed that I.C.E. would guard its border by radar, in much the same way that the British guarded their island during the late war. Just as we had detected the entry of enemy aircraft, so I.C.E. were detecting the entry not simply of aircraft, but of people too. Of course, it was a much harder technical problem to pick out a slowly moving person from a mass of ground reflections, but it was a problem that would easily be within the reach of this fantastic organisation.

"I'm sorry, my dear, but we'll have to turn back," I said to Cathleen. "We'll surely be caught if we go on."

When I had explained, she said, "It's to work inside the Barrier that I'm going. I care not whether I am caught or no."

"But they'll simply throw you out again, instead of letting you stay and work."

"Knowing what I know, I do not think so."

Looking at her as she then looked, hair fluttering in the same breeze that had blown away the morning mists, I did not think so either. St. Peter may turn her away from the Gates of Heaven, but I do not think so.

"They certainly won't let *me* in, my dear."

116

"That is likely enough. It would certainly be a great mistake for *you* to go on."

I was too amazed and aghast at the thought of our parting to make any reply. She took me by the hands.

"This is the way of it. Me heart tells me that everything between the two of us is wrong, it was all wrong from the first day." Impulsively she kissed me. "I won't be forgetting you, Thomas Sherwood. I won't be forgetting what you did for me back there in the hills."

The capricious mist was down again. In a flash she had darted away and was hidden with an agonising swiftness. I raced after her but I was too late. I called her name but my voice was choked by the white wall.

With tears in my eyes, I continued to shout her name, running the while in the direction she had gone. Then of an instant I saw that she had the rights of the matter, and like an automaton I turned back towards the east, back in the direction we had come from. A few moments before, we had passed this way together.

The mist was now swirling in patches. Once I had a clear view to the west and thought I could see Cathleen. But I did not turn again, for the case was plainly hopeless. She had the right when she said that everything between us was wrong. On the literal plane I had still thrown away her brother's estate—his wretched manuscript—and I had made no immediate move to save her from the torture of the Canon. Back in the hills, the trumpets of Florestan had sounded too late.

Bitterly, I saw that a consistent pattern runs through all the great love stories. The heroine must never be allowed to suffer physical distress, while above all the hero must be quite inept. If Orpheus hadn't been an inept ass, if he had recovered his Eurydice, who would have had the slightest interest in their continued marital bliss? Consider the simplicity of good solid muscle-men like Naisi and Tristram, tricked by the most transparent devices. Sorrowfully, I realised that my talents were more suited to the city page of *The Times* than to literature or grand opera.

Less remote ideas were crowding into my head. In response to them I put on the most tremendous pace as I ran downhill to the north-east. The sun and wind were fast dissolving the last of the mists.

I heard the helicopter while it was still some way off. I found a space between two boulders and dived into the heather face-down. With the lifting of the mist, the pilot was able to come quite low. The noise of his engines rose and fell consistently. I realised that he was systematically sweeping the moor strip by strip.

An intense roar made it plain that the fellow must be hovering almost overhead like some gigantic hawk. I made not the slightest movement. My rough clothing would blend with the heather. Reason told me that my camouflage was excellent. Emotion told me that I would stand out like a sore thumb.

The helicopter moved steadily towards the west. Now I could hear more noises and I knew that there must be more than one of the darned things at work. At length I heard distant shouts, and paradoxically I felt a fierce elation. For at last I knew I was dealing with an opponent who was both clever and rational. This was not an organisation of bunglers like poor Papa Parsonage. It was not an organisation that could be fooled by a pinch of magnesium powder or destroyed by a pint or two of petrol.

The I.C.E. plan was clever and straightforward. As soon as the mist cleared a fleet of helicopters had landed a squad of men who were now scouring the mountainside. The helicopters in the meantime were again aloft and were presumably in communication by radio telephone with the search party. If I attempted to move I would surely be seen from the air and the ground forces would instantly be instructed to pick me up, or off.

Yet the odds were pretty even. It isn't easy to search ten square miles or more of rough ground. And I had one enormous psychological advantage, for I must be outside the main area of the search. From the moment I had reached the eastern slope of the mountain I must have been hidden from the radar scan, and my very swift movement down the eastern flank must be unknown to the searchers. It was rather like looking for a small object in long grass—it becomes very difficult of discovery if it lies not quite where one expects.

I lay still and silent, hour by hour, in a dull afternoon sun. Many times I heard voices, and twice there was the sound of boots scraping over the rocks. Probably their owners were at least a hundred yards off, but I could have sworn they were nearer. I did not look up, or behind as Orpheus would assuredly have done. Cathleen must be caught by now in this finely spun web. I wondered how much she would tell them, probably not too much.

Slowly the day wore on to its close. The light was failing and at last it seemed safe to move. But beyond easing my aching muscles I did not shift from the safe position between the boulders. And it was as well that I maintained caution to the end, for a helicopter came over yet once more, using the very last of the twilight. It was brought home to me that I was not only dealing with a clever and powerful opponent, but with one that was implacable and entirely unrelenting.

The events of the afternoon had settled a point that had given me cause for worry earlier on. I could not understand why the frontier of I.C.E. territory was so poorly guarded. I had expected to encounter trouble even ten miles or more back from the border. But now I knew why it was made to look so easy: to encourage the unwary into an impossible position. Luck and the mist had saved me.

The advantage lay now on my side, however, for I was moving back into practically unguarded country. A forced march through the night would put me beyond the range of the frontier patrols, or at least so I hoped.

The hours of confinement between the boulders had provided an excellent opportunity for putting in some serious thought on this matter of I.C.E. There were three possibilities: to attempt to sneak through the wild areas of moor and mountain; to use the main routes, depending on bluff and trickery; to attack from the sea. I had now satisfied myself that the first alternative was difficult almost to the point of impossibility. Nor had I any confidence in the second. From all I had seen and heard of I.C.E. it was plain that this particular alternative should only be tried as a last desperate gamble.

So by a process of elimination it followed that I must now explore the chance of a seaward landing into the forbidden area. This at least had the advantage that there was no uncertainty about my next move. I must drive as fast as possible to the north-east, then to the north, swing around Limerick, and turn lastly to the west, to the coast of Clare somewhere in the region of Kilkee. There I could contact certain of our agents among the fishermen, agents whose names I had noticed in Colquhoun's notebook.

But all this was still very much in the future. For the present I had a long night's tramp ahead, which was not to be made any more pleasant by the thin, cold rain that started about nine o'clock. I will not attempt to describe the hours of slow walking, again by compass, for there was no moon or stars. It was essential to proceed with great caution. Several times I had to make detours to avoid extensive areas of soft bog. By daybreak I was still five miles or more to the south-west of Mallow.

I was sorely tempted to continue into the town, as I was now in great need of a hot meal. But this would manifestly be the height of stupidity. My boots and trousers carried certain evidence that I had just crossed the mountains and the marshes. And Mallow would be the first place where they would look for me, if indeed they were looking for me.

Soon I was to find that a search was being prosecuted with great thoroughness. A mile away I gained an extensive view of the main Dublin road, the road that Cathleen and I had driven along two days before. I had not watched for more than a few minutes before I saw that patrols were active everywhere. Cars and buses were being stopped. Every passer-by was being questioned. Possibly I could have crossed the road successfully, but the risk did not seem worth taking. The alternative was to lie up until dark.

My guess is that the search had nothing to do with I.C.E. directly. What presumably had happened was that I.C.E. had contacted the ordinary police, and the police were determined to make a real show of their efficiency.

The day was worse than unpleasant. The rain became heavy and continuous; I had little food left; and I was stiff and cold. Perhaps I should have continued with Cathleen? Perhaps I should have made a genuine offer of my services to I.C.E.?

But if I'd taken a job with I.C.E. I would really have been morally bound to drop the whole business, and this I was not prepared to do. It was the intellectual problem, the problem of finding out just what it was that made I.C.E. tick, that was really driving me along. It was the determination to solve this problem that hardened me to withstand the unrelieved misery of the day and of the following night.

The road was crossed safely once darkness had fallen. At first I intended to continue right through until dawn, but a strong cold wind went a long way towards knocking the stuffing out of me. I also crossed the northern road from Cork to Limerick at a point about equidistant between Mallow and Buttevant. About a mile to the west of Doneraile I stumbled on a stretch of woodland. The partial shelter from the wind tempted me to stop for the remainder of the night, it being then nearly three of an appalling summer morning. In a hollow, well sheltered by trees, I built as large a fire as I dared.

Outside the glow of the fire there was unrelenting

blackness. The police, or some curious farmer, or the Devil himself for that matter, might be lurking out there preparing to seize me. The wind, shrieking in the trees, sounded like the cries of the damned; and I was insistently reminded that two nights previously I had killed three men.

The rain began heavily again with the coming of dawn. Without food I started out north towards the Ballyhoura Hills. I made no great pace as I struggled over the rough bog. It was well past midday by the time I reached the maze of small roads to the south of Kilmallock. Come what may I was determined to seek the shelter of some wayside farm.

I had once decided that the right thing to do was to travel through Ireland like a tinker. Now I looked a tinker; wet, grimy, smeared with bog, unkempt. In truth the downpour was now to my advantage, for it provided some excuse for my appearance.

It must have been nigh on three o'clock when I came upon just the right sort of place, near a cross-roads.

"Ah!" exclaimed the woman, "and its yourself that looks as if you'd rolled the way through the bog from Kilfinnane."

"My car broke down up on Ballyhoura. I tried to put it right and got all dirty, I'm afraid."

She showed me to a small bedroom. The rain was beating a perpetual cannonade on the window.

"And have you no clothes to put on while your things are dried?"

"I travelled all through the night, and I'm pretty tired. So I'd be glad of a rest until supper-time. Could you dry my things before then do you think?"

"By the saints, it's a wonder that you young people do not all come to grief and disaster. But I'll send Paddy up to fetch your clothes in a few minutes' time."

Since she took me for a scatterbrain I decided to play in character.

"I forgot my razor when I left Dublin, and I've had so much trouble with the old car that I haven't thought about anything else."

"So it's a razor you want to borrow. Well, take good care you do not mistake it for your neck-tie." And she went out with a chuckle.

Quickly I slipped the money out of my trousers and hid it between the blankets, where no doubt it would dry out during the night. It took but a few moments to strip down. Paddy, evidently the husband, collected my dripping garments—is there anything more repulsive than dripping clothes? He left shaving soap, brush, and a cut-throat razor. I washed and shaved most gingerly. I was asleep almost before I tumbled into bed.

No more than a second later it seemed, Paddy was knocking to say that he had brought my clothes and that supper would be ready in a short while.

How good it was to put on warm, dry clothes again. I made the bed carefully, because of the money, before I went downstairs. A shock awaited me, for it was soon apparent that I had chanced not only on a farm, but on a boarding-house. There were other guests. One indeed was in the hall taking off oilskins and depositing fishing tackle. He was a small, stocky, humorous-looking man. And he was dressed as a canon of the Church of Ireland.

CHAPTER TEN

Journey to the Coast

All the guests sat down to supper together: the Canon, his wife and two children, two rather silent young women school teachers, and myself. When the introductions were made I claimed to be a research student in mathematics from Trinity, Dublin, not Cambridge. There was no other alternative, for by now it would be nearly hopeless to maintain that I was from England. My accent was an obvious difficulty, but I dealt with this problem by remarking that I had chosen Dublin as a place of study to make easier my intended entry into the services of I.C.E.

The danger of this tactic was that the Canon would almost certainly turn out to be a Trinity man himself, and he might trip me with some quite innocently intended question. I deliberately accepted the risk, however, because later on it was possible that I would be obliged to tell the same story to a more searching audience.

But this consideration was irrelevant, for no sooner did I mention I.C.E. than the Canon climbed upon a hobby horse.

"I would ask you to think very carefully indeed before you take such a step," said he.

I was a little startled by this remark; it was far too reminiscent of the false Canon. I took exactly the same line as before, saying that I saw nothing amiss with the activities of I.C.E. But now I received a far more coherent reply.

"Thirty years ago a great World War was fought. And it was fought to suppress just such a régime in Germany as we have here today in Ireland."

"There may be a parallel, sir, between the two cases, but if so I'm afraid it doesn't seem very obvious."

"The parallel is one in which a few men are able to impress their will on the rest. It may be that what is being done now is not the same in detail as it was in Germany a generation ago, but the principle is the same—a few at the top decide what shall be done, and the rest are forced into abject obedience."

The Canon's wife kept staring at her husband as if to stop so dangerous an outflow, but I had no intention of allowing this promising spring to dry up. For here was the first remark I had yet heard that seemed to bear some relevance to the real problem—the driving force behind I.C.E. Not to appear over-anxious, I steered the conversation slightly away from the matter in hand:

"I can't quite see why you go back thirty years for an example. Wouldn't the Russians serve the same case?"

The pudding was brought in at this point. Apparently the Canon was trying to lose weight, and with this course of the meal of little interest to him, he addressed the table freely.

"A most interesting point," he observed with relish. "The Russian system is no less obnoxious, my dear fellow, but it is subtly different. In Russia it is the creed itself that dominates; everyone must obey, high and low alike. But here in Ireland it is the high-ups themselves who decide the creed."

"Well, I suppose I must admit that I've never given much thought to who I'd be working for. Are these people at the top of I.C.E. really like Hitler and his gang? I mean personally."

"That I cannot answer, because I've never seen any of these people myself."

"Then . . ."

He interrupted with a wave of his right hand: "How do I know they exist—eh? Well, well, Mr. Sherwood, I've lived in the west of Ireland for almost twenty years. My work brings me into contact with many people, both inside and outside the Church. I saw the first small beginnings of I.C.E., and I've seen it grow step by step over the last ten years." Now he lifted a finger to emphasise his remark: "And throughout all this time I've never yet come across anyone employed by I.C.E. who really made the important decisions in his own job. They're all slaves, Mr. Sherwood. And that's exactly what I had in mind when I said that you ought to think very carefully before you decide to throw in your lot with these people."

"Then everyone must be acting under instructions, except of course for those who give the instructions. But have you any idea how all this obedience is achieved, sir? It almost sounds like an army."

"It is an army, precisely so. Quite literally, there is a considerable army at work behind the Barrier. But I hear darker stories whispered, stories of drugs, even of the use of bacteria. Men are said not to be the same after they have passed through the hands of this I.C.E. medical service."

"Now, John, that's quite enough!" exclaimed his wife. "And at dinner-time too," she added to cover her alarm.

The Canon's remarks had a considerable, if not profound, effect on me. The remark about drugs, although probably guesswork, did fit with Parsonage's statement that I.C.E. somehow managed to take very few agents into its employment. It had always puzzled me to understand how they could take on so many trustworthy scientists (from their point of view) and so few untrustworthy ones. Perhaps this was the explanation. At all events there seemed even less prospect of my being able to bluff myself into the inner councils of this incredible organisation.

"But one must agree that the ordinary people of Ireland are much better off now than they used to be," observed one of the teachers.

"One must admit that we are a good deal better off in some directions and a great deal worse off in others," answered the Canon.

"There was none of this police surveillance in the good old days," he went on, "no road patrols making endless inquiries, no day-time curfews, no harrying of every stranger in sight."

The teacher silenced, he turned back to me, at last changing the subject:

"Paddy tells me that your car is broken down. To-morrow I'll be going into Limerick for a few hours. Is there anything I can get for you?"

I thanked him and said that it was a new cut-out I

would be needing. Then after supper I went along to the lady of the house, Mrs. O'Callaghan, to ask if I could use the telephone. This done, I rejoined the others in the small sitting-room. Meanwhile the storm shrieked across the hill-side at the back of the house.

We built up the turf fire in a splendid fashion. Conversation never lagged, for the Canon turned out to be a supreme raconteur with a vast fund of spine-tingling stories. As the evening wore on, he progressed from ghosts seen at third-hand to ghosts seen at second-hand, and at last to ghosts that he himself could vouch for upon affidavit. The ladies became decidedly jumpy and, truth to tell, I was little better, for the re-emergence of the Canon had been distinctly unnerving. Here was the darned fellow again, not a charred bag of bones as I had supposed, but as large as life, telling a sequence of most ingeniously contrived supernatural stories.

It grew so hot in the small room that we opened the door. Still the fire burned brightly, and the rain pelted fiercely on the window. But there came a quite sudden moment of silence, and in that moment I saw from the corner of my eye a streak leap out from the bright-red pile of turf in the grate. In a flash it seemed to cross the room and to be out by the open door. Simultaneously there were piercing screams from the women; the teachers leaped across the room, ending their flight by pinning me completely in the bottom of my chair.

The Canon was white about the gills, for I suppose he achieved his skill as a story-teller by half believing his gruesome yarns.

"Now I wonder just what that could be?" he said with a commendable attempt at a calm unconcern.

"I wish I could look around a bit," I answered from the depths of my prison. With muttered apologies the school teachers removed themselves from the scrummage—their screams had amply compensated for their erstwhile silence.

"It may have been a cat," suggested the Canon.

"And how would a cat come to be in the middle of the fire?" countered his wife with implacable logic.

The upshot was that we—the Canon and I—went off to consult with Paddy. He assured us that the household kept no cat. In a shaking voice he insisted that it was no cat we had seen, but 'Himself', a view that the Canon, with his Protestant tradition, was not disposed to accept. The two of us tramped about the house but we could find nothing. We returned to the sitting-room.

"Ah well, it is no matter," remarked the Canon with ill-concealed anxiety. "It only shows that we should have been away to bed long ago." He pulled out a watch and flicked it open. With horror I looked for the imprint of a crown, but there was none that I could see.

The mists of sleep were gathering around me when there was a soft thud on the bed and a subdued miaow. It *had* been a cat, after all.

The wind fell during the night and the rain died to a light drizzle. The Canon was already at breakfast when I came down.

"It *was* a cat," he exclaimed in triumph. "I saw the little beggar on the stairs. It must have been seeking shelter from the storm, got into the chimney somehow, and skated down into the room—like an Eastern firewalker. Used up half its nine lives at one go, I'm

130

thinking." He laughed uproariously, and one of the teachers smiled rather wanly.

"Doesn't the cat have a very special significance in the practice of witchcraft?" I asked.

No one seemed to have the stomach to pursue this subject. The Canon indeed made a sharp turn-about: "I expect to be leaving for Limerick at about ten o'clock. Would you like to come with me, or can I pick up whatever it is you want?"

I said I would like to go along with him because I wasn't sure of the precise specifications of the cut-out, but that I would recognise it when I saw it.

The problem of explaining to Mrs. O'Callaghan that although I would be returning for my car I might not be returning to her house proved a little tricky. Fortunately she still took me for a scatterbrain to be humoured. So I managed to pay my due, and the Canon and I were away by 10.50 a.m.

About six miles south of Limerick we were stopped at a barrier.

"There's going to be a curfew," remarked the Canon with surprising complacency as he brought the car to a stop. A guard handed him a green slip of paper.

"Show this if you should want to go out again, sir. I expect you've got your papers with you?"

"Yes, of course," answered the Canon.

"And you, sir?" The question was addressed to me.

"Yes, of course," I replied.

The car picked up speed, and I was now trapped in a city under a daytime curfew where all strangers were hunted on sight. Not for the first time I deplored my lack of Irish identification papers. I had not wished to

carry such papers through the Dublin immigration—
and Seamus Colquhoun had been a broken reed. My
British passport would be a sadly inadequate document. The bad error had been to accompany the
Canon, but the lift to Limerick was nearly half-way to
my destination, and after the long miserable tramps of
the previous days I had allowed myself to be seduced
by his offer.

The Canon dropped me in the city, saying that he
would meet me again at about four, outside the Hilton
Hotel. I was sorry not to be able to say good-bye, for I
had no intention of being outside the Hilton Hotel at
four.

Without delay I sought out the Pan-American Air-
ways Office.

"I phoned yesterday, booking an evening flight to
London," I said to the clerk.

"What name, sir?"

"Sherwood, Thomas Sherwood."

He looked through his list, and then nodded in con-
firmation. "Could I see your passport, please?"

The misgiving I felt in handing it over was tempered
by the realisation that if I couldn't deceive an airline
clerk my case would indeed be hopeless. He glanced at
the photograph, ripped a counterfoil off my visa, and
handed the passport back. I suppose it must have
seemed very natural that someone with a British passport should be travelling to London.

He filled in a ticket and handed me a green boarding card. I paid for the ticket and asked:

"I noticed that you gave the fellow before me a
yellow boarding card. Why was that?"

132

The clerk dropped his voice. "We're instructed by the police to issue yellow cards to anyone who books a flight *after* a curfew is announced. You'll be all right with your card, sir. If I may give you a bit of advice I'd take an early bus out to the airport."

"Why?"

"Because the police like everyone with valid papers to get out of the city as soon as possible. That makes it easier for them to deal with the rest."

I climbed into the bus, thanking my lucky stars that by some sixth sense I'd had the wit to make a booking by phone the previous night. Almost the worst that could now happen was that I should find myself back in London. I hadn't really fulfilled my mission, but at least I'd have a tolerable story to tell. At all events I could make things a bit easier for anyone who should follow me.

It was probable that the police would notice that I was seriously off-beat so far as my itinerary was concerned. It was possible that I'd be held for questioning, but I couldn't see that any serious charge could be sustained against me. If they had grounds for really strong suspicion, then by good detective work there was little doubt that the whole course of my activities could be reconstructed, but there wasn't the slightest reason why they should go to such lengths. The most likely thing was that I'd be kept under close watch until I boarded the plane—that I wouldn't be allowed to slip away at Shannon Airport.

But I was saved by my companion in the bus. He was a little man, I judged of sixty-five, dressed in a blue wind-jacket that boasted the insignia of the New Jersey

Sno' Club. He told me that he was a small manufacturer from the town of Elizabeth, on his first visit to Ireland. When the police boarded the bus and were looking through the papers of the people in front of us, he began deploring this undemocratic activity in a loud voice. The police kept glancing at us, and heads were constantly being turned. Then the little fellow announced:

"And what's more, I haven't even been allowed to see anything of this I.C.E. business. From all I hear they've quite a few things that we could make use of back home in the States."

When the police reached us, he scowled at them: "Always hustling innocent people about. I'll have a few questions to ask when I get back to New Jersey."

In their anxiety to get at the old fellow, the guards somewhat naturally were rather superficial in their examination of my things. My green card, passport, and visa stamp were all they bothered with.

But they put the old chap's effects through a fine-tooth-comb, luggage and all. He never ceased to complain the whole while. He would write to his representative in Congress. He would get his wife to complain to the local women's club, a threat which two other male Americans assured the guards to be serious. The police retired at last, baffled men. I had the impression that I wasn't the only person in the bus to sigh with relief.

I was not averse to visiting the airport. On the face of it the easiest way into I.C.E. territory would be to land at the airport and then to take a small boat down the Shannon, eventually landing somewhere on the south bank. Quite apart from espionage, it was certain that profitable smuggling of I.C.E. products must be taking place through the airport. I once read the precept that wherever an economically profitable racket exists, it is a certainty that such a racket will receive full exploitation. If so, there surely had to be a route through Shannon Airport into I.C.E. Land.

Manifestly I should learn little from hanging about the main lounge, and it would be unwise to go roaming about the airfield until I knew the lay-out better. I had once worked for a month during the summer at a Strathpeffer hotel, spending my earnings afterwards in climbing the north-western Highlands, so I had some slight knowledge of kitchen and restaurant work. I knew that there are always cleaning jobs that no one likes to do, and I resolved to present myself as a new recruit to one of these jobs. I looked the part, something of a ruffian, and I knew that my credentials would not be over-anxiously surveyed. I knew also that it was unlikely that I would be given any job that brought me into contact with the public. Such jobs are always sought after, because of the chance of tips. It was unlikely therefore that I would run any risk of recognition by my companions in the bus.

I had a few suitably grimy sheets of paper taken from the Unicorn Hotel in my pocket. On one of them I scrawled the following ludicrous message:

This is a recommendation for Joe McCloy. He is a good man to have around.

Shaun Houseman,
Manager.

135

As I expected, the kitchen manager gave me a job. It was also the sort of job that I expected, and I set about it with the expected measure of inefficiency.

The time of my flight came and went, which gave me a rather greater degree of freedom. They might be looking for Thomas Sherwood, the precise, pedantic student, back there in the lounge, but they wouldn't notice rough, tough Joe McCloy unloading supplies outside the kitchen door.

I struck up the acquaintance of a boiler-man with the improbable name of Rory Parnell, and as he was able to find me very rough sleeping quarters I decided to stay on for a while in my new guise. I bought shaving equipment, a block of soap, and a clean shirt, the latter a villainous green check affair that looked quite the part.

It was three days later, some time after ten o'clock in the evening, when one of the waiters in the lounge pulled me aside.

"Joey, me bhoy," says he, "I'm after getting away for a few hours. I'm asking you to take me place like a true friend."

Since this was the first time we had spoken together, it was hardly clear how I came to be his true friend, but, nothing abashed, he went on: "And it's only a few wee orders for tea and coffee that you'll be getting, and maybe an odd glass of whiskey. And it's the tips you'll be pocketing."

I acted the part of wooden obstinacy to the point of stupidity, and only when the fellow had offered quite a considerable bribe did I accede. Either he was engaged on some nefarious activity, or he was visiting a girl; so much was clear from the size of the bribe. I put on his white jacket and took over.

The job was of course quite easy. Each new flight brought in a fresh crop of customers. In the abstract, I was surprised to see how much in the way of tips I was beginning to accumulate. No wonder these jobs were sought after, and no wonder their holders soon develop a bland and debonair confidence.

I imagine it must have been about 2.30 a.m. when I noticed a lone man signalling me from an alcove. I went over to take his order. Our eyes met, and I saw it was the New Jersey Sno' man, but now without his wind-jacket.

"And so we meet again, young fellow. Would you be good enough to step outside? I've a proposition to make and I don't want to be overheard by every busybody."

When we had found a quiet spot he went on: "If they think Hiram Q. Savage is going to be beaten by all these rules and regulations, well, they're going to learn something different, doggone it. I said I would see this I.C.E., and see them I will. I don't aim to become a laughing-stock back home in Elizabeth, no sir! But I'll need your help, young fellow."

"How can I help?"

"This is the deal. I have a boat all ready, moored in the river, right near here. I was mortified when I learned that I couldn't use a motored craft because of the noise, and I'm too old now to row very far."

"So you want me to row you across the river?"

"Right. Maybe I ought to say that I've got an idea that you aren't quite what you claim to be. Maybe I ought to go right back in there and tell 'em what I think. But I won't. I'll make you a fair offer instead."

We haggled for a few minutes, and in the end he offered me fifty Irish pounds to land him on I.C.E. territory. Two things were plain, one that he was very innocent and the other that he must want to get through the Barrier rather badly if he was willing to risk a hazardous river trip. For I had no doubt that, quite apart from the patrols that must be operating on the river, it would be a risky business to try crossing the currents of the Shannon during the night hours in a small boat.

Of course he might be an *agent provocateur*, but I thought the chance sufficiently slight for it to be worth while following his proposal a little further. My idea was to use his boat not to cross the Shannon at all, but to cross the wide mouth of the river Fergus. This would save a long detour by land. If I could get ashore in the neighbourhood of Kildysart, it would only be an easy day's walk into Kilkee.

"How do you know I won't go back in there and tell 'em about you?" I asked.

"When a man has lived as long as I have, and when he's done as much business as I have, he learns to be some judge of character. Either he learns or he goes out of business, and I'm not out of business yet."

"How did you get hold of this boat?"

"And he learns not to give his friends away. Don't forget that, young man."

"Very well. Let me see your boat."

I cached my white overall; it was obviously too conspicuous. We skirted the airfield, the little man leading the way with the sprightliness of a gnome. At length we reached the east-west channel that separates the mainland from an island to the north. Instead of a waiting posse of guards there was indeed a small boat moored near the western end of the channel. The oars, I noticed, were muffled. I reckoned it would be reasonably safe to assay the crossing of the Fergus estuary. This opinion was backed, I might say, by an extensive experience in the VIIth eight of the First and Third Trinity Boat Club.

There was no moon but sufficient starlight for me to have a clear view of my passenger as I sculled out from the shore. I saw him take a round instrument from his pocket, which I realised must be a compass.

"You're far too much to the west. Turn to my left until I give the word to stop."

Of course I was keeping to the west as closely as I could judge from the stars. I followed my original course without deviation. Now he pulled a second instrument from his pocket, however. I caught a glint of starlight on it and knew it for a revolver.

"There will be no nonsense. Turn the boat as I tell you."

Once again I realised that I had blundered. I set the boat on its new course, and said: "You realise that what you're trying to do is extremely risky?"

"Of course I realise it," he answered with scorn.

"But it's mad. It means going through Tarbert race."

"Of course it does, but the tide will be in our favour, if you get ahead and don't talk so much. Come on, take her along faster."

"You're welcome to try if you think you can do

139

better. I tell you it's crazy. There must be some far easier way of getting into I.C.E. territory."

"If there is I haven't found it, and I've been trying for a long time."

"That doesn't justify such an extreme risk."

"In my case it does. I'm an old man with not many more years to live. If I were in your position, young fellow, I might of course think differently."

"I do think differently."

"But you aren't doing the thinking," he answered with a chuckle.

Would he shoot if I changed course? Probably the risk was about the same as the risk from the river. If we made the trip to the I.C.E. shore I should be where I wanted to be. So on balance it was probably best to head down-river, but I didn't like the way the current was already beginning to grip the boat.

"Surely you weren't relying on a chance encounter to provide someone to row for you on this trip?" I remarked out of curiosity.

"Surely I was not," he replied. "The young man whose job you had taken at the airport contracted to accompany me. He received a considerable payment on account, so that when he refused to make good the bargain I was obliged unfortunately to deal rather severely with him."

"And how did you decide to put your proposition to me?"

Again the chuckle. By now the boat was moving at a fair pace, and the water was getting a bit heavy.

"I knew you were compromised. I guessed it already in the bus."

"Then I have you to thank for what you did. I'll repay you by offering a piece of good advice." I paused to readjust the boat, which seemed to have been pushed somewhat off course.

"And what is that?" he asked.

"Get rid of the pistol. In my experience pistols always cause trouble for their owners."

Again he laughed. "Well, well, we shall see."

It was now high time to stop talking, to give all my attention to the boat. We were approaching the main stream of the Shannon and there were a number of islands on the westward flank. We rounded them successfully and began to move down-river. I kept the boat on the northern side, for I wanted to avoid the central current as long as possible.

The tug of the current was indeed now very obvious, and I think we must have been approaching Foynes when a bright light flared up quite close to us. It was the searchlight of a patrol boat lighting up, not our little craft, but a larger one with a whole group of people—maybe six—in it. I recovered my wits quicker than the old fellow, and in a flash I brought the blade of one of the oars across the hand that held the gun. Luckily it was knocked into the water without going off. In an instant I turned the boat and pulled hard towards the northern shore.

It was a long grinding struggle but I made it by the first faint light of dawn. I was pretty spent and the old chap was growling that I had broken one of his fingers. Crossly I waded through shallow water and brought the boat in to land. As I helped him out I remarked:

"There was never any chance of getting through that

way. Don't you realise that the whole river is endlessly patrolled, and that those boats are equipped with radar? And, for another thing, I told you it was unlucky to carry a gun."

I fixed up the old fellow's hand as best I could—it wasn't seriously damaged, and got him on to the road for Kildysart. As soon as I decently could I stopped at a small farm for breakfast. Although this improved me a great deal, I was pretty tired, partly from the long row and partly from walking with wet feet. I was therefore quite pleased to see a motorist at work on his car—this was perhaps five miles from Kilrush.

"Can I give a hand?" I asked.

There was something vaguely familiar about this motorist. He was peering into the engine and he now looked up at me. The shock of seeing Houseman and the false Canon together on that fateful morning back at Slievenamuck had been no greater than this. The true Canon's belief in ghosts was vindicated. For here was none other than Seamus Colquhoun.

CHAPTER ELEVEN

Beyond the Barrier

"Well, well, Mr. Colquhoun. And how does it feel to be raised from the dead?"

"So it's Mister Sure-Fire, trying to be funny."

Of course the report in the *Irish Times* hadn't mentioned Colquhoun by name. I had simply jumped to what seemed a reasonable conclusion. I did what I could by way of explanation.

"Now isn't that just like Mr. Clever Dick? Was there nobody but meself in the whole of Dublin on whom the guards might be wanting to set a hand?"

"The time and place seemed singularly appropriate."

"They did, did they?" Colquhoun rose threateningly, a spanner in his right fist. "And where would me note-book now be?" he asked.

"With Mr. Houseman of the Unicorn Hotel, Longford, of course."

"You shrunken pin-wit," he roared, "you should have found out that the man was sold to the Divil!"

"As a matter of fact I did find out, but orders are orders. Mine but to do and die, you know."

"You'll be dead before your time," he growled, taking a step towards me.

"Quit fooling, Colquhoun. If you don't drop that

spanner I'll knock all Hades out of you. When I found Houseman had thrown in his lot with the P.S.D. crew, I burned the book. It's fertilising some farmer's field."

He put down the spanner and leant against the car.

"Is that the truth of it?"

"Of course."

"What a shocking pity you didn't keep it!"

"Stop being a pin-head yourself. I might have been caught half a dozen times this last three weeks. Did you want the police to get hold of the damned thing?"

"No, I suppose for an amateur you did the best you could," he conceded.

"What news do you hear of Houseman?"

"The best," he answered. "There is a good chance that he may have departed from this vale of tears."

"How did you come to hear that? I had quite a bit of trouble with the man."

"Listen to little Mr. Wren, the King of Birds. Listen to him sing! He had trouble with the man!"

"It looks as if you'll be having quite a walk, Mr. Colquhoun, unless you can get your car running again."

"It is a strange tale. A horrible huge mountain of a fellow appears one day in the town of Tipperary with a cracked skull."

"Which strikes me as one of the most unlikely statements I've ever heard."

"I'm telling you again, and for the last time, not to be always interrupting me. As I was saying, this horrible fellow appears in Tipperary with multiple fractures of the cranium. What makes this such a noteworthy incident is that this same fellow is known to be bodyguard to the moguls of P.S.D."

144

"Which doesn't seem to me to make the story any more probable. Surely you can see that for yourself?"

Colquhoun was now getting thoroughly angry. But he ploughed determinedly on:

"A strange story this fellow tells when at last they get him to talk."

"Who gets him to talk?"

"The guards, of course. Then up they went to a high mountain farm, where they found a most terrible scene, a scene of shocking debauchery. Apparently the whole party was carousing and became so drunk that the place was set on fire, and all were burned to ashes before anyone could notice the approach of death."

"Colquhoun, you're a grammarian's nightmare. Don't you think it would be a little more profitable if we were to get the car started? Was Houseman one of the party?"

"That is not known for certain, but it is my belief that he was. Little was found to identify the Divil's party, except this."

I could not restrain a cry of astonishment. The object Colquhoun held in his hand was a portion of a watch. The metal had partially melted, but an imprint of a crown could still be distinguished. Colquhoun clicked his tongue in a deprecating fashion.

"What would you do without your nursemaid, little feller?" he said. "I had to remove the metal frame of a rucksack from that fire, one that was made in England. The guards might have been a wee bit curious about that rucksack."

He roared with laughter, for I suppose I looked uncommonly like a stuck pig.

"But . . ." I began.

"How did I find out? Your young lady friend, of course, Mr. Know-it-all. She got in touch with me after that business back at Longford. Unfortunately she wouldn't wait to have me to join her before she was after trying to hit Houseman for six, and got herself caught for her pains. I had to follow on several days behind, but I kept your trail all right."

"Did you expect me to head in this direction?"

"Don't flatter yourself that I'm consumed with interest about what you may be doing, although I'll allow that I'm a bit curious to know how you managed to split that feller's headpiece."

"And I suppose you know what happened to Cathleen?"

"She's gone to take her brother's place behind the Barrier. And would there be anything else you might want to know, me infant prodigy?"

Was this possible? Did these people spend the whole of their lives living some part or other?

"I suppose you're trying to pull together the remnants of your scattered organisation?" I asked.

"And by what mighty mental process did you arrive at that conclusion?"

"I didn't, I'm asking."

"Then you may ask."

I moved over to the car. "What's wrong?"

"The engine isn't firing properly."

"I'll bet it isn't, and not only the engine, if you ask me."

"I'm not asking," grunted Colquhoun, waggling his spanner in a hopeless fashion.

146

I got to work on the machine. Some minutes later I straightened my back, now rather stiff from the rowing, and said:

"It's no use, your cut-out has gone."

"What does that mean, Jacko?"

"It means that you'll have to get a new one and get your battery charged, it's hopelessly flat. And it means you'll have to walk. Got any dry socks?"

"What should I be wanting dry socks for?"

"You're not, it's me that's wanting 'em."

Colquhoun complained so strenuously throughout the walk into Kilkee that his sentiments became quite contagious. In spite of the socks, I was quite tired by the time we arrived there. During the last mile or so my companion became silent, however. With complete assurance he strode into the little fishing port. Although to my eye an incongruous figure, he seemed to attract no notice as we walked through the groups of men and animals that thronged the streets. An occasional lorry or car hooted its way through the mêlée. This was plainly the Ireland of old. Only a few miles to the south, across the estuary of the Shannon, lay the most modern industrial development that the world had yet seen.

Colquhoun turned down a side-street, took a crooked path to avoid dogs lying on the pavement, and stepped inside an open door. Although I didn't realise it explicitly, I must have allowed him to take the lead, for I followed without question. It never occurred to me that the Guards might be waiting for us.

They were not, but our entrance into the house nevertheless had a small touch of drama about it. A powerfully built dark-haired young fellow, obviously a fisher-man, was at a very late breakfast. A good-looking girl seemed busily engaged at a fireside oven. We were greeted with looks that might possibly be translated into these words: "The past is back to haunt us. Dear God, must we go on being persecuted for ever just because we were once foolish enough to make a small, wee mistake?" Manifestly, Colquhoun and I were not welcome.

I took no immediate part in the following conversation, which at the same time proved to be both animated and disjointed. Stripped of the unnecessary verbiage that appeared to be inseparable from any talk with Colquhoun, the situation was plainly that Mike and Mary O'Dwyer, husband and wife, had worked for Colquhoun in the past, but now were anxious to break an embarrassing association. Indeed they had been hoping until our arrival that the connection had come to an end in a natural way with the disintegration of Colquhoun's band. Colquhoun for his part was anxious to re-forge his chain, and O'Dwyer was a necessary link, for it appeared that O'Dwyer was the acknowledged expert at getting agents into I.C.E. territory. In short, O'Dwyer was exactly my man.

It wasn't difficult to understand O'Dwyer's point of view. He owned his boat, and there was a ready market to the south for all the products of legitimate fishing. He could be entirely prosperous without risk. Indeed it was obscure why he had ever become involved with Colquhoun in the first place. Maybe that was how he came to own the boat, or maybe it was the excite-ment.

At all events the excitement had no appeal now for O'Dwyer.

"I tell you it just cannot be done, Mr. Colquhoun," he exclaimed repeatedly. "It's not like the old days when I could take the boat into any beach or cove. Every place is now watched by electric waves. Even at night the patrol boats are able to hunt down anybody who comes within five miles of the shore. And there are submarine nets across all the bays, so that underneath the water there is no way either."

I thought it time to join in: "This is all true except in heavy weather. When the sea-waves are high they reflect the radio transmission like a whole mass of little ships. Then it's quite impossible to separate a true ship from the sea-waves. That's why an attempt from the sea is much more likely to succeed than one from the land—always provided it's made in bad weather."

"Is it that you're supporting his argument?" exclaimed Colquhoun.

I felt that much more of this sort of remark would drive me straight to the madhouse, for one simply could not discuss any question with Colquhoun in a normal way.

"I'm not supporting and I'm not denying an argument," I exclaimed with some exasperation. "I'm not concerned with argument, I'm *telling* you what the situation is."

Mary O'Dwyer set an appetising plateful in front of me, and I realised that at any rate a part of my irritation was probably due to hunger.

"Maybe what you say is right enough," said Mike, drinking tea from a large mug between his words. "But

149

who is to take a boat in heavy weather into such a coast? Nobody but a madman, I'm thinking."

"Could you manage to carry a small motor-boat without its being seen?" I asked.

"It might be done."

"Then there's one way in which the business could possibly be managed. Instead of carrying a passenger right in to the coast, you might set him down at sea in the motor-boat, maybe four miles or so out. Then you would simply leave it to the passenger to find his own way safely."

O'Dwyer looked curiously at me.

"All very fine, except for one thing."

"And what's that?"

"The sea. Do you know what bad weather on the Irish Coast is like? Two winters ago a lighthouse keeper was drowned, washed by a wave off the rocks at a place certainly 150 feet above the normal sea level."

"Then we're talking at cross-purposes. I'm not asking for a storm with waves fifty feet or more in height. Waves of about fifteen feet would hide an ordinary fishing-boat from the I.C.E. radar. Waves of as little as six feet would hide a small motor-boat."

O'Dwyer was still not convinced.

"It would be very risky for a stranger in a small boat to attempt a night landing, even with the sea calm."

"*You* wouldn't be taking the risk."

"That is true, but I see the danger. And where would I be getting the motor-boats? Every time, a new one would be needed."

"That's Colquhoun's business. If he wants your help, he ought to supply the equipment."

"And isn't it nice for me to have me affairs all fixed and decided by a young cock-sparrer? So I'm to supply the equipment, am I? And what are you going to supply, Mr. Smart-Wits?"

"I'm going to take the risk. If you'll get the motor-boat, and if Mike will take it on, I'll undertake to see whether this business can be managed or not."

"And now I know how a toy-soldier gives his orders. Just like little Mr. Twopence-Ha'penny here."

I don't often lose my temper, but now I quickly leant across the table and banged the inner edge of Colquhoun's plate with my fist. The plate rose like a wooden 'piggy', turned over in the air, and deposited the food down the front of his suit.

"If you'd really like to learn how I split that fellow's skull, I'd be happy to give a demonstration," I said.

Colquhoun's dislike of me was, I thought, the dislike of the professional for a cocky amateur. And he was smarting sufficiently under recent reverses to be glad of some showdown that he might hope to win, for I had no doubt he was pretty handy with a knife. But O'Dwyer gave him no chance.

"I'll have no brawling in the house," O'Dwyer roared. He was amply big and active enough to beat the daylights out of the pair of us, and I couldn't help wondering why Colquhoun's sudden appearance had disturbed him in the least degree. How does an Intelligence Service keep its agents? Through the fear of being denounced?

I stood up to go. "Thank you very much for the meal, Mrs. O'Dwyer. I'm sorry I made such poor use of some of your food."

"And where would Mr. Suck-and-Blow be going?"

"To buy a couple of pairs of socks," I answered, biting back an obvious retort.

I bought the socks and a bag of apples, which I munched strolling about the pier looking over the fishing-boats. Except for riding a real storm they appeared eminently seaworthy. There was a seat against the sea-wall. Before I realised it I was asleep in the sun. A somewhat unkempt figure placidly snoozing would hardly excite any grave suspicion in the breasts of the local constabulary, not in this corner of Old Ireland, with its mingled scent of fish and horses.

I revived some three hours later, feeling that I needed to stick my head under a water tap. The first thing to do, I thought as I strolled back along the pier, was to get a job on one of these boats; not likely to be much difficulty in that, because there was a shortage of labour everywhere, so much was being absorbed by the industry to the south. Perhaps I should try O'Dwyer first. At least there'd be no danger of his giving me away to the police. In any case I must return to his house to pick up my things.

When I got back to the O'Dwyer home I found that Colquhoun had left—an indescribable relief, for I was really very tired indeed, what with only one proper night's sleep in an extremely trying week. It worried me out of proportion that I couldn't return the socks.

"Would you be needing a new hand, Mike?" I asked.

"And what would I give out about ye?"

"That I'm a student from Dublin, working on a summer job for a few weeks. Name, Thomas Sherwood."

"How d'ye do, Tom me bhoy. Any experience?"

"Very little, I'm afraid, a few trips out from Bideford."

"Well, well, that will not be unlike a student from Dublin," he said with a chuckle. "Old Slugeamus has a spare room where ye can sleep. Ye can trust him with the life of ye. I'll be after showing you the way to his cottage."

"Ah, he cannot go there," objected Mary O'Dwyer. "They say the flies is as big as bees around his cottage."

"Away with ye, woman. He'll be as right as rain," answered Mike.

Seamus McCarthy, known as 'Old Slugeamus', turned out to be a more or less permanent member of O'Dwyer's crew, a fellow who managed to fish all night and drink all day in a most amazing fashion. At first I thought that he never slept, but later I discovered that even in sleep he did things by excess. When the weather was bad, he would often sleep the clock around, twice. His cottage was in indescribable confusion, a pulsating scene to which a vociferous parrot made due contribution. In the two weeks I spent at Kilkee I managed to get no more than a superficial semblance of order into the place. In any case I suspect that the task would have proved rather like painting the Forth Bridge; that a stage would have been reached where Slugeamus spread wreckage and destruction as fast as I was able to establish order. This stage was never reached, Slugeamus always being several orders of magnitude ahead of me.

In appearance he was fairly tall, stoutish, with sandy hair and complexion to match. He wore a huge black sweater, rubber boots, and cap. I suppose he had a shirt too, but I never saw it, since the roll of the sweater came high on a short neck.

I must have made a great hit with him. One evening, in his cups, he produced a small waterproof canister.

"Taken from a stiff," he announced proudly.

"Who, what, and where was this stiff?"

"Santa Maria, hear him talk, like a powerful great book! This feller was all swelled up by the sea, been bobbing and floating out there a dozen Masses, no less."

"He means that the corpus had been afloat for nigh on two weeks," translated O'Dwyer.

"Bobbing like a wee porpoise between the rocks," agreed Slugeamus, grampus-like.

"And what was in the canister?"

"Aren't we waiting to hear what the professor has to say?"

This seemed a cue, so I managed to open up the thing. Inside was a small roll of paper. Written on it was a short cryptic message:

Twin helices. Senses opposite.

The only twin helices I could think of were the helices of the Crick-Watson theory of DNA. But why should a 'corpus' be bobbing around the ocean carrying a message that related to the structure of nucleic acid? In any case the statement 'Senses opposite' was obscure. This seemed to be just another of those minor mysteries of life that one is not destined to solve. But in thinking so I was wrong.

After the shocking weather of the previous week it would have been reasonable to expect heavy seas. Perversely, day after day was now fine and the sea quite calm. The rhythm of a new life became established. We would leave port about an hour before sundown, the boat driven by a powerful diesel engine. As one looked back towards the land, the whole bay would seem to be overflowing, like a blue basin filled to the rim.

So we would throb our way out towards the great glowing red ball that hung low in the western sky. I would look assiduously for the 'green flash' at the last moment of the declining sun, but never with certain success. Then would come the casting of the net, and the inspection of lobster pots. Strange that our modern industrial civilisation seems to have contributed so little to the technique of fishing. The locomotion of the boat is modern, of course, but the actual method of fishing is largely unchanged.

During the night we would cook some succulent fish, or a lobster, which we would wash down with mugs of tea, our digestions being good. After dawn the net would be taken in, and the fish sorted into boxes during the journey back to port. Back at the jetty would come the handling of the boxes on to the quay and into a waiting lorry. And on occasion the net would have to be mended, an art in which I was instructed by Slugeamus. I don't think that I could ever match the deft swiftness of his fingers, even if I were to practise for a generation.

But it was easy to see how the method of handling the boxes might be improved. It seemed possible to mount a temporary derrick on one of the masts, and then to use a pulley block to lift the boxes directly from the hold of the boat on to the back of a lorry. I mentioned the idea to Mike O'Dwyer.

"Aye, that's the way of the Picts. But how would it be worth while with a catch as small as ours?"

"But there's every reason to be thinking of increasing your catch, now that there's no lack of a market."

"And that's true enough," he agreed.

It came about that there was never any opportunity to put this idea into practice, however. One day Mike showed me a small motor-boat about ten feet long, well designed to avoid flooding of the engine by breaking waves. I concealed my curiosity as to where the new boat had come from, for I had no real doubt that it was a peace-offering from Colquhoun. Without unnecessary discussion I spent a couple of afternoons taking down and reassembling the motor. Although I would dearly have liked to make a few trips into the Bay, it would manifestly be foolish to advertise either the boat or myself unduly.

Shortly afterwards we had news on the radio of heavy weather blowing up from the south-west. Only three other boats put out along with us on the fateful night. The rain was falling and the quay was almost deserted, so that Mike decided simply to tow the little craft behind us. Even so it did not entirely escape notice. A jibe from another crew was met by Slugeamus:

"What should it be, me bhoy, but our lifeboat?"

I hoped that he had the rights of the matter.

Our plan was straightforward. A glance at any map of Kerry will show that a boat may be taken well into Dingle Bay without ever coming within five miles of the shore. Somewhere south of Dingle the motor-boat would be released, and I would head on a north-east course, using the sea and the wind to set me on the northern shore of the Bay, a shore mainly without cliffs.

The trip was a very long one for O'Dwyer, almost a hundred miles each way. Reckoning on a maximum speed of twelve knots, this meant at least sixteen hours of continuous pounding, even if the weather got no worse. It meant that he couldn't hope to regain the shelter of Kilkee harbour until ten or eleven the following morning. I mention this to exonerate O'Dwyer from all reasonable blame for what was to follow.

The weather worsened. We were now south of the Shannon, somewhere on ten miles to the seaward of Kerry Head. It was a difficult decision. Should we turn back, or should we go on, now that we were so close? We decided to go on, O'Dwyer declaring that he would have the sea and wind with him on the return— and if a storm should be blowing up he would run for Dingle. The crew would then of course be arrested, but on a fair claim of bad weather he would surely be eventually escorted back to waters north of the Shannon. In the latter case I would leave the trawler and head for the south side of Dingle Bay.

About four in the morning O'Dwyer at last decided that the moment of parting had arrived. He also declared that he would attempt to return by the way we had come. Slugeamus put a wet arm around me: "Let's hope we won't be weeping for you," he shouted.

The sea was heaving most unpleasantly. We pulled the little motor-boat in as near as we dared. By the light of an electric torch it seemed nearly impossible to board her. One moment she lay in the trough of a wave, the next half-way up the trawler's side. But this was the moment I had been asking for, so there was no use fussing. The thing to do was to jump when the boat was at its highest.

I tied a rope about my waist in the fashion of a mountaineer—I did not wish to be too encumbered by a lifebelt. O'Dwyer was at the wheel, attempting to keep the best distance between the trawler and the motor-boat. So I gave the rope to Slugeamus, making sure there was the right amount of slack. Then I stood, torch in hand, watching the boat coming up, down, up, down, up again for the last time, and I jumped. Painfully I moved my arms and legs in turn to make sure that I was only bruised.

As soon as they saw I was safely in and able to move, O'Dwyer allowed the distance between the craft to increase, but he didn't give the order to cast off until I had the engine started, which in my cold, numbed state took quite a while.

The little vessel bobbed like a cork. No radar could detect me, at least that much was quite certain. It was essential to run the engine slowly, so I concentrated simply on maintaining direction—the gathering storm from the south-west would drive me in, for I felt sure now that a storm was coming.

I steered by compass pretty well to the north, rather than to the north-east, since I felt that the sooner I got away from the middle of Dingle Bay the better. There can be no doubt that I owe my life to this slight change of plan.

No words can describe the stark horror that can be compressed into a single moment of time, so I shall not attempt any gaudy description. The plain facts are that I was cold, bruised, soaked to the skin, sick from the motion of the boat, when after an hour or more I heard above the wind the sound of waves breaking ahead. Nor was it the sound of waves breaking on a beach, but the roar of great waves hitting the base of a high cliff.

There was nothing to be done but to turn about and to give the engine full throttle. With the thought that O'Dwyer had taken me too far in and that I must be somewhere in the region of Annascaul, I turned to the west. Now I was side-on to the waves and it was only a question of time before the engine would be swamped.

With the feeling that all was surely finished, and that O'Dwyer had given me fair warning, I now concentrated only on finding calmer water and on keeping away from the cliffs. I suddenly realised to my surprise that the engine was still firing and that the motion of the boat was distinctly less. Checking on my compass, I found I was heading south-south-west, out to sea again! I was too confused to perceive the true explanation of this singular situation. I knew only that every minute was carrying me into calmer water.

The night was intensely black and I had no warning, except perhaps the clearer note of the engine. The boat struck hard against a rock. I was too shaken to make a move and it wasn't until the heaving sea had taken the vessel off and then impaled it for a second time that I made a frenzied leap for safety. I kicked furiously, banged my knees and tore my nails, and at last found myself on a rock ledge with the water sucking below.

Slowly I edged up the rocky wall. If I could climb

ten feet or more I might be safe from a rising tide. Soon I found myself crawling rather than climbing. A few moments later I felt grass under my hands. Evidently I had reached the flat top of some small rocky outcrop. I continued to crawl until the noise of the sea became muffled. Then I lay down, exhausted, to wait for dawn.

Dawn came. I saw a long rising stretch of grass to the south. Shivering violently, I went cautiously back to the sea. The apparently steep cliff resolved itself into a very easy climb, for the boat had crashed in a comparatively shelving rocky bay.

Slowly I trudged up the turf and as I did so I came more and more out of shelter into a driving wind. The storm was still blowing, still blowing out of the southwest.

With the strengthening light the explanation of the night's events became obvious—I could see cliffs rearing high into low clouds, three or four miles away to the north-east. They were the cliffs of the island of Great Blasket. O'Dwyer had been more delayed by the wind and sea than he realised and had started me not south of Dingle at all, but a full ten miles farther to seaward. And I was now on the low flat island of Inishvickillane. It was clear why I.C.E. had discontinued the lighthouse on the Tearaght. Had it been working we should never have made this mistake.

Feeling that somewhere I had heard of a similar situation, I began to explore the island. It was maybe three-quarters of an hour, but it seemed longer, before at last I found a substantial house. I walked towards it, gloomily realising that although I had got myself successfully beyond the Barrier my position was completely hopeless. Then I remembered it was in Stevenson's *Kidnapped* that David Balfour had simply been able to walk off Earraid when the tide went down. But there would be no walking off Inishvickillane. My boat was a wreck, and I must give myself up, right at the beginning. I was 'run-out' without receiving a single ball.

CHAPTER TWELVE

The Cliffs of Inishtooskert

It was pointless to struggle further, cold, wet, and hungry. 'I might as well give myself up immediately,' I thought as I walked up the winding path to the stone house. Whoever lived here wasn't going to enjoy being wakened at this early hour, but this was clearly the occasion to be hanged for the sheep rather than the lamb.

In response to my hullabaloo, the door was opened by a sleepy-eyed, middle-aged fellow in a dressing-gown. I suppose I had expected to find a local small farmer, tending a flock of sheep with a little fishing as a side-line, and the story I had prepared was designed for the consumption of such a person. It was accordinly very disturbing to hear an American voice:

"Where the hell are you from?"

"Oh, I'm more or less an ordinary devil washed up by the sea."

"Well, in that case come inside. But how did you get here?"

"From the sea, as I've just said."

"But for God's sake, you don't mean you were shipwrecked, on a night like this?"

"There's no other way I'd be standing here. Our boat went down."

"How many of you are there, for heaven's sake?"

"Two others drowned in the sea, I'm thinking."

My manner must have been suitably grave, for in truth I was seriously worried about Mike and Slugeamus. The great thing was that they could always stand in behind Brandon Head. This would give shelter from the south-west, so that the odds would be in their favour.

"Well, we must look for 'em without delay."

"And what would I have been doing this hour past but looking for me friends?"

The man left me for a moment to return with a dressing-gown.

"Take this robe. The bathroom is the second door to the right. When you're through, come into this passage. It leads straight to the kitchen."

With muttered thanks I did just as he advised. It was a terrific relief to get off my salt-drenched clothes. I had to run the water quite cool at first to avoid smarting. At length, feeling very tired but very much better, I returned to the kitchen, wrapped in the dressing-gown and carrying my dripping things. There was the smell of frying bacon.

"I've got an air-search started. There's no reason to give up hope yet."

This was a nuisance, for I had no wish for Mike to be spotted. Several things were clear. From the excellent fitments in the bathroom and kitchen this was no farmhouse. Rather was it a farmhouse converted into a luxury residence. Plainly I had stumbled on a comparatively influential person, as I could judge from his last remark. Equally plainly, my story would sound painfully thin, but I was sufficiently exhausted to be past caring.

As I ate ravenously, the fellow looked me over curiously.

"I'm baffled to understand how you came to be at sea. Where are you from?"

"Kilkee."

This shook him, as I expected it would.

"But that's fifty miles outside the Area! How did you ever get yourself as much lost as this? Boy, you're in the wrong ball-park!"

"Poaching."

"I'm sorry, I don't get it."

"The best sole on the coast is to be found in Dingle Bay. When the weather's bad, but not too bad, we often come down here to get what we can. It doesn't pay really, but it's a sport with all of us fishermen outside the Barrier."

"You weren't expecting this storm, I suppose."

"No sir. The reports were of a choppy sea and a strong breeze, but no storm."

"All this is news to me."

I had no doubt at all of this. It was a preposterous story, but my presence there at last gave it some slight substance. If this amiable fellow didn't like it he was welcome to think up a better for himself. The true explanation looked preposterous too.

My host produced a pair of pyjamas and showed me to a bedroom, as soon as I had finished breakfast. It was now about 7.30 a.m. I tumbled into bed and fell asleep.

It was dark when I awoke. With the light switched

on, I found that clothes—not my own—had been put in the room while I slept, and also a razor, soap, and toothbrush. By the time I was ready to go downstairs I looked reasonably respectable, pretty well for the first time in the last two months, in fact since I left Dublin.

Perhaps I should explain that there seemed to be six or more bedrooms upstairs, but that downstairs, apart from the kitchen and the bathroom I had used in the morning, there was just one single very large room.

I made my way to the latter room, and was very surprised and disturbed to find six people there. There was the American of the morning; two girls and a man, all of curiously mixed colouring, dark skin, light hair; a third girl, a good-looking genuine blonde; and a third man, apparently of about thirty.

There were no introductions. The third man said:

"So this is your fellow from the sea, eh, Homer?" Then he turned to me with tones of command:

"You may go into the kitchen and cook whatever you fancy."

"Thank you, sir."

I left for the kitchen feeling well pleased, in spite of this abrupt and contemptuous dismissal. The genuine blonde followed me.

"I'd better show you where the things are to be found," she said.

It was a little embarrassing to display a hearty appetite when my companions were supposed to be entombed in a watery grave. Worse, the blonde began to ask questions about how I came to separate from the two of them, and about the final landing on the island.

165

I took the line of answering in monosyllables, and blew my nose vigorously. Eventually the girl left, so that at last I was able to settle down to a really good meal.

There were indications that the storm was blowing itself out, which was all to the good. Mike and Slugeamus would surely be away towards home, even if they had been obliged to stand to during the day. I washed up the dishes in good heart, for I had received a slice of the most tremendous good fortune. Even by the light of early morning the American had looked familiar. He was of course Homer Hertzbrun, the Nobel Prize nuclear physicist. More important still, the third man, the man who had ordered me peremptorily to the kitchen, was none other than Arthur Mitchell, F.R.S., the chemist from Cambridge. This was the man that I had been told to look out for particularly, a possible key to the organisation of I.C.E.

This being the case, I had no intention of remaining immersed in the domestic quarters. Whatever it might require in the way of cheek or brass, I was determined to get back there into the lounge. Turf burns quickly and is soon used up, especially on a stormy night. A new load is always welcome to any company. So I looked around until I found the supply dump and a large basket. Then with a full load of the stuff I opened the lounge door and walked in with the best confidence I could muster.

Two other men had evidently joined the gang. Probably they had been outside, walking the island, when I had first appeared. I closed the door quietly on the inside and began unloading the turf. Soon I was quite forgotten, however, for a tremendous argument seemed to be going on. I sat unmoving by the side of the fire, listening.

At first I could make out little of what was going on. The argument was clearly very one-sided, however. There seemed to be five against one, with two sitting out. The genuine blonde and one of the new men were the sitters out. The solitary fighter was one of the two half-blonde girls.

The five were very sure of themselves. The solitary girl was equally sure. Whatever abstruse physical (or mathematical?) question was under discussion, she gave all the indications of knowing exactly what she was talking about. She had an odd appearance, a jolly-looking face, but a face that decidedly wasn't jolly. This 'jolly-girl-that-wasn't' began to get very exasperated, as one might do in talking to a crowd of exceedingly dull, obstinate people. The five, with the confidence of the majority, kept firing all manner of objections at her.

The scene was fast becoming acrimonious when the mental fog in which I had been immersed suddenly cleared away. I saw where the trouble lay. Perhaps I had better explain.

In two dimensions a circle divides the plane into two parts, the 'inside' of the circle and the 'outside', both parts being simply connected. All this is obvious enough. The same result is true for any closed curve in two dimensions that can be put into a continuous one-to-one correspondence with a circle. So far, so good.

Now the majority of five were generalising this theorem to higher dimensions in the course of their argument, and I knew this to be already wrong in three dimensions. Without pausing to heed the consequences, in the bright clarity of the moment of perception, I said so.

The half-blonde girl nodded a curt approval. "It's nice to find somebody with a little elementary common sense," said she.

"What do you know about it?" snapped Mitchell.

"In science and mathematics it doesn't matter who speaks, only what is said," I answered.

"I did not expect a fisherman as an ally."

Then I saw the enormity of what I had done. But I was a mathematician first and an agent a long way second, and this I had no wish to alter.

Even as they moved to attack, I saw that my one hope of deception lay in keeping within a hair's breadth of the truth.

"Let's get this right. You did say you were a fisherman, didn't you?" asked Hertzbrun.

"Of course I did."

"And it is common these days for young fishermen to be well informed on the finer points of topology?"

"Look here, sir, you wouldn't expect me to blab out on your doorstep the whole story of my life. I had to make some sort of selection, and the relevant selection was that I happened to be a shipwrecked fisherman. Remembering that I expected to find a shepherd or a fisherman here and not a scientist, it seemed pointless to explain that I was a student temporarily employed as a fisherman over the summer."

"And where would you be a student from?"

"Cambridge."

"See here, Mr.——?"

"Sherwood, Thomas Sherwood."

There was a slight silence. Then Mitchell went on: "See here, Mr. Sherwood, as a fisherman there are two very queer things about you: one that you're shipwrecked in forbidden territory, and the other that you seem to be a singularly well-informed mathematical student from Cambridge. What I want to be clear about is the connection between these peculiarities. I imagine you're not going to pretend that there is no such connection?"

"Of course not. There's the perfectly obvious connection that any self-respecting undergraduate would do his damnedest to get into a place like this. As soon as you forbid him to do something he'll do it for sure, just for devilment."

"That explains the psychology but not how it was done," said the half-blond man, with the same slightly peculiar accent as the mathematically-minded girl. It had rather the sound of someone who speaks Gaelic as a first language.

"Did you get permission to visit the west coast?" asked Hertzbrun.

"Naturally not. I got permission to visit Dublin and various points to the east. But I worked my way over to the west, not taking the various rules and regulations very seriously, I'm afraid. When I found that fishermen outside the Area were in the habit of poaching down this coast, just as I said this morning, I decided to join the ranks. There's quite a shortage of men, you know, so I'd no difficulty in landing a job. My idea was to get as near as possible to what you're pleased to call 'forbidden territory'. Sooner or later I felt there'd be a chance to get in."

"And are we asked to believe that you just happened to be wrecked by chance and your companions drowned?"

"Of course not. I soon saw that the right way to get in would be with a small motor-boat. I persuaded the skipper of my trawler to let me make a shot with an old boat that I managed to put together. Unfortunately we were seriously out of position, due to the gale, when I started—far too much to sea down the Bay. I expected to land near Dingle instead of here. And indeed I feel very badly about this miscalculation, since it has led me into abusing your hospitality, I'm afraid."

"You can repay us by giving details of this trawler that carried you so close into our coast."

I shook my head. "You must know that I can't do that. For consistency with what I said this morning, let me only say that there were three of us and that we were out from Kilkee."

I felt this to be well-managed. They wouldn't believe my last glib statement, and that was Mike's best insurance. Kilkee would be the last place where they would look for the errant trawler. The inquisition ended with a sarcastic laugh from the jolly-girl-that-wasn't. The other half-blonde girl turned to her also with a laugh: "Fanny, this looks like quite a chance, doesn't it?"

But what the chance was I couldn't guess.

As often happens after a summer storm, the next day was bright and clear. When I came down to breakfast, the genuine blonde was alone in the kitchen.

"They're having a business meeting today," she said. "I'm not in on it," she went on, "so I thought we might go off in the boat, if you haven't finished with boats for good and all?"

It was a nuisance to hear that I couldn't spend the day with the whole party, for I knew in my bones that I was now within a stone's throw of the solution to the whole problem. Still, if they were having a meeting I could hardly barge in, and there would always be the evening anyway.

"And where have you a mind to go?" I asked.

"There's some quite nice scrambling on one of the islands. I see by your boots that you're a mountaineer. How about going over for an hour or two? The rock is surprisingly good."

We packed lunch and set off. The boat was a far more powerful affair than the one I had wrecked. It forged easily through the still heavy sea, driving from wave to wave, the sun sparkling all around us.

"This is where one of the galleons of the Armada came through," shouted the girl as we made the passage between Blasket and the mainland. The Tearaght appeared to the west, and the cliffs of Inishtooskert lay ahead.

I was now feeling as well as it was possible to feel. After the weeks of walking, and after the lifting and hauling of nets, I was exceedingly fit. The world around me was ablaze with colour and light, and I had an exceedingly pretty girl to spend the day with.

We found an anchorage on the south side of Inishtooskert.

"Go ahead," I said. "I'll just check the mooring ropes again."

The girl led the way, almost at water level, until the

cliffs steepened above our heads. Then she unslung a nylon rope.

"Let's start with this. It's quite easy really."

We tied on and the girl took the lead, climbing very easily up the first pitch of thirty feet or so. I had made three trips with the Cambridge Mountaineering Club, and although I am no expert climber, it was without misgiving that I followed behind. The climb was no more than 'moderate', and in any case I had the moral support of the rope.

At first I had made no attempt to 'lead' because evidently the girl knew the climb. But soon I realised that she was a couple of grades better than I was. As we moved up the cliff I had the exhilarating experience of following an expert on a climb that was within my capacity. It was possible to imitate her light, delicate, almost dancing movement. Under these conditions one invariably climbs at best, indeed often beyond one's real ability.

We made three separate ascents of the whole cliff, all by different routes; one a strange pinnacle on the west side of the island, surmounted by an eagle's nest. Then at the island's summit we sat down to lunch. This was a day of colour. The main-land was aflame—the bog, the stubble fields, the avenues of rowan trees, blue, except where it shone and sparkled like a vast the line of Eagle Mountain. The sea was deep jewel.

After lunch, the girl said: "Just one more climb, and then I think we ought to start back. They should have finished their meeting by the time we return."

The new route lay to the east, near the 'fin' of

the island. After a tolerable first twenty feet, it became difficult. But behind such a leader I had no worries. We struck the first 'severe' pitch about a third way up. This was beyond my real ability and by rights I should have protested and returned. But what young man would make such a protest to a very beautiful girl who climbed with such effortless grace? I would be all right with the rope as safeguard! She took the pitch like a Greek goddess heading for Olympus.

The next pitch, a long one without any adequate stance, was no better. It started from a good foothold, going at about sixty degrees up a long smooth slab. The holds were very small, no more than little knobs in the rock. Even the start was exceedingly awkward, a step up from the foothold on to a slight excrescence situated almost at shoulder height. Had this come at the beginning I would have pocketed my pride and said 'No' very firmly. But now it would almost be as bad to return as to continue. I got up somehow. A pitch no more than 'very difficult' followed. I used far too much brute strength on it.

By now we were some 200 feet up, not too far from the top, thank goodness. But there was still trouble ahead, a shockingly steep climb over a projecting nose, with holds that were just adequate. I was panting pretty hard as I came up over this nose on to a wide stance. The girl was taking in the rope, a smile on her face.

"Jolly good," she said. "That's the last bad bit. I know it's pretty awkward the first time. There's just the boulder now."

We were in a not too steep gully, jammed by a huge

boulder. At first sight there seemed no way over this last obstacle. It was true that the boulder projected out of the gully on one side and that tolerable holds could be seen far out on that side, but they could not be reached.

"How on earth does this thing go?"

"Impossible for one, easy for two. A perfect argument against solitary climbing," was the answer. "You give me a shoulder, so that I can reach the top and haul myself up. Then I secure the rope from above so that you can swing out on to those good holds over there. You'd better use an absailing position so as to be absolutely safe."

And of course by this combined tactic it was perfectly straightforward, if not 'easy'. It was certainly a far simpler matter than the pitches we had just come up. So I gave her a shoulder, and with something of a struggle she managed to heave herself over the rounded top of the boulder. 'Harder for her than for me,' I thought, as I looked at my holds four yards away to the left. They looked rather good.

"I'm up," she shouted, as she started to take in the rope. She kept taking in slack until the rope tightened between us.

"That's too much. Give me about three yards," I shouted back. The rope slithered on the rock, and I saw an end come down, not the usual end, but an end that had been neatly cut. Equally neatly, I had been limed and snared.

I was now alone with an unclimbable boulder above and an almost unclimbable cliff below. And with devilish forethought the girl had left me with only twelve feet of useless rope. I shouted furiously, but there was no reply. I heard the faint sound of boots on rock, and that was all.

I find it difficult, even months afterwards, to write of this situation without my feet sweating. The route up the cliff must have been chosen with appalling cunning. My first move, if I was to descend, lay over the steep nose, and this is the one sort of pitch that it is genuinely more difficult to descend than to ascend. The trouble with descent is to find holds for the feet, since they cannot readily be seen. When the rock is steep and the holds are small, one is only too likely to be left scrabbling vainly with the feet, hanging by the fingers—for a little while.

This I realised as I looked stupidly at the severed rope. What I did not realise was that all the clues were now in my hand, all the clues necessary for solving the mystery of I.C.E. Yet I wasn't to arrive at the solution for nigh on another year, perhaps because I was to be led away from the main issue by clues apparently more patent, but in fact misleading.

Right now, however, I was congealed on the cliff, unable to move up or down. And as I stood immovable and irresolute I became acutely aware of the boom of the sea striking the bottom of the cliff 250 feet immediately beneath my feet. I tried not to look down but my eyes seemed ever drawn to the blue water. I watched it heave and burst into masses of foam.

I expected to become crag-fast, a state of paralysis in which the climber loses all sense of balance. He clings desperately to the rock until exhaustion comes and at last he falls to his death. Instead I became furiously angry. Suddenly I had a desperate desire to catch up with this hell-cat of a blonde. I would knock all Hades out of the girl once I did.

It would help to descend in stockinged feet, for then my toes could feel the indentations in the rock. I managed to get my boots off, but one of them slipped. It hit the cliff-face once on its journey to the sea, disappearing with a slight splash. My morale must have been greatly improved by the flaming rage that consumed me, for deliberately I also dispatched the fellow to a watery grave. The faithful boots in which I had walked through Ireland were gone, and with them a chapter closed.

Although I was now almost anxious to begin the descent, there was one thing more to be done. I have a good photographic memory. I willed myself to review all the holds by which I had climbed. I made a mental map of each of the separate pitches. Then at last I started downward.

The bulge was terribly difficult. I forced myself to take the weight on my toes. I would explore downwards with one foot, find at last some indentation, and then gradually transfer the weight to the lower foot. The climbing was very slow, the danger and temptation was to make too much use of the hands. Even at a distance in time of nearly a year, as I write these words I notice little beads of perspiration on my thumbs.

The 'very difficult' pitch seemed easier than on the ascent, and no wonder after the steep bulge I had just come down. Then I reached the top of the great slab. But now it was less difficult to see the holds, and I had two advantages that I didn't have in the ascent. My stockinged feet were more sensitive to the nicks and knobs in the rock, and the friction of any clothing on the rock provided a useful upward force. The last step down the slab on to the ample foothold below proved exceedingly awkward, however. I was trembling very markedly when I reached the foothold, the trembling coming from muscles that had been taut and strained for too long.

But now I knew that I would get down. There were still two shortish severe pitches before I reached the lower easy rocks. I took the pitches without undue haste, but I went down the lower rocks very quickly.

'Now, my girl, you can look out for yourself,' I thought as I felt in my inner coat pocket. My fingers closed on the distributor cap of the motor-boat engine. I had removed it before we started off in the morning, when I was pretending to look to the mooring ropes; for, as I have said before, I am of a suspicious mind. The girl had cleverly taken me in, I must admit, but now the score was even. She couldn't start the boat, and my turn was to come, very shortly.

CHAPTER THIRTEEN

The Industrial Corporation of Eire

In a fine old temper I scrambled rapidly along the rocks that bordered the sea, in haste to get back to the anchorage. But I was still a way off when I heard a familiar roar, a damned helicopter again. Somehow the genuine blonde must have got word across that she was marooned on the island. Obviously they had come to pick her up.

I raced up the slope, trying to reach the top of the island before the girl could be taken off. But human muscles compete poorly with the internal combustion engine, and I was still some way from the summit when the helicopter rose again and moved away over the sea. I had to be content with the futile and ineffective gesture of shaking my fist at the wretched thing as it passed almost overhead.

There was no point on this occasion in trying to conceal myself, since my safe descent of the cliff would be obvious as soon as the boat put out from the island; if the boat put out, that is to say, for there was just the possibility that the blonde might have put the engine completely out of operation. There seemed little reason why she should have done so, but I was apprehensive as I made my way downhill to the mooring spot.

'How easy is a bush supposed a bear.' My fears were groundless, nothing in the boat had been touched except that a small W/T set had been taken from its container. This was how the girl had managed to bring help so quickly. I had been foolish not to have noticed this little piece of radio equipment.

It took but five minutes to replace the distributor cap, turn on the petrol, and start the engine. Although I was in a tearing hurry to get back to Inishvickillane, I made a detour to the end of the island, to a point where I could see the horrible climb on the cliff. For a quarter of a mile out to sea it seemed impossible that even a fly could have come down it. With a shiver I realised something that had not occurred to me before—this part of the cliff was indented in such a way that it could not be seen from the mainland. If I had stayed stuck to the rock I wouldn't have been seen, and there would have been no real hope of rescue.

The boat pitched and rolled quite considerably as I drove her at full speed into the waves. It was rather like taking a car rapidly along a road covered in pot-holes. But I cared nothing for the boat, only so long as it got me back safely to the island. What I wanted right now was an interview with Dr. Mitchell and his friends. I was too mad at the time to appreciate the methods of I.C.E. If the girl had got me to swing out to the boulder, *and then cut the rope while I was swinging*, nothing could have saved me. But that would have been murder direct, and apparently they drew the line at this. A fine sense of delicacy persuaded them to put me in a position where I would kill myself, where I had only myself to blame, a position from which I ought to be able to extricate myself—for it is a cardinal rule of rock climbing that nobody should ascend a crag unless he is competent to descend it.

Why had they decided to get rid of me? How had I given myself away? My impression was that I had told my story reasonably well. It was possible, and even likely, that they would still be suspicious, but there is a great margin between suspicion and certainty. And surely only people who were absolutely certain would commit murder? Attempted murder it had been morally, however one might play on words.

Then I saw where my mistake lay, glaringly obvious now. When I had stripped off in the bathroom the previous morning and taken my wet things to the kitchen I had unwittingly handed over my trousers without removing Colquhoun's money. And the money had given me away. No student would carry anything like so much. I cursed myself for a wet fool.

Now I was a mad fool. I drove the boat, slapping and racketing along the same course that the galleons of the Armada had travelled four hundreds years ago, and then I turned to the south-west heading directly towards Inishvickillane. The boat ran more smoothly as she came into waters that were sheltered from the south-west wind. I brought her in quickly to the landing place, made fast, and started up the path to the house.

In a powerful rage I opened the door without knocking. There was nobody in the kitchen, nobody in the sitting-room, nobody upstairs. It was plain that the birds had flown, probably taken off by helicopter or some such device. I went back to the kitchen and found my trousers still hanging before the fire-place. A quick inspection showed the money to be still there, but I did not draw the correct inference. By now I was shunted on to a logical side-track.

I had just decided that my trousers, the ones hanging there, were distinctly inferior to the ones I was now wearing, and I had just transferred the money, when I was startled by a voice behind me.

"Mr. Sherwood, I believe." I swung round, to find a small, oldish fellow, to my jaundiced eye a little weasel of a fellow, standing in the doorway leading to the lounge. The adrenalin was still flowing strongly, so that my instinct was to pick him up and shake him soundly. I took a couple of steps forward, and then, only then, noticed the dark silhouettes of three massive men standing beyond the weasel. The four of them stepped into the kitchen and I saw that the weasel's companions were in uniform. These were members of the I.C.E. police. The flow of adrenalin stopped, and discretion dominated.

"Yes, Mr. Sherwood? Shall we talk in here, or would you prefer the lounge?"

"There is little to be gained by disturbing ourselves," I said taking a seat.

"Very well, then. Now I think we ought to have a quiet talk. Let me introduce myself. The name is Earnshaw, Howard Earnshaw."

This was superfluous, for Howard Earnshaw, some-time Professor of Metallurgy in the University of London, was another of the people that I had been warned to look out for. "A wild man, a fanatic," Parsonage had roared at me.

"My name is apparently already known to you," I remarked.

"Your name, and your career. If I may say so, you have the beginnings of a very fine career."

I bowed, and this rat-catcher of a fellow went on:

"But why, oh why, Mr. Sherwood, must you go about things in such an odd and roundabout way? Why not come straight to the front door if you are interested in I.C.E., and I gather by your presence here that you are? We are not in the habit of turning promising young men away empty-handed. Just the reverse."

"Well, you see, there's the possibility that I might stay on at Cambridge and take a Ph.D. But I thought it wouldn't do any harm to have a look around before making up my mind."

"And didn't it occur to you that there might be some objection to your 'taking a look around'? Suppose every prospective candidate for a job at I.C.E. were to decide to snoop around as you've been doing. Don't you think that would be rather unpleasant for us?"

"I'm afraid it just didn't occur to me to look at it in that way."

"Well now, Mr. Sherwood, I'm going to speak quite frankly. Normally we deal very severely with people who deliberately make an illegal entry into Kerry. But I'm the first to admit this would be somewhat absurd in your case. To be shut away would do you no good, and it would do us no good either. So what I'm going to do is to treat your case exactly as if you'd made an application for a post directly from Cambridge."

Somehow I managed to avoid any show of surprise. During the last few minutes it had gradually dawned on me that Mr. Weasel could know nothing at all about the business on the cliffs of Inishtooskert. But what did it all mean? Who in their senses would first try to kill a man, and then, when the attempt failed, would immediately turn round and offer him a job? The correct explanation actually occurred to me, but I dismissed it without much thought. I had become hopelessly confused, which was precisely what the real authorities of I.C.E. wanted.

Aloud I said: "That seems a very fair offer in the circumstances, sir. But I think I ought to warn you that I'm rather an individual sort of worker."

Plainly I was now back to winning small points again.

"I think you'll find that I.C.E. has sufficient elasticity to provide the right sort of working conditions for even more curious people than yourself, Mr. Sherwood."

"You said that you'd treat my case as if I'd applied for a job in the normal fashion. Can you tell me what this means?"

"It means that you'll be entitled to the normal salary scale, for entrants with a good university degree: 1,500 Irish pounds per annum. That'll be your case. Subsequent salary increases will be largely a matter for yourself. If you are good to the Corporation, the Corporation will be good to you."

"That seems a very decent proposition."

"I wonder if you realise what sort of organisation it is that you'll be joining, Mr. Sherwood?"

"To be frank, sir, it's just because I can't answer this very question that I hesitated over joining the Corporation."

Earnshaw sat back and grinned in the manner of a death's head, no doubt imagining that he was unbending in a pleasant style.

"Many people seem to think that there lies a mystery where in fact there's no mystery at all. I.C.E. is *science*, science in control of itself, an organisation run by scientists. In the world at large, science is forced to serve many masters. Here scientists are asked to serve only science itself. This is the real explanation of why we are forging far ahead, of why in a few short years we shall have none to rival us."

"That makes everything a good deal clearer."

"I am glad of it. Let me put things more crudely in terms of money. The great nations of the world value science so poorly that less than one tenth of one per cent of their productivity is spent on basic scientific research. In contrast we spend approximately twenty per cent. In fact we are now spending more in total on basic research than all the nations of the world. This may seem an astonishing statement but it is true nevertheless, for the expenditure of the rest of the world is only a little more than £100 million per annum—a trifling sum, my dear fellow."

I said that it all sounded like a great opportunity for a young man to have.

"A very great opportunity. There is no telling how far an able young man like yourself may be able to rise."

In this at least the man was prophetic. Had he been able to foresee the course of events I think he would have expired instantly.

"Well now," he purred, "this is all very satisfactory.

I have a few papers here which I'll sign for you. Then you can take off straight away for Headquarters." He handed me the papers. "Now let's hope you'll have no more trouble, Mr. Sherwood."

Two of the policemen led me outside, to the beautiful grassy plateau of the island. As if to maintain the theme, a helicopter was waiting. There was still the possibility, remote admittedly, that some 'accident' was to be staged.

We took off and gained height over the Bay. Everywhere along the coast was a line of foam, a reminder of the passing storm. The islands were similarly girdled as they lay in blue water. There were high clouds, streaked by upper winds that were still strong, and the bright purple colour of the mainland seemed even more intense than I had remarked earlier in the day.

But it wasn't to this scene of wild beauty that my attention was mainly directed. An aerial trip provided a unique opportunity for getting an idea of the lay-out of the I.C.E. industrial plants, as they ranged over the flat boglands around Cahirciveen. Now I could see them clearly on our right hand, so vast and extensive as to suggest interesting notions. It was very easy to pick them out because of the great roads with which the whole system was linked.

But it was the new city of Caragh that really took the eye, built in the beautiful valley some five miles to the south of the lake from which it takes its name. Instead of the greys and dull browns of the average city seen from the air, Caragh is ablaze with colour. Instead of standing apart from the surrounding countryside through its drabness, it is distinguished by its brilliance.

This is achieved largely by the cultivated flowers which occupy much of the total area of the city. The buildings themselves are chiefly noticeable from the air through the flashes of reflected sunlight, mainly a golden effect achieved by some translucent dispersive material.

The buildings become more dominant as soon as one lands, their colours more alight. Caragh is not a vast unwieldy collection of small hutches, like other cities of the world. It contains but sixty-odd buildings laid out in great avenues, no more than seven or eight to any particular avenue. Taking advantage of the natural slope of the land, and of the ample water supply, small rivers run past the buildings. At night the whole city is lit by a soft diffuse light.

Let me dispose now of my own petty affairs. On landing I was directed to a place which seemed to be a species of high-grade recruiting office. I was given a temporary room in what I suppose might be described as an hotel, and was handed a preliminary cash advance of twenty pounds, not that I had any real need of the latter. I bought various necessaries and a volume of Shakespeare's Comedies. Then I sought out the best restaurant in the city and treated myself to a wonderful meal, by way of celebrating an entry into a new life.

After dinner I spent a couple of hours walking entranced through the city. At last I was where I wanted to be—I was 'in'.

Now I must deal with a question that might possibly trouble a reader of this report. Wouldn't it have been vastly more simple to have reached Caragh by the straightforward method of applying for a job with I.C.E.? Why go to all this fantastic trouble?

There were three reasons for my apparently indirect, roundabout approach, each a strong one. It is not in my nature to be actively deceitful. I simply couldn't have set myself to work against an employer who had accepted my services in good faith. I would, moreover, have reached Caragh without any real confidence in myself, a solitary individual pitted against an enormously powerful organisation. This was of course the situation now. I *was* a solitary individual pitted against a powerful organisation. But curiously I felt no misgivings. The successful descent of the cliffs of Inishtooskert seemed to have given me an enormous confidence. Moreover, this latter affair had left me fighting mad, and this was perhaps the most important of the three reasons. If I had not been in a deep, cold rage I would soon have been seduced by this beautiful city. I would soon have taken off my coat and worked in earnest for I.C.E.

At length I returned to my room. Before turning in I read a couple of acts of *Twelfth Night*. 'This gives a picture of the apex of society as it was four centuries ago,' I thought. 'There are many things that we can't do nowadays; we can't write like Shakespeare. But of a certainty no earlier generation than ours could have built such a city as Caragh. The society of four centuries ago would have thought themselves on another planet, if by some magic they could have been transported here. Indeed to people of our own age it almost looks like authentic science fiction. But Caragh is something strange but real, for it is the city of the third millennium, the city of the future.'

CHAPTER FOURTEEN

Some Inferences

In my conceit I imagined that the logical tap-root of I.C.E. would soon be exposed. Now that I had reached the nerve centre of this great enterprise I even began to think about ways and means of getting out of Kerry once I had accumulated the necessary information. I little suspected that I was embarking on the most baffling section of the whole affair.

Luckily, during the first months at Caragh I started to work quite genuinely. For some time I'd wanted to learn about modern field theories in physics, and as the winter progressed I became more and more engrossed in this subject. So I was able to preserve some degree of sanity as difficulties began to pile up all around me.

But I did make odd scraps of progress. One day I had occasion to refer to a paper in the *Astrophysical Journal*. In flicking through the volume in question I noticed a place where a couple of exclamation marks had been inserted in the margin. I was too bound up in the thoughts of the moment to pay much attention to this minor detail. A few days later, however, I needed to look up the same paper in order to settle a remaining small point. I remembered the exclamation marks and decided to see what they were about. But the marks in the margin were nowhere to be found.

Feeling still only mildly curious, I then looked for traces of rubbing out, but I couldn't find any. Luckily I have a good memory, as I think I've mentioned before, and there was no doubt in my mind, within a page or two, where the defacement had occurred. The surface of the paper in the margins was entirely smooth, in a way it couldn't possibly have been if a rubber had been used, even very lightly. This was an entirely different copy of the volume but in a similar binding. Why?

Naturally I read through the paper that happened to be situated at the place where I believed the marks to have been inserted. It dealt with the problem of electrical pinches in the solar atmosphere. The general idea was that the solar atmosphere is pervaded by tubes of magnetic force, rooted below the photosphere. These tubes become twisted through the motion of the dense material at their roots, but this twisting doesn't in itself produce any serious instability. If for instance a tube becomes so seriously twisted that contraction sets in at any place, the very action of the pinch itself increases the pitch of the helix, and so restores stability.

The idea of the paper was to let two such tubes come together at a particular place. Then if the fields penetrate each other at the point of contact a violent contraction must occur when the helices are so wound that the longitudinal components cancel and the circular components of the magnetic field augment. In this case a region of instability is held firmly out from the solar surface by the strength of the stable supporting arms of the tubes, which act as the filaments of an arc.

In a flash I remembered the 'corpus' floating in the sea—what was it? Twin helices, senses opposite! This might well be the clue to the thermo-nuclear reactor. Here was a way in which a high-temperature region could be held away from the boundary of a vessel, on magnetic springs.

It was obvious what had happened. Some informed person had noticed this paper, containing unawares the germ of the right idea. Unable to restrain himself he had added the exclamation marks.

Another point was equally obvious. My movements must be under very close surveillance. Even so, this business with the *Astrophysical Journal* had been rather clumsily managed. I reinserted the exclamation marks and returned the volume to the shelves.

I think perhaps that I ought to give some outline of my ideas about the real nature of I.C.E. as I had them at this early stage. In certain respects the general picture didn't turn out to be too far wrong, although the most essential step was still completely beyond my comprehension. Here, then, is the position as I saw it.

Starting with straightforward matters, it appeared that I.C.E. employed about half a million persons, working and living for the most part on the south side of Dingle Bay. I was curious at first to understand how this large population was housed without its being necessary to construct at least one large city.

I suppose that in ordinary homes each person has a space allowance of roughly 100 cubic yards. A large building, say with a volume of 200,000 cubic yards, suitably shaped to be divided into apartments, would house about 2,000 persons. It followed that the whole population could be fitted into about 250 such buildings, which together would cover an area of only some 400 acres. Since the area of land available must be some 30,000 acres it was clear that an impression of enormous spaciousness could be achieved—each building could be surrounded by more than 100 acres of garden, woodland, and sea-shore.

In my opinion a lot of nonsense is talked about lack of privacy under such conditions. There is one overriding prerequisite, complete sound-proofing. Provided this is satisfied there is no reason why one shouldn't feel just as private, just as remote from one's neighbours, in an apartment as in a detached house. I had learned this when I lived for three years in College at Cambridge.

The often-heard argument that apartments are unsuitable for families with children is of course correct if the apartment block is set in a city, surrounded by busy streets. But the argument is scarcely true for an apartment block set in woods and fields, with a near-by stream.

So I had to reckon on half a million well-paid, well-satisfied employees of I.C.E. This number of people may seem large at first sight. Yet it was plainly out of proportion, in the sense of being small, compared to the industrial activities of I.C.E. This could only mean that enormous use must be made of automation.

Now let me say something of the scale of this industry. By now I could see clearly the difference between I.C.E. and the older-established industries of Europe and America. The latter grew up around specialised mineral deposits—coal, oil, metallic ores. Without these deposits the older style of industrialisation was completely

191

impossible. On the political and economic fronts, the world became divided into 'haves' and 'have-nots', depending on whereabouts on the Earth's surface these specialised deposits happened to be situated.

Britain ran ahead, first of Spain, then of France, because Britain was more of a 'have' than her rivals. America ran ahead of Britain because she was still more of a 'have'. Russia based its rise to dominance not so much on the invention of new techniques as on the deployment of hitherto unused resources. Sweden was a 'have', Austria was a 'have-not'. All this was in-dustrialisation of an early primitive kind.

In the second phase of industrialism, the industrialism now apparently perfected by I.C.E., no specialised deposits are needed at all. The key to this second phase lies in the possession of an effectively unlimited source of energy. Everything here depends on the thermo-nuclear reactor, the clue to which had fallen so recently into my hands. With a thermo-nuclear reactor, a single ton of ordinary water can be made to yield as much energy as several hundred tons of coal—and there is no shortage of water in the sea. Indeed the use of coal and oil as a prime-mover in industry becomes utterly in-efficient and archaic.

With unlimited energy the need for high-grade metallic ores disappears. Low-grade ores can be smelted —and there is an ample supply to be found everywhere. Carbon can be taken from inorganic compounds, nitrogen from the air, a whole vast range of chemicals from sea water.

So I arrived at the rich concept of this second phase of industrialisation, a phase in which nothing is needed but the commonest materials—water, air, and fairly common rocks. This was a phase that can be practised by anybody, by any nation, provided one condition is met—provided one knows exactly what to do. This second phase was clearly enormously more effective and powerful than the first.

Of course this concept wasn't original. It must have been at least thirty years old. It was the second concept that I was more interested in. The concept of information as an entity in itself, the concept of information as a violently explosive social force. Put two or three hundred engineers and chemists back in old Roman times and let them be given a chance to show what they could do! Within a decade or two they would have turned Roman civilisation topsy-turvy and made a mockery of the apparently important issues of the time.

It was here that I came to the big problem. How came it that I.C.E. possessed this great block of new information, while the older industrial nations did not?

There was one solid argument in favour of the Earnshaw point of view. It was certainly true that the major industrial nations were spending only tiny proportions of their national incomes on acquiring the new block of information—on basic research, that is to say. In the case of the U.S., for instance, the amount spent was only 1/30th of one per cent. Earnshaw had been dead right about this.

Why should a nation drag its feet in such a way? Why should it refuse to press on towards the rich rewards that the second phase of industrialisation would give? I believed I knew the answers to these questions.

Our ordinary ideas about social and economic

stability depend upon new knowledge not being injected into society at too rapid a rate. Could it be that older industrialised nations, when faced by a choice between scientific advance and preserving a social *status quo*, all preferred the latter alternative? If so, this was certainly a big point in favour of Dr. Weasel's opinion.

Even so I couldn't believe it to be the explanation I was looking for. Scientific advance at a maximum rate would cause one nation to forge slowly ahead of a less progressive nation. The gap between the two would widen gradually decade by decade; the gap would eventually become very great, but only after a generation or so. There would be none of the explosive advance of I.C.E. This could come only from a massive, sudden injection of a large volume of new information. From where? This was the rock on which I foundered whenever I tried to think the matter through to a conclusion.

194

CHAPTER FIFTEEN

Caged

Naturally I would dearly have loved to get back into the northern peninsula of Kerry again. But this peninsula, together with the part of the southernmost peninsula west of Adrigole, was absolutely out of bounds, not only to me but to everyone else with whom I came in contact. This entirely confirmed my suspicion that much of what I wanted to know must lie with Mitchell and his friends. Try as I would, however, I simply could not pick up the track of these people.

It was a great temptation to try my former raiding methods. I thought of attempting to force a route through the mountains to the north of Dingle. I thought of taking a boat down the Kenmare river and of sailing around Valencia Island and thence across Dingle Bay. I even thought of stealing a helicopter. But a moment's thought showed all these ideas to be mere wild-cat schemes. Such methods had proved exceedingly difficult even when I was outside I.C.E. territory, even when I was unknown to the I.C.E. security police. Now that I was obviously under close watch—as the incident of the *Astrophysical Journal* plainly showed—it would be outright nonsense to try any more cloak-and-dagger stuff. The moment had come for sheer logical reasoning.

195

As far as material considerations were concerned, I had no cause for complaint. I had a very pleasant apartment in Caragh. I was able to get a quiet cottage in Ballinskelligs Bay, to which I often went down at week-ends.

I made many acquaintances but no real friends during the three months before Christmas. It was quite staggering to find everyone wholly incurious about the underlying organisation of I.C.E. The general disposition was to follow the statements expressed to me by Earnshaw. Beyond this, nobody seemed to care. Why be curious when one is on to a good thing? Why dissect a goose that is laying eggs of gold?

Or was there a more sinister explanation? It seemed rather unnatural that none of the young fellows of about my own age seemed in the least bit worried about the logical problem that was plaguing the life out of me, the problem of what was really at the bottom of this I.C.E. Moreover it was quite clear that nobody was being allowed to talk with me too much. I would strike up a short friendship with someone, we might spend a couple of week-ends together, perhaps in the mountains or by the sea, then invariably the man would be shifted to some other job, or he simply wouldn't turn up for an appointment. This happened time and time again, and although I was angry at first, I eventually came to accept the situation. I had done all I could to reach Caragh, and it was obviously no good fussing now that I was here.

I remembered the remarks of the true Canon, the ones about the I.C.E. medical service. Was it possible that all these people around me had been conditioned in some way? I looked carefully at the work of my young colleagues. Was it more competent than original? Frankly, I was too inexperienced to be sure, but more than experienced enough to be suspicious. At all events I was glad that my health was good. I resolved to give nobody the opportunity of shooting any drugs into me.

My one weak spot was food—not eating too much, I hope, but having to eat at all. I was at pains to think of a plan that would make it exceedingly difficult for anyone to tamper with my food. I made a rigid rule that I would take everything from large self-help restaurants. I never took any dish that wasn't on display and that wasn't reasonably popular, for it was most improbable that a large number of people would be dosed with some noxious stuff just to get hold of me. And I made the situation much more complicated by varying the place where I ate and the timing of my meals in a random fashion—I got some slight amusement by using the non-recurring decimal representation of π to make my choices, two digits for each meal.

There was one exception to the disruption of incipient friendship: a young fellow called Womersley persistently kept inviting me out to dinner. Although I had no hesitation in refusing him, I managed for a time to make reasonably polite excuses. When, however, in the face of this discouragement he still kept on, I decided at last to avoid further embarrassment by putting the matter to a test. This really was a mistake, even though I managed to win the first round without difficulty.

I met Womersley, a tall, pale fellow of about twenty-eight, one evening in early December. We drove in his car to a restaurant about three miles outside Caragh. As I expected, *hors d'œuvre*, salmon, and cold meat dishes were on display, so it was not at all awkward to get past the first courses of the dinner with reasonable safety. The sweet and the coffee would be altogether another question.

Womersley droned on about the merits of the wild duck he was eating. I answered by saying that the only dish I would have preferred to the salmon would have been curried mutton. The point was lost on him, however, since he was obviously no student of the great Holmes. Before choosing my salmon I had left Womersley for a moment to make a telephone call to the Caragh Information Office. I asked the office to call me back in half an hour with some tolerably complicated information about vacant cottages in St. Finan's Bay, and I gave Womersley as my name.

My companion ordered chocolate ice-cream and coffee, and I did exactly the same, hoping that my timing would be reasonably accurate. I was lucky. I kept Womersley talking for a couple of minutes after the waiter had brought the order. This was sufficient. The man came back with the news that Dr. Womersley was wanted on the telephone. I interchanged the ice-creams and coffee.

Womersley was bound to be suspicious, if he wasn't the simpleton he pretended to be. I might possibly have been spotted changing the sweets, although I did this pretty quickly and our table was fairly well out of view in a corner. But these considerations didn't trouble me very seriously. Womersley must now eat the sweet unless he wanted to make an issue of it. And somehow

I didn't think he would dare to make a fuss. My impression is that he was under orders to be discreet in public at all costs. Anyway, he ate the ice-cream and drank the coffee—not quite all the coffee, I noticed.

I insisted that we return to my apartment, since I preferred to drink my own brandy to risking Womersley's. We started a game of chess, probably the strangest I have ever played, both of us expecting the other fellow to fall sick. I studied Womersley's face carefully as he made his moves, and he for his part stared at me as I made mine, which I did quickly.

The transition was amazing. One minute the man was studying the board, the next he was staring at me, his face contorted with an odd mixture of anger and apprehension.

"You tricky bastard," he yelled, "you'll get yourself fixed good and proper for this!"

Then he jumped up and made for the door, but I seized him by an arm and spun him quickly into a chair. I noticed little drops of perspiration on his forehead. He tried to get up but I pushed him back.

"I must get to hospital. Don't you understand?"

"I understand all right. You'll get to hospital in good time. But first I want to know who put you up to this business."

"I don't know."

"Stop playing the fool. Who was it?"

"I don't know. I tell you I don't know," he moaned. The drug was taking effect at an alarming rate. I suppose it would have served the man right if I had kept right on bullying him, but his distress was now so obvious that I simply couldn't bring myself to persecute him any longer. I rang the hospital and told the Duty Officer that Thomas Sherwood was sick.

It took very little time indeed before a doctor arrived, a man I would say in his late thirties, to my notion not a very pleasant fellow. He marched into my apartment, asking "Where is he?" in what I took to be an unctuous tone.

"In there," I indicated.

"You had better go downstairs. There will be an ambulance in a minute or two. You can show the men where to come."

Without going out of the apartment, I slammed the outer door. Then I tiptoed back to the living-room. The doctor was injecting something into the wretched Womersley. The faint groans died away, and I heard the man say:

"Well, well, Mr. Sherwood, quiet at last! Now we shall see what we shall see."

Then I saw red. I took hold of the fellow and slammed him really hard against a wall.

"May I introduce myself? My name is Thomas Sherwood."

"But . . . I thought," he stuttered.

"You thought that this silly fellow here was Thomas Sherwood. You know you medical people are so full of your wretched drugs and needles that you seem to have no idea of how unpleasant a physicist could be if he were so minded. I might get you to eat a little boron, for instance."

This took him by surprise.

"But boron isn't . . ."

"Boron isn't a serious poison in small quantities? It

would be after exposure to a moderate flux of neutrons. I'd take you where the neutrons wouldn't hurt me very much, but where they'd cook the insides out of you." Then I grabbed him again and slapped him hard with my open hand.

Was I getting as bad as the wretched Tiny? No, I think not. This whole affair smacked of concentration camps and secret police. But something really had to happen now. I.C.E. Security simply could not take this incident lying down. Besides, the cards were on the table, and discretion was no longer of much importance.

Just as once before in Marrowbone Lane, I made my plans in a flash. I was out of the apartment in an instant. The ambulance attendants were still in the road outside the building. I told them to go up to Apartment 619. My first intention was to drive away in the ambulance, in some respects an ideal vehicle to escape with. But then I realised that Womersley might be really ill, it might be important to get him to hospital quickly. The drug had certainly acted with an astonishing swiftness, perhaps indicating a serious overdose. I decided to get away by bus to Killarney and thence on foot.

This might appear a wholly precipitate change of plan, but I had long ago made up my mind about the terms on which I was prepared to carry on the fight against I.C.E. I was willing to do what I could single-handed against this powerful organisation. I was willing to be jailed, I was even willing to take a severe physical beating, but I was not willing to risk any change in my personality. I am an unrepentant sinner. I would prefer to go to Hell as I am, rather than to Heaven as I am not.

It would be the best part of an hour before the bus left, so I dropped into a fairly crowded café. I would then be far less likely to be picked up than if I spent the hour standing around at the bus station. I was shown to a table where a man was eating a sandwich and coffee. I wasn't hungry, but for the sake of appearance I also ordered coffee and a sandwich.

The best plan seemed to be to cross the frontier at the place I knew so well in the Boggerath Mountains. The whole nature of the frontier defences made it much easier to get out than to get in. I thought that if I could get as far as Killarney I would have a sporting chance.

Suddenly I realised that the man at my table was studying my face rather intently.

"I wouldn't try it," said he.

"You wouldn't try what?"

"I wouldn't try making a get-away on one of the buses, on the one to Killarney for instance." Then he laughed in my face. "You haven't got a chance, my boy. I followed you right from Building J." Superfluously, he went on:

"As soon as I saw where you were heading, I slipped in here ahead of you, and told the waitress to show you to my table. Very simple, eh?"

"Commendably so. If you need any recommendation for promotion I shall be happy to act as a referee."

"Shall we be going, or would you like to drink your coffee first? I need hardly say that it would be quite pointless to make any attempt to escape. We have you surrounded, and the roads can be blocked at a moment's notice."

'Ah well, back we go to winning small points again,' I thought to myself. Aloud I said:

"I think I'll finish the coffee, if you don't mind?"

"Oh, not in the least."

With bowed shoulders, and a slow gait, I went ahead of the man. But as soon as we were out of the door I whirled on him, as I had once whirled on the wretched Tiny. But this was a vastly easier proposition. The first punch was beautifully placed. The fellow went down soundlessly like a fairground dummy. In an instant I was away down the road, heading towards the centre of the city. There was more than a chance that the man was bluffing and that I was not surrounded at all, at any rate not for the moment. There had scarcely been time for one person to get on my track, let alone a whole squad.

I had gone about two hundred yards when two cars came towards me. They passed by, heading for the café. I cursed myself for a fool in wasting time over the coffee. Plainly my only hope now lay in an outrageously wild-cat scheme. There was a helicopter landing-square very close, and I headed at speed towards it, hoping that I might find a machine in readiness for take-off. I had no idea at all about flying one of the brutes, but this was obviously the moment to learn.

I now had a fantastic run of luck. I was nearing the place, when I heard one of the wretched things coming in to land. With complete assurance I walked to the square. I managed to get in without any challenge. I saw two passengers alight. The pilot got out on some errand or other, and without the slightest hesitation I walked towards the machine. Still without any challenge, I fumbled with the catch on the door. It seemed to be very stiff and far more difficult than it should have been. At last there was a clear space in front of me, and I was hauling myself into the cabin. But now I knew only too well that something was wrong, badly wrong. The coffee that I had insisted on drinking had been drugged. I slumped down into the pilot's seat. My last thought was to try to will myself to bridge the gap of unconsciousness that I knew was to follow.

I had just one vision, of bright lights, of voices, and a startlingly clear impression of the half-blond man whom I had seen on the island of Inishvickillane. Then I found myself awake and perfectly well, back in my own bed in Apartment 619, Building J.

I knew it to be a Sunday. So I shaved, took a shower and dressed in leisurely style. It was a little surprising to find no Sunday papers to read over breakfast. I was also a little surprised to find that although I was thirsty I seemed to have little appetite for food. I packed a picnic lunch thinking to go walking for three or four hours. Plainly I was in need of a blow of fresh air.

It was only when I reached the road outside Building J that the situation became clear. This was not a Sunday. Everything was wrong, the sky was too dark, the air too chilly, and there were no flowers. This was more like a day in December than one in early October. I bought a newspaper and found that indeed the date was 9th December 1970. For some reason there was a gap of more than two months in my memory. My last clear recollection was of arriving from Dublin by air in early October.

Although I was somewhat mystified by the situation I wasn't seriously worried. I had planned to go for a walk, so off I went. I caught sight of the sun at about two o'clock and from its low position in the sky it was manifest that the December date was correct.

When I returned to my apartment I made a search through my papers to see if there was anything to throw light on the missing months. I found letters from I.C.E. addressed to Trinity College in which the terms of my appointment were clearly stated. Sure enough, there was a copy of my own letter saying that I would arrive by air on 2nd October, just as I remembered it. There was the stub of my airline ticket from London.

The problem was cleared up by a doctor, a jovial old boy, who came to see me in the evening.

"Ah, it's nice to see you back in the land of the living," said he.

"And why shouldn't I be in the land of the living?"

"My boy, you've had a really bad blow on the head. Lucky you've got a skull made of steel."

"Where did it happen?"

"You've forgotten?"

"A whole two months seem to have dissolved away."

"Ah well, that's scarcely surprising. Temporary amnesia is very common in such cases, although I'm a bit surprised that it extends over as much as two months. The thing to do is to keep absolutely quiet for the next few weeks. Perhaps a little gentle walking, but don't go out too much. I'll make arrangements for food to be sent up here to you. And there are various

205

sedatives that you ought to be taking twice a day. Try to get some sleep after lunch. It gives any ruptured blood vessels in the head a chance to heal."

"But what in heaven's name was the trouble?"

He lifted a finger and wagged it in a fatherly manner. "You aren't the first young fellow that I've had to caution. Avoid fast cars, my boy. The next time you may not be so fortunate."

This explanation took quite a weight off my mind, and feeling distinctly sleepy I went to bed about nine o'clock.

Once again I turned the matter over in my head when I awoke the following morning. I was glad to find my memories of the previous day perfectly clear and sharp, so my brain evidently wasn't impaired except by the loss of two months, which after all wouldn't be a very serious matter.

Instead of taking a shower, I filled the bath. Lying in the water I suddenly noticed the marks of hypodermic needles in my thighs. Idly I wondered why one should be given injections for the treatment of a blow on the head. Perhaps there had been lacerations too. I looked myself over but couldn't find any. There were no bruises either. Odd! Except for my head, which surely must be badly bruised. I felt slowly and gingerly. No pain anywhere. Distinctly odd! I increased the pressure and still no pain. I certainly must have a skull of steel, just as the old fellow had said. Thoughtfully I shaved.

After breakfast, I looked again through the file of letters, those that I had written and those that I had received from I.C.E. Two more odd things. One of the I.C.E. letters mentioned physics and I had done no physics in my Tripos. And as long ago as May I had made arrangements to change my rooms in Trinity from Bishop's Hostel to Great Court. Yet my letters were addressed in August and September from Bishop's Hostel.

It seems incredible that I sat for an hour trying to reconcile all these facts before the first seeds of real suspicion entered my head. When they came, they came with a rush however. Suddenly I knew with certainty that there had been no motor accident. I knew with compelling certainty that the missing months had been crammed tight with crucial incident. And with these certainties there came the suspicion that the letters in my file must be false, and that I might not have arrived in Caragh City from Dublin by air on the second of October. How I had arrived I could not say, for my mind had not only blankness in it, but many things that were false. Yet I had won my first victory. My curiosity was aflame.

The old doctor came to see me once again, bringing exactly the same advice as before, together with more medicines. Instead of accepting them, I went to the bathroom to fetch the first consignment of whatever stuff it was that he was trying to persuade me to swallow. I handed it back to him, saying that perhaps he would have better use for the material than I had. He smiled in a rather kindly way as if to say 'Good luck', bowed, and left the apartment without further comment.

For the only time in my life I came near mental breakdown in the days that followed, for try as I would

I could gain no entry to my missing memories. I was convinced that they were tucked somewhere in my brain, but nothing I could do seemed to wake them into consciousness. It was like the frustration of trying to remember a forgotten name, but a thousand times worse.

I had papers in my files relating to the cottage in Ballinskelligs Bay, and on the third week-end after my awakening I decided to go down there. Friday was fine, so instead of using the bus, I walked along the hills overlooking the mouth of the Kenmare river. From the upper slopes of Mullaghbeg I lay on a rocky ledge watching the ever-changing swell of the sea breaking endlessly over richly coloured rocks. My fingers touched a rough boulder and in an instant the memory of the appalling descent of the crags of Inishtooskert became alive again. Like the island itself, this solitary memory reared up sharp and clear out of a sea of oblivion.

A fine day is often followed by wind and storm. So it was on that particular week-end. At the height of the gale I put on oilskins and made my way down to the edge of a roaring sea. Foolishly I went too close to the water and was hit by the flying top of a great wave. Even as the spray was driving furiously into my face I knew that another chord had been set in vibration. I knew that I had arrived in Kerry by sea, and in just such a storm as this.

After supper I built a great turf fire. Over a pot of coffee I worked away to extend the two breaches I had now made into the world of black uncertainty. Sluge-amus was my next victory, and with him came Mike O'Dwyer and then Colquhoun. There was no longer any frustration. Methodically, like a jigsaw puzzle, I fitted the whole picture together. I worked both backwards and forwards rediscovering detail after detail. Occasionally whole blocks of experience would suddenly click back into place. It was 4 a.m. in the morning when I retired to bed, exhausted but triumphant.

My memories continued to sharpen in the days that followed, until with the passage of a week the whole story had become every bit as clear as it had ever been. But I knew that I was only half victorious. I knew that in some subtle respect, one that I could put no name to, I had been changed. Something was different in me, and my agitation of mind was not decreased by a sense of mysterious uncertainty. I am the first to admit that I was appallingly slow in finding the solution to the major mystery of I.C.E., but I feel no shame at my failure to deduce the nature of the change that was even now taking place within me. At all events it was not a change that reduced my determination in the least degree.

CHAPTER SIXTEEN

Chance Pays a Visit

As January passed to February, I came more and more to feel how completely I had been isolated. 'Birds of a feather . . .' Unfortunately there were no birds of my particular feather anywhere to be found in Caragh City. My only appreciable conversations were with the farmers I might meet in a day's tramp among the hills, or with fishermen in Ballinskelligs Bay at week-ends.

One afternoon, however, I happened to be in a store, when I caught sight of a familiar head.

"Well, be the saints if it isn't Thomas Sherwood!" exclaimed Cathleen. "Bull, me husband, often speaks of you," she added.

"Bull?"

"Me name's Bradley now."

Then I remembered Bull Bradley, an experimental physicist from my Cambridge days. He was so named, not from his sexual proclivities, but from the roars with which he used to lead the forward line of the Clare College rugby fifteen. He was just the fellow to have tackled the monster back at Slievenamuck, and to have got his head broken for his pains.

Cathleen invited me to dinner at their apartment, where Bull Bradley greeted me with great heartiness:

"Sherwood, old boy, nice to see you." Then he roared with laughter. "You remember that manuscript of Cathy's you threw away? Well, it wasn't any good, you know. A deliberate piece of nonsense. We turn 'em out by the dozen in our department." This remark persuaded me to keep the conversation at a purely social level.

The evening passed pleasantly and at the end I naturally returned the invitation. But although the return was accepted, it never in fact came to pass. Cathleen rang me up one afternoon asking if she could see me for a few moments. Later she said:

"Thomas, I'm wondering about coming out with you on Thursday. I'm wondering for Bull's sake, you see."

"There's been some talk about me in Bull's department?"

She nodded. "They suspect you very much, Thomas. You must be careful." As we parted for the third time, she put her hand on my arm.

"It's sorry I am about those papers."

Colquhoun had been very confident about Cathleen. Was it possible that this partnership with Bull Bradley had more to it than met the eye? In any case my acquaintance could only be an embarrassment to them, so it was clearly right that I should keep myself out of their way.

In fact this was my last attempt at any form of social life. I saw that I must accept the position of Ishmael, my hand against everyone. After all, this is what I had asked for, and this is what I had got for my pains. As the months rolled on I was to become bitterly lonely, but at least there was one profit to be rung from the

211

situation: I was able to work at a furious pace. Otherwise it would have been only too easy to have succumbed to the unaccustomed luxury in which I was now living.

The weather was rarely good these days, but very occasionally the week-end would be clear and fine and not too cold. Then I would walk to my cottage by the sea. A singular affair arose out of one of these trips to Ballinskelligs Bay. I should perhaps explain that my cottage was set aside by itself in a rather lonely spot. It had often occurred to me that if I.C.E. really wished to dispose of me nothing could be easier—but then the blonde girl might have settled the matter back on the cliffs of Inishtooskert simply by cutting the rope at the right moment. In some curious way I had the belief that an intellectual battle was really being fought—that the authorities in I.C.E., whoever they might be, preferred to use psychological rather than physical weapons.

One Saturday evening at about eleven o'clock there came a knock on my door. A man fell across the threshold as soon as I opened up. His head was heavily bandaged, his clothes torn, and he seemed to be suffering from multiple flesh wounds, not too serious as far as I could judge. But his left knee joint was giving him much pain, so that he had been obliged to crawl a considerable way to the cottage.

The poor fellow revived somewhat after he had lowered a large tot of whiskey.

"Would your name be Thomas Sherwood?" he asked in a Devon accent that warmed my heart.

"Yes, it would."

"D'you have any identification?"

212

"Letters, books, a passport. But I might have all these even if I wasn't Thomas Sherwood."

"Which is true enough. But you answered the description all right. I haven't much time, so I'll have to take the risk."

"You seem to have taken plenty already. Before taking any more, perhaps you'd better explain why you've come here."

"Because I happen to have the same boss."

"Meaning who?"

"During winter storms the waves beat heavily on the western strands."

"This is the right moment to buy vegetables on the London market."

"Or fish, for that matter, if you have a taste for it."

"I see. And how did you know that I was down here at this cottage?"

"Sherwood, you're a suspicious devil, I must say!"

"It's just that I like to get the picture clear."

"I believe you have some acquaintance with Cathleen O'Rourke—a Mrs. Bull Bradley she calls herself now. Anything more?"

"I see what you're driving at, Mr.——?"

"Chance, John Chance."

"Very well, Mr. Chance, what d'you want with me?"

"If you look outside you'll find a rucksack. Better take a torch."

I found the rucksack. It was stout and very heavy. I carried it into the cottage.

"That's exactly what I want you to do."

"I don't understand."

"I want you to carry the rucksack for me, nothing more, about seven miles to the St. Finan's Bay Road. There'll be a car waiting when you get there."

I poured him another whiskey.

"Suppose you tell me a bit more. What's in the sack?"

Instead of replying, he took large swigs at the whiskey. I unfastened the top of the rucksack and managed to slip my hand down the side.

"Wireless equipment, eh? I thought as much, from the weight."

"You haven't learned much discretion, have you?"

"Not very much, I'm afraid. But unless I learn a lot more about you and about this rucksack, Mr. Chance, I'm certainly not going to carry it a single yard."

"Still not satisfied with my credentials, eh?"

"Perfectly. I simply want to know what game you're playing."

"And suppose you get yourself caught. Don't you think it might be better for you not to know what game I'm playing?"

"Maybe so. But it's not my way of doing things."

"All right, then, Tom, you've asked for it. I suppose you can guess that I got in here by parachute. Crocked my knee, damn it."

"Where did you land?"

"Towards the top of Coomakista Pass. I had the devil of a job getting as far as this."

"By why go carrying a sack of radio equipment around the countryside?"

"That's our alarm clock. It must be got to St. Finan's Bay before dawn."

"You mean it's a trigger?"

"It's a hell of a trigger, Tom lad."

His face twisted with a spasm of pain. "Some more whiskey, please. This damned leg is giving me merry hell."

"Where's the bomb?"

"Near Castletown of course. That's where I.C.E. has all its defence precautions. Once they're blown sky-high we can simply send our chaps in at leisure."

"I can see that. What I don't see is why a wireless transmitter had to be dropped by parachute. If our men have been able to assemble a bomb, surely they could manage a transmitter?"

"Ever tried to smuggle anything out of the Castletown area?"

"Couldn't a time device have been used?"

"I imagine it was considered, but that wasn't thought to be the best way. I'm not the General, you know. I'm just a chap in the trenches who does what he's told."

"But why take all these risks? Why not trigger the bomb from the air?"

"To make certain of the coding. That's why this thing has simply got to be hoofed to St. Finan's Bay. They have the final code-setting there, brought across by boat."

It was just the sort of muddle-headed situation that fitted my own experience. But it had a horrible chance of succeeding. I picked up the rucksack.

"Where exactly is this car? I'm going to be darned tired by the time I reach it."

I trudged slowly along the road. Each time a car

came past I slipped off the rucksack, putting it down out of sight at the roadside, then I continued walking without it. Once the car was past I returned to pick it up again. The main danger was in getting through Waterville. Here I simply had to risk being seen. It was a spine-tingling ten minutes before I was safely on the far side of the little town.

By now I could appreciate Chance's point. There were situations in which it was not wise to know too much. Tens of thousands of people were going to be killed. The problem of I.C.E. was going to be solved, not intellectually, but by battering it out of existence. And suddenly I knew it was not going to happen. There was soft bog to both sides of the road. In a few minutes I had moved a hundred yards to the left. I slipped off the heavy load, ripped out half a dozen metal boxes and sunk them one by one into the squelchy ground. Returning to the road, I walked another mile before abandoning the rucksack itself.

I was too hopelessly miserable to turn for home, too hopelessly miserable to do anything but impale myself on the guns of the desperate men who were waiting in the car a couples of mile ahead.

The St. Finan's junction appeared at last. The dark shape of the car was just visible against the light-coloured road. I walked quickly towards it. There was nobody inside. I turned to see a dark figure rise from the roadside. A light flashed in my eyes. I was just on the point of hurling myself forward when a vaguely familiar voice rang out:

"And what might you be doing here, sir?"

The light went off. I flicked on my own torch, and

saw a guard from Waterville with whom I had a passing acquaintance.

"Oh, Mr. McSweeney, I didn't recognise you. I'm on a late tramp, and getting pretty tired too. I saw the car as I passed the junction and wondered if by any chance I could get myself a lift along the road."

McSweeney was joined by a second guard, who asked: "And who might this be?"

"It's Mr. Sherwood. He lives on the other side of Waterville."

"This is a late hour to be on the road."

"That's true too. I'll be glad when I can climb into my bed," I replied.

"Would you have seen anybody walking the road?"

"I was passed by an odd cyclist, and by several cars."

"Which way have you come?"

"Over the Ballaghossian from Caragh."

"A powerful distance."

"That's what my feet are saying."

"Would any of the cyclists have been carrying a great rucksack?"

"Not that I could see."

"Well, well, it can't do any real harm if we take Mr. Sherwood home. Get into the car, Mr. Sherwood."

I was relieved to find both guards climbing into the front seats. I might be under suspicion but I was not yet under arrest. More alarming, what if these were John Chance's confederates, the men I was supposed to be meeting? Plainly I must prevent the guards from entering the cottage at all costs. I could deal with Chance, but I could scarcely hope to deal with three desperate and angry men.

I got out of the car at the entrance to the little lane that ran down to the cottage. The guards got out too.

"We'll see you down the lane, Mr. Sherwood. Just to make sure that everything's in order," said McSweeney.

"That's very kind of you but I shall be perfectly all right. I'm only tired, not crippled, you know."

"Some pretty queer customers are abroad tonight, and not the good people either," said the other guard with a chuckle.

"We'd like to see you home, Mr. Sherwood, as much for our satisfaction as for yours," added McSweeney.

So I had no choice but to lead the way. Thank heavens the cottage was in darkness. I opened the door —it was actually unlocked, but I rattled my key to make it sound as if I were unfastening the place. I switched on the light, thanking my lucky stars that I had been tidy enough to wash up after supper. The whiskey bottle and Chance's empty glass lay on the table. I grabbed two clean glasses.

"Have a snifter before you go," I remarked, slapping out the spirits in generous quantity before they had time to reply, for I was scared they would smell the stuff.

"Well, it isn't an Irishman's habit to refuse."

I noticed they darted glances about the place as they drank. But it wasn't easy to tell that I had already arrived at the cottage from Caragh during the late afternoon—if Chance kept quiet everything might still be saved.

"Thanks for the sensation, Mr. Sherwood. We'll be going our way, now that you seem to be all right here."

They stepped outside and I accompanied them,

ostensibly to offer further thanks for the ride. They moved off towards the lane. I returned to the cottage, but I waited with the door open listening to their progress down the lane. I heard the car start up and drive away, but of course only one of them might have gone and the other might be returning, so I locked the door and drew the curtains. I put a kettle on the stove, which would be the normal thing to do after a long tramp. The temptation to run upstairs or to shout was almost irresistible, but I realised that Chance might not have drawn the curtains and that an injudicious use of light might easily make him visible from the outside.

I waited as long as I could—perhaps half an hour, until the tension became unbearable. Then I took the bull by the horns. I switched on an upstairs light, going quickly from the one bedroom to the other. Chance had gone. I am half ashamed to say that I looked under the beds and in the wardrobes, but Chance had vanished, game leg and all. I am not a solitary drinker, but on that occasion I gulped down the last of the whiskey.

I fell asleep after lying for about an hour turning and twisting the incredible events of the night, trying to fit them into a pattern that had at least some semblance of rationality. It was just greying dawn outside when I was wakened by the loud ring of the telephone. In some apprehension, I went down the steep cottage stairs as quickly as I could. A girl's voice asked if it was Mr. Sherwood speaking. When I answered that it was, she simply laughed and immediately rang off.

By now I was quite hungry, so, gloomily, I cooked breakfast, thinking that from the moment I left Cambridge I seemed to have been surrounded by a raving pack of lunatics. If I could have viewed the happenings of the last eight hours without preconceptions I think I could have made sense of them. But the only line of reasoning that seemed to hold the slightest consistency led to such an apparently monstrous contradiction that I was not bold enough to follow it to an end.

The thing that worried me most about this strange affair was a strong feeling that this wasn't the first time I had seen Mr. John Chance. But where and when I first met him I could not think. My memory might still be playing an odd trick, of course.

CHAPTER SEVENTEEN

Break-through at Last

I am going to pass over several months' happenings rather quickly, not because this was a fallow period—I do not remember ever having worked so hard—but because most of my work was of only personal relevance.

Among the scientific activities that I discovered, two might be very briefly mentioned. I saw many more 'moving mountains', of the sort I had first glimpsed in Dublin. These machines, of the size of small ships, were of course nuclear-powered. Popularly known as the 'Neuclids', they were used for vast earth-moving operations. One day I watched them at work as they levelled and flattened the *Magavilé an Diail* to the east of Cahirciveen.

A great deal was apparently going on in the biological field. One point over which it was easy to get information deserves especial mention: the extermination of flies and insect pests in general. There may be some who will regret the passing of the mosquito and the midge, but I am not to be numbered among them.

In my attempt to catch up with Mitchell and his friends one of the obvious dodges I tried was attending the main weekly scientific seminar at Caragh. There was no security involved, so I'd no trouble in gaining

221

entry. But even though these meetings were well attended by the higher grades of scientific personnel, Mitchell and Co. never appeared.

This was the beginning of an important train of events, however, events that started in a small way. I was anxious to cause all the disturbance and disruption I possibly could. Outright defiance of restrictions seemed foolish and unprofitable, since the odds were obviously too much against me. But there was no harm in trying to inculcate a sense of inferiority in the scientific personnel, and I thought I saw how to do this.

I noticed a curiously contradictory feature of these weekly scientific meetings. Anyone who could ask intelligent questions of the lecturer of the day gained great prestige. And if the lecturer made an error that one could correct, then better still. In spite of the reputation that could be won in this fashion, nobody took the trouble to prepare himself in advance—apart from the lecturer, of course. Nor was it at all difficult to prepare oneself, because the subjects of the meetings were always announced at least a week beforehand.

So in addition to my own work I deliberately began to read up carefully in advance on all manner of topics. Sometimes the subjects were fairly mathematical. These were not only the easiest for me to cope with but they were also the greatest prestige-winners. I had more trouble with experimental physics and with chemical and biological topics. Yet a day or two's reading was usually sufficient to suggest a question or two. The great thing was that nine of the audience out of ten would be following the lecturer only rather vaguely. Then if one could ask some precisely formulated question the effect of a complete understanding was created.

I took up a position in the middle of the second row, leaving the front row for men of established reputation. It was astonishing how quickly the system took effect. Within a month the high and mighty were looking at me with averted vision. Within two months they were nodding openly. Within three months I had a recognised seat on the front row.

This policy had two effects. The more immediate, and the less important from a long-term point of view, was that I was asked to give a seminar myself, i.e., to be the lecturer on a certain day, the subject to be of my own choosing. Now it was indeed lucky that I had been hard at work during the past five months; for I did have something new to talk about—not completely developed, it is true, but interesting. I chose the following topic:

"*The Interpretation of Electric Charge as a Rotation.*"

One day I had a conversation with one of the older scientists. Would I undertake the solution of a set of equations that had proved very puzzling? They were of a non-linear partial type that could only be tackled numerically on a high-speed digital computer. I agreed to this proposal because I particularly wanted to gain some experience in the use of such a computer.

The special difficulty of the equations was that derivatives with respect to each of the variables became so large in certain ranges of the variables that it seemed impossible to store a lattice with the usual property of small changes of the functions from one lattice point to the next.

Once I had agreed to tackle the problem, I set about

it with great energy, if only to prevent my new-found reputation from sagging. The first step, and the most difficult, was to decide the mathematical method of attack. Then came the job of coding for the computer, which was of the ultra-high-speed, superconducting variety. Naturally I started by building up a stock of sub-routines. These I tested separately until they were working properly. Then came the big job of fitting all the individual pieces together and of writing the logical program for controlling their operation.

It was well past high summer before everything was working properly. I was now ready for producing results. This meant that instead of needing the computer for a few minutes at a time I would be requiring long 'production' runs, each lasting an hour or more. Clearly I should soon find out whether I.C.E. was really serious about this problem, or whether the idea was merely to keep me busy and quiet. In the latter case, they would soon jib at providing adequate time for these long runs on the machine.

As things turned out, I had no serious complaint to make. I got a fairly adequate ration of time on the computer—not as much as I'd have liked, but then nobody ever gets as much as he would like. Since the program worked pretty well I was soon on good terms with the machine manager and with his staff. I had an arrangement whereby I'd take over the computer whenever it happened to be free. This was fairly often, because plans for machine operation made in advance frequently go awry. So it was with many who were officially scheduled to use the machine. Things would go wrong, the instrument would lie unused, and then I could step in. By this device I was able to extend considerably the amount of time for which I was able to operate the computer.

I mention all this to explain why I got into the habit of examining the machine schedules pretty closely. It annoyed me that no shifts were normally worked over the week-ends. The waste of the computer seemed scandalous, if not downright wicked. But I was told that there simply wasn't enough work to justify the extra staff that would be necessary for week-end operation. I suppose this was right, for with a computer of such great speed the amount of calculation that could be done in a five-day week was fantastically large. Still, it seemed a shocking waste.

On Monday, Tuesday, and Thursday the computer was run from 9 a.m. to 6 p.m., and from 8 p.m. to 7 a.m. The intervening short periods—viz. 6 p.m. to 8 p.m., and 7 a.m. to 9 a.m., were used for engineering maintenance. On Wednesdays and Fridays the computer was run from 9 a.m. to 4.30 p.m., and there was no night shift. Naturally I was curious about this difference, and my curiosity was sharply augmented by my complete failure to find any explanation for it. When I mentioned the matter to the machine manager, he jumped so violently that I was very careful to say nothing more.

The obvious tactic was to try to get a run that would last right up to 4.30 p.m. on one of these days. It was a long time before success came my way, and then only as a result of a double accident. The manager was on holiday, and his assistant's wife was expecting a baby. One Friday, the assistant phoned to say that the computer was available from 3 p.m. to 4.15 p.m., but that on no account must I continue to work after 4.15 p.m. Foolishly he told me that he himself would not be in the laboratory that particular afternoon. This meant that I had only the young operator to deal with, and I knew he would be anxious to get away for the week-end, probably with his wife to the sea.

It was something of a dubious trick to assure the young fellow that he could leave at 4 p.m. I made all the necessary motions to indicate that I was packing up and told him to go off, saying that I would set a new roll of paper in the 'printer' as soon as I had all my tables, cards, and tapes collected together. By now I had learned how to operate the machine pretty well, and I had worked with this particular operator fairly often. So, being Irish, and therefore no instinctive stickler for rules and regulations, he left me to my own devices at about 4.5 p.m.

I restarted the computer with a scarcely ruffled conscience. When 4.15 p.m. came I continued to let the machine calculate. Slowly the minutes slipped away. I was on tenterhooks lest someone should come in. The following quarter of an hour provided the first case of a lack of security that I can recall since my entry into the services of I.C.E. Someone should certainly have been detailed to make sure that the computer had been vacated. It is strange, indeed, how easily a simple security precaution can be overlooked at the end of a week in the holiday season, especially on a really beautiful day.

The clock came to 4.30 p.m. and still there was no interruption. The computer went merrily along,

chattering out its results. Then I was aware that someone had come in quite quietly. I was examining the
results at the printer, and I forced myself to go on doing
so for maybe half a minute.

"Oh, I'd no idea the machine was in use."

"No, you can have it straight away," I replied.

"If there's something you want to finish . . ."

"No, no, I can output the calculation on to tape, and
pick it up later."

I flicked a switch, and one of the magnetic units came
immediately into motion.

"All right, I'm finished now."

I moved over to retrieve the tape with my unfinished
calculation on it, intensely conscious that I had just
managed to win a round in this long-drawn-out game.
For the intruder was none other than Fanny, the half-
blonde girl who had been right about her topology
when the other five were wrong, back so long ago on
the island of Inishvickillane.

I watched out of the corner of my eye as her deck of
cards went into the 'reader'. Plainly it was a very big
program, some three times my own. Since the difficulty of a program depends about on the square of
the number of instructions, this had roughly ten times
the difficulty of mine. 'Pray heavens it doesn't work,'
I thought uncharitably. 'Otherwise I'll be getting the
inferiority, not I.C.E.!'

The machine worked for perhaps ten seconds and
stopped. The girl, swearing quietly to herself, keyed in
a manual instruction and immediately a group of
numbers was hammered out on the printer. Then the
girl retired to study her program together with the

numbers. Time crept on. Five o'clock came and I was in an agony lest someone in authority should find me there. I was sorely tempted to seek some redress for the day on the cliffs of Inishtooskert, which I had by no means forgotten. But I kept at a distance while she worked away. I think the computer must have been lying idle for some forty-five minutes before she got up with a long sheet of new instructions that had now to be inserted manually into the machine. In this way it was possible to modify the programme at an enormous expense of operating time.

"You'd better read out the instructions, and where you want 'em to go, while I do the keying," I said.

We worked for about half an hour flicking the keys. I concentrated really hard, determined not to make an error, which is only too easily done. Then we cross-checked all the changes, reading from the machine as it was now modified against the girl's list. When at length she was satisfied, one more instruction was keyed—to start the computer calculating again. 'It can't possibly work,' I said to myself, 'not after all this agony.' But it did. At least it didn't stop this time.

The girl sat over the printer, watching the numbers that were tapped out from time to time. She compared them with a hand-written table taken from a file.

"It looks to be working all right now—as far as I can tell."

"Well, well, I must say for a fisherman you seem enormously versatile," she added.

"I'm afraid my program is a very modest affair compared with this," I said, indicating the machine and its present calculation.

"What are you doing?"

I gave a brief sketch of my own problem.

"You know," she said, "I had an idea you were around Caragh when I saw a notice of a seminar on the nature of electric charge. Perhaps you could tell me about it over dinner? I want to get about another hour's work done. You don't mind waiting?"

In the circumstances waiting was the last thing I minded. When the machine had been switched off and we'd gathered together our respective belongings, I asked the girl where we should go. With the first grin I'd seen from her, she answered:

"One of the public places."

We packed our things in the back of a car parked close by the lab. While the girl drove, I guided her to a good restaurant about five miles to the south, one that wouldn't be too noisy. Our entry was marked by some curious glances from one or two of the tables.

I took this to be a tribute to the girl's appearance, which in truth was very remarkable—violet eyes, light hair, and a skin that looked as if it had been deeply tanned by a month of climbing on sunlit snow mountains. She appeared to be in her early twenties, but I had a suspicion she was older.

There were obvious reasons why I didn't want to talk physics. But by the time the edge of hunger had been assuaged, the girl's demands to hear about the nature of electric charge had a curiously commanding ring. So there was nothing to be done except to let the conversation swing to technicalities, away from the matters that were on my mind.

I drew pictures and jotted down various equations on

the back of a menu. When I was through all the explanations, she said:

"You'll get a fair measure of success with that approach, but it's very ugly."

"Can you suggest one better?"

"Yes, of course, but not without quite extensive changes. The whole way of writing the theory needs inverting. Instead of using space-time for the basic variables, put field quantities as the independent variables in the equations that describe the particles."

"Which is something I've vaguely wondered about— getting space-time as a derived quantity, getting it from field variables with a degree of arbitrariness equivalent to the usual invariance conditions."

"Well, you'd better stop vaguely wondering. I'll show you later how to get started, although I really oughtn't to be telling you all this."

The waiter brought the dessert. I waited for him to leave before asking the obvious question:

"And why shouldn't you be telling me this?"

She answered in a quiet voice: "Because according to what I'm told you happen to be a most desperate and dangerous fellow." She laughed quite unaffectedly.

"You must have been told a whole lot of nonsense."

"Oh, I don't think so. About a month ago I read through quite a long and entertaining dossier about you." Again she laughed, and like a fool I couldn't see the joke. "When you came here to Ireland what was it you were looking for, Mr. Fisherman?"

"Maybe you."

"Well, and now you've found me what do you propose to do?"

230

"Find out about those equations, of course."

"You don't like being laughed at, do you? You're every bit as bad as the others."

"Did you have a hand in that business on the cliffs of Inishtooskert, by the way?"

This stopped the laughter.

"No, I didn't know anything about it at the time. That particularly futile brain-storm was cooked up by Arthur or by his wife. But I did make sure that nothing of the sort was tried again."

"For which my thanks! The blonde climber was Mitchell's wife?"

"Is, the tense is wrong."

"He's welcome to her, the——"

"Tsh-sh."

"And what was so futile about the idea of leaving me hanging on to that damned cliff?"

"It was obvious you'd get down. And if you didn't you didn't deserve to, being taken in by a ninny like that!"

"When you've need of it you seem to have access to a pretty fair fund of irrationality, don't you?"

"Look, I think we'd better get back to the car. I dislike having to cross to the island after dark, although with you there, Mr. Fisherman, I suppose I really shouldn't worry. You'd better pay the bill. You do pay the bill, don't you?"

"Yes, I pay my debts."

"That's rather what I thought. I do too."

The girl drove the car rapidly northward towards Killorglin.

"I suppose you know that the northern peninsula is

out of bounds for me?"

"Scared? Do you want to get out?"

"The answer to both questions is no. I mention it because I shall have to depend on you to get me through the security checks."

"Do you suppose the thought hadn't occurred to me?"

"A while back you mentioned a dossier. Have you any idea where the information in it came from?"

"If I wanted to be unkind, to baffle you, to keep you quiet for a few minutes while I concentrate on driving this car, I'd tell you that Seamus Colquhoun happens to be one of our best agents—we have some, you know. Does the name mean anything to you? I think I've got it right."

Here was a minor mystery cleared up. Now I knew how Mr. John Chance had got hold of Parsonage's passwords, and with this knowledge I remembered exactly where I'd seen Mr. Chance for the first time. Now I understood the motive for his visit to my cottage. It boiled up inside me, not anger, but helpless laughter.

"So you have a sense of humour after all!" she remarked.

"Then it was pretty well a miracle that I got anywhere at all."

"It was utterly astonishing. We never reckoned that anybody would have the hardihood—or should I say the foolhardihood?—to bring in a boat on a night like the one on which you came to Inishvickillane. You see why I said it was ridiculous to think that you could be finished off with that cliff trick. When someone shows himself to have the luck of the devil, a sensible person draws the obvious conclusion."

"How did you come to get hold of the dossier?"

"I suppose I'd better explain a few things. I never intended to leave you kicking your heels around Caragh for so long. But for some months I was terribly busy, and by the time I got round to it our people had made a silly sort of game out of teasing you."

"Would you call making me lose my memory a piece of teasing?"

"When you come to hear the full story of the memory business you'll see there were two sides to it. I think you'll agree that you've really made a pretty good bargain."

"And Mr. John Chance?"

"Yes, that was rather well done, wasn't it? But trying to isolate you, to keep you odd man out wasn't at all sensible. After what had happened already it was perfectly clear that you'd manage to fit everything together sooner or later. The interest of the game was to see how you'd do it, just where you'd pop up. I could have died of laughter when I saw you in the computer room today. But I'll say no more, or you'll be getting conceited, if you're not that already."

There was no danger of adding to my conceit, for this was one of the most deflating remarks I'd ever heard. If this incredible girl had been laughing at me, how had she been able to correct such a huge difficult program on the computer?

We took the road through Milltown and turned off for Dingle at Castlemain. There were three security controls at various points, but the girl and the car were apparently well known, for we passed through them almost without stopping.

The clouds flared red in front of us as we left Dingle behind. I think both of us were conscious of chasing the declining sun as we drove up the incline to Bally-ferriter. In spite of the matters that were insistently running through my head, it was impossible not to be overwhelmed by the blazing western sky. We stopped the car along the road between Ballyferriter and Dunquin, and climbed away on to the rough moorland. The sea below us was alive with a liquid fire.

The girl was shaking with violent, uncontrolled sobs. By now I was immured to most occasions of surprise, but this was utterly beyond expectation. I slipped my arm around her. She tried to shy violently away, but I held fast and soon she stopped protesting.

We returned to the car and I took it the last part of the journey to Dunquin Harbour. Because of the ideas that danced in my head I found the driving horribly difficult, for the incredible solution to the main mystery had suddenly leaped into the glaring light of consciousness.

CHAPTER EIGHTEEN

Inishvickillane Again

The light was fading quickly as we moved out from Dunquin, headed south of Blasket. There was much on my mind, above all there was much that I wanted to ask this strange girl. But this wasn't the right time or place, what with the noise of the engine and the sound of the sea slapping hard on the boat-side.

Besides, I was still half unnerved by the deception of Seamus Colquhoun. Not that this was a matter of much importance any longer. But what a fool I had been to be taken in by the wretched man! True, I had always felt somewhat uneasy in my talks with him, but this very agitation had somehow contrived to mislead me. The amazing thing was that he had never tried to find out who had sent me, or anything about my mission—he didn't even seem to know my name. If he had ever shown the least curiosity my suspicions would probably have been roused—at least I hoped so.

Then in a further flash I saw the reason. Because anything I could have told Colquhoun was already known to I.C.E. How, and from where, I still couldn't say. Percy Parsonage? I doubted it—I simply had to doubt it, otherwise my reason must have given way. Mr. Rafferty? I doubted this too. Rafferty wasn't in the right class. But then, if I'd misjudged Colquhoun, why not George Rafferty too? No, no, this was beyond possibility.

Then I saw the whole business as it must have seemed to I.C.E. First, the fantastic business on the train to Fishguard. Papa Percy's blood had got me into Ireland all right, but not at all for the reason he expected. Who would have had the heart to keep me out after that affair? How they must have laughed! But I suspect the Homeric aspects of the matter probably wore a bit thin during my first week in Dublin. My small-minded antics, in museums, at 18 St. Stephen's Green, with Sam Lover and Buck Whaley, were not at all to be favourably compared with the robuster concepts of the ticket-collector, Karl, Inspector Harwood, and the imaginary body.

As I say, I think I.C.E. lost patience after that tame first week. I think they decided to pull me in as soon as I appeared at Marrowbone Lane. And not to be outdone by Parsonage's affray in the train, I think they put on a similar ribald show, with Liam and the Irish stage character, and with the posse of police. But for the first time I won a few points in the game; I wriggled out of the net, and in a way that could hardly have been guessed beforehand.

After that, I was manifestly given a fair amount of rope. And why not, since Colquhoun must have known about Houseman and P.S.D.? He must have known that in sending me to Longford he was playing a masterstroke.

Yet from the moment I stepped off the bus at Tang the game swung more and more in my favour. I think they lost my track as I walked my quiet, gentle way through the lanes and fields of Ireland. I think the appallingly unlucky coincidence at Slievenamuck with its ghastly outcome was more than they bargained for. I think that they only picked up the trail again at Shannon Airport, almost certainly because of my booking of the flight to London. No wonder Seamus Colquhoun was waiting there on the road to Kilkee!

This raised another of my failures. The cut-out on Colquhoun's car had definitely been wrong—a delightful subtlety on his part, not a chance coincidence as I had supposed. In fact I ought to have deduced Colquhoun's duplicity from this one incident alone. Obviously the true Canon had been questioned, and had given the purchase of a cut-out as my reason for visiting Limerick.

Yet the shipwreck on Inishvickillane won a major victory for me—I knew it even at the time. But my one moment of supreme triumph was quite missed, the moment in which I had blandly announced my name. This must have come on them like a bolt from heaven. I remembered now the silence of that moment, and I knew that if I had hit hard in exactly the right direction all could have been settled within the space of a single hour. Instead, I had told a pettifogging, feeble story. After my topological intervention, this must have seemed a pitiful anticlimax. It explained Fanny's sarcastic laughter, and it allowed Mr. John Chance to regain the initiative.

The mere thought of Mr. Chance filled me with a deep shame. Oh, it was so easy to make excuses in plenty: that I had seen him only once before for an odd hour in a poorish light, that I was suffering from a loss of memory, that the bandage on his head made an excellent disguise, that his voice was brilliantly changed. But back in Parsonage's office I had read a dossier on Arthur Mitchell. I knew perfectly well that he was born in Devon, at Barnstaple in 1925. I knew that he won a scholarship to Winchester, which meant that he would have an accented and an unaccented voice both readily at his command.

The boat was approaching the little harbour on the island. In a few minutes I should probably be seeing Arthur Mitchell again. I resolved that on this third occasion the honours of the encounter should be divided a little more equally between us. I would have been quite aghast to learn the margin by which I was to lose this third exchange, for I had still to learn that there is no better way to drown a serious argument than by the popping of champagne corks.

Now we had reached the anchorage. We made fast, climbed the little cliff, and started along the path to the stone house.

"And have you got everything sorted out, Mr. Fisherman?"

"Not quite, but I'm making some progress."

"You're an odd fellow."

"Are you thinking of any particular one of my oddities?"

"There aren't many people who know anything about us, but those that do, when they first find out . . ." She paused in mid-sentence.

"Recoil?"

"Not so much physically as mentally."

"And I didn't?"

"No."

"Was it because you thought I might that you never tried to seek me out?"

She took me by the arm. "Look, my fisherman friend, it's nice that you're very intelligent, but there is no need to be quite so clear-headed."

'They' were waiting for us: Mitchell and his wife Harriet, Hertzbrun, and the other half-blonde girl— the man apparently was away. It was interesting that our coming must have been advertised, either by the restaurant or by one of the security controls.

The girl Fanny had evidently entirely recovered herself. She introduced me with obvious relish:

"Arthur, meet Mr. Sherwood. Two old Cambridge men together. You'll be able to have quite a talk."

"I hope the knee is better," I said.

"Very much better, thank you. Did Fanny tell you?"

"No, he guessed all by himself. And here is Harriet, Arthur's wife. But of course you're old friends, aren't you?" The two girls stood side by side, of about the same height with hair of nearly the same colour, one with light skin and the other with dark, one with blue-violet eyes the other with green—a couple of cats watching each other.

"Homer Hertzbrun—Mr. Sherwood. Homer, you should hear what Mr. Sherwood has to say about the geometry of electric charge." Then she turned to the other half-blonde. "And now meet my twin—Mr. Sherwood—Mary Ann."

"Well, Fanny, so you decided to get him after all."

"Do you have to sound so predatory?"

239

"I'm not predatory, I'm just delighted that we shall be able to have some peace now."

It would have been easy to be misled by this innocent conversation. I'd again been astonished by Mitchell's youthful appearance. 'He certainly looks no more than thirty,' I thought; 'yet the man must be approaching forty-five.' There was just one possible explanation. These people must have solved the very difficult bio-chemical problem of arresting the ageing process.

Strange that the old legend should describe the Land of Youth as an island off the Kerry coast. Suddenly I realised what Fanny had meant by the other half of the bargain, and I knew at last just what it was that I felt to be different in me.

Hertzbrun quickly produced a tray with drinks and glasses.

"That's exactly what I need, Homer," exclaimed Mitchell. "I'm going to drink to the end of my responsibilities."

"I don't get it."

"Of course you get it. I'm going to put my feet up, I'm going to get rid of my ulcers, I'm going to have one long, glorious holiday. Homer my boy, pour me a large tot, a very large one."

"But—"

"No buts. It's perfectly obvious. Here's young Sherwood, twenty years younger than me in actual years, and as strong as a horse. Why shouldn't I let him do the worrying? He knows almost as much about science as I do, and he's much more ruthless, in fact he's quite an ugly customer."

"If I might offer an opinion . . ." I started.

"You may not. Yes, much more ruthless. Besides, he's got Fanny's ear, and I haven't. The next phase of development depends on Fanny, and the two of us have too many rows."

Mary Ann laughed, and another small mystery was cleared away. This was the laugh I had heard over the telephone, on the morning after the visit of Mr. Chance.

"Poor Arthur, if you think they're not going to have plenty of rows you're very much mistaken. Either there will be some splendid rows or Fanny will simply gobble him up."

"Now look here, you're all taking too much for granted, especially Mitchell," I objected.

"It may seem very precipitate to you, Sherwood, but it isn't really. I wonder if you've any idea what it means to start an organisation like this absolutely from scratch, to build everything step by step. It's like bringing up a child. At first you think all your worries'll be over in a year or two, but they're not. Then you think everything will be plain sailing after ten years, but it isn't. Then you realise you'll never be out of trouble, however long you go on."

"Stop wailing," said Mary Ann. "Some women bring up six children."

"I'm not wailing. I'm showing Sherwood why it's been on my mind for some time to find someone who could take over the responsibilities. I've had my eye on Sherwood right from the start, or at any rate from the time he finished off those absurd P.S.D. people."

"Right from the start? So you have agents in London?"

"Why be so naïve? Of course we have agents in

London. Is that very surprising?"

"It would relieve my mind a great deal to know who it was in particular that forwarded the information about me."

"I don't know that I ought to gratify your morbid curiosity. But you may take it that we knew all about you, several days before you left London."

"It wouldn't have been Parsonage by any chance?"

"Oh no, not Papa Percy. He's a regular fire-eater, the poor old fellow. I had a lot of trouble with him, until I managed to place a very capable girl in his office, one whom you were kind enough to take out to dinner, I believe?"

I moaned aloud.

"Are you feeling all right?" asked Mary Ann.

"Hands off! Or you'll get—" began Fanny.

"In heaven's name, will you two stop it! Cat and dog, always cat and dog," exclaimed the green-eyed Harriet.

"Now, I wonder which is the cat," answered Mary Ann, displaying a full set of teeth.

"Ladies!" exclaimed Hertzbrun.

"You should say 'fair ladies'," I remarked absently.

"Of course he should," nodded Mary Ann. "Why don't you say 'fair ladies', Homer?"

"When the wind blows, never ask it to stop. Just let it blow itself out," groaned Fanny.

"How did you find out about the petrol bombs?"

"Oh, after we got our first report, from one of our men—a Seamus Colquhoun if you're interested—we sent in our experts. I think they pieced together what had happened pretty well. Incidentally, why did you use two bombs? Wouldn't one have been sufficient?"

"I used two because I'm an ugly customer."

"Which is rather what we thought. Well, as I was saying, I became very interested in you at this stage, particularly when you got away from our frontier patrol in the Boggerath Mountains. I still can't see how the devil you managed to do that, or how you split the skull of a man seven stones heavier than yourself."

Mitchell began to laugh.

"Look at him, Homer! Sitting there as large as life, imagining himself to be a placid, docile, law-abiding, young man."

He went on with a rush, plainly to stop the irrepressible Mary Ann: "Of course I expected you'd be caught trying to get into Kerry. We put out special alerts to all our patrols. I was flabbergasted when you did get in, and to Inishvickillane of all places."

"Couldn't you have kept a watch on me at Kilkee? Then you must have known that I'd try from the sea."

"We expected you to try from the sea. But we never contemplated either that you'd come in on such a wild night, or that you'd be mad enough to risk this part of the coast." He paused for a drink. "When you appeared out of the sea, and told such a convincing story with the aplomb of a bishop, I realised that you were probably my man."

"So you promptly arranged to have me killed on the cliffs of Inishtooskert?"

"I must admit that we were all a little at cross-purposes over that business. But it was no serious matter."

"No serious matter!"

"Of course not. If you hadn't had the determination to get down that damned cliff you certainly wouldn't have been our man."

"And if I'd ended by falling into the sea?"

"Well, even more certainly you wouldn't have been our man, would you now, my dear fellow?"

"Didn't I overhear you say something just now about me being ruthless?"

"I said you were more ruthless than we are, which I think is true. Look, Sherwood, answer me fair. If you'd tried to kill somebody on those cliffs, would you have given 'em the slightest chance of getting away safely?"

"I'd never try to kill anyone in that way."

"No, you'd feed 'em boron, I suppose—it was boron, wasn't it?"

"I never heard anything about boron," said Hertzbrun.

"Oh, it was just another example of Sherwood's methods. He threatened to feed a boron porridge to one of our men. Then, having terrified the poor fellow, he proceeded to cuff him soundly."

"Well, Arthur, I must say I certainly question the wisdom of handing things over to such a bloodthirsty young devil as Sherwood seems to be. Boron and neutrons, eh? A very nasty idea, I must say."

"No, I think you're wrong, Homer. Our policy needs to be more aggressive. Sherwood is just the right man to put a real edge on the weapons we've been forging. Look, Sherwood, do you mind if I ask you a straight question?"

244

"No, no, ask anything. How many pints of my blood did you say you wanted?"

"There's no need to take umbrage, man. What really surprises me is why it took so long—almost a year—for you to get back to Inishvickillane. You see, this was a point of some importance to me, because I'd made the decision to carry on until you got back here. I've been getting quite impatient. In fact I even had to come out and look you up myself, in Ballinskelligs if I remember rightly."

"I hope I behaved to your satisfaction on that occasion?"

"Entirely so, but really you should have recognised me, you know!"

Then, just as I thought I must burst apart, Fanny laughed and took my arm. "In case you may not have noticed it, he's pulling your leg. You'll have to get used to this appalling madhouse. Let's go for a walk by the sea."

CHAPTER NINETEEN

At the Strand's Edge

The tide was down, so that we could walk the sand by the margin of the sea.

"Don't be misled by Mary Ann. She's really very clever."

"I wasn't misled at all. Was it she who solved the ageing problem?"

"You don't miss much, do you? I suppose it was fairly obvious from Arthur. But how did you guess it was Mary Ann?"

"Oh, just bits and fragments of talk, and a good deal of intuition. But that was a very ingenious piece of rough-housing. Did they think it all up while we were driving from Caragh?"

"Most of it, I expect. But you took it very well."

"I took it very stupidly. I just didn't seem to have a single decent card to play."

"Well, it wasn't entirely nonsense. Arthur is very tired, and it has been a long struggle. It's a hard struggle for everybody."

"Why is it so hard?"

"It's hard for Arthur because he's got all the donkey work to do. It's hard for Mary Ann to take anything very seriously. And it's hard for me because I get depressed."

The night was beautifully clear. At last the moment had come to ask the first of the questions that were thundering in my head:

"Can we see it from here?"

The girl pointed to the chain of stars lying between Delta and Omicron Herculis. "It doesn't seem very much," she whispered, "just a faint thing that you'd scarcely notice without a telescope."

I gazed up at the sky. So this was where it had come from, this bolt of knowledge, this bolt that was going to turn our little human world head over heels. Small wonder I hadn't thought of it before.

"What was the trouble? Increasing heat?"

"Yes, we were slowly cooked alive as our star became brighter and brighter. As generation followed generation we adapted ourselves as best we could. We lived in vast refrigerators, but in the end nothing could keep out the fierce blast.

"The rocks became fluid with a liquid fire—it was like the sea tonight when we got out of the car. That's why I was so upset. What is beautiful here was extermination for us. Our planet was wiped clean. An evolution that had taken a thousand million years to develop suddenly ceased to exist."

Once again I slipped an arm around her. This time she laughed.

"You wouldn't be doing that if you knew what I once looked like. Not at all like a human."

Now I saw the point more clearly. It would be futile to send a physical body hurtling across space. The essential thing was to send the information, the bolt of information. This would be much easier to do in any case.

"So you changed your body—the chemical part of you. But the electronic part is the same. In computer language, your old brain program was written on to a human brain."

"It was rather like taking a program from a very large computer and attempting to write it into a small computer, like trying to pour a large volume of precious liquid into a tiny vessel—great quantities spilled and wasted. Imagine trying to compress your own degree of perception into the brain of a dog. Everything becomes dim and vague, like a clear landscape suddenly enshrouded in mist.

"After all, we were beings of somewhere between the third and fourth orders."

"Sorry, I don't understand third and fourth orders."

"Oh, just a rough measure of intelligence. We could handle problems needing somewhere between a thousand million and ten thousand million units of information. Now I'm reduced maybe to around a hundred million."

"Divide units of information by a million and take the logarithm to base ten, eh?"

Fanny quickly stamped hard on my toes. "Stop talking like a child."

"You've got a lot of power in that darned leg of yours. How did you come by it? I mean, were you assembled from raw materials—water, ordinary carbon and nitrogen and so forth?"

"I'm pretty sure not. To construct a human directly from inorganic materials is a problem of the fourth order, and this I think would have been too difficult. It would be much simpler to get the bodies produced in the ordinary way and then to write the information on the brain. I'd guess this to be no more than a third order problem, if as much as that. But you'd do better to ask Dicky. You haven't really met him yet, but it's much more in his line. You see, the three of us are pretty complementary to each other—Mary Ann and Dicky got the chemical and biological knowledge, while I got the physical. Obviously it's better like this than if we'd all been the same."

"So in the early chemical days of I.C.E. it was the others who supplied the main drive, while now you're responsible for all the new physical development."

"You may say that if you wish."

"So if I were to dump you in the water my job as an agent would really be finished, wouldn't it? Remember what you said about me being a dangerous fellow."

I just managed to get my other foot out of the way in time.

"You don't like being laughed at, do you?—as bad as the others."

"I don't like being taken for a fool."

"Stop being so appallingly human," I said.

She laughed loud and clear above the noise of the sea.

As we walked slowly arm in arm the thoughts chased themselves in my head. Before the moment of extinction arrived a dying race had somehow managed to transfer a little of its experience and knowledge to another planet. So much was clear. But how had it been done?

The transmission of information from a planet moving around one star to a planet moving around a quite different star was clearly not out of the question. It probably wasn't very much beyond our own present-day techniques. This girl Fanny was manifestly an ordinary human on whose brain the information from another race had somehow been written.

A baby isn't born with a knowledge of physics and mathematics. This comes to be impressed on the brain as the baby grows up; from reading books, from listening to the words of one's teachers, and of course from observing the world around us. In some way I still didn't understand, this normal process had been replaced by a more powerful method, a method controlled by an alien race. The motive of this race was clear—to pass on some memory of itself, to avoid a complete oblivion.

The waves were falling gently on the sand. We stopped for a moment to watch.

"It's very beautiful here. You know, I don't think we had much idea about beauty—there wasn't much of it in our world, I suppose, just a blazing, glaring slag-heap." She kicked a stone into the water. "We weren't angry, just resigned to passing on what we could. But now in some queer way I seem less resigned. What's the point of it all? It'll be just the same here. The Earth is already half-way along exactly the same road to extinction. The Sun will get inexorably brighter as the years roll by, just as our star did, and life on the Earth will just as surely come to an end."

"I suppose that some reasonably sensible game is being played all right, if only we were clever enough to see it."

"But how clever? It's the lack of detailed balancing that really astonishes me—the Universe has an enormous effect on us, but we seem to have no reverse effect on the Universe."

"I think we might have if only we knew enough."

"To see the complete logical design?"

"To see a logical design better than the actual one. Then I think that something might happen."

"Which may well be true. But we know nothing of the level of intelligence that would be needed."

"Except that humans fall far short of it. Your race fell short, perhaps by a little, perhaps by a lot. It may come at what you would call the fourth order, or at the tenth order, or at the millionth order."

"And I suppose that if a species doesn't get far enough ahead it's simply wiped out, as we were wiped out."

"You weren't wiped out. What you've now got in your head survived. It may save humanity a century, or a millennium. It gives us a push onwards down a long road. In our turn we may get nowhere. We may have to end by passing what scraps of information we can to some other creature. But maybe in the end someone will succeed where all the rest have failed."

"All right, Mr. Fisherman, I understand the lesson. It's only when I'm depressed that I become stupid."

We made our way up from the strand. It is a narrow way up the cliffs, but somehow we managed to climb the path, together.

Epilogue

The Cointreau was finished, the reading done, the coffee cold, the fire out, but Geoffrey Holtum sat on, scratching his head.

October the First is Too Late

To the Reader

The 'science' in this book is mostly
scaffolding for the story, story-telling in
the traditional sense. However, the discussions
of the significance of time and of the
meaning of consciousness are intended to be
quite serious, as also are the contents of
chapter fourteen.

Fred Hoyle, 14 July 1965

1 Prelude

I had been invited to compose a piece for the Festival of Contemporary Music, Cologne, 1966. My intention was a set of variations in serial form. I chose the serial formula, partly as a technical exercise, partly because I had a fancy to end each variation with the sound of a farmyard animal.

The first three variations went smoothly enough but I got stuck on the fourth. I decided a change of air was needed to get me out of the rut. My decision to go for a week down to Cornwall was the trifling beginning of a sequence of momentous events. It was as if I had crossed a more or less flat watershed that nevertheless separates rivers flowing to quite different oceans.

I was lying on the clifftops in the sunshine trying to puzzle out exactly how one might imitate the whinny of a horse. I must have dozed off to sleep for perhaps ten minutes. I woke with a tremendous tune, the melody of a lifetime, running in my head. It flowed on and on, statement and response, question and answer, seemingly without end. It began with a series of rocking chords in the bass. Then the first phrase came in the treble. From there on it took off with a momentum that never seemed to die, the kind of *perpetuum mobile* you get in the first movement of the sixth Brandenburg concerto. Quickly, I scribbled the cascade of notes on a piece of score paper, for this was not a case in which I dare trust to memory. How inevitable a melody is while you have it running in your head, how difficult to recapture once it has gone.

On the way back to my lodging at a local farmhouse I passed several horses grazing but the thought of my fourth variation was gone now. Late into the night I pondered on the ramifications of that tune. It is rare indeed for a long melody to go well with harmony. To produce striking orchestral effects one normally uses a mixture of several scraps of melody, mere fragments. But this case seemed different. Orchestral ideas grew naturally around it. The instruments thundered in my head, their individual qualities, their distinctive tones, became ever more clear, ever sharper. The people of the farm must have thought me a queer fish, I dare say. I sat all day writing for the fever of creation was on me. By the end of the week the piece was essentially finished. There was still routine work to do but nothing more.

I was already on my way back to London before the problem of the Festival recurred to me. It was obvious the variations would never be finished in time. It wasn't just a week that was lost. In the past few days I had burnt up a couple of months of normal effort. I wondered about using the new piece. Reason told me no, emotion told me yes. I desperately wanted to hear the new sounds from the orchestra. I had given it everything, maximum sonority. Yet this was exactly where I would run into trouble. A considerable quantity of electronic music would quite certainly be played. My piece, coming late in the programme, would unfortunately look like an all-out attack on other composers. When compared with the full blast of the true orchestra, their stuff would inevitably sound thin and wan.

Then there were two points of conscience. I don't have any rooted objection to the *avant garde*. While the new fashions have nothing very great to recommend them, they do at least contribute *something* to music. Classical methods work wonderfully well for the positive emotions, for sentiments of epic proportions. But the less pleasant emotions cannot be described at all in classical terms. It was beyond the resources of even the greatest of the old musicians to display genuine anger for instance. So really I had no quarrel with modern styles as such. My quarrel was with a fashion that claimed those styles to be everything, as if a craftsman were to insist on always working with a single tool.

My second worry was whether my piece could really be described as 'contemporary'. Of course it was contemporary in the sense that it was recent, not more than a week old, but there is a sense in which the word represents form and technique rather than chronology.

The choice evidently lay between withdrawing and going ahead with the new piece. After something of a struggle with myself I decided to go ahead. There was a lot to be done, parts to be copied, and then mailed way to Germany. The orchestra was to be the Mannheim Symphony.

The journey to Cologne was uneventful. Two rehearsals were scheduled for me. After a few misunderstandings I managed to get the playing into tolerable shape. My time was an evening of the second week. As it came round I was motivated in the following way. My thoughts on the piece had dulled in the intervening weeks but the sound of the orchestra reawakened something of the fury I had felt in that week in Cornwall. This, and the fact that several people had heard my rehearsals and had already spread critical rumours, put me in a combative state of mind by the time I walked on to the platform to conduct.

All worries disappeared at the first surge of the music. For the next seventeen minutes I was totally committed to the vision I had had on those faraway Cornish cliffs. In rehearsal I deliberately held the orchestra back. When an orchestra becomes excited with a new work it is good policy to wait until the first actual performance before giving them their full head. I not only gave it them now I drove them with an intensity I had never shown before. In a sense it comes ill of a composer to speak well of his own work; but it is all so far back now that I think I can be reasonably objective. As the melody surged into the final fanfare I knew I had in no way disgraced myself. I also knew I had contributed little to music except a stirring fifteen minutes or so. The musician's problem is stated very simply: how to display the more worthwhile aspects of human nature differently from the old masters. Modern styles have concentrated in part on the meaner side of things, as I have already remarked, in part on the purely abstract. Modern styles are no solution to the problem but neither was my piece. It was an extrapolation of the old methods. It faced the challenge of comparison with the composers of the past – for fifteen minutes. It pointed no way to anybody else.

This criticism I would have been entirely willing to accept if the audience had admitted the straightforward merit of what had been done. They didn't. There was scattered applause mixed with boos and hisses. Momentarily nonplussed I failed to take a quick bow and to make a quick exit. The hissing increased. Suddenly I became coldly angry. With an imperious

257

gesture I turned to the leader and shouted loudly, 'Bar one!' Such is the respect of a German orchestra for its conductor that the players all obediently turned back to the beginning. Before anybody in the audience realized what was going to happen the rolling bass chords started again. The shouting behind me held its own for a little while until the orchestra picked up volume. Then as the full chords broke loose the mob amounted to little more than a whisper in a storm. At the end they had their say, or rather their shout. This time it was quite full blooded. I was in no doubt of what to do. I bowed around the hall twice, shook the leader's hand, patted him on the shoulder, and walked out.

As I made my way back to the hostel I fully intended to quit Cologne the following morning. Yet when morning came I saw no reason to run away like a whipped dog. I found it much easier to behave normally, as if nothing had happened, than I would have expected. My fellow musicians were only meeting me in small numbers at a time now. Perhaps for this reason they had lost something of the confidence of the evening before. Several of the critics went out of their way to tell me, more or less out of the back of the hand, how much they had enjoyed my piece. Well, well. I remembered being told, as a youngster, that if universal approbation represented a hundred per cent on a scale of appreciation, then to be universally well known, but disliked, was already worth fifty per cent. To be entirely unknown corresponded to the zero mark.

I did leave the Festival two days before its end, not under any compulsion, but because I got bored. Two weeks of caterwauling was more than I could take. So midway through the afternoon I found myself at the airport. It chanced that Alex Hamilton had decided to get out too. We travelled back together. Alex is the untypical Scot. He has a remarkable gift for floating through life. His musical style is modern, abstract, technically very good. His great gift, outside music, lies in avoiding doing the things he doesn't want to do. He couldn't understand why I had gone so deliberately out of my way to make trouble for myself. He didn't criticize me directly. We sat together, Alex making lighter conversation than I was able to do myself. Every now and then he would stop talking and begin shaking with silent laughter. I stood it as long as I could and then said, 'I'm glad you think it funny.' It wasn't a very worthwhile remark but it sent him into still more violent contortions. Then he patted me on the shoulder and said, 'It was marvellous, just marvellous.'

We got into London airport more or less on time. Quickly we were into the reception hall and through immigration. Then came an unconscionably long wait in the customs hall. If the trend towards faster aircraft goes on long enough we shall end up by taking more time to unload the baggage than for the flight, I thought grumpily. A sudden slap on the back caused me to turn sharply, a cross look still on my face. It was a slim dark-haired man in his early thirties. Recognition came in perhaps half a second. 'Thank goodness it's you,' he said, 'for a second I thought I might have slapped the wrong back.'

It was John Sinclair. We'd been at school together. We had won scholarships to Cambridge in the same year, his in mathematics, mine in music. Besides his mathematics Sinclair had a natural liking for music. In our university days I was as much interested in the piano itself as in composition. The larger part of my musical education I got outside the lecture-room, by playing great quantities of music. I developed in those days the habit of riding through a composer's works totally, symphonies, quartets, as well as straight piano music. John Sinclair used to spend many a spare hour in my rooms.

We were both interested in mountains. Already at school we had been out on one or two walking tours together. We kept it going at university. At the end of our third year we made a great trip to Skye. A party of four of us camped in Glen Brittle. We had a magnificent couple of weeks climbing in the Cuillin. The penultimate day was very wet. We spent it in the tents, cooking and talking. Our talk centred on what we were going to do the following year. Sinclair and I came to the tentative conclusion that we'd make a trip to the remarkable sandstone mountains of the extreme north-west. This plan never came to fruition. I won a scholarship to Italy in the following year. By the time I returned Sinclair was away in the United States. Although we had only met twice in the intervening years I had followed his career with more than a passing interest. The Royal Society just managed to scramble him into its Fellowship, at the age of twenty-nine, in time to forestall the award of a Nobel Prize. I followed what was going on as best I could in magazines like the *New Scientist* and the

259

Scientific American. I knew he had contributed a decisive step in the physics of elementary particles, something of a highly algebraic nature.

I made the introductions.

'Where are you in from?'

'New York. And you?'

'We're just back from Cologne. Music Festival.'

Our bags came at last. Alex and I checked them through customs. I said to him, 'Let's wait.' It was some minutes before Sinclair joined us. 'How about a taxi into town, and having dinner together?' he said. This was fine by me. I'd been a little shy suggesting it. When you haven't seen a man for six years, when he's gone a long way in those six years, you never know exactly where you stand. But it seemed that John hadn't changed much, in spite of his towering success. He was thinner now than he used to be, and I would have said he'd got a slightly worried look about him. We took a taxi to my place, ostensibly for a drink. We had several drinks.

Dinner began to seem less important. Alex had developed quite a sway. He sat firmly down in the largest chair, gave a flowing gesture, with the hand that was not holding a glass, and said, 'Music.'

'What? Any preferences, anybody?'

'Anything, anything you like.' He turned to John, 'We don't have preferences, do we? What we want is, music!'

I had not the slightest idea of what was going to come out as my hands came down on the keyboard. It was a Chopin nocturne, one I couldn't recall having played for years. True I used to go quite a lot for Chopin in my late teens. Quite a bit has been written on the techniques of seduction. My not very humble submission is that most of such stuff is plain nonsense. For every girl of eighteen who can be broken down by feats of muscle power on the football field there are ten who will swoon into your arms at the sound of a Chopin waltz or mazurka. I have no doubt the same system works just as well at later ages, but for me at least it had come to seem too cheap and easy. Seducing a girl with your own music is all fair and aboveboard. Doing it with someone else's had come to seem not quite proper, like shooting a sitting bird, or fishing with maggots. Anyway, out came the nocturne, somewhere from my subconscious memory. The alcohol stopped any worries about forgetting the way it went. As the piece glided to its end I had the feeling I had never played Chopin more perfectly. No doubt this was the effect of the alcohol too. Yet it is a mistake to think in terms of absolutes. It's the way you feel, the way your audience feels, that really counts. Alex was getting quite high now, 'More Choppy, please. More Choppy.'

They kept me at it for two solid hours. Whenever I tried to leave the stool Alex would have none of it. 'Keep playing,' he yodelled. Where the stuff came from I simply couldn't say. It just seemed to well up in the fingers. There was a great mazurka. I couldn't even remember its number. The notes came unbidden. I began a piece which at first I couldn't place. Then I realized this was the calm beginning of the tremendous polonaise-fantaisie. For a while I had fears I could never remember the magnificent second half. Then I began to listen intently to the music itself. I became lost in it. Not until my fingers came down on the final crashing chord was I aware of any passage of time. They were both on my shoulder now. For a moment I thought Alex was going to weep. I jumped up and said firmly, 'Time for food.'

There were eggs in the refrigerator. Within twenty minutes we had a big omelette all piping hot on the table. John and I ate while Alex talked, his mouth full the whole while. Somehow it sounded very witty. Wit, like love, evidently lies in the ear of the listener. We had some fresh fruit. Then I went off to make coffee.

When I came back Alex was nowhere to be seen.

'He's gone, apparently.'

That was Alex all over. He had the gift of appearing out of nowhere and of disappearing without the slightest explanation. He was the nearest human embodiment of the Cheshire cat I had ever met.

'Has he really gone?' asked John.

'Oh yes. He never goes in any other way.'

'What an odd fellow. Well, Dick, how have you been these last few years?'

Perhaps I should explain that I was christened Richard and that my nose, broken in a boyhood accident, somehow dominates my appearance. With this formality out of the way, let me return to my story.

We settled ourselves comfortably as we drank our coffee.

The conversation turned naturally on memories and anecdotes of our earlier years. No third person would have been much interested in the talk. By the time we had done it was half past one. I didn't know where John had been intending to stay the night but it was obvious that he should occupy my spare room. I got out towels and bed linen. Half an hour later I was asleep, blissfully unaware of the strange events that even the near future was to reveal.

2 Fugue

We were nearly through breakfast the following morning when John said, 'How about it?'

'How about what?'

'The trip we once planned to the north-west. Liathach, An Teallach, Suilven, and the rest of 'em.'

'When?'

'As soon as you're ready.'

'I'm ready now. What shall we go in?'

'I can borrow a car easily enough.'

'That wasn't what I was thinking. This time of year the hotels in the Highlands are certain to be full.'

John thought about this for a minute and got up from the table. 'I'll see what I can do. Where's the phone?'

It was half an hour before he reappeared. 'Well, it's all fixed.'

'What?'

'I've got hold of a caravan with a car to pull it.'

It wasn't a very great achievement, not for a Nobel laureate, but he seemed quite proud of it.

After breakfast John went out, took a taxi, and disappeared. I set about cleaning up. I telephoned a few people to say I would be away for about ten days. Then I searched for my boots and other items of mountain equipment. The boots looked just about serviceable. I hadn't kept them as carefully as they deserved. Rucksack, a bit of rope, anorak, socks, breeches, I scattered them over the floor. I packed and was ready when John returned. It was nearly one o'clock by the time we headed our outfit through St John's Wood on to the A1.

The journey to the north became an unmitigated bore. It was dark when we reached Scotch Corner. We turned off the fast highway, taking the smaller cross-country road to Penrith. By the time we reached Brough we had both had enough. So we drove away on the moorland road which leads from Brough to

Middleton. It was certain there would be patches of open ground on which we could park the caravan for the night. So it proved, after we had climbed up towards the moors for maybe a couple of miles. We ate a simple but ample meal from provisions we had bought on the way. A mug of tea each, with a big dollop of rum in it, was the last manoeuvre before getting down into our bags.

There was a good deal of rain in the night, so we had no great hopes for the weather the following morning. But when I put on the kettle at about six o'clock it didn't look too bad. Although there was mist on the high ground it seemed as if the rain might hold off. I woke John with a cup of tea and asked him how he would feel about stretching his legs. He said that would be fine, so I cooked about six slices of bacon. Instead of eating it there and then we wrapped it in a piece of aluminium foil. This, a knife, a loaf of bread, and a hunk of cake, went into a rucksack. By a quarter to seven we were away. We took the car along the road until John, who was studying the map, announced that the point of attack had been reached. We laughed at the thought of an attack on Mickle Fell. Yet we knew, gentle as the hill might be so far as height was concerned, there would be plenty of really hard walking before we reached the top. Hard because the ground was broken by big tussocks and by peat hags. The mist wouldn't make navigating easy.

We made the top of a little ridge. The line ahead didn't look right to John. It was characteristic of him that he wouldn't move on until we had fixed the exact point where we were now standing. It was pretty damp. I began to grow cold as we argued. At last we had the contours on the map fitted correctly to the mile or so of country we could see ahead. It was now clear what the trouble was. We hadn't started at quite the point we intended. We had left the car almost a mile short of the right spot. John grumbled to himself, to the effect that he must be losing his grip. Next we got into an argument about which was the best line to take, not so much from a point of view of arriving at the top, but of avoiding the worst of the broken ground. We decided to move leftward in order to avoid the green soggy depression below us. After about half an hour we came on a wire fence that seemed to lead in the right direction. Looking at the map it occurred to me that it might mark the

264

boundary between Westmorland and Yorkshire. If it did it would lead us to exactly where we wanted to be. The time seemed about right for breakfast. We cut two or three slices of bread, munched up the bacon, and started off again, each with a lump of cake in his hand.

We made good progress along the fence because the ground was somewhat smoother along its line than it was in open country. About eight o'clock the mists lifted. Mickle Fell was dead ahead of us. Now it was only a simple walk to the top. As soon as we were on the limestone, or what seemed to be limestone, there was a delightful change of vegetation. Gone was the acid peat bog. Now we had grass beneath our feet and sheep were grazing on the long back of the fell. We made quick progress to the east down a longish ridge to a mine perched near a lake under the hillside. By eleven o'clock we were on the road again.

We were anxious to continue our journey to the north as soon as possible. It was nearly three miles back to the car, the best part of an hour's walk, so we decided to try to get a lift from a passing motorist. Because there wasn't too much traffic, and because most cars might only have room for one of us, we split up. I went about four hundred yards ahead, climbed up a steep little bank and lay out on its top, leaving John to deal with the motorists. Within ten minutes he had a lift. He gave a triumphant wave as the car passed by. We had been wise for there certainly wasn't room in it for me.

The minutes lengthened to half an hour. Every so often a car came around a corner in the road about two hundred yards ahead of my little bank. I could hear them before they came into view. Each one I expected to be ours. An hour went by and still no sign of John. Obviously our borrowed car had failed to start. There was nothing for it but to walk after all. As I stumped the hard road I wished I had not given John my rucksack, not because it was heavy, but because I could have changed into rubbers and then I could have trotted the distance in twenty minutes or so.

The car was there, exactly as we had left it. John was not to be seen, plainly he had gone for help, probably to a garage in Brough. I sat down to wait and another hour went by. What the hell was going on? Why hadn't John left a note, or left the keys so that at least I could get into the damned car? I began

265

to curse these impractical scientists. Reluctantly I set off to walk the further mile to the caravan. John had the key to that too but we had left a window open and I managed to climb in without much trouble. Thereafter, I washed and tried to soothe my nerves with a big pot of tea and a further chunk of cake.

But this wasn't funny any more. By three o'clock I was striding my way into Brough in a high old temper. I found two garages and drew a blank at both. It was another hour before I could persuade a mechanic to drive me to our car. He somehow opened it and soon had the engine going. I paid him £1 and he drove away plainly thinking I was daft. What to do now? I had heard of motorists in the United States who gave a lift and then beat up and robbed their unsuspecting passenger but I could recall no such case in Britain. Yet something like this must have happened. I drove to the place where we had come down off the ridge of Mickle Fell, then back again the whole six miles to Brough, very slowly. At that stage I reported the whole business to a police sergeant. He took it all down in a grave manner which I suspected to be routine. He asked where I was staying and I told him the position of the caravan up on the moor. The police, he said, would get on to the matter immediately and someone would come up to the caravan as soon as they had any information.

There was nothing to be done now but drive back to the van. It was coming up to six o'clock by the time I got there. I was in two minds about cooking dinner. Underneath I was hungry but the worry of the situation dulled my appetite. I decided to stretch out on a bunk for half an hour or so before starting preparations for a meal. As far as I was aware this was exactly what I did. It wasn't until I had eaten and washed up that I saw from my watch it was already nine o'clock. Shortly after, there came a powerful knock at the van door.

It was an inspector in plain clothes, from which I guessed this had become a C I D matter. He asked me a lot of questions about myself. They were not taking John's disappearance lightly now. His reputation as a scientist would in itself have forced them to take it seriously but I suspected there might also be a security aspect to the matter. Hence the questions about myself. I guessed the police wanted to satisfy themselves that I had no part in the business, whatever it was. After about an hour of the questioning the man prepared to leave. I remembered to check my watch with his before he did so. There was nothing wrong with it.

Darkness came on and I settled down for the night. If I had been thoroughly fit I suppose I would quickly have fallen asleep. Now I tossed around uneasily wondering about John Sinclair. Of course I didn't know much about him as he was now, only as he used to be. It certainly seemed as if the intervening years had never existed. We had resumed the old free and easy days of school and university. Yet the intervening years were real enough. John's life must have become more complicated, professionally and socially, than it was when I knew him. To me he might seem the same person but to the world at large this would not be so. These speculations, sensible enough in themselves, got me nowhere.

Suddenly my attention was caught by approaching footsteps. I wriggled out of my bag, found a box of matches and started to light the little gas lamp over the kitchen stove. I was still fumbling when the door opened. Then the light came on and I saw it was John, his face not a foot from mine. The slightly worried look, which I had already remarked the first evening, was more obvious now.

'Where in the hell have you been?' I asked.

He came into the van, slumped on to his bunk, and began to unlace his boots.

'I haven't the slightest idea, Dick. That's the truth.'

It was my impulse to press the matter further. But if what John said was indeed true, if he really had no idea what had happened, it was pointless to argue. Probably it was some kind of blackout. I didn't know whether he had become subject to temporary losses of memory but it was at least a possible explanation. Hard exercise, taken suddenly without any previous training, might have brought on some kind of attack. Anyway he was safe, which was the main thing.

'Hungry?'

'Devilishly so.'

I had a feeling that what he wanted was silence and food. I wasn't averse to another snack myself. With an impressive display of energy I had the table set. Wild and wonderful smells pervaded the caravan within a few minutes. John ate more or less silently. I had a big mug of tea and a piece of cake. I told John about the police. With his agreement I drove to a phone box about half a mile down the road. I put through a 999 call telling the constable on duty that John had turned up and that he seemed to have suffered a temporary amnesia but was quite recovered now. When I returned to the caravan I found him in a deep sleep.

We were very late up the following morning. Partly for this reason, and partly because we had another visit from the inspector, it was on midday before we resumed our journey to the north. What was said between John and the inspector I do not know. They went off for a walk together, returning after about an hour, an hour which I spent cleaning up the van. At all events the inspector seemed satisfied now, which was all that seemed to matter.

We took the outfit straight through the centre of Glasgow. Because we were slow-moving this was probably the quickest way. We managed to find the road to Loch Lomond without much difficulty. We passed various camping sites intent on reaching Glencoe if we possibly could. It seemed a long pull up to Crianlarich and the distance to Tyndrum was somewhat longer than I remembered it. Then we were out on to the beginning of Rannoch Moor. John who was driving muttered something about the caravan being wrong. The outfit began to weave rather violently. He brought it to a quick halt. Inspection showed a puncture on the nearside back wheel of the car. As we got out the jack and spare wheel clouds of midges descended on us in their thousands. We were back in Scotland. It took less than a quarter of an hour to change that wheel. Yet we were practically eaten alive.

We had been fighting time to get to Glencoe in the light. I knew the exact spot where I wanted to go, on to the old road which crosses the new road about two miles the other side of Kingshouse Inn. By the time we reached the place the last of the light was gone. It was impossible to execute any complicated movement with the caravan. All we could do was simply drive straight ahead on to the old road. This meant the caravan would be the wrong way round for making an exit. We would have to turn it by hand. Worse, the car was wedged in on the wrong side. After uncoupling, there was no possibility, because of the narrowness of the road, the unsurfaced old road, of getting it back on to the highway. We would need the car itself the following morning to drive about four miles

268

down the glen to the beginning of the ordinary route up Bidean nam Bian. Sufficient unto the day is the evil thereof.

We were early astir. After a quick cup of tea, cooking bacon, packing the rucksack, it was still only 6 a.m. by the time we were ready to be off. The morning was perfect, not a cloud in the sky. But now we had to tackle the problem of the car. The simplest solution seemed to be to continue along the old road, for the best part of a mile, until it joined the surfaced road again. We took it very slowly indeed. Even so it was a wild ride. This was an occasion for a jeep or a Land-Rover. There was a good deal of scraping of the undercarriage but finally we made it without incurring disaster. Ten minutes later we had parked near the rather gloomy Loch Triochtan.

The track up the mountainside appeared unpleasantly steep Yet once we made a start it turned out to be not as bad as it looked. We followed the bed of a stream for quite a way up a little valley which lay back into the mountain more than we had expected. After maybe a mile we decided to cut out of the stream bed, up to the left. Once again the slope was not too bad. By eight o'clock we reached a little corrie which I guessed to be about a thousand feet below the summit. Ahead of us was a fine rock buttress, presumably the famous Churchdoor Buttress. In the floor of the corrie there were wonderful pools of clear cold water. It was now quite warm and we spent a good half-hour over a leisurely breakfast. For the first time we appreciated the advantages of the caravan. It was much to be preferred to a tent because of the midges. It was to be preferred to an hotel because of the wonderful early start we could make from it. Down in the hotel at Kingshouse, or at Ballachulish, we should only just now be sitting down to breakfast. It was true we *were* having breakfast, but at nearly three thousand feet, with most of the day's climbing already done.

We were off again just before nine o'clock, on to a rather loose slope of scree and broken rocks. It took us up for about five hundred feet. Then we were on the summit ridge in bright sunshine. The rocks here were firm and warm. We mounted quickly to the top. It was going to be hot and a haze was already rising. To the north the Mamores and Ben Nevis looked tremendous. To the south were the ragged peaks of Glen Etive. We had no need of hurry, we spent a good hour on the top. In my capacity as quartermaster I produced my *bonne bouche*, two tins of orange juice. Then we set off along the ridge at a steady easy pace. We went just as we felt like it, down the long shelving ridge towards Glen Etive, then up again to the beginning of the Beinn Fhada ridge. Then down a steepish short slope, up again over a couple of bumps or so, to a little col. Here our route lay down a steep, broken hillside on the left. There was roughly a thousand feet of it and it didn't look inviting, to untrained men. We had a friendly disagreement as to which was the best way down. John chose a gully between rocky walls, a kind of stone shoot. I thought the more open ground to the right would be better. When I had gone down it for perhaps a hundred feet I realized I was mistaken. As I struggled downward I lost contact with John. When I next saw him he was a long way below me, maybe two or three hundred feet. I stuck at it and at last came to where he was lying resting on a boulder. I suggested we keep going down the widish scoop that lay on our right, that it would take us down to the stream in the big corrie into which we were descending. John laughed. He asserted the scoop would take us down to a cliff edge. I couldn't see how he knew this but after my mistake on the slope above I didn't think it wise to argue.

The bottom of the corrie was an amazing affair. It looked as though it was going to be a flat bottom. Then at the last moment the hillside plunged steeply into a little gorge. The gorge ran for more than a mile along what looked like a flat valley. This was the hidden valley I had heard of many times. Whether by luck, instinct, or sheer skill, I don't know, but John led the way to a point where there was an easy breach in the cliffs where we could get down to the stream and to its opposite side on which we could see a good track.

I was hot with the ridge walk and and the steep descent. I suggested we have a bathe in the stream. The idea took on. Within five minutes I was down into one of the clear pools. Being cold is a strange experience when you come to think about it. Being really cold is unpleasant but it isn't a sharp agonizing business. Cold is a stealthy, unrelenting enemy. The only pleasurable aspect of it, to my knowledge, is when you come piping hot down a mountainside and jump into a pool of icy water. The pleasure lasts no more than thirty seconds. You stick it for another minute and then out you crawl as fast as you can. This was exactly what we did. It was while we were drying off in the sunshine that the odd thing struck me. Back at school we had often stripped our shirts off after football. I knew perfectly well John had a strawberry birthmark, about the size of a half-crown, in the small of his back. There was now no trace of it.

3 Intermezzo

Birthmarks and suchlike, 'marks prodigious' as the old wizard
of Stratford had it, aren't quite the stuff of polite conversation.
Back at school I would not have had the least inhibition. Now
it took some effort.

'Hey, John, didn't you have a birthmark in the middle of
your back?'

'Yes, of course. What of it?'

'Well, it isn't there any more.'

'Of course it's there.'

'I assure you it isn't.'

'Must be the strong sunshine. There's no contrast out here.'

We made our way to the throat of the valley. There was an
amazing tangle of great boulders. Threading our way through
them we came to easy slopes of grass that led down into
Glencoe itself. When we were back in camp I put the kettle on
for the much needed cup of tea.

John said, 'You'd better check that mark.'

I had been right. There wasn't the least trace of it. Foolishly,
I said, 'You haven't had it removed or anything?'

'Of course I haven't.'

John made no further comment. His face was knit in a tense
expression, one I had seen often enough before when he was
engaged on some awkward problem. I knew better than to ask
him to explain. He scribbled on a big scratch pad as we drank
our tea.

I left him at it and drove down the valley to the sea. I took
the left fork towards Port Appin. I didn't quite know what to
make of John and his troubles so I put them out of my mind as
best I could. I began wondering about the possibilities of a sea
symphony. It was certainly an idea but perhaps not a very
good one. There is of course great beauty and drama in the
sea. Yet the subject is unattractively amorphous, far removed
from human problems. In a way it seemed just an escape

formula, an excuse for a display of flashing orchestral effects. I doubted whether there was much more scope in this direction.

It was half past six when I returned to the van. John was still figuring. I poured both of us a generous woof of a drink. By the time we were through it I said we'd better be off to the hotel at Ballachulish unless he was keen to cook the dinner.

'Let's go then. I want to use the phone.'

I hadn't expected the hotel to be so full. With mild apprehension I asked if they could manage dinner for the two of us. A woman said she would see and would we like a drink in the meantime? We had the drink and the woman came back. Yes, they could manage dinner but we'd have to wait until about a quarter past eight.

'I'll do my phoning now,' grunted John when she'd gone.

He left me in a milling crowd, apparently talking for the most part about their experiences on the road. There seemed not the slightest appreciation of the magic of a wonderful day spent in one of the most beautiful places on Earth. At half past seven somebody started bashing away at a gong. All but three or four of the company drifted out of the bar. There was an upright piano along one side of the room. I opened the lid and fingered the keys in an idle fashion. 'Do you play?' asked a middle-aged woman. For answer I pulled up a chair and settled into a number from one of the latest shows. The piano was of the honky-tonk variety which I never can resist. It was gloriously out of tune. I meandered through two or three numbers and they loved it. The woman's husband, or so I took him to be, said, 'Have a drink?' I asked for half a pint of bitter. I was sipping it, making polite conversation, when John returned. I could judge nothing from his face.

At last our turn for dinner came round, none too soon, for I was hungry. We were put at a table by ourselves.

'Any idea of what you want to do tomorrow?' I asked.

'I'm afraid we'll have to call it off, Dick. But don't let me drag you back to London.'

'Is there anything I can do?'

'Not explicitly. How are you fixed?'

'In what way?'

'Have you any engagements, ones it would be difficult to break?'

'Not really. Why?'

273

'I'll have to go back to the States. If you're free I'd like you to come along.'

I laughed. My bank manager was just going to love the suggestion. 'What would I use for money?'

'There's no problem. You travel on contract.'

We closed the subject at this point until we were back in the van. Then John began, 'I suppose I'd better tell you a bit of what's going on. It won't make much sense I'm afraid.'

I put a pile of clothing under my pillow, to make a backrest as I stretched out on my bunk. My legs were beginning to stiffen up.

'I suppose you've followed the general outline of the things that have been turning up in space research?'

'Yes, more or less, so far as it's possible from newspaper reports.'

'One of the aims of the space programme is to take a look at the outside world in unfamiliar parts of the spectrum.'

'You mean things like X-rays and gamma rays?'

'That's right. But of course X-rays and gamma rays are at the high frequency end. There's a lot of stuff in the far infrared, stuff that gets absorbed in our own atmosphere just like the X-rays do. I'm talking now about wavelengths roughly a hundred times less than the shortest radio waves.'

'What's the point – curiosity?'

'It started that way. The first idea was to pick up radiation from the Sun, to check that it had the intensity everybody expected it to have.'

'Did it?'

'Within a reasonable margin of accuracy. It wasn't something to hold a press conference about. Yet interesting, technically. That was all, or nearly all.'

'It doesn't sound as if it would make the girls swoon.'

'What was odd though was that some of the electronics, not in this experiment itself you understand, but electronics connected with other things that were going on, went badly wrong. It seemed as if they were suffering from pick-up troubles. Naturally there was a hell of an inquest about it. Nothing sensible could be found. All the circumstantial evidence pointed to a modulation in the region of a hundred megacycles, a modulation on the current output from the new infrared experiment. On the face of it this seemed impossible. Well,

274

to cut it short, the lads just had time to modify the gadgetry before the next shot went up. The circumstantial evidence unfortunately turned out to be right. There *was* a modulation at nearly a hundred megacycles.'

'Could it have been a pick-up as well?'

'Everybody felt it had to be. Well, the inquest grew now to major proportions. It was still going on when I left the States. I'm not involved myself very directly with this stuff. It happens the chap in charge of the experiment is a friend of mine. The last thing I heard was that they had a proof it wasn't the Sun itself, at least they thought so. They thought they'd demonstrated it had come from the rocket. Yet nobody had any real idea of why or how.'

'You think it might be the Sun after all?'

I knew how John's mind worked, at any rate psychologically. I had a pretty good notion this was his opinion.

'I don't know – yet. Back at the hotel I put a call through to this friend. I couldn't get him personally but I got one of his chaps. They're going to ring back with some information I need tomorrow morning. Then I'll be in a much better position to say.'

I lay awake that night for a long time. It astonished me how easily John had been able to fall asleep. I could hear him breathing deeply and quite regularly as if there was nothing in the world to worry about. I had a general idea of what he had told me. Yet for the life of me I couldn't see its relevance to the disturbing incidents of the last three days.

The following morning John went back to the hotel. It was half past ten by the time he came back.

'We'll have lunch at twelve. There's a plane from Glasgow to London at three o'clock. We should have time to catch it.'

'How about the car and the caravan?'

'We'll take the car to Glasgow. I've made arrangements for the van to be collected from here.'

'What else?'

'Can you manage the midday plane to New York on Friday?'

This would give me three days to put my affairs to rights in London. It wouldn't be easy but I could make it. 'I suppose so.'

'Good, I'm going to put in an hour's calculation.'

John worked quickly and keenly. I could see it was nothing but algebra and arithmetic. As I watched I was struck by the difference between the mathematician and the musician. When I had worked myself with a similar intensity a few weeks ago, back in Cornwall, I had been in a kind of trance. There was nothing trance-like about John. With a swoop like an eagle he came to a stop. I didn't need to ask him if it had turned out successfully. So much was obvious. Nor did I ask him what it meant.

'Satisfied?'

'Yes.' He sat for a minute and then added, 'Funny.'

'How?'

'The conclusion. I have demonstrated the correctness of a hunch – at the expense of an appalling conclusion. Oddly enough it seems more satisfactory this way round, better than being wrong and having a sensible, straightforward answer. It shows the important thing is to know your reasoning powers work properly. *Where* they lead you is really unimportant, which I suppose is why human beings are able to achieve completely new things. Basically, it's why we're no longer swinging by our tails from trees.'

That was all I got out of him.

The journey back to London was uneventful. We parted at the air terminal, each to make his own arrangements. We didn't meet again until an hour before the plane to New York was due to depart on the Friday morning.

The intervening days were busy enough for me. Actually I must admit that I was quite glad to get out of London. Frankly, I had got my personal affairs into something of a tangle. I managed to track down Alex Hamilton, not an easy exercise. I asked him to keep an eye on my place, to use it if he wanted. I told him a little of my difficulties, lest in occupying my simple apartments he should find himself assailed by too many girls on too many sides. This sent him into another of his prolonged fits of silent laughter. He asked me if I had any spare unwanted cash to lend him. I said emphatically I had not.

We grew mellow in the transatlantic plane after a couple of cocktails. The hours slipped away and John and I soon found ourselves through American immigration and customs.

We took a taxi from Kennedy airport to an hotel whose

name I have forgotten. It was somewhere mid-town. At dinner that night, which we ate in a near-by restaurant, I at last got round to asking John what his plans were. He answered:

'We're going on to California as soon as I'm through the things I must do here. It'll probably take about three days. I think it's simpler if I work it out alone. Do you think you can keep yourself happy for a day or two?'

I said I had no doubt I could find plenty to do. He went on:

'I'm going to turn in pretty early tonight. I find it's a good idea to take the change of clock in at least a couple of bites.'

It may seem strange that until then I had no idea of exactly where we were going. It is my practice in life to take as little account of times and schedules as I can. I like to be as little tied down by commitments. Surprises are the spice of life. Surprises rarely come to those busy fellows who are always consulting their engagement book. As I got into bed that night I had no idea what I was going to do in the next two or three days. It turned out they were quite uneventful. For one thing I felt tired, more exactly, drained of energy, I suppose by the five-hour shift in the clock.

If I had known I should never see New York again, I would have made an effort to do much more in the way of sightseeing during those three days. On the evening of the second day I found a note from John saying we were booked to San Diego on an eleven o'clock flight the following morning and that he would see me at the flight-gate half an hour before take-off.

We were met at San Diego airport by a young man, apparently a graduate student at the university. He drove us north about ten miles to an hotel in La Jolla. We were shown up to our rooms. I decided I was in need of sleep, a wise move in view of the party to which we were apparently invited that night.

I got up at about five o'clock, shaved and dressed, and then took a stroll on the beach. This was my first sight of the Pacific. I was to see much more of it in the days to come. The beach stretched to the north for a mile or so. Beyond were cliffs running into the distance as far as I could see.

A car arrived for me at half past six. The driver introduced himself – I am sorry to say I immediately forgot his name. We chatted without the least trace of embarrassment as he drove up through a complex of small roads on to the side of a steepish hill. It occurred to me that one would never have got into such an immediately casual relationship with anybody back home. We pulled up outside a single-storey house.

John had arrived already. There were one or two women there so it seemed this was to be a social occasion rather than a work conference. But the conference developed all right. If I had been more experienced in the American way of life I would have realized how inevitable this was. Work conferences always develop at every dinner party provided the men have some common interest. We started with drinks, which were enlivened by the arrival of a spritely fellow wearing an incredible hat. It was of the trilby variety. It looked as if it had been treated by being first buried in the ground for a year or two, then by being thrown as food to an army of hungry mice. His name was Art Clementi. I did not forget the name this time.

There seemed plenty to talk about. John was apparently well known in these parts, so drinks took quite a while. They dissolved imperceptibly into a buffet supper. When the women learnt I was a musician there were the usual demands that I should play. Many musicians detest being invited to the piano at times when they feel they should be off duty. I have never developed a hard and fast dividing line between being on and off duty so playing at odd moments never worries me. I rattled off a couple of Scarlatti sonatas. Then a big fellow standing, somewhat unsteadily, a glass in one hand, by the piano, said, 'How about that Tchaikovsky thing?' He hummed a few notes. Evidently he meant the first piano concerto. I threw off the big opening chords and said, rather unkindly, 'Now you do the orchestra.' They all laughed, the big man as well, not in the least embarrassed. So I began the incredible Tchaikovsky Opus 1, No. 1, incredible because it was Tchaikovsky's first work. When I came to the storming finish I heard the big man mutter, 'Christ!'

A few of the people left. The women seemed to melt away, at maybe half past ten. I noticed the time because I was beginning to feel sleepy again, in fact I was wondering how soon we would get away. Apart from John and me there were six of them. I guessed Clementi must be the friend John had spoken about back in Scotland. He wanted to know what had brought us hot-footed from England.

'Because I know where the modulation is coming from.'

'Then just give us a hint,' said the big man.

John was almost irritatingly precise. He took three quite simple diagrams out from his briefcase. On each there were just three lines meeting at a point. On each line there was an arrow, two pointing away from the point of intersection, the other towards it. The angles between the lines were marked.

'We've had three cases where vehicles have changed directions. In each of them I've shown the direction of the Sun, at the moment of change.'

'As seen from the vehicle?'

'Right. Now you'd better check my facts because a lot depends on them.'

Clementi took up the sheets, studied them, then shook his head. 'We could do that tomorrow. I'm sure you'll have it right.' He turned to the others and grinned, giving them a wink.

John went on, 'Everybody believes something in the rocket is at fault, because the frequencies changed when the rocket changed.'

'That seems to settle it.'

'Then why are the frequencies somewhat different in the three cases?'

John pulled out a fourth sheet. On it were four columns, three numbers in each column. He pointed to the first. 'These were the frequencies on the three occasions before the change of direction was made. You see they're not the same. What should cause the difference?'

'I don't know. But for that matter why the hell is there a change whenever the course corrections are made? The mere fact there *are* changes shows there must be a connexion with the rocket.'

'I'm not doubting it. But the connexion is with the direction of the rocket not with the electronics inside it.'

Clementi winked again, not I saw by way of derision but to fire John with a little emotion. He didn't succeed. John went on in the same irritatingly precise fashion, 'I'm sorry it's so triflingly simple. The whole thing turns on the direction of the rocket relative to the Sun. In the second column I've divided the frequencies in the first column by the sine of the corresponding angles. You see the numbers are still different.'

'I'd expect them to be different,' grunted one of the men.

'Then I noticed that if I normalized everything to the speed of the rocket something very interesting happened. The speeds were about twenty per cent different in the three cases. I took one of the three as standard and divided this time by the speeds. These are the numbers in the third column here. They're very nearly identical.'

I didn't understand what all this was about. But I did see, elementary as it all looked, that it produced a sharp reaction in the local boys.

'I did exactly the same for the frequencies measured after the shifts of direction.'

John produced another piece of paper, again with four columns. He pointed to the third and said, 'You see they're the same, not only the same among themselves, but the same as before the changes were made.'

'What's the fourth column for?' asked Clementi.

'The numbers in the fourth column are just a little more nearly equal than those in the third. The difference is very slight. It was a check, a sort of clinching factor.'

'Clinching for what?'

'For the Sun. Those last figures include the Doppler shift correction, the shift due to the rocket motion in the solar direction.'

There was a long silence. Then Clementi nodded gravely, 'That's what I was afraid of, right from the beginning. You're telling us it's the solar radiation itself that's got this modulation on top of it. Granted you haven't gone crazy and cooked the numbers that's certainly what it looks like.'

'What does it look like?' I asked.

Clementi turned on me. 'It looks as if the Sun is emitting a sharply directed beam of infra-red radiation. The modulation was due to our rocket cutting across the interference fringes.'

'But how the hell can the Sun be emitting a directed beam? It's impossible,' burst out one of the men.

'If you'd asked me an hour ago I'd have said it was impossible. But the facts are clear. It's preposterous and outrageous but it must be true.'

I could see John too was beginning to feel tired. He yawned

280

and stretched himself and said, 'Well, at least there's something to be done.'

'There's a hell of a lot to be done.'

'I can't see any point in having a directed beam of radiation – and this must be fantastically directional – unless it's used for transmitting information.'

'By whom, for God's sake?'

'How the devil should I know. The thing to do next is to look for some intrinsic form of modulation. We've got to filter out this effect of the interference fringes. Then we must look for some genuine source modulation.'

Quite spontaneously everybody began to consume strong drinks at a very rapid rate. In spite of their comparative reticence, John's disclosures, simple as they might be, had produced a profound sense of shock. I didn't understand what had been said with any great clarity so I suppose things weren't as sharp to me as they were to the others. Yet I gathered that someone, or something, was using the Sun as a signalling device.

4 Tempo di Minuetto

I lay awake for a little while that night. A remarkable conclusion had obviously been pieced together from the simplest
fragments, like a crushing position in a chess game built by a
master from a series of seemingly trifling moves. It was the
pattern, the sequence, that really counted, not the intrinsic
difficulty of any particular step. The data John had used were
no doubt well known to hundreds of people, if not to thousands, but the relevant facts had been embedded in a million-
and-one irrelevancies.

No doubt entirely due to chance I had become involved in a
tremendous situation. It hardly needed special knowledge to
understand the implication of what I had heard. Every single
one of the men involved in tonight's discussion had sought an
alibi, either in understatement or in flippancy. They were
trying to avoid the significance of the situation. Not of course
permanently but to get themselves used to it by slow stages.

The following day I received a cheque for $1,500, paid on
account, through the University of California. I turned it
straightaway into travellers' cheques. I hired a car from a local
agency. The next two days I spent driving along the coast and
into the back country. Possession of the car gave me a new
dimension of freedom. The effects of the journey, particularly
of the time switch, were passing off now. In short I was beginning to enjoy myself.

On the third day I was asked to present myself at ten-thirty
the following morning at such-and-such a building on the
university campus. I was shown to a pleasant office overlooking the sea. It was rather like looking down from the
Cornish cliffs, except the light was stronger here. John came in
with a man of about fifty-five. I was asked to describe exactly
what had happened on our trip to Scotland.

I gave a simple factual account, answered a few questions,
and that was that. John went out with the man. A few minutes
later he returned alone.

'Sorry, Dick, I've been so much occupied. We'll meet for dinner tonight. Not here, in Los Angeles. Let's say half past six. You've got a car?'

I nodded.

He produced a map. 'This is the place here, at the intersection of Wilshire and Santa Monica Boulevards.'

I drove to Los Angeles during the afternoon. It would have been quicker by the inland freeway but I decided to keep on the coast road through Long Beach. I wanted to see the various coastal places I had read about. They didn't live up to my expectations. I was glad by the time I reached Santa Monica.

I wasn't familiar with the district or with the traffic conditions. Yet it was less bewildering than I would have expected. Without too much trouble I reached the restaurant. John was late but not grossly so. Yet to be late at all was unusual for him.

'We'll get away from science for one night,' he said as we sat down at a table, which he had apparently booked beforehand.

'I've been pretty hard at it ever since we got into New York. To be frank I'm damn tired.'

'What's the general pitch?'

'Well, it's obvious we need a new vehicle out there with special instrumentation. There's nothing difficult in it at all. Not experimentally I mean. But it's the devil to get anything unusual done. The whole space programme is going ahead like some enormous juggernaut. Only with the highest priority can you get anything changed.'

'I suppose if you know exactly what you want to do that's the most efficient way.'

'If you know what you want to do, beforehand. Which of course means you're not going to find anything of very much interest.'

'Did you get your way?'

'Yes, with Art's help. We've been up at J P L – the Jet Propulsion Lab all day, arguing. Once they were convinced, everything went smoothly, but they took some convincing.'

'When's it going to happen?'

'More or less immediately. A new vehicle was practically ready for launching. It was designed to go a long way out so it's got pretty sensitive controls. It'll do our job very easily. The problem is to get the right packages ready in time.'

283

'The right black boxes?'

'Yes. The lads will be working night and day on it. Here's the point as it affects you. We're going to use the big receiving dish out in Hawaii. It's out in the islands because there's not much man-made interference. Would you like a trip?'

I said I'd be delighted to make a trip to Hawaii. Then a waiter bore down on our table with a multitude of dishes.

Conversation was somewhat spasmodic for the next half-hour. The meal, an excellent one, deserved justice.

Over the coffee I asked, 'Is this Hawaii trip a joy ride or is it strictly necessary?'

'Not strictly, if by that you mean absolutely essential. But well worthwhile from my point of view. We'll get the data hot off the line. Art's coming with us. The station on Hawaii is his show.'

'When do we take off?'

'I was planning to travel the day after tomorrow. But there's no reason why you shouldn't go on earlier if you want to. By the way I've got an invitation for tonight.'

'More science?'

'God forbid, I'm in need of a rest. This is a friend of a friend of a friend, out in Beverly Hills. We can always leave early if we get bored.'

'Where are you staying?'

'I've got a motel back in Pasadena. You might as well stay over here by the sea though, it's quite a bit cooler.'

'Then I suppose I'd better find a place before we go to Beverly Hills.'

'Oh, I wouldn't bother. The motels are open all night. You can get one any time. Besides you never know where you'll end up.'

On this remark John paid the bill. We went out to the parking place.

'You'd better follow me, we might as well take both cars. I'm not exactly sure of where to go but I know the general direction.'

I kept faithfully on John's tail through a succession of boulevards and streets. Then we were in a twisting mass of side-roads among large houses. We both came to a halt. John was muttering imprecations. It seemed he was more disturbed by not being able to find the place than he had been by the scientific situation. We started off again. After two more tries we at last drew up outside a prosperous looking domicile. A dozen cars were parked in the roadway outside. Inside, a good-looking woman pressed two large drinks on us, with a welcoming smile, and no questions asked.

We pushed our way into a large room. Perhaps thirty people were in there, talking loudly. I had the impression it would have been possible for almost anybody to have walked in.

In the general bedlam of a cocktail party I am lucky to have something of an advantage over my fellow men. My hearing is abnormally acute so I can still make out what is being said at a stage where the average person is pretty well deafened. I plunged fairly confidently into the morass.

After a quick, not inexpert, survey of the female company a dark-haired girl caught my attention. I thought her face the most interesting of the female element. It was a face of some considerable character. I moved over into her general environment. Because I could just make out what people were trying to say, I soon found a place in the local conversation. The girl I judged to be in her mid-twenties, a few years younger than I was. There came a lull during which a man, who was probably the host, got himself launched into a description of how he had just bought an estate of vast acreage up near Ojai.

I was able to get the dark-haired girl away to myself. Our talk was trivial in the extreme as it was bound to be. I said I was just out from Britain, a simple, not very effective ploy. Her attention became a little warmer, however, when I told her that I was a musician. It seemed I was on the way to Chopin waltzes and mazurkas again.

We were joined by an older, rather handsome woman. The girl drifted away at the first opportunity, perhaps because she was glad to be rescued or because she didn't like the handsome woman. The woman took me on one side, saying confidentially, 'Have you met her before, Lena I mean?'

'No, but I've seen her somewhere I'm sure. Who is she?'

'Do you mean you don't know?'

'Cross my heart.'

'Helena Summers. She was in the film, *The Passionate*.'

'The passionate what?'

The woman laughed, 'No wisecracks.' Then she became still

285

more confidential. Taking my arm she murmured, 'Lena's in bad shape, plenty trouble there.'

There was no opportunity to ask what the plenty trouble was because a handsome, virile man of about my own age suddenly held the stage. I had seen him before so I was pretty sure he must be in the acting world too. He not only had the attention of the others, he had mine too. Astonishingly, he was talking about the effect of Chopin waltzes on young women.

There were two open pianos back-to-back at one end of the big room. The man began to look through a pile of music evidently with the intention of playing himself. I was becoming combative now, rather like a dog whose territory has been infringed. He started on the big Chopin waltz in A flat Major. The interpretation was quite good, the technique somewhat faulty. I found myself appreciably irritated to see the women crowding around the piano.

Then I had the good sense to feel rather ashamed. After all, a lot of practice was needed to play as well as that, which showed my handsome friend must have a very genuine affection for music. Yet I found it difficult not to be jaundiced by the way he switched in a flash to Beethoven's short E Minor sonata. I resisted entering the discussion that followed. But then the girl Lena broke in with the remark that I was a musician. So I was thrown into the pool. I was introduced to the man. His name, Roger Berard, was just about as vaguely familiar as his face. I did my best to pretend to know it well for anything less would have seemed impolite.

'How about playing four hands? Mozart?'

I said that would be excellent. But they couldn't find the right music. Berard picked up the score of Mozart's K488 concerto. 'Do you think we could manage this?' he asked.

I said we'd have to use both pianos.

Two experts with an understanding between them could have managed on one piano. We would have got ourselves into a hopeless tangle of hands and feet.

'There's only one copy. You haven't got another?' my partner asked the man I had guessed to be the host. 'Why the hell should I keep two. I can't even play one.' This brought a chorus of after-dinner laughter.

'We can use both pianos,' I said. 'If you take the solo part, I think I can manage the orchestration.' This was more vicious

286

than it may sound. I knew Berard was in a show-off mood. I suspected he was interested in one of the girls, not apparently the dark girl. By choosing the orchestral accompaniment I naturally had the heavier part. Besides, this was the music I cut my teeth on.

It went as I had expected up to a point. I omitted the orchestral introduction, letting him lead off with the solo part. He began aggressively but with the volume of tone I was able to roll out it must soon have become clear that there was no profit at all for him in a competition. About half-way through the first movement he stopped the nonsense. He began to listen to what he was playing. Then the whole thing went off reasonably well. On a concert platform a four-hands performance is never very attractive. Yet under casual circumstances like this it can be quite exciting, especially if it is unrehearsed. Nobody minds the hesitations and misunderstandings between the two players. It all adds to the fun. We were pressed to continue.

Surprisingly, Berard wanted me to play solo. He got out a volume of Beethoven sonatas talking avidly the while about the late ones. His instinct for music was genuine enough. I saw the artificiality of his earlier remarks really came from the society in which he was living. The world is full of frustrated musicians, people who would have liked to be musicians but who by ill chance had been forced into some other profession. I've met scores of them. They have one characteristic in common. By not being musicians they've done far better for themselves in all material respects than they'd have done as musicians.

I played the Opus 111. There wasn't a great deal of applause at the end but the warmth was obvious. They spoke now in quiet voices, not at all like the uproar that had been going on when John and I came in earlier. It was clear they wanted me to go on but it wasn't easy to think of anything to play after the Opus 111. Almost idly I rattled off the waltz theme of the Diabelli variations. Then I was into the variations proper. There was no turning back now. Once again my memory, or perhaps the thought of the dark girl with plenty trouble, served me well. I got through to No. 33 with a sprinkling of wrong notes but without serious mishap. It was more than enough. They were overwhelmed, crushed. Well they might be. Given the slightest musical sense it is impossible not to be staggered emotionally by the greatest works played at close range. This was the way, at close range, in which the old composers intended their solo works to be heard, intimately, not from the platform in a large hall. More and more, I have come to realize just how unsatisfactory public performances on a piano are. Even the most exquisite playing comes over weakly, attenuated, and thin. It is all rather like eating a well-cooked dinner with a strong smell of antiseptic in the air.

Emotionally I had had enough now, at any rate on the piano. We got into small talk of no concern. John whispered discreetly in my ear, 'Great stuff, Dicky. This is my phone number, give me a call tomorrow morning.' Then he was away. At last I got a chance to talk to Lena. Her face was animated and responsive now. Odd the way it goes, I thought, mazurkas at eighteen, Beethoven sonatas at twenty-five. I wondered what the trick would be at fifty – aleatoricism? More or less spontaneously we decided to leave. This was a community in which you arrived when you pleased and left when you pleased. It would have suited Alex Hamilton. The hostess – I still didn't know her name – asked me to call up any time I was free. It was all aboveboard and genuine. She kissed me as I left. I thought of poor John on his solitary way back to Pasadena or to wherever he was going. There was nothing like science for the good clean life.

Outside, I took Lena's arm. She said, 'Can I drive you some-where?'

'Yes, I'm looking for some place to sleep.'

'How am I intended to take that?'

'Quite genuinely. I've got to find a motel.'

'There are plenty.'

She guided the car with a sure hand through the labyrinth of small roads. I was glad I hadn't been left to make my way out at this time of night. It was warm, the car was open, there was a pleasant fragrance in the air. She said, 'I'd like to drive by the sea.'

We parked at the top of a cliff. Below us the sea spread out in a huge luminous phosphorescent arc. I turned to Lena. She smiled at my inquiring look.

I remember very little of where we went, of slipping out of the car into the house, or of the trivia of the bedroom. But I do remember lying there afterwards listening to the roar of the sea. I remember that enough light came through a long window for me to see Lena's face. There were tears standing on her eyelashes. When I brushed them away she smiled. A moment later she was asleep. I lay awake for a little while more, at peace, still listening to the sea, before I too fell asleep.

It was late the following morning when we woke. The house was built very close by the water. The beach was fairly steeply sloping, the sand was good. A few minutes after getting out of bed I was tumbling in the surf. After a quick dry off I padded into the kitchen for breakfast. I had decided I wasn't going to Hawaii, not unless Lena would come too. There seemed no point in my tagging along with the scientists like a camp follower. Over coffee I asked Lena if she had any wish to go out to the islands. 'I'd like to go, but next week I'm working. If you're going to be there for some time I could join you later.' This seemed to be the right compromise.

I rang John during the morning to say I'd prefer not to travel with him the following day but rather come on by myself at the end of the week. There seemed no point in my hanging around in Los Angeles once Lena started at the studios.

The next few days passed all too quickly. We drove around, we swam, and made love and made music. Neither of us had any reason to feel there was anything unique about those days. I was not a soldier going to the wars, someone who might never return. After all, we would meet again in a week or two, if not in Hawaii, in Los Angeles. Yet we parted one morning at the airport with sudden sadness.

The mood lasted with me all the way to the islands. Three hours later I saw them standing up boldly out of a blue sea. I took a taxi from the airport into Honolulu. Soon I was booked into an hotel at Waikiki, close to the sea.

From there I put a call through to John who I knew would be on the island of Hawaii itself. I didn't reach him first shot so I had to leave a message to have him call me back. This forced me to hang around the hotel. When John at last came through, quite a while later, he said it would be best if I made the island hop the following morning. Why didn't I hire a car and take a look around Oahu? I said this was fine by me. It was mid-afternoon by the time I had the car which meant there wasn't a great deal of the day left for sightseeing. I asked at the hotel desk which was the most spectacular beach. The girl suggested I might like to go to the north side of the island to Sunset Beach.

It was warm and sticky as I drove over the twisting mountain road. The beach itself was tremendous, yet somehow I couldn't really get interested. I wondered if this was the way you became old, nothing excited you any more. I drove back by the east coast. After checking my car, I had an early dinner and then went straight to bed. I couldn't sleep. I lay wide awake for an hour, then I got up, dressed, and walked out to the sea.

As I strolled along the flat sand I was in the grip of a fit of loneliness such as I had rarely, if ever, experienced before. It came gradually upon me how much loneliness was increasing in our modern society. I realized it had been a dominating factor in almost all the people I had played to the other night.

I wandered back along the beach wondering whether these ideas, which had a deep validity, I was convinced, could somehow be expressed in sound. Anything new, for it to be worthwhile, must come out of my inner feelings. It couldn't be developed as a mere logical plan. The grandeur of Bach's music came out of his religious impulses, not from his technique. He worked to develop the technique because of the inner convictions, not the other way round.

To the west, away from the city, stars filled the sky. As I looked up to them my senses were suddenly acute and overwhelmingly strong. Reason suggests there could be nothing to it. Yet, knowing now what was to happen, I sometimes wonder whether the future at that moment did not touch me like a cold wind across the face.

290

5 Allegro Assai

The mood was gone the following morning. The trip from Honolulu to the big island of Hawaii was, I suppose, about one hundred and fifty miles. I was met at Waimea by a car. The country hereabouts was surprisingly flat, considering the fourteen-thousand-foot high Mauna Kea was only some fifteen miles to the south. The journey to the field-station was a short one and soon I was dumping my bags into a room in the sleeping quarters. Although the buildings had a prefabricated look about them they were, nevertheless, very well appointed inside. I had barely finished unpacking when John arrived.

'Just in time,' he said. 'We're beginning to get results. It's already clear the signal is genuinely modulated.'

'You mean the beam really is being used for conveying information?'

'That's what it looks like.'

About midday a party of five army and navy officers arrived. Over lunch everybody started to talk. For a while it was all much the things I knew already, apart from some technical interpolations which didn't interest me. John explained his ideas. Clementi quickly went over the general experimental set-up. The officers got the drift, more or less as I did. They asked questions about the interference fringes, questions I was too shy to ask. Clementi drew a series of loops, by way of answer, looking somewhat like a bunch of bananas. There was a lot of talk about near-fields and far-fields but this was beyond me.

The essential idea seemed to be one of phase. If you have something that oscillates up and down the precise position where it happens to be at a given moment is the phase. What it came down to was this: if you chose a particular moment of time, and then considered the phases over a very big area, they all had to be the same, in order to explain the observations. When he was asked how big the area had to be, John replied:

'According to my calculations about ten times the radius of the Sun.'

291

'But how can you get a phase correlation over such an enormous area?'

'That's what we all want to know,' muttered Clementi.

The big man padded around and stated sententiously, 'Control phase, and you control the universe.'

'But that's what we do with our radar, isn't it?' asked an elderly, blue-eyed naval officer.

John nodded. 'That's exactly the right way to put it. It's just as if there was a big antenna, measuring ten times the radius of the Sun. Apparently it's beaming a message out into space.'

There was silence for a while.

'What would be the directivity, with an antenna as large as that?' asked another of the officers.

'At a big distance, quite fantastic. The beam would go out into space as an extremely fine pencil.'

Someone had a bright idea.

'What's the chance of our being in the direct beam?'

'Remembering that we are in the near-field, it works out at somewhere between one in ten and one in a hundred, provided the beam is directed more or less along the ecliptic. Less than that if it's directed at random.'

'Isn't it a bit surprising that we just happen to lie in it?'

'We're not necessarily lying in the main lobe. I've thought quite a lot about this point. From a climatic point of view, I mean.'

John had their attention now.

'There must be something like a ten per cent difference in the solar radiation according to whether we're in the main beam or not. Of course we can't know anything directly about this infra-red stuff down here on the surface of the Earth. The infra-red never gets through the atmosphere. But it would have the effect of increasing the boundary temperature of the Earth.'

'By how much?'

'Anything up to ten degrees I would say. What I've been wondering is whether all the mysterious climatic fluctuations the Earth seems to suffer – the ice-ages for instance – could be caused by our relation to this beam. You know, it may not always point in the same direction. Sometimes the Earth could pass through it, during the year I mean. At other times we might miss it entirely.'

Clementi made a kind of humming sound. He wasn't winking. 'A few degrees up, or a few degrees down, is really all that might be needed to make quite big changes of climate. It could be at that. But look here, John, old chap, old fellow, old scoundrel more like, are you hinting that this deal up there might have been going on for thousands of years?'

'I should have thought it extremely likely. If it was something that had just started up right now, well, wouldn't it be ridiculously improbable?'

'Yeah, I suppose so.'

Several of the men were pacing like caged beasts up and down the lounge floor.

There was a silence which everybody seemed reluctant to break. At last, the naval officer with the blue eyes spoke:

'Gentlemen, it's time we came to the real issues. I don't know whether my colleagues and I can be described as having anything more than a watching brief here. But the questions that stand out in my mind are, first, how's it being done, second, what's it for? I must admit I'm personally in a smoke screen but maybe Dr Sinclair has something he'd like to add.'

This was quite a formal speech. I wondered how John would react to it. He shrugged his shoulders and began:

'I think anybody's guesses are as good as anybody else's at this stage. For myself I can't remotely conceive how this phasing trick is being worked. But being worked it surely is, so for the moment we'd better accept that, and go on from there – if we can. We've tested the deduction that the beam is being used to convey information.'

'What information? What the hell is there to send, where and to whom?'

One of the army officers grinned and suggested, 'Maybe it's a TV relay.'

Most of them laughed at this. I noticed John didn't. When the laughter had died down he simply said, 'Could be.' Everybody looked at him, so he went on:

'It may sound crazy but what else can it be? Oh, I don't mean a TV relay strictly. Think of the colossal amount of information that's probably being sent out, of the order of a hundred million bits a second. In a year, that's several thousand trillion bits. Something like a hundred million textbooks a year. What sort of traffic would you need to fill a channel like that?'

'You mean there'd be no point in sending out such a lot of stuff unless there was really something to send?' Everybody laughed at this.

After a further short pause John went on:

'There are two speculative possibilities. This might be an interstellar, or even an intergalactic, relay station. Granted the enormous directionality of the system, the fineness of the pencil beam, these signals could be received at an enormous distance away from us.'

Clementi had obviously been thinking along the same lines. 'The details really aren't as fantastic as the thing itself. But as John says, we know the thing exists, so there's no getting away from it. It's easy enough to do an intensity calculation. If this really is a relay station, if some guy at the other end has even a moderately sensitive detecting device, say only a millionth part as sensitive as our big radio telescopes – as this thing out on the hillside here – then these signals can be picked up – where? Come on, freshman physics! Not just 'in our own galaxy, but anywhere, out and beyond anything we can see with the biggest telescopes.'

'You mean this is just about the most...' The naval officer broke off whatever it was he was going to say. It was clear to him, as to me, that the wonders of science had gone beyond all reasonable bounds.

I was back in my room that night, jotting down one or two musical ideas, when John tapped on my door. 'Would you like to go for a stroll?'

We slipped out of a side door.

'I don't want any of the others to join us just for the moment.'

We had walked along for two or three hundred yards before he came to the point:

'I've been thinking it would be a good idea if you were to write everything down. I mean from the beginning. I think it would be a good idea to have an account from an unbiased person.'

'You mean a non-scientist?'

'If you like to put it that way, yes.'

My story is built from notes as I made them following this incident. Unfortunately my diary wasn't remotely detailed enough as it has turned out. So perforce I have often had to fill in as best I can from memory – this will explain how it comes about that sharp accounts of what took place are sometimes juxtaposed with obvious lapses of memory – my failure to recollect odd names for instance.

I began to see now why John had more or less press-ganged me into coming along with him. I also felt freer to ask questions with a clear conscience.

'It's all very well to avoid the problem of how this incredible thing is being done but do you have any idea at all about what's really happening?'

We walked on for a little way.

'Not with any precision. The obvious inference is that someone is doing it. I suppose the most straightforward explanation would be to say that it's some creature, some intelligence, on one of the other planets.'

'A major boost to the space programme – eh?'

'As you say, a major boost to the space programme.'

I guessed that John really didn't believe this. When I asked him point blank he replied:

'It's an outrageous explanation fitted to a fantastic situation. Yet anything else seems worse. It's all a question of the way you look at it. When something really new happens most scientists take the line of least resistance. They accept the explanation that involves the least change from their preconceived notions. Which is what I'm doing now.'

'But you don't believe it?' I pressed.

'With me, believing or not believing a particular explanation is more a matter of method than of emotion. If I were emotional I'd be almost certain to plump for what I've just told you. The way I always work is like this. If I find things turning out much as I expect then I follow the line of least resistance, exactly the same as everyone else. But if I find my deductions going wildly wrong it's my instinct to explain my shortcomings by saying that I just haven't got hold of the right idea at all. I don't try to do a patchwork job, to choose the explanation that requires the least possible change from my previous position. I throw the net wide, just as wide as I can.'

By now my eyes were accommodated to the dark. We were able to pick our way across the open grassland with more precision.

'I suppose it's really not fair to twist your arm any further but what does this wide net look like? My own imagination just boggles at the idea of there being something still more strange and unusual than creatures on another planet.'

'I've got nothing definite to go on, except the day on the moor after we came off Mickle Fell.'

'You still think that amnesia business might have had something to do with it?'

'I don't know. What I do know, is that every explanation I can conceive of for that gap of thirteen hours, and for the mark that used to be on my back, is much more weird than this planet business. It suggests to my mind there's a real danger of our concepts going wildly astray.'

'In what sense?'

'Consider the usual science-fiction story. Let me anatomize the situation for you. Science-fiction is a medium that concerns, above all else, life forms other than ourselves. The real life forms of our own planet belong of course to natural history, to zoology, so science-fiction purports to deal with life forms of the imagination. Yet what do we find when we read science-fiction? Nothing really but human beings. The brains of a creature of science-fiction are essentially human. You put such a brain inside a big lizard, and bang-wallop, you have a science-fiction story. Or if you can't be bothered with the lizard-like aspect of the story, you simply put the human brain in a human creature, and call it a humanoid. To make the story go, the humanoid is usually set up as more intelligent than ourselves, with a better technology. Then the story turns on how the dear old magnificent human species manages to deal with the alien threat. It boils down to a new version of indians and cowboys.

'Let me be a bit more serious. If these rather simple-minded notions stopped at science-fiction it wouldn't be so bad. But as soon as we try to think quite seriously about intelligence outside the Earth that's exactly the way our concepts go.'

'So when you talked about a creature on one of the other planets you were really inventing a science-fiction story?'

'That's the way it seems to me.'

'Yet what else could there be?'

'Very hard to say, isn't it? If your brain doesn't have the right concepts you can't really force it to develop them. I'm quite willing to agree there may be lots of creatures more or less similar to us distributed up and down the universe, or even among the stars up there. What I doubt is whether there are any such creatures on Mars or Venus. Even if there were, I don't think they could perform this trick with the Sun.'

'You think it's too big? The Sun I mean. That a creature stuck down on a planet could hardly do anything to a star?'

'I'm more or less sure of it.'

After a short pause, John went off on a new tack. 'In physics, we accept a lot of mysterious things.'

'Such as what?'

'Well, it's very mysterious that our consciousness enables us to take decisions which turn out to improve our description of the world – in circumstances, mark you, when improvement ought to be impossible according to our basic physics.'

'Sounds the sort of thing our religious friends would be glad to hear.'

'They can read it in any textbook if they like. Let me give an example. You take a number of radioactive nuclei of a particular kind, the number being chosen so that there's an even chance of one of them going off in a certain period of time, say ten seconds. Then for ten seconds you surround them with counters, or any other detecting device you might like to use. At the end of the time the question is, has one of them decayed or not. To decide this you take a look at your counters. The conventional notion is that the state of the counters decides whether a nucleus has gone off or not.'

'What you're saying is that if you did this experiment a lot of times your calculations require that in a half of the cases a nucleus will have decayed and in the other half there will have been no decay?'

'Right. But my problem now concerns an individual case. Has there been a decay or hasn't there? How do you decide?'

'I would suppose by looking, which is what you said a moment ago.'

'Of course. But here comes the rub. It is perfectly possible to put your counters, or your bubble chamber, your camera, all your gobbledegook in fact, into your calculations – and we know quite definitely that any attempt to get a definite answer out of calculation will prove completely fruitless. The thing that gives the answer isn't the camera or the counter, it's the actual operation of looking yourself at your equipment. It seems that only when we ourselves take a subjective decision can we improve our description of the world, over and above the uncertainty of our theories. I'm talking about quantum theories now.'

'So you've got a real contradiction?'

I waited as John paused again. He lifted his hand in a gesture. 'There's one possible loophole. We could be wrong in comparing ourselves as physical systems with a camera or a counter or anything like that. The essential thing about a camera is that it's local. Its operation can be described by a strictly finite number of variables, its activities are restricted to a limited volume of space-time. It could be that when we make subjective judgements we're using connexions that are non-local. If this is right the logical ramifications are enormous. It means we can have connexions ranging all over the universe.'

'What's the relation to this business?'

'This affair could have nothing at all to do with our own local planets. It could be on a vastly bigger scale. It needn't have anything to do with human brains in lizard heads.'

'You've one or two fairly definite ideas?'

From long experience I knew that John would not have got himself into this conversation unless there was more than general guesswork behind it.

'There's one thing. You remember we talked about the purpose of this phased infra-red stuff. For God's sake don't tell anyone I don't really go along with that relay station idea. There's another more remarkable possibility. I've got a feeling the more remarkable possibility has a better chance of being right. Think of the enormous volume of communication that must be involved here, the incredibly detailed information. What kind of thing do we know about that would need such a capacity? This is the question I keep asking myself. What was it, a hundred million major textbooks a year? The sort of physics we study needs nothing like that. If you know how, you can put all our basic physics into one book. I suppose you could put most aspects of our technology into a hundred books. The only things I can see around me needing anything like this volume of information are biological organisms, our brain processes for instance, or the information needed to construct a human being.'

The following day I went for a drive round the island. I

went to Volcano House and took a look at the active Kilauea crater. I saw sugar plantations, pineapple fields, rain forests, the sea and the mountains. When I got back to the experimental station I found the place in a wild panic. Somebody told me war had started and that Los Angeles had been destroyed.

went to Volcano House and took a look at the

The personal crowded out the general. My first thought was of
Lena. I was dry in the throat. I began rushing around with the
others, in the hope of finding John or one of his friends. I
couldn't really believe the news was true but it didn't need to be
true to be frightening. Of course I knew there was a bad
situation in south-eastern Asia. Yet I hadn't remotely credited
it could blow up into a major war, if that was what this really
was. Then I remembered war always seems to come as a
surprise to civilians, at any rate it had in 1914. At last I ran
into Art Clementi.

'Is there any truth . . .' I began.

'Can't say yet. But something serious seems to have happened. A few of us are going over to Pearl City. We can
probably manage to tuck you in if you want to come along.
John's going, the Brass want him down there.'

I packed my things as quickly as I could. In a sense, rushing
over to Pearl City was a form of panic, a desire to do something, to avoid sitting still and waiting. That's the way terror
got you, you just ran aimlessly around in any direction.

It was only when I walked with my bag out to the car park
that I found John. I was glad to see he didn't look too worried.

'I find this very difficult to believe. Something's happened all
right but it must have become exaggerated. We'd better go over
and find out exactly what it is.'

Scarcely a word was spoken on the journey to Hailo airport.
Nobody said very much there either. We all got on to the plane
in silence. It put down for a short stop in the island of Maui
and then went on to Honolulu. A big station wagon was waiting for us. There was very little traffic on the road as we made
our way to the naval base. Then came a hold-up when it was
found that neither John nor I was an American citizen. After a
delay, in which I suppose a number of phone calls were put
through, we were separated from the others and told that a car

300

would be made available to take us to a downtown hotel. After the best part of an hour a car did appear and we made away in it. In the car John said, 'I told Art we would go to the Waikiki.'.

We got rooms at the hotel. I tried to ring Los Angeles but found all lines engaged. Then I lay flat out on my bed in a quite blank state of mind. I had a call from John on the house phone at about six o'clock suggesting we meet downstairs in the bar for a drink. It seemed as good an idea as anything else. After the drink we went to dinner in the hotel restaurant.

'I wonder if I could have a talk with you chaps?' The speaker was an Australian. We told him to pull up a chair. Clearly he had finished dinner. We were only half-way through the main course. We introduced ourselves, and took stock of our new acquaintance. It struck me I had become far more suspicious, far less free and easy, in the last few hours. I felt as if I was on some kind of an assignment. The Australian had an athletic look about him. His manner was pleasant and open.

'I heard you talking and realized you were a couple of Britishers.'

The clans were certainly drawing together. Our exclusion at Pearl City and now this.

'How about a walk on the beach when you've finished? I'll be in the bar.'

Then he was gone.

Not long afterwards Art Clementi appeared. We naturally wanted to know the news:

'It looks bad, real bad. There's no doubt the west coast has been attacked.'

We tried to get more out of him but either he knew nothing more or he wouldn't say. It was all very odd. It was also odd that Clementi went off without eating dinner with us. He excused himself by saying he had already eaten but I knew from the way he looked at the food that this couldn't be so. What the hell did it mean, the contrast between this frigidity and the uproarious welcome we had received only the other day in California?

We got the beginnings of an answer from our Australian acquaintance. He waited until we were well away on the beach before he would talk. The man was a QANTAS pilot. He had been on a regular flight from Honolulu to the United States.

As he approached the international airport at Los Angeles a message had come through directing him to return.

'There was something crook about it.'

'In what way?'

'It didn't look right. In fact it was all wrong, just as wrong as it bloody well could be.'

'Things wouldn't look very pretty after a nuclear attack.'

I had told John nothing of Helena Summers. In the poor light I don't suppose they could have seen my distress.

'That's just it. If I could have seen a lot of damage, a lot of smoke, I wouldn't have been surprised.'

'There must have been smoke.'

'Well, there wasn't. It was a clear day. Of course I was nearly fifty miles out to sea. Yet as far as I could tell there was nothing.'

We stopped in astonishment. The surf broke loudly, not far away on our right. We waited for the rippling noise to die away.

'Nothing?'

'Not a bloody thing. I could see the whole Los Angeles basin. And I tell you there wasn't a bloody thing there.'

'I tried to ring Los Angeles this afternoon. They told me all the lines were engaged, so there must be something there.'

'Do you think they'd tell you if there wasn't?'

'Didn't you get any signals from the control tower?'

'Not a damn thing. Not a peep. I thought the radio must be out of action. We couldn't pick up anything, not from San Francisco either, or from the control stations to the east. I told the wireless operator to keep trying. He did a big search over the whole shortwave band. Do you know what he came up with?'

'If the war's really started all long-range stuff will be off the air. Local TV stations and news stations will be on, probably.'

'Well, I'll tell you this. I got the control back here, exactly as usual. And I got some shortwave stuff from Britain. And that was it, nothing anywhere else.'

'You got the usual British channels?'

'As far as I could tell. We're a long way off here. So I only got odd snatches. As far as we could judge it was about what was to be expected in a normal way.'

We walked on for a while before John said, 'Could that be

the trouble do you think? It seems incredible but if Britain's really on the air in any normal way she hasn't been attacked.'

'It could be.'

'Did you get anything from the west, the other way?'

'From Fiji, nothing from Sydney.'

It didn't make sense, except perhaps for one ray of light.

'Do you think they imagine we've gone neutral? If Britain is more or less normally on the air that's what it looks like.'

'I'd thought of that,' answered John. 'It would fit. If they think we've ratted on them it would be natural enough for them to treat us pretty distantly. Yet it seems fantastic. British policy and American policy are in it together. I would have thought we couldn't keep out even if we wanted to.'

We headed back to the hotel. I asked, 'What are you going to do? With your plane? Go back to Australia?'

The pilot paused for a moment. 'I've given quite a bit of thought to that. I'm supposed to be on a through flight Los Angeles to London, with a refuelling stop in Canada. I suppose if I insist they'll let me take off as long as I agree to keep over Canadian territory all the way.'

'Isn't that the natural thing to do?'

'I suppose so. But I'm leery about it. I can't say exactly why, but I'd prefer it if I could go right through in one hop.'

'I thought the new planes could pretty well do that, at any rate from California. Can't you make it with a light load?'

'I've got one of the old jobs.'

'Pity, because we ought to be getting back home – at any rate if the atmosphere doesn't get warmer around here.'

'Day after tomorrow we have a long-distance plane coming through. It could make the trip. I'll have a word with the captain if you like.'

We said we thought it might be a good idea.

By now we were nearing the hotel. After a drink at the bar I decided to turn in. Sick at heart I took one last look out over the sea before I climbed into bed. Unpleasant emotions seemed inseparable from this damned place. I lay there thinking about Lena. I could remember the tears and the smile which followed them.

What the devil did the Australian mean by saying there was nothing? Not even the dead and the dying? I little realized that I had become separated from Helena Summers by much more than death.

I was wakened the following morning by the phone burring in my ears. It was John saying he was going out to Pearl City, that the climate seemed to have changed back just as suddenly as it had shifted yesterday. I asked him why, but he didn't know. When I came down to breakfast in the coffee shop I found the blue-eyed naval officer waiting for me. We sat down together. I ordered a stack of wheatcakes and coffee. He ordered coffee.

'I'm afraid we owe you a very sincere apology. Yesterday we didn't know where we were, not that we're much better today. But we can see things a bit more clearly now.'

Then he went on to tell me, rather haltingly, much the same as John had already guessed, that radio communications from Britain, apparently still covering the normal radio waveband, had convinced them Britain had somehow managed to stay out of the war. This had made for a peculiar situation so far as we were concerned. They had thought the best thing was to do nothing and say nothing. I said both John and I had appreciated what the situation must look like and we quite understood his position. He became less embarrassed but no less worried. I told him I had a close friend in Los Angeles and could he tell me anything of what had happened there. He looked about him, to see whether anybody was listening, and then said, 'We can't understand it, we just can't understand it. We've sent planes over and – well, there's nothing there, nothing at all.'

I asked if this could be some strange new development in war technique. Yet even as I asked the question I realized it was absurd. The officer shook his head. He looked tired and old and I could see the situation was quite beyond him.

'It may sound horrible. If it had been war, the kind we expected, I would at least have understood what was going on. It looks like a nightmare, as if we were all dreaming. I keep hoping I'll waken up. That sounds kinda silly.'

'Don't you think we ought to stop trying to understand it, at any rate for the time being. Perhaps we ought to get back to the way we were when we were kids. We all took the world the way we found it. Only later as we grew up did we try to make sense of it.'

'Yes, I suppose so. But at my time of life it isn't easy to learn new tricks. You get set in your ways as the years roll past. You see I had a son and daughter-in-law and two kids in Los Angeles.'

We shook hands sadly and he left.

For the next two days I sat in my room writing as hard as I could go. I wanted to get all the old, more normal, stuff down before my standards of judgement became distorted by this strange new world. I knew John and his colleagues would seek me out as soon as the next move was decided. As I say, I was given two days' grace. I emerged from my room only for meals. My fingers grew stiff with writing, always writing, twelve hours a day.

John appeared at last late on the second day. He had not eaten at lunchtime so I went with him back to the restaurant, although I had already had dinner. I asked for the news.

'Fragmentary in the extreme. The balance of opinion still favours war of some sort. Nobody can fit the facts together. It seems quite certain that Los Angeles really has ceased to exist. We don't know much about the rest of the States. In Britain it seems to be just as normal as it is here. There's some activity in Europe, although it doesn't look normal there either. From Russia there's as big a blackout as there is from the American mainland.'

I waited. It was an old trick with John, the dramatic pause.

'Back home they're in just the same mess. We managed to get a message through. They wanted news, saying they're just as much in the dark as we are.'

'I had the old naval chap in again this morning. He doesn't like it at all.'

'The devil is that everything is so normal here. It's only the outside communications that are crazy.'

'Could it be some sort of hoax, some ridiculous psychological experiment, connected with the military programme? To determine the population reaction.'

'Well, if it is, we shall soon know. You remember the Australian. He told us a plane was coming in from Fiji, one that might manage to get through to Britain in one hop? It's here now, it came in yesterday evening, and it's the only real long-range plane in the islands. So they've decided to send it over the States. It can get to somewhere in the region of

305

Denver or Chicago and still manage to get back here to the islands. The military people have commandeered it. After a bit of argument I've got the two of us included on the trip. I've given them the idea I might come up with some explanation of what's going on.' John ran his hand through his hair and added, 'Some hopes.'

At breakfast the following morning I realized a strange thing had happened in the preceding days, the days in which I had been shut away in my room. From the beginning, from the moment the war rumours first spread, smiles had disappeared, there had been less talk, less laughter, fewer vehicles on the street. Now there was an almost complete silence. Everybody spoke quietly, as if someone or something was listening to what was being said. In these islands of sunshine it was weird and unnerving.

We got to the airport at about nine o'clock. I would say about forty persons, mostly service officers, were already assembled there. I looked around for Art Clementi, hoping to straighten out the misunderstanding and embarrassment of our last meeting, but he wasn't there.

'Looks as though we're taking a very light load,' I said.

'To give as big a range as possible.'

A few minutes later we climbed up an old-fashioned ramp into the rear door of the plane. An Australian girl smiled at us as we enplaned. A few minutes later we were in the air.

We settled down in our seats. The hostess brought us quite large glasses of fresh orange juice. It was a welcome change from the inevitable coffee.

'Australian idea,' said John. 'Genuine stuff, not artificial muck.'

'What's been going on the last two days?'

'I got involved in two things. Damn queer, both of them. I was out at the university, at the seismic department. On the face of it not very exciting. Simple equipment and so on. I'm not familiar with the details of that business so I had to accept what they told me.'

'And what the devil did they tell you?'

'Well, the general background of seismic disturbances – you know there are always slight earth movements going on all the time – has gone up enormously in the last four days.'

'I didn't notice any earthquake.'

306

'Oh, this was below the subjective threshold. But it was much above the usual noise level by several orders of magnitude.'

'Maybe there's been a big earthquake somewhere, a long way off.'

'It couldn't be just one earthquake, it wouldn't last long enough. More like a succession of them. And even that doesn't fit the pattern properly. From a single earthquake, particularly a big one, you get a pretty clean-cut record. This stuff is all confused, it looked like real random noise.'

'What could be doing it?'

'Nobody has the slightest idea. It isn't very dramatic, not like the other things, but I thought I'd mention it. Often it's the non-spectacular things that lead you in the right direction.'

'You said there was something else, two things you'd been looking at.'

'Right. Signals from the rocket have stopped. Art Clementi's boys are getting a blank record.'

'How long did you expect to go on getting a signal before the rocket got too far away from the Earth?'

'Oh, for several weeks more. The natural interpretation is that a small meteorite has hit something in the electronics. It was a rush job so we couldn't take every precaution we would have liked to have done. Yet it's queer to find the signals stopping only a few minutes before the war was announced.'

Several officers and the pilot came to talk to John during the flight. It struck me as odd how much status depends on the social situation. War had reduced us to persons of no account. The present situation, with all its weird implications, taking one as far as the shifting frontiers of science or even beyond that, made John a commanding figure. He was the most distinguished scientist available for consultation. On his coat tails, almost literally, I managed to get into the cockpit as the plane approached the American mainland.

There were a lot of us jammed in there. Yet I could see a great deal more than was possible from an ordinary passenger seat. I gathered it was the Los Angeles basin ahead. The air was completely clear. There was nothing of the banks of brown smog I had seen when we came in from New York two weeks ago. Was it only two weeks ago? It needed no more than the most casual glance to see there was no city here.

'Take a look along the Sierra Madre. Look for the Observatory.'

We were coming lower now, to an altitude of about ten thousand feet I guessed. There were mountains below us, heavily wooded. I noticed there were no fire-rides. We flew immediately above their crests, sharp and jagged. The trees covered the very topmost point. If this was Mount Wilson, there was no observatory here. We left the mountains and came back to the flatter land by the coast, dropping down still further, to only a few thousand feet. It was then we caught brief glimpses of habitation in the woods. The woods were now covering places where only two weeks before there had been great sprawling boulevards, streaming with traffic, swarming with humanity.

But there were signs of life below us and this lifted our spirits to an astonishing degree. The trouble was we couldn't land the plane. An enormous runway was needed for that and no such thing as a runway was to be seen in the wilderness below us. We came low enough to notice a few cultivated patches of land and this was all. Whoever was down there was keeping out of sight.

The itch to get to the ground was overwhelming, I think, to everybody on the plane. Since we had plenty of fuel we did the obvious thing of heading east, into the American mainland. Sooner or later we all felt it must be possible to find an airstrip. Two weeks ago every town of any appreciable size had its airport, with runways extended for the new jets. The day was so clear that even after we climbed back to forty thousand feet we could still see the ground below quite well.

As we flew on we all kept a sharp lookout for towns and roads. We saw neither in the usual sense. There was an occasional rough track through the mountains. Now and again we thought there were further signs of primitive inhabitations. Whether or not there were houses we couldn't say. Further east, and ever further, we went. The search for a place to land was becoming fruitless. We tried Phoenix, or what used to be Phoenix, then Albuquerque, then at last we were over the central plains. We came down very low over Denver. It wasn't entirely easy to be sure we had located the correct place. There were no radio beacons to guide us. All navigation had to be done with the compasses, and even by the old-fashioned

308

method of simply looking down on to the ground. Denver was a good place to look for. The big sudden rise of the Rockies lies only thirty miles or so to the west. That landmark was quite unmistakable, so all we had to do was to fly on a north–south line until the crew felt convinced they had found the right place. Once again we came low, to a thousand feet or so. Below us there were open grasslands. There were no signs of growing crops. Manifestly, the vegetation was in a natural state, a natural ecology.

With the present light load the plane was expected to have a range of between eight and nine thousand miles. So far, we had done about three thousand. Perhaps it would have been wise to have turned back. Yet the desire to find a landing spot was so strong in all of us that we felt impelled to make one more try, in the direction of Chicago. We wouldn't have a great deal to spare in the matter of range, but by taking a more direct route back to Hawaii the pilot thought he would be all right.

We picked up a powerful tail wind. Quite strong radio signals were coming in now from the east, probably of European origin. We found nothing at Chicago, except endless lakes and woods. Then came the critical discussion, to go on or to go back. The big advantage of going back was we knew exactly where we were going. The disadvantage was that we didn't have a great deal in hand in the way of range. We would have to fight the head wind, although this wouldn't matter too much as long as we found a reasonably direct route. The advantage of going on was that radio-guidance systems seemed to be working more or less normally somewhere to the east. And we still had the tail wind so range would be no problem that way. Besides it was manifestly desirable to establish actual physical communication with whatever it was that lay to the east.

Truth to tell, I think everybody wanted to take a look at New York. It was much the same story as we flew over the Appalachians in the fading light. But there were far more signs of life here, far more primitive shacks, it seemed. It all looked as America might have looked around the year 1800. Darkness came on. We saw little more, except twice there were flickering lights below us, fairly obviously camp fires. Then we were out over the Atlantic.

By now we were back in our seats. The stewardess served us with a meal. There wasn't much conversation, and what there was of it was pretty terse. John and I sat silently, each immersed deeply in his own thoughts. The irrational feeling swept over me that somehow the plane had become a world closed in on itself, that it would go on and on flying for ever. We had frequent reports from the pilot, however, to say that radio communication ahead was entirely normal. But perhaps this was just another monstrous deception? Emotionally, I felt we must go on and on until at last we came to our starting point, back in Hawaii; that we would find everything wiped clean even on the islands, just as it was on the American mainland.

I saw John looking repeatedly at his watch. Like me, like all of us, he was finding the passage of time excruciatingly slow. We had still three hours more to go before the next stage in the drama would unfold itself.

In retrospect I am not sure whether the innocence of my mind was an advantage or not. To build any rational explanation of what had happened, of what I had seen, was utterly beyond me. So I was left only with monstrous images and grotesque explanations.

After an age, in which every ten minutes seemed stretched to an hour, as it does in childhood, the little speakers above our heads crackled. The pilot's voice came over to say we had just passed the west coast of Ireland, that we would be landing at London airport in about three-quarters of an hour. Even the harshness of the speakers failed to conceal the relief, the emotional tones, in his voice.

All the evidence was that London airport was working normally. From the tilt of the fuselage you could see we were coming down now. The moon was shining on banks of clouds below us. Then we were down to the clouds and into them. These were the clouds that hang so frequently over the British Isles, blotting out the sun, giving the grey skies I knew so well. The clouds were astonishingly thin, the layer couldn't have been thicker than a few hundred feet. We broke suddenly below it. There on the ground was a multitude of lights. The sheer normality of it, the roads we could now pick out, set up a sharp reaction. I returned quickly to my seat and lay back feeling I might be sick. It wasn't air-sickness, rather that of faintness. Then I saw we were going down to the ground at last. The landing wasn't a good one, there was a big bump as the wheels hit, but at least we were down. Within a few seconds I felt all right again.

As we taxied along the runway I had the odd thought that maybe I had been dreaming. Perhaps I had snoozed away the whole of a perfectly normal flight. It was hard to believe otherwise as the pilot manoeuvred the plane into its final resting spot.

There was an unconscionably long delay before steps appeared and the rear door was opened. We stood up, collected our belongings, and waited in the aisle in precisely the usual fashion. The people ahead began to move slowly. A minute later I was in the open air. We were shepherded by a girl into a waiting bus. There was another delay and then the crew joined us.

I expected to be taken to the usual assembly hall, or waiting hall, or whatever they called it, prior to immigration and customs. But the bus came to a gate that led off the airfield. The gate was opened. While we were halted two policemen got in. Away over on my right, in the distance, I had the impression of an airport crowded with thousands on thousands of people. It was as if they were waiting there, in the hope of seeing planes coming in to land. Soon we were at a traffic light that led out on to the highway. Then we were speeding into London. Here too, as in Honolulu, there was very little traffic. It was a fair guess that we had been brought this way to avoid the crowds, perhaps to avoid reporters and television cameras. Quite evidently, I had not been dreaming.

7 Adagio

We were taken to what was obviously the headquarters of some intelligence unit. Men in uniform, men in civilian clothes, were walking around in a strained, taut way. The American officers were quickly separated from the rest of us. In fact only John and myself and the Australian crew were in civvies. We were shown into rough sleeping quarters. John took this without comment. With a grin he said to me, 'They'll soon change their tune.'

The following morning, after an unappetizing breakfast, two officers came looking for John. They asked him to follow them, or more politely to go with them. John insisted I should go along too. They were doubtful, but once he had told them I knew as much about the business as he did — a gross exaggeration — they made no further objections. We were taken to a waiting car. In the front, beside the chauffeur, was a fellow whom I took to be a plain-clothes officer of some species or other.

The car headed out into west London. It kept on into the country for an hour or thereabouts. At last we turned in at the gates of a pretty flossy place. The house was vaguely familiar.

'Chequers,' grinned John. 'I told you they'd change their tune.'

We were received courteously by the Prime Minister himself. There were a number of other guests, quite a mob of them. The Prime Minister introduced us round. There was the Foreign Secretary, the Chancellor, the Minister of Defence, the Chief of Staff, and about half a dozen other high-ranking service officers. They were drinking sherry. A glass of the stuff was pressed into our hands.

John explained my presence by saying I had been making a complete record of everything that had happened. This seemed to please everybody, as if a record is equivalent to an explanation. I also noticed how easy it is for a scribe to get himself into even the most intimate conference. It comes I supposed from the laziness to which all flesh is prey. I also noticed the heavy preponderance of the military. It struck me wryly that whenever the unusual happens the stock of the military always seems to rise.

Before lunch John gave an excellent and precise account of what had happened in California, in Hawaii, and on the flight back across America. His narrative was put together so concisely and with such logical consistency that his audience listened without comment or question until it was finished. Then everybody waited for the Prime Minister to comment:

'Obviously you've been thinking of explanations for all this. You've given us the facts. But what do they mean?'

'It's too early to say, sir. It's common dictum I believe among lawyers that one must wait for all the evidence to be in before forming an opinion. I've been waiting for all the facts. You must have an awful lot of things we don't know anything about.'

'We've got plenty of facts, but I don't mind telling you we haven't the slightest idea what they mean. You've given us a pretty succinct account of the American situation. Here's what's happened to us. As far as we can make out everything is quite normal in Britain. From the American mainland we've had absolutely nothing, which doesn't surprise me in view of what you've just said. From Europe too there's been a blackout except in the last few hours.'

'When did the blackout start?'

'Oh, nearly two days ago.'

'At 10.37 p.m.'

One of the officers had consulted a notebook. I felt there must be something wrong here. John was looking puzzled:

'That's only about thirty-six hours. It happened four days ago with us.'

It was their turn to look surprised.

'You mean you lost contact with the American mainland four days ago?' asked the Chancellor.

We both affirmed that this was so.

'Very strange, very strange.'

The Prime Minister was drumming his fingertips on the table.

John went on, 'That's another interesting fact. You were talking about Europe, what's going on there?'

313

'We don't know.' This from the Minister of Defence.

'You mean it's just as blank as the American mainland?'

'No, it isn't. We've been getting wireless messages but they're strange in every conceivable respect.'

'Why haven't you sent planes over?' I broke in.

The Prime Minister looked at me for a few seconds. I saw his eyes were dark and troubled. 'Of course we sent planes over. They never returned.'

On this new and sombre note we sat down to lunch. A short menu had been typed. I was engrossed in my own thoughts, hardly listening to the discussion, significant as it might be. Idly I looked at the menu. It was dated September the 19th. Of course it must be a mistake. I waited until there was a lull in the talk and then asked, feeling very foolish, whether the date on the menu was right. The triviality of the question riveted everybody's attention. A few seconds went by in which I had the impression they were all ticking off the days in their minds. Then someone said, 'I think it's right.' Another added, 'Of course it's right.' The Prime Minister looked at me and asked, simply, 'Why?'

'Because according to my reckoning it should be somewhere in the middle of August. I think the 13th, certainly within a day or two of that. What's your reckoning, John?'

'Somewhere about that, within a day or two. I've been so heavily occupied that I've really lost precise contact. Yet there isn't the slightest doubt we're still in August. At least Dick and I are in August.'

At this very dramatic point the girl serving the food whispered something to the Prime Minister. He nodded and she went away. A moment later a young lieutenant in uniform appeared. He went to the Chief of Staff, stood behind his chair as if to serve some dish, saluted, and handed him an envelope. The Chief of Staff turned and said, 'Thank you. You can wait outside.'

Everybody watched the envelope being slit open very precisely with a knife. I would have ripped it open with thumb and finger myself. We watched the Chief of Staff reading with growing astonishment. Then he got up and took the papers to the Prime Minister. He stood behind the Prime Minister's chair, waiting for them to be read through. Then the Prime Minister said:

314

'It's jibberish. Here's a sample:

My views are known to you. They have always been 'defensive' in all theatres but the west. But the difficulty is to prove the wisdom of this now that Russia is out. I confess I stick to it more because my instinct prompts me to stick to it, than because of any good argument by which I can support it.

Where the devil did this stuff come from?'

The Chief of Staff handed the Prime Minister another sheet. The Prime Minister went on:

'Apparently a man in uniform approached the Dover dock authorities this morning. He was in a distraught frame of mind. He insisted on being provided with transport to take him to London, to the War Office. Police took him in custody and found this letter on him. That all?'

'That's all I have here.'

'Why the hell should we be bothered by some lunatic? There must be thousands of them around just at the moment.'

This point of view commended itself to me for every crackpot in the country would now be at work. I could see the ranters in Hyde Park predicting the end of the world.

'There's something very familiar about that passage,' said the Minister of Defence in a puzzled voice.

'Yes,' nodded the Chief of Staff, 'and I think I know where it comes from.' He turned to the Prime Minister, 'If you'll excuse me, sir, I'd like to take a look in the library.'

We all followed him to the library. He looked at the shelves, here and there, for a while. Then with a satisfied grunt he pulled out a volume. He flicked through the pages until at last he came to what he wanted.

'Here it is, the exact passage. You can see for yourselves.'

He held the book down on the table. It was indeed there, exactly as I remembered the Prime Minister reading out a few moments before. It was part of a letter, the rest of which I supposed the Prime Minister hadn't bothered with. Then I noticed the volume was an official war history.

'It's part of a letter from Sir Douglas Haig to Sir William Robertson, written 27 September 1917.'

Coffee was served in the library. We sipped it silently until John said:

'I wouldn't take this as a hoax.'

315

'How would you take it?' asked the Prime Minister.

'That's another matter. What I mean is our natural impulse is to take it as a hoax because that's the way we'd like to see it.'

'You're not suggesting we should take it literally?'

'I think we ought to know more about it. What about the man they got the letter from? You say he was dressed in uniform. What was the uniform? Surely the people in Dover can tell us. And where did he come from? Did he come from the sea? Why not find out before we get into an argument?'

The Chief of Staff went away. He came back half an hour later, his face ashen grey.

'The man was dressed in a sergeant's uniform, exactly as he would be in 1917. He did come from the sea. They found the boat. There were more than a hundred other passengers. They're all dressed in the uniforms of 1917, or rather they were before they were moved *en bloc* to the local mental hospital. Every one of them swears we are in the year 1917.'

John banged his hands together for a few seconds, 'That's what I expected was going to happen. On a small scale it's the only explanation that makes sense. There's one thing I'd like to find out before coming to the point though.'

There was a phone in the library. In a bemused state of mind I heard John's voice – apparently involved in a technical discussion. After the call was finished, he said:

'Yes, there's been a lot of Earth movement here too, not much below subjective threshold. The noise level is much higher than it was in Hawaii. Normally this is one of the quietest parts of the Earth.'

'What do you get out of that?'

'Nothing in itself. But that was the way it had to be for consistency. I think I know now *what* has happened, although I haven't the slightest idea of *how* or *why*. In fact it's pretty obvious, isn't it?'

We were leaning forward in our chairs. John went on:

'I'll put it as crudely as I can. We've got ourselves into some kind of time-machine. Remember the old Wells story?'

The Chancellor smiled wryly, 'You mean about the fellow who invented a black box in which you could travel either forwards or backwards in time?'

'That's right, a remarkable black box it was. But our time-

316

machine is much more singular. It's not just a case of our being precipitated into other moments of time. And I don't think anybody else has been either. I think everybody, all over the Earth, will have the impression they're living quite normally in the present, as they understand the present. Nobody has noticed any sudden shift of time and nobody will do so, except in the way Dick here did while we were at lunch.'

The Prime Minister pulled a face and threw out his arms in a wide gesture, 'Let's try to see through a glass a little less darkly. Is there any reality in the discrepancy of a month, or are you under some hallucination, or are we under an hallucination?'

'Neither. We're both right. There is no inconsistency in it's being 19 September here in Britain, and the year being 1966. And there would have been no inconsistency to us in the time being the middle of August if we had stayed in Hawaii. It was only when we got together that the discrepancy came out.'

This touched them all off into animated comment. The Chancellor's voice stood out above the rest, 'You mean there are different times in different places on the Earth?'

'That's right. That's the way it must be. In Hawaii it is the middle of August 1966, in Britain it is 19 September 1966, on the American mainland I would guess it is somewhere before the year 1750, in France it is the end of September 1917.'

This was enough for the Prime Minister. 'If there's any possibility you're right we've got a lot of things to do, and without delay. I'm going to suggest we meet back here in four hours, shall we say?' There were nods around the room. Without further ado the Chief of Staff got up and went out. He was followed by the other officers. It was clear the Chief of Staff, the Chancellor, and the Minister of Defence, also felt the need for action, so John and I went out into the garden. After pacing around for a while we decided to go for a walk.

'I see everything fits together, that way. But every instinct, every emotion I've got, rebels against it,' I said with some warmth as we strode out along a country lane.

'Because, like all of us in our daily lives, you're stuck with a grotesque and absurd illusion.'

'How's that?'

'The idea of time as an ever-rolling stream. The thing which is supposed to bear all its sons away. There's one thing quite certain in this business: the idea of time as a steady progression from past to future is wrong. I know very well we feel this way about it subjectively. But we're the victims of a confidence trick. If there's one thing we can be sure about in physics it is that all times exist with equal reality. If you consider the motion of the Earth around the Sun, it is a spiral in four dimensional space-time. There's absolutely no question of singling out a special point on the spiral and saying that particular point is the present position of the Earth. Not so far as physics is concerned.'

'But there certainly *is* such a thing as the present. Without the ideas of the past, the present, and the future we could make no sense at all out of life. If you were aware of your whole life at once it would be like playing a sonata simply by pushing down all the notes on the keyboard. The essential thing about a sonata is the notes are played in turn, not all at once.'

'I'm not really trying to say the present is without validity. Rather that it can't have any validity in physics.'

'Then physics isn't everything? A big admission for a physicist, isn't it?'

'Remember the night we were out walking, back in Hawaii? I said then there were parts of our experience which simply defied physical law. I can develop those ideas a lot further. In a way I'd sooner get it off my chest now, rather than later. It sounds too crazy to put before a lot of people. Yet I'm sure something along these lines must be right. I'm going to put it in terms of a parable. Suppose you have a lot of pigeon holes, numbered in sequence, one, two, and so on ... up to thousands and millions, and millions of millions if you like. In fact the sequence can be infinite both ways, if you prefer.'

I said that I didn't mind. John went on, 'All right, let's come now to the contents of the pigeon holes. Suppose you choose one of them, say the 137th. You find in it a story, as you might find one of those little slips of paper in a Christmas cracker. But you also find statements about the stories you'll find in other pigeon holes. You decide to check up on whether these statements about the stories in the other pigeon holes are right or not. To your surprise you find the statements made about earlier pigeon holes, the 136th, the 135th, and so on, are substantially correct. But when you compare with the pigeon

318

holes on the other side, the 138th, the 139th, ... you find things aren't so good. You find a lot of contradictions and discrepancies. This turns out to be the same wherever you happen to look, in every pigeon hole. The statements made about pigeon holes on one side are always pretty good, those made about pigeon holes on the other side are at best diffuse and at worst just plain wrong. Now let's translate this parable into the time problem. We'll call the particular pigeon hole, the one you happen to be examining, the present. The earlier pigeon holes, the ones for which you find substantially correct statements, are what we will call the past. The later pigeon holes, the ones for which there isn't too much in the way of correct statements, we call the future. Let me go on a bit further. What I want to suggest is that the actual world is very much like this. Instead of pigeon holes we talk about states.'

'I understand what you're saying. You have a division into a number of states. Choice of any one of them constitutes the present. My problem is, who decides which pigeon hole to look in, the one that constitutes the present?'

'If I could answer that question I'd be a good half-way towards solving everything. Before I say anything about it let me ask *you* a question. Suppose that in each of these states your own consciousness is included. As soon as a particular state is chosen, as soon as an imaginary office worker takes a look at the contents of a particular pigeon hole, you have the subjective consciousness of a particular moment, of what you call the present. Think of the clerk in an office taking a look, first at the contents of one pigeon hole, then at the contents of another. Suppose he does this, not in sequence, but in any old order. What is the effect on your subjective consciousness? So far as the clerk himself is concerned, he's jumping about all over the place among the pigeon holes. So your consciousness jumps all over the place. But the strange thing is that your subjective impression is quite different. You have the impression of time as an ever-rolling stream.'

We walked on for a while. I saw that if the contents of a pigeon hole could never be modified then John was right. It would be possible for his clerk to look into a particular pigeon hole a dozen times or more and you'd never know about it. All you could be aware of, on his idea, was the contents of a pigeon hole, not when or how it was sampled. But there was one thing that bothered me:

'Doesn't the idea of a sequence of choices on the part of your clerk itself imply the flow of time? If it does, the argument gets you nowhere.'

'I'm sure it does not. A sequence is a logical concept in which time doesn't really enter at all.'

I saw in a general sort of way what he meant. Yet I was troubled. 'But if you have a rule that requires you to pass from one pigeon hole to the next, like passing from one number to the next, isn't it really exactly the same as a smooth flow of time?'

'If the rule were the one you say, yes certainly. But you could have rules that didn't require the next number to be the succeeding pigeon hole. Look, suppose we do it this way. We could choose number 1, then number 100, then number 2, then number 99, and so on until we've had every pigeon hole from 1 to 100. Then we could do the same thing from 101 to 200. That would be a different kind of rule. In fact there are infinitely many ways in which you can lay down rules, if the sequence itself is infinite. Any particular rule establishes what we call a correspondence between the pigeon holes and the choices. If every pigeon hole is chosen exactly once we have what mathematicians call a one-one correspondence. If every pigeon hole is chosen many times we have a one-many correspondence. The crux of my argument is that you get exactly the same subjective experience whatever the correspondence you choose. It doesn't matter what order you take the pigeon holes, it doesn't matter if you choose some or all of them a million times, you'd never know anything different from the simple sequential order. All you can know is the original contents of the pigeon holes themselves.'

'So really the choices could be an incredible hotch-potch. You could have youth and old age interlaced with each other and you'd never know?'

'Not only that, but you could experience your youth a million times over and you'd never know. If the clerk were to put a note in a pigeon hole whenever he used it, then of course you could know you'd had a certain experience before. But as long as he leaves no note you can never know.'

'I suppose so. Where have we got to now?'

'Quite a way. We've got our sequence of pigeon holes, that's the physical world. We don't think of one pigeon hole as having any more significance than another, which agrees with what I said before. We don't think of one particular state of the Earth as having any more significance than any other state of the Earth. We've completely eliminated the bogus idea of a steady flow of time. Our consciousness corresponds to just where the light falls, as it dances about among the pigeon holes. It lights up first one, then another, in some sequence that is quite irrelevant.

'Now let's come to the hard part. What is this light? I'm no longer talking in terms of a clerk in an office, because I don't want to get bogged down in human images. All our pigeon holes are in darkness except where the spot of light falls. What that light consists of, where it comes from, we know nothing. It lies outside our present-day physics.

'You remember I told you that it's possible to defy our own present-day physical laws and still to make a clear gain in our assessment of the world. You remember the radio-active nuclei with the counters surrounding them? We wanted to know whether or not in a certain period of time a nucleus had undergone decay. I said there was only one way to find out. By looking. In other words by using the spot of light in our pigeon hole. My strong hunch is that it's the spot of light that permits decisions which lie outside the laws of physics. This is why I'm so sure something else must be involved. It doesn't need to be anything mystical. It may be subject to precise description, to law and order, the same as in our ordinary physics. It may only be mysterious because we don't understand it.'

'There's certainly a lot of things I don't understand. This light of yours, or whatever you like to call it, how does it decide that you are you and I am me?'

'That could be another illusion. Look, along one wall of our office we have one complete set of pigeon holes, all in their nice tidy sequence. Along another wall we have another set of pigeon holes. Two completely different sets. But there is only one light. It dances about in both sets of pigeon holes. Wherever it happens to be, there is the phenomenon of consciousness. One set of pigeon holes is what you call *you*, the other is what I call *me*. It would be possible to experience both and never know it. It would be possible to follow the little

321

patch of light wherever it went. There could be only one consciousness, although there must certainly be more than one set of pigeon holes.'

I found this a staggering idea. 'If you're right it would be possible to be a million people and never know it.'

'It would be possible to be much more than that. It would be possible to be every creature on every system of planets, throughout the universe. My point is that for every so-called different creature, for every different person, you need a separate set of pigeon holes. But the consciousness could be the same. There could even be completely different universes. Go back to my decaying nucleus. Hook up a bomb which explodes according to whether you have decay of a nucleus or not. Make the bomb so big that it becomes a doomsday machine. Let it be capable – if exploded – of wiping out all life on the Earth. Let the whole thing go for the critical few seconds, you remember we were considering whether a nucleus would decay in a particular ten seconds? Do we all survive or don't we?

'My guess is that inevitably we appear to survive, because there is a division, the world divides into two, into two completely disparate stacks of pigeon holes. In one, a nucleus undergoes decay, explodes the bomb, and wipes us out. But the pigeon holes in that case never contain anything further about life on the Earth. So although those pigeon holes might be activated, there could never be any awareness that an explosion had taken place. In the other block, the Earth would be safe, our lives would continue – to put it in the usual phrase. Whenever the spotlight of consciousness hit those pigeon holes we should be aware of the Earth and we should decide the bomb had not exploded.'

We walked on and on. There were weird implications here.

'You speak about completely different worlds, different universes. Do you think there was a world in which everything went normally? I know I'm not using words perhaps in the way you'd like me to, but I think you can get the idea. Was there a world in which none of these queer things happened?'

'I don't have any doubt about it. There was certainly a world in which, on 27 September, the men in the trenches in Flanders had Lloyd George as their Prime Minister. We know what happened in that world. It remains to be seen what will happen in this one.'

I thought about this for a moment and then burst out, 'You don't mean to say those men out there are going through the same experiences that men actually went through in 1917? All the mud and the shellfire?'

'Yes, of course. We're not in a pretty world.'

'But don't you see what it means? Damn it all I had an uncle killed in those Flanders battles. For all I know he's out there now.'

'For all you know he may not be killed this time. For all you know you may see him. It's fifty years on or thereabouts, so I don't suppose there'll be many queer cases. I mean of men being alive twice.'

Incredulously, I realized what he meant, someone who had survived the trench battles might still be living. There might be two of them, a young man out there in 1917 and an old man here in 1966.

'But it's fantastic. There can't be two of you.'

'You don't seem to take much notice of what I've been talking about. Remember the states of consciousness, remember the subjective impression of consciousness is not the same thing as the pigeon holes of the physical world. The consciousness of the man in the trenches is not the same as the old man living over here. The pigeon holes are different and they can never be lighted up by the same spot of light.'

'You mean the spot could dance about between the two of them but so long as the pigeon holes are different there would be the subjective impression of their being totally different individuals.'

'Exactly the same as you and I have the impression of being different.'

We walked back in silence. I think both of us were overwhelmed, not only by these ideas, but by the situation that was soon to develop.

We got back to the garden. Then an odd detail occurred to me, 'What was all that stuff about seismic disturbances?'

'My idea, only a fancy if you like, runs something like this. I've told you we're living in a new physical situation. A new bunch of pigeon holes. The game, as I see it, is that the new pigeon holes are similar in most respects to some of the pigeon

323

holes in the other system. It's as if the present world were built out of copies of bits of the old world. Do you remember the day on the moor below Mickle Fell? Don't you realize it was a copy that came back to the caravan that night? Not quite a perfect copy, the birthmark was missing.

'Well, this whole world is a copy of some of the bits from another, the more normal world. This world may be queer by every standard we're used to but the bits must have a proper relation to each other.'

'You mean there's nothing supernatural in it?'

'You might put it that way. Well, look what's involved. Think about the Earth. Things change slowly as the years pass. Landforms are not quite the same now, in 1966, as they were in 1866. So if you copy the part of the Earth that corresponds to the England of 1966, and try to fit it to the Europe of 1917, and to the America of 1700 or 1800, things won't exactly match.'

An idea was working itself around in my head. 'You'd need a lot of information, wouldn't you, to make copies like that?'

John paused as we entered the house. 'Right you are, Dicky my boy. A lot of information. Remember what I said about that infra-red transmission. It was taking an awful lot of traffic.'

'Traffic needed for the copying.'

John nodded and added in a whisper, almost as if he were afraid of being overheard, 'Needed for the copying. We still don't know *how* it was done but at least we know *why*. Different worlds remembered and then all put together to form a strange new world. We shall find out more as we go along. This isn't the end of it.'

8 Allegro Molto e con Brio

As soon as we returned to the house John was collared by one of the service officers. I had spotted a piano earlier in the day. I went to see if there was any chance of my being able to play. Luckily the room with the piano was unoccupied so I shut the door and began to run my fingers over the keyboard. I was horribly out of shape and the first few minutes were pretty bad. I can't remember exactly what I played. Fragments here and there mixed in with a lot of improvisation. I was pretty wound up. For me this was the best way to get any tensions out of my system.

I became aware that someone had entered the room. It was the Prime Minister.

'I hope you don't mind my playing a bit. There didn't seem to be anybody about.'

'Not in the least. It's a relief to hear something different from this appalling situation we're in.'

'Is it true then? About Europe I mean?'

'There doesn't seem to be any doubt about it. Evidence is coming in from all directions. By radio, and by ships coming into port. The whole thing's a fantastic chaos. Whenever a ship comes in, both sides, those on board and those on shore, think the other is completely mad.'

'What are you going to do?'

'That's what we're going to decide. We must put an end to it somehow.'

'Sinclair thinks the situation is real. So far as the soldiers in France are concerned it's real, nothing different from what it was.'

'I don't know which is the more surprising thing, the facts, the situation, or the whole psychology of my own position. It's all completely changed.'

'I can see everything's changed, but what especially worries you?'

325

'Well, it's not unlike a rather delightful and remarkable story I once heard. About a wagon train crossing the United States during the last century. Two children happened to survive an Indian attack, their parents and friends being killed. One was a boy of twelve, the other a girl of three. The little boy took on the responsibility of getting his sister to California, and somehow succeeded. A complete change from dependence to responsibility. For the last two decades we've been drifting here in Britain in a thoroughly aimless fashion. There was nothing we could do to have any real effect on the world. After the responsibilities of the nineteenth century we'd suddenly become peripheral. Of course we've been pretending, I've been pretending, that we could have influence in other countries, and so influence the course of events. But it was a pretence really designed to keep up our own self-respect. Now everything's suddenly changed, just as it did for those two children. It seems as if what's happening in Europe, and what's going to happen, depends utterly and completely on us.'

The Prime Minister paced rapidly up and down the room. There was suddenly a decisive air about him, an attitude far removed from the bumbling policies of the last few years.

The number of visitors at Chequers had increased sharply during the afternoon. In addition to the politicians and the military there were now economists and two professors of history from Oxford. Messages from the outside world were constantly arriving, replies were constantly being sent. A buffet supper had been arranged. We took platefuls of food to a long table, sat down, and the discussion began. The Home Secretary said an immediate policy decision must be made, within the hour.

'We've reached the stage where something really definite must be said to the people. It can't be very long before the truth gets known. The strong westerly winds of the last few days have dropped. People in the south, particularly in Kent, can actually hear the gunfire in Flanders.'

The Prime Minister agreed to make an appearance on television, to make a frank statement about the whole position. Messages to the B B C and I T V were instantly dispatched.

Then the meeting got down to the problem in everybody's mind, how to stop the tragedy in France. Not a single person round the table had any thoughts otherwise. At all costs the disastrous attacks of early October, the attacks inevitably leading to the mud of Passchendaele, had to be prevented.

With the superior technology of 1966 it was at first sight easy to force a dictated peace on all the combatants. But how could the deadly weapons of the post-nuclear era be explained to minds still immersed in the second decade of the century? A simple display of force would be almost meaningless. Nor was there any prospect of peace being imposed through conventional weapons. In fact the conventional weapons at the disposal of the Prime Minister and his colleagues were negligible in total weight compared to the weapons possessed by the European armies. Guns and tanks were now vastly more refined, it was true, but their numbers were far too small to have any real effect. Only with planes and bombs could anything be done in this line. The air marshals confidently asserted that with complete mastery of the air it would be possible to destroy railway communications on the German side. In this way it would be possible to cut off all supplies to the German side of the fighting line. It was generally agreed, however, that this would only be done as a last resort, if the Germans were unwilling to take an immediately negotiated peace seriously.

The historians were called in at this point, to assess the German attitude to the war in 1917. There was a lot of talk about German political parties, the Social Democrats, the Centre, about the army and the Junkers. Surprisingly perhaps, the opinion was that negotiation might be easiest with the Junkers. It was said their chief motive in fighting the war, besides maintaining the prestige of the German army, was to hold on to their estates in East Germany. The Social Democrats were apparently wrong in the head, expansionist in outlook, and the Centre was worse than impossible.

The French position was plainly tricky. Their country had been violated, their army was passing through a difficult psychological phase, and their only dream was the eventual defeat of Germany. It was open to question whether the French would take kindly to a negotiated peace. The Prime Minister must visit Paris without delay, it was agreed.

At this point the problem of communication with the continent came in for discussion. It was pointed out that the first planes sent from Britain had failed to return. Perhaps the crew members had been taken for madmen, or perhaps the planes had been shot down? I saw the hint of a smile on John's face and knew he had a different explanation. Later he told me those planes had simply flown into – nothingness, before the different zones of the Earth were fully joined.

The opinion was that there would be no difficulty in landing in France provided a strong force of planes was sent. Then the problem of what to do about the British army came up for discussion. This was a matter of some delicacy. Yet even the Chief of Staff agreed that the commanding officers, particularly Sir Douglas Haig, must be recalled without delay. This would be a matter of difficulty, it was realized. The simplest method might be a letter purporting to come from Lloyd George, which would involve forging the old gaffer's signature. Arrangements were immediately put in hand.

Lastly it was agreed to mount an intense psychological campaign. Scores of heavy transport planes would be sent over the fighting line with thousands of tons of leaflets. There would be leaflets for the British, the French, and the Germans. They would say the same thing, they would tell the common soldier to stop it, not to fire another shot, another shell. This would be on the full authority of the British government.

As I heard these preparations being put in train I wondered to myself what it was that had changed in the British government between 1917 and 1966. Here was the Prime Minister in much the position Lloyd George had been in in 1917. Yet, whereas Lloyd George's thoughts had been wholly on how to prosecute the war more efficiently, we were now discussing it on the basis of an instant ceasefire. Nobody around the table had the slightest doubt of what must be done. I saw the difference came from the condition of our minds. In 1917, 1917 in Britain, nobody had been able to think outside the war situation. No doubt everybody wanted the war to stop. Yet everybody in 1917 had lacked the confidence to take the necessary steps. In 1966 our minds were completely outside that situation.

Everybody now had an inner confidence that the situation could be dealt with, somehow. This confidence, I saw, came from the technology of 1966. If our high-speed planes had been taken away, if there were no nuclear weapons in the background, if our industries were not enormously more efficient than the European ones, then we might have found ourselves thinking differently. Our escape from the mentality of 1917 really came from a lack of the fear that haunted the British government in 1917.

When the economists began to speak I realized that our situation in the long term wasn't any too favourable, however. Our technology depended to a considerable extent on large imports of oil. These would no longer be forthcoming, if the world of 1917 existed also in the Middle East. Here it transpired that absolutely nothing had come from the armies in the East, nothing from Egypt or from Mesopotamia. It was agreed this should be looked into forthwith. There would have to be a large-scale conversion back to coal as an energy source. And our coal reserves in 1966 were not too good. Above all, where would we get food imports? With the United States and Canada out of the picture, there was no simple answer to this question. Nothing was known yet about Australia. So there was still some hope of food from the Antipodes. But this was only a hope. It was manifest that the only satisfactory policy for the world of the future was to use the manpower of Europe. With the war ended, every available part of Europe must be put to food production. Oil production must be started in the Middle East without further delay.

I wasn't clear where John and I would come into this picture. When the meeting broke up for a short rest, at about nine o'clock, John got me on one side. He told me he had made arrangements, with the Prime Minister's approval, to get a survey of the world started. If it was 1917 in Europe, about 1750 in North America, there was no telling what it was on the rest of the Earth.

We would use one of the big long-distance planes, at any rate in the first instance. We would make a survey for possible landing places. If there were none, then at a later stage we would have to use flying boats, which could quickly be made available for our use. With these we could land on water, more or less as we pleased, provided the weather was fine. All this was clearly an excellent idea and I was not at all disappointed to be in on it. Yet the situation in Europe, its inner psychology, fascinated me. I hoped we would remain fairly close to events as they developed.

The Prime Minister left to make his speech to the nation. Everybody crowded around a television set as the time for the telecast at last came up. It was a good clear account of the situation, gravely delivered. I could not help wondering what the effect would be on the average viewer. Two months ago it would have seemed raving madness. But now the people would be partially prepared for it. I remembered the crowds back at London airport the previous evening. For all I knew, an end to uncertainty would prove more a relief than otherwise.

We also watched the programme which followed the Prime Minister. With their usual pertinacity, the news agencies must already have discovered the truth. A B B C team of commentators had managed to get across to France. Well-known faces appeared. They had lost their usual smooth technical competence. Wild and distraught now, they were with the British army at Ypres.

We learnt that most of their number had been arrested by the army authorities but a film of what they had found there had been smuggled out of France, presumably with the aid of a light aircraft. To me, the First World War has always had the aspect of a nightmare viewed from the comforting light of the day. Here it was displayed in all its nightmare qualities with the urgency of the present about it. The camera spared us neither the mud, nor the shellfire, nor the wounded and the dead. There were interviews with the living, conjuring up visions of hell. Then quite suddenly it was all over. With mature perception, the B B C announced a complete closure of all its services for the night; for nothing in the way of a normal programme could possibly have followed what we had just seen.

The next day there was an outcry from the Press. *The Times* demanded that whatever was going on in France must be stopped, instantly, without delay. The cry was echoed on every hand. It was clear that action must be swift and immediately effective if the government was to survive even for a week. The irony of the change in outlook of the British people over fifty years escaped almost everyone.

For the next month little useful work was done by the population at large. Most people spent a large part of their time within range of a television set. Everybody in any way immediately involved in the crisis itself worked, however, with a furious intensity. The day after our conference at Chequers we were told to proceed on our voyages of exploration. So we were back at London airport, back with our Australian friend

330

and his plane. We took off early on the morning of 21 September, as the date was here in Britain. Our mission was to proceed east, to the battlefront between the German and Russian armies. It occurred to me that the Tsar was still in power in Russia, Lenin and the Bolsheviks had not yet appeared. This would have given great satisfaction to the Americans if they had been there to appreciate it. Of course there was still Hawaii. This was another ironical situation, for the fiftieth state had suddenly become the first.

I wondered whether the pilot would make a deliberate excursion into northern France. I was rather glad he did not. I needed no further convincing about what was going on there. We were soon across the North Sea and over the southern part of Denmark. Then we headed more or less due east. At our height we were quite immune from any primitive anti-aircraft fire. Our immediate objective was Berlin. Although we had no radio guidance, apart from the fixes which we got from stations back in Britain, we found the city without undue difficulty. There, thirty thousand feet below us, was the city of the Kaisers. War stricken now, its people ill-clad and hungry, dreading the approach of winter, the fourth winter of war. Twenty-five years earlier we should have been dropping bombs. Today we dropped some twenty tons of leaflets which had been printed in a high priority rush job the previous day. I was fascinated by the thought of what the people would think when they read:

BRITISH GOVERNMENT DEMANDS CESSATION OF WAR

There followed a precise statement of the numbers of the dead, wounded, and missing. They were given month by month, for the different battlefronts. To the authorities in Germany they would appear quite fantastically accurate, for they had been compiled from the Germans' own post-war records. The leaflets fluttering down through the air below us were likely to prove vastly more effective than a plane load of bombs could ever be. There would also be the fantasy generated by the sight from the ground of our plane, monstrous by the standards of 1917. The shattering effect of all these factors was clear to me.

Clouds gathered as we flew further east. We could see

331

nothing of what lay below. Our mission was to discover the state of things in Russia, if possible to report on the eastern battlefront. To do this it would be necessary to go down to lower altitudes to break through the cloudbank which now obscured our view. There seemed no particular reason to fear anti-aircraft fire.

We must have been somewhere near the Russian border when the pilot set us on a gentle glide. To begin with it was very much the same as it had been coming into London airport on our flight from Hawaii. There we had come down on to a sea of clouds, had gone quite quickly through it, and had at last come out with a clear view of the ground. It had been exactly what we expected and hoped it would be. Now as we came out through the clouds we saw a great flat plain stretching away in all directions, brown and desolate, without the slightest trace of vegetation. It was a wilderness of bare rock.

We flew on towards the east. An hour later we were somewhere over the position of Moscow. The clouds were clearing. To our astonishment what looked like a vast ocean lay ahead. Yet it was an ocean such as none of us had seen before. As we came clear of the clouds we were dazzled by an intense light from below, coming from the direction of the Sun. The ground was evidently a far better reflector than the waters of the oceans. Compared to the intense light towards the south, the north was dark, a dark purple. Once we had learnt to avoid the southern glare we were amazed by the profusion of colours the sunlight was bringing out in the material below us.

We came down low, to about five hundred feet on the altimeter. Still we could see nothing but a smooth plain. There were no familiar landmarks from which we could judge our height, it all looked the same from any height. There were no trees, houses, no rocks or boulders, nothing.

Still we flew on. Two hours later we were over what should have been the Ural mountains. The level plain was unbroken. There was neither hill nor valley. There was always the iridescent plain below us. We discussed the possibility of landing. There was no problem about finding a flat place, it was all flat. What we didn't know was whether the surface was firm or soft. If it were soft we should simply bog in. Take-off would be impossible even if the pilot managed the landing safely. To be marooned in this trackless waste was certain death. We were

332

well into Siberia by now, more than a thousand miles from the nearest inhabitation. We could never cross this great plain on foot. Nor was it easy to see how we could possibly be rescued if we got ourselves into trouble. If a landing was impossible for us, it would be impossible for any plane sent out to our help. Yet we all felt something had to be done. Somehow we had to find out what this thing below us was. We could go back to base, of course, and make plans for tomorrow, or for the following week, but it was hard to see how this would get us any further.

One thing was favourable, there was almost no wind. This meant we could go down in a smooth gentle glide if we wanted to. Our Australian pilot was not to be put off. 'I'm going to have a crack at the bastard,' he said. 'We'll go down until our wheels touch, then I'll bring her up again. We ought to be able to tell from the hydraulic shock on the wheels whether we're dealing with soft or hard ground.'

Now we were down to a thousand feet, then quickly down to five hundred. The last seconds seemed interminably long. The jolt was much harder than I expected, really because the pilot didn't quite know where the surface was. As we came up again it needed no examination of the hydraulic system to know that we had hit hard ground.

Our line was to the north so as to avoid the glare of the Sun. After stabilizing the aircraft and checking the instruments we came down again. This time we made a normal landing. There would be nobody here to wheel a flight of steps out to the plane. We would have to hang a ladder of some sort. The crew got out a lightweight metal job. I was glad of this, because the rigidity of the metal would make the climb back into the plane reasonably easy. We opened the front hatch and let out the ladder. A couple of minutes later I was swinging down it.

I stepped gingerly on to the ground, then away from the ladder, and down on to my hands and knees. I ran a hand over the surface. It was completely smooth. I tried to dig into it with a fingernail, but it was quite resistant. The colours were more vivid down here. By turning round in a circle from the direction of the Sun in the south to the anti-sun in the north, and then back again to the south, it was possible to go through a whole cycle of changes. It was a vivid yellow towards the Sun, then green as one swivelled round towards the west, then

333

a pale blue in the north-west, purple in the north, and back through the same colours in a reverse order as one turned through east to the south again. It was the same wherever one stood.

I walked away from the plane to a distance of about three hundred yards. The difference between looking towards the plane and looking away from it was quite fantastic. Looking away from it one had no impression of scale whatsoever. It was impossible to know whether you were looking ten yards, a hundred yards, or even a hundred miles. The effect was bewildering and distinctly frightening. It was far more weird than the kind of white-out you sometimes get on a snowfield in the mountains. Yet as soon as you turned round, there was the plane – the whole scene jumped instantly into scale.

John came up to me.

'What do you make of it?' I asked.

'It's a kind of glass. We're on a huge glass plain stretching for thousands of miles.'

'But how, how the hell did it happen?'

'Heat. Heat from outside. The surface has been melted and fused. It's a kind of glass, rather like a tektite. except it's much more homogeneous, and far less brittle.'

'You said heat from the outside. What could cause that?'

'It's a bit like the glass you get after the explosion of a nuclear weapon. But there doesn't seem to be any radio-activity, from the Geiger counters in the plane.'

This explained the equipment I had seen John fiddling with during the flight.

'How far do you think it goes?'

'God knows. Perhaps all the way to China.'

'That's going to take out a big slice of the land area.'

'You know it's very strange. . .'

John stopped, as he always did, when he was in the middle of some important statement. Now he went on, 'How smooth it all is. You'd expect the surface to be scratched, by blown sand or bits of grit. It should have a short of sand-blasted, matt finish.'

'You think that's important?'

'Well, it must mean there's never been any bits of sand or grit, there's no other explanation. The point I think is that

334

everything's been melted, every damn last bit of surface rock. Nothing was left over.'

'If we follow up your idea about different parts of the Earth belonging to different ages, do you think this could refer to a time after a disastrous nuclear war?'

'It could, I suppose. If it were a few centuries or more afterwards, I suppose the radioactivity would mostly have died down. We'd better dig up a chunk of the stuff and take it back with us for analysis. That should tell us if there's any long-lived artificial radioactivity in it. Probably it isn't much good speculating until we know the facts.'

When we attempted to quarry the material we found the ground quite extraordinarily hard. We laughed at our fears about making a landing. The whole plain, millions of square miles of it, was just one ideal, perfect airstrip.

It began to grow chilly as the Sun fell lower in the west. We decided to eat a meal before taking off. After a short argument it was decided to have it out of doors. The food was handed down the ladder by the crew. Soon we were munching sandwiches and drinking hot coffee. We took a last walk around the plane. A quarter of an hour later we were back in the air. Turned towards the Sun we were on our homeward journey.

We managed just about to hold our own with the rotation of the Earth, so the Sun maintained its position pretty well constant in the sky as we flew westward. Scattered clouds began to appear, then there was a thicker cover below us. An hour and a half later we were back over eastern Germany. I wondered what furious interchange of messages was going on down there, what diplomatic activity.

It was about six o'clock when we landed at London airport. We were almost smothered by reporters and cameramen. A posse of police managed to make a way for us. It occurred to me that not one of the newshounds around us could have suspected, eerie and odd as this new world might seem to them, that we had come back from something still stranger and more remote.

We discovered there was no possibility of getting the plane serviced soon enough for us to be able to make another exploratory voyage the following day. So I returned for the night to my own apartments in London. I found Alex Hamilton glued to the television set. He asked me what I knew about the situation. I told him a little, not too much. Then I asked him for his opinion. He said it was very interesting that, with America out of the way and with Europe back in 1917, we were way ahead of Webern and Schoenberg. All we had to do was to murder all the musicians in Britain, to destroy all the libraries, and we would be made. I said I thought he was completely on the wrong lines. These new events called for an epic style, not for abstractionalism. At this he fell into one of his laughing fits. 'So you're thinking of reviving the Cologne piece.'

I said I was thinking of much more than that, but along the same lines. In fact I was bursting with ideas and would be glad of the following day to jot a few things down.

I made dinner while Alex went on watching TV. Afterwards we both watched it. The B B C seemed to have moved into France *en bloc*. They reported that the Prime Minister had seen the French Prime Minister, Monsieur Briand. According to the reports the French were proving difficult. They were insisting that honour be satisfied. Then we learnt the Germans were sending their Foreign Minister to London, a man of the name of Kuhlmann. The British commanders in the field had been replaced by modern officers who were preparing a general retreat from the trenches.

At this stage I must put my own experiences aside in order to relate at secondhand how it came about that the war situation in France simply collapsed like a pack of cards. First the men themselves, the ordinary fighting soldiers. In the last months of 1917 they were in a curious psychological state of mind. They had come to see the trenches as the real world, they had come to regard the situation back home as an unreal dream. It was as though they had walked out of the ordinary world into hell and now hell was the place which really counted. If they thought at all of the people back home, then apart from their families it was with a dull sullen hatred. This was true as much on the one side as the other. So when instructions came to cease from the horrible slaughter the men had not the slightest compunction about obeying. It was what they wanted anyway. It had been the *outside* that had been impelling them. Suddenly it seemed as if a miracle had happened somehow on the outside, which was the way it had to be. What they had gone through could only be made good by a miracle. They had paid enough in agony for any miracle. If there was little element of rationality in this point of view it was backed by intense emotion. To the men it was a heaven-sent deliverance. The psychological effect of discovering a hiatus of fifty years seemed more or less in tune with the horrors of the battlefield itself.

On the German side there was little will to continue the fight. Kuhlmann had in any case been on the point of proposing peace terms himself, similar to those which the British government now suggested. And the German High Command was shaken to its roots by the situation in the east and south. Nothing at that stage was known in Germany of the existence of the huge Plain of Glass, but all communication with the East had mysteriously ceased. The railway tracks to the east continued normally to Warsaw and somewhat beyond that. Every town, every village, down to the smallest hamlet, seemed to be entirely normal up to a certain point. Then it all simply vanished. The railway tracks ceased. The vegetation ceased. Not a single person could be found. It was just a complete desert. Those who knew these facts, and there were not many at this stage, had the bottom knocked out of their self-confidence. Hindenburg and Ludendorff knew of course, as did most of the High Command. It could only mean that what was being said in the west, in Britain, was true. Added to the already bad state of the war, to the privations in Germany, it was decisive. It was agreed that Hindenburg should travel to London for the proposed conference.

A cease fire was already in effect by the time the conference was held. The biggest card in the hand of the British government was of course the military weapons of 1966. The immediate problem was to bring the strength of those weapons over to the German mind. An actual physical demonstration was to be avoided if at all possible. But in the game of political manoeuvre it is known, at least in the world of 1966 it was known, that even the strongest card will have no effect unless you take steps to acquaint your opponents of its existence. There is little point in keeping a card secret and then playing it as a sudden surprise. Almost exactly the reverse. Playing a strong card always alters a situation so it is never the same at the end as it was at the beginning.

The problem was solved in a simple fashion. It was solved by using one of the most remarkable feats of 1966, but one quite unmilitary in character. It was done simply with a high fidelity gramophone. Delegates from the continent were ushered through a room in which an old-fashioned tinny machine, the sort you wind up, with a little horn, was playing. It wheezed out its feeble sounds as the delegates assembled in the conference room. The delegates were at first surprised at this apparent eccentricity. Then they were shattered by a sudden switch to full volume on the 1966 equipment.

All that needed to be done was to draw a simple analogy. The Prime Minister just pointed out that the weapons of his own day, of 1966, bore the same relation to the weapons being used in France, as did this new powerful gramophone to the little whining horn of 1917. He asked the German staff officers to compare their own weapons with those of the year 1860. Then perhaps they would understand how things stood. He wasn't telling them this in order to claim a victory. He wasn't interested in a victory as they would understand it. The important thing was to get down to a discussion of acceptable peace terms. All that was needed was a rational, reasonable approach to the problem. It was rather like a headmaster scolding a group of naughty boys.

Two days after our first flight of exploration we made a second one. Our aim was to discover the state of affairs in the Mediterranean, the Near East, and the Middle East. Our plan was to fly out over the Balkans, then over Turkey, Armenia, into Persia, and back via Palestine, Greece, and Italy. We wanted to find out how far to the south the great Plain of Glass extended. It was the same crew and personnel as before.

As we climbed aboard the plane I was in a divided state of mind. I had a host of musical ideas hammering away in my brain, but I was dead set to make the trip for I was utterly fascinated by the strange new geography of the Earth. Also I was baffled and intrigued by the psychological problems that were going to occur when the men from 1917 came home to the world of 1966. How were the two worlds to collaborate with each other? What would happen when a man, perhaps of thirty, back from the trenches, met his own son in the year 1966, his son at the age of sixty? And how of the strangest cases of all, those in which a man appeared twice, both young and old? Questions such as these seemed so weird and singular

338

that I would have been astonished to learn as I walked up the steps into the aircraft that I was on the verge of a trip which would take me still farther away from the sane, stable world of a month ago. I still had no conception of how deep the waters were to run.

9 Andante con Moto

We flew out across the battlefields. From our height, about
twenty-five thousand feet, the devastation had a pitiful aspect
about it. After our flight across America, and our recent flight
in the East, the scale here seemed very tiny. It was tragic to
think so small a fragment of the Earth had cost so many lives.

Within an hour we were over central Germany, then over
Austria–Hungary, as I supposed it must now be called. The
sharpness of the transition in the Balkans was obscured by the
mountainous country. By the time we emerged into the flat
lands of Rumania all was changed. Gone were patterns of
organized cultivation. Plainly the line of demarcation between
1917 and something quite different occurred somewhere in the
Transylvanian Alps.

We came down low. There was no absence of vegetation
here. It grew in abundance. It was all utterly out of control,
without organization. It looked as though man had never set
his hand on the forests and grasslands which lay below us.

We flew over the Black Sea to the Turkish coast. Not a single
ship or craft of any kind did we see. It was the same story in
Turkey, wild vegetation without any sign of human activity or
interference.

By now I was greatly impressed by how vast the Earth really
was compared to the limited regions of which I had any knowledge myself. At first the changes in these regions had seemed
of enormous significance. Yet Europe had shifted by only fifty
years, America by only a couple of hundred years or so. Over
most of the Earth the times might well be utterly different.

We flew on over Armenia to the Caspian. Then on the far
side of the Caspian we saw one of our objectives, the shining
Plain of Glass. Evidently we were again near some line of
demarcation. We found the actual line running just south of
what used to be the Aral Sea. Of that sea there was not the
slightest trace. We turned south in the direction of Tashkent

and Samarkand. The glass gave way to sand quite suddenly as if the fusing agent had extended to a particular point and then no further. Here there was straightforward desert, sand.

We must have been somewhere near latitude 40° when we picked up the first traces of humanity. There was not much of it, only an occasional very tiny village. Yet we were enormously encouraged by this modest discovery. We found nothing at all in the place we took to be the site of Tashkent. So we turned west again with the intention of exploring Baghdad and the Tigris–Euphrates valleys. We found more scattered evidence of human habitations, all on a very tiny scale. Even before we reached Baghdad I think we realized we were not looking down on the world of 1917.

On the site of Baghdad – there could be no doubt about the site from the contours of the river below us – there was only a small collection of hovels. Again we found only minute villages on the banks of the great rivers. This was not a part of the world I had been in, or over, before. So I had no real standard of comparison. But there seemed more water than I would have expected. Our pilot was in no doubt of it himself:

'A bloody great swamp down there, almost like the mouth of the Ganges. Completely changed. Pity we don't have a flying boat.'

We flew quite low on two or three occasions but could see no people. Perhaps this was not surprising for anybody down there must surely have thrown themselves into hiding at the roar of the plane. Our failure to find anything of interest as we travelled back to the west depressed us more and more. Nothing was to be seen in Mesopotamia of the armies of 1917. We flew on towards Palestine. Our intention was to locate the city of Jerusalem. This we could easily do once we found the Dead Sea, simply by flying on a westerly course from the northern end of the Sea.

We missed the Dead Sea on our first run. Since we were operating on our compasses we could always expect to be a hundred miles off course due to the wind. We did indeed come over a large expanse of water but it was clear we had reached the Mediterranean. So we turned south along the coast of Palestine in the direction of Egypt. We kept on until the coastline turned due west. This we knew must be the neighbourhood of Gaza. From there we found the Dead Sea quite easily. We carried out our plan of flying west from the northern tip. In five minutes or so we were over what should have been Jerusalem. There seemed to be signs of habitation but once again it was just a few hovels. There was no sign of the city of David, captured around the year 1050 B.C. It was plain the Hebrews had not, and now never would, reach the lands below us. Into this new world Christ would not be born.

We headed out over the Mediterranean. Very soon we were over the wine-dark seas of Greece. My reveries were sharply interrupted by a sudden grip on the arm:

'My god, look down there.'

The sea was breaking around a headland twenty thousand feet below us. Standing proudly on the headland was a temple. At once we were all animated. We flew round in circles coming lower and lower.

'Look, it's complete, it's not a ruin.'

'Where do you reckon we are?' I asked the pilot.

'I think we're just south of Athens.'

John had been looking at the chart. 'It fits the Attic peninsular. There's this island here off the east coast. Its shape fits that long one down there, doesn't it?'

There wasn't any doubt about it. We flew lower and lower. Now we could just make out people below us. They were running to the temple. I realized it was the temple of Sounion.

We said nothing as we turned up the coast to the north-west. It took only a few minutes before we were over Athens. Standing complete on the Acropolis was the Parthenon. Close by was an amphitheatre full of people. The city was not very large but at least it was a city. Whatever the time was down there it obviously had little to do with the twentieth century. The time had to be somewhere between the date of construction of the Parthenon, which I remembered to be about 450 B.C., and the date at which the temple at Sounion fell into ruin, which it must have done in the first centuries A.D. There seemed little doubt that we were looking down on the Greece of classical times.

We would have liked to have flown around for a long time, to have come as low as we dared, but we all realized it would be better not to do so. The people down there would see the great bird in the skies as a visitation from the gods. There would be panic and a wailing and gnashing of teeth. The sooner we were away the better. So regretfully we headed west towards Corinth. Naturally there was no canal cutting through the narrow neck of land which separates the Peloponnese from the land to the north. We saw a multitude of small boats as we flew along the Gulf, propelled it seemed by human muscle power, by oarsmen.

A further surprise was in store for us. Very naturally we were heading for Rome. We were doing so in the full expectation of it being classical times everywhere throughout the Mediterranean. The situation in Rome would allow us to date the epoch more closely. We were due for a sharp disappointment for over the Italian mainland there was nothing but vegetation. We flew on and on and it was the same everywhere. No city of Rome at all. No towns, villages, or hamlets Only as we came north of the Alps did the wild country change. Quite abruptly we were in a modern society with its towns and streets and its factories. It was probably 1917 down there but we all felt we had suddenly come back to our own times. It was the same all the way from Switzerland across France. Then we were over the English Channel. It was hard to believe as we flew over the neat fields of Kent that the other regions of the Earth were so grotesquely changed.

To say it felt like waking from a dream is an admitted cliché yet there was a dreamlike quality about it all. Even now, I thought as we moved in to land, we have seen only a fraction of the Earth. We don't really know the Glass Plain extends right through China. We had no idea of the situation in Africa, or in South America, or anywhere in the southern hemisphere for that matter.

After the sandy deserts of the Middle and Near East, after the missing city of Jerusalem, Greece had seemed real enough. Now I was back in London it all seemed wildly ridiculous. Could one seriously credit that out there it might still be the third, fourth, or fifth century B.C.? Yet the fifth century B.C. had been just as real and sharp as 1966.

I had dinner the following night with John. We discussed at length our next moves. It was clear the flights of discovery had to go on without hindrance or delay. It was imperative to get a general idea of the new layout of the whole Earth. One of us at least must continue on those trips. The problem was to decide whether we should both go or whether we should split up, one to continue the general survey, the other to investigate details, perhaps details of the situation in Greece. This would have to be done with the greatest care. The Greeks would not be alarmed by the arrival of strangers, provided they came in a fashion that seemed normal, by boat from the sea. But not in a modern boat with thumping engines. John told me preparations were already being made along these lines. The government had asked the navy to send in an expedition. Did I want to be included in the party? If I did it would be necessary to drop my name in the right quarter, and without delay. I said I would sleep on it. We agreed to meet again at lunch on the morrow.

The decision was an awkward one pretty well evenly balanced. I was completely fascinated at the prospect of seeing classical Greece at first hand. This would be the real thing not a cruise organized two thousand years after the event. Yet I had the feeling I would be pushing myself out of the main stream of events. The trip must surely be a leisurely one taking weeks if not months. I would lose contact with John. I would hence lose my entrée to the high-stepping circles in which I had moved of late. This was entirely a matter of unbridled curiosity not at all of snobbery. I wanted to know what was going on. Quite clearly the intricate dealings between Britain and Europe would be utterly intriguing to observe at close quarters.

Ironically these considerations were grossly wide of the mark for the mainstream of events was not at all where I supposed it to be. As it came about my decision made no difference to my arriving at the true mainstream, but in the ultimate outcome it did make a critical difference, that of my arriving independently not by John's much more direct route. No thoughts of this kind were in my mind of course when at last I came down on the side of the Grecian expedition. It was music which swayed the balance. For one thing, here was the chance to settle all the controversy and arguments about ancient music. For another, I was more and more feeling the need of leisure to give expression to my own creative impulses. The flights, the discussions, marvellously intriguing in themselves, were consuming the whole of my time and energies. A reduction of tempo was needed.

When I told John of my decision he was a little doubtful:

'Things have changed a bit in the last twenty-four hours, I'm afraid. The government is getting itself bogged down more and more with the European situations. They're really not in a position to give much priority to the Greek business. It was agreed yesterday to keep things pretty well on ice for the time being.'

'You mean the expedition is off?'

'Not entirely but it's only going to be a small show.'

I have an obstinate streak in me. When I'm thinking about any issue I like to hear the opinions of other people. I like to collect as much information as possible. But once I've made a decision I like to stick to it. Once I've made up my mind I hate to be 'advised'. I passed off John's entirely good-tempered warning. I'd made my decision. I told him so and without further ado he regarded the matter as closed.

'They've put the whole thing under an old naval boy, Admiral Cochrane. You'll be hearing from him pretty soon.'

Throughout lunch I could see John was bubbling over with something or other. Until my problem was out of the way he wouldn't say what it was. Then he chuckled and let it all out:

'Remember we were talking the other day about what would happen when a man in 1966 came face to face with himself in 1917? Well, it's happened, in a way.'

'How d'you mean, in a way?'

'Not a direct confrontation, as of yet.'

'Go on.'

'A most exalted member of the government. They've managed to hush it up so far, but it's bound to come out.'

'Why shouldn't it come out?'

'They're still keeping the identity of the exalted member secret but I don't think I would need more than one guess.'

'I wish I could guess what it is you're driving at.'

'We were thinking in terms of a man from the trenches coming back and meeting himself. Remember?'

'For heaven's sake, out with it!'

'It's not the man that's come back from France, it's the mother.'

'I'm getting in deeper, into a bog.'

'The mother was in the VAD. She's come back. So the son has met his mother, aged twenty, thirty years or so younger than he is.'

'Very touching I would imagine.'

'You're still not with it, I'm afraid. The point is the mother was, more properly *is*, of a kindly disposition. She took pity on a young officer. Natural enough in the circumstances, considering what's been going on in France. In a curious way, death always tends to breed life.'

The preposterous implication hit me. 'You mean the *alter ego* is still in the womb!'

'Right. You could hardly imagine a confrontation more curious than that, could you? I thought I'd covered most of the possibilities but this one got completely past me.'

On this ludicrous note John and I parted, the one of us as it turned out to follow the high road, the other the low road. Not to Scotland, to somewhere very different.

10 Entr'acte

While the events of this narrative were still happening it was difficult to separate the trivial from the important. It was also difficult to perceive any general structure underlying the whole affair. Yet looking backward it is easy to see that the structure was rather like the two acts of a play with each act divided into two scenes. The experiences in Scotland, California, and Hawaii constituted Act 1, Scene I, the juxtaposition of the Britain of 1966 with the Europe of 1917 constituted Act 1, Scene 2.

The second act remains for me to describe. My point here is that the two acts were connected by occurrences whose very ordinariness quite concealed the inexorable transition which took place from the still more or less normal world of Act 1 to the utterly new and strange world of Act 2.

Outwardly nothing more was involved than the transport by sea of a small party from Britain to Greece. In the spring of 1966 it had been easy to breakfast in London, to lunch in Athens, the flight by air took a mere two hours. By 28 September, the day we left Portsmouth Harbour, there were no flights. The number of planes now existing in the whole world was quite few. There were no airports in Greece any more. There were no rail tracks, no roads even, across the Alps. Every available ship had been diverted to the European crossings. There was no simple way of reaching Greece any more, and those ways which apparently were open, like our sea route, became closed only a few days later. We crossed a barrier on 30 September as we steamed south off the coast of Portugal. The following day, 1 October, would have been too late.

The day after my last talk with John Sinclair I had a call from Admiral Cochrane. I learned the party was to be under the 'command' of a Captain Morgan Evans, a one-time classical scholar of Balliol. An anthropologist, also with a

347

knowledge of ancient Greek and also from Oxford, had been chosen. I believed I had heard of Anna Feldman, a formidable battle-axe as I recalled. Two other members from an intelligence unit remained to be assigned to the expedition. The general idea was to take a naval vessel to a point south of Greece and just west of Crete. A small boat would then be launched and would continue to the Greek mainland. The boat would be equipped both with sail and with auxiliary engines. Following a discussion of such details the Admiral suggested the whole party might meet for dinner that night, would I be available?

Outwardly there was nothing about Anna Feldman to suggest the tempestuous virago, inwardly it might be another matter. To the eye she seemed a pleasant-looking woman in the middle thirties. I took immediately to Morgan Evans. I judged him to be about fifty. I also judged him to have a real Welsh temperament underlying the reserve of the naval officer. Of the chaps from intelligence there was still no sign – I presumed they were lying doggo until the last possible moment.

Dinner was over before nine o'clock. It seemed a bit early to break up so I suggested we might all proceed to my apartments after making the usual apologies for untidiness and disarray. We flagged a taxi and drove through the nearly empty streets.

I had been chosen for the expedition because of my presence on the original discovery flight. Only when the Admiral noticed sheets of manuscript scattered over my piano did he realize I was a musician. The old boy turned out to have a regular passion for Schubert. I started with the *Rosamunde* ballet music, then the Opus 90 impromptus. Whenever I play any composer's works I always become increasingly enthusiastic as I go on. More and more Schubert poured forth, the Schubert of the popular image, with wonderful tunes and rustling accompaniments. Then I remembered the other Schubert, the Schubert of fire and grandeur, a Schubert almost unknown to the world at large. I hunted quickly among stacks of music. At last I found what I wanted, the three posthumous sonatas. I started on the F sharp Minor.

What can one say of the Andantino in this sonata? Why call it Andantino, why refer to a shattering achievement as if it were a child's piece? How the devil did the man do it? How did the composer of *Rosamunde* suddenly become the composer of the F sharp Minor? How did extreme subtlety suddenly become combined with a consuming flame of passion and tragedy?

I continued to ponder these questions in the weeks and months ahead. I came at last to understand far more of what I now believe to be the essence of music, more than I ever gleaned from my teachers or from my own endeavours as a pianist and as a composer. Great music has nothing really to do with technique or even with an honest determination. Technique, skill, experience, determination, all these are necessary factors, but they are only peripheral. For every musician who has achieved anything truly great there must have been hundreds with adequate technique and keen determination. The missing component was the inner well-spring of emotion. Unless the inner fires burn with a fierce intensity the rest serves only as a gloss, like an automobile standing there with its paintwork and chrome all polished and shining but without any engine to drive it.

I have always had barely hidden doubts about much of contemporary music. I understand abstract music, I know what composers are trying to do: I have myself written quite a lot of abstract music but always I have had a sense of unease. Now I see why. Abstract music represents an attempt by very highly skilled people to eliminate from music the essential component which they themselves lack, the emotional fires. Abstract music is an attempt to make technique sufficient, an indefensible position I think. For why on this basis should one not be a mathematician? Music is the wrong profession for the purely abstract.

The difficulty of course is that you can't conjure emotion, sexual emotion perhaps, but not the deeper emotions. Schubert wrote those posthumous sonatas because he was impelled to do so. But not by thoughts of box office or of the plaudits of the world. There must indeed have seemed every likelihood that his manuscripts would even be thrown away, that every note would be lost to oblivion. Yet this was of no consequence, for Schubert wrote in his last year, with the figure of Death standing clearly over him. These sonatas were his dialogues with Death. They were his inquiry, a musician's inquiry, into the meaning of life and death. The world, in the sense of 'success' or of 'recognition', had no part in them.

349

Perhaps here we have a clue to why the Andantino was so named. Perhaps it did seem like a child's piece when taken in such a grim dialogue. I played the Andantino with very little pedal. At the end the Admiral was so affected that for a moment I thought he had been overcome by a heart attack – in a sense he had, but of a favourable kind.

The evening with Schubert had two consequences. For one, everybody wanted a small piano to be included in the expedition's equipment. Stowing a piano aboard a ten-ton yacht would create problems but the Admiral was keenly determined on their solution.

Two days went by in which we found ourselves hanging around still waiting for the chaps from intelligence. Cochrane at last told me he was having 'difficulties'. Intelligence was more than fully occupied in Europe. It was now felt impossible to release anybody for our 'show'. This brought home very sharply the extent to which I had allowed myself to be shunted on to a side-track, very much confirming John's warning. Yet the obstinate streak in me was still dominant. I had no thought of withdrawing. I asked the Admiral if he would come along himself. Regretfully, the answer was the same, European commitments. So rather as an afterthought I asked if there would be any objection to a friend of mine, another musician, being included. This was how it came about that Alex Hamilton was aboard when at last we steamed out of Portsmouth Harbour. The second outcome of the Schubert evening.

Our ship was not very prepossessing, it was a workaday ship. It had to be because of the equipment needed to launch our boat. By the evening of 30 September we were off the coast of Portugal. The days slipped placidly away. Beyond Gibraltar now, we steamed steadily east towards the isles of Greece. We would sit on deck until far into the night. The sea was calm. Surrounded by the darkened waters, stars filling the sky, anything seemed possible. Jason and the Argonaut might have glided by.

During the next days we familiarized ourselves with the gear on the yacht. Launching was a somewhat hectic process. We anchored in as shallow water as the captain dared. Then the men built a good-sized slipway. I had visions of the yacht getting out of control as it went down into the sea but everything passed off quite well. Held on powerful ropes, the boat

350

moved slowly foot by foot down to the water, not at all the swift dramatic launching I had expected. With its auxiliary engines started, the crew quickly had it away from the edge of our ship to a safe distance. The last step before we ourselves embarked was to check with our captain on the rendezvous we had arranged for two months hence. Greece might well be flooded by tourists and newsmen long before two months were up. Yet if this should not happen we intended to make our departure as inconspicuously as possible. We would simply reverse the procedure of our arrival. We had sufficient fuel to return to the neighbourhood of Crete where we would be met by our naval escort.

It was early morning when our yacht was launched. By nine o'clock we were on our way. We waved good-bye and within an hour we were alone in an open sea.

Really all we had to do was to run almost exactly due north. Inevitably this would bring us to the Attic peninsula. From there we could navigate simply by eye. Timing was something of a difficulty. Arriving at a modern port in the evening with modern electrical illumination was one thing. Arriving at an ancient port more or less in darkness was another. We decided it would be better not to rush things, to go slowly and to arrive the following morning. This we could easily do by changing to sail. There was a lot of sense in this because we needed practice with the sails. We were distinctly clumsy in our work. We kept the engines running at low revolutions until we got the hang of it.

By nightfall we had been going nine hours. I reckoned we must have come some fifty miles. We took down the sails and started the engines again. Our course now was somewhat to the east of north. Twelve more hours at five knots should put us just about right, providing the weather held. Luckily it did. I slept very well indeed considering the circumstances and the occasion. In a queer way it had all come to assume the aspect of an everyday experience. Saturated by the new and the strange, I was ready simply to accept whatever chanced to come along.

I woke to the smell of cooking bacon. Anna had a primus stove going. Soon I was washed and dressed and munching happily. Then it was time to stop the engines and to go back to sail. This time we managed with less incident and argument.

Except that Alex almost got himself knocked overboard by a swinging boom. In the harassment of the moment I reflected that he might keep away from his sudden exits, at least for the next few hours.

By ten o'clock we could see land all the way ahead of us. The island of Hydra lay on the left. This was as it should be. Throughout the morning we sailed on, coming ever nearer to the coast ahead.

Now occurred the first event to signal our passage to a new world and a new era. We came up on a boat such as I had never seen before. It was of about the same size as our own but undecked. Although it had a single large crude sail the main contribution to its speed came from oarsmen, about ten to each side of the boat. We started the engines as a precaution, for we had no wish to fall foul of a pirate ship. Then we went in to hailing distance. There was an interchange between the men in the boat and Morgan, of which I didn't understand a word. We accelerated away from them. When we were about a quarter of a mile ahead I asked, 'What did they say?'

'Only that they're on their way to Athens too. I said we were strangers which must have seemed pretty obvious. I said we'd go in ahead of them.'

'I suppose it wasn't the right occasion to find out what's going on?'

'I've been thinking about that, you know. We'll have to be extremely careful in our inquiries. Remember the Greeks date their years from 776 B.C., the year in which they started the Olympic Games. The best thing will be to ask them for an explanation of how they count the years.'

Then Morgan and Anna fell into an impassioned discussion about what the men in the boat had been saying. Classical scholars of the twentieth century were going to have their troubles, it seemed. Suddenly Alex gripped my arm and pointed ahead. We were getting quite close in now to what I took to be the port of Piraeus.

'Look, aren't those the Long Walls?'

We were all gazing at the seven or eight miles of unbroken wall, a wall that swept from near the sea away to the north-east. Athens we knew must lie at the northern end.

'The wall is complete,' whispered Anna. 'It must mean we're somewhere around the time of Pericles.'

352

Now came the worst of our problems, to tie up the boat without using the engines. The harbour lay ahead. We could see more open boats, charmingly and somewhat impracticably designed. We took the simple line of taking down sail, throwing out an anchor, and waiting for the people on shore to come to us. This worked out exactly as one might have expected. Soon there was an excited throng at the water edge obviously wondering at the strange lines of the new vessel which had appeared from the sea. Within a few moments half a dozen boats were rowed out to us. Morgan somehow managed to convey the idea that we wanted a tow to a safe spot. A dozen or more men took our rope. With much argument and laughter they hauled us about two hundred and fifty yards to a sheltered spot where there was a draught of about ten feet. Once again we put down anchor. Morgan and Alex rowed ashore in our dinghy. They made fast with a rope. Within a few minutes we were all safely landed. I realized now that our story of being strangers from the north, the land of giants in Greek lore, would seem entirely true. I was a full head taller than any of these people.

11 Vivace

It would be easy to become deeply involved in the very many detailed differences between modern society and the times in which we were now immersed, but an encyclopaedic description of the situation would only obscure the wood by the trees. It was the differences of principle which really counted.

Take the height of the people. I found it hard not to think of them all as children, simply because they were ten inches to a foot shorter than I was, a difference of only some fifteen per cent when you think about it. My reaction came because I was conditioned to think of significantly smaller people as children. Yet these people were just as clever, just as much driven by strong emotion, by the desire for power, love, intellectual achievement, as we ourselves were.

Everything about us was hand-made, every movement – at any rate on the land – was provided by muscle, either animal or human. While most things were meaner, evidence of better taste was to be seen in almost every article. Nothing in our modern society could exceed, or perhaps even equal, the finest women's dresses I was to see here. Yet these dresses demanded enormous effort, a far greater fraction of the productivity of the community, than was the case in modern society. This meant that fine clothing could only be worn by privileged persons and then only on special occasions. The everyday dress of the average citizen was rough and crude by our modern machine standards. It would have been impossible for it to be otherwise in a society of such limited resources.

The same was true of the buildings. On the whole people lived in houses little better than hovels. Only the wealthiest members of the community approached what we would call average middle-class comfort. Yet public buildings, the Parthenon, were of a magnificence our modern society could not equal at all. Indeed the situation was exactly reversed in the world of 1966. Private homes could be spacious and tasteful.

354

Public buildings, public offices, hospitals, the whole gamut of state enterprises, were nearly always painfully sordid.

It took a little time both to notice and to get used to these differences. Immediately after our landing we were concerned to ensure the safety of our boat and to see our few important possessions adequately locked away below deck. No doubt hundreds of pairs of inquisitive hands would work themselves over every exposed inch of the yacht. Yet it seemed doubtful they would actually break in through the closed hatchways. At any rate we decided to take the risk. There was no car or bus to carry us the eight miles to Athens. We simply walked along the great fortified wall of the city.

We were met three miles out by civic dignitaries. I could tell nothing of what was said, for in the beginning I had only the crudest knowledge of the language, picked up from Morgan and Anna on the few days of our voyage from Britain. Morgan took on the task of explaining our position. He spoke clearly and slowly. His inflexion provided the populace at large with a considerable source of amusement. Yet his commanding height, combined with a Welsh flair for erudition, had a disarming effect on his audience. Clearly we were well received.

All I could tell was that we were escorted under favourable circumstances into the city. We arrived at length at an open area where about a thousand people had quickly gathered at the news of our arrival. The place of our congregation was a discussion arena, of the name Agora, I learnt later. There seemed to be nothing for it but that Morgan should give an account of the manner of our journey from the north, through the Pillars of Hercules, the western Mediterranean, and thence to Athens. I was surprised at the length of his speech. Only later did I realize that time was a commodity not in short supply in this community. It would have been taken as an insult, when so many were gathered together, to have spoken tersely. Morgan knew this from his classical studies. Later he told me he addressed the throng something along the following lines:

At this time of the year the days in the north are short, the Sun lies low in the sky. Our fields and our houses are battered by the strong wind which blows everlastingly from the west. Rain clouds fill the sky with an ever-present threat of violent storms. So you may understand the thoughts of my countrymen turn often to the

355

lands of the south, for it is a belief among our people that southern lands are warmer, winds lighter, that in every way the natural elements are less destructive of human comfort. It was to discover whether this was so that we commenced our journey.

I give only this short example of Morgan's discursive style. It would be painful to attempt even a partial repetition of his speech, of the manner and construction of our vessel, of the nature of our rivers and harbours, of the terrors of the open sea. He described our farewell to our native land giving them a Greek version of John of Gaunt's speech from Richard II. Then the sights we had seen on our journey, the birds and fishes, the Rock of Gibraltar. The words flowed on and on until I wondered if he was intent on talking the whole day away. Not a sound came from the audience. Although, as I say, there was upward of a thousand of them, everyone seemed able to hear. The excellent acoustic properties of Greek theatres, always such a marvel to the modern world, came from the fact that the spoken word, discussion and argument, had absolute top priority. In days before the microphone and loud speaker, acoustics simply had to be good. Soon I was to realize that to be able to speak clearly, with persuasion and reason, was equivalent to power in this city.

Everybody listened in rapt attention. I expected a barrage of questions at the end. Yet there were no questions, only applause. Later I realized that questions were regarded as perfectly proper in any argument or disputation, but questions were not asked at the end of a free speech.

It was not until about two in the afternoon that we left the Agora. We were taken to the house of one of the wealthiest inhabitants. A meal had been prepared. For the first time I was aware of the existence of slaves. Not in any violent way but by the manner in which certain people were addressed; the voice tone is unmistakable in any language. The food was simple but of good quality. The mutton with which we were served was very far from being the everyday diet of the average Greek. The bread likewise was something important and precious. The bread was served by itself as a separate course. We were given a cup of liquid which turned out to be olive oil. Luckily I have a liking for olive oil and so did not suffer the torments which afflicted Alex. The meat was served with wine, which soon cut away the greasy taste of the oil. The oil in its turn prevented

356

any strong intoxication. The meal ended with fresh fruit of a quality I had never tasted before.

Through the meal Morgan and Anna had of necessity to take on themselves the whole interchange of information. I noticed there was no interest at all in what we did. I was never asked what I was, and I think the notion of my being a musician would have baffled them. Everybody here was what they wanted to be, what they were interested in. This was among the leisured classes, for it was taken for granted that we ourselves must be wealthy persons. Only the wealthy could contemplate a voyage such as we had made. Our hosts were concerned with the structure of the seas beyond the Pillars of Hercules, with what we believed about the nature of the world. How was our political life organized?

They didn't like the idea of elected representatives of the people. To them it was important that every free adult member of the community should be permitted to vote on every specific issue. It was impossible to explain that the very size of our population precluded their own democratic system. Morgan pointed out that our people were scattered in many cities, that it was impossible for them to be constantly travelling in order to discuss things together. It was essential for each city to appoint its own representatives and for the representatives of all the cities to confer together. I was surprised and rather alarmed by the serious, chilled manner in which this was received. The idea of a number of cities working together on terms of equality was apparently repugnant to them.

After the meal our party divided up. We were taken separately to the house of some wealthy person. My own host got little out of me, I am afraid, for in the beginning I could do no more than smile and nod. It is true my ears were already picking up the sounds of this new language. I was listening keenly, and watching the manner in which the sounds were made by the mouth, but it would be several months yet before I would be able to converse with any freedom. It came as a surprise to find how soon after sundown everybody retired for the night. I quickly became used to this aspect of life, however. Indeed, a reverse reaction set in, it became difficult to understand why the possession of artificial light persuades modern society to outphase the day. Within a week I came to think of the practice of staying up, out of bed, after the Sun has long

357

since set, and of then staying in bed after the Sun has long since risen, as entirely absurd.

The following day I managed to convey to my host that there were certain things on the ship I would like to fetch. Lots of people wanted to help. Nobody seemed to think anything of a sixteen-mile walk, eight miles there and eight miles back.

What I wanted was the piano. It was a devil of a problem to get it out of the yacht's cabin on to the shore. There were willing hands in plenty. We took it to pieces as far as we could. It was not particularly difficult to get the smaller pieces across, the legs, the keyboard, and so forth. The trouble came with the main iron frame. Yet it is surprising what a sufficient amount of muscle power will do. I was haunted by the fear of the whole thing ending up at the bottom of ten feet of clear water. But these people knew how to lift weights. Their major buildings were an astonishing tribute to their abilities in this respect. The essential thing was not to be in a hurry. So far as possible they never made a move which could not be reversed. The first thing was to distribute the weight over the maximum possible area. The trouble with an iron frame taken by itself is the sheer concentration of its weight. So what was done was to build a kind of wooden raft to which the frame was securely tied with many ropes. Then on to the raft long poles were securely lashed, so the whole thing could be moved more or less like a passenger in a sedan chair. The long poles allowed a dozen men or more to take part in the lifting operation. First they lifted it from the yacht into one of the big open boats. Then they manoeuvred the boat close enough to the shore for men wading to reach it. After this the rest was easy. They managed the full eight miles back to the city in less than three hours. I spent the afternoon and the following day carefully reassembling the parts with an apparent infinity of helpers.

Tuning was something I wasn't at all used to. I had taken the precaution of bringing a number of forks, which ensured the fundamentals of the job. Then I simply trusted to my ear. There isn't any difficulty in knowing when a piano is in tune or out of tune. The difficulty is to know exactly what to do if it's out of tune. You have to judge what move you must make next. My advantage over a professional tuner was time, I had plenty of it, I didn't have to rush on to the next job in order to earn my living. In fact I took the whole afternoon of the first day and the following day before I had it to my liking.

At this point I should mention that Alex plays the violin with great competence but like a solitary drinker he would usually only play to himself. Yet I noticed he had brought his fiddle with him. In fact I'd been quite envious of the ease with which he packed it and the ease with which he got it ashore. It struck me how much the shape and size and weight of musical instruments are related to their origin. Violins, easily carried, from itinerant players. Flutes and reed instruments, also easily carried, the possessions of wandering shepherds. Drums, not easily carried, the prerogative of courts, of pomp and circumstance. Double basses and pianofortes, not easily carried, the inventions of later ages when transport had become highly organized. I was acutely aware that, whereas Alex would be able to carry his violin from house to house, city to city, into the country if need be, I would be more or less stuck here in Athens with my piano.

Of course there were compensating advantages. Harmony and counterpoint could both be given full range, or nearly full range, on a piano. On the violin only simple harmonies could be achieved, and then only by superb playing. Counterpoint was hardly to be thought of on a single violin. This wasn't the end of it. I had the whole of musical literature, not merely piano music, but symphonies and quartets, available to me.

I began to play the second afternoon of our arrival. So many people gathered around that it was necessary to move out of doors, into a fairly extensive courtyard. My audience was obviously amazed at the intricacy of the whole thing. I realized, as it turned out correctly, that their ears were not tuned to complex sounds. So I kept to simple lines. It was natural for me to play a selection of operatic arias. I played just what came into my head. There was a considerable proportion of Mozart in it. Naturally I was curious as to how the music would be received by my audience. In a quite strange way, mainly with argument. At the end of a number there would be a crowding round the piano, there would be a lot of gesticulation, and there would be a great deal of talk. I was soon to realize that the two things taken most seriously here were war and speech. Both were far ahead of sex in the estimation of the people. In fact sex was like food, a regular necessity but not to be fussed about. Talk ranged over the whole gamut, from private groups of half a dozen people up to the great oratorical speeches to many thousands. An immense amount of time and care went into the big speeches, for as I have already remarked persuasion was equivalent here to power. You were not permitted to murder a neighbour whom you might detest, but if you could persuade your fellow citizens that your neighbour was a danger to the community then the city itself would turn on him, imprison him, exile him, deprive him of his rights and property, and in extreme cases might even execute him. The gift of the gab was a matter of no small importance. It extended even to music.

It wasn't long before two flutes and a lyre appeared. They were very simply but well made. A sturdy, bright-faced young fellow of eighteen or nineteen began to pipe away on one of the flutes. Soon he was joined by a girl at the lyre. She used a small piece of wood to pluck the strings. The music was in a simple 4/4 rhythm. It was highly modal in its melodic structure. That is to say the notes used depended on the pitch of the octave in which the melody happened to lie.

Let me add a word here on different systems of musical composition. They all depend on some kind of restriction. In the modern style, modern in the sense of the twentieth century, there is no restriction at all on the notes you can use. They all have equal weight. The restriction comes on the order in which the notes are to be played, the restrictions being determined in part by the order which the composer himself lays down at the beginning of his composition, and in part by certain standard rules. In tonal music, the music of the eighteenth and nineteenth centuries, the restriction comes on the notes to be used. Only seven out of the twelve notes in the octave have equal weight. The other five appear only occasionally as accidentals. The manner in which the restriction to seven notes is made is also subject to certain rules, your particular choice being called the key in which you elect to operate. Once you have restricted yourself by a choice of key you are free to arrange your seven notes in any order you please. You are free to use the same seven notes in any octave you may please. And at any time you may change your restriction, you may modulate into another key. The style of this Greek music was more akin to

360

the key system than to the modern serialization. It restricted the notes to be used to seven, but you had no freedom over which seven, you couldn't choose your key to suit yourself. The seven notes were decided by the pitch of your octave. I think the practice probably came from the manufacture of the instruments themselves. The instruments produced certain notes better than others, unlike the piano which produces all its notes equally. The general effect was rather plaintive to an ear grown accustomed to the key system.

The young man turned over his flute to someone else, took hold of one of the girls, and began to dance. The motions were simple, rather static, but graceful none the less. When they had finished I went back to the piano and played three or four waltzes. There was much laughter as several of the bolder spirits tried to find the right steps. I stopped the music to give them a short demonstration, first alone, then of the positions of the two partners, with my young friend's girl, then of the real speed of the dance with an imaginary partner. Back at the piano I played the dances at first quite slowly, then with increasing speed. The dancing was more or less a fiasco but everybody enjoyed it for all that.

This was the beginning of a reputation which I soon acquired for myself and of which I shall have more to say later on. It was made clear that I didn't have to go to bed by myself if I didn't want to, but I did want to. To me, it was still not much more than a month since the tragic affair in Los Angeles. The memory of those few whirlwind days was still sharp and clear. In what had started as a more or less casual liaison I had perhaps made the mistake of giving too much of myself. At any rate I was still numb from the sharp catastrophic end of a passionate situation. I saw it would be a good idea to spread the intelligence that I was suffering from a grievous bereavement. I resolved to ask Morgan to put this story around the following day.

Before dropping off to sleep I mused on one small item of information I had gleaned from the talk around me. The young flute player's name had been Xenophon. Was this the Xenophon who was later to rescue a whole Greek army from disaster in Mesopotamia? I had no means of knowing how common the name might be so there was no clear answer. I had also discovered the name of my host, Andocides. I had a feeling the name should mean something to me and I resolved to ask Morgan about it on the morrow.

As it turned out I had no need to seek out the others, they were waiting for me the following morning. Morgan knew now exactly where he was. He knew the year and the time of year. It was 425 B.C.

'Man, we're right in the middle of it.'

I was still sleepy and wondered vaguely what it was we were in the middle of.

'The war, the war between Athens and Sparta.'

'Then why are there so many men about?'

'Because winter is coming on. These things run more or less on a strict time-table. You know we ought to do something about it, to put an end to it.'

He was very excited, understandably so. To the classical scholar the fall of Athens in the Peloponnesian War must seem utterly tragic. Yet this was a different world now. It was inconceivable that a war between two tiny Greek cities, with a population of only a few hundred thousand, would be permitted to drag on year after year. The situation was tragic all right but not in the sense Morgan seemed to think. He had immersed himself so much in classical literature, he was thinking so much in the ancient Greek language, that he seemed to have forgotten the barbarians from the north who would soon be arriving here. Soon this delicate civilization around us would collapse like a house of cards. Financially the people would do all right of course. There were not very many of them, only a million or two, I suppose. With their great tourist attractions, the standard of living would rise sharply, but the civilization and culture would soon be lost. Above all the confidence would be lost. This was the problem, not the problem of Athens and Sparta.

An odd thought occurred to me, what was it Morgan had said? We must do something to stop it. Wasn't that exactly what the Prime Minister had said, about the situation in Europe? In many ways we had the same situation here. A disastrous war knocking the stuffing out of both sides. In one place the year was 1917, in the other 425 B.C., but the pattern was really the same.

Morgan had now drawn up a list of prominent Athenians, men whom sooner or later we could expect to find in the city.

362

Socrates, Euripides, and Aristophanes were the names which meant most to me. At the distance of the twentieth century these men seemed more or less contemporaries. From Morgan's list I realized their respective ages were forty-five, fifty-five and twenty. 'Socrates is out of town. With the army in the north.'

In the next few days the general picture of what was happening gradually came into focus. This was indeed a city at war. We had been deceived into thinking otherwise because the fighting during the last few months had gone almost uniformly in favour of Athens. Standing out above a number of minor victories, there had been a major success at Pylos, on the far side of the Peloponnesus. A Spartan peace offer had been refused, and the peace offer had been followed by the arrival in Athens of a couple of hundred Spartan prisoners. It was a pathetically minor affair compared to what had been happening in Europe, yet it accounted for the apparently carefree aspect of the city. Nobody had any doubt that the war with Sparta would soon be brought to a victorious conclusion, least of all the commanding officers. Yet we knew that if it were to follow its own course the war would last for another twenty years and would result in the defeat of Athens. But how was one to convince them of this?

Morgan, with the enthusiasm of a Welsh revivalist, made a shot at it. He made more progress than might have been supposed, partly because of his impressive height, partly because he knew from his historical studies more or less what the Spartan envoys had said when they had come to request peace earlier in the year. The coincidence between his arguments, the arguments of a complete foreigner, and the entirely reasonable point of view of the Spartans, made an impression. It accorded with one section of Athenian opinion. But it fell foul of the influential generals. After their recent success at Pylos, these men, Cleon and his friends, were riding the top of the wave. There was little Morgan could really do except make us thoroughly unpopular. Indeed our respective hosts began to find us something of an embarrassment. With some relief they seized on my suggestion that we acquire a house of our own. Everybody, friends and those not so friendly, made an effort to get us installed in congenial quarters. We were given half a dozen slaves and left to look after ourselves. So much for Morgan's preachings.

I didn't have much enthusiasm myself for this stop-the-war project. I was quite convinced that things would change drastically and catastrophically for the reasons I have already given. What I did have strong feelings about, however, were the slaves. I had no objection to hiring the middle-aged man and woman, the three girls, and the boy, as paid servants. So I conveyed to them that henceforward they were freed, although they could continue to work for a wage if they so pleased. All but the boy decided to stay.

This move increased our unpopularity, as I suppose it was bound to do, since it touched the whole Greek society at a sensitive point. The former owners took the point of view that we had spurned a generous gift. In answer to this there was nothing to be done but to pay for the slaves. I offered seven gold sovereigns for each of them. The money was taken with not very good grace.

There were some who were intellectually curious about our point of view, however. I remember in particular a man of the name of Protagoras. I gathered he was some kind of teacher, so perhaps he had a professional interest. Quite a crowd assembled when we started to argue. What none of them could understand, even the most reasonable ones, was how we got menial tasks performed in our country if we had no slaves. To the answer that we either did such tasks ourselves or paid some poorer but still free person to do them for us, they expressed frank disbelief. There was so much to be done they said, in the fields, the factories, and in the home. Surely we couldn't do it all ourselves? The argument was pressed home quite skilfully and at considerable length. The gist of their point of view was that if you didn't have slaves you'd have no leisure whatsoever. Plainly we were men of leisure. How else could I play the great lyre-in-the-box so skilfully?

There was really nothing for it except to explain that much of the manual work, which they found so necessary, was performed by machine in our society. This they couldn't understand, so I was pressed into giving descriptions and details. The bog got deeper and ever more sticky. As they took me more and more for a foolish liar I became angry. I asked them if it was possible to propel a boat without sail and without oars. Of course not, they insisted.

So it came about that we made a journey to our yacht still anchored in the harbour at Piraeus. We had been in the habit of going over there two or three times a week, to make sure everything was all right, and gradually to transfer various articles of which we might have need. Lately we had managed to make the journey without too much in the way of an attendant retinue. Now however there was a huge procession as we walked the eight miles of the wall to the harbour. Quite a number of the foremost citizens turned out. There was my former host, Andocides, Cleon, the people's leader, a sculptor of the name of Myron, and an old boy who turned out to be none other than Sophocles. Everybody apparently wanted to give the lie to these boastful strangers.

I said we could manage to take half a dozen of them. Cleon and half his retinue stepped forward, setting themselves immediately above the rest. I left Alex to sort out the job of who was going to go with us. Morgan and I went out to the yacht. We spent some time working at the engine, making sure there was adequate fuel in the tank. When the motor had spluttered a few times, and was clearly on the point of starting, I signalled to the party on shore to come aboard. Nothing ever seemed to put Alex out of humour. As if it was all a big joke he somehow managed to limit the number to the specified six. Somehow he kept the others back as the six climbed aboard, the politicians I noticed.

The engine sprang to life. We soon had the anchor up. Then we were out in the bay. Morgan took the wheel and immediately made the mistake of turning north, into the straits between the island of Salamis and the mainland. As a naval officer he obviously had a fancy to see these straits, where the great Persian fleet had been defeated less than fifty years earlier. The mistake was that we were headed towards the city of Megera, an enemy city, in some ways the cause of the war itself. To those on deck it must have seemed as if we were determined to hand them over to the enemy. Only by locking ourselves in the little cabin could they be prevented from taking over the boat. We put on speed to about ten knots, which astonished the natives. There were ships in the straits.

We went quite close to them and swished past with contemptuous ease. The whole trip around the island took I suppose
about five hours.

On the way back, when it was realized that we had no unpleasant intentions, the atmosphere thawed a good deal.
Everybody seemed in good spirits as we made our way back to
port. The crowd on shore had grown even larger. I expected
something in the way of a great cheer, such as might greet a
troopship coming into harbour. Instead there was a curious
silence. We prepared to return to shore. This was not to be,
however. The boat was invaded by determined men. They
wanted to see exactly how the trick was done. What was it we
had up our sleeves? Men swarmed everywhere. There was
nothing for it but to show them the engines. We started them
up again. We showed one group after another, in a seemingly
endless sequence, the rotating propeller shaft. I think they
realized how the boat came to be propelled through the water.
What they couldn't understand was what was going on inside
the engine.

I knew exactly what was going to happen. We should never
have control of our boat again. At any rate not until they had
taken it entirely to pieces. Perhaps when they couldn't put the
engine together again, or if they ran out of fuel, they would
call on us for help. Everybody was very pleasant and polite,
but now it was they who wanted us back to shore.

We had in the cabin a transistor radio receiver and transmitter. It was obvious we should take them with us, to enable
us still to contact our naval friends. Indeed we had agreed to
make radio contact, since it was always possible the weather
would turn out to be too bad for us to make our agreed
rendezvous. So we returned to Athens carrying the radio
equipment ourselves. Two days later we were told our boat had
been commandeered by the city. I was not surprised. With so
much speed its uses in the war would obviously be very great.
All along I had realized it would be unreasonable not to expect
something like this to happen. I blamed myself for not keeping
my big mouth shut. In a way I had been just as foolish as
Morgan.

The incident did improve our popularity however. I no
longer had the feeling we might be thrown into prison at any
moment. This had not been an idle fear. Only seven years

earlier the great Phidias, the designer of the Parthenon itself, had died in prison.

Now within the space of a fortnight two remarkable things happened. Messengers arrived from the north. There was great excitement in the city. We thought the long awaited penetration into Greece from the Balkans had occurred. We were wrong. It was the Delphic Oracle. The prophecy was that a continuation of the war would prove the ruination of Athens, a disaster to Sparta, and to the whole of Greece. This was the meaning, it was said, of the great roaring bird which had appeared in the sky at the time of the solstice.

Nobody in Athens had ever referred to the day when we had flown directly over the city. Many tens of thousands of persons must have seen our plane. Yet not a soul had said a word about it. To mention it was to court ill-luck apparently, to tempt providence, to give substance to the portent. Now the meaning was made known. The oracle's words had far more effect than I could have expected. The discussions that went on in the Agora, in the hall of Poikile, had every aspect of rationality about them. Yet not far beneath the surface there was a deep instinctive belief in the supernatural. The old beliefs were not very far away, just as the Middle Ages were not really very far away from twentieth-century Britain.

An important effect for us personally was that our standing was enormously improved. The very reason for our previous unpopularity, Morgan's uncompromising advocacy of peace, was now the word of the oracle. Why I wondered had the oracle spoken in this fashion? None of us could recall any mention of it in classical literature.

With our new-found popularity there was a lot of music making. Alex had suddenly lost his inhibitions about playing in front of people. I guessed it might be the girl with whom he was now living, a Corinthian of great beauty, named Lais. She was taller than most of the Greek girls, fair like many of them. This was something that had surprised me, how much fairer the general population was than I'd expected. It was of course the Dorian strain which had come in from the north a century or two earlier. Anyway Alex had got himself a succulent specimen, and good luck to him, I thought. At about that time he developed a passion for Hungarian gypsy music. It proved surprisingly popular with everybody. We used to bash away at the stuff. Somehow Alex got them all whirling around like dervishes.

I played my part adequately but without real gusto. I was now seriously worried by the fact that we still heard nothing at all from the outside. It scarcely seemed credible. And there was a second queer thing.

Soon after the episode of the yacht we tried out our radio receiver. Not a sound could we get on it. Convinced the electronics had gone wrong we switched on the transmitter. Whereupon we almost blew the receiver. One afternoon I set out on a long walk. About ten miles from Athens I turned on the transmitter which I had managed to bring with me without attracting notice. On my return to Athens I found Morgan had easily picked up my transmission. Of course it was one thing to pick up a transmission from only ten miles away and quite something else to receive signals from stations a thousand miles or more away. But the transmitters back home were vastly more powerful than our little piece of equipment. It could all be explicable in terms of a lowered sensitivity of the receiver. But it could be something quite different.

The others had not been through the strange experiences of August and September in quite the way I had. Probably for this reason I was more sensitive to the situation than they appeared to be. My fear was that another gross shift had taken place. It looked to me as though the juxtaposition of different worlds and different times might have come to an end. Those different worlds might have come together for a brief spell and then separated again. It could be that we had managed to transfer ourselves from the twentieth century to the fifth century B.C., and now there was no simple retreat. It could be our naval friends would never appear off the coast of Crete, not in this world anyway. Otherwise it seemed to me quite impossible to explain our continued isolation from the outside world.

These thoughts filled my mind. I was in a stormy, gloomy mood as the time for our visit drew to an end. As it turned out the weather itself was stormy, the seas rough, and there would have been no possibility of our putting out in the small yacht. We had heard nothing further about it so presumably it was still in the hands of the shipbuilders. I was hardly worried about this aspect of the matter. Our main reason for leaving by sea had been to avoid disturbing the people here too much. If they wanted to take an awkward line that was just too bad. Now we should just have to wait until the external world arrived here, if it ever did. If there was no external world now, then there was little point in our putting to sea.

More and more as the days passed an explosion boiled up inside me. I tried to get it all out of my system, in long fierce sessions at the piano. Our house was not large and these violent sessions soon became wearying to my companions. Increasingly I thought of moving somewhere by myself, to some place where I could play to myself, not always to an audience. Another thing, I was becoming fed up with always being odd-man out. There was Morgan and Anna who made a pair, Alex and his girl friend, and myself, alone. Somehow it didn't fit.

12 Largo Appassionato

The others greeted the suggestion that I might go off for a few weeks to get some composition done with an ill-disguised enthusiasm. The question was where to go. I wanted space. In summer when it would be possible to spend much of the day outdoors these small houses would be fine. Now in winter it was altogether too cramping. Yet where was I to get space? The city was obviously overcrowded, everywhere. We started to make inquiries. The solution came in a curious way.

My stormy sessions at the piano had not passed unnoticed. There was the madness of Dionysus in it. And the dances, the gipsy music, the gay music I somehow contrived to play for our numerous visitors, was also the music of Dionysus. I was told of a temple to the god some fifteen miles down the peninsula. It was said to be in a pleasant spot overlooking the sea. Why did I not go there if I wanted to be alone? I could take two slaves, or rather two servants, to see to my needs. To the Greeks it was a logical solution.

I visited the temple. Space there certainly was. I had no quarrel with the site, only with the winds that blew there. Yet there was plenty of wood, colossal quantities of it, within easy range. It would be easier to build magnificent fires here than it was in the city. All in all the solution seemed a possible one.

The transition from the city to the temple was made smoothly and easily. I was once again amazed by the ease with which the piano was transported. The middle-aged couple came with me. It was from them, during the coming months, that I gradually acquired reasonable proficiency in the language. Isolated down the coast there was nobody else to speak to. Not that I had any overriding desire to talk but the practical matters of everyday life had to be attended to. There were the fires to be built in the right places, tables where I could write, and so on.

For now a great fever of composition was on me. I had

always composed before out of a sense of duty, really because it was my job. I had made plans of the kind of music I would write and then more or less carried them out. This time I needed no plans. The sounds simply filled my head of their own accord. What I had to do was to order them and to write them down. Only later did I realize that this was the right way. When you feel compelled to write music you write good music. The compulsion came from the experiences of the previous months. The shock and tragedy of the beginning of the whole affair. The thoughts of men who emerged from the trenches into a clean and decent world again. The landing on the great Plain of Glass with its wonderful shimmering colours. Then this delicate but deadly civilization in which I was now living. The agony, the loneliness, and the grandeur were all there in my head, above all the mystery of it. The emotions were there. Gradually the sounds built themselves to give expression to the emotions.

I worked at an ever-increasing intensity. The Greek couple were quite convinced I was mad, and in a sense I was. Never had I been so entirely gripped by the task in hand. I would go to bed utterly exhausted in the evening. Strangely enough, I had little difficulty in falling asleep. Perhaps even more strangely I wakened early, feeling quite refreshed again. Time passed almost without my realizing it. A whole symphony grew until everything was there, orchestral sketch and all. Only the more or less mechanical details of the final copy remained. While the fever was on me there was no point at all in taking up time in a straightforward job. So I rushed on to other ideas, which were now forming. Two sonatas simply tumbled out, more properly sonata-fantasias. The urge to break the bounds of all the forms proved irresistible. The symphony had structure but it wasn't a structure I could put a name to.

Then I began the work that was to consume me for over two months. It was for orchestra and chorus. I fretted and fumed for a while. I had no literature. I wanted words to give expression to the kind of feeling I now had within me. I had thrashed around for several days before the obvious solution occurred to me, first to conceive the music and its moods, then to write appropriate words myself. It was the species of work all composers want to write, what in the old days would have taken the form of a Mass, set to the standard text. My lack of

371

belief in the text, the usual Credo for instance, would have made a mockery of a formal Mass.

By this new method I was entirely free to build the musical structure as I went along. I was not inhibited by the need to set meaningless words. It was the creation, the meaning, the purpose of the world that had significance. It was the tragedy of man, the tragedy that he can sense such problems but not solve them, which overwhelmed me. The last thing I wanted was easy solutions beginning with the words 'I believe'. It was the juxtaposition in all of us of the primitive with something better that troubled me.

Early on, my friends and the people of Athens came out to see me quite often. I was so ill-mannered at these interruptions that the visits became less and less frequent. By the time of the first spring flowers I had become almost a hermit. Even Alex hardly came any more. Only in retrospect did I realize this for at the time I was entirely preoccupied. Undoubtedly in the popular mind I was now well-placed, a mad priest in the temple of Dionysus. Gradually the work came to an end, the fires began to damp themselves down. I looked around me and realized where I was. I began to think again about the everyday world. There seemed no doubt now but that my wild prognostication was correct. The different ages of the Earth which had come momentarily together had somehow separated again. Otherwise there would have been evidence long ago of the vibrant, harsh civilization of Europe.

As the spring days lengthened I became more and more fretful. Once again I had the need of human company. I decided the time had come for a return to the city. One day I made the journey alone. After the quietness of the winter the noise of the city startled my ears. I came at last to my friends' house. For a moment I had the irrational fear that they too would be gone leaving me alone in a new existence. But there they were, heartily glad to see me apparently safe and well.

I was all agog to hear the news:

'Have you heard anything at all from our people?'

'Not a thing,' answered Morgan.

From his face I could see that at last he too was worried. 'What does it mean? Man, they must have been here before now. How is it that nobody comes?'

'We'd better face it I think. Somehow this world, this time,

372

has cut adrift again. I don't know how. I don't know how it happened before, how they ever came together. But we're adrift now, that's the only way it can be.'

Alex was the least perturbed of the three of them, he still had his girl friend apparently. Anna began to weep, almost silently. Morgan went over to comfort her as best he could. Then he came back to me:

'What's to be done? We've just got to decide on some course of action.'

'How about the boat? Have they said anything about it?'

'I gather they've loused it up. The engine I mean. Still we might put it in shape again, if we're lucky.'

'Maybe we should go into the prophecy business. We ought to do pretty well in that line.'

We chatted on for several hours. I decided I was moving back to the house. It would really have been more sensible to have spent the winter in the city, then to have gone out into the country now in the spring. But this would be to order one's life by rational argument. The period I had just come through was not the sort of thing one could legislate for. We began to discuss details. The best thing would be to move back in two or three weeks' time. There was still quite a bit of work to be done. It was more or less plain sailing now. But I would get through the scoring quicker by myself than in the middle of an uproar. With this settled I returned to the temple.

When I came to the reasonably straightforward parts of my work I became restless. I found it impossible to devote the same long hours, ten hours or more each day. I found it best to put in five or six hours in the morning, to take a long walk in the afternoon, and so early to bed. I came to move more and more about the peninsula. Not that I could yet go very far. I began looking forward to the prospect of longer trips. I decided that in April and May I would make a journey into the Pelopponesus, if circumstances permitted it.

One day I came on a large temple on the slopes of the mountain of Aegaleos. This was the hill from which Xerxes was said to have watched the defeat of his fleet at Salamis. The temple was to Apollo. It stood on a flat grassy knoll covered with a profusion of wild flowers set in a beautiful meadow. After winter in my rougher accommodation down by the sea it seemed just about perfect. The day was almost unaccountably soft up here. I remembered the strange oracle from Delphi. That too came from the temple of Apollo. From the god himself according to the beliefs of these people.

The immediate approaches to the temple were carefully kept. I walked up the steps out of the sun into the darkened interior. At the far end there was a door, or rather an opening, into an enclosed garden. Flowers were to be seen everywhere in the garden. I was looking generally around when I heard a quiet sound behind me. I turned quickly to find a girl looking down at me from the top of a short flight of steps. She was instantly different from any girl I had yet seen. The hair was of the usual light brown, but the eyes were grey. At first I thought she seemed tall because she had the advantage of the steps. Then I realized that indeed she was tall, of almost my own height.

'This is a beautiful day on which to meet a beautiful girl in such a garden as this.'

My Greek was still not very fluent, but I hoped it would be good enough.

'Not many come here. You are welcome.'

I found this difficult to believe, with such a girl as this. Yet possibly she was too tall to be attractive to the average Greek male.

'I fear I came without any knowledge that you would be here. So I brought nothing to sacrifice to the god, or even a small gift to please you.'

'I see from your face you are a stranger.'

'It would be a lucky man on whom you would look with favour.'

The girl threw back her head and laughed. Then she became serious and said, 'You forget where you are. We are not now in the temple of Dionysus.'

There was nothing unfavourable in this. By now I knew enough of Greek customs to realize what was meant, or at least I thought so. Two advances, two retreats, then a decision. Enough dalliance to satisfy the human sense of dignity, not so much as to be an undue waste of time. The enormous death rate from disease and war demanded a high birth rate. I felt I knew exactly where I stood. I took the girl's hand in mine, prepared to make a pretty speech, when to my surprise she said:

374

'What you would have must be worked for. I must remind you again what place this is.'

Of course she meant she was a priestess of Apollo. Yet I was unaware of anything inhibiting about such an occupation. Perhaps the time of the year was wrong.

'All worthwhile things must be earned. It will be my pleasure to do whatever you wish.'

'Are you not the strange man who for months past has sacrificed himself to Dionysus?'

I was a bit sensitive to this suggestion. Just because I had been forced to use the temple down by the shore, to avoid living in a rabbit hutch, was no reason why I should be thought insane. Yet I had some idea of what the girl meant. I had been puzzled in the beginning by the attitude of the Greeks to their gods. On the face of it religion did not seem to be taken very seriously. But in at least one important respect the gods were still thought of in terms of reality. The gods represented a quintessence of human emotions and abilities. Madness, wild actions, lack of restraint, moderated by genuine spontaneity, those were the qualities of Dionysus, the qualities I appeared to possess. In a way the judgement was fair enough. Here in the temple of Apollo the idea was of controlled form, aesthetics in general. This was the place where beauty did not need to be sensual.

'You practice your art without licence. *This* is the abode of music.'

Now I saw what she was driving at. Apollo of course was the god of song and music. By not making obeisances in the temple of the god I had in effect set myself up in opposition to him. I was guilty of sacrilege, at any rate in the eyes of his priestess. If I hoped to make any further progress with her it would plainly be necessary to carry out some act of appeasement. A further assessment of the situation persuaded me appeasement would be worthwhile provided it was not too serious. I was wondering just what to suggest when she said:

'You will remember what happened to the satyr Marsyas?'

I racked my brains as to who this satyr fellow might be. Clearly I was being compared to him, not flatteringly I suspected. Then it flashed through my mind that the fellow was supposed to have engaged Apollo in a musical contest, the one

375

on the lyre, the other on the flute. I had a notion he came to a sticky end.

'I would be ready to engage in any contest that seemed fitting.'

'You are haunted by a foolish pride.'

I could not help smiling for the thought of a contest between a primitive lyre and a modern piano seemed ludicrous.

'You cannot really mean such a contest is possible?' I asked in frank incredulity.

For answer the girl took me into the temple. She showed me a lyre measuring about a yard across. She played a melody on it. The inference was obvious. The girl, or some other person in the temple, was indeed willing to engage in a musical trial of strength.

'It will be necessary for me to fetch my own instrument.'

'That was expected. You will come two days before the next full moon. You may bring what you please and you may bring whom you please. We shall begin half-way through the last third of the day.'

We walked amicably out of the front entrance of the temple. We strolled through the field to the beginning of the pathway down the mountain. There were still one or two points to be settled:

'Who is to be the judge?'

'We shall be the judges, you and I.'

'And the stake? What is the winner to receive and what the loser?'

'You have already made your request clear. What the penalty might be I will leave you to reflect upon during the coming days.'

I started down the path in excellent spirits. My only worry in such a contest would have been the judges. Anything might happen if untrained ears were permitted a vote. This way, with the girl and myself as judges, the worst that could happen would be a stalemate.

I sat down at the piano to recover the melody the girl had played. It was a beautiful thing, a little sad, but a great deal better than anything I had yet heard since coming to Greece. Someone at the temple, if not the girl herself, was very much out of the common run. I supposed they were aware of it. No doubt this was why the challenge had been issued. I began to play variations on the melody. It was certainly a beautiful thing but no better than hundreds of other melodies that could be conjured up. With the whole of European musical literature behind me there could be no question of the outcome of the contest.

I walked into Athens the following morning. My story put Alex Hamilton once again into fits of laughter. 'Wonderful, that's quite marvellous.'

Of course everybody soon knew about it, Alex saw to that. To him it was the joke of the year. I was not surprised to find the Greeks taking it more seriously. One or two of them, particularly I remember a chap of the name of Diagoras, came and congratulated me. They said it was high time the old superstitions were broken. From the gravity of their manner, I realized the superstitions went deeper than even they themselves supposed.

I suspect I would soon have had an ugly situation on my hands if the people hadn't felt the god to be entirely capable of looking after himself. It was as though I had desecrated a temple, not a trivial offence.

My worry that too many people would flock on to the hill was apparently shared also by the Boule, the council of the city. A decree was quickly passed that nobody outside my personal party was to approach the temple within ten stadia, that is to say within a mile.

Only on the morning of the day itself did the full implication of the situation really become clear to me. The way I had fixed things with the priestess this was to be a private affair. There was no suggestion of a public contest. In fact that had been exactly my worry. I wanted to avoid a contest by popular acclamation. Yet in a sense this was exactly what it had become. Even worse, how could I possibly win? Even if the priestess were to come down on my side she could hardly say so in public. The populace would tear her limb from limb. And the stalemate, which I had fondly imagined would be the worst that could befall me, would become a mockery if those at the temple should declare against me. I saw I was in really serious trouble. I also saw the priestess had probably planned this from the beginning. My crime against the god was probably a serious one in her eyes. I started up the pathway in the middle morning with far less enthusiasm than I had come down it four days before.

My forebodings proved very accurate. Even in the early afternoon a considerable crowd was already gathered on the flat ground in front of the temple. They obeyed the orders of the city fathers up to a point. They were keeping about three hundred yards from the temple. I had no doubt the city fathers themselves would come even closer. I was accosted by a small, ugly-looking man:

'Is it really true you are to engage the god in a contest?'

'Is it really true there is a god?'

'I see it is true.'

He looked me over for a long time. Then reflectively he added, 'Well, well, it should prove interesting.'

I looked him over carefully. 'Can I ask you a question? Are you sure of anything?'

'I am sure the summer is hot and the winter cold.'

'And you are sure your fellow citizens have too many pre-conceived opinions?'

'Of that I am also sure. They say the last one to challenge the god was flayed alive for his pains. Of that I am *not* sure.'

'Thank you for your encouragement.'

I left him at the foot of the temple steps. I had reached the top, when as an afterthought I shouted, 'By the way, have you paid that cock to Asclepius yet?'

Nuts, I thought, as I walked into the temple. This just can't be true. But the stone pillars were hard enough and the piano was real enough. It was a meeting of two different worlds.

By now I had some experience of the best place to site the piano in order to get the best resonant effects. The men who carried it up knew nothing of this so it had to be moved. I had to go out again to get the necessary help. Once I was satisfied with the position, my helpers cleared off just as quickly as they could.

I still had a long tuning job. I wanted to make the best possible job for the acoustics in the temple were wonderful.

Already we were in the third part of the day, the third division of the day, so I wouldn't have much longer to wait. I strolled outside and came on Alex, Morgan, Anna, and a few Greek friends who were still willing to stand by me.

Alex was somewhat contrite at the commotion he had

caused. 'Don't worry, just play,' he said. 'You can't lose, except by being too ambitious.'

I suggested it would be best if they came through the temple to the little inner garden. The piano was placed towards that end and they would hear better from there.

'I think it's going to be a good evening,' said Anna. This might well be true. The remarkable carrying power of sound was one of the secrets of the Greek open air theatre. On many evenings the sound travelled horizontally instead of upwards, as it tends to do in northern climates.

The light inside the temple was not very good. It was fortunate I had decided to trust my memory. As the light gradually faded it would have been difficult to read notes inside here. Actually I had no fears upon the musical side, the troubles were political. I guessed the whole thing was a trick organized by the politicians we had offended soon after our arrival.

So far nobody from the other side had shown themselves in the temple. Now at last a priest appeared. He was of a similar colouring to the girl priestess, light brown hair, and he was similarly tall. In the subdued light I could not judge the colour of his eyes.

'Is it your wish to proceed with the contest?'

I suppose in the circumstances it would have been sensible for me to have called it all off. There was no point in running my head into a political noose. Yet this was ostensibly a musical contest. How could I retreat from a trial of strength in my own craft? Perhaps it was pride which impelled me to go on but I think not.

'Yes, I wish to continue.'

The priest then withdrew. Some five minutes later the first sounds came. I say came because I had no idea as to their exact source. It had to be from one or other of the three side chambers opening out from the main floor.

The melody was the one the girl had played for me four days earlier. The melody was the same but the instrument was not. It had a far clearer, more penetrating, quality. It was played with much greater decision. If this indeed was the girl then she had been fooling me before. The melody was followed by a complex variation from which it emerged again as a single line. But now the line was changed, in a fashion I couldn't

379

exactly determine. There were three more variations, each rapidly and lightly played. Following each one came the melody, always with changes. It was as if the tune were made to evolve through the intervening sections of complex structure. This was all I could make out in the beginning. It lasted for some six or seven minutes.

Now it was my turn. I decided to match the light rippling music I had just heard. I think it was Liszt who referred to shooting the octaves out of one's shirt-sleeves. I played four Chopin studies. This I felt was a fair return. Even though I had kept things very light and delicate it was clear the piano was more wonderful than whatever instrument was being played behind the scenes. Even so I was amazed at the quality of what I had heard. It was really beautiful miniature stuff, enormously superior to anything I had heard in the city. Who the hell was playing it I began to wonder.

The next round was instantly more serious. The texture was fuller and louder. Yet the precision of detail was still there. A casual listener would have judged there to be long and short notes, exactly as in our own music. Yet this was not so. Every note was short. The impression of a long note was given by several short notes played very close together. You can't do this at all on a piano, no matter how quickly you move your finger. It takes the key so long to respond that by the time you press it for a second time the total volume generated by the first note has already fallen so far that the second one stands out as a quite separate pulse of sound. In this case, when a long note was desired the second pulse came before the first one had died more than a little way. There was a slight dying effect of course, otherwise the note would have been long and uniform, exactly the way it can be on a violin. Here you could just about detect the separation of the pulses. This indeed was one of the things which gave the music its quite novel sound. It was as if somebody were plucking a string at an enormously high rate, as if the string were responding instantly. So much could I make out of the individual notes themselves.

It still baffled me as to exactly what restrictions were being placed on the choice of the notes themselves. This was not twelve-tone music, all the tones were not being used. Yet it wasn't tonal in the sense of our system of keys. The structure was more complicated than anything I had heard before. I had the strong impression of rules depending somehow on the form of the work itself. It was as if the rules, the restrictions, depended on the place in the piece. The rules at the beginning and those at the end seemed different, and different again from those in the middle. It was as if the large-scale development of the work influenced its manner of construction.

I mention all this to show why it wasn't in any way easy even for a trained musician to grasp instantly what was going on. Plainly I had to deal with a subtle and complex form. My last thought of the people outside was that they could hardly find the music of the god easier to comprehend than my own. I think it was at this point, as the second of my opponent's sections came to an end, that the first chill of apprehension swept over me.

My response was essentially automatic. I made my choices from *The Art of Fugue*. I made them instinctively, allowing the music to well out of the fingertips. As I came to an end I no longer had any idea of playing to the crowd outside, or even to my friends in the little garden, but to whatever it was that lay out of sight somewhere in the darkening temple.

With the beginning of the third trial all was changed. The music was now full-toned, slow and majestic. Its quality and power was a fitting tribute to the gods. This was no simple priest or priestess, or even a thousand of them. A power was abroad here that could not be denied. It was a power hitting at me, not at the crowd. There was no appeal to popular taste, even the popular taste of the twentieth century. It was exactly what it claimed to be, Apollonian in stature.

Although I was far more concerned to listen now than to analyse, I was overwhelmingly impressed by the tonal ambivalence, by the difficulty of deciding what note or chord would come next. Even before the end was reached I knew there could only be one answer.

I began the Adagio Sostenuto from Beethoven's Opus 106. I took the tempo as slow as I dared. The movement, long as it is, had now to be stretched to the limit. The sonority was wonderful, every note rang out true and clear. The minutes passed and the music flowed everlastingly on. It might be the god himself who was opposing me, yet he should learn something of the depths of human agony. I was already playing the arpeggiated bass chords that bring the movement to an end when the fantastic risk I had taken flashed through my mind. But the memory I had always relied on so heavily in the past had not let me down. Nor could I have ever been reconciled to myself if it had.

There came a long pause. It did not signify the end, I knew. A pause was necessary for aesthetic reasons. I was sitting waiting when a light step caused me to swivel suddenly and apprehensively round. It was the girl, the priestess, dressed in a quite beautiful long gown. It had no relation to the dresses of the women of Athens. It buttoned around the neck in a manner reminding me of the costume of a Chinese woman.

'It is necessary for the last part that you should play only the music you have written yourself.'

After this calm command she was gone.

So the ground was swept from under me as the first notes of my opponent's last section rang out loud and triumphantly. It was altogether bigger in its proportion than the previous rounds. It was quite symphonic in scale, although there was no suggestion of orchestral instruments. Everything was built out of plucked notes. It lacked something of the colour of an orchestra but this can be my only criticism. How much of it I failed to appreciate with my ears untrained to the basic style I do not know. Yet enough of the splendour of it was clear to me for the near hopelessness of my position to be obvious. Yet it was only at the end that desperation seized me. While the music played I listened with bowed head.

I knew I could only answer one vision of creation with another. I needed full orchestra and chorus, all I had was a single piano. I sat for a little while, the sweat dripping down my face. Then I began with the slow maestoso section of my last work. A lifetime's discipline of listening to what I was playing steadied my nerves. The ideas came back more and more. Gradually the intense fury of those winter months reasserted itself. How long I played I could not tell. It was quite dark now, apart from shafts of moonlight coming through the entrances to the temple. I came at last to a convenient stopping point. Then I just sat, silently waiting.

The girl came to me. Without seeing any clear-cut gesture I realized she wanted mè to follow her. I kept two or three paces behind as we crossed the main floor. We came out of a side

382

entrance into the open moonlight. The scent of flowers seemed overwhelmingly strong.

'You may sit here if you wish,' almost in a whisper.

I sat down, not because I was tired, but because it was the easiest way to unwind myself.

'What is your verdict?' she asked.

So they were sticking to the bargain, whoever they were.

'I can say nothing about the end, my last piece. You asked for it to be my own. Nobody can give a fair judgement of his own music. Of the other three parts, I do not think I lost.'

'Do you wish to claim victory, even apart from the fourth and last section?'

I thought for a long time. All my instinct told me that nothing could equal Bach or the finest of Beethoven. Yet the mere fact I hesitated showed it would be wrong to claim too much. I knew the works of Bach and Beethoven as I knew the back of my own hand, so I was familiar with their tremendous merits. I had heard this new music but once. It was inconceivable I could have distilled out of a single hearing all that was in it.

'No, I do not wish to claim victory. But you, what is your opinion?' I asked.

In a soft voice, the girl replied, 'I am content to take the same view.'

The load lifted instantly from my mind. It was the proper verdict. The styles were too different for a judgement of better or worse to be made. Only similar things can be compared in a direct fashion, only when they set out to obey the same rules and restrictions.

'So we end as we began. Except I hope you will no longer think of me as an uncontrolled madman.'

'I never did, I simply wanted to hear you play.'

The cool effrontery of this reply shattered my growing complacency. The girl went on. 'Because you make no claims for your own work, I will give you that which you asked for.'

She took me a few steps further into the little side garden, to where I could see a flat couch. I was rather surprised she paid no heed to the crowds outside. I suppose she thought the people would be so frightened at what they had heard that there could be no danger of them entering the temple. She laughed quite openly as I began to kiss her.

The night was a subtle compound of many ingredients.

Moments of high passion, of whispered conversation and laughter bubbling along like a stream in the woods, of the scent of the flowers, of snatches of sleep, and of long intervals lying quiet – the girl in my arms – looking up at the sky above our heads. Time was measured not on my watch but by the changing positions of the stars. It was not until the glow of morning was spreading upward from the eastern horizon that at last I fell into a deep sleep.

I awoke with the instant conviction of having slept long and wonderfully well. With languorous disappointment I realized the girl had gone. It was not until I heaved myself into a sitting posture that the first shock came. I was inside some building. It was obviously not the temple. For a flash I thought I had been carried away to prison. Then I saw this could be no prison, it was far too comfortable.

Not only that but I was dressed in a queer garment. It could be said to be a pair of pyjamas, or more accurately pyjamas, because as far as I could see I was completely fastened up in the damn thing. It was all in one piece and there seemed to be no possibility of getting it either on or off. The material too was strange. It was coloured in a multitudinous and expensive manner. It somehow suggested Joseph's coat, yet the colours were delicate rather than garish.

Quickly I jumped out of bed. Then I saw it wasn't a bed. It was simply a flat piece of the floor of the room itself, but raised two or three feet above the rest of the floor. The carpeting, or whatever it was, was extremely soft to the tread. I didn't bother to examine it but moved quickly to the opening out of the room – there was no door. I came into a very large room indeed, a room which was odd in the extreme. To begin with, there wasn't a single chair, not a single item of furniture, in the usual sense. The floor was in the same deep blue material as the bedroom. It was everywhere uneven. It had raised and lowered portions in no particular pattern that I could discern. The walls and the ceiling were coloured in a fashion both gay and restrained. The dominant colours were different on the different walls, one had green and yellows, another was tinged largely with gold, another red. The overall shape was rectangular. Generally speaking the walls were vertical. Like the floor, however, there were few strictly plain surfaces. The effect was pleasing and soothing. One side of the room was open, and I could see sunshine beyond a curtaining material. I tried to get through the curtain but I could find no means of pulling the material aside. It took some minutes before I got the trick of it. I noticed that one could simply put one's hand through it, as if the whole fabric were rotten. Then I walked through it. Instead of the tear being permanent the material closed up behind me.

I was out on a large balcony. The house was built on the side of a hill. A smooth path came towards it from a near-by clump of trees. This was the only sign of a road I could see anywhere. Apart from the hum of insects it was quite silent. Everywhere over the hillside, running for miles in all directions, were banks of flowers and trees. I saw an occasional glimpse of some other house. Below me in the distance lay green fields. In the very far distance the mountains rising high into the sky were snow capped.

13 Allegretto e Sempre Cantabile

My first thought was that I had awakened at last from a long nightmare, or more likely from some fever. It was in Hawaii everything had started to go wrong. At a first glance here I was back again in Hawaii. The quality of the light, the high mountains, were superficially similar. Could this strange building be some kind of isolation hospital?

The pyjamas I was wearing might also at first glance have been taken for some exotic Hawaiian garment. But the material wasn't right, it was much too expensive in its weave and colouring. Then nobody I had ever known had conceived of a house like this, not even in the wildest dreams. Besides it couldn't be Hawaii. Those mountains must be at least fifty miles away. The visibility was tremendous. At such a range on Hawaii I would have been looking out over the sea but there was no sign of an ocean. There had been many flowers on Hawaii but nothing to compare with this luxuriant profusion.

Step by step I went over recent events. The night at the temple was last night. I was convinced of it. Yet this was quite certainly not Greece. The style of the house, its spaciousness, the countryside, and above all those mountains, were definitely not Grecian.

Although strange and singular things had been happening, up to this point they had not happened to me personally. This was the first big jump in my own personal consciousness. Subjectively I felt quite normal, yet objectively it seemed as if I must be as nutty as a squirrel.

I decided to search the house. I saw a second curtain opening off the balcony. As it was of the same material as before I simply walked through it without experiencing any sensation except a gentle brushing against the cheek. There were further rooms, smaller but designed in much the same fashion as the big room. However in one of them there was a table. It was the only article of furniture to be seen anywhere.

On it was a considerable pile of musical manuscripts. The briefest inspection showed they were the works on which I had spent the winter, in the little temple of Dionysus. At least in that respect I was not crazy. I flicked through the pages. My memory was right in every respect, all the details were in place, exactly as they should have been. At least some things were right, inexplicable as the basic facts seemed on the face of it. I went back to the large room. Sitting there on the floor was John Sinclair.

I collapsed by his side and said weakly, 'What the hell's going on?'

'I thought you might be getting worried. I've been round twice before but you were asleep. It's incredible you managed to get here.'

'Incredible?'

'You'd better tell me exactly what happened, before you woke up to find yourself here I mean.'

I started to give a general outline of my experience in Greece. John would have none of it. He demanded I should go through everything in complete detail. I came at last to the night in the temple. At the end of my description of the contest with the god, John began to laugh delightedly.

Remembering the ordeal I said, sourly, 'You're not the only one to find it funny. By now the whole of Athens will be laughing hysterically about it.'

'Piqued, eh? You know it's ironical. While I would have been quite incapable myself of putting up any sort of musical performance, I could have told you straightaway what it was you were dealing with.'

'What the devil d'you mean?'

'Isn't it perfectly obvious? It was the music of the future.'

I sat digesting this as best I could. He went on, 'Perhaps now you can realize why I was so keen to look everywhere, all over the Earth. Don't think I didn't want to come with you to Greece. I would have loved it, but I was convinced that the Britain of 1966 wasn't the last moment of time to be abroad on the Earth. Remember all the different periods we saw, perhaps five thousand B.C. in the Middle East, four hundred B.C. in Greece, the eighteenth century in America, 1917 in Europe, why stop at 1966 in Britain? There had to be something more.'

'So you went on searching?'

'High and low. We drew a complete blank everywhere in the southern hemisphere. I can't be entirely sure about South America because we ran into terrible weather there. You remember the Plain of Glass?'

I nodded and he went on:

'You see that just had to be the distant future, far away in the future.'

'Why?'

John made no immediate answer. He took a small box-like device from his pocket and pressed what seemed to be a switch. Instantly the floor became everywhere very soft, as if one had sunk into a feather bed. Because of the rises and hollows it was easy to get oneself into a comfortable position. Then he did something again to the box and the floor went quite hard again, at least hard compared to what it had been a moment before. I found myself sitting in what might have been taken for an extremely comfortable chair.

'So that's why they don't need any chairs?'

'That's right. Would you like some food?'

Now he came to mention it, I was damned hungry. I said so.

'Come on then. I'll show you some other gadgets.'

He led the way to one of the subsidiary rooms. He pressed a small button. Instantly a panel slid by and what seemed to be a typewriter keyboard appeared on one of the walls.

'What would you like?'

I said I would like fruit juice and bacon and egg.

'I'll do the best I can.'

John tapped the keyboard as if he was writing a message, then gave one final flourish, pressing what seemed to be a master button. About ten seconds later a kind of hatchway opened and out came a metal arm on which were two trays. On each tray was a large glass of yellow juice, which I took to be orange juice. There was also what seemed to be a slice of bread or toast covered in some reddish fluffy stuff.

'What the hell is this?'

'Your bacon and egg. I think I got it right.'

He dipped his finger into the froth and tasted it. Then he nodded and said, more seriously:

'Let's go back and talk.'

Somewhat bemused, I followed him. We took up our respective positions on the floor.

John explained: 'You see these people don't eat animals, so all the food is either vegetable or synthetic. There are literally hundreds of these preparations. I haven't sampled more than a small fraction of them yet.'

I tried the orange juice. It was excellent, in fact I couldn't recall tasting any better. Then I addressed myself to the froth. I had no complaint about that either. It wasn't bacon and egg by any means but it fell into the right kind of savoury class. 'Where the devil does the taste come from?'

'Well of course it's artificial in the sense the chemicals are produced synthetically, but they're the right chemicals, the ones you really get in the sort of food we're used to. Incidentally, you'll find the calorific value is quite low. You can eat bags of this stuff without growing fat.'

And then we were back to more gadgets. John had a piece of his bread and froth left. He smeared the froth on to the carpet material and chucked the piece of bread to the far side of the room. 'Time to get the sweeper out,' he remarked cheerfully. 'Better come over to the doorway.'

He took out his little box and fiddled again with it. There was a sort of blowing noise from the sides of the room, from what would be the wainscoting in a normal house. A white strip started at one side. It moved slowly across to the other side, where it finally disappeared. In its wake there was nothing but clean carpet. The whole process took about thirty seconds. John was like a boy with a toy. 'Not much trouble about housekeeping, is there?'

He stopped clowning and we went on to the balcony. He produced what looked rather like two deck chairs. Thank god for a touch of normality, I thought.

'You were talking about the Plain of Glass. Why does it belong so obviously to the future?'

'Because it's been melted, everywhere, smoothly. You know the Sun is going to get hotter and hotter as time goes on. There'll be a stage when the whole surface of the Earth melts. After that the Sun will cool. Everywhere over the Earth there'll be smooth glass. You remember what I said about it's not being etched by blown grit or sand. There couldn't be any sand with everything fused. Besides at that stage there would be no atmosphere, no wind. The Plain of Glass is the ultimate fate of the Earth.'

I sat for some time sipping my orange juice, letting all this sink in.

John went on. 'You see, it was a fair bet that if the distant future were represented here, there ought to be something in between, between 1966 and the far-off future. That's why I was so convinced it was worth going on searching.'

'Didn't you expect these people of the future would show themselves?'

'Not necessarily. Remember your own point of view about the Greeks. You were worried at the mere idea of mobs of our own people streaming into Greece. You wanted to leave it as much the way it was as you could. The future could be quite shy of appearing among us for exactly the same reason. They couldn't simply declare themselves as strangers, in the way you could when you arrived at Athens. The same thing in London would be impossible.'

'Yet they must have appeared in Greece.'

'For exactly the reason I've just given you. One thing I don't quite understand is how they've managed to keep Europeans out of Greece. You must have been lucky enough to get through their barrier before they closed it.'

'You think that's why our own people never arrived?'

'Fairly obvious, isn't it? Somehow the communication lines must have been cut. I can't quite see how, but we must realize these people are at least as far ahead of us technologically as we are ahead of the Greeks. I don't think there's much profit in worrying too much about practical details. If the Britain of 1966 could put an instant stop to the war in Europe, with only a technological lead of fifty years, a society with a lead of thousands of years wouldn't have too much trouble in hiving off a bit of the Earth. In any case that's exactly what they've done with their own country.'

I looked away towards the mountains. 'Where are we? I was trying to puzzle it out before you came. The nearest I could get was Hawaii, but that didn't seem right.'

John looked at his watch. 'It's not very far from midday. If you were to sit here for several hours you'd see the Sun move from left to right. Now work it out for yourself.'

The Sun moved from left to right, did it? I thought for a few minutes. This must mean we were in the northern hemisphere, because the Sun had to be south of the zenith. As far as

390

I could judge, there was an angle of about twenty degrees between the direction of the Sun and the vertical. So far so good. Then it was early spring, at least it had been only the beginning of April in Greece. If it was the same here it meant the angle between the Sun and the vertical was pretty well the geographical latitude, evidently twenty degrees north or thereabouts. My next thought was of the Himalayas. Could these mountains be the Himalayas? Then I remembered the Himalayan range is much further north than one usually supposes. In fact the equator goes south of the whole of India, the mountains come at thirty degrees north. I looked up again towards the Sun, the angle couldn't be as much as thirty degrees. Mentally I ran along a parallel of latitude, first into Burma. Obviously Burma wasn't right either, unless the vegetation was completely changed. Then I thought about Arabia and Africa. None of it fitted. The solution came to me last of all. The twentieth parallel must cut through America somewhere about Mexico City. The clarity of the air, the feeling I had of altitude, the mountains, were right.

'Mexico, of course.'

'Very good.'

'How did you get here yourself?'

'A good question, considering the way *you* got here. Damn it, I know what I'm looking for and I have to comb the whole Earth before I find it. All you have to do is to walk up a hill to a temple and what happens, you run slap bang into these people of the future.'

I had a clear memory of the priestess standing on the steps looking down at me in the little garden. So that was the explanation of why she seemed so different, why she was so tall. Melea, she had told me her name was last night, if it was last night.

'You know, John, my manuscripts. When I came up to the temple I didn't bring them with me. I left them back at the place where I was working. Somehow they must have been retrieved.'

'Oh, I'm sure you're definitely *persona grata*. After your musical performance. You see it's very likely they've lost all of our music. It must have come as quite a shock to them to hear it. I'm all right myself now, but it wasn't easy in the beginning. We got here during a storm. Otherwise I'm sure they would have misled us through the radio. We found a place to land and came down.'

'What happened to the rest of the crew?'

'I'll tell you about them in a moment. Of course the people here wanted to know who we were, all manner of detail.'

'How about language difficulties?'

'You'll see how they cope with that, all in good time.'

'So you got to the place where you wanted to be?'

'I was agog to find out what they knew. I was curious about a lot of technical problems in physics, obviously. It was like doing a puzzle in a newspaper. You're told the solution is on page eight, column four. If you find you can't do the puzzle, the natural thing is to look at the answer, which was the way I felt about a lot of things. I asked a lot of questions in return, which was lucky for me, otherwise they'd have dealt with me the same way they did with the rest of the crew.

'We had to go back in their textbooks quite a fair way before we reached the things I know about. One of my own discoveries I found under somebody else's name. Naturally I didn't take at all kindly to this. When I pointed it out, they instantly changed their tune and became very friendly. All doors were opened to me as it were. Well, two or three days after our landing, I learnt the plane was being sent away. I didn't want to go myself for obvious reasons but I did want to send a message. So I sought out the crew.'

John stopped at this point, his usual habit, just when he had reached the decisive point.

'Well,' I grunted.

'They didn't know me, they damned well didn't know me from Adam. There was nothing wrong with them physically. Of course when they made no move to recognize me it was clear the people here didn't want any message sent. I saw it wasn't a good idea to press the point. So I simply let the plane go.'

'Why didn't they recognize you?'

'Well, it's perhaps not really so surprising. What we can do with drugs, anaesthetics and so on, would seem astonishing to the Greeks, wouldn't it? I don't think they had been harmed in any way, except they would lose their memory of the whole incident. It would be a kind of artificially induced amnesia.'

'You think that's why I remember absolutely nothing between the temple and here?'

'I would say so. Probably they didn't want you making a fuss.'

I decided I would have another glass of orange juice. For some reason I was extremely thirsty. John gave me a description of which button to press and I went to the kitchen alone. With a bit of fiddling I got what I wanted, but I got plenty of other stuff as well. I took the whole lot back to the balcony, for I was getting hungry again. I had in fact lost weight during the winter. For the most part I had lived on fish and on a kind of cake made out of honey and flour. After such a pleasant but monotonous diet, the profusion of tastes coming from the machines in the kitchen had quite a fascination

'How advanced are these people, technologically I mean?' I asked as I munched the odd concoctions.

'Considering they're something like six thousand years beyond us, not as much as I would have expected. At the development pace of the nineteenth and twentieth centuries, I'd say they're about five hundred years on. Of course that's impressive enough. It's about the gap which separated us from the fifteenth century. They've apparently been able to put into practice things we could only just conceive of. For instance they can produce enormous captive magnetic fields. You do this with a superconducting material, which prevents you from having ridiculous heating problems. Our trouble was that we couldn't get sufficiently rigid materials, and we had to fuss with very low temperatures. Somehow they've got rigid serviceable materials. Very strong magnetic fields have become a standard part of their technology, like the electric motor and dynamo are with us. You'll find their vehicles look at first sight like a hovercraft. They float over the ground. But they don't do it by blowing air. They simply ride on a magnetic field. The logistics of it work just like a railway system. They've got tracks laid out all over the country. But the tracks are magnetic, nothing at all like railway lines. The great thing about it is that it's all silent, and it's all computer controlled. Apparently you ring up for a vehicle in the same way as we might ring up for a taxi.'

'But with travelling as individual as that, like taxis, I'd have thought there'd be an almost impossible crush.'

'I think the secret of it is that there just aren't many people. We think in terms of tens or hundreds of millions. I haven't found out yet exactly how many of them there are, but it can't be anything like a twentieth-century population.'

It was all very intriguing. Already I had a fancy to do a bit of travelling around myself.

'How did you know to come up here?'

'I had information you were here.'

'You realize what that means?'

'I don't think it's as bad as you think. Look, who were your special friends in Greece? You give me an answer because I've asked an entirely reasonable question, not because I force an answer out of you. That's probably what you did. There may be nothing more to it.'

'And I've since forgotten all about it?'

'I thought we agreed about that. Anyway they told me you would be here. Something more, they're going to put on a special film show for us. To give us an idea of the things that have happened in the span of time between our day and theirs. I gather it'll last for quite a time, although they apologized for the sparsity of some of the material. They said we would realize why when we'd seen it.'

We went back inside to the main room. John hunted around until he found a master switch. When he pressed it the same thing happened as in the kitchen, a panel slid back and a kind of typewriter keyboard appeared. Only this time there were many more keys on it. John took out a piece of paper:

'I've got the code here, at least I've got instructions about which buttons to press. Until we get used to it we'd better do what they tell us. Otherwise we may find ourselves inside the washing machine.'

He pressed I suppose about half a dozen keys. On one of the flat pieces of the wall there appeared a picture. It was a pleasant country scene in colour, no more. 'That must be the call signal.'

We made ourselves a couple of comfortable armchairs in the floor and sat down to wait. There was a sudden commotion outside. Then in streamed my priestess, Melea, followed by another girl. I kissed Melea, and for good measure the other girl too. They were strikingly similar. Noticing the picture on the wall Melea said something in a strange language. She went to the keyboard on the wall and punched a few buttons. The picture disappeared. Something else must have happened, for there were a few small clicks, but I didn't notice anything by eye. Then Melea made quite a little speech, again in the strange language. A second or two after she had finished I was astonished to hear her voice again in the room. I say in the room because it didn't come from any particular place. I suppose there must have been a lot of small speakers distributed everywhere over the walls. The astonishing thing was that the language was English, with a very curious pronunciation, but English nevertheless.

'This is my friend Neria. She too was in Greece, at the temple of Delphi. That also was a temple of Apollo. It was she who made the prophecy about the war between Athens and Sparta. Will you not introduce your friend?'

I began to speak in my not very good Greek. She interrupted me:

'It will be much better if you speak in your own language.'

So I made the introduction. Immediately I had finished there came my own voice, I would have sworn it was mine, in a language of which I didn't know a single word. Naturally I was pretty dumbfounded. The girls stepped forward and kissed John, one after the other, which must have surprised him as much as the language business did me. Off his guard, he turned to me and said:

'Did they behave in Greece like this?' Immediately after he had finished, his voice was heard everywhere throughout the room in the new language. The girls made the incident into a joke which helped break the ice. I've noticed before that when you've been close and intimate with a girl you haven't known for more than a short time the second meeting is always a slight embarrassment. One can never be sure whether the situation is still the same as it had been. So I was glad this moment of embarrassment was out of the way.

Melea turned to me and smiled. 'We have brought you a present. In fact we've brought you two, one from each of us, but we are only going to let you see one at a time.'

The translation system made for very accurate understanding but I could see it was going to be a bit stilted. It wouldn't be right over breakfast.

Now it was Neria who went to the keyboard. With a

deliberate flourish of the hand she tapped away at two or three of the buttons. I was quite unprepared for what followed. I suppose I expected some kind of picture to appear on the wall. But no, in through the doorway from the direction of the kitchen an object glided into the room. It made no sound as it moved. Neria pressed a button and it stopped not far from the exit on to the balcony. I realized they must have the magnetic tracks John was talking about even under the damned floor itself.

We all turned our attention to the object. At the touch of a switch on its side the top folded back. There underneath was a keyboard, a piano keyboard, with the usual eighty-eight keys. At the right-hand end there was a small metal lever, and nothing else.

The two girls stood waiting like expectant children at a party, just after the conjurer had arrived. For me, some conjuring would be necessary it seemed. There was no piano stool, no pedals, and the box itself just wasn't big enough to contain any appreciable length of string.

'Where do I sit?'

'Haven't you got an adjuster?'

'No,' said John, before I could reply.

The girls laughed. 'Then he is going to be very uncomfortable unless we fetch one from the storage room.'

We all made quite a business of adjusting the shape of the floor to fit the position of the box. It was every bit as impressive as the usual adjustment of the piano stool. At last I decided I was comfortable enough and that my hands were in the right relation to the keyboard.

The three of them were sprawling on the floor, Melea actually at a height above me, so contoured was the room. I felt as if I was in a kind of arena. I began to play a Handel chaconne. The effect was indescribable, indescribably good and indescribably bad. Sometimes the music came through with a really wonderful tone. Then an instant later there would be the most horrible overload effect, the volume would become enormous. I stopped for a moment.

'You'd better either adjust the control or play more lightly,' said Neria.

I tried moving the lever. As I did so, the pressure needed on the keys to give the same volume of tone changed. I began to experiment with single notes. It was the pressure on the key that decided the volume. Any increase of pressure after a key reached its bed, any key-bedding, produced a grotesque increase of output. The mechanics of striking a single note were completely different from a piano. On the piano you get maximum output at the moment the hammer hits the strings. From that moment on, the volume of tone sags badly. A long-sustained note is impossible if you judge by an objective criterion. The thing which makes piano music possible is the curious subjective effect by which you continue to think you hear the tone after it has really sagged. Of course the manner of striking the strings makes some difference but the appalling fall-off of tonal quality is always there. Here the situation was quite different. The volume could be held steady, for seconds if necessary, simply by keeping a constant downward pressure on the key. In fact by increasing the pressure you could increase the output, exactly as a violinist can.

It took a lot of experimenting before I had the feel of it. Indeed it would be weeks or months before I would be able to get maximum effects out of this new system. In a sense it was a little like switching from piano to organ, in that the sound stopped as soon as you took your finger off the key. Unlike the organ, however, you could get a surge of tone in the middle of a note, like the thrill a violinist can produce.

When I had got the hang of individual notes I found the general tonal structure had interesting differences and interesting possibilities. It was sharper, less vague than a piano. This seemed to come from control over high harmonics particularly in the treble. The general effect was a greater clarity and a more legato quality. The harsh percussive effects of the piano could not be reproduced, they were quite lost. I found by adjusting the general output control that I could either play with the usual kind of heavy pressure, the strong finger effect I was normally used to, or I could go over to quite light fingering as one does on a harpsichord. Either way I could get the same big volume of tone. This made it possible, using light fingering, to play passages both very fast and very loud.

I had to be almost literally pulled away from this new box of tricks. Apparently a meal was ready. Incredibly it was set on the floor. The girls had made all kinds of indentations to hold the various articles and dishes. The colours of the food stood out sharply against the dark blue flooring material. It looked exactly as if a bed of flowers had been laid out. The effect was so remarkable that I felt it could not be due to chance.

It was all entirely vegetarian food. They didn't eat animals John had said. Yet you wouldn't have known it. The tastes were there. In fact my only problem was there seemed to be too many tastes, almost as if you were getting the whole of a large menu all at once. The wine was very good. Apparently a span of ten thousand years made little difference so far as wine was concerned.

'How do you like your little present? You haven't thanked us for it yet.'

'He is exactly like a child with it,' said John with a tinge of jealousy.

I pressed my advantage. 'You said you had two presents.'

'None for me,' muttered John. At this the girl Neria stroked his face.

'There are better presents for you than a little black box,' Neria smiled.

I saw John was going to have his troubles, and especially because of the way the translation system operated. It suddenly struck me how much the pronunciation of English by the girls had changed. It was now very much more like normal everyday English. My curiosity flowed over and I had to ask how it was all done, although I realized we were pretending that nothing seemed unusual to us.

'Oh, it is really very simple,' said Melea.

'I would not have thought you would have had any difficulty with that,' grinned the other girl.

John took up the challenge. 'Let me make a guess. First you have a system of language translation set up in a computer. As well as grammatical rules, synonyms, and so forth, you have a library of mouth sounds. When a word is spoken it is analysed for its sounds, taken to pieces. Then it is put through the translation procedure. The same is done for the translated word, in reverse. It's a matter really of having sounds as well as a dictionary. But how did you manage to change the pronunciation as you went along?'

The same thing was puzzling me.

The girls laughed: 'Your own pronunciation was analysed, of course. As you spoke each word, the sound formation was taken to pieces. After that, when the same word was used in the translation of something that we said, it was put together in the way you had used. Now do you understand?'

John nodded, and I think I got a pretty good idea myself.

But there was still one thing that worried me. 'How do you get the voices to sound so right?'

'Because each of us has a library in our computer of the way our voice sounds. Not just in our own language, but of all the sounds that can be made with the human voice. By doing this our voice could be translated into any language whatever, even though we ourselves could not understand a word of it.'

'You haven't a library of our voices?'

'No, we are not really using your voices at all. We've used the voice of one of our own people, not anybody we happen to know well personally. Otherwise it would be very strange.'

By now we had finished the meal. I was again astonished by the speed with which it was all cleared away. Just the same carpet-sweeping procedure that John had used. The really striking thing was when the white strip reached the position of the piano, or rather the piano-like box of tricks, the whole thing lifted up off the floor, and the white strip went underneath it. Thirty seconds and the room was clear. Dinner was finished.

Both girls went out. Several minutes later they came back carrying two large parcels which they put on top of the piano. With smiles they bowed at me and said: 'They're yours.'

They were the most normal articles I had yet seen, apparently straightforward parcels, wrapped in what looked uncommonly like paper. I undid the first one. It was just a large metal disc about two feet in diameter and an inch thick.

'Handle it very carefully, please.'

John came over: 'It must be hollow, or layers of metal. Otherwise it would be much heavier.'

It had seemed heavy enough to me. I undid the other parcel. Here there were three discs of the same diameter but less thick. The girls were watching us with amusement. John and I talked about it for some time. It was obviously connected with some sort of electronic device. But what? They were like huge, weighty gramophone records, the sort of thing a stone-age man might have produced, only they were made of bright metal not stone. We gave it up.

Melea took the biggest of the discs, while her friend went to the keyboard on the wall. I was beginning to wonder what these people would do without their walls and floors, when a metallic arm moved smoothly and slowly out of the wall. Melea fitted the disc into it and the whole thing retreated completely from view.

There was a lot to be said for not cluttering up the room with chairs and tables and a hundred and one other articles. The room might have been expected to look bare but it didn't. This was due to the shape and the colours which somehow conveyed the impression of being out-of-doors. I realized what it was that had struck me as being so queer in the first place. Normally when you go into a building you change your sense of scale. Rooms that would seem ridiculously small if they were out-of-doors become tolerably large. What happened here was that you didn't make any change of scale, you had the same sense of size as you have in the open air.

I just had time for these reflections before the music started. I was transfixed at the first chords. It was the beginning of the Mass I had taken three months of the winter to write. It was all there, the whole orchestra. At least it was very nearly the orchestra as I knew it. Very nearly, but not quite, the harmonic balance of the individual instruments was a little different. The music flowed on and I lost all sense of calm judgement. Listening to one's own music is a little like listening to one's own voice, you do it with a sense of wonder, fascination, and horror. You can't believe it really sounds like that. The wonder now was that the instruments were all there, the notes all correct. I could detect no mistake of pitch or of timing. Indeed the timing was if anything too accurate. When the chorus came in the words were English. They were my own words.

Now we were at the section I had played in the temple, the section I had conceived of in an agony of mind. It held me now, playing on my emotions as if I, its creator, were no more than a keyboard. The pain and tragedy dissolved at last into sunlight and the work came to an end, after what seemed like a vast span of time. It was I suppose about two hours.

I knew of course what was on the other discs, the symphony and the piano pieces. I had no thought to hear them now, I wanted no more music that day. I took hold of Melea and we went out on to the balcony. There were no lights anywhere on the ground but the sky was incredibly full of stars. It was even clearer, more remote, than the Grecian sky had been.

It was like the night we had passed at the temple, last night so far as my memory was concerned. Even so there were a thousand and one questions I wanted to ask which still perturbed me, but this was not the occasion for them. The morning would come soon enough.

I woke first. Melea was still there, her face close to mine, her long hair entangling her shoulders. I lay without moving for some time, not wishing to waken her. The feeling was in part selfish for I wanted to study her face. There was natural beauty in it but not a trace of glamour. It was a face that could not have existed in the year 1966.

The eyes opened at last. There was the usual fleeting fraction of a second while the eyes come into focus and the brain comes to life.

'Today will be a happy day,' she said, a little sleepily. There was an emphasis on the word today which I could not understand.

It was indeed a good day. We started early, not long after sunrise. It turned out there was some reasonably shaped clothing in the house, a kind of shirt and trousers. Fashions can't change too much simply because of the shape of the human body. The odd thing about these clothes, however, was they had no buttons or fastenings of any kind. You put them on after the style of a boiler suit, except they were very well cut and there was no zip-fastener. There was a special kind of cloth along the fastening which simply pressed against the cloth on the other side of the seam. It was like scotch-tape, except you could use it time and time again. You simply pulled it apart with a good stout tug.

After the usual frothy breakfast we called up a taxi. Unlike the taxis I was used to, it wouldn't come to the house itself, only to the nearest taxi rank, a good mile away. There had been a heavy dew during the night which was still covering the trees, bushes, and flower beds as we walked down the hillside. The vehicle was already waiting for us. I can best describe it as a squashed sphere. The lower third of it was opaque, the rest was made of some translucent material. There was a little kiosk near by. Melea beckoned me to follow her. I watched while she tapped out what I took to be our destination on one of the inevitable keyboards. A slip of material, translucent, about six inches long by one inch wide appeared. Set within the material were about a dozen characters, apparently in metal. We got into the vehicle. Melea pulled out a rectangular sheet about two feet long. Into this she inserted the smaller slip and then replaced the sheet. Neria touched a button and instantly we began to move.

I could see now as we moved away the reason for the squashed appearance of the sphere. The vehicle itself was about fifteen feet across. The walls were rather like the kind of shop window that doesn't seem to have any glass in it. You had the impression you were looking straight out. There was no rattle or rumble as we picked up speed. Very soon we were whistling along at what I guessed to be about eighty miles an hour. It took about two hours to our destination. We went towards the south. I could see the big mountains I had glimpsed from the balcony. They were volcanic cones, not unlike the mountains of Hawaii in fact.

'One of them will be Popocatepetl, I suppose,' said John.

'They must have cleared the whole of the jungle that used to occupy these parts,' he added.

We passed mainly through green fields. Every now and then I could see little valleys filled with flowers, like the one we had come from. I thought I could glimpse houses. Also in the distance I caught flashes of vehicles similar to the one we were travelling in. At an intersection of the pathways, or magnetic tracks, or whatever they were, we came quite close to another vehicle. The occupants waved and we waved back.

As we approached the mountains it was obvious the jungle had indeed been cleared. We went quite smoothly and silently up the mountainside. Eventually we passed from fields to grassland. It was for all the world like an alp, except there were no animals.

'What has happened to all the animals?'

I asked this in Greek, for Greek was now our only means of communication – strange we had to work through a language that lay two thousand years in the past for me, eight thousand years in the past for the girls.

'The situation is very sad. All the major animals were wiped out and became extinct long ago.'

'How about the domestic animals?'

'We no longer have any need of them. They are not here, not in our country anyway. We turned them loose in places suited to them. Many exist in a wild form like cattle and sheep, but the animal population of the Earth has become very poor. At least it was so until these new events occurred. Now we have collected them again.'

We reached our destination high on the grasslands. I could feel the altitude quite appreciably, which meant we were probably above eleven thousand feet. Grass still grew at this elevation because of the sub-tropical climate. For about three hours we climbed along a pleasant track. At last we came to rougher ground. There was a hut where we had lunch. We took exactly what we needed. I was now keenly aware that nobody ever paid for anything.

When I remarked on this to John he said, 'Obviously this is a high-powered civilization with very few people. I imagine they could make far more than they need, so why worry about paying.'

'To make sure people work.'

'It's obvious they have so many machines, so much automation, there isn't any need for anybody to work, not in our sense. I imagine their problem must be leisure not work.'

Another party arrived, a party of six. They looked at us curiously and I thought a little sadly. I couldn't make out why for I didn't feel sad myself. The newcomers had a remarkable family resemblance to the two girls. These people must all look pretty much alike. The man who had appeared for a brief moment back in the temple on the mountain, he also had been remarkably like Melea. I saw now why the girls didn't bother to glamorize themselves. If everybody looked more or less the same, there really wouldn't be any point in it.

I asked Melea how many people there were in total. She told me about five million.

'Over the whole Earth, only five million?' I asked in astonishment.

'We don't live over the whole Earth, only in this country here.'

'You mean the rest of the Earth is empty?'

'Not empty but wild, in its natural state. Why should we want to live everywhere? Five millions is quite enough people

403

to know. How many people do you know in your country, more than five million?'

'Of course not. We make a choice of those we wish to know.'

'There is no point in us making such a choice. Why should we want to know one person and ignore another?'

The view away to the north was tremendous as we walked back again downhill by a different path.

'I think we must hurry,' said Neria.

This was translated to us, with the explanation that there would be a thunderstorm about four o'clock in the afternoon. We got back to our taxi barely in time. It was a wonderful ride down the mountainside through the driving rain and the flickering lightning. Several times the lightning struck at points not far removed from us. Neither of the girls seemed at all worried about being hit ourselves. John noticed this and whispered, 'They must have some protective field, lowering the potential a bit, near the track.'

It was amazing there was so little noise inside our sphere.

Once we quitted the vehicle back at our own valley we soon got thoroughly wet. The girls didn't seem to mind in the least and strode along, uncaring. We followed them to a house which wasn't ours. Quite a few people were already here. One of them showed us to what seemed to be a changing-room. There was a strong hot-air blower that dried you off completely in a couple of minutes. Then we picked ourselves a selection of garments and sealed ourselves up inside them. We took less than ten minutes but it could have been done in under three or four.

About twenty people came in that evening to what was evidently a party. It was not quite as free and easy as a party can be where everybody speaks the same language, because quite often we had to go through the translation system. Yet it was all far, far easier than attending any sort of function in a foreign country in the world of 1966. I had been right about the preparation of meals. They all made a big thing about the arrangement of the colours, into patterns like flower beds, and about the shape of the floor. They divided into two halves and had a kind of race. From the gun it took about ten minutes.

During the meal a sly game went on, of softening up the floor under one or another of us. It may sound ridiculous but it

404

certainly looked funny, especially after a modicum of alcohol. Although everybody talked twenty to the dozen there was no appalling volume of sound. The floor, the ceiling, and the walls, were evidently sound absorbing. Yet when I had played the previous night I hadn't had the impression of playing into a sink. It seemed as if the reflecting qualities of the room must be changeable.

After dinner the little piano suddenly appeared. It came in by itself through a doorway. There was nothing for it but that I should sing for my supper. There was a very good reason why everybody wanted to hear me. What I had already begun to suspect, that nobody in this society played any musical instrument, was confirmed. Music could be put together so readily using electronic techniques that incentive was quite lacking for anyone to go through the long years of drudgery so necessary for proficient performance.

The evening reminded me in a curiously vivid way of the party back so long ago in Los Angeles. I found myself beginning the waltz theme of the Diabelli variations. I had not played them since the night in Los Angeles. Until now I had associated Beethoven's great masterpiece with a different time, a different age. But now the variations emerged with as much freshness as ever, and with more power than I had been able to produce on the instruments of that apparently far-off epoch.

14 Grave e Mesto

The following morning the party had quite dissolved. When Melea and I appeared for breakfast we found John talking to a white-haired man of about sixty. Melea instantly became serious. She said:

'This morning it has to be different. It is about the film we stopped you from seeing the other afternoon. You will soon understand why it was better left until the end.'

This made me uneasy.

'What do you mean, by there being an end?'

'I think you must see first. After that you must hear what we have to say. Then we can decide.'

The two girls and the man left us. The beginning of the film appeared. Evidently the others didn't want to watch it.

The showing took upward of four hours. It was the longest documentary film I had ever seen, naturally enough for it dealt with a time span of six thousand years. We covered time at an average rate of a century to each four minutes. There was no place here for intricate involvements, or for the niceties of politics. Yet it was all too easy to follow. The black record of the human species swept remorselessly on as the minutes and hours ticked away.

It was a shock at the beginning to be very quickly out of both the twentieth and the twenty-first centuries. The first quick point was a transition from poverty to affluence in the undeveloped continents of the twentieth century, Africa and Asia. A homogeneous civilization swept with incredible speed over the whole Earth. There were brief flashes of the people, of their machines, their customs, their political leaders. It was all done visually. We sat in silence watching, our ears free of the cacophonous uproar of the usual sound track. It was easy to comment to each other on what we saw, not that we had much to say beyond the occasional exclamation.

Earth teemed with people. Cities spread out farther and

farther until they became joined to each other. Urban populations covered an increasing fraction of the land surface. At first it was only one per cent, then five per cent, then twenty-five per cent. The technological drive went irresistibly on. Land became of more and more value. There was no room any longer for any animal save man. So we watched the gradual extinction of the whole animal world. Even the bird population declined and withered away.

We saw something of domestic life. We saw the standardized little boxes in which almost everybody was now living. The insistent question formed in your mind, what was it all good for? What conceivable reason could there be to prefer a thousand little boxes to one dignified house? The same of course for the people. What was the advantage of this appalling fecundity of the human species?

Soon we were in the twenty-fifth century. Angry voices began to be heard. The pressures were mounting, competing with the technology. The technology itself was kept going by the most rigorous demands on individual freedom. It was indeed a veritable ant-heap. The average person became restricted to a life that lay somewhere between the freedom of the twentieth century and the lack of freedom of a man serving a life sentence in prison. Nobody travelled now, except on official business – I mean travelled to distant parts. Everything was provided in one's own locality, food, amusements, work. The work itself demanded little initiative. The people were leading what can only be described as a punched-card life.

The technology wasn't working too well any more. Food was mostly of poor quality, mostly factory produced. At that stage, in the twenty-fifth century, the seas were essentially swept clean of fish. The land animals had been the first to go, then the birds, now last the fish.

The first disaster happened with amazing suddenness. What had seemed a more or less homogeneous civilization split into two, like the division of an amoeba.

'It's a point of instability,' whispered John. 'Look, the whole thing's going to grow exponentially.'

Whatever he meant, this vast gargantuan, sprawling, tasteless, in every way appalling, civilization exploded in a flash. It started with bombs and rockets, with fire. The film, so far silent, now came alive, not with any synthetic sound track, but with the crackling of the actual fire, with the shriek, instantly cut short, of a woman enveloped in a cloud of burning petrol. Then it was all over. It was quiet everywhere. Death and decay swept at an incredible speed, like some monstrous fungus, everywhere over the Earth. There was no movement, no transport, no food distribution. The intricate organization which had itself fed on the efforts of a large fraction of the whole population was dead. Everything which had depended on it, including the lives of the people, now died too. We could hear the whine of infants, the despairing cries of children. The abomination came at last to an end. It seemed as if the human species, having wiped everything else from the face of the planet, had now itself become extinct.

Miraculously this did not happen. A dozen or more specially favoured, especially lucky, small centres of population managed to survive. They were already beginning their recovery by the time we saw them, I suppose because no camera had been there to record the worst moments. Indeed the technique of photography suddenly became very crude, almost the way it had been when photography was first invented.

We saw the slow steady expansion of one centre after another. The population increased, the technology improved. We saw the people happy and smiling again. We heard them talking in a new language. We saw them attempting to recover the relics and treasures of the past, particularly books and manuscripts. We saw how they made every effort as they improved to absorb the culture of the past. Amazingly, a great deal survived.

By now we were almost a thousand years on. The new civilization was becoming exuberant. There was nothing of the deathly, machine-like quality of the situation before the first upheaval, the Great Disaster as it came to be known. People were individuals again. There was hope for the future once more.

The different centres were by now overlapping each other. They were in argument. There was a period of war, astonishingly short it seemed to us on this kaleidoscopic record. The war turned out to be no more than a kind of lubricant that allowed the hitherto separate regions to join up with each other into a coherent whole. With a growing sense of horror I realized it was all going to happen again. There was going to be a second disaster. It became so completely inevitable as one watched. Century after century went by. Each brought its contribution to the elephantine growth. Gone was the zip and zest of the first pioneers of this new civilization. We were back again in a punched-card era. It all happened with horrible predictability. The first and second catastrophes might have been interchanged and you couldn't have told the difference.

So it was with the reconstruction. We saw it all beginning again. There was a longish sequence belonging to North America, in what used to be the United States. It had a vaguely familiar look about it. John burst out loudly, in contrast to our previous whispers:

'That's it, look, that's it! That's what we saw, when we flew across America from Hawaii!'

So it was. What we had seen was not the America of the eighteenth century. It was the America of the fourth millennium.

The record was relentless. I could see now why the girls and the white-haired man had not wanted to stay. Added to horror of intimate detail, I had the feeling of a whole species in some monstrous, unclean cycle from which it could never escape. Each cycle was occupying a little less than a thousand years. Always during the reconstruction phase we could see the same bland confidence that this time it would be different. Because these phases were reasonably long drawn out, over three centuries or so, it always seemed as if the disease had been cured. Then quite suddenly, almost in a flash, the monstrous expansion started again. It was a kind of shocking social cancer. Then came the major surgery of flame and death, and so back to endeavour, to a temporary happiness, and to unrequited hope.

Yet at last something different did happen. At last, when it seemed as if extinction had finally come, just two centres managed to survive. They grew to a reasonable and moderate size, and at that they stopped, or almost stopped, for nearly a thousand years. The film became quite detailed. An important point had evidently been reached.

Always when a centre of population expanded from a small beginning the people were far less heterogeneous than the kind of human population we were used to. Now we had a rather

409

uniform situation. Yet there were still the two population centres.

There was no suggestion of war, however. The people, looking much like the people of the future, were restrained and reasonable, they had learnt the lesson of the past. The two centres maintained a quite friendly rivalry, with the aspects of a favourable situation about it. The rivalry seemed to prevent complacency, it seemed to provide an incentive to achievement. Yet as time went by I could detect a slow steady growth in both population groups, caused apparently by the friendly competition between them.

Both groups were quite well aware of what was happening. They noted the growth, yet they decided after considerable thought that the situation could be kept within bounds. So it was for a long time. Quite suddenly, however, control seemed to be lost. There was a stage beyond which expansion simply could not be prevented. This stage was reached before anybody expected it. From then on we watched a wretched society being forced along a road down which it did not wish to travel. It seemed as if everybody knew what was going to happen, yet nobody could prevent it.

'They've got beyond a point of instability. It's inherent in the organization. They can't get back.'

John's prognostication was right. The controlled rivalry disappeared. In its place came an unrestrained rivalry. The groups grew, merged together, after the usual momentary outburst, and so the disease spread to its inevitable conclusion.

At the next re-expansion phase there were three groups. When they reached a very moderate size, about a million people each, discussions took place between them. The outcome was that all three groups merged voluntarily, not to cover the whole Earth, but to contain themselves in a small portion of it. So the people of the future at last appeared. I saw clearly now why they lived in only one place.

How long had they been in their present state? It turned out, upward of a thousand years. In that time strikingly little change had taken place. They believed a genuine stability had at last been achieved, and their belief had more substance to it than the facile, arrogant claims we had seen so often in the earlier parts of the film.

We sat for a long time in silence. There did not seem very

much to say. Maybe an hour later, the girls and the white-haired man returned.

'I think the time has come for us to speak seriously,' said the man.

I could see something of the appalling predicament that he and his people were in. It was clear the Earth, with its different centres of population, might already be beyond all control. John was evidently thinking along the same lines, for he asked:

'What plans have you made, about how you're going to organize the Earth?'

The white-haired man answered simply: 'We have no such plans, because none are possible.'

The horror of the situation was at last becoming clear to me. It wasn't so much that we, the remnants of the twentieth century world, were inevitably condemned to a catastrophic future, with its rhythmic disasters, but that these people, the people of the future, were condemned to return to the agony of the past.

I could see the hopelessness of trying to impose any kind of control. It might last for a few years, even for a few generations, but from what we had seen there could be no permanent stability. Sooner or later the same grotesque swings, from arrogant expansion to pitiful collapse, would occur. It could only be prevented through the gross annihilation of the whole of the past. I had no doubt the technology of these people would enable them to carry through such an annihilation. Yet this was just as impossible as any attempt at control. It would destroy, psychologically, the annihilators. It would be a complete negation of all that these people stood for.

John had been silent for a while, evidently in perturbed thought. Now he asked, surprisingly, 'Have you seen the situation in Africa and in the southern hemisphere?'

'Yes, we have made a survey.'

'What did you find?'

'Nothing, the same as you.'

'Isn't that a bit odd? I know you have elected to live here in this part of the world. But surely some of your people, if only small expeditions, must have explored other parts of the world fairly frequently?'

411

'You are wondering why neither you nor we have run into any of our expeditions. The point has not escaped us.'

'What's your explanation?'

'We know of nothing definite.'

John was pacing about restlessly. He was evidently much agitated. Dramatically he turned. 'You know what I think, I think both Africa and the southern hemisphere belong to the future, like the great Plain of Glass. I don't think they're your contemporary world at all. Otherwise there would be unmistakable traces of your people somewhere.'

The white-haired man smiled a little sadly.

'You are very intelligent, Dr Sinclair. There seems to be little that has escaped you. Yes, it is possible that those regions may represent the future, the future even to us.'

'You realize the implication?'

'Naturally.'

I could contain myself no longer. 'For heaven's sake what does it mean?'

John turned on me. 'It means that in the future, in the time belonging to those lands, the human race has become extinct. It has all come to nothing, the great experiment of animal life on this planet. Nothing has survived except a few insects.'

'I do not see why you should be so perturbed, Dr Sinclair.'

'It is a confession of failure.'

'I cannot see why. In that sense, failure must come in any case, quite inevitably. You yourself have stood on the great Plain of Glass. You know what the whole Earth will come to in the end. The only question is whether it comes later, or sooner.'

I turned incredulously. 'Extinction! It doesn't worry you?'

'In the sense of a serious critical problem, no. It will be hard for you to understand our point of view. In your time, everything of importance always lay in the future. You worked for the future, you were dominated by a sense of progress. The path along which you walked was always less important than the view around the next corner. Our philosophy is quite different. We have strong ideas of how life should be lived. If the conditions we believe to be necessary can no longer be met we would prefer there to be no future. You see, we do not believe in time as an ever-rolling stream. We believe all times are equally important, the past is not lost.'

I looked quizzically at John, for this was much what he himself had said one afternoon back in England. I remembered his argument about consciousness and about rows of pigeon holes, except I couldn't remember the details. Whether because he actually agreed with the white-haired man, or because he thought I had detected him in some inconsistency, John now took a different line.

'I could sympathize with your point of view if you could be sure extinction will come quickly. Do you think that will be the way of it? Surely there will be a long slow downward trend, at any rate to begin with. The degeneration will occur by slow creeping degrees. Things will go just a little wrong at first, then more wrong, then catastrophically wrong. We have seen enough today to be sure our species will not die easily. Extinction will be a long-drawn-out, agonizing affair. Surely you can't maintain that living through such an experience would be in any way pleasant? Surely it is to be avoided, if it possibly can be?'

The white-haired man fell silent. I could see John's point had great force with him. The girl Neria took up the argument:

'These are exactly the questions we have been occupied with during the past months. We have only come to a decision after much discussion.'

The white-haired man continued. 'It is only fair to tell you that what we are now saying is being heard by all our people.'

He pointed to the walls of the room as if to signify their qualities as receiving and transmission systems, qualities that were really obvious from the translations we were receiving.

He went on, 'I tell you this to make it clear that I am not giving just a personal opinion. These are the considered views of our whole community.'

'So what it comes down to,' said John, 'is that you're not going to do anything definite. You're going to continue in the same way as before?'

'You are correct. We have weighed the likelihood of extinction against all the other factors. We see that a general mixing of ourselves with the people of Europe might be said to give the human species another chance. But it would only be a blind chance.'

'It may be better to take even a blind chance.'

413

'With the certainty of a repetition of what you have just seen?'

We were back at the dilemma.

'Is there no way of proceeding slowly, of making experiments as you go?' I asked. For answer, the white-haired man went on:

'It is necessary for me to tell you something further, which I do not think you have yet appreciated. This strange world, this world with different ages living side by side, is not going to last permanently. Soon we shall revert to where we were before, or very nearly to where we were before.'

John nodded. 'Yes, I've been having suspicions in that direction. The question is, whose world is it going to be?'

'There can be no doubt at all about that. It will be ours. The play is already complete so far as you are concerned. There is no possibility of changing your society. It is we who are balanced on the knife edge.'

Deep within me I had the concept of there being some sort of plan.

When I said so, the white-haired man answered, 'The concept of a plan involves the idea of working to a specified end. You have in mind an ultimate El Dorado, which some day you may attain. Yet there can be no such El Dorado for the Earth. You have seen the final state of the Earth, out there in the great Plain of Glass. Perhaps you may think we could escape to some other planet moving around some other star. Yet that star too will die. So it will be for our whole galaxy. Ultimate continuity, in a physical, material respect is impossible.

'It is possible that gradually, inevitably, a huge intellect is being built from the creatures evolving on trillions of planets, everywhere throughout the universe. What in these circumstances you wonder would be our personal contribution? Perhaps if we were lucky we might contribute some small fragment to the sum total. More likely, we should contribute nothing. In all respects duplication occurs on an enormous scale, galaxies, stars, planets, living creatures, all in vast numbers. Stars like each other, living creatures like each other, all doing more or less the same thing, many indeed following almost exactly the same course of evolution. Yet, like the occasional mutation, something a little different may happen in exceptional cases. Perhaps in one case in a thousand a new facet may emerge. The question we have asked ourselves is whether this small chance is worth all the agony. Is it worth even the few thousand years you have observed this morning? Was the long process of evolution, lasting hundreds of millions of years, perhaps still to go on for hundreds of millions of years, worth the eventual small chance of life here on the Earth making a fragmentary contribution to some higher level of attainment, of which we can barely conceive? To an imaginary planner, the answer would of course be yes, because the planner would be interested only in the higher levels being built from the lower, just as we ourselves are pleased to have evolved from more primitive creatures. Yet to the creatures themselves the answer may be no.'

I saw now where the argument was leading. 'Your answer I take it is no?'

'Our answer is no. If we hold firmly with the utmost determination to our present point of balance we may hope to deny what we believe to be the normal course of evolution.'

John was walking up and down. 'Can we come back now to the how and the why of it?'

'There are several interpretations. It could be an opportunity to repair some biological defect in our heredity. We may have lost some essential component which your population has still within it. It could be a punishment, by showing us our own extinction, to cause us distress. It could even be an experiment to see how we react in the face of both these things.'

'Surely we're faced now with a situation that doesn't concern you alone? Your technology is naturally better than ours, but there are now at least twenty times as many people in our world as there are in yours.'

'That is quite incorrect I am afraid. Your people exist only in a ghost world. For a little while your world may have a vivid reality, but very soon now, now that we have made our decision, it will be gone. It will go in a brief flash, just as it arrived.'

I found it difficult to conceive of myself as a ghost. 'I would not have said there was anything ghostlike about the two of us.'

'Not in the least, you are real enough.'

Melea spoke for the first time. 'The different zones of the Earth will change back to what they were before. The Greece

415

in which we met, the temple, will be gone. It will be gone far more completely than even the ruined remains of your own time. It will be gone almost without trace. It will be gone, except for the records in our libraries. Europe too will be gone, so will the great Plain of Glass. It will only be this zone here that will remain.'

The man nodded and went on, 'So you must decide. For the people of your country there is no decision to make. For us, we have made our decision. But for you it will be difficult. If you leave here you will disappear, into oblivion. If you stay, you will continue to live out your lives among us. The decision you will take must depend on your own thoughts and emotions. We cannot guide you further. Between you there is both reason and emotion. You must find where *your* balance lies.'

Before they left, Melea came to me and said, 'I will not stay with you tonight, because I do not want to influence the way you will decide.'

The three of them, the two girls and the white-haired man, looking almost infinitely sad, left us to our thoughts and deliberations.

My first reaction was to question what had been said. 'Is there any possibility of it not turning out the way they think? I mean about Britain and Europe simply disappearing. It seems preposterous.'

'Well, it's only the inverse of what happened before. If it was possible to go one way, it must be possible to go the other.'

'But everything back home, John, it was real enough. Those weren't ghost people, they were people with real feelings.'

'Of course they had real feelings, but they were apparitions nevertheless. For us it's different. We shall live out a perfectly real life if we stay here, but only if we stay here.'

'Well, there can't be any doubt about it. Going back – to oblivion I mean.'

'That was the way I felt until I began to think about it. What you must realize is, you really wouldn't be going back to oblivion, you'd be going back to one life not two.'

'I don't understand, even faintly.'

'Surely you could see from the film we've just watched that we've already lived our proper lives. Our lives exist – you remember the pigeon hole business – lives in which we quitted

Los Angeles for Hawaii. Somewhere in Hawaii there was a forking point. Instead of a single set of pigeon holes, suddenly there became two sets. One of them went along perfectly normal lines.'

'You mean the lines we expected, a life in which we returned to the Los Angeles of the twentieth century?'

'Yes, of course.'

'Why don't we know anything about it?'

'Because the two have separated, they've forked apart. There's no connexion between them. You're either in the one or the other. It's the sequence all over again. Whichever you're in you never know of the other. In this sequence you can never know what happened when you returned to Los Angeles. In that other sequence you can never know even a single thing about this one. The two are utterly separated. In the other sequence, neither you nor I will know about the future, about the film we saw this morning.'

'Then what does it come down to? What's the decision?'

'The decision is whether we want this particular sequence to end in a kind of cul-de-sac. We can either prolong it out into the usual lifetime or we can simply chop it off.'

'What would be the sense of chopping it off?'

'Because we might find this sequence intensely painful. Let me put it to you this way. You know you've got two lives to live. One life is perfectly normal and pleasant, but in the other you commit some serious offence, an offence which carries either the death penalty or a penalty of life imprisonment. You have the choice of which it shall be. If you only had one single life you might well choose imprisonment, in order to be able to go on. But with two lives do you really make that choice? There would be a lot to be said for avoiding the continual agony of being cooped up in prison, without any possibility of escape, year after year for several decades. You might well say to yourself – remembering you know about the other more or less pleasant life – let's make an end of this one, let's make it into a cul-de-sac. You see my point?'

'Except I don't see any parallel between being in prison and being here.'

'That's exactly the thing we've got to decide. That's exactly what our friend meant by saying we've got a difficult decision. I'm going to argue in favour of us both leaving. You take the

417

other line. Then we must sleep on it and each make up his own mind about it.'

So we started. It was a long talk, very long, so I will give only a condensed version of what John said.

'Try to see what we're in,' began John. 'We're in a fossilized society. They've decided, completely as a matter of policy, that they're not going to change. They're not going to seek after progress. They're satisfied with the way life is. For them this may be fine but to us it would be a living death. We have a drive that forces us towards further achievement. Of course it may be quite illusory, probably it is. But being the way we are I think we would find it very much an imprisonment.'

'I don't see there's anything to stop us from going on doing the things we want to do.'

'I see plenty. I've got several thousand years of scientific development to learn before I could possibly get down to any really useful work. Of course it would be interesting enough to begin with. There'd be the solution to the problems that I know about. In a way it would be marvellous to read about it all. But just think of the years of grind and drudgery that would be needed before I could do anything at all creative. It's likely I'd never succeed. You've got to begin as a child, with a child's ability to learn, if you're to break through the wall of an entirely new civilization. I'm afraid I should be reduced to a useless potterer.

'You yourself may be a little better off. The kind of music you know of has some validity. In fact you've got more or less a completely open field. Yet even your position wouldn't be too good. These people may have a liking for music, they may be able to compose it, but none of them can actually play. You can see for yourself that everything is done electronically. Perhaps you would get them to sing but that would be about all. You would never hear a real orchestra again.

'These are the bigger issues but think of the smaller ones. There are a million and one simple things these people take for granted. Yet they'd all be strange to us. It's fine enough for a few days, but think how it'd be for a whole lifetime. We'd never really belong. We'd never again hear our own language spoken, except through an artificial electronic device. Remember Art Clementi and his boys. Remember the night you were first in La Jolla. It was all very wild and woolly maybe com-

418

pared to these people. But wouldn't you come to ache for some of the zip and zest of that old life? In a way it was very squalid, but it had a vigour we should miss terribly. Remember we're not just walking out into nothingness. We're simply saying that this is a life we don't want to live, just as these people themselves have refused to follow a life of what we are pleased to call progress. Logically I can go along with them, but emotionally I'm not conditioned to their sort of existence.'

This is the main substance of what he said. I lay awake a long time that night. Even when I did get to sleep it was a troubled sleep. It was clear to me that John had already made up his mind to leave. If I stayed I'd be entirely alone. The point about never again hearing my own language hit me heavily, more than some of the logical arguments. It was true that within a few months or a year I would learn the language of these people, just as I had learnt to get along in Greek. But obviously there would always be a hankering back to the language of my youth.

I saw I would make pilgrimages back to my old home. There would be nothing but wild country. The glens of the Highlands would be much the same as I had known them. The shape of the hills would be the same. There would still be the hidden valley down which John and I had walked, apparently only a few months ago. But there would be no people, anywhere. I would make one or two such pilgrimages. Then I would go no longer, for the sadness of it all, the knowledge of what had happened, would be borne in on me too heavily. If I stayed here I would be in a kind of psychological no man's land. On the one side there would be a civilization which I liked but which I was not really a part of, on the other side there would be the vivid memories of my own people, and the knowledge of what they had come to suffer.

The following morning Melea and her friend were there. John told them we had decided to leave. Melea said that transportation arrangements had already been made. It was a sad little breakfast we had together. The time for departure came. We all agreed that delay would be bad. I took one last look around. There was the electronic box, the thing I had come to think of as a piano, looking now strangely pathetic. I had a strong urge to play on it for one last time. I told the

others, saying I would prefer to be alone, that I would follow
in a few minutes. Melea answered:

'Don't be too long. There isn't much time.'

I began to play. I realized that only in music could I find the
answer I was seeking to the questions of the previous evening.
Argument I could follow, it weighed with me, yet I could
decide nothing from it. I did not know exactly what the music
was, it was an improvisation not so much on a musical theme
as on the agony of the destiny of man. I continued to play on
and on, aware at last that I had made my commitment. I was
playing the Schubert Andantino when Melea returned.

15 Coda

The prognostications were correct. Within a few hours of the departure of John Sinclair the world reverted to 'normal'. The England of 1966, the Europe of 1917, the Greece of 425 B.C., all vanished just as remarkably as they had appeared. I have not seen John again, nor do I think there is the smallest possibility I will ever do so.

Although much more science is known here than was known in the world of 1966, the detailed operation of the singular mixing of epochs is not well understood. As I make it out, issues involving time-reversal were involved, but the physics of the matter is not within my competence. What *is* quite certain is that the affair was brought about from a higher level of perception than our own. That such levels exist seems reasonable. That we ourselves are unable to comprehend the thoughts, the actions, the technology perhaps, of an intelligence of a higher order also seems reasonable. Disturb a stone and watch ants scurrying hither and thither underneath it. Can those ants comprehend what it is that has suddenly turned their tight little world upside down? I think not. It emerges very clearly that humanity can also be stirred up at any time, just like ants under a stone.

Two years have passed since these events. I have learned the new language. I no longer speak any English. For the most part this causes no distress. Yet occasionally a pang sears through me, an overriding desire to hear the old sounds again. I began this present narrative while in such a mood, feeling that if I couldn't speak my native language with any purpose I might at least write it.

In these two years I have composed a great deal of music. I do not compose nowadays for plaudits, for box office, or to please critics. I compose simply to please myself and my friends. I have returned to Europe, to England and even to Glencoe. I have climbed Bidean nam Bian again, followed the same ridge and come down into the same hidden valley. There is no village of Glencoe, no Macdonalds and Campbells to feud with each other, no motorists touring the glen. The country is entirely wild and still more beautiful.

More and more the old life has become vague and remote, like the memories of distant childhood. This gradual evaporation of a life which at one time was so intensely vibrant has come upon me with profound sadness. In these pages I have been able in some measure to give a sense of reality to what are now mere outlines in a gathering mist. Yet one detail stands out harsh and stark.

The day John Sinclair was missing from the caravan on the moors below Mickle Fell, I myself had the impression of a time gap of about two hours, between six and nine in the evening. I bitterly regret that I did not mention this impression to John. Of course I couldn't be at all sure I hadn't simply nodded off to sleep. I didn't want to appear to be dramatizing myself. Then subsequent events soon swept the incident out of my mind. Yet I suspect this small detail – reconsidered in the light of all that followed – assumes a deep significance. Accepting a bifurcation of worlds, accepting the copying process which John himself believed in so strongly, accepting his view that it was an apparition, a copy of himself, who returned to the caravan after the gap of nine hours, could it have been a copy of myself who was waiting there to receive him, another apparition who cooked the meal when he said he was so devilishly hungry?

After the bifurcation there were two worlds, the straightforward world of 1966 in which nothing particularly unusual happened, and this strange new world belonging to the people of the future. Which of these worlds got our copies, which got the 'originals'? We both took it for granted that the copies went to the new world, copies of everything, of the Prime Minister, of our Australian pilot. This presumption may well have been correct except for the two of us. For us it may well have been the world of 1966 which had the apparitions.

Why the two of us? Why should just the two of us be different? Because we were just the two who managed to penetrate into the territory of the people of the future. John always thought of this penetration as accidental. He laughed about my getting through to Greece, about my encounter with

Melea in the temple on the hill. But was it really an accident? Hardly I think, for it fits too smoothly into a pattern, a pattern that would have been completed if John had elected to stay here, a pattern in which 'copies' vanished and 'originals' remained.

After the bifurcation in Hawaii, I was in the company of John Sinclair for a mere ten days. If at any time during those ten days I had looked for it I strongly suspect I would have found John's old birthmark. The birthmark was a tell-tale clue giving away the whole story. An opportunity did indeed fall our way, perhaps was even deliberately put in our way, the day of our trip to Popocatepetl, the day when we all got so very wet on the return journey. But for the sexual distraction of the two girls being there as we dried off, the mark would very probably have been noticed. I have no doubt now it was the real John Sinclair who was sent out from here – into oblivion. The irony and tragedy is that to the two of us it was the world of 1966 that was the real cul-de-sac.

Fifth Planet

Fifth Planet

Preface

The very nature of the plot has forced us to set this story in the more distant future than we would otherwise have preferred. It is hardly possible to foresee the shape of society a century or more ahead of one's own time, and we have not attempted to do so. Instead we have been content to extrapolate those social trends that can plainly be seen at the moment. The story was written in August 1962. We mention this to bring out the prediction – we take a little pride in its apparent correctness – at the foot of page 22. We do not know whether to hope or fear that other predictions of the story will turn out to possess a similar validity.

The basis of the plot is to be found on pages 208 to 210. However, to avoid too much interruption of the narrative, the ideas mentioned in these pages have been shortened as far as possible. Physics regards the world as four dimensional. All moments of time exist together. The world can be thought of as a map, not only spatially, but also with respect to time. The map stretches away both into the past and into the future. There is no such thing as 'waiting' for the future. It is already there in the map.

Two problems arise out of this. The first is the so-called 'arrow of time'. Events occur in the map in definite sequences. Light emerges from a torch after you press the switch. The emphasis here is not on the word 'after' – it would be possible to turn the map round, to count time backwards, as we do in counting years B.C. Then one would say that light emerges from the torch *before* one presses the switch. This is simply a trivial inversion. What is not trivial is that light does not emerge *both* before and after the pressing of the switch.

Events do not occur symmetrically with respect to time. In the case of the torch there is an asymmetry whichever way we elect to read the map. It is this asymmetry that we refer to as the arrow of time. The 'future' part of the map is radically different from the 'past', and this is true whichever way we turn the map.

Physics has made a good deal of progress in understanding this problem. The arrow of time may not be completely resolved, but at any rate it is being grappled with. The same cannot be said for the second problem.

What constitutes the present? Provided one considers oneself as something apart from the physical world, the answer does not seem difficult. The present can be thought of as the particular place in the map where you happen to be. It is your subjective presence at a particular spot that defines the present. But you cannot have your cake and eat it. You cannot consider your subjective presence as being outside the physical world and in the same breath consider yourself as a part of the map.

According to science, a human is an animal. He takes his place in the map along with all other physical events. In fact the events that constitute the human are confined to a four-dimensional tube, a world tube, that threads its way over a finite portion of the map. What then is the subjective present? It is certainly not the whole collection of events inside one's own personal tube, otherwise we should live the whole of our lives all at once, like playing a sonata simply by pressing the whole keyboard. Stated more precisely, the subjective present consists not of the complete collection of events but of a certain subset. How is the subset defined?

Certain clear technical issues now appear. Is the subset such that one particular member has a time-like displacement to all other members? In that case the other members could have a causal connexion to the particular member. But if so, how is the particular member of the subset chosen?

There seems to be no way of coping with issues such as these except by admitting that something else besides the four-dimensional world tube is needed. Something else outside what science would normally describe as the animal itself.

This approach need not be mystic. The required subset could be defined mathematically as the intersection of the world tube with a three-dimensional space-like surface. Thus a surface

$$\phi\ (x^1,\ x^2,\ x^3,\ x^4) = c$$

for a particular value of c, and with $\partial\phi/\partial x^i$ $(i = 1,2,3,4)$ a time-like vector, serves to define a subset of points in the world tube. Changing c changes the subset. We could be said to live our lives through changes of c – i.e. by sweeping through a family of surfaces.

It is plausible that the subjective present has a mathematical structure of this kind. But what then are the ϕ surfaces? Could they be derived from known physical fields, for example from the electromagnetic field? That is to say, is the subjective present really controlled by normal sensory data? An obvious way of testing this possibility would be to keep the known external fields constant and to consider whether the subjective present can be considered to change.

Our impression – no more than an impression – is that changes of the subjective present do occur under conditions where the external electromagnetic field, for example, is essentially unchanged. As a rather imprecise example of what we mean, suppose two visits separated by many years are made to a particular place – say, to a mountain – and suppose the weather and the lighting conditions are generally similar on the two occasions. Exact identity of condition is of course impossible, but we find it difficult to believe that major differences of the subjective present, such as might be felt by an individual, are determined by slight, and perhaps even unnoticed, changes in the external conditions – e.g. by the slight shift in the disposition of grass and boulders on a mountainside.

The ϕ surfaces we feel must have the property of not being closely reproducible in the sense of this example. The fantasy of the present story lies in the properties we have ascribed to these surfaces, in fact to the functional behaviour of ϕ.

6 April 1963   **F. H.**
                                                         G. H.

Contents

Contents

Chapter One

Night Thoughts

Hugh Conway shifted uneasily. An hour before his wife had come to him with such fervour that he knew she must have been unfaithful again. He could hear her soft breathing, a more regular rhythm than his own. It wasn't surprising, not with Cathy's beauty, the completely flawless beauty that you couldn't take your eyes off; the sort of beauty that you had to see, that couldn't be described, photographed, or painted. They had been married for ten years, and still Conway couldn't keep his eyes off her even though he knew it annoyed her. Even other women, women who might spend hours in front of a mirror, acknowledged it. For compensation they shook their heads and said sharply it was a pity Cathy had not been equally blessed with brains.

For ten years Conway had been on the hook. For ten years they had staggered from one domestic crisis to another, from one social absurdity to another. Things had seemed to be going better during the last few months, but now this new affair had started. The odd thing was that in the abstract he valued intelligence more than beauty. In the last few years there had been half a dozen other women that he'd liked, that he could talk sensibly to, and that he'd have been happy with. More than once he'd made up his mind to put an end to the inane, futile life with Cathy. But then, in some unguarded moment, he'd be riveted again; the old chemistry would start up in his blood, and that would be it. He wondered why Cathy herself didn't break it up. She only despised him for his weakness. Probably she regarded him as a convenient base from which to conduct her operations.

Literary types had always written their own variations on

the theme of 'Love and War'. But only a hundred years ago they'd been talking about there being two cultures. Now the old literary culture was dead, and the scientific culture, if by that you meant physics, wasn't in much better shape. Their places had been taken by a new culture.

What a tiger he'd have been if he'd lived in the middle of the last century, and known what he knew now. Conway allowed his thoughts to play with the prospects. It was, he decided, the confusion of the present that was the devil. Being a good scientist didn't help. It only made you more keenly aware of the uncertainties of the future. The 1960s was the time when they'd first thought of going to the moon. He could have told them exactly what they'd find when they got there. There'd been quite a bit of argument about whether they'd find dust or lava. As it turned out they'd found both. Funny to think now that that first trip to the moon has set the whole world alight. It had been the touchstone of national prestige. Now it was just a pinpoint in the past. Today the world was alight again. Everybody said it was the biggest thing ever; and for once, Conway thought, everybody was right. Funny too to think that in 1960 they hadn't had the slightest suspicion about it

Even as recently as a hundred years ago the astronomers had known almost nothing about the proper motions of the stars. The line of sight motions were, of course, known from the Doppler shift. But the transverse motions, even of quite near-by stars, only caused them to change their directions by a few tenths of a second of an arc each year. It hadn't been until the coming of high-quality satellite telescopes that angles as small as this could be measured in any particular year, although over twenty or thirty years it would have been possible to measure the cumulative effect from the ground. But nobody had been willing to start a programme that wouldn't pay off results for thirty years. So, not until the nineties of the last century did the proper motions begin to be really well known. Not until then was it possible to decide just how each individual star was moving in space.

The same sort of measurements, parallax measurements, had given accurate distances to the stars – at any rate, for distances up to a thousand light years. And with the distances and motions fully known, it was possible to build a model of how all the stars were moving in the neighbourhood of the Sun. With the solar system at the centre, you could imagine each star represented by a little dot. Attached to each dot was an arrow, the direction of the arrow showing where the star was moving, and the length of the arrow showing how fast the star was moving. That was the first stage. Then you had to make a correction. If you wanted a model of the stars as they are now at the present moment you had to allow for the fact that we do not see the direction of the stars as they are, but only as they were at the moment when the light started out on its journey to us. If you want the model as it is now you have to move each star a bit along the direction of its arrow. The amount you have to move a particular star depends on two things – its speed of motion and its distance. The distance, because there has been more delay in the light from a distant star than from a near-by one. And the speed for the obvious reason that a star moves more out of its position every year the faster it is moving.

Suppose that all this has been done and that you have a model showing the positions and motions of the stars as they are now. Then by following each star in turn along its appropriate arrow you can find out where they will all be a year from now. Or ten years from now. Or a hundred years from now. In fact, you can find out whether any two arrows will meet each other. If any two arrows do meet each other you know that some time in the future those two particular stars will come near to each other. Of course they can hardly be expected to collide, for stars are very tiny things compared to the distances between them. A direct collision is vastly improbable, but a close approach is quite another matter.

Conway began to figure the probabilities. Assume an approach within twenty astronomical units, the distance of the planet Uranus from the Sun. That gives a target area of ten to the minus eight square parsecs. Taking thirty kilometres per second as the average speed of the stars relative to any particular star, and taking the mean density of the stars as one per cubic parsec, the chance of an approach to any special star was just ten to the minus eight for every thirty thousand years. So over three billion years the chance was one in a thousand. In the lifetime of the solar system there had been one chance in a thousand of just such an approach of another star, and this really wasn't very long odds. Taking all stars together, there had been more than a hundred million approaches between pairs of them during the whole history of the Galaxy.

All this the men of the twentieth century would have followed. And they wouldn't have been particularly surprised to learn that the Sun was going to be one of these hundred million cases. The unexpected thing was that this particular moment – the late twenty-first century – was the time of the encounter. It wasn't a billion years ago, and it was unlikely to be a billion years hence. It would be now, the year 2087.

A special name had to be found for the approaching star. At an early stage, helium lines were detected in the spectrum, so it had seemed obvious to use the Greek name for the Sun, Helios. This was towards the end of the twentieth century, before the last remnants of a classical culture were lost.

Of course, it wasn't clear to begin with just how close Helios would approach the Sun. The target area was very small, so that small errors of measurement led to big errors in the answers. The first estimates gave a distance of closest approach that exceeded ten thousand astronomical units, that is, about three hundred times the distance of the farthest planet, Pluto. Then a half century of unremitting effort showed that the approach was to be a good deal nearer than this. By the year 2025 the best estimate was a thousand astronomical units, 961 to be more precise.

The mounting interest of the public had helped to maintain the popularity of the physical sciences at a time when nuclear physics and the study of elementary particles were steeply in decline – the latter because it had become too difficult. Fundamental astronomy was once more in vogue. As Helios came closer it became easier to make accurate measurements. During the sixties, excitement mounted furiously as it became more and more clear that Helios would actually move inside the orbits of the outer planets. By 2070, a definitive value was obtained. At its closest, Helios would be a mere twenty astronomical units from the Sun. It would be 15,000 times brighter than the full moon, although at that distance it would still have only a fortieth of the brightness of the Sun itself.

The orbit of the Earth would be disturbed, but not enormously so. After Helios had receded away again the Earth's path around the Sun would be more elliptical than it was before. This would be the main effect. The result would be an accentuation, not enormous, but certainly perceptible, of the seasons of the year. And the year itself would certainly be changed from the immemorial $365\frac{1}{4}$ days. But nobody knew yet exactly what the changes would be.

If the effects on the Earth's motion were to be comparatively slight, this was manifestly not the case for the outer planets of the solar system. Helios would exert as big an influence on these as the Sun did. Indeed there was a likelihood that the three outer planets, Uranus, Neptune, and Pluto, would be stripped away entirely from our system.

Because Helios was to penetrate our system it was clear that we should penetrate the planets of Helios itself, if the incoming star had any planets. Astronomical theories showed that this was a marginal issue. The larger mass of Helios was a point against the existence of a planetary system. But it was quickly pointed out that Helios was spinning around only very slowly, like the Sun, and this scarcely seemed credible unless a system of planets had indeed developed. In the event, just at the turn of the century, two planets were in fact detected observationally. They were large fellows, like Jupiter in our own system. Their American discoverers named them Hera and Semele.

This was before the development of quantitative social studies had changed our cultural and intellectual standards, before those philosophers of the nineteenth and twentieth centuries who had inquired into the nature of man's thinking had attained a popular distinction exceeding Newton and Einstein. The new fashion was to have its opportunities, however. For when, forty years later, two further planets were detected, of about the size of our own Uranus, they were named Hegel and Kierkegaard.

And now a fifth planet had been found only a few months ago, by Conway himself. It was much smaller than the others and had therefore been difficult to pick up against the background glare of Helios. It was much more like the earth in size. Apart from this simple fact, little so far was known about it. Conway's mind ranged over plans for the future. There was a tradition that whoever discovered a new planet had the honour of naming it, like the rule that had operated a century or more ago in the naming of the chemical elements. Conway smiled to himself in the darkness. Because he was British and because the British, according to the rest of the world, were still immersed in the twentieth century, he had refused widespread international pressure to adopt the name Spinoza. Instead he had called it – Achilles.

Chapter Two

Tight Little Island

Hugh Conway scraped a fragment of butter over a piece of hard half-burnt toast. Cathy made a pretence of reading *The Times*. The financial page too, Hugh noticed, as he cocked an eye over the top of the paper. He studied the flawless complexion and the pile of dark, soft chestnut curls, thinking, for perhaps the millionth time, that he was an ass. She put down the paper and looked at him squarely with deep-blue killer eyes.

'Well?' she said.

'We're having another conference. I'll probably be away about five days. And I was wondering if you'd like to make a trip up to Town.'

That was the last thing she'd been expecting. With a wary flash she came back at him, 'How much? How much can I spend?'

Hugh knew that a few days in London, spent in the intimate company of some new boy-friend, was exactly what Cathy had been scheming towards. By offering her the trip on a plate he'd forced her back on to her final line of defence – money. He smiled wryly.

'I'm overdrawn at the bank. And I'm not paid till the end of June. If you look up at the top of the paper you'll see that it is still only the middle of May.'

'Bob Shaw doesn't have any difficulty about money,' returned Cathy with the merest twitch of her nose, 'and he's only a rag-bag of a fellow, as you always say.'

Hugh snorted, 'Property development. Property development in Slough.'

'Well, why not?'

'I'm not putting my slender resources into any development in Slough, even if the Americans are taking to the place.'

Elbow on table, Cathy cupped her chin in her right hand, 'You could do something better, couldn't you?'

Hugh smiled now. 'It is my job to do something better.'

He paused for a moment. Then shot it straight out, 'Well, who is it this time?'

She looked blankly across the table, the soul of innocence. 'What do you mean?'

'You know damned well what I mean. Who is it?'

Cathy giggled, 'I thought it was a mouse. It turned out to be a tiger.'

'Stop being absurd.'

'I'm not being absurd.'

Hugh put his second boiled egg into the cup and absently began to crack the top.

Cathy now had the bit between her teeth. 'I don't ask you who you sleep with when you're away.' She smiled broadly, and Hugh felt the old, but still sharp, pangs of jealousy.

'I don't sleep with anybody,' he exploded.

'Don't you, darling? Well if you did I wouldn't want to know about it.'

Cathy leant back in her chair so that her hair fell backwards, as if to suggest that the subject was closed.

'You know perfectly well we're not talking about me.'

'No? If I should sleep with another man, what does it matter to you, so long as you don't know about it.'

'Of course it matters.'

'Why?'

'Because it affects both of us.'

Cathy pondered this for a moment. Then wrinkling her face to show that she was making a serious effort she said, 'If you don't know about it, it can't affect you, can it? If it was to affect me, then it would be wrong. But I don't allow it to affect me, do I?'

With a vicious stab of his spoon, Hugh sliced the top off the egg. It was hard-boiled.

'It's hard-boiled,' he yapped.

Cathy looked down at the egg as if she had never seen one before. 'You're always making a fuss about things that don't matter.'

'But the first one,' he nittered, pointing to the bits of shell on his plate, 'the first one was soft-boiled. It was so soft-boiled that if I'd held it up the whole egg would have run out.'

Cathy stretched herself lazily, 'Just like the two of us, dear. You hard-boiled, me soft-boiled.'

Fuming helplessly, Hugh jumped up from the table. He stalked from the breakfast-room to his study, stuffed a pile of papers which he had been reading the previous evening into his brief-case, walked back to the kitchen, and shouted, 'Those eggs are substandard.' Then he stormed out of the house, thinking that, in an age of female emancipation, the arguments of patriarchy were no match for those of matriarchy.

When he had gone, Cathy took on an air of set purpose. She went to the telephone, dialled, and got a wrong number. Deciding that she was using the wrong code, she consulted a small red notebook. Very deliberately, reading the numbers as if they were some strange hieroglyphs, she tried again. A voice answered.

'Will you put me through to Mike Fawsett, please?'

There were two ways of going between the Conways' house in the sleepy village of Alderbourne and the Helios Project Centre at Harwell, the site of which had been a nuclear research establishment in the dim distant days. There was the super-S highway, or the winding, tree-shaded lane that had not changed much since the eighteenth century. In fact, the whole English countryside had not altered much since the eighteenth century. In the last hundred years the population of the British Isles had risen from fifty to seventy millions, but the increase in building had been almost entirely in the cities. In spite of their growth, the cities hadn't managed to achieve quite the same sprawling, amorphous character as had their American counterparts; Los Angeles had now stretched out as far as Albuquerque, which perhaps explained why Americans were favourably disposed towards a property development in Slough.

Hugh decided that he was too furious to risk driving along the highway and took the country road. The may hedges were in blossom, and it was all quietly beautiful as he followed the ridge of the Downs. By this route he came into the Helios Centre from above. On impulse he parked the car and got out to stretch his legs. Then, squatting on the grass, he gazed down on the Centre, the Centre where the decisions affecting man's greatest adventure would be made. He sighed softly as he contrasted the grandeur of the world of ideas with his own petty domestic squabblings. The buildings below shone brightly in the sun, reflecting gold mixed with opalescent blues.

Ten minutes more brought him to the parking-lot, the one sordid spot in the Centre. Five minutes' walk, and he entered a long, curving, strip-like building, made of glass and metal. The staircase had the sweep and magnificence of an eighteenth-century manor house. His feet made no sound as he walked up the steps. A light ahead beckoned him as he strolled, silently, down a long, curving corridor. Turning off the corridor, he went into a room that almost defies description. It was not small, but neither was it very large. It was not barely furnished or decorated, but it would be difficult to say just what materials had been used in order to set it out. It was entirely silent to the tread, as had been the corridor and the staircase, but it was not entirely silent. There was a faint hum of electric motors. There was a magnificent old table in the centre. But the dignified effect was spoilt by a dozen or more absurd pads of white paper spaced at regular intervals around it. This was the Committee Room.

By this time all important decisions affecting the structure

of human society were taken in committee. Everybody knew
that the system was wrong, but by now no one had the power
to stop it. No committee was willing to vote to destroy itself.
In the early days a few men had found themselves, more or
less by chance, to be possessors of the power to persuade their
colleagues – they were natural intellectual salesmen. And
like good salesmen, who can dispose of anything under the
sun, they could get their way on any matter, however absurd.
What had begun as a purely amateur sport had gradually
developed into stark professionalism. Nowadays one did not
become a good committee man by chance. One became a
good committee man by sheer unremitting effort in which
every working moment was spent in planning and scheming
how to operate. But not all committee men were good. There
had to be some who were bad, simply because some members had to possess an adequate knowledge of the essential
facts. It was by now quite impossible both to be a good committee man and to know anything. The trouble, of course,
was that those who knew what they were talking about
never got their own way, although supporters of the system
claimed that this was a good thing.

Hugh was one of the first to arrive. He busied himself in
a futile, unprofessional way with his papers. Even though
there was something he wanted from this particular meeting, his mind wandered from the business in hand. He jerked
his thoughts back from Cathy. He must try to remember that
only one other member of the Committee would be British.
He must try to remember the motives and opinions of the
other members, to put himself inside their skins. Above all,
he must try to make use of the complex of emotions that had
led to the Helios Centre being built in Britain.

The common man of the twentieth century would have
been surprised to have learnt just how far the trends of his
own day had been carried through into the twenty-first
century, just how far the logic of ideas had been pressed. The
development of the deterrent is, of course, an outstanding
example. To our innocent ancestors, civil defence meant

443

exactly what it said, defence to protect the civil population, to protect the man in the street. To us now, this is an outrageously archaic notion. In fact, two-thirds of the way through the twentieth century, a few perceptive pioneers had already realized that civil defence was to become the outstanding weapon of aggression. With ruthlessly effective civil defence a nation could afford nuclear war – almost. And if the other side couldn't afford it at all, you could bully him just as much as you pleased. So what started as the sole concern of the individual became a matter of major national policy, in America, in Europe, in Russia, and China. Refusal to take part in effective civil defence programmes became a treasonable crime. It seems laughable now to think that at one time civil defence consisted merely of building a shelter in one's own garden. As we all know, effective defence lies in evacuating whole cities at a moment's notice, in fact at the very worst and most inconvenient moments. And, of course, one cannot be said to be prepared to do this unless one actually does it. Remorselessly. This means that the times of evacuation cannot be announced beforehand, it is the essence of the matter that people must not be prepared. The warning comes in the middle of a wedding, a funeral, a confinement. It causes the restaurants of the Champs-Elysées to disgorge their diners into the street, gourmets with their napkins still tucked into their collars. All this in the interests of *l'honneur*.

Through a series of accidents the British had escaped all this. In the sixties of the last century their politicians had at last realized that power had become a shadow. A little genuine power could be won, however, by joining in a United Europe. This they earnestly strove to do, but their efforts were thwarted through a series of mischances, an intransigent French president, the conservatism of their own people at home, and the lack of conservatism of the people abroad. At all events, the British were kept outside, and power vanished for ever from Whitehall. Gone was the need for expensive military budgets or for the remorseless logic of the deterrent. The British slept in their beds, the forgotten men of the twenty-first century.

Or not quite forgotten. For to the harassed American, the ulcerous Russian, the thought of a few weeks' holiday in London became indescribably precious. New York became almost entirely automatized, Paris became the city with thoughts only for the glorious future, in Moscow puritanism lay like a dead hand on the people. Only in London could one dine in peace. Only in London could one follow dinner with a little play that didn't matter at all.

Because of its enormous attraction for tourists Britain was extremely prosperous. Other parts of the world, Africa in particular, split themselves asunder in their rivalries, in their attempts each to become the workshop of the world. Small financial crises triggered each other across the globe like falling rows of skittles. And throughout all this the British lent money here and there on profitable terms, as the Swiss had done a century earlier.

The Swiss at last abandoned their neutral position and threw in their lot with Europe. Communication through radio and the aeroplane, prosperity and power, achieved what invading armies could not do. It was the enormously rising prestige of Europe that did it. The Swiss gained status by joining, it was like marrying the daughter of a noble house. One effect was that the various small international organizations that had made Switzerland their home felt obliged to seek new quarters. Britain by now had become the obvious place. After all, what was Britain except a raft afloat in the sea, a raft exposed to the wind and weather, populated by a calm people who went about their business without ever realizing that the world was a serious place to live in? It was just the place for bored international secretariats to move to.

The decision to build the Helios Centre in Britain was a more serious affair, however. This was not a small matter. Its ramifications affected every major nation in the world. And just for this reason it could not be placed in any one of

445

those major nations. Quite obviously the Russo-Chinese bloc would not permit the Centre to be sited in the territory of the Euro-American bloc. And, of course, vice versa. Africa was too hot, dusty, and industrial. South America was a serious possibility, but the fact that most interested parties were in the Northern Hemisphere, the attractions of London, and the precedence established by other International Agencies, swayed the day. So the Helios Project came to be established at Harwell.

Around the year 2040, the British Government made an attempt to get itself back into the power complex in a small feeble way. The belt of power spreads in an ominous girdle across the northern latitudes of the Earth. The two division points, one in the Bering Strait, the other to the east of Germany, unified during the short period of Western ascendancy in the 1990s. The West is the West, America and Europe, and the East is the East, Russia and China. The leaders of neither group want war, for war would put an effective end to the exercise of their power. But neither do they want a cessation of tension, for this also would produce an important down-grading of their functions. Besides, it had been proved mathematically by the social scientists, now dominant and rampant, that a world without tension would be a world in decline. The problem is to live with tension without allowing it ever to break loose. Our main safety factor lies in our ability to predict, again with mathematical precision, just what the other side will do in a given set of circumstances. Unpredictable behaviour by either side would soon lead to disaster.

All this was first recognized, long, long ago by the scientists of the Rand Corporation, a decade or so before that organization took over the effective control of American policy from the Pentagon. To begin with, the fly in the ointment was that one side didn't quite know the basis on which the other side made its calculations. Without this knowledge things could go wrong – they could become unstable, as the mathematicians said. Nobody at first had the impudence to suggest the obvious solution. But little by little steps were taken towards it. A hundred years ago the most closely guarded secrets were those that concerned methods of calculation, military logistics as it was then called. Then secrecy was gradually relaxed. Papers on the subject began to be published quite openly. Finally, after a series of seventeen summit meetings, the answer was reached, the answer that an intelligent child might have arrived at after five minutes' study. The military planners of both sides should get together to discuss their suppositions and hypotheses. So it came about that biannual meetings between the planners and mathematicians of both sides were arranged. The meetings would allow them not only to make sure they understood each other but to arrive at a common basis for future developments. The seminar was the answer. But the question immediately arose where the meetings should be held. It was here that the British Government made its bid. The meetings should obviously be held in Britain, that raft in the middle of the ocean, beholden to neither side. But, of course, this was not to be. It was decided that the meetings be held alternately, first on the one side, then on the other. That is why they were arranged biannually, and have been so ever since.

'Gentlemen, the meeting is integrated,' boomed the voice of the Chairman, 'the time is half past nine.'

Conway wrenched his mind back to Helios and today's meeting. He thought to himself, not for the first time, how screamingly boring it all was. How boring compared with the world of ideas!

Chapter Three

First Preparations

Conway had known that this would be a critical meeting. He had never before had to sit in on anything quite like it. Very difficult decisions had to be taken, and lives would depend upon them. And the meeting wasn't properly constituted; it didn't have the right technical knowledge, it was too high-level for that. There were still higher levels, of course, but it was unlikely that anyone would have the energy or determination to change what this committee decided.

The first part of the meeting, up to coffee-time at eleven o'clock, was taken up mainly by four speakers. There was Dr Hoddas, a Hungarian. Conway, as he drank his coffee, would have been in some difficulty to remember a single word that Dr Hoddas had said. For Conway had long since learnt the art of not listening. If you listened to everything that was said you became utterly exhausted and were unable to take effective part when the really important issues came up for discussion. In fact, the exhausting of a meeting with pretentious inconsequential nonsense was a part of the technique of a good committee man. It was also part of Dr Hoddas's technique to speak in a guttural French. He was equipped with a large dictionary in which he insisted on looking up words and phrases.

Professor Bombas from Tanganyika had urged that, whatever decisions were taken, the small nations should not be left out. Conway wondered just what he meant by this. Perhaps that the metal coils be made in Togoland, the graphite chambers in Colombia, the computer in Greenland, and the whole thing assembled by a friendly consortium of Americans and Russians. If so, God help the crew.

Doctor Leyburn, the economist, wanted decisions to be taken as soon as possible, so that exactly what was involved financially could become known to the respective governments. Conway also wanted the decisions to be taken, but for a different reason, because Helios and its retinue of planets was approaching them by seventy kilometres in every second, and the later they started the harder would everything become. Irichenko wanted parity. Whatever the West was going to do, the East would do and, of course, vice versa. He emphasized this critical observation with an enormous blow on the table, and was on the point of raising his fist for a second time when he remembered that emphasis was regarded as bad form in the West.

The after-coffee-pre-lunch session was worse. They spent it discussing whether they would go for a landing, instead of simply sweeping in orbit around the planets of the Helios system. They decided they would go for a landing. Conway had known that would be the decision. It was so inevitable that it could have been decided in thirty seconds.

The next question, which they closed in on after lunch, a lunch of five courses and four wines, was – which planet? There was of course only one possibility, Achilles. But nobody was going to admit this. Long reports on the four big fellows, Hera, Semele, and the two philosophical planets, were read out. It was just as impossible to make a landing on them as it was to make a landing on Jupiter or Saturn. So it all came back to Achilles. The point of course was that Conway, as the discoverer of Achilles, had to have his position devalued. It was a basic rule that no technical expert should be allowed to get on top of a committee. It was time for him to speak up: 'Mr Chairman, there is an important point that I'd like to draw the Committee's attention to,' he began. 'Really we know very little about the surface of Achilles. It may be just as hostile as the surfaces of the other four.'

There was a staccato burst of Russian from Irichenko. It was translated to Conway as, 'Why don't we know?'

'Because it's a small planet, and it's still very far away.' Conway allowed a silence to fall. He knew they must come back to him. The Chairman writhed in his seat, squirmed his neck, and said, 'Well, Professor Conway?'

'My point, sir, is that the whole question is so uncertain that it might be better if we contented ourselves with a purely orbital flight.'

There was a shocked silence. Heads turned in his direction.

'But, Professor Conway,' said the Chairman in an unnaturally soft voice, 'we've already decided that. We've already decided that we're going to go for a landing.' He spoke as if to an idiot child. Everybody felt superior to him. Within ten more minutes they'd decided to make a landing on Achilles.

That was as far as they got the first day. As they walked out of the room, mumbling as they went, it didn't seem to occur to them that perhaps the most momentous decision in the history of mankind had just been taken. For quite certainly the decision had now been taken, irrevocably taken. In theory the decision could be revoked by higher authorities, but it wouldn't be. In theory all decisions were in the hands of a few men, but those few couldn't possibly be familiar with the details of every problem. They were obliged to take advice from below. Provided a committee was properly constituted, provided all relevant matters were fully discussed, advice was never refused. Society had worked itself into a position where it was as much as the top men could do to rubberstamp the decisions of those below them.

If Conway had been a good committee man, he would have gone with the rest of them to the hotel, he would have dined with a few selected colleagues, and he would have tried to lobby them on the matters he knew must come up for discussion the following day. But because he was not a good committee man he decided to go home, to see whether Cathy had taken up his suggestion of a visit to town. To his intense chagrin he found that she had. Furious, he poured himself a stiff drink and bit savagely into his lonely sandwich.

Cathy paid off the taxi-cab. She allowed it to drive away before making sure that the man had brought her to the right place. The lighting outside the restaurant was subdued rather than bright. She could just make out the name, La Riviera. It was the right place, it had never occurred to her that it mightn't be.

Mike was waiting for her. He was a big powerful fellow, with shortish hair, handsome rather than good-looking. In his official dossier he was described as well coordinated, and the figures given for his reaction times were very good indeed.

He grinned affectionately. 'Hello there, Cat. How about a drink?'

If Conway had seen them move together to the bar he'd have grinned wryly and thought that Cathy always chose them that way, so as to give him a sense of inferiority. But perhaps she worked things the other way round too, perhaps she used his brains to give the Fawsetts of this world a sense of inferiority.

Conway, grimly chewing his supper, thought about the sacredness of the committee system as he did so. 'Why do I feel it's my duty to be there again tomorrow morning?' he demanded of himself. All they would do would be to spend three hours deciding that they'd gone as far as they could go, and that the next stages lay with the technical committees. And after a lot of talk the technical committees would decide that the next stages lay with certain individuals. And at last, when the work lay with individuals, something would get done. What will it matter in forty years' time if I don't go to that meeting tomorrow morning, he thought to himself. I'll probably be dead then anyway. Better to do something that's really important to me, to go straight up to London and bring Cathy back by the scruff of the neck. The decision taken, his mind began to race: how was he to find one person in a city of ten million people?

He felt rather ashamed of himself as he went through the papers in Cathy's desk. But he had to find some sort of a clue as to where she might be. There wasn't much to go on, bills from London stores, cheque stubs – Cathy was astonishingly careful about money – and, surprisingly, a batch of newspaper cuttings. They were all about space expeditions and activities. The news of his own discovery of Achilles was there amongst them.

It took him barely an hour to reach the outskirts of London. When he stopped for petrol he noticed a small café, with the usual mechanical and electronic amusements, where he managed to find change for the phone. Driving along he had been turning over in his mind how best to find Cathy. It would be useless trying to comb endless restaurants and night-clubs, so he dismissed that possible line of inquiry. His original thought of telephoning some of Cathy's favourite dives didn't seem such a good idea either. Why should she go to any of the places they'd been to together? What's the use? he thought to himself, feeling rather ashamed of hunting his wife. Why should he worry? – but he did worry.

He came back to reality just in time to avoid a taxi. He found he had crossed to the south side of the river and was driving aimlessly through Lambeth, heading for Greenwich. He parked by the bridge and spent half an hour staring moodily over the water. Up river, London glowed like a monstrous aurora. He wondered idly about information theory, about exactly how one would formulate his present predicament in a mathematical way. One tiny piece of information, that was all he needed, and he'd be able to find Cathy within half an hour. Without that bit of information he had to go about things in a tortuous elephantine way. Even the police could do no better. There was something terrifyingly anonymous about a really big city.

Still, when you considered that it seemed to be the aim of

society these days to reduce every individual to the status of a punched card, perhaps it wasn't altogether a bad thing. He began to speculate on a future where every place, London even, was controlled by a gigantic computer. It would be obligatory wherever you went, every shop, restaurant, or hotel, even when you walked along the street, to put your own identification card into an electronic scanner. It would be a crime not to do this every quarter of an hour or so. Then the computer would know where everybody was at all times. And you could ask it questions: where is Cathy Conway right now? A small tug hooted as it swirled under the bridge at his feet. Conway shivered as he walked back to his parked car; he had a terrible feeling that he'd just had a vision of the future. It would be easy to justify such a system in the interests of defence and security. The way it would start would be with a few selected individuals, individuals of special importance, who would be flattered by the constant interest in their movements, who would for the most part fall in with the system. Then it would work its way down through the social ladder. People would feel it gave them status. Come to think of it, royal families had lived under the system for centuries.

Conway crossed the river by the Greenwich Bridge. As he wandered along the bank he heard the sound of upbeat music coming from a small dockland pub. He stepped up to the solid oak door, which silently opened.

The dense smoke fumes made his eyes water as he tried to focus on the milieu. A band was playing 'Undecided', a jazz tune from the early twentieth century.

At the bar stood a large blueblood. A red scar ran from his left eye to the corner of his mouth. Leaning against the far end of the bar was a sultry but attractive girl.

Conway threaded his way through empty plastic beer mugs to where the girl was sitting.

'Two Scotches,' he said to the barman. 'Make 'em doubles.'

The girl smiled. The strong liquor began to make him feel

453

more human. She turned and faced him. He could now see that she was slight but well covered, with warm brown eyes which looked at him sympathetically.

'Hey, what's the trouble,' she said, pulling her stool nearer.

'A slight case of jealousy,' replied Conway. 'Two more whiskies, please.'

Conway's troubles began to disappear as he relaxed. He forgot about his mission and concentrated on the girl in hand. She didn't seem very interested to hear his theory on following people's movements.

At the fourth whisky Conway came into his own. He started to talk flippantly about committees and how ridiculous they were.

The girl looked up suddenly and put her finger to his lips. 'Not here, people might get the wrong idea about you.'

'What wrong idea?' Conway said savagely.

'Oh, forget it, would you like to dance?'

As he stood up he felt the pub rocking gently. Somehow he was manoeuvred to the dance floor, where he sagged into the girl's arms.

'Come on, Conway, we can't have this,' he grinned happily to himself.

He felt soft hair brushing against his cheek, like Cathy's. He floated off with the memories of Cathy and himself. Now when she danced like this it was a cover-up for something.

'Ouch, mind my feet.'

'Sorry, I was dreaming.'

'I know,' she smiled resignedly.

'La Jalousie.'

He felt himself being taken back to the bar.

Seated again, he felt more secure and bent solemnly towards her. 'What do you do? I am a physicist.'

'I help people,' came the tart reply.

Conway chuckled, 'That's amazing. I'm glad there are people who still help each other.'

Conway's chuckle echoed as though he were in a large auditorium.

'It's not closing time, is it?' he said to the girl, but she'd gone.

The silence was broken by the scar-faced tough, who was standing over the pianist.

'I said, I don't like it.'

The man at the piano took no notice.

The control in the big man's voice snapped.

'I don't like it,' he screamed.

Conway rose slowly.

'I don't like you or the tune, so why don't – '

The impact on the floor was terrific as Conway hit it. He started to laugh, but stopped suddenly as a boot caught him on the thigh.

Pulling himself up on to the bar-stool, he saw the girl standing by the door with his jacket. Infuriated by the kick, he swung the bar-stool into the crowd gathering next to him. Thud. Silence. Then all hell broke loose.

It was some time before Conway realized that it was not himself but the band who were being attacked. Smiling he slowly unscrewed the pump-handle from the bar and started hitting heads in all directions.

They blurred in front of him. The floor and the ceiling contracted and expanded like a concertina until a grey light seemed to fill the room.

The girl tried to pull this windmill out of the confusion. Finally she succeeded. Outside she heard the first wail of the airborne police.

Conway was still flailing his pump-handle as she pushed him into her car.

She drove quickly through the silent streets, listening for the sirens.

The car stopped. Conway stumbled out and saw a plate-glass window. He tried to hit himself.

The girl took him firmly up to her apartment, where he collapsed into a chair.

Conway woke with a furious hang-over. Vaguely he

remembered getting himself into a tough spot, and he remembered something about a girl. Involuntarily he looked to the other side of the bed. With a faint sense of relief he saw it was empty. Struggling upright he found his clothes thrown carelessly over a couple of chairs. There were various feminine items about the place. So his memories weren't far wrong. Gingerly he dressed himself, thrust his face close to a mirror, put out his tongue and said, 'God, I look awful.'

He tried to keep his head still as he walked out of the bedroom.

'How do you feel?' she asked.

'Terrible.'

She handed him a couple of pills with a cup of coffee. His unsteady hand shook the liquid in the cup round and round, making him feel giddy.

'Any better?' the girl asked sympathetically as he finally managed to sit down.

'I feel like a bloody goldfish in a revolving bowl,' replied Conway.

The girl grinned and went out, leaving him alone with his aches and pains. His mind fought its way through the mercifully thinning alcoholic haze. Does doing the job one is best suited for also apply to being a good prostitute? he wondered.

Of course, one had to draw the line somewhere. The question was where. Didn't that depend when you lived and where? You drew the line one place today and another place tomorrow. Conway decided it was all a hypocritical conspiracy.

Somewhere a shrill persistent ring bore in on his brain.

'God, must that telephone always ring,' he moaned to the girl as she came back into the room.

'Oh, belt up,' she said angrily, 'that telephone call was to tell me to get out of this flat.'

'Why,' asked Conway, rather startled by the outburst.

'Because of the little fracas you had last night. May I

456

remind you?' She handed him the pump-handle. Conway looked at it in surprise, remembering nothing.

'Now, if I don't leave the district they will have me beaten up like the band last night,' she explained rather coldly.

'You could go to the police; they would straighten the matter out.'

'Like hell they would! What do you think I'm running here – a Sunday school?'

Conway was beginning to focus more clearly. Suddenly he dug up what he'd been trying to remember – the sound of an Australian voice, a voice offering him a flat, not far from here on the other side of the river. One of the rocket engineers, Henry Emling, was going off to Cape Canaveral for a year. He'd been too busy to take much notice of the offer. But then he really couldn't . . .

Conway stopped in mid-thought; there was no let-out in that direction – Emling was a wild fellow, who gave not a damn for status, form or respectability. He'd hardly be more than amused if he knew that the girl had got the flat.

'There's a flat on the south side of the river that I might be able to get for you,' said Conway, to save himself from being a hypocrite.

Later that morning Conway stood outside the dress shop where Cathy bought most of her clothes, thinking up an excuse for going in.

He didn't learn very much except that she was with a friend, a man called Mike.

To satisfy his curiosity he went round to the bureau of information. His hunch was right. The man was obviously Mike Fawsett.

Conway took a second taxi back to his own car, which he had left near Regent's Park. He was in a grim mood as he drove out of London to the west. He knew now why Cathy had the pile of newspaper cuttings, dealing with the exploits of astronauts. With a sinking feeling he knew that this was not just a casual affair.

Chapter Four

The Rocket

It was blowing hard and beginning to rain by the time Conway reached home. He loaded a large pile of wood into a big wicker basket and began to light a fire. The smoke was rising in the grate when the telephone rang.

'Is that Hugh, this is Alex. How did things go today?' Alex Cadogan was one of the foremost rocket engineers at the Centre. Much would depend on him in the months to come.

'I'm afraid I didn't get to the meeting today. I woke with a lousy headache.' Absolutely true, thought Conway. There was a short shocked silence. Cadogan could hardly believe that anyone would fail to attend a Higher Committee Meeting, even if he did wake with a lousy headache. Conway had more than a suspicion that Cadogan would dearly have liked to attend Higher Committee Meetings himself, good engineer that he was. Funny the way that people who could do a job superlatively well always wanted to be doing something else. 'Why don't you come over for a drink tonight,' went on Conway. 'Oh yes, I'm feeling all right now. By the time you get over here I'll have found out what happened today.'

After Cadogan had rung off, Conway put through a call to his secretary, Edith O'Malan.

'Oh, Professor Conway, what happened?' she asked.

'I had a bad head all day I'm afraid,' he answered.

'But we've been ringing your number all day.'

Ye gods, thought Conway, they can't leave you alone even when you are ill. He wondered whether there was anybody, anywhere, today, who could count his life his own.

Only a couple of centuries earlier there were fox-hunting, fire-eating squires in plenty who would have gobbled up on sight whole handfuls of these committee-sitting wallahs. But nowadays not a single fire-eating squire was to be found. The nineteenth century was almost as far back in time as – well, as the time of Achilles.

'I've been having a few of these turns lately,' he excused himself lamely. 'So I really thought that I ought to go up to town to see my doctor.'

This seemed to satisfy her. It had come to a pretty pass when one had to satisfy one's secretary.

'I hope it's all right,' her voice faltered.

'Probably a tumour or something,' he said.

'Oh no, Professor Conway, it's not as bad as that.'

Conway wondered if it was as bad as that. 'What happened today? Did the Chairman send any word through to the office?'

'They decided to refer things to the technical committees. I think there was quite a discussion about it.'

Of course there had been quite a discussion about it. So they had decided to refer things to the technicians after all – perhaps some day they'd really do something for themselves.

Alexander Cadogan arrived about half an hour later. He was a slow-spoken, heavily-built chap, born thirty-five years ago in the State of California, just about a hundred years after California became the rocket-building centre of the world. His head for alcohol was prodigious.

'I'd like you to meet an old friend, Chuck Lamos – Hugh Conway.'

'Glad to meet you. Have you eaten?' asked Hugh.

'Not yet, but a sandwich will do us fine.'

'A sandwich is all you'll get, Cathy's away.'

'Off on a trip?'

'A few days in London. Help yourselves to a drink, boys. I'll see what I can dig out.'

'Aren't you going to tell us what happened?'

'Oh, they decided to refer things to you chaps after all – amazing, isn't it?'

'Which doesn't surprise me.'

'How soon will we get the green light?'

'You know it will have to go right up to the top before you can get that,' answered Hugh. 'You might as well assume you've got to go ahead and carry on right now from there.'

'I reckon that's right, they're not likely to start wiring up the motors themselves,' grinned Lamos.

When Conway came back with the sandwiches he found Cadogan pacing up and down with heavy steps in front of the fire, 'Hugh, it's going to be one hell of a job,' he said.

'The century's understatement,' grunted Lamos. 'It's the double requirement that's the very devil. Big momentum change and rapid momentum change. I suppose there isn't any chance you've got your speeds wrong?' he asked.

'Come off it,' grinned Hugh. 'You know we've got things nailed down to within a few per cent – except for the precise velocity of escape from Achilles. But it's probably not much different from the Earth, give or take a few kilometres a second.'

'Say ten down and ten up, with the necessary safety factor about thirty kilometres a second under high-thrust conditions. How much under low-thrust?' asked Lamos.

'About two hundred,' growled Cadogan, as he bit into his sandwich. 'Not a very nice prospect, is it?'

'As Alex says, it's going to be one hell of a job.'

The problem was a far more formidable one than anything that had been attempted before. At first the two engineers were reluctant to accept the fact that there was a basically new situation here. But as the hours passed Conway's arguments gradually convinced them. It wouldn't do to use the normal techniques, it wouldn't do to make the normal sort of trip, like the one to Uranus. Normally it was possible to arrive in the outer parts of the solar system with a practically zero velocity. But if they did this, the Helios system would sweep past them at about seventy kilometres a second. It would be like running to a railway track only to see the express train thunder by. Somehow they had to get aboard. And since there was no stopping this particular train it would be necessary for their rocket to develop the same speed. It would be rather like driving a car alongside a train and attempting to jump across from the car to the train the moment the car had exactly the right speed.

And, of course, when they wanted to come back home, it would be necessary to do the whole exercise in reverse. Otherwise the landing party would simply be swept away with Helios on its journey through space. All in all, they figured out that a total momentum drive of at least two hundred kilometres per second would be necessary for the whole trip. This was ten times greater than was necessary for a trip to the Moon. Reckoning on a final returning pay-load of ten tons, the all-up weight would exceed 10,000 tons, even if they could manage an exhaust speed as great as twenty kilometres per second. Moreover the trip could not last for more than a few months. So this meant that they couldn't use an electro-magnetic ion rocket. They'd have to use a free-floating nuclear engine, free-floating in a magnetic field. And, as Cadogan said, those things were real buggers. Especially if you had to have a big thrust, such as they would need to land on Achilles.

'We'll just have to have two of 'em,' said Lamos, 'one inside the other.'

'It's damn well going back a century,' grunted Cadogan. 'I want to be sure there's no way of avoiding such a bastard.'

But they decided there wasn't. There was also the problem of getting started. Somehow they would have to get their machine into orbit around the Earth to begin with.

'That means the best part of a 100,000 tons of lousy chemical fuel,' mused Lamos. 'We can do it, but it isn't going to be a picnic.'

'That's your worry, not the Committee's,' grinned Conway, as he squirted soda into a glass.

461

'Damn all committees, and their mothers, and their grandmothers,' muttered Cadogan. 'They wouldn't be so free with their decisions if they had to do the work.'

'When we've got her in orbit,' went on Lamos, 'We'll have to strip all the rubbish off her.'

'I see,' said Conway, 'so the crew will be able to start with a nice clean ship.'

'That's right, and I can tell you one thing – they'll take it for granted.'

'At least we'll give 'em some work to do after they've landed,' Cadogan's lips twisted as the thought struck him as mildly amusing. 'They'll have to get rid of the bigger reactor, and that won't be a nice job,' he added.

The plan was to have a two-stage nuclear device, the first stage to get as far as Achilles, and to make the landing. The need for the big thrust wouldn't do the delicately suspended reactor much good. So the idea was to get rid of it and of all the outer fuel tanks before starting on the homeward trip. Effectively the crew would then have a new rocket unencumbered by excess weight. But the job would be a tough one, even if the atmosphere of Achilles should turn out to be more or less normal. And even if there wasn't anything to hinder the work – or anybody!

Who might there be? This question was outside the terms of reference of Conway's committee. Otherwise he would have been more interested in attending their meetings. But he knew that the general view was that there would be no trouble from an alien intelligence. And any bacteria or viruses there might be were likely to be so different from their terrestrial varieties that there would be little or no interaction. No radio signals were coming from Achilles. This was already known. This meant, according to the military, that there was no highly intelligent life on the planet. It was just possible that there might be a civilization like that of ancient Rome, not quite sufficiently developed to have discovered the advantages of radio communication, but certainly advanced enough to overwhelm the landing party by sheer weight of numbers. However, the sociologists estimated that the chances against this were about a million to one. It was known, they said, that civilizations such as those of Greece and Rome were transitory, lasting for no more than a few thousand years. Even if developments on Achilles were similar to those on the Earth, it was most unlikely that the present moment would just happen to coincide with the brief existence of such a civilization. The arguments looked good. Even so, Conway thought, it would hardly be pleasant to have dinosaurs breathing down your neck while you were trying to do the delicate technical job of stripping your rocket.

It was to be many months before Cadogan would be able to show Conway the fruits of their conversations that night. But a day was to come the following April when Alex would show him through the gigantic hangars where the Achilles rocket was being assembled. He would see the vast tubes with their thick graphite walls, surrounded by super-cooled magnetic coils. These gave an enormous pinch to the magnetic field at two points on the axis of the rocket. They were necessary to prevent the reactor from simply drifting away into space, or from drifting the other way towards the inner guts of the rocket. The reactor, in fact, was held captive between the two pinched points. Laterally it was held captive by a weaker field. This was maintained by an outer solenoid. The field could be weaker towards the graphite walls simply because there was no way through it. In contrast there had to be small openings of the field along the axis. The hot plasma surrounding the reactor had to be reflected as it approached the openings, and this of course meant a strong pinch.

The problem was to prevent the walls from being burnt up, and this was solved by the injection of liquid inert fuel over the whole wall. The rate of injection was controlled by feedback devices which adjusted the flow in accordance with the energy output of the reactor. The greater the output, the faster the flow. What happened was that radiation, intense radiation, from the reactor first vaporized and then ionized the inert fuel, which then streamed outwards along the wall and ultimately formed the jet of the rocket.

As regards the inert fuel, what they wanted was a low molecular weight, not too low a boiling point, and a high density. Unfortunately the spending of hundreds of thousands of millions of pounds over the years had not succeeded in changing the laws of chemistry, whatever priorities the committees put on their projects. So the best inert fuels were exactly those that could have been deduced from chemical handbooks a century earlier. Ordinary ammonia was as good as anything, with its three atoms of hydrogen to one of nitrogen. After ionization it gave a molecular weight only a little above two. Hydrogen itself would have given a much better molecular weight, but the density was hopelessly low, and it was also difficult to keep vast quantities of hydrogen in a liquid state.

Successful rocket design had proceeded by increasing the temperature of the sheet of gas close to the walls as it sped on its journey into space. Operating temperatures were now in the neighbourhood of a hundred thousand degrees, which gave the best exhaust speed of about twenty kilometres per second. With such a high operating temperature the walls had to be shielded to prevent evaporation of the graphite, and this meant that they had to be protected by the outflowing gases themselves. If the sheet of gas should become too thin, the walls, and eventually the controls of the motor itself, simply burnt up. If the rapidly-flowing sheet of gas was too thick, more than sufficient to protect the walls, then the inert fuel was used uneconomically. There had to be a fine balance, and this was why the feed-back devices that controlled the flow were so crucial. The reactor itself, suspended in its magnetic field, was of course of the gaseous variety, controlled in its operations only through the magnetic field.

A further complication had been added to the Achilles ship. To avoid carrying unnecessary weight, storage tanks had to be jettisoned as the inert fuel was used up. The problem was one of geometry. The motors had to be at the rear of the rocket. How does one jettison the fuel storage tanks without jettisoning the motor itself? The problem could not be solved with the motors in a fixed position, they had to be moved steadily backwards as the rear part of the rocket was stripped away. This was done by mounting the whole reactor system on a central shaft, the shaft being screwed backwards as the flight proceeded. Towards the front, but buried deep inside the gigantic structure, was a second smaller, but otherwise identical, rocket. It weighed perhaps a thousand tons. This would be used for the homeward flight. Inside it were the crew's quarters. There was no question of any observations through port-holes. This was quite unnecessary, for at the front in the extreme outer skin of the rocket was a host of electronic devices, arranged to transmit their information to the crew inside – radio aerials, television cameras, ultra-violet and X-ray 'eyes', and three telescopes, one of eighty inches aperture.

When, many months later, Conway was shown over this vast conglomeration of electronic and nucleonic devices, it seemed almost impossibly complicated. It seemed almost impossible that it should all work correctly. Yet on paper it had looked very straightforward. But Conway knew himself to be one of those strange people to whom calculations on paper appear a lot simpler than the real thing. It always amazed him how complicated a simple electric plug could be made. If he stopped really to think about it, the coils that produced the pinch effect, so critical to the correct operation of the whole affair, were just an application of elementary electricity. Yet, with their cooling equipment, their voltage controls and other feed-back devices, they seemed strange, menacing, and enigmatic.

Although he could hardly believe it, Conway realized that to most people things were the other way round. It was usually the calculations on paper that seemed obscure. To most people calculations only acquired a meaning when they were translated into material terms. It was a question of the way you saw the world. Conway saw it in terms of the abstractions of the mind, not in terms of concrete everyday things.

Chapter Five

Personnel

Mike Fawsett looked himself over carefully in the bathroom mirror as he shaved. He was trying to decide whether Cathy could properly be described as demanding. He decided that she could. He heard a disturbance in the bedroom, a waiter was bringing breakfast. He showered quickly, rubbed himself down, slipped on his dressing-gown and pushed open the door.

'Coffee's almost cold, darling.'

Cathy was sitting up, her back to the bedhead, a large cup cradled in her hands. She smiled, not because she was amused, or because she was welcoming Mike, but because she was utterly at ease. She looked him over, smiled again and, without realizing it, stretched herself slightly.

'I don't mind it cold,' he said.

'The one thing they never seem able to do is to get the coffee hot. The best hotels are the worst.'

These self-contradictory remarks were somehow typical of Cathy. He wondered if he should broach the subject on his mind. He knew that his name was on the list of possible candidates for the flight to Achilles. But the list was certain to be a long one, and four men would be chosen. He also knew that every candidate would have a completely first-class record, not only of expeditions into space, but also in their medical and psychological histories. He knew that a straw would decide between those who were chosen and those who were not. A single dissentient voice would be sufficient to rule a man out. This was bound to be the case when someone equally good was available to replace him. One possible, and even likely, voice was that of Cathy's husband. He wondered if Conway was a vindictive man. After all, he wouldn't need to be particularly vindictive. It would only be ordinary human nature. He wondered for a moment whether perhaps Conway might not find out; then, looking down at Cathy as she buttered a roll, he dismissed the thought. Nobody he had ever met was more open than Cathy. You took her or you left her. She didn't care.

'Jam or honey?' she asked.

He ignored the question. 'Cathy, you know I'm up for the big trip?'

'I know. I saw the list among Hugh's papers.'

'You don't think he might do something to stop me?'

'He won't. I'll see to that. He'll do as I say.'

Cathy leant forward and pushed away the breakfast trolley. She put her hand round Mike's head and pulled him towards her.

Tom Fiske was brought up without any difficulties on the sand lots of Scranton, Pa. His parents were entirely unknown, apparently having decided at an early stage in young Tom's career to part company from him. After spending eleven of his first twelve years in an orphanage, Tom decided to chance his luck as a free-lance operator. He worked in the evening and attended high school by day. So unwilling nowadays are the inhabitants of the highly prosperous countries to engage in any form of physical activity that Tom found very little difficulty in eking out a bare living. In summer there was any amount of gardening to be done. Winter was more difficult, but there were the mails around Christmas time, there was the snow to be cleared in front of people's homes, and after a couple of years of experience he found that doing leg-work for professional debt collectors could be tolerably profitable. He had a good nose for sniffing out information, he was not regarded with a suspicious eye, his skin was thick perforce, and his legs were fast.

As he grew older, as he became interested in the other

sex, he came to realize that these activities were not very profitable, nor did they carry status. He thought hard about being a professional ball-player, and if the big-time clubs had given him a fair try-out it is possible that he would have made it.

At the age of eighteen he had a serious discussion with himself. Candour compelled him to admit that he was getting nowhere. It was true he was eating, but only in hamburger joints, reeking of evaporated fats. There seemed no hope at all of making the sort of moolah that would enable him to buy a house on one of the hills to the west of the town, where he might raise a family in peace, and in contemplation of the American scene. Actually this was not entirely true. Tom's real enemy was not the under-privilege of birth but a genuine ignorance of what to do. He was handicapped neither by physical shortcomings, nor by low intelligence, but by sheer lack of know-what. There had never been a time since about the year 1950 when a 'young man who knew' could not make himself a million dollars by the time he was twenty. Luck made no difference, but know-what certainly did.

So it came about that the U.S. Army found itself with a raw recruit on its hands. Tom enlisted, and so avoided the draft, shortly before his nineteenth birthday. At that age he was a rather gangly youngster, just about six feet tall, with a close-cropped head that would have grown a shock of red hair if it had been given time to do so. His face was mildly freckled, and his ears stuck out sufficiently to give him a slightly aggressive look, without being really noticeable. The psychological tests he was given were really a waste of time, for the readiness of his smile in the face of past experience manifestly showed that he had the right temperament. At that time there was a gap in his front teeth – one of them had been knocked out in a gang fight about five years earlier.

But they did give him tests, physical as well as psychological. Although the results, especially the physical results, were abnormally good, nobody took very much notice of

469

that. His whole background was too amorphous for him to be taken seriously at that stage. He was first sent on a tour of duty in Bolivia. This did little to help his future career, except perhaps to give him a catholic outlook on things in general. Then he was hauled back to the U.S. and given an eight-months' training as an electronics maintenance engineer. He survived the course and got the first break of his life by being sent to winter at the Mount Erebus station in Antarctica. After three summer months he volunteered to see the winter through at this remote spot, according to some the nearest in its inhospitality to the satellites of Jupiter. On the way back to base camp the following spring he and three other colleagues were overtaken by a series of furious storms. These would not have mattered but for a series of freakish mishaps to their equipment. Even in this day and age it is possible to run close to disaster on the Antarctic Plateau. They managed to make base, but only after a desperate struggle. The doctor who examined Tom was first astonished and then suspicious. His condition when compared with that of the other three men appeared to be too good. At first it seemed to indicate that Tom had somehow managed to avoid pulling his weight. When further investigation proved this to be by no means true a thorough report on Tom was made to Washington. The report rated an electronic check-over. This meant that the whole of Tom's past history, so far as it was known to the Army, that is to say so far as it had been committed to punched cards, was fed into an electronic computer. The computer delivered its report; Tom was well within the range of physical and mental characteristics required for a candidate to space school. He was accordingly sent to the Department of Space Medicine at Santa Barbara, California.

The normal physical tests, endurance and reaction times, showed up nothing particularly unusual, nothing much different from hundreds of other well-coordinated cadets. But the results were sufficiently satisfactory for him to proceed to more advanced training. This meant acceleration tests. It was then that something really unusual began to emerge. It wasn't that Tom liked being accelerated at x times gravity any more than anyone else, but his recovery time was quite abnormally quick. After prolonged acceleration he could return to coordinated physical and mental activity long before the normal recruit. From the emergence of this freak ability it was only a question of time before Tom got his first trip into space. It was a routine flight to the Moon, in which he performed well enough to graduate as an astronaut.

Now it was a question of the long haul. Lots of young fellows had started equally as well as Tom, but it was another matter as the flights became more numerous and longer in duration. Tom simply took it all in his stride. A gap in performance slowly opened out between him and the average man. The longer time went on, the wider the gap became.

It seems whatever the human race sets itself to do there will always be a few rare individuals who manage to perform almost unnaturally well, as if they were not members of the species at all. So far as space flight was concerned, Tom was one of these. He was a natural, his name a cert for the trip to Achilles. He wouldn't be the leader, he didn't have the right educational or social background, but if anyone stood the course it would be Tom Fiske. And if he needed any further recommendation, he now had a girl, 36-25-36, five feet six and a half inches, green eyes, fine hair dyed blonde, the secretary of a big noise in the top organization, the Rand Corporation. This was judged by the psychiatrists to give him additional stability.

During the months that followed Cathy Conway had several assignations with Mike Fawsett. Inevitably serious rows with Conway followed in the wake of these arrangements. For his part, and for his own sake, Fawsett kept the affair as much throttled down as he could. He knew that the moment of decision was not far away.

471

Hugh Conway had no intention of raising the matter of the choice of the Achilles crew with Cathy. He intended that she should raise it herself. All he had to do was to leave the relevant committee papers lying around in his study. She would be sure to find them.

It worked out as he planned. She did raise the subject, but in a manner that simply took his breath away. Late one evening, when they were going to bed, Cathy turned to him, entirely naked, candidly and boldly, and said, 'You're going to make sure that Mike gets in, aren't you?' Strangely, it shattered his confidence. He himself might be a clever fellow, but surely his wife was unique. Had any woman ever before had the sheer gall to look seductive simply to demand – yes, demand – that her husband should do a favour to her lover. Conway doubted it.

'I'm not going to lift a finger to help that Fawsett stumble-bum, if that's what you're getting at.'

'You know what it means, Hugh. It means we're finished if you don't. I'm not going to go on living with a mean-minded man.'

'You think it's mean-minded to refuse to help a man who's seduced my wife, do you?'

'He didn't seduce me,' began Cathy indignantly. Then her voice trailed away as she realized that she had fallen into a small trap.

'You're quite shameless. Look at you now,' went on Conway.

'If I can't undress in front of my husband, who can I undress in front of?' It was the usual story. In any matter sexual Cathy had the perfect defence, on anything else she was worse than hopeless. 'But you're quite right,' she went on, 'the way you stare at me it isn't decent. After ten years it's abnormal. There must be something wrong with you.' Acting up the part she grabbed a dressing-gown and slipped it around her shoulders.

'How can you expect things to go on working if you're always sleeping around with some nuke or other?' he asked.

Cathy's face reddened slightly, 'I don't sleep around with nukes.' And of course she didn't. 'If you're going to be nasty, I'll tell you this. If you'd sleep around a bit we would get along a lot better. You ought to see a psychiatrist. It ain't natural the way you are always looking at me. Anyway, how can you know I'm so good if you never go out with anybody else?'

Conway didn't know whether to get mad or to laugh.

'And you know what I'm like. You've known right from the beginning. You can't make a leopard change its spots.'

There was justice in this. He had known. Before he married Cathy various people had told him in measured asides that she was classified in her psychological record as a pseudonympho. He'd never really known the technical meaning of this term – by now he'd simply come to associate it with someone like Cathy. He'd known perfectly well what she was like and he'd made the masculine error of supposing that he could change her. In this he had really been unfair. It was perhaps because he could think so that their marriage had lasted for so long, three times as long as the average. Many of his friends would also have subscribed to the view that he was abnormal.

'Don't you realize that I couldn't get Fawsett into the party even if I wanted to. I'm not choosing the crew.'

'Rubbish!'

'I mean it. You know perfectly well that these things are only settled at the top.'

Cathy pondered this for a moment, and then said, 'But you could do your best.'

'All I can do is to promise not to do my worst.'

She sat on the edge of the bed looking down for a moment and shook the mop of brown curls. When she looked up at him her eyes were ablaze with indignation, 'But it's *your* planet,' she burst out.

Instantly the shadow of Mike Fawsett vanished like a puff of smoke. Cathy's lips were as compulsive as they had ever been. Afterwards, she fell almost instantly asleep. Conway was left with his brain racing.

There was nothing for it but to go back to his study again. He moved the light blanket gently around Cathy's shoulders and tiptoed from the room, pausing for a moment to listen to her breathing as he always did. It was as steady and regular as that of a child. With a clear perception he realized that Cathy was abnormal in the sense that she lived more in the present than a normal person. The past had some meaning for her but not a great deal, while the future was still dim and inconsequential. Once Fawsett was on his way across space she would forget all about him. But of course the trouble would arise again with increased emphasis on his return, if he returned. Conway would have found this analysis ironic if he had known just what was going to happen to Cathy.

Down in the study he rummaged among his papers. Because his private estimate was that the crew of the Achilles ship had no more than a fifty per cent chance of survival, let alone success, his inner wish had been to recommend Fawsett strongly for a place in the crew. But he had been tormented inside himself by the story of David and Uriah, except of course that things weren't quite the same way round in this case. After all, Fawsett wanted to go. But this had hardly seemed sufficient. It seemed somehow wrong to send a man to what might be his death when you yourself stood to profit from that death. So until tonight he had been balanced in his mind as to what he should do. But now he was decided. Cathy had settled the matter for him. He was damned if he was going to lose his wife because of a scruple, for he knew that she would surely leave him if he should black-ball Fawsett.

Conway's doubts were based on many arguments, none of them very conclusive, but adding together to a solid amount of evidence. Now he had one more thread, a thread as yet unknown to anyone else. He had a crucial new result from his observations. If it had been almost anyone else, the news would already have flashed around the world. Since about the year 1960 scientists had announced their discoveries almost before they had made them. Not that Conway was close, but he believed in having a little time to digest his own work before it was mauled over in public. He knew what the newspapers would do with this one. Shuffling his notes he came to what he wanted. To the inexpert eye it was just a pen tracing, a thin line that rose and fell in a complicated and apparently unpredictable way as it moved down the length of a long strip of paper. It was the spectrum of Achilles. Most of the complicated behaviour of the line towards the right-hand end of the strip was due to the presence of water vapour in the atmosphere of Achilles. What Conway had been looking for were slight modifications of this water vapour pattern. His finger found the relevant place. There really couldn't be any doubt about it. They were the bands of chlorophyll.

Chapter Six

The Russian Ship

Conway's discovery caused a major stir, as he had anticipated it would. It meant that there must be some sort of
plant life on Achilles. Previously they had only had the very
green colour of the planet to go by, strongly suggesting the
presence of plant life, although there was just the bare
possibility that it might come from a green inorganic
salt.

Speculations on the possibilities of there also being animal life were now rife. The lack of radio signals was of course
again given prominence, but it was pointed out that weak
signals could not be detected because of the masking effect
of Helios itself. The angular separation of Achilles from the
star, as seen from the Earth, was only about three degrees.
Radio waves emitted by the star, random noise without any
coherent signal, slopped into even the biggest radio dishes,
producing a completely effective jamming of any weak signal from Achilles. So there was this possibility, but it wasn't
taken very seriously. After all, a terrestrial television transmitting station could easily have been detected, if it had
been sited on the approaching planet.

But although the public wasn't much worried, military
planners took matters more seriously. It was inevitable that
they should do so, for it is the nature of military planning
that one must take all possibilities seriously, however absurd
they may be.

The argument was: if there was someone on Achilles who
was planning an invasion of the Earth, then that someone
might have deliberately damped down all forms of radio
emission. They might not wish to give their presence away.

When it was pointed out that the Earth itself had given its presence away, for instance by more than a hundred television channels in Europe and the United States alone, the psychologists pointed out that this was an outcome of terrestrial tension. A more developed society, with less tension, might well have stayed its hand. It might have waited to see if it could pick up any signals from the other fellow before making any signals of its own. There were no radio astronomers among the military planners or psychologists, otherwise they would have pointed out that that was precisely what they themselves had been trying to do for over a century.

It was therefore inevitable that plans should be drawn up to meet a potential invasion from space. The Achilles project was not only exploratory, it took over the functions of an advanced patrol. And the crew would be briefed accordingly.

A beneficial result of all this was that some genuine cooperation between East and West was plainly desirable. In fact, it is well known from psychological studies that adjustments in human society take place in such a way as to maintain a state of constant tension. In plain terms, if for some reason current problems disappear then new ones must quickly be invented. Similarly, if troubles mount up, the new ones proceed to devalue the old ones. Knowing all this could be demonstrated by strict mathematics, everybody at the top suspected that the danger of a space invasion would be over-emphasized. The top generals felt that the mathematical psychologists were taking them for a ride, and the psychologists themselves thought that this was probably so, although they couldn't be sure. This is not as absurd as it may sound. Mathematical psychology is of course based on what used to be known as the theory of games. And it is essential to the theory of games that there should be at least two sides. This assumption runs through the whole mathematical structure. The trouble in the present case was that no one knew whether there was another side or not. Nobody quite knew how the mathematics went, strictly speaking, if there was complete uncertainty about the existence of an opponent. The result was a state of confusion. Everybody suspected that they were being taken for a trip, but no one was quite sure how.

It was inevitable that there should be summit meetings. For many, many years these had been disguised as intimate family gatherings. The Russian President, at the moment Vladimir Kaluga, would depart from Moscow for New York or for Paris accompanied by his two sons and three daughters, the daughters being accompanied by their husbands and their children, and their servants, interpreters, general hangers-on and advisers. They would be met at the airport by the Euro-American President and his wife, in this case Lee and Martha Kipling. It was an interesting difference of culture that the Russian President was always a widower and the Euro-American President always a married man. In their respective territories these qualities were regarded as a sign of vigour.

The party would be moved safely, to Nantucket Island perhaps, or to some château on the Loire. There they would get down to business, their families forgotten. It was the only way to achieve a comparatively sane interchange of ideas. At an official summit meeting, held in the full glare of international publicity, all previous positions must necessarily be maintained. All official contacts were reduced to the state of intellectual trench warfare. Only when they were ostensibly in the bosoms of their families could the leaders of either side deviate by a hair's breadth from the implacably straight paths along which they were set by their respective communities. Even if you lost your shirt you must still preserve your face, as one highly-paid political commentator put it.

Even so, world publicity would do what it could to impede their every movement. Wherever they were situated, whether in the fastness of a Rhineland castle, or on a farm near the banks of the Shenandoah, newsmen would

478

swarm into the district, and helicopters would plant television cameras on every available vantage point. A small child, at the age of innocence, would not be allowed to pick a bunch of flowers without its picture being instantly transmitted to the waiting multitudes in the pulsating world outside. In spite of the modern newfangled devices it was all very much as it had been in medieval times. Except that monarchs were then described in a flowing language of some magnificence; they were not referred to boldly as Lee, Vlad, and Marty.

It was at one of these homey, fireside parties that the West first divulged its list of astronauts for the Achilles expedition – Fiske, Fawsett, Larson, and Reinbach. Larson was to be the leader, with Fawsett as his second in command. Kaluga carried the news back to Moscow.

It is not known who was responsible for the Russian stroke of imagination, almost of genius. But it is pleasant to think that somewhere behind a dull grey wall of concrete somewhere in Moscow, and behind the flinty exterior of some close-cropped Russian committee man there lurks a touch of romance. The Russo-Chinese list for their expedition was announced about a month later. It was: Alexander Pitoyan, Nuri Bakovsky, Ivan Kratov and Tara Ilyana.

The United States fell slap-bang into the propaganda trap that had been prepared for the West. Once Americans had digested the incredible news that a woman was to be sent on the Russian expedition it was quickly pointed out that the performances of Russian women athletes closely approached those of men. It was broadly hinted that Miss Ilyana would turn out to be practically a man in all her essential qualities. Visions of rough, tough, Russian women breaking stones along the road to Archangel were conjured up. The remnants of the once-powerful Hearst Press even went so far as to publish the headline COMMIES TO BLAST THREE-HUNDRED-POUND WOMAN INTO SPACE. The editor in question was allowed twelve hours of self-congratulation before the trap was sprung. Ilyana turned out to be a curvaceous blonde with a high I.Q.

Somewhat more than a touch of inspiration had gone into Ilyana's selection, however. Without the work of Nicolai Popkin, a young mathematician from Rostov, a proposal to include a woman would have been regarded as an amusing and welcome joke by the higher committees, but it would not have been taken seriously. Inevitably sex was always a difficulty where long space voyages were concerned. Young men cooped up in a space-ship for months on end naturally found themselves turning lightly to thoughts of love. The strange result proved by Popkin, subsequently to become famous as Popkin's Theorem was, that there would be far less talk and thought about sex if a woman were included in the party. A few laymen had doubts about this result but their views were brushed aside, for mathematical rigour could not be gainsaid. Rigour there seemed to be – at least the mathematicians said so. Three Academicians, consulted as referees, found Popkin's argument both elegant and satisfying. It was said that the shock-haired young man had used a particularly subtle lemma.

Once decided on their course the committees proceeded with ruthless efficiency. It was immediately clear that a major propaganda victory could be scored. The thing to do was quite obviously to choose a girl who in her appearance might have been taken as an ideal representation of American womanhood. So the hunt was on. The search was of course confined to members of the Young Communists Party. It was also restricted by the requirement of an excellent educational background. But after that, the Russian authorities were only interested in vital statistics, and in those qualities that were literally superficial.

Thousands of dossiers, in the form of neat packets of punched-cards, were sent from the provinces to Moscow, where they were analysed with the aid of a computer. The computer was of course supplied with a programme of selection, the gate of which was very narrow. Almost fifty girls managed to pass through the gate, Ilyana being one of them. There is no telling how she was chosen out of this short list but Tara Ilyana was certainly a pleasant young woman with a well-integrated personality.

It would have been hard for anyone from the twentieth century to understand the shattering effect of Ilyana's inclusion on American public opinion. Everywhere one heard the gloomy prognostication that now 'they' were finished. The social temperature had continued to rise in an unbroken steep curve ever since the middle of the twentieth century. By 2087 everybody lived in the way that film stars used to live a century ago. Marriages lasted on average about a year.

It was the discovery of how to prevent children in broken homes from becoming insecure, made about seventy years ago, that really produced the difference. It was one of the few really genuine social advances, to stop the furious fighting that used to take place in the law courts over the custody of children. No wonder they felt insecure when such things were going on. Now this was all altered. The old tribal structure had come back with the young being thought of as members of the tribe, rather than as belonging to a particular person. But woe betide the child who didn't belong to the tribe – who didn't belong to the right social bracket, like young Tom Fiske. Then things were really tough, but no worse than they used to be. Anyway, with the kids getting married at thirteen or fourteen – entering the sexual parabola as the psychiatrists call it – there wasn't much childhood to worry about.

It is of course well known that astronauts are a great success with women. The pattern has been with us for more than a hundred years, ever since the absurd early idea of sending married men on the first trips into space was abandoned. By a like token it was clear that Ilyana was going to be a great success with men, even before she ever set her well-shaped foot into the Achilles ship.

The second most interesting member of the Russian team

was Alex Pitoyan. A slim dark young man, he was the only Muscovite in the team. Seven years earlier he had graduated from Moscow University with excellent marks in Physics and Mathematics. Different from other able young men of his time, he showed no taste for mathematico-psychological studies, but became interested in complex orbital calculations. The field was not a particularly difficult one, since the use of computers had largely obviated the tricky analytical work of previous centuries. Within five years Pitoyan had become a master of the subject and of the use of computers in general. Now it was perfectly clear that the orbits of the Achilles ships could not be pre-set. They would have to pass through very complex gravitational fields, and no one could say exactly what initial orbit was the correct one. The available data were not good enough for that, and were most unlikely to become good enough, even though observational measurement was becoming more and more accurate as the Helios system approached our own. Inevitably the orbit would have to be altered while the ship was in flight. The crew would have to play it by ear and make appropriate corrections as the need arose. One possibility was to send all available information back to Earth for the terrestrial laboratories to make the necessary calculations, and for the appropriate corrections to be sent back to the ship. This was precisely the Euro-American plan. The Russians on the other hand decided for safety's sake to include a computer in the ship. They also decided to send a genuine scientist, not someone with a merely superficial training. Pitoyan was a good effective choice; medical reports showed that while he was not in the class of the normal astronaut, he could be expected to survive the rigours of take-off and landing, and from a mental point of view it was quite likely that he would more than hold his own.

Soon after the announcement of the composition of the party he decided that it would be nice to make Ilyana's acquaintance on a rather more informal basis than had been possible on the occasion of their meeting at the House of Astronauts. The affair prospered for a little while but was then brought to an abrupt halt by the authorities, who warned him very sternly that if this behaviour were to continue he was out. The behaviour was sharply terminated. Alone in his tiny flat, fifty yards off Tchaikovsky Street, he shrugged and grinned to himself. It would be simpler after take-off.

It is an old idea that there might be somebody in the world exactly and precisely like oneself. Add a sinister touch to the situation in which you happen to meet that person, and what do you do? According to tradition you are supposed to crack up. Actually nature is very prolific. Essentially the same individuals are constantly being born, often simultaneously, and often in widely different parts of the earth. The circumstances of birth and the different conventions of the societies in which they are brought up proceed to clothe these individuals with a façade that hides their basic similarity, but like is apt to ally itself with like if they are brought together under basically the same circumstances. No one could tell exactly where the ancestors of Tom Fiske had come from, judging from his appearance probably from Norway or Denmark via the south of England. The ancestors of Ivan Kratov and of Nuri Bakovsky had probably moved into Russia from the direction of the Pripet marshes about fifteen hundred years ago. Whether their forebears at a still earlier date were ever associated together must of necessity be a matter of doubt and speculation, but certain it is that all three were basically the same individual. Laid over one of them were the doubts, miseries, and uncertainties of a free society. Laid over the other two were the inflexible certainty, the pride, and the boredom of a culture that thinks it knows exactly where it is going.

An observer from entirely outside the human race would indeed have discovered much about their respective cultures, their behaviour would have allowed him to measure the merits and demerits of the societies that had raised them.

To the Westerner who claims that the case of Tom Fiske was not a fair one, that Tom Fiske was not a fair representative of their culture, it must be said that if Fiske had been brought up as the Westerner imagines in theory that all children should be brought up, then he never would have made the grade, he would never have got within the remotest sighting distance of the Western party to Achilles. The comparison is of necessity a fair one. And the conclusions our imaginary observer might reach are not clear. Which system they would favour is quite uncertain.

Suffice it then to say that Kratov and Bakovsky were basically courageous tough men. Where Fiske had been dragged up, not brought up, they had received the most careful of graduated trainings. They had both started life at a crèche. They had been told that Russia was the greatest nation on earth, and because the people who told them this provided food, warmth, and shelter, they saw no reason to disbelieve it. They were not intelligent enough to think outside the carefully organized social structure in which they were embedded. They saw no reason to behave in any way differently from the other boys around them. In all respects they were exactly the same as the others, except in their ability to survive physical discomfort without appreciable mental strain. So that, at the time they were chosen for the Achilles expedition, they were undistinguished individuals, their characters essentially unformed, precisely because they were not unique and because their education had been designed to suppress, not to bring out, all small differences between one person and another. Once again, if they had not been chosen, those who were would not have differed in any sensible respect. They were the products of a system, a system that had erected a tiny gate through which only men of a very restricted type could pass. On the voyage itself their qualities might begin to mark them out as real people, not as packets of punch-cards to be fed to a computer.

There was an ironic similarity in the design of the Russian rocket. Just as the men were essentially the same men, so the rocket was essentially the same rocket. And just as the men were overlaid by superficial differences, of no real consequence at all, so the rocket looked different to the casual eye. When mounted in its outer container, the container of the chemical fuel that was to get it into orbit around the Earth, it measured a hundred feet across the base and was five hundred feet in height. The American rocket on the other hand measured only sixty feet across the base but was a thousand feet in height. The Russian looked squat and ugly, compared to the pencilled elegance of the American machine. But basically they were exactly the same job. They were powered in the same way, and the logic of their construction was the same. It had cost the best part of a hundred thousand million pounds to produce the superficial differences. It was however, exactly these differences that everybody was proud of. They said that they were 'essentially' Russian or 'all' American as the case might be.

Chapter Seven

The Launching

Mike Fawsett marched up and down the brightly lit hall as he waited for the Atlantic shuttle, which was already an hour late. The timing of really big flights was absolutely precise, to the second. Funny that they couldn't run a three-thousand-mile hop efficiently.

Mike himself was equally at home on either side of the Atlantic. His mother was American, his father British. His early education had been in England, but he'd come over to the States for graduate training, and had spent most of his life there since. To get himself into space school he had taken out American citizenship, and by now the difference between him and a native-born American was mainly that the law still prevented him from ever becoming President. But this scarcely worried him, for with his inclusion in the Achilles crew he had achieved the ambition of a lifetime, of more than a lifetime. He was marching up and down now not because he was nervous or impatient at the delay but because of an over-abundance of physical energy. This constant desire to be moving, to be flexing his muscles, had always been a difficulty on flights into space. It was a bit odd he thought to himself that they chose physical types for these jobs, when an armchair man might find things a lot easier.

He hadn't seen Cathy for three months. It had been absolutely essential to stick unswervingly to his training. The new ship was quite a bit different to anything he had ever been in before. Now that they were getting near take-off they'd been given the green light – to make the best of their last week-end. The more he saw of Cathy the better the authorities would be pleased. They'd know about it of course, they'd have her dossier. The main point was that he was in the clear.

The speaker announced that the Atlantic ferry was in. The waiting crowd moved closer to the exit gate. Then he saw Cathy coming, one of the first out – she must have simply floated through all formalities. He kissed her, 'Cat, darling, you're late.'

'Oh, am I? I can never get the time right when it changes.'

'I've got everything fixed.'

She looked up at him, thinking that she too had got everything fixed. Hugh had gone down to the south of Florida for the big launching. This left her quite free to spend the last few days with Mike.

They took the monorail into Manhattan. They passed high above the Triborough Bridge and above the East River. It was really much more impressive than actually flying. It was nearly 4.30 on a November afternoon, and the lights of New York were just coming on. The whole sight of it delighted Cathy. It wasn't that she was unsophisticated, or that she hadn't seen it before, but that her memories of the past – of her last visit to New York two years earlier – were now dim and vague. Mike's arm around her shoulder was the reality.

Their section of the car branched off the main line at Fifty-second Street. Within thirty seconds they were standing on the pavement of Fifth Avenue. Mike carried her bag along one of the cross streets and they were almost instantly inside a block of expensively furnished apartments.

'I didn't know you'd got a place in New York, Mike.'

'I don't have, but I've got a friend.'

'Look what I've brought for you.' Cathy was already beginning to spread her things over the bedroom. She opened up a package, and there was a large soft toy. It was a donkey with big black hoofs, a black top, and a white patch for its mouth and nose. The ears were long and sagged down the back like a lion's mane. The eyes had a quizzical look. 'It's a mascot. You can't keep your pyjamas inside it.'

He looked at the absurd toy with an embarrassed grin, wondering where he could get rid of it quietly.

After the past months he had a great desire for Cathy, but when he tried to kiss her she pushed him away quite firmly. Of course, it could be the journey that had tired her, but Mike had more than a suspicion that she was levelling the score for his neglect of her during the last few weeks.

With the coming of night the people who thronged the streets of Manhattan during the day mostly retired to their homes, down the Jersey coast or far up the valley of the Hudson, or into Westchester and beyond to Connecticut. Those who provided services and entertainment stayed behind, apart from the very few who actually lived in the city. It had changed a good deal over the last century. Nowadays there is no land on Manhattan, not even the smallest patch, that is available for cheap living. The whole island, from the Battery in the south to its northernmost tip, is now solid with office premises. The only exceptions are the eating-houses, the theatres of Broadway, hotels, and a very few private apartments grouped around Central Park. Looking backwards over the whole history of the development of New York one notices a consistent pattern. The amount of the island developed for business administration simply depended on the state of the economy of the Union. In the very early days only the southernmost regions were used. The rest of the island was available at small cost to anyone who wished to live there. By the middle of the twentieth century, the movement to the north had reached almost to Sixtieth Street. Beyond were about thirty more streets of prosperous residences and hotels. Then came Harlem, and the cheap tenements of the Puerto Ricans. All this has long since gone. Everywhere, north to south, east to west, stand the office blocks, medium sized by New York standards. It would be easy to erect buildings of the size of the old sky-scrapers, but the removal of such edifices is unduly costly.

Strangely enough the stresses to which the modern New

Yorker is subject in his daily life are probably less than they were a hundred years ago. For nowadays nobody living there conceives that life could be in any way different from what it is. To the great mass of commuters it seems entirely natural that one should spend the whole of one's life in commuting. The very first memories almost are of the daily routine of making the school bus. The alarm bell at seven o'clock, the hurried shower and breakfast, the short walk to the end of the street to join the others. This was now the universal pattern. Nowhere was a child to be found who ambled along alone, happy in a world of his own imagination, content to arrive late at school and not thinking it important. The psychologists said it was a good thing that there were no such children, for they would have lived unhappy lives themselves and produced tensions and unrest in others.

Fifteen hundred miles away to the south, Conway was standing looking out over sandy land-locked pools towards the sea. He was dressed in shirt and slacks, the shirt open at the neck, the November night pleasantly warm with a slight wind blowing from the sea. The count-down was on. If everything went well the first of the two gigantic rockets would take off in two hours' time. There had to be two of them, one for an emergency. Both would be put in orbit around the Earth, engineers would strip away the outer covering – the sardine tin as they called it – and both would be given thorough final tests. If both passed these tests then he supposed that some committee or other would spend a half-day deciding which was to be used for the actual flight. Both would not be used, for one must be kept in reserve in case of a disaster. He had driven out from the launching area to get away from the rising tension. It was an amazing phenomenon, some ten thousand men – engineers, electricians, electronics experts, service personnel, scientists and mathematicians – all of them gripped by one single complex of thoughts, the launching. Not a single one of them could think outside that pattern. Not even to save their lives. If danger was to threaten, men would risk their lives without even knowing that they were doing so. Conway decided that it must have been a bit like this in the old battles. It was a common thought process that simply took charge and directed a man towards an end that was not his own personal one. Conway shivered as he wondered whether it would ever be possible to control in a pre-directed way these cooperative thought structures. They grew only by chance now, by trial, sometimes they developed, like this launching business, and sometimes they didn't – but suppose you could control whether they developed or not. Then you really would have an ant-heap. He turned round and looked towards the aura of light where the work was now going on. Was there any real difference between an ant-heap and what was going on over there?

Conway drove back to the control area. Up to a certain point the lights ahead of him seemed to brighten, but after a certain stage, through some physiological quirk, they appeared to reach a constant level, even though he was drawing nearer to them all the time. He could now see the lights glinting on the thousand-foot-high metallic outer casing of the first rocket. He glanced briefly at his watch. Within little more than an hour this great flashing needle would be streaming upwards on the first stage of its journey into space. He braked the car to a standstill by the roadside and got out for a moment to stare across at the thing.

Could one doubt that this was a magnificent achievement? It was a question that Conway had often asked himself before. He had never been able to give a satisfactory reply, and now as he looked across at the shining streak of light, still three miles away, he found himself as far away as ever from an answer.

When you came down to the bare bones of it there was no denying that here was a magnificent expression of the abilities of the human race. It wasn't just the ideas, it was

the organization too. Then why somewhere deep in himself
did he revolt against it? Perhaps he himself had a malfunction. He knew that that was what the psychologists
thought about him. He knew that in the files he was said to
be badly adjusted and unstable, he knew that no one at the
top would take the slightest notice of any sociological pro-
nouncements he might make. They would listen to him
on technical issues, but that figured. It was well known that
a brain suffering from abnormality was more likely than the
normal to show streaks of brilliance. In fact it was well
known that thorough analysis of the lives of all those whom
Conway himself would have placed as great men showed
them up as socially sick men. Perhaps they were right and
perhaps they were not. Perhaps it was an attempt of little
men of small consequence to devalue their betters.

This in a way was the root of the matter. It was really the
contrast between the frenzied importance that was attached
to this rocket here, and the systematic devaluation of
achievements of comparable magnificence when they happened to come from one or two people. For the great
achievement by an individual was always harder to understand and conceive of and to appreciate, whereas this rocket
business was obvious to everybody. It was really the mentality of the society that had produced the thing, rather than
the thing itself, to which he objected. It was because they
did it all so seriously. The decision to go to Achilles had
been taken as a matter of policy, not of adventure. Policy
should never have been allowed to cross the threshold into
the world of ideas.

Somehow it was all there in the things that were around
him now. The millions of kilowatts that were being burned
in the launching-field away to the west, the glint of metal
in the distance, the smell of gasoline from the road, the beer
cans that also glinted near his feet, and the star Helios that
was now rising to the east. Soon it would dim the lights of
the launching-field.

The guard checked very carefully through Conway's

papers – he couldn't understand why anyone with Conway's priority status wouldn't be already on the field.

'You're kinda late, aren't you, sir?' he asked.

'It's not due up for another hour or more, is it?'

The guard shrugged and allowed him to go on. Conway wondered how in the middle of all this hysteria they managed to get the damned thing off the ground at all.

He parked and walked very deliberately towards the spot where he knew the senior engineers would be assembled. When he found Cadogan he saw that the burly Californian was in one hell of a temper. Conway would have given heavy odds that Cadogan was suffering from a bad headache. He couldn't understand why, for the development engineers had long since been out of the active side of the job. First it was the turn of the development engineers, then of the production team, and now, at the actual launching itself, of the operational engineers. Cadogan wasn't allowed even the slightest of decisions at this stage. Perhaps that was what was making him mad.

Conway turned away lest they should see him grinning in the grey light that now suffused the whole area. The pattern was consistent, the way every profession despised the others. The theoreticians, the chaps who worked with mathematics on paper, despised them all. The observers and experimentalists despised the engineers, and the development engineers despised every other form of engineer, and so on along the whole chain. Yet society couldn't get along for five minutes without the whole bunch of them. It was really that they were all like children, perplexed and apprehensive of what they didn't understand.

'How about a drink?' he asked Cadogan.

'Best idea we've heard around here.'

'What'll it be?'

'Straight Scotch.'

It took Conway ten minutes to find the bar, and he had to assure the bartender that the drinks were not for anyone on ops. He carried them back across the compound in a

492

small hand refrigerator. He glanced at his watch. Cathy would be in New York by now, probably dining somewhere about West Forty-seventh Street. He wished he had doubled the size and strength of his drink.

In place of the electronic signals coming over the loudspeakers a human voice began to count off the last seconds. A flicker of light developing instantly into a ring of fire appeared at the base of the rocket. As always, Conway had the sickening feeling that it was never going to move. It seemed to stand there for an eternity. When he had almost given up hope it began to move very slowly upwards. Suddenly it accelerated away from them leaving a patch of yellow flame in the sky. It seemed a miracle that such an enormous thing could be moved without toppling over.

The roar lessened to a less painful level. They waited without moving, dreading that the speakers might announce some malfunction. But when the announcement came it was to say that the ship was already in orbit; it was in the right orbit, and within an hour the team of five hundred engineers would be stripping away the now obsolete outer casing. Conway looked once again towards Helios, but only for a flash. For although Helios was not overly bright, he knew that if he looked at that fiercely blue point of light for too long it would burn out a spot on his retina.

None of them had eaten, so they made their way to the restaurant. They began by ordering a long row of ice-cold double Martinis.

'God, how I hate that old-fashioned chemical stuff,' said Cadogan. 'I was all goose-pimples as it went up.'

'It's a pity one of the old-timers couldn't have seen it,' someone said.

'That's right. They didn't know what they were starting.'

By morning the whole world knew that both the first rocket and the second reserve were safely in their parking orbits. Fawsett and Cathy heard it over breakfast.

'How long does that mean we've got?' she asked.

'Another day, Baby.' He saw Cathy wince and realized that his transatlantic switch was a mistake.

'I don't know exactly when we shall be taking off, but certainly within three or four days after that.'

'But why can't they tell you when you'll be taking off?'

This was the sort of question that Cathy was always asking. It defied an answer, it was the way that things were done.

'They'll be giving us our final briefing.'

'But they've been briefing you, or whatever it is they do to you, for months now, haven't they?'

Mike sighed, 'Well, something unexpected might have turned up.'

'But it hasn't. I don't see why you shouldn't go straight to the place. I do if I want to go anywhere.'

Fawsett really couldn't see either, but he knew he wasn't going to start breaking new ground now. Besides, he was doubtful if he could stand up to another three days with Cathy. He found himself wondering how Conway managed it.

'Well, we'd better make the best use of the time we've got,' she said.

By now he was coming to realize that Cathy was using him, not the other way round. It had never happened to him before. He began to wonder how it came about that her marriage to Conway seemed to go on and on for ever without breaking up.

'We could always have stayed in bed,' he said.

'You said there wasn't any breakfast service. So we had to get up,' answered Cathy, taking a long drink of orange juice. He noticed that whereas she had an aversion to fattening foods she always managed to maintain a hearty appetite. This seemed typical of her.

'I'm ready now.'

He felt it would be unmanly and unmasculine not to lead the way back to the bed. But when they got there it was she who pulled him down on to her. With her arms round his neck she whispered, 'We must get the most out of every single minute, darling.'

The light was greying dawn. During the night there had been an early snowfall. For the most part the flakes had simply melted as they reached the ground, except that there were two inches of wet brownish slush everywhere along the side of the pavements. Mike slowly dressed himself. He had about two hours before he must report. And he had a headache, not the thick fuzzy headache of a hang-over either. Cathy was still sleeping peacefully. He moved about the room making more noise than he need have done. Still she slept on, almost without moving. God, he thought, does she do nothing but eat, sleep, and fornicate.

If Cathy had been awake and if she could have read his thoughts, she would have told him that if one wanted to be vulgar there were words that one could use more tastefully. And she might have added, if she had managed to formulate the thought, that in a man's world what else was there for a woman to do.

Eventually he shook her by the shoulders. When she opened her eyes they were quite blank for a moment. Then they seemed to focus, she put her arms around him and said, 'Oh, Mike.'

'No, no, not now, Sugar.'

This made her let him go.

'I've got to move very soon. I wanted to say good-bye.'

The thought that Mike really had to go rushed in upon Cathy. She jumped quickly out of bed and cried, 'I'll have my clothes on in a moment.'

Again he took her by the shoulders, 'No, for God's sake, no. I hate that sort of good-bye. Let's make it now, here.'

Cathy's face was alive with emotion, 'Promise me Mike, promise me that you'll come back safely.'

As if he could promise anything of the sort, as if he wouldn't do his damnedest to come back. 'It's all going to be very simple. You know I've been out there scores of times before.'

'But this isn't really the same, is it Mike?'

'It isn't exactly the same, but it's the same sort of thing. It's going to be maraschino cherry,' he added.

She clung to him at the door, and there were tears in her eyes as he waved across to her from inside the elevator. On the way down he knew that Cathy had not been acting a part. It was just that she was – well, he'd better face it – a bit physical. It was a cold, raw morning outside. A lousy morning to be beginning such an adventure, and he still had the headache.

Cathy sat for perhaps an hour after he had gone, staring vacantly in front of her. Then she went to her bag and found to her relief that she hadn't forgotten her little red address book. She found the number and began one of her usual battles with the telephone company. It worked out all right in the end; eventually she was put through to Hugh, 'Can you meet me if I come down today?' she asked.

Conway used every ounce of influence he could muster to find a good place near Miami. His luck was in, a friend turned out to be a friend of the President of Reactors Incorporated, who had a bungalow on a private strip of beach. The key to it was sent down to the rocket base by helicopter. It was mid-afternoon when he met Cathy at the Miami airport. As usual she kissed him as if absolutely nothing had happened. In the car she moved across the seat towards him. It seemed incredible but she really behaved as if she had forgotten the whole business. When they reached the bungalow he took a shower and then busied himself mixing drinks. He found Cathy outside, changed into slacks and a shirt, sitting in a deckchair looking down at the slope of the beach towards the sea. 'It's nice to be here,' she said, 'it was horribly cold and wet in New York.'

They kept them waiting around for the best part of two days. There was absolutely nothing for them to do at the assembly sector, except to drink endlessly, and to talk about the girls they'd spent the last two days with. Reinbach had spent them with an actress in her cabin on Malibu Beach. She'd been hot stuff, but not quite so hot as she thought she was. Still, he hadn't had a bad time, not when he reckoned what they were in for, except that he'd had to go into some big surf to pull out a young kid and had got himself a belly full of salt water, which he could still taste in his mouth. Larson had spent his leave with a couple of sisters and made a big point of the need for recovery. The first day he slept for fifteen hours, the second day he did three sessions in the gymnasium. Fiske and Fawsett were more reticent. Fiske had been with his girl from the Rand Corporation. She had tried to pressure him into marriage, having a shrewd suspicion that he was an easier proposition now than he would be on his return. When he pointed out that there was a rule against married men she said they could get married secretly. But Fiske wasn't falling for that one at this stage of the game. He wasn't going to risk losing at the last round. Mike listened to the chatter about girls, said as little as he could, and thought that they didn't know what they were talking about.

After the fourth Scotch, the night before take-off, he suddenly had a big idea. It would be worth millions if he could exploit it – just his luck to be off into space at this moment. For he'd discovered the secret of sex appeal. When you considered what girls were willing to pay to cosmetic manufacturers, mere pedlars of daubs and rose-water, what would they be prepared to pay for the real thing? The trouble was that the real answer was too simple, once you saw it it was obvious. He realized it from thinking about Cathy. What was it that made it for her? Her looks – yes, partly. But even without her looks she'd still have been dynamite. It was this that gave him the answer. Sex appeal wasn't a mysterious quality, a subtle alchemical conjuring trick, it came just from being interested in sex, as simple as that, genuinely interested in sex. A pretence, however cunningly disguised, could never compete with the real thing. This cleared up a point that had always puzzled him.

He'd often wondered why so many of his friends with the marriages that worked best were married to quite plain girls. He saw it now. The plain girls had discovered the same answer.

The space shuttle had them out in orbit in half an hour. Several hours' manoeuvring followed as they made small corrections to their orbit. The idea was to bring them alongside the ship that was to carry them into the depths of space. It is strange to recall how the first orbits of the Earth, around the year 1960, were greeted with world-wide excitement. For now not one of the four astronauts deigned even to look outside. Larson, the leader, was concerned with a mass of official papers, Reinbach and Fawsett read paper-backed novels, while Fiske concerned himself with the sporting press. Yet when they were brought alongside, all four crowded to the viewing tube.

'Boy, what a beaut,' muttered Fiske. And a beaut she was, sleek and powerful, ready at a touch to hurl them on their journey towards the unknown planet.

The Russians waited until it was known that the four astronauts were safely transferred to the big ship before announcing that their own ship had already been in flight towards Helios for two days. The West groaned, and earnest commentators on the television networks assured viewers that the East had scored yet another propaganda victory; they were always ahead.

Actually the Russians had had their difficulties. The inclusion of Ilyana in the party was all very well at the stage when everything was on paper. It was a useful goad for pricking the capitalist warmongers of the West. But as the project took shape and neared completion it was gradually borne in on the Russian planners that they really were committed to sending a woman into space – and on the most difficult and hazardous journey that had yet been attempted. The mathematicians demonstrated very plainly that any withdrawal would lose more ground than had been gained by the original trick. So Ilyana had to go. When the matter was referred to the engineers they made light of it. After all, it would be possible to take the girl out to orbit under quite low acceleration. This could easily be done in a specially designed transit vehicle. It wouldn't be a bad idea to take Pitoyan that way too for he wasn't a professional either. The accelerations of the main ship as it moved away from its parking orbit around the Earth would in any case be quite gentle. The only dicey part would be the actual landing on Achilles, and Ilyana would simply have to take her chance. Nobody in Moscow would have dreamt that Ilyana was to come out of that particular episode rather better than the others.

A small, but not negligible, advantage was to be had from leaving the parking orbit quite quickly, at a moment when the direction in the orbit was parallel to the Earth's motion around the Sun. This meant that a fairly powerful acceleration had to be used, in fact as powerful as the reactor motors could reasonably stand without risks being taken. Both Pitoyan and Ilyana had had a rather bad passage during this phase. When it was over, but while they were still feeling groggy, Pitoyan was rather annoyed by the excessive attention that Kratov and Bakovsky were giving to their female colleague. He consoled himself with the thought that, once recovered, he should have little difficulty in cutting out such a pair of corn-growers.

Bakovsky set the ship on a slowly ascending climb out of the plane of the planetary orbits. Helios was not moving in that plane, so it was essential to move upwards at about 45° in order to make the interception at the right point, at the right point if they were ever to be able to return safely, that is to say. Pitoyan quickly recovered his self-respect by checking that the course had been correctly set. This was his line of business, and the others acknowledged it.

Ilyana had been thrilled by the sight of the Earth as they had moved up to their parking orbit. She had made a tape recording, in pleasant flowing terms, describing it all. The tape was returned to Moscow where tens of thousands of copies were made. These were sent out, throughout the length and breadth of the Russo-Chinese Union. They were played in schools to earnest-faced children, children who spent the summer herding goats in Uzbekistan, to slant-eyed children on the river Lena, and to girls with pigtails in Odessa. Ilyana was very proud.

The Earth had looked very beautiful as it receded away from them, now it was a rather small distant disc. Ilyana spent many hours at the viewer, entranced by the beauties of the colours and by the ever-changing patterns. She watched a storm developing in the Atlantic and wondered whether the effects would reach as far as Moscow. On the dark side of the Earth she could see the lights of cities, and this sent shivers down her back. It was improper to think it, but she couldn't help thinking it – of all the things that were going on in those cities, of how important the Earth seemed to the people down there, and of how little it looked in the telescope – no bigger than a firefly. She thought it was rather like being a god to look down on it, and then despised herself for such bourgeois thoughts.

She liked it when the region of her birth around Kiev came into view, and was exasperated that the picture was not a great deal clearer. Pitoyan told her that it was the refracting effect of the Earth's own atmosphere, and this of course was correct. She knew she would have a bit of trouble with Pitoyan. Not that that would have mattered very much in itself, but it would upset the other two, whom she thought of as being very nice and sweet and rather harmless.

It was also fascinating to look at Mars and Venus, and Jupiter and Saturn. It was true that she had seen them just as well in books, but somehow it seemed infinitely more exciting actually to see the planets. Everywhere it was black except that the stars shone as beautiful points of light. Along the Milky Way there was an endless carpet of star-dust. It reminded her of childhood stories, of the diamonds in the

Tsar's palace. But the Sun seemed alive, she could see things wriggling on its surface like snakes. She saw the lances of the corona as they streamed out many millions of miles into space and felt an overwhelming fear of the relentless tongues of flame.

Pitoyan found that things were not as easy as he had expected. He had thought that there would be lots of times when Kratov and Bakovsky would both be thoroughly and soundly asleep. But the way it turned out the lights were always on, and there always seemed to be someone thoroughly awake. The situation was impossible, the opportunities nil. What Pitoyan had not reckoned on was Popkin's Theorem. All this had been taken account of in the calculations. And Popkin was perfectly right, the amount of talk on sex in the Russian rocket was absolutely nil in contrast to that in the American rocket, now two and a half days behind.

They were travelling at this time at about thirty kilometres per second. This meant a distance of about two million miles a day, so that the Russians were some five million miles ahead. But there was still a very long way to go. It was like winning the first couple of matches in the baseball season. It meant little or nothing.

To both rockets there was a constant flow of information and of questions from Earth. The time for a message to get through was still only about a couple of minutes. Later on, when the time would widen to about eight hours, they would have far more privacy. Only genuinely important information would then be sent.

Chapter Eight

The Voyage

For the most part the messages were concerned with technical data, but there were also more personal messages – what
was the crew eating, how were they sleeping, how did they
manage to occupy the time. It had all been gone into a score
of times before, but the public wanted to know about it
again, especially since for the first time a woman was in
space. The bulletins concerning Ilyana swept the headlines.
When it turned out that her pulse counts, her electro-
cardiogram, and so on were entirely normal, there was an
outcry from women's organizations all over the globe, particularly from the United States. They asked why a woman
had not been sent into space before. Governments dis-
dained to answer this question, for there really was no
answer to it.

The public maintained its interest for as long as the
public is capable of maintaining interest in anything at all,
that is to say, about ten days. Interest waned and withered
and was replaced by the remarkable story of a gorilla living
with a harem of human women in the Massif Central of
France. Investigation failed to reveal any gorilla, but it did
reveal the existence of three good restaurants, the proprietor
of which was a very smart businessman from Paris.

The four professionals in the Western rocket spent no
time gazing at the star-dust along the Milky Way. They
went about their business with a slow unhurried precision.
They too set their ship on an inclined path up from the
plane of the solar system. Just as the basic design of both
was the same, so they moved along nearly parallel paths.
It was true that the slight divergence might carry them a

502

few tens of millions of miles apart, but this was only a small fraction of the total length of their journey, which was to be measured in thousands of millions of miles.

Life in the ships was almost indescribably inactive. There was of course the routine checking of instruments, the preparation of the messages to be sent back to Earth and the reception and interpretation of incoming messages, the careful checking of themselves – heartbeats and the like – but this took only a small fraction of the twenty-four hours of each day. By the standards of the first space-craft they were luxuriously housed, but by any terrestrial standard they were packed like peas in a pod. It was here that one of the two essential qualities of the long-trip man showed itself. The first necessity was the obvious one, of being able to take big accelerations, of being able to take a physical beating, and still react quickly at the end of it. The second was in some ways more difficult, simply to lie there for weeks on end, in this case for months on end, doing nothing. It was even worse than being a prisoner of war in the old days, for there was no compound to trot round for a bit of exercise. For the most part a man didn't talk to his companions but just lay there reading, thinking, sleeping, or resting with a vacant mind. The ability to keep quiet was an absolute must for any long-distance astronaut. One chatterer in a ship and you'd had it, either you throttled him and chucked him out into space, or in a couple of months you were all prime for the nut-house. You spoke either in monosyllables or else tersely in highly-developed space slang. Exceptionally, Larson and his crew did in fact do a certain amount of talking from time to time, their subject being the inevitable one, the presence of Ilyana in the Russian rocket. Their visions of what must be happening there were lurid in the extreme. They cursed their own authorities at some length for not having the same idea. It was the best idea since the old chemical fuels went out.

Actually the situation in the Russian rocket was becoming more tense. Gradually the tiny container became the whole world, became the whole universe. The combine-harvesters sweeping across the landscape of his native steppes now seemed much less real to Kratov; the great crowds in Red Square began to evaporate in the mind of Nuri Bakovsky. The effect of the pounding and kneading that their personalities had received almost from birth was perceptibly weakening. They began to cast covert glances at Ilyana. At first they felt guilty about it. Nothing such as the Americans were imagining was taking place, but the tension was building up. Popkin, if he could have been there as an unseen observer, would have had less confidence in his Theorem.

The rockets had been on their outward journey for about a month when the first slightly disturbing incident took place. A burst of radio waves was detected from the Helios system. There was a major scare on Earth.

It was generated in the following way. The radio waves were first detected at the European Radio Astronomy Centre in the Aosta Valley north of Milan. The science correspondent of the Parisian newspaper *Le Figaro* happened to be there at the time and heard about it over lunch. Within an hour he was in Milan phoning through to his friends in all the major capitals. Radiating from the capitals, telephone lines were set tingling to a score of internationally-famous scientists, some of whom made the mistake of answering the phone. They were told that a burst of radio waves had been picked up from Achilles. What did they think of that?

The news was so shattering that most of them answered the question instead of slamming the receiver down. Conway said it was bad and that he didn't like it at all; others expressed much the same opinion. Within a couple of hours it was on the news-stands everywhere throughout the world. Conway had just time to see his name in large type before he received a call from officialdom. An angry voice told him that the radio burst wasn't from Achilles at all, it was from the star Helios. But it was a good scare whilst it lasted.

Conway kicked himself for being so foolish as to fall into

such a silly trap. Over the hundred years during which Helios had been intensively observed there had been three comparatively short periods, of a year or two each, during which the star had become a strong emitter of radio waves. It started with the emission of a few isolated bursts, but then the bursts became more frequent until they overlapped each other. At this stage there was a continuous roar of radio noise from Helios that had proved a most serious nuisance to radio astronomy. Then after a while the bursts became less frequent, they no longer overlapped each other, and gradually the whole thing died away. It was obvious that Helios was running into another of these episodes.

Over the last hundred years more information had been accumulated about Helios than was available for any star, except of course the Sun. The mass was fifty-two per cent greater than that of the Sun and the brightness was almost ten times greater – Helios being not only more massive but more evolved, as the astronomers said. This meant that, whereas the Sun had a future of about eight billion years in front of it, the future of Helios was limited to about one billion years. But long before that time was over, perhaps after only another five hundred million years, any animal life that existed on Achilles would be fried to a crisp. It had occurred to Conway, as well as to the military planners, that any such animal life – if it was in a position to do so – might consider that a switch of planets would be advantageous. But does one bother about what is going to happen a few hundred million years hence?

Because it was more evolved Helios was not quite as blue in colour as it would otherwise have been. The effective temperature at its surface was about 6,500°, which meant that the maximum of its spectrum fell in the green region, not in the yellow as with the Sun. Helios was a blue-green star and Achilles was a green planet. The distance of Achilles from its star had of course to be considerably greater than the distance of the Earth from the Sun, otherwise everything on Achilles would already have been fried to a

505

crisp anyway. The much greater brightness of Helios would have seen to that. In fact the whole system was just a little bigger than the solar system in every respect. Its planets were just that bit more spread out. It was as if the scale of our own system was rather more than doubled, as if the orbit of the Earth were moved somewhere out beyond Mars. It wasn't at all a big change, our own system could easily have been like it. But then the Earth would have been much too cold. The oceans would have been permanently frozen and, instead of plant growth covering the rocks, the land masses would have been grey, black, and brown. That is at the present stage of course. Eventually the Sun would evolve; it would get hotter; and a time would come when even a more distant Earth would warm up until the waters melted and life might begin in the resulting slime.

But if the burst of radio waves from Helios had not signalled the presence of little men with antennae, it did create a difficult problem indeed. The West had gambled, apparently unjustifiably, on a more or less constant interval of thirty years between these seizures of the star. The last one had been nineteen years earlier. So it had looked as though the next wouldn't happen until Helios had swept on its way past the solar system. Yet here it was, beginning again after only nineteen years, and this was extremely awkward. The noise emissions would jam the messages from the spaceships back to Earth. There was no problem to begin with, there was still a large angle between the directions of the ships and the direction of Helios, but later on the angles would become much less – not much more than 3°. The difficulty arose in the transmission from the ships to the Earth, not the other way round. This could be serious because, unless the ships could signal through their precise positions, speeds, and directions of motion, the appropriate orbits could not be worked out by the terrestrial computers. Then it was more than doubtful whether they would be able to navigate themselves through the tricky gravitational fields.

The authorities did their best to keep these issues hidden. But in the West secrecy can only be kept if a very large number of people are willing to keep it. Except where dire punishment can be enforced, a large number of people are never willing to keep a secret, not with enterprise the key-note of success. There was an almighty hoo-ha when at last somebody blew it.

Nobody of course could be blamed for the behaviour of Helios. But the Western administration could be blamed for not showing the same foresight as the Russians in sending a scientist on the voyage. There was more than a chance that, whereas the Western rocket would go astray or be forced to return empty-handed, Pitoyan would be able to work himself through the difficulties. People fumed to think that the Russians had done it again. It was clear that Lee and Marty Kipling would not win the next election.

At first sight one might wonder why any jamming at all should occur. After all, the big dishes, the ten-thousand-foot dish in the Aosta valley, for instance, would be pointed towards the ship, not towards the star. There should be $3°$ or more between the directions of the ship and the star, so why any jamming? This was the question that the com-mittees wanted a clear answer to.

They got an answer, but to them at least it wasn't clear – sidelobes. Nobody could quite understand this. It was pointed out that if a telescope was pointed at an object, one simply did not see things that were three degrees away. The scientists said this was perfectly right, but that radio waves weren't the same as seeing things. The answer came back that committee members had always thought light and radio waves to be really aspects of the same thing. Were the technicians trying now to say that this was not so? The technicians said that it was so, but that the frequency of radio waves was not the same as for light and this made all the difference. Indeed the same phenomenon did exist for ordinary light but normally it was too small to be noticed. There was a big difference due to the frequency and of course due to a profusion of star-spots on Helios. It was all a question of sidelobes. The word became bandied about the corridors of power – after all, an election depended on the darned things, whatever they were – these sidelobes.

The big question was what were they going to do about it. The problem of the sidelobes had simply got to be licked. The cost was irrelevant. The committees became irritated and appalled by the dunderheads of scientists who claimed that the problem just couldn't be solved. It didn't matter what you were willing to pay – it still couldn't be solved. That seemed incredible.

Then at last it all boiled down to there being one slight loophole. A dish of thirty thousand feet would be about ten times better than the present ten-thousand-footer in the Vale of Aosta. This might help, although the engineers pointed out that unless a bigger dish could be made with the same precision as the present ones as much would be lost as would be gained. This also seemed incredible but there it was. Orders were given for the instant construction of a super-S dish. Cost was immaterial. Conway nattered and raved about it. 'Can't the fools see they can't win this way,' he stormed. 'A gain of ten will be useless. The blasted star is bound to win out. They'd need a million-footer to beat it.'

Nothing was said to Larson and his crew. There was no point in upsetting them – sufficient unto the day is the evil thereof. So the flight went inexorably on. For every second that the committee men talked, for every second that the constructional engineers worked at the monstrous new project, the ships moved another thirty miles towards their destination.

The situation was tense indeed in the Russian rocket. It was being temporarily stabilized by Pitoyan, who had to switch from his former tactics and play the part of the disinterested party man. He let the other fellows see that he disapproved of their glances at the girl's legs. He studiously looked the other way whenever she undressed. His unspoken chiding served to return Kratov and Bakovsky to within the perimeter of their training. Such feedback effects among the psychological currents had been correctly foreseen by Popkin.

George Larson and Uli Reinbach were on a sleeping jag. It sometimes happened on a long trip that the sheer void in your own mind caught up on you. Then you would sleep maybe for a week at a time. In fact you'd quite likely just go on sleeping and sleeping unless there was someone there to waken you. They'd all have gone to sleep endlessly if it hadn't been for the small sounds that were artificially generated in their cabin. The utter silence of space did that for you. Before the effect of the silence, and of the long wait, became well known, there had been cases of whole crews drifting into a hypnotic sleep. There had been bad tragedies, failures to correct orbits at the right moment and of ships passing for ever out of the solar system, ships that would continue to hurtle through the void for as long as the Galaxy itself should last. That was why Mike Fawsett and Tom Fiske remained awake while the two others slept. There always had to be two of you awake, just in case one should go to sleep. It was a danger that they knew all about and, being professionals, they knew how to deal with it.

Mike Fawsett was filling the latest details on micrometeorites into the log-book. There were instruments on the outside of the rocket that detected an occasional impact of these very tiny solid particles. They were still to be found around them, even though they were well up from the plane of the solar system. One good feature of being up here was that it cut out the risk of being hit by a great chunk of rock. This was always a worry when you were down in the plane, on a run past Jupiter, especially when in the asteroidal belt, which consisted of chunks of rock resulting from the original break-up of asteroids. The particles that they were getting now came, very likely, from comets which moved as much out of the plane as they did in it. Mike wasn't thinking very much about it all, however. He was thinking what an idiot he'd been not to make absolutely the most of his week-end with Cathy. He remembered something in Shakespeare but he couldn't quite recall the exact words – it was something about being cloyed with a surfeit of sweetness. Well, he could do with a bit of sweetness now. Tom Fiske was thinking much the same thoughts as he read through the latest message from Earth. But then the message caught his attention.

'Scan this,' he said to Fawsett.

The message read: 'Return if difficulties encountered. Stop, repeat stop. Correct orbit uncertain. Return, repeat return at your discretion.'

Mike read it through twice and he still couldn't understand it. For the past two or three weeks they'd been getting messages that were all a bit off-centre. It was as though nobody down there was taking any notice of what they said, as if they weren't receiving transmissions from the ship.

Mike made a series of checks on their bearings. It wasn't very difficult out here on any of a thousand of the distant stars that stared unwinkingly from the black depths. It seemed as if they were trying to read into the innermost corners of the mind. After being brought up on the Earth, after looking at stars that twinkled in a friendly way, this steady glare was disconcerting. It was rather like eyes without lids. One never got used to it.

The stellar bearings checked with those of the gyros. There was nothing the matter with their course. Mike had had the idea that perhaps they'd somehow got themselves exactly on to the line joining Helios to the Earth. Then it wouldn't have been surprising if the terrestrial receivers had been unable to pick them up against the background of the star. But everything was perfectly O.K. They were a good two and a half degrees outside that line.

He decided to do something they should have done weeks ago, to turn the aerials round towards Helios instead of towards the Earth. Of course they had kept a close watch

510

out for all forms of flare activity and of the emission of streams of particles, but it had never occurred to any of them to worry about radio emission, not while they were receiving Earth. They hadn't bothered to do this before because they expected only meaningless noise.

The receiver saturated instantly. There was no gain setting low enough to stop it overloading. So Mike quickly turned the aerials off the star. This was the source of the trouble, although like the committees he couldn't see why. They woke Larson and Reinbach. Once he'd washed down a couple of pills with a glass of water and once he'd understood what it was all about, Larson began to swear steadily.

'It means we blueblooded well can't make it,' he ended.

'We could try,' said Fiske.

They all sat silently for quite a while. Each man knew what a 'try' would mean. It would mean they'd lose momentum, and in correcting their mistakes they'd waste fuel. The margin of safety was small enough as it was. If they wasted twenty per cent of their momentum drive they couldn't get back to Earth.

'There's two things to be done,' began Larson at last. 'We try for it, and maybe we lose twenty kilometres a second. All right, then we can just park around the job instead of going down on to it. That'll save us what we lose. Or we can go right ahead and down and make land. Then we don't get back. But we can get back far enough for our fellows to find us, once this scintillator has gotten itself out of the way.'

They thought about it for a while. That was the way it would be on a normal trip. But one of the things that had been hammered into them during the months of training was the danger of judging by past experience. The difficulty was that the gravitational fields changed faster than you moved. What looked like the right orbit now would turn out to be the wrong one by the time you got there. None of them was very clear as to why this was so, but they'd been put through tests of exactly this sort, tests in which they were asked to guess orbits in advance and in which they'd been completely fooled. In their hearts they knew that it would be easy to lose, not just twenty kilometres of momentum, but the whole of their fuel supply. It would be dead easy to find themselves attached to Helios instead of to the Sun at the end of it all and for them to be swept out of the solar system altogether.

An odd idea was forming in Mike's head.

'We could always contact the Russes,' he began. 'They've got a boff and a computer in their job. Why couldn't they compute our orbit for us?'

'Jesus, we'd never hear the last of it,' said Reinbach wiping his face. 'They'd radio straight through to Earth and we'd be for the plank when we got back. It would be better to turn back right now.'

'They can't radio back to Earth,' answered Fawsett. 'They'll have the same trouble as we have.'

'That's true too,' acknowledged Larson. 'They couldn't say anything until afterwards, and I reckon afterwards will be too late.'

They pondered this for a while. There was a lot in it. Face-saving and face-losing is a game in which correct timing is absolutely essential. The master stroke of today looks old hat by tomorrow.

'They could always give us the wrong orbit,' grunted Larson.

'That's a problem we can come to when we reach it. We haven't got the orbit yet.'

'And I'd say there wasn't much chance of them giving us it.'

'Well, we can't do any harm by trying. What do you say?'

They decided after talking it out to try to raise Earth once more. If that failed then they'd make their appeal to the Russians.

Pitoyan had some difficulty in deciphering the message from the Americans.

The appeal for help didn't surprise him at all because they had already had information from Earth that communications were not being received. The very frankness of the Russians on this point can be regarded in the light of self-congratulation, emphasizing that no matter how far the unexpected might arise they would still be masters of the situation.

Pitoyan's prestige had of course risen enormously. Without him the rocket could not reach its destination. Previously he had merely represented a measure of safety, of insurance, but now everything turned on his knowledge and skill in calculating the orbit ahead of them. And now the Euro-American capitalists had been obliged to turn to him for help. This impressed and overwhelmed Kratov and Bakovsky more than anything else could do. To them, as to all ordinary Russians, the West was a fairyland, steeped in delicious vice. To keep up their self-respect Kratov and Bakovsky still continued to send back their diurnal messages towards Earth. To Pitoyan this was futile and ridiculous, and he felt himself now to be the effective leader of the expedition.

Pitoyan felt like ten men when he awoke. He awoke because Ilyana's hair was tickling his nose. He dressed quickly in order not to excite the suspicions of Kratov and Bakovsky. Then he turned to his work with a zest. It was just because of this that two days later an orbit was sent out from the Russian ship and was received some two minutes later by Tom Fiske.

There was really nothing that the Euro-Americans could do but accept the orbit as it was given to them. They set their ship on the prescribed course and determined to keep the strictest possible check on future developments. It had surprised them a little to be given the complete orbit. They'd expected the Russians to give them only the starting speed and direction. This way they'd have a better chance of checking that the Russos weren't up to any tricks. It didn't occur to them that as far as tricks were concerned they were thinking along quite the wrong lines.

By now they were about equidistant between Helios and the Sun. When Conway had gazed at the star across the gasoline-tainted pavements of Florida it had seemed a small, distant, blue-grey disc. But now it was clear which star was really the monarch of the skies. The Sun was a dull faint orange disc. One of the most frightening things about these long distance trips was the way in which the Sun faded into comparative insignificance. In comparison, Helios was a brilliant object projected against a black sky. It is a matter of some difficulty to know what colour one should call it. One might say that the Sun is white and Helios a white steely-blue, but the human eye is a most primitive colour-measuring device. In fact Helios shone out a magnificent turquoise blue.

The weeks continued to pass, and the distant glittering disc imperceptibly grew larger and larger. Comparing one day with the next there seemed to be no change but gradually a new splendour emerged, of brilliance and light, of sparkle and of awe. As they moved into the Helios system the blazing ball in front of them was growing rapidly bigger, dramatically bigger. It was approaching the Sun's normal size but was apparently incomparably brighter. It is true that scientific instruments revealed the cold fact that it was only ten times brighter, but it didn't seem so to the now almost silent crews of the approaching ships. Its surface detail was almost indescribably complex. There were the crimson-red tongues of flame, prominences similar to those of the Sun but on a larger scale. These could be seen only at the limb where they lifted themselves hundreds of thousands and sometimes millions of miles above the surface of the star. The darker areas of the surface glowed orange almost like the surface of the Sun. These areas were quite small patches lying embedded in brilliant blue seas. For once they felt lucky to be cut off from communication with home, for they knew their words would be totally inadequate to describe what they saw. It was better to take films which would show things as they really were.

The accelerations of their ships were surprisingly gentle. There was none of the sound and fury of a take-off from Earth. They had to change speed by fifty kilometres per second, but since they had at least a couple of weeks to do this in they did not feel the gentle push that was bringing their motion into consonance with that of the Helios system. Below their feet the suspended reactors pulsed at a low level. The inert fuel was injected steadily along the cylinder walls, where it was heated into a sheet of rapidly streaming gas.

So far they had paid little attention to Achilles itself for it was still only a point of light. For a long time the outstanding planets were Hera and Semele. But now there came an inversion. Achilles was growing brighter than its rivals. This could mean only one thing. They were closing the distance. It was only at this stage that Larson and his crew became sure that they had not been sold down the river. It had always been possible that the orbit they were following was a false one. It had been hell waiting to know whether they were in the right orbit or in an orbit that would throw them back where they had just come from, in one that would leave them permanently attached to Helios, or in an orbit that would take them entirely out into space away from both stars. But now they knew that the Russians had played it square.

These days they were to be found more and more at the telescopic viewer. Achilles filled a good-sized television screen, and the image was reasonably clean. There were two overridingly dominant colours, orange and green. The strange thing was that although the picture was good they could still see no details. It wasn't that the atmosphere of Achilles was blocking their vision, as is the case for instance for the planet Venus, it was just as if there didn't seem to be any details. There were large green areas, and there were large orange areas. Occasionally they picked up a flash, however, and this they knew to be the reflection of sunlight in a liquid, almost certainly in water. Simple measurements now confirmed what was suspected about the mass and size of the planet. In conformity with the general pattern of the Helios system everything was just that bit bigger than in the solar system. The mass was one and a quarter times that of the Earth, and the radius was also a trifle larger. Gravity would be a bit greater than on Earth, but only slightly so, certainly not enough to be of the slightest worry to them.

The composition of the atmosphere they already knew pretty well. Almost twice the oxygen density of the Earth, a little less nitrogen, water vapour and carbon dioxide. And they said to themselves, they'd seen it all before. To men who had stood on the surface of the Moon and on Mars, it looked pretty good. As Reinbach said, 'If the Earth was like that it would just about be perfect.'

Larson moved over to the controls. Any fool could manage it now. He set the dials, checked them, pressed the re-set and, with gentle pressure from the main control lever, started the ship down towards its parking orbit.

Chapter Nine

The Landing

A difficulty about making a landing on any planet, which
was not realized in early days of space flight, when everybody was only too keen to make a landing at all, was that
you only get one bite at the cherry. If you put down at what
turned out later to be the wrong place – well, then you'd
had it. You couldn't simply blast off again and make a
second try. It cost too much fuel. And an ordinary simple
aeroplane, if you were to take the trouble to carry one with
you, suffered in the same way – it needed too much fuel.
But they did have very fine mobility machines. Machines
that walked on eight great padded legs. They had been
found enormously more serviceable on broken ground than
caterpillar tractors. The first time down on a planet, or at a
particular spot on a planet, was always a tricky matter. You
never knew whether you were going to find yourself on
steep mountain slopes or on hundreds of miles of soft quick-
sand. A combination of the two was the worst – quicksands
lying on top of large boulders, and covering small rock
precipices.

The range of their land vehicles again depended on fuel
– not on the fuel they could carry in the rocket this time, but
on how much each vehicle itself could carry. With a full
load each vehicle had a range of about five hundred miles.
This you could extend, perhaps to two thousand miles, by
carefully laying a chain of dumps. It was rather like the
methods used by the old polar explorers. You used big
machines to carry supplies for smaller ones, and it was
enormously wasteful and tedious. A more brilliant method
was to lay the dumps already from the parking orbit. The

517

rocket disgorged capsules containing fuel for the machines and food for the men, and oxygen too if that was needed, at regular intervals along its orbit. When it worked it was fine. But there was more than a chance that a capsule might burn up as it streaked like a meteorite into the atmosphere of the planet. And as the old explorers knew perfectly well, one failure along the chain of dumps was sufficient to cause disaster.

On an expedition such as this, far from home, away from any possible relief from Earth, the sensible thing was to choose a particular spot and not to attempt to explore more than a circular patch around that spot, say to a distance of five hundred miles. This meant they had to choose their landing place with care. If you were doing the same thing on the Earth you would obviously be unwise to put down in the middle of the Gobi Desert. Or on the tundras of Lapland. So when they got down into the parking orbit they were in no hurry to make their next move. They wanted to make quite a number of circuits of Achilles. This way they could be sure they hadn't missed all the interesting places. And they had plenty of time to debate which was the best spot.

By now the surface was only about three hundred miles below them. They had never seen anything remotely like it before. There just wasn't any detail, anywhere. The green areas faded smoothly into the orange. They knew now what these orange regions were. They were sandy lakes, mainly of about fifty miles in area. Their shapes were highly variable, some being more or less circular, others long and thin, some curved, and some straight like canals. In places they formed a huge series of interconnected pools. It was rather like the system of pools that one might see on a sandy beach immediately after a spring tide, except that these systems sometimes stretched for a thousand miles, the pools being laid out below them in a fantastic mosaic. These were obviously the oceans of Achilles. Probably they were not very deep, perhaps only a few hundred fathoms. There were clouds dotted below them like a patchwork quilt. They looked rather like strange ships sailing a vast series of land-locked lagoons.

The green areas worried them. They still couldn't tell what the darned stuff was. For one thing the green regions were unbroken, there were no outcrops of bare rock. In fact there didn't seem to be any outcrop of rock to be found anywhere on the planet. This didn't mean there were no hills; their measurements showed them that there were rises and falls of as much as ten thousand feet. But the green stuff went over the tops just as smoothly as it covered the lower slopes. At first they had thought they were rain-forests. But at this distance the telescopic viewer would just about show up tall trees, and it didn't. And although they could see many places where rain was falling, there seemed to be nothing heavy enough to maintain a rain-forest. They decided it must be some sort of dense scrub. It looked as though it would be pretty well suited to the mobility machines.

By all the rules there should have been a sense of exaltation inside the rocket. But hour followed hour with the men almost silent. The trouble was that their training hadn't fitted them for anything like this. They had been trained to step out into a stark landscape, a landscape drenched perhaps by ultra-violet light and X-rays, an environment utterly hostile to human life. Here there was no reason why they shouldn't breathe naturally as they did on Earth. There was plenty of atmosphere, plenty of ozone to shield them from all damaging rays, blue as the star Helios was. They weren't used to this. It was too gentle. At each orbit they shifted their position somewhat, so that they would be able to take a look at the whole surface, to make sure that they hadn't missed something.

On the seventeenth circuit Reinbach, who was at the viewer, exclaimed, 'They're down.' Far below them they could see the gleaming needle of the Russian rocket.

'Why are the bastards always first, even when it doesn't

really matter. It would have been better if they'd waited,' Fawsett muttered.

'Wow,' grinned Larson mirthlessly, 'it settles our problem for us. We'll go in on the far side.'

That seemed the reasonable thing to do, then they'd each have half of the planet to play with, exactly as they had on Earth.

Their brief vision of the gleaming needle below them had told the Westerners nothing of what had happened. It was a remarkable indication of the technical equality of East and West that the initial gap of two days, of some ten million miles, had been maintained almost entirely throughout the flight. Because Pitoyan had been a little more careful with the orbit of his own ship than he had been with that of the Westerners, the last stages of their route had been slightly more economical. They had then widened their lead to about five days. But they had taken up the best part of three of them in orbiting Achilles. After their tenth revolution these tactics began to seem unnecessary to Ilyana and Pitoyan. Pitoyan felt that now they'd seen a fair sample of what was below them, and if it was a question of a decision it would be best to throw a coin for it. Both he and Ilyana, in spite of their diversions, were utterly weary of the journey. It was like being on a ship moored a mile from land after a long voyage. They were impatient to make a landing. But Kratov and Bakovsky knew better. For all any of them knew some creature down there might be waiting for them. Sooner or later such a creature might make a false move, giving itself away. So the two Army men maintained their unwinking vigil at the scanner. The slightest flicker on it could be important.

At wearisome last Bakovsky decided to go down. He insisted that Ilyana and Pitoyan, as amateurs, should strap themselves down safely in their bunks before he set the ship into its gentle downward glide. Pitoyan looked up from his bunk at the cabin lights. He hadn't realized before how much he'd come to hate them. In a minute or less the retro drive would come into action. They'd have to take the best part of ten kilometres a second on the retros. There could be no question of braking down through the atmosphere by friction, they couldn't make a fireball of the rocket, not with all the delicate equipment in it, necessary for the homeward trip. He didn't like the big drive, the drive that seemed to flatten him into a thin sheet of jelly. He was just aware that it was coming on – then his thoughts were abruptly cut off. This was the black-out, blacker than a black-out in fact.

Pitoyan was next aware of someone peering down into his face. His head pounded furiously and his body felt as if the drive were still on. But it couldn't be because nobody could be standing over him if the drive were still on. The mist cleared a little, and he could see, still rather vaguely, that it was the face of Bakovsky. He was aware that Bakovsky was undoing the straps that held him down to the bunk. He tried to move, but his right arm hurt him like hell; it pierced his nerve centres in spite of all the other aches that were being signalled to his brain. Now he could see that the whole cabin was a complete and utter shambles. Not a thing seemed to be where it should be. Incredible as it might seem there had been a crash. 'Kratov is dead,' muttered Bakovsky. The thought of Ilyana, that perhaps she was dead too, gripped him, and somehow he managed to struggle to his feet. His right arm hung limp at his side. He knew it must be broken. He knew why Kratov was dead. The body had been flung across the cabin and lay mutilated against the wall. He staggered towards Ilyana's bunk and heard her moan before he blacked out again.

When he came to his senses again the body had disappeared. The cabin was still closed to the outside, so somewhere along the corridor leading from the cabin into the interior of the rocket there must be a place for the dead. Then Pitoyan remembered that there had to be such a space morgue in case of accidents. It was a place where the body would be frozen, so that it could be returned to Earth for the medical people to look at. You weren't allowed to leave a body in space because the medical people might find out something from it. It wasn't like the old-time burial at sea. Almost irrationally Pitoyan wondered if the refrigerators were still working.

Then he remembered Ilyana. With a shock of relief he saw that the girl's eyes were open. And they were focused on him, not staring vacantly. 'Can you help me?' she whispered. The straps were undone, Bakovsky must have done that already. With his good arm he managed to help her to sit up. He had a horrible fear that he would see her limbs bent at some impossible angle. There was blood across her face and neck, but he realized that this was only from cuts which would heal. Her face was twisted in pain as she stood and made two or three tentative steps across the cabin. 'I think I'm only badly cut about and bruised,' she muttered.

So the score was two badly bruised, one broken arm, and one dead. Pitoyan judged that they must have struck the ground at no more than sixty miles an hour, otherwise none of them would have known anything about it. He grinned wryly at the thought that they'd been talking about drives of a hundred kilometres a second, gaily talking about it for the last year, when a collision of only one per cent of that speed could bring their little world down into ruin. Almost literally, they were nothing but bags of water, and the repositories of shrieking nervous systems.

Ilyana had of course graduated in a course of nursing. As soon as she was slightly recovered she began to tend Pitoyan's arm. She gave him a strong shot of pain-killing drug, then cut away the sleeve of his jacket, made the best set she could and fixed him up with splints. She didn't like to use a cast because the set might not be good enough. Then she collapsed back on her bunk.

Bakovsky meanwhile had managed to get the outer hatch open. In the shock of the moment it didn't occur to him to put on a space-suit. The atmosphere ought to be right and he just risked it, something that every raw recruit at space-school would have told him was wrong. But there was no harm done, the spectroscopes had been right. He looked down at the ground four hundred feet below him. He tried to get the automatic ladders to work but they wouldn't. Either they were jammed or the power had gone. With a resigned shrug he got out an old-fashioned rope-ladder and paid it slowly out until he could see the end begin to curl up as it rested on the ground. Then he stopped paying out the rope. It was an absurd thing to do, but even now in the face of disaster he couldn't quite shake himself loose of a lifetime of obedience to instructions. After all hostile natives might attack the rocket, in which case it would be quicker to haul up the ladder if it wasn't all paid out. It never crossed his mind that the presence of natives, even if hostile, might be preferable to their present situation.

It was a long way down to the ground and his arms hurt, and the big bruises hurt, before he reached it. It was going to be a hell of a climb back to the rocket but he thought he could make it. He realized that Pitoyan would never do it. Certainly it would be possible to lower Pitoyan to the ground, but not even he, Nuri Bakovsky, was strong enough to lift a full-grown man through a clear height of four hundred feet. So if Pitoyan came down he'd have to stay there.

He could see that the end of the rocket had driven into a hard sandy material. They had come down at a point quite close to the edge of one of the strange lagoon-like seas. He noticed for a moment that the sky was very, very blue. The rocket was projected against it, towering now high above his head. He saw that it leant drunkenly at an angle of about ten degrees to the vertical. With a sinking heart and a tightening in the pit of his stomach he realized that it would be almost impossible to trim it for their homeward flight. He saw the odds piled up against them. Buried deep inside this mass of metal, stuck there in the sand, was a smaller, but entirely new rocket. It had all its own motors and fuel. It had its own living quarters, smaller than the ones in which they had travelled two thousand million miles across space, but nevertheless sufficient for their purposes. It had its own motors and fuel supply. But how was he to strip down to it? How was he to get rid of the outer, now useless, exterior. There were only two men, himself and a weakling with a broken arm. And even if there were ten of them like himself, there was the obvious danger that the whole structure would topple over while they were working at it. They didn't have any cranes to straighten it. The whole theory of stripping down was based on the assumption that you had made an absolutely perfect vertical landing. He looked up again at the yawning structure above him, grunted to himself, and began to climb the ladder.

It was a long bitter struggle and he was shaking violently by the time he reached the hatch. The ladder seemed almost impossibly heavy as he hauled it in. It didn't occur to him that, but for the higher density of oxygen in the planet's atmosphere, he would never have made it at all. Bakovsky was nearer to collapse than he realized. He returned to the cabin and began to do what he had to do. At the moment it seemed quite senseless but then you never knew what might happen. It was always possible that they would get back to Earth, and if that should happen the first thing that his superiors would demand would be a report on the accident. The report had to be written at the earliest possible moment, and that meant now. It was one of those things that had to be done however ridiculous it might seem.

The effect of the drug was beginning to wear off. Pitoyan's mind was slowly clearing. His reasoning was better now that his arm wasn't hurting quite so much. He didn't need to make the trip down to the ground to know how things stood. It was a miracle that they were standing up at all, even at an angle of ten degrees, and not lying flat out on the ground. He knew with a minimum of thought that unless they had help they were finished. It wouldn't need hostile natives to see to that. The Westerners were the only hope of help. Messages to Earth would not get through, and even if they did it was doubtful whether a reserve rocket could reach them. It wasn't at all like an appeal sent from the Moon or from Mars. Now they were attached to the Helios system, sweeping with it through the solar system.

With Ilyana's help he managed to get the reserve electric generator working. The main radio transmitter didn't seem to function properly. But there was also a reserve for that. He got it operating and began to send out endlessly the international distress signal.

Meanwhile Bakovsky worked away at his report. He checked and back-checked all the technical data. He didn't work quickly and it took him quite a while to finish. He signed the sheets, looked up the automatic calendar, and dated them.

'Will you read this through and sign it if you agree with it?' he said abruptly to Pitoyan.

While Ilyana took his place at the radio transmitter Pitoyan read carefully through the dozen or so sheets of paper. Bakovsky had a clear, very direct style that it was not possible to misunderstand. By now Pitoyan was somewhat curious about the accident. Of course there had been cases of this sort of thing happening, but in modern times it was very rare. It was almost the last thing that he'd expected when he'd thought over all the possible disasters that might hit them. He could see nothing wrong with Bakovsky's description of events before landing. They agreed with his own memory, although it was always possible that shock was producing some distortions. At the last he came to the pages of technical data. He almost decided to by-pass them and sign the document, but there was a dead man to answer for, so he thought that maybe he'd better finish the job properly.

It was all routine stuff – checking pre-set dial positions against the entries Bakovsky had made in the form of routine tables. There were the conditions of various switches, and these he came to last of all. They too checked against the report until he came to the switch that controlled the servo settings for the final landing. It was obviously impossible to predict with extreme precision how much retro drive would be necessary to make the final touch-down. So as the rocket approached the ground there was a device that measured how fast it was coming in; if the speed was too great the drive would increase appropriately. Without this feed-back mechanism it was almost impossible to avoid striking the ground at a moderate speed of, say, fifty or sixty miles per hour, just as they had done. He stared down at the final page and then stared again. It was completely obvious what had happened. The fools had failed to activate the feed-back mechanism. In his fury Pitoyan forgot the pain in his arm. According to Bakovsky's entry the servo switch was in the 'On' position. Pitoyan looked across at the control board again. The switch was manifestly in the 'Off' position.

He looked again over the other tables. Bakovsky couldn't have made all those entries simply from memory, he must have consulted the control dials. So why had he marked the servo switch wrongly? If he'd wanted to lie about it all he had to do was to turn it into the 'ready' position. In fact the whole of this cross-checking was a bit absurd if Bakovsky wanted to cheat. Probably he'd taken it as so obvious that the switch must be 'On' that he hadn't even bothered to look.

His mouth tightly drawn, his face grey with the pain that seemed to fill him, he went out of the cabin, staggering as he did so, and made his way into the bowels of the ship looking for Bakovsky. He found him contemplating the magnetic clamps that held the inner rocket – the one they hadn't used yet – in position. 'Would you come back to the cabin. There's something in the report that I don't understand.'

There was a slight air of belligerence in Bakovsky's face as they climbed back to the cabin.

'Well, what is it?'

'The switch for the servo of the retro.'

'What's wrong with it?'

'You've marked it as being in the "On" position, whereas

it's "Off". That's the cause of all the trouble, you blasted idiot.'

Bakovsky's face reddened. This was the sort of thing you hit a man for. He glanced at the control board and then turned to Pitoyan and said angrily, 'But the switch is in the "On" position. Can't you see for yourself? Haven't you got eyes, little man?'

The Westerners had made their decision. Like the Russians they chose a spot within a green area but not far from one of the orange seas. They wanted to be able to explore both kinds of region. And they didn't want to go too near the seas, for they suspected that the ground would be sandy and perhaps awkwardly soft for a landing. Their chosen place was almost at the opposite side of the planet from that of the Russians. Being professionals they did not start their ship immediately downwards once they had taken their decision. After all they had spent eight months getting there, so a few more hours wasn't going to make much difference. So they continued to circuit the planet for a while. And all the time as they moved they sent out radio waves which were bounced back by the surface below them and picked up in their receivers. This not only gave them their height from the ground, it also gave them rough information about what the ground was like.

'Funny, we're getting interference.' Fawsett was at the receiver.

'What sort of interference?'

They were all round the receiver now.

'Looks more or less like C.W.'

The image in the display tube was blurred, but then for a moment it became clear as if the interference had ceased. Then it blurred again, and so it went on for perhaps fifteen minutes.

'Looks as though we're out of it, whatever it was.'

'We'll still see if it's there when we come round again.'

'Could it be the Russos?' asked Reinbach.

'What the devil would they do that for?'

'I don't know. But we're fairly close to the place where they landed, aren't we?'

An hour and a half later they were back again. The signals were still there, and they were only there on the particular frequency they were using. Now they were on the right track it didn't take them very long to figure it out.

'It's the distress signal. For some reason their modulation can't be working. The Russos are in trouble.'

'What trouble?' asked Fiske, not addressing anybody in particular. 'They can't have blown up the landing. That sort of thing just doesn't happen any more.'

They chose a spot for landing, decently clear of the Russian ship, about a hundred miles away. They checked and cross-checked all the necessary details for making the landing, made three more orbits of the planet, and only then started up the motors again, still very gently. The rocket began to bite into the atmosphere. As the temperature of the outer skin rose, so the motors came more and more into action. The crew were on their bunks now. This was what they had come for.

Larson was the first man up. His first move was to check the stabilizers. It looked O.K., well within tolerance. He checked the condition of the motors. They weren't bad, although it didn't matter much because they'd be having new motors for the trip back. Pity in a way that they couldn't use the old motors to get them back into the parking orbit. Then they could have used the new ones only under low thrust, except of course for the final landing back on Earth. But that hardly figured. It wouldn't be possible to strip the ship down in orbit. They weren't equipped for that.

'Everything O.K.?' asked Fawsett.

'I'm told so,' answered Larson, still looking at the dials.

They prepared to test the atmosphere. It was all right, it just had to be all right, that's what the spectroscope said. But you didn't take any chances with things like that. First they evacuated a capsule, then opened it to the outside so that the atmospheric gases would rush in. They sealed it again, carried it back to their working quarters and worked through a series of standard tests. The tests gave the same results as the spectroscopic analysis had done. They had to, of course, but somehow you trusted the results more when you actually had a bit of the stuff inside your own rocket.

They filled a transparent airlock with more of the stuff. Reinbach got into it, wearing a space helmet and still breathing their own oxygen supply. Slowly and carefully he took off the helmet. From outside the others saw a smile spread across his face and he gave them the thumbs-up sign. A few minutes later they opened the main hatch and allowed the air to enter the rocket. Nothing happened. It was all right. Fiske threw the switch that sent the ladders down to the ground.

'Mike, you're in charge.' Larson set his foot on the ladder and began to climb down. Reinbach and Fiske followed, leaving Fawsett behind, just in case. All three of them laughed when they reached the ground. Now they knew what the green stuff was. Nothing but grass. Grass that stretched away from them in all directions, over hill over dale. It came about up to their calves and it had a nice soft pile. They weren't botanists so they couldn't tell whether it was any different from the grass back home. After all one grass looks pretty well like another. Embedded in the grass were flowers which they couldn't recognize. Even so it all looked pretty much like a clover field. There was a light wind that produced a slight stirring of its surface. They walked a few hundred yards away from the rocket. The sky, they noticed, was very blue, a little richer than on Earth. The wind and the grass were producing a very gentle whispering sound.

Uli Reinbach climbed back into the rocket. Fawsett and he soon had the first of their vehicles ready. With a small crane which they projected from inside the rocket the vehicle was lowered to the ground on a sling. It was a rather primitive arrangement but somehow it seemed always to work perfectly well. With it they lowered a consignment of stores. Now Larson had to make a decision. He wanted more than anything to make the trip across the rolling hills ahead of them. But as leader it was his job to stay by the rocket, at any rate until they had really cased the joint. Reluctantly he gave orders for Fawsett to come down. Mike swung his way quickly hand-over-hand down the vertical rigid ladder. He knew that this meant that he was going to make the trip, not Larson.

'You're going to take her, Mike. Got the bearing?'

'Yes, I've got it. How far do you reckon they are away?'

'Between ninety and a hundred miles.'

'Pity in a way we didn't come down a bit nearer.'

'You can make it, there's twelve hours of light. We don't want to be breathing down their necks. It might cause trouble later on.'

Larson waved and there was a faint halloo from Reinbach high in the rocket as they made off. Mike let Fiske take the driver's seat. They hadn't gone half a mile before they'd complimented each other on how sweetly the motor was working. The excess oxygen concentration of the atmosphere saw to that.

They'd never seen ground quite as smooth as this, their great centipede-like machine was simply chewing up the distance. After climbing steadily for fifteen hundred feet or so, they began on a long gentle switchback about five hundred feet up and five hundred feet down, and always the grass, about nine inches to a foot in height, stretched ahead of them. They had no fears of being benighted. The length of the 'day' on Achilles was nearly thirty-six hours, and it was still well before noon at the place where they had landed. Large white fleecy clouds were dotted over the hills, and Mike realized that it would only have needed a flock or two of sheep for him to have persuaded himself that the whole thing had been a dream and that he was really back home. But there were no sheep; in fact, as far as they could see, there was no animal life at all on the planet. That was one of the odd things about all this grass. There were no small insects weaving their ways amongst it. The faint drone of a terrestrial landscape was missing. There was just the wind whispering in the grass.

They ran into a few showers of light rain. Mike put his hand out into it. He looked at the little transparent drops in the palm of his hand. It was water all right. Even the rain here was gentle.

The only discordant element in the scene was the rasping noise of their exhaust and the thud of the eight metal feet as they pounded into the earth. It was a mere three and a half hours before they sighted the gleaming column of the Russian ship. They saw it from the top of one of the rises, still an hour and a half's journey away from them. They could also see the gleam of water far away on their left. It revived memories of many places on Earth, but it wasn't really like any of them.

The rocket was standing at the bottom of a long decline. They clawed their way down over three miles of flat, softer ground without difficulty. At first they couldn't tell what had gone wrong because the rocket was inclined directly towards them, but as they veered to the right to avoid a shallow pool they saw it leaning there, like a fantastic tower of Pisa.

'Jesus, how did they manage that?' grinned Fiske. 'You'd think they'd been using a guidance system from out of the Ark.'

They reached the open space in front of the rocket. There was no sign of any movement.

'Looks as if nobody's home,' said Fiske.

They set up a hideous din on their hooter, and after a couple of minutes a door high in the wall of the rocket opened up. They could see a white face, which disappeared, to be replaced by two faces. They shouted up asking what was the matter, and didn't understand what was shouted back in reply from above. The faces withdrew, but after a

- - -

moment a wriggling coil of rope began to descend towards them.

'Jeez, they must be pooped if they're using a thing like that.'

Nobody started to come down and there were more shouts from above.

'Looks as though they want us to go up.'

'Am I under orders?'

Fiske was grinning. Mike had a feeling that he wanted to try out the rope ladder.

'You are. I reckon you can't make it in five minutes.'

Fiske went up the first fifty feet very quickly, then up the next fifty more slowly. By the time he was two hundred feet up, half-way from the ground to the door above, his legs were beginning to tremble. He stopped a moment and then did what he should have done from the beginning, climbed slowly and deliberately without thinking about it. At least he did have one thought, that he could always manage to go down again if he had to. Fifty feet below the door he saw that the twisting of the ladder had caused him to get on the wrong side. Moving his hands gingerly round one by one to the other side, grasping a rung firmly he hooked one foot around and then quickly threw his weight to the other side. He caught sight of the ground and sweated even more than he had been doing. He found the last few feet very hard going, but a strong arm at last hauled him through the opening.

'What the hell's the trouble?'

The short stocky man who had pulled him in said something he didn't understand. Then he caught sight of a slim dark fellow, his arm between splints.

'My name is Pitoyan. It was I who sent you the orbit. We need your help now.'

Pretty direct, thought Fiske. 'You'll have to come along and see the Captain.'

It was obvious that this particular machine would never lift itself again off the ground – not with the sort of treatment they'd be able to give to it. The stocky man was sorting over a coil of rope. It made him mad to think they hadn't given him a guide-line.

Then he saw a fair girl standing in the shadow.

'My name is Tara Ilyana,' she said. 'I hope that you can help us. We are in great difficulty.'

Like hell they were, he thought.

They put a guide-line on Ilyana and with its support she didn't find the descent to the ground too bad. Mike received her with open arms. He wished he'd had a shave and a clean-up before starting out, but Larson would have given him no peace. He could now see a figure being lowered like a sack of potatoes. Pitoyan could not manage the ladder and it was simpler that way. Next came a bundle wrapped in a strong white plastic sheet. At last both Fiske and Bakovsky were also down. Incredibly Bakovsky had managed to shut the door by sheer brute strength.

Mike signalled Bakovsky and Pitoyan to climb into the cabin along with him. He started up the machine and set out towards the nearest of the hills. It took them twenty minutes to get there. There was an unspoken question as they dismounted. The two Russians looked slowly over the place, then turned to Fawsett and nodded. Returning the way they had come, Bakovsky and Fawsett lifted the bundle into the machine. Ilyana and Pitoyan were put into the cabin, the others climbed on to the outside of the vehicle as best they could, and they moved away. Back at the hilltop everybody again dismounted. Mike made an adjustment that reversed two of the large metal feet to form a digging instrument. It took only a couple of minutes with this improvised bulldozer to scoop an adequate grave for Kratov among the gently waving grass. They all saluted. Before climbing aboard the machine Bakovsky walked away alone. He turned towards their rocket and saluted again.

Pitoyan found the pounding as they thudded up and down, over and above, down and under, more than painful. There was a constant hammering in his ears and in his head.

He was in poor shape by the time they got back to the
Western camp. They took him up into the rocket and Ilyana
came with him. They took off the splints and put his arm
in some sort of machine.

'Instant bone-setter,' grinned Reinbach.

Even through the mists of pain he could not help wondering at the ingenuity of the Americans. He was given sedatives and put to bed. Before sleep overtook him he called
Larson to his side and said, 'You must watch that man
Bakovsky. He is quite mad. He did not set the landing
servos.'

'You mean he deliberately crashed the ship?' asked
Larson.

'I do not know. You see he thinks that the switches were
set correctly. Even when I showed him that it was not right
he still could not see it. When the switch was off, he said it
was on. In front of my eyes he deliberately changed the
switches round and said "Now that is off". I am not a fool.
When he said he had put the switch off he had really put it
on. There is something changed round inside him, he sees
that switch the wrong way round. It is the beginning of madness. You can see that I am right because the ship did crash.'

The others hadn't caught these ramblings of Pitoyan's.
When they asked Larson about it he said, 'He says this
Bakovsky fellow has got bugs. We'd better watch him.'

After the months spent in the rocket they would all have
liked to sleep outside. But although it was ludicrous to
imagine an attack, security demanded that two of them at
least should stay with Pitoyan, now in a deep sleep inside
the rocket. Because he and Fawsett had already had many
hours in the open, free of worries, Reinbach agreed with
Larson that they should be the unlucky ones. They also
decided that it would be a good thing to keep Bakovsky
outside the rocket as much as possible. There was no telling
what he might do if he was bugs.

As Helios sank below the horizon they drank a last mug of
coffee and climbed into their sleeping-bags.

Ilyana liked this sleeping out under the stars. As she lay on her bed she could see the whole arch of the Milky Way stretching from one side of the horizon to the other. It was funny that the constellations looked exactly the same as they did from Earth, except that the Pole Star wasn't the Pole Star. The whole heavens seemed to revolve around a point somewhere near Arcturus. Now the starlight had gone the wind seemed louder. And the rustling in the grass seemed louder. Before she fell asleep she realized that a patch of light in what she had come to think of as the East was growing lighter. It couldn't be dawn already, that must be twelve hours away. Then she realized that it was the Sun. It was now an almost ridiculously tiny dim ball.

Chapter Ten

Exploration

By now they were approaching the most difficult problem of all. It was always the way on a big expedition. To begin with there were the plans back home, the building of the equipment, the expenditure of tens of thousands of millions of dollars. Then came the space run itself, with all the uncertainties and possible dangers. The landing place had to be found, the actual landing itself made, and the tricky business of leaving the rocket – of changing one environment for another. After that you came to grips with the biggest problem. What were you to do?

Take their present situation for instance. They could report that the atmosphere of Achilles did in fact have the same composition as the spectroscope said it had. They could take back pictures of the rolling green slopes around them, and the films they'd taken while the rocket was still in orbit. The pictures would show fleecy clouds and perhaps a rainbow if they were lucky. They would show the orange-tinted sandy lakes. But there were cynical bastards back home who would say that one didn't need to come five thousand million miles, and spend gillions of dollars, to get pictures of orange-tinted lakes. So there they were, back with the problem: what exactly were they to do?

To begin with, at any rate, there wasn't much difficulty in answering this question. The first thing to do was to strip down the rocket. This they set about the day after the landing. The job was made easier by the presence of the Russians. Bakovsky, bugs as he might be, was a willing and experienced worker. Ilyana was a willing and welcome worker. And although Pitoyan with his damaged arm was almost useless, he would later become a most valuable member of the party, when it came to navigating out again through the gravitational fields of the Sun and of Helios. This problem had worried Larson even before they landed. It was true that the problem wasn't quite as difficult as getting in had been. But it had plenty of possibilities of disaster. Now, with Pitoyan, they had their insurance. The future looked pretty good.

They had a clear-cut routine for stripping down the job. The precise order in which every operation had to be performed was laid down in the manual. Every stud, every electro-magnetic clamp, had its appropriate moment. They had powered winches and pulley blocks; the outer part of the rocket became a crane which they used to handle the inner parts. In fact as the rocket came apart they used one bit against another in a cunningly designed dismantling programme. The result after three weeks' work was a sleek, slim job about four hundred feet high, with its motors brand new and almost as powerful as the first motors had been. It stood there ready to swish them back home, its posterior ready to spurt a jet of blue-violet flame.

Strewn around the camp was the wreckage of the old ship. They set to work to tidy it up. They unbolted one section from another, so that the original thousand-foot-long strips of gleaming metal separated into more manageable lengths. These they dragged away with their vehicles and built into neat junk piles. One particular piece of junk they handled with extreme care however. This was a long, closed cylinder containing the highly radioactive motors. They dug a long deep trench and buried it. They checked carefully with geiger counters that nothing dangerous had managed to escape out of it. When everything was finished they had a party. As Larson said, 'This is where we begin to enjoy ourselves.'

They had two vehicles, both of them running well. Since they could maintain radio communication with each other there seemed to be no reason why they shouldn't send out two separate exploratory parties. Somebody of course had to stay with the rocket. Pitoyan's arm, although much easier now, would make extensive cross-country pounding unpleasant, so it was obvious that he should be one of those left behind. The Westerners drew lots. It fell to Mike Fawsett. He consoled himself with the thought that this was only the first exploration anyway, and that he would get a chance later. They set out early one morning, soon after the rise of Helios. One party set off to explore the shores of the first lake, which they guessed to be about fifty miles away. They could also take another look at the Russian ship on the way back. It might just be worth salvaging a few things from it. Bakovsky went with that party. The other was to explore away from the shallow seas, directly into the large green area on whose fringe they were encamped.

The division of the personnel was Larson, Bakovsky, and Ilyana in the seaward party, Fiske and Reinbach in the landward one. They set off to a good deal of shouting and to a good deal of ribaldry addressed to Larson, which Bakovsky did not understand. Fawsett felt like stretching his legs. He took a ride with Reinbach and Fiske for about five miles and began to stroll back towards the rocket. Eventually the din of pounding machinery faded, and he was left to swish his way along, calf-deep in the grass.

He sat down not because he needed to rest but to take it in better. He plucked several stalks of grass and made a crude dissection of them with his fingers. He couldn't have told that it wasn't terrestrial grass unless he'd known. He fancied there were some differences but he wasn't sure. He plucked several flowers and did the same thing. They'd take plenty of specimens back and give the botanists a ball. He lay back, cradling the back of his head in his hands, and lazily allowed his eyes to wander over the thin streaks of clouds, thirty thousand feet up they must be. Then his eyes caught the green sward rising and falling in front of him. Just like a golf course he thought. What a hell of a time a golfer would have in this place. An idea struck him and he

538

realized it should have occurred to him before. It might have done if they hadn't all been so busy working on the rocket. How fast did this grass grow?

It obviously did grow. The thickness and softness of its pile showed that. It didn't seem to have changed much whilst they had been there, maybe it was an inch or so higher than it had been when they landed. He couldn't even be sure of that. The colour of the planet, observed over the long months of their journey, had scarcely changed either. It had stayed a steady light-green; it hadn't shown the same sort of seasonal changes that take place on Earth. There couldn't be any seasons here on Achilles.

Forty miles away Fiske and Reinbach stopped for a mid-morning break and a cup of coffee.

'It's queer but that thar grass doesn't seem to grow,' observed Reinbach. 'Maybe somebody keeps it cut.'

They laughed at this of course.

'God, think what it would be like to be a cow. Sort of cow's paradise, isn't it?'

'Funny there ain't no flies and no beetles.'

'And no 'quitoes. Makes me feel creepy.'

They lolled down in the grass and smoked. Reinbach's cigarette hung from a corner of his mouth, 'Did I ever tell you about 'Frisco and the Golden Gate?'

'Did you ever stop telling me about it?'

'I had a swell time for the three months I was there. Used to get in twice a week from Palo Alto. Used to eat on Fisherman's Wharf. They said it was the same as it had been two hundred years ago, but that was a lot of damn lies. It was full of big modern restaurants. You used to sit in there and drink highballs. You could look out over the bay, and sometimes it was clear and sometimes it was misty. Sometimes the water was as blue as that thar sky. And they brought you whacking great plates of fish. Outside in the harbour you could see the boats they used to catch 'em in.'

'You're making me hungry again,' said Fiske.

'I used to look down at the little bastards, oysters, and

scallops, and bits of halibut, and wonder where they'd all been a month ago.'

Fiske yawned. 'Swimming around thinking fishy thoughts.'

'Yeah, one of 'em might have been up as far north as Seattle, some of 'em right there just outside the Bay, and others – like abalone – right down south.'

They watched little funnels of smoke rising and dissipating. 'Kind of funny,' went on Reinbach, 'all those fish swimming around.'

'So what's funny about that? It'd be real funny if they weren't swimming around.'

'I mean swimming around and not knowing anything about us.'

'Not until you'd chawed 'em up. Then I expect they knowed all about you. Time we was moving.'

'Yeah, time we was moving. Otherwise I'll be getting bugs.'

Fiske looked up at the bright sky and along the grassy ridge on which they were standing. 'You going crazy or something? There's nothing wrong here.'

'No, there's nothing wrong here. It's just a funny idea I had.'

'Nuts. Let's get started.'

'I was just thinking what if it's the same with us.'

Fiske started the motors. The roar crackled out and startled even their noise-trained ears.

'What's that?'

'I got to thinking,' shouted Reinbach in return, 'what if it's the same with us.'

Fiske leaned over and cut the motors. 'What if what's the same with us?' he asked.

'Well, what if we're like those bloody fish, swimming about our own little pond, and not knowing something else is very near us.'

Mike Fawsett woke and realized that he must have dozed off for a little while. He opened his eyes, focused on a cloud, and then raised himself to a sitting position. He saw Cathy walking towards him from the grass. She was dressed in the same flimsy negligee she had worn the last week in New York. Instantly he knew it was a ghost and he wasn't particularly frightened. He scrambled to his feet expecting to see it disappear. But it didn't. It kept straight on walking towards him. He tried to shout or to speak but somehow or other words wouldn't come. When she was ten yards away she smiled and said, quietly but very clearly:

'Hello, Mike. You don't look very pleased to see me.'

'How did you get here?' His voice sounded unnaturally hard.

'Oh, I've been here all the time, ever since you landed.'

'But how did you get here?' His voice was stronger now, although his heart thudded furiously in his ears.

'I came with you.'

It was Cathy to the life, voice inflections and all. But it couldn't be. It had to be a ghost. A thought occurred to him.

'You're dead, aren't you?'

The old smile, exactly the old smile, came over Cathy's face. Her hand undid the two buttons of the coat, 'I'll show you if I am dead. It's beautifully quiet here, isn't it?'

For a second he thought he'd found the explanation. They'd used the reserve rocket. But then he realized that this was grotesquely absurd. How could they have caught them up, why should Cathy be in it, and how had she managed to find him here. The sweat was streaming down his forehead. With a tremendous effort of will he stepped towards her and lifted his hand to take hold of her. She had to be a ghost. She had to vanish now. Convulsively he moved his hands to grip her shoulders – they were met by solid flesh.

'Now are you satisfied?' she said. And she flung her arms around his neck. Her lips were on his, fierce and possessive, and he could feel her body through the flimsy coat. Something snapped. It was all wrong, madly wrong. With a wild cry he broke away from the clutching arms and began to run. But he was little faster than a drunken man and she easily caught up with him. In a moment they were down on the grass and she was on top of him, her face very close to his, 'You can't get away. I've got you completely now.' His mental resistance weakened and as it did so his physical strength returned. It just had to be Cathy, he could feel every bit of her. With an exultant cry he flung his arms around her and pulled her towards him. There was a wild moment, different from anything he had experienced before. Then he seemed to be falling, endlessly falling.

Twenty minutes later Pitoyan found him. He was holding convulsively to the grass, his fingers dug into its roots, and he was sobbing helplessly.

Fiske brought their machine to a clattering halt.

'We've been at this place before. I wish you'd watched those gyros.' He looked at Reinbach accusingly. 'You and your bloody fish.'

Reinbach was indignant. 'I have been watching the bastards. Are you thinking I'm bugs?'

'I'm not suggesting anything, only watch 'em this time.'

'Why don't you let me do the driving. Then you could set the course.'

This seemed like a good idea, so Reinbach moved over to the driver's seat. Within an hour they were back at the same spot.

'Who's not been watching the mockers now?' asked Reinbach.

'But it can't be,' protested Tom Fiske. 'I haven't taken my eyes off 'em.'

'Well, for God's sake, look where we are !'

They decided to stop for a spot of lunch and to cool off a bit. When they started again Reinbach was still in the driver's seat. This time things seemed to go better, it seemed as if new country was opening before them all the time. It was the same sort of country, the everlasting rise and fall of the green slopes, but they had a feeling that in spite of the downs they were gaining height steadily. In fact the altimeter showed they were. It was clearly a high point they were approaching. When they reached what they thought to be the top there were about two hours to go before Helios would dip below the horizon. Reinbach cut the engine and they got out to stretch their legs. Within fifty yards was the can they had thrown away at lunch-time.

'We're in it. Don't you see, Tom, we're in it, we're in a groove, we'll never get out, we're just going to go on round and round for ever. Remember what I told you – about maybe there being something close that you and me didn't know about?'

Reinbach's chatter was wild and it annoyed Tom.

'Shut up, or I'll fix you.'

Fiske didn't like it but he still had a full grip on himself. 'We'll kip down here until after the shiner's down,' he said, indicating Helios. 'Then we'll go by the stars. There can't be anything wrong with them. It's the gyros that are wrong.'

They walked away from the machine, just to get away from the smell of gasoline. They sprawled down in the grass and set themselves to wait. For a time Reinbach kept glancing back nervously to the machine as if he expected it to vanish. But it was always there, solid and reassuring, and after a while he calmed down and felt better. Of course it must be the bloody gyros.

They waited until Helios was down and the stars came out, the old familiar stars. It was as if the strange world about them had suddenly dissolved and they were back home among their own people. They set off in good spirits. It couldn't be more than three hours' drive back to the rocket and, after retanking and replacing the bloody mockers, they'd start out again tomorrow.

They drove for practically four hours and they still couldn't see the signal beacon that must be burning on top of the rocket. Fiske had an idea. They tried the radio, but they couldn't raise the rocket with that either.

'We must have overshot somehow,' muttered Reinbach.

'Yeah, I reckon that's it.'

'What do we do now?'

'We'll just lay up till dawn. It's a goddamned nuisance to lose time like this but I reckon that's the best thing to do.'

They got out their sleeping-bags and cots. It was pleasantly warm inside the bags, there was a gentle breeze blowing, and within an hour both men were asleep. Helios was already twenty degrees up into the sky when they awoke.

'Jeez, we've overslept.' As Fiske wrenched himself quickly out of his bag something caught his attention. Sickened he stared away down the ridge. Reinbach joined him and they both stared for a long time. They walked towards the thing. It was the can again. Reinback was beginning to tremble uncontrollably. Fiske looked at him and saw that nothing could be done. Reinbach would break up quickly from here on. He walked alone for about a hundred yards feeling very near to breaking point himself. It seemed to him that the whisper in the grass had grown louder.

Larson drove his vehicle hard the first day out. He had brought Bakovsky along because back there in camp he'd felt it would be better not to make a pass at the Russian girl. Now he wished he'd sent Bakovsky with Fiske's party. It began to seem a bit ridiculous to worry about the complications that could arise when you got back home, if you got back home. Perhaps he'd manage to find some way to get rid of the fellow.

The sand began before they got to the water and before the grass stopped. In fact there seemed to be a strip of about twenty miles where the sand and grass overlapped each other. This was why they hadn't been able to see any clear line of demarcation between the green and the orange regions from above. They were graded into each other – you could almost say, carefully graded into each other. Before dark the first day they reached a long sandy beach. It stretched away as far as they could see. The machine made about fifteen miles an hour along it, grinding its rows of feet smoothly and systematically as it went along. They actually drove out into the water and found that it deepened very slowly indeed, as Larson had expected it would.

They made camp by the water's edge. It was real good that there were no insects, no mosquitoes, but it was rather a pity there were no sea birds. The water was salt as they'd expected.

It wasn't until they were in their cots that a thought occurred to Larson, a point he should have noticed days ago. It was queer that they'd seen no rivers. The grassland must absorb all the rain. That must be the way of it. And it must be a question of soil. The sand wouldn't grow anything, so the water accumulated there. At least it formed sheets of water. The whole surface of the planet must obviously be controlled by different soil conditions. Larson wondered how the grass and the flowers in it managed to fix nitrogen from the air if there were no bugs in the soil. Or perhaps there were some bugs. So far they hadn't really made a thorough examination. It was one of the things they'd better look carefully into, or they'd get into trouble when they got back home. He found himself looking over towards Ilyana.

They drove on the next day, still following the margin of the sea. It continued exactly as it had begun. The second night Larson decided they'd gone far enough and maybe they'd better turn round in the morning. But when the morning came he decided to push on a bit farther, with the idea that the important things always lie just around the corner. When by midday nothing new had appeared they unanimously agreed to retreat. That night they used the same camping spot as they had the previous night. Nothing was changed, there were still the same light ripples on the surface of the water.

They had made perhaps forty miles back along their tracks the following morning when Bakovsky raised his arm and pointed in excitement.

'He says he can see something over there,' translated Ilyana.

Straining his eyes Larson thought he caught a flash of light. Through their glasses he saw that indeed something was shining. It was situated in a direction away from the water, perhaps ten miles away. Perhaps even more, for the air was very clear.

'We must have been blind to have missed it.'

'I think we might have missed it now but for Bakovsky's keenness of eye.'

'Yeah, that's right sweetheart.'

But Larson knew they should have seen it on their way out. The way they were going now made it a lot harder. He supposed they must have been tired when they did this stretch.

They heaved and clawed their way across the sand towards the bright shining thing. Come to think of it why hadn't they seen it from above? They began to make better progress after climbing a ridge on to the firmer ground. The gleaming thing seemed quite steady. By now Larson was pretty sure that it must be an artefact. How come, he wondered to himself.

It seemed to grow brighter as they came nearer. In fact it seemed so big and bright now that he was more than ever puzzled as to why they had missed it. He kept whispering to himself, 'What the hell is it, what the hell is it?' as they closed the distance. Even when they got to within half a mile he still couldn't make it out. It seemed like just a set of vertical transparent sheets. They were set in a row one behind the other down a long line. He guessed they must behave rather like huge windows. If you were in the right direction you got a big blast of light from them, but if you weren't you saw nothing. They drove the vehicle to within about two hundred yards of the nearest sheet.

'I reckon you'd better stay back here, honey.'

Ilyana said something in Russian and Bakovsky nodded at Larson, evidently agreeing with him. Larson opened up a container in the back of the vehicle and took out two automatic rifles. One he handed to Bakovsky, and the two men began to walk slowly and carefully towards the strange structure ahead of them.

Larson stopped in front of the first. He noticed out of the corner of his eye as he gazed up at it that Bakovsky was watching the ends of the sheet in case something should come round there. He couldn't make it out at all. It was just a plain sheet of translucent material mounted there like a huge bill-board, an enormous bill-board. He couldn't see the slightest point in it unless it was a bill-board. They made their way very cautiously around the ends. Beyond the first bill-board there was an absolutely identical second bill-board. Then a third, then a fourth, and so on. They stood there like a row of dominoes set up on end, and it was all utterly absurd.

They must have made their way around a score of the things when they came upon something different. But it didn't make sense any more than the bill-boards had done. It was just a box, almost cubical, made of exactly the same material. And beyond the box there was an identical row of bill-boards again.

Larson became aware of Bakovsky at his side. It was almost as ridiculous that he should be wearing an American uniform and Bakovsky a Russian one. Maybe this thing was some sort of customs barrier. That was about as much sense as he could put on it. They spent a good hour walking in and out, through and between, as if they were in a maze. Then Larson had an idea. He went back to the machine. It had some boff stuff in it. He didn't understand exactly what good they were, but he knew that the boffs used them for measuring electric and magnetic fields. On the far side of the vehicle he took hold of Ilyana and kissed her long and hard.

'Me and you'll work this out later, Baby,' he whispered.

Then he started back to the thing. Bakovsky was waiting for him in front of the first bill-board. Larson handed over some of the things that he had slung around his neck, they were getting a bit heavy. They turned the dials, pressed a few switches, thumbed through a manual when nothing seemed to happen, made a few adjustments and at last got some sort of reading. They didn't know what it meant but at least it was something. At least it meant that the bill-boards did something and that was satisfying in itself.

When they passed from the first bill-board to the second the reading on their instrument got bigger. And it increased still more when they passed to the third. So it went on until they reached the box in the middle. All around the box something or other, whatever it was, was darn'd strong. As they started to walk along the row of sheets beyond the box it grew less and less strong until it faded out altogether at the far side. There was a pleasing symmetry about the whole business.

Larson knew that this meant that Achilles could not be quite the simple place it appeared to be. But apart from what he could see around him, which he didn't understand at all, he had absolutely nothing to go on.

They marched up and down, backwards and forwards, looking at the boff instrument. It always did exactly the same thing. The readings got bigger towards the middle and less towards the outside. That was it, and that was all of it.

Now that they had found something both Larson and Bakovsky began to think along the same lines. Theirs was the natural human reaction. What could they do to change things? They didn't understand it, but perhaps if they could fiddle with something or other, something would happen, and then they would begin to understand it. Fiddle with it first and think about it afterwards. That was the thing to do.

The simple thing to do would be to heave a stone at one of the transparent things, but there were no stones lying around. In any case that would be rather silly. What they must do was something electrical. It didn't much matter what, but it must be something electrical. It occurred to

Larson that if they could electrify the air between two of the
sheets then maybe something might happen. Something
rather like a lightning stroke. The question was how to
electrify the air. They hadn't any sources of high voltage
with them. But then he noticed that Bakovsky was carrying
a hand-grenade, a high-temperature hand-grenade; with
the oxygen concentration as high as it was the grenade
would burn splendidly. It would make quite a fair packet of
ionized atoms, if they should throw it in exactly the right
place between two of the sheets.

He explained as best he could the idea to the Russian and
Bakovsky nodded in agreement. So they walked back to the
middle where the electricity was strongest. They chose two
of the sheets nearest to the big box in the middle. Bakovsky
insisted on throwing the grenade and Larson could hardly
object since the Russian knew the exact weight of it. Off the
little sphere went and Larson and Bakovsky ran as far as
they could in the second or two before it exploded. Crouched
down, with their heads away from the explosion, they heard
it go off, and, almost simultaneously it seemed, there was a
crack like thunder. They were momentarily blinded as they
looked up by a flash that seemed to race repeatedly between
the innermost and outermost sheets.

'My God, look at the box,' shouted Larson.

There, inside the box, was a bluish-green light, pulsating
wildly. At its brightest it was a fine, steely point of light, at
its most diffuse it filled the whole gigantic box. Fascinated
they watched as it went rhythmically through these cycles
about every five seconds. After four minutes or so the colours
began to change, first to a lemon-yellow and finally to
orange-red. Then to their intense regret the whole spectacle
faded slowly away. Larson gave Bakovsky a friendly pat on
the back and the Russian looked up at him and smiled.

Larson wondered if they could do it again. Only the row
of sheets on the far side of the box had discharged. There
was a chance they could manage it again on the near side.
So they took their instruments to the two sheets nearest to

the box on the near side – that is to say on the side where the vehicle and Ilyana were waiting. To their delight the instruments were still giving the same high value. Larson held up his hand in a knowing gesture, and while Bakovsky waited he walked to the far side of the box with the instruments. Sure enough there was nothing there. They'd fixed that side good and proper.

When he got back to Bakovsky, Larson nodded, and the Russian proceeded to unhook another grenade. Suddenly it seemed to Larson that his whole personality, his very self, was lifted upwards and dissipated like a puff of smoke. It was as if he could feel himself trailing away into nothingness.

Ilyana was astonished to see a man running at full speed from out of the inside of the thing. He ran at an angle to her so that he passed about two hundred yards away on her right-hand side. It was Bakovsky. She said afterwards that he looked like a man who was being chased by something. But that couldn't be true because she could see for herself that there wasn't anything behind him.

Bakovsky ran for nearly half a mile, his face strained with the utmost terror, until he reached a place where an arm of the sandy lake could be seen. At first the water only covered the tops of his boots, but even though it rose up to his knees and to his thighs he still plunged on, not slackening his frenzied thrust until the waters at last closed over his head.

Ilyana ran to the machine. She had watched Larson drive the vehicle and managed to get it started without much difficulty. The controls proved more awkward, but at length she was moving towards the water. She found footprints leading to the arm of the sea but the water was transparently clear and empty. Bakovsky had disappeared completely.

Puzzled and frightened, Ilyana drove the machine back and walked slowly towards the bright shining screens. She knew it was foolish to go in there, but she was determined to find out what she could. She knew perfectly well she'd been sent on this expedition for political reasons – as a toy, a cat's paw, of the men in power. She must behave at least as bravely as a man.

She found Larson at last. He was obviously dead. The expression on his face terrified her. It wasn't a look of horror, such as she felt must have been on Bakovsky's face as he raced past her in the distance, it was a look of complete vacancy and blankness. It was a complete negation of life. Very slowly she walked the whole length of this thing, whatever it was, with its awful power. She saw the places where the discharges had torn jagged holes in the transparent sheets. She saw that the inner box was not quite transparent, the walls were very slightly discoloured. She found Larson's body again, and was considering how she should best bury it, when a strange numbness overcame her. It lasted, as it seemed, for only a fraction of a second, but when she recovered she found herself outside the whole structure, halfway back to the vehicle itself. And she knew quite certainly that she must not return inside.

Driving to the spot where they had parked before, she got out the camera. She must take what photographs she could, otherwise who would be willing to believe her. Certainly not the hard-faced men in Moscow.

There was something there that could kill a man without a blow, that could drive a man out of his senses. For some reason the thing that had killed her two companions had spared her, but if it wanted it could kill her too. She had no doubt about that.

Feeling helplessly inadequate and suddenly very much alone, she sat for a while thinking what she should do.

As she raised the camera she had a horrible certainty that something was going to happen. But nothing did. Whatever it was in there didn't object to the pictures being taken. It was her upbringing that had frightened her, an upbringing in which it was an offence to photograph almost every object on sight. She took a dozen pictures, realizing vaguely that if the camera were faulty the number of pictures wouldn't help.

Pictures wouldn't help her either unless she managed to get back to the American rocket. Like most passengers she hadn't taken any real notice of the way they'd come. She had only a general idea of the direction. There would be enough fuel in the vehicle for the return trip by the most direct route, but there wouldn't be much to spare for trial and error. She started up the motors and set off. As the machine moved over the ground with a rattle, roar, and thud, she looked back over her shoulder, fearful of what she had left behind.

She gave up all thoughts of making a detour to her own ship. It was useless. It would never soar into this blue sky above her head. Momentarily distracted she made the mistake of looking up towards Helios and was instantly blinded. The amount of light from the star was pretty close to that which we normally receive on Earth from the Sun. But the disc of Helios had only about a quarter of the apparent area, so it could easily blind anyone looking at it for more than a brief flash.

She waited impatiently until the bright lights in front of her eyes disappeared and she was able to see around her again. She had instinctively braked the vehicle to a stop, and now she turned round in the cabin and looked back over the way she had come. The thing with its huge transparent sheets had vanished. Nothing remained but peaceful rolling grassland.

She began to shiver. It wasn't just shock. Being frightened didn't describe the way she felt. It was almost like being without limbs altogether. She could still think and that was about all. She could not feel the wheel in her hands and the vehicle seemed to go where it wanted. It went on after Helios had set beyond the distant horizon, it went on pounding and thrashing throughout the night, the crackling exhaust shattering the air as it passed by. After three hours the sun rose in what might have been described as the East. As it moved up into the sky its glow sent a strange red radiance over the whole countryside. It was as if she were driving through a sea of liquid fire.

Pitoyan saw the vehicle coming in about an hour after dawn. He was more than glad to see it returning, for the condition of Mike Fawsett worried him. For the most part Fawsett was in a feverish condition, but every now and then his temperature would fall and he would become quite coherent. But the questions he would ask were strange even to Pitoyan who knew that he didn't speak English very well. So he was glad that the big American, Larson, was coming back. He was also glad that Ilyana was coming back. He managed to descend the fixed ladder with his one good arm. The vehicle was only half a mile away now and he ran to meet it. He could see Ilyana, strangely enough in the driver's seat. The machine stopped almost in front of him. He opened the cabin door and Ilyana tumbled out. She stared at him wildly for a moment, then threw her arms around his neck, and burst into uncontrolled, but healthy, sobs.

Fiske knew that he was reaching the end of his control. His nerves had been almost unbearably frayed by Reinbach's breakdown. Twice more they had tried together to get away from this same spot. Twice more they had found themselves back again. Then Reinbach had refused to go on. In a way, if you were always returning to the same bloody place, there was a sort of crazy sense in that.

But you couldn't give up. If you gave up you were finished. So he'd made a try by himself. He'd concentrated on every inch of the way, concentrated until he felt his eyes would jump out of their sockets. He'd been sure that it was all different this time, until he came over a little ridge and found Reinbach lying there in a more or less unconscious state.

By now most of the fuel was gone. They'd simply wasted it in just driving round and round, driving round a circle with about a ten-mile radius as far as he could judge. He estimated this from the time it took and from the speed of the machine. It was as if they were in the bottom of a bowl, just going round in circles, only they weren't in the bottom of a bowl.

Tom Fiske wouldn't have cared if it had been the machine that had been leading them wrong. He wouldn't have cared if the gyros had gone stark-naked screwball. But the thing that really did frighten him was that they'd tried to make their way by the stars. Tom Fiske knew that you can't play about with the stars, nothing could do that. Yet it had been just the same, they'd come back exactly to the same bloody place.

It meant that you couldn't trust your own eyes. Fiske smoked for a moment and thought that one over. That was just about it, that was the truth of it, you couldn't trust your eyes. He remembered Bakovsky and the servo switch. Wasn't that what had happened to the Russian ship? Surprisingly this calmed him a bit. Somehow it seemed better to think that it was they who had gone crazy and not the world outside.

He thought of telling Reinbach about this idea and went across to him. At first he thought that Uli had fallen asleep, but then he saw that his eyes were open and that he was staring up to the sky. He shook him gently by the shoulder and said, 'Hey, I've got an idea.' And a hell of an idea it was too. To his relief the fever which seemed to have been growing on Reinbach had gone down. He could see that when Uli looked at him.

'Shouldn't we be getting back to the ship?' The poor devil seemed to have lost his memory. Probably some sort of nervous protective device.

'We'll try again as soon as it's light.'

'I'm sure we can make it now. It's all pretty smooth going.'

Well, if that was what Uli wanted they might as well make another circuit, thought Tom.

After an hour and a half's driving they ran at last out of fuel. Tom jumped down from the cabin fully expecting to find himself back to square one. But as far as he could see this wasn't the place. Then he remembered that what he saw didn't signify. Reinbach had come down from the cabin. 'What is it?' he asked.

'We're out of fuel.'

'Then we'd better walk.'

This was what had been worrying Fiske all along. Sooner or later they'd have to walk if they were to get out of this place. But they might just as well find themselves walking in circles as driving in circles. The mad idea occurred to him that maybe in some way all this was connected with the vehicle and not with themselves. Maybe they could walk out. It didn't figure, but then nothing he could think of figured. The danger of course was that they couldn't carry much food and water. For the first time it occurred to Fiske that there were no streams. The rain just fell on to the grass, where it was absorbed into the roots until the moisture evaporated again. He wished there had been streams. He remembered that he'd always liked the sound of running water.

They started to walk, still following a course set by the stars. The Sun came up, and they found themselves walking through the same liquid fire that Ilyana had driven through. Reinbach was going well now. There were times when he would plough ahead, and then Fiske was worried because Uli didn't seem to take much notice of the course he was trying to set. Reinbach had the air of a man who didn't care much where he was going so long as he got to hell out of the place. The trouble was that they didn't know how to get out of the place.

But about three hours before dawn Reinbach broke down. It was obvious that his temperature was soaring up again. There was nothing that Fiske could do except to let him lie there in the grass. It looked as though there was nothing that either of them could do. For Fiske knew that they would never find their way back to the machine. He tried to put his own jacket around Reinbach, but in his delirium the sick man kept throwing it off again. A bright star rose above the horizon. Tom realized that it couldn't be a star, there wasn't a bright star in that place. He realized it was Jupiter, one of their own planets.

When dawn came he looked around him. To his intense relief there was no sign of the can, or of the machine for that matter. At least so far they hadn't gone round in a circle. His eyes scanned the horizon and at one point he caught a distant flash of light. His mouth was dry with a growing excitement as he realized that it must be the rocket. The terror seemed to fall away from him in the morning light. He knew he would make it now.

The only trouble was Reinbach. He was obviously in a bad way and couldn't be expected to do more than stumble a few yards at a time, at best. Tom thought about leaving him and going to fetch help, but then he realized that it would be next to impossible to find him again in this featureless countryside. So he did the only thing possible, he slung Reinbach across his shoulders and set out slowly but steadily towards the welcoming point of light. It would take a long time, but he would make it.

Ilyana had told her story to Pitoyan. Although he said he believed her he'd asked for the camera and had gone to process the film. Sitting waiting in the grass she saw him coming down the ladder from the rocket holding a bunch of prints in his bad hand. With a sinking heart she knew that they'd be blanks. There wouldn't be anything on them at all. And that was the way it was. They were all just useless blanks.

The way he looked at her it was obvious that he thought that she was mad, the same way that the American, Fawsett, seemed to be mad.

Then Pitoyan told her that he knew the two men had been killed in a very different way. They had been killed in fighting over her, and that she might as well admit it instead of producing a ridiculous story. Ilyana, seeing that she would never convince him, admitted it. She told him that the American had attacked her, which in a sense was true. Bakovsky had come back unexpectedly, and in the ensuing fight the American had killed him, but not before Bakovsky had exploded a grenade. It sounded silly to her but Pitoyan seemed to believe it. It came within the range he could believe whereas the truth did not. And Ilyana saw that this would be the way of it when they got back to Earth, if they ever got back. By now she didn't seem to care very much. She thought of the endless, anonymous grey buildings in Moscow, and decided it was unimportant what they believed.

Pitoyan began to climb back into the rocket. It was funny the way he seemed to spend almost all his time inside the thing, thought Ilyana. He even slept there, as if he were afraid of this new world around them. Ilyana shivered as the memories of yesterday came back to her. Even about those memories there was something strange. They weren't as clear or as sharp as they should have been. They should have been etched indelibly on her mind, but it was more as if they had happened three years ago. In a way she was glad of this, for it prevented her from being frightened out of her wits, of having the same trembling fits as the American, Fawsett, had.

She began to think about the Americans in the other vehicle. She hadn't thought much about them before, but now, suddenly, she was quite sure they must be in trouble. She started up the ladder after Pitoyan, intending to ask him to try to raise them on the radio. At the top she paused for a moment to gaze out over the green countryside. It was then she saw two men moving very slowly on foot about five miles away. In a few seconds she was on the ground again, starting up her machine. She drove it, threshing and thudding, up the incline towards the distant hills.

Tom Fiske was now staggering very badly. The weight on his shoulders seemed to press him into the ground, his ears were thudding with the sound of his own heartbeats. For a while he couldn't believe that the noise really came from a machine that seemed to be coming towards him. For a moment he had the wild idea that somehow his own machine had managed to get started by itself, but this one pulled in alongside of him and the pretty Russian girl climbed down from the cabin.

She helped him up with Reinbach's inert body, and they moved off. He sat in a stupor. He didn't have to carry anything any more, and within an incredibly short time they were back in front of the rocket. Again he had to make a big effort. He had to carry Reinbach up the long vertical ladder, he couldn't expect the girl to help with this. Somehow he got him into one of the bunks, and he and the little Russian fellow shot him full of drugs. Uli ought to be all right now.

Pitoyan told him what had happened. He told him about Fawsett, and it was obvious to Tom that both Mike and Uli had gone down with the same sort of fever. It was equally obvious that the expedition was over. The sooner they lifted the rocket up into the sky and were started back for home the better. But first he had to check up on Larson's death. This was absolutely necessary because of the inquiry there would be back on Earth. He went down and re-tanked the machine. Then he went to Ilyana and said, 'I've got to make a check-up. I'm sorry but you'll have to show me the way back.' Ilyana nodded dumbly. She climbed into the cabin along-side Fiske. It all seemed so similar to the way that she, Bakovsky and the big American had started out four days ago.

By the time they had gone about ten miles, and were traversing what looked like an undulating grassy road, she realized that it was quite useless. She doubted if she could really find her way back, and even if she did find the proper place she doubted if they would see anything at all. It would be just as blank as the pictures had been. She motioned Fiske to stop for a moment and got down from the cabin. Tom quite misinterpreted her reason for this, and he allowed her to lead him about two hundred yards along the track to a spot where they could just see the machine. She sat down in the grass and motioned him to follow. Then she began to tell him what had really happened. She spoke in slow, precise English, and he saw the picture gradually unfold itself – the sandy seas, and the gleaming transparent sheets.

'Well,' he said when she'd finished, 'it figures.'

'What does that mean?'

'It means that if that's the way it happened, that's the way it happened. I believe you.'

He told her his own experience of the strangeness of this new world, of the useless and unending circling they'd been condemned to, how they'd just gone round and round like flies walking around a window-pane. When he'd finished she took his hand in her own and began to stroke it. 'You must say that you ran out of fuel. It is better to be thought a fool than to be thought mad. But I know that what you say is right.'

It seemed the most natural thing he'd ever known to take this fair-haired girl into his arms. For the first time in his life he found himself to be making love without congratulating himself that he was doing so.

Chapter Eleven

The Return

The ship lifted itself swiftly an d smoothly out of the atmosphere of Achilles. They made ten orbits around the planet. Without telling the others, Tom Fiske and Ilyana looked for the gleaming translucent sheets, but none could be seen. Pitoyan obtained the data for the first crude setting of their orbit and Tom set the controls and opened up the motors. The ship seemed lighter and easier to handle than on the outward journey but this was probably just an illusion.

A day later they were almost a million miles out from Achilles. It was still a remarkable sight, the green areas looked just the same as they had on the way in. Two days ago Fiske had cursed the endless grass slopes, but now as he looked at them for almost the last time there was a strange tightening in his throat. He remembered what Reinbach had said about the fish off 'Frisco Bay and he had a feeling that that's what they'd been – a lot of fish that didn't know what was going on around them.

The cabin had been laid out for a crew of four, which meant that either they'd got to improvise or that two of them had to share the same bunk. Tom Fiske and Ilyana shared the same bunk and made no bones about doing so over the whole of the long trip back home. Pitoyan, furious at first, realized that even without a damaged arm he wouldn't be a match for Tom. He thought about taking his revenge by refusing to calculate the orbits. That would have been fine if he'd been in another ship, but any disaster to this ship was a disaster to himself. So he calculated the orbits and with equal correctness reckoned that he would have no difficulty in finding girls back home. He had achieved something worth talking about and had every intention of taking complete advantage of it.

The sick men caused them a lot of trouble. It wasn't just the careful nursing they needed at times, it was the way they seemed to become queer when they recovered for a while. A lunatic was the last thing you wanted to have on your hands in a space-ship. And they seemed to have two lunatics. Luckily they never seemed to be at their best at the same moment.

When the fever went out of them they behaved as if they were somehow vacant. Both of them would climb about the rocket asking questions as if they'd never seen a ship before. It was as if they were back in childhood, although when you looked them straight in the eye they didn't look at all like kids. Their eyes looked more like deep pools, and it was a bit uncanny the way each of them seemed to know what was wrong with the other. When one of them was more or less all right and the other was in a high fever the one who was all right would sit around endlessly just looking down at the other fellow. It was a sort of medical game of tag, and it gave them the creeps. They got into the way of leaving Reinbach and Fawsett to look after each other more and more. But for this the final tragedy would probably not have happened.

It occurred at a time when Reinbach was in comparatively good shape. Fawsett was in a high fever and was shouting incoherently – shouting the usual name of Cathy. When he was in this state it almost looked as if he thought he was talking to somebody. He would reach out his hands as if to take hold of something or somebody. The three of them got into the way of keeping as far off as possible when these attacks were on him, especially if Reinbach was there to watch. One day, about four months out from Achilles, they found Fawsett sprawled on top of Reinbach. His hands were clamped around Reinbach's neck and they had to open his rigid fingers to pull him off. Reinbach's face was black and the sight made Tom Fiske sick. Fawsett was still shrieking for Cathy, so Fiske hit him hard on the jaw, and this put a stop to the nonsense for a while.

By rights they should have put Reinbach's body in the freezing compartment. But Fiske felt that Uli's death might be easier to explain if they got rid of the body. It didn't seem as if it would be much harder to account for four deaths on the planet instead of just three. Why stop at three? So they placed Reinbach in a long metal cylinder, sealed it, and ejected it from the ship. It occurred to Fiske that if anybody ever recovered a body from space, with the lack of oxygen it would probably be perfectly preserved.

After this they kept a close watch on Fawsett. Secretly they all felt that they wouldn't be sorry if this shrieking maniac were to put an end to himself. In their closely confined circumstances it was a continuous waiting nightmare. The trouble was that you couldn't get on terms with Fawsett, even when he seemed to have recovered for a time. The strange thing was that he seemed to be mad with them about Reinbach's death – as if they'd caused it. The sooner they got him into a bug-house back on Earth the better they'd feel.

Back on Earth they had news of the returning ship. The bursts of radio noise from Helios were weakening somewhat, and the angle between the direction of the ship and of the star was widening. So at last, after almost a year, they had news.

The problem to those in the ship was what to do by way of explanation. They decided, without formulating any plan or purpose, essentially each for himself, to be as vague as possible. Fiske sent out transmissions on the Euro-American wave-length, while Pitoyan sent out communications on the Russian wave-length. So both sides thought that their ship was returning.

Of the endless stream of questions to which they were subjected they answered some and ignored others. For the moment at least they could claim that transmission was faulty. Pitoyan had the inspiration of doctoring their transmitter, so that it deliberately garbled their messages. He spent a lot of effort doing this in a way that he hoped the experts would find difficult to understand when finally the rocket landed on Earth. It would have been easy to have put the transmitter out of action altogether, but it was necessary to keep Earth accurately informed on one point, namely when and where they would be coming in to land. Later on, as Pitoyan said, they would have to play it by ear.

Both Washington and Moscow were unbearably frustrated by these tactics. The two Governments wanted full and accurate information themselves, although they still hadn't informed their respective publics.

They had a sound psychological reason for this. It would still be three or four months before any ship could return, there was still the long coasting section through the orbits of Saturn and Jupiter. And they knew that the populace at large simply cannot maintain its interest in any topic for three months. There would be an intense newspaper, radio and television publicity for perhaps ten days, and after that the public's appetite would fall off quite steeply. But if they held their horses until about three weeks before the landing, then interest instead of falling could be whipped up to fever point. After all, this was a sort of gladiatorial show – except that, instead of putting up a million or two for a building like the Colosseum in Rome, this had cost them more than a hundred thousand million. Both Governments intended to see they got good value for their money.

Of course the news could not be kept from the public if the publicity services hadn't been willing to cooperate. There were certain to be scores of official leaks. This was particularly true in the West. But the plan of the Governments was really in the interests of the publicity services themselves. Responsible people soon saw that. To prevent a break occurring it was made very clear that whatever syndicate attempted to jump the gun would have all its official privileges withdrawn. So although it would have been possible for any one group to have scooped the others, the gain – while undoubtedly large for the moment – would in the long run have been more than compensated through the long-term loss of facilities. No group was willing to run such a risk and all leaks were plugged before they could spout their delicious liquid into the mouths of the waiting public.

So those who were in the know were aware of the return some three months before Fiske finally put the rocket down neatly and squarely in the south of Florida. Conway was one of those who knew, and it was hardly possible for him to keep the news from Cathy. During the past year their marriage had worked a little better than it normally did. Cathy had made no reference at all to Mike Fawsett. But with the news of the impending return she instantly shed another mental skin, in just the way she had done on the day of Fawsett's departure. Now Conway did not exist at all for her. She seemed to live in a dream world of her own. Conway realized that the moment of the landing would be the culmination of her affair with Fawsett. It was in fact more a vision than a human relationship. The great rocket would stream downwards from the heavens, its exhaust belching the familiar orange ring, and it would fall more and more slowly until with infinite grace it came to rest on the huge ten-mile-square asphalt area. There would be a surge of vehicles towards it, the ladder would come down, the public would be martialled by hundreds of police, those with priority passes to the fore.

Then at last the astronauts would begin their majestic descent from above. They would swing athletically down the vertical ladder. The first to touch the ground would be Mike Fawsett. And no sooner was he there – the cheers deafening his ears – than Cathy would run forward and throw herself into his arms. So they would stand for all the world to see, Cathy and her hero from space. That was the dream.

The Earth could now be seen as a vast ball in the telescopic viewer. Fiske knew they would be there within the week. The moment had now arrived, the moment they had been putting off for months. It would be best now to send out a terse description of the basic facts, that only one rocket was returning, that only a half of the original complement of both ships would be returning. Fiske decided that there was no point in explaining at this stage. Pitoyan agreed with him. So they sent out a bare, cold statement of the true position.

The consternation that this message produced in all major capitals may well be imagined. For three weeks past now the news had been out, both in the West and in the East. Every child throughout the vast region from Smolensk to Peking knew that their beloved heroes were returning. Arrangements had been made for the parades. In Moscow itself there was to be the biggest super-S parade of all times. The factories had turned out many millions of yards of the best banner material. The cream of the fighting services would swing their way along the vast flower-decked avenues, they would be followed by schoolgirls in phalanxes, phalanxes of cunning design, schoolgirls with pigtails who had listened avidly to the reports from Ilyana. Finally, in the rear, the parade would end with an impressive platoon of wise men.

In the West things had been managed differently, but equally effectively. All round the preimeter, in fact all round the outer three miles of the asphalt area, stands were being erected. The stands would rise gradually, tier by tier, from ground-level at the front to a height of four hundred feet behind. It would be a stadium of vast proportions with the latest and most up-to-date loudspeaker system. The central region, some twenty-five square miles in area, would be entirely carpeted. Although it was not known at the time, the carpet was of substandard quality and the Corporation involved would undoubtedly have found itself in legal difficulties if it had not been for the events that were to follow the landing of the rocket. Tickets for a seat in the prepared stands were originally issued at an average price of fifty dollars apiece, but only a lucky few managed to acquire them at this low figure. By the time Conway and Cathy left London for New York the scalpers' price had risen to almost five hundred dollars.

It can well be imagined that the news from the incoming ship filled the corridors of power in Moscow with dismay. The mere notion that their ship had pooped was enough in itself, but the information that two of its crew were being brought back like sacks of rye by the Western vice maniacs, was just too much to swallow. In the West, on the other hand, the propaganda weather appeared rosier. Their ship had made it, and the squat Russian craft had not. The propaganda advantages of the situation would outweigh the fact that two boys had been lost. After all, boys had been lost before, in one way or another. Still there was a lot of explaining to be done, and the men of Washington, of Paris, Berlin and of the Rand Corporation smacked their lips, especially those whose job it was, or whose pleasure it was, to evaluate the conflicting tensions of the human psyche.

Conway had remembered the beach bungalow to the north of Miami. Fifteen months earlier he and Cathy had spent the three weeks following the departure of the Achilles ship there, and things had gone perhaps better than at any other time in their marriage before or since. He had a futile idea that perhaps if they were to go there again, now before the ship made its landing, perhaps the same thing would happen again. So he'd moved heaven and earth to get a place, and spent the best part of ten thousand dollars in renting a bungalow for the critical month. He felt he was moving into the top bracket.

But Cathy was living in a sort of trance, like a sleep-walking princess. There was no friction between them – there was just nothing. Conway felt as if he had been reduced to the status of an equerry. He knew that Cathy had come with him because by doing so she avoided all the tangles concerning tickets, passes, schedules, hotel bookings and the like, into which she inevitably fell every few hours. She spent two days in the beauty salons of New York, which was ridiculous because she didn't need it.

At the bungalow she didn't actually complain but it was clear she thought the Sun was destroying her complexion. Naturally she had her own room and Conway had his. Conway estimated that it was just about fifty-fifty, taken over the eleven years, the time they'd spent in a room together and the time they'd spent in different rooms. There wasn't any particular pattern about it, it wasn't as if they'd started off together and finished apart. It was all jumbled up, higgledy-piggledy, in a way just like all Cathy's arrangements. Later he was quite sure they'd be back on the single arrangement. He calculated that the Fawsett business would last for about two weeks.

Forty-eight hours before the estimated time of landing every road into Florida was choked with traffic, the American Automobile Association estimated that the mean rate of flow was less than ten miles an hour. The trouble was that the blockage wasn't quite complete. If it had been the drivers could have quitted their cars, they could have got out their cots and slept for a while by the roadside, but because every few minutes they were able to move a mile or two this was not possible. So the drivers had to keep awake right round the clock, and beyond that. You couldn't even pull off the highway into a roadside diner, because every place was always full. It just went on for ever, or more accurately for six or seven hundred miles. It was the traffic pile-up of the century.

Conway had expected it, that was why he'd come in to Miami by air. It was hopeless to get a hire-car, of course, but he had friends. They were good ones because they managed to get him a vehicle of sorts. It reminded him of the ancient Cadillacs in the museums, the sort of things that looked like travelling saloon bars. They had been in vogue at about the turn of the century. When he heard the highway statistics on the radio he was glad he'd also had the foresight to get a permit to use one of the official ferries. It took him and Cathy nearly a couple of hours to get from the beach to the airport, but once they were there things went very smoothly. A boy in uniform drove the car into a waiting plane, they followed themselves, and within a few moments they were in the air. The short trip was quite terrifying. In the usual commercial plane you couldn't see very much of what was going on around you, but in these ferries it was possible to see out over a wide arc. There seemed to be planes everywhere; it was like being in the middle of a huge ball of flies. The crew made nothing of it so Conway supposed that it was more or less normal. Cathy didn't even notice it. Once again they got the car off very quickly and they drove along the side-road to the main highway. It took them twenty-five minutes before Conway could find a place to turn out into the main stream of traffic. It was unbelievably nerve-racking, but since they had only ten miles to go it didn't take them more than another couple of hours. Conway calculated that there were about fifty lanes of traffic, crawling ever onwards like beetles.

His official passes took them on to the carpeted area. For the moment they had to keep to the outside because nobody could be sure that the rocket would manage to land at the exact centre. It had to be given room to manoeuvre. So even the most privileged, and there were many of these, had for the moment to stay on the outside, although, of course, on the carpet. Later, after the landing, they would be allowed to move forward to within a few hundred yards of the ship. The President and other Heads of State, and Generals from four stars upwards, would be driven, the rest of them would have to walk. Comfortable pullman-like chairs had been provided for them to sit, and there were large umbrellas under which they could shelter from the sun. Trucks toured around the carpeted arena, staffed by uniformed waiters who dispensed the coldest of Martinis, mixed with the approved ratio of four-point-seven-five. Conway ordered a consignment and motioned Cathy to sit down.

'Why have we to come so early?' she asked.

'Because two hours from now everything in here is going to be closed, except to the top brass.'

This seemed to satisfy her. It was basically true, although Conway had an idea that he could have managed to get in later if he had really wanted to. They had some thirteen hours to wait. He felt that sitting around throughout the late afternoon and the night would take a little of the gloss off Fawsett's return.

It all looked rather like a gargantuan ball game. The outer bleachers with their infinity of seats were beginning to fill up. In fact over an angle of more than 120° away on the right the stands were pretty solid. Popular music played incessantly on the loudspeaker system. At dusk the lights came on. They bought dinner and more drinks from the travelling trucks. A monstrous massed band, there must have been many tens of thousands of them, marched into the arena, plumes flying and trumpets braying. This was something that Conway hadn't bargained for, especially the girls dressed in scanties, who wheeled past in line abreast. Their flimsy garments were covered in sequins that winked knowingly in the blazing lights. Every now and then the girls simultaneously threw short silver-coloured sticks high in the air, and whenever they did so the crowd let out an enormous whoop.

In spite of it all, Cathy fell sound asleep at about eleven o'clock. Conway felt that this was her best performance to date. Even with her head thrown back at an awkward angle she was still dangerously beautiful. In fact the submission implied by the sleep, the submission to life as it were, made her more dangerous in repose than when she was awake. The sequined girls, during interludes in their antics, looked Cathy over with obvious disapproval.

Some of them came and sat at his table. They talked and he bought them drinks and still Cathy went on sleeping. It was obvious that everything about her was irrelevant to the vision.

The festivities and the music died away about three hours before dawn. Conway dozed off fitfully and woke up with a taste in his mouth at the first light. The band and the girls had apparently brought cots with them, they could be seen stretched out in little plots right into the distance. Some of the plots were of mixed sexes, but he noticed that for the most part the girls slept together, as if to give themselves mutual protection from invaders. A little clump had gathered around his table, perhaps because Cathy's presence guaranteed safety. It wasn't long before Cathy herself awoke. She went through her usual routine of lazy stretching. Then she ran her hands repeatedly through her hair, massaging her scalp as she did so. After these preparatory manoeuvres she got up and looked around her. When she had taken in the little crowd around them her nose wrinkled, 'You collect them, don't you?'

'I should have thought I rated a modicum of comfort,' he answered.

This was a mistake, for it caused Cathy's mind to click into focus. She remembered now what she had come for, and with the returning memory she retired into herself once more. By the time she had finished her toilet and had visited one of the mushroom-shaped buildings, apparently constructed of bamboo, that had sprung up overnight, breakfast was being served from the trucks.

The girls were waking up now, they were sitting up and grunting to each other, and examining their feet – a gesture which Conway could appreciate, for all this tramping around on the asphalt base could not have improved their condition. The girls bought a strange variety of foodstuffs from an exceptionally large truck that drew itself to a screeching halt almost on top of Conway's chair. With ungrudging amazement he watched them consume hot dogs and pop, bits of hamburger on a skewer like a shish kebab, and milk shakes thick with ice-cream. One girl had brought a stove on which she boiled water. Fascinated, Conway watched her add the steaming water to a dehydrated bacon and egg *mélange*. It started by being quite small, and then it grew and grew. She took a quite spherical piece of bread and separated it into two halves. The interior was hollow and into this she fitted the stuff, clamped both pieces of bread together with her hands, gave it a powerful squeeze, and began eating.

Two hours later a large flotilla drove into the arena. Out came firstly the brass, then a large group of Russian Army Officers, and lastly the Heads of State. Conway could see Lee Kipling and Vladimir Kaluga, and he knew that the end was near.

It came incredibly quickly. The masters of ceremony, most astute of mortals, must have kept a road open, they must have held back the flotilla till the last possible moment, and then in the very nick of time they must have sped at breakneck pace to the appointed spot. For although those at the top may be kept waiting, they must not seem to be kept waiting.

It was all incredibly well managed. The band was now in formation, and the girls had taken their places. Mysteriously the cots, the stoves and the mushroom bamboo buildings had vanished, and at this exact moment there came a roar from the sky.

571

Chapter Twelve

Dulce Domum

Fiske had never brought a ship in to land before, for he had never been the captain or vice-captain of a crew, although of course he had made thousands of dummy landings on the equipment at space-school. He knew that he must trust the instruments implicitly, and forget all about the ground below. A day before the landing he made careful study of a list of the order in which he must make all the settings. He checked his list carefully against the manuals. During the last hour he went over each of the items one by one for the third time. Finally he checked that Fawsett and the two Russians were properly secured. Then he went to his own bunk, fastened himself in, and waited.

The retro action began and the pressure built up. Just as he felt he couldn't stand any more, it miraculously began to ease off, as it always did. That was the way the ship was designed, to take advantage of the maximum you could stand. Now the motion was so gentle that he couldn't tell whether they were still moving or whether they'd landed already.

The indicators above his bunk, now the Captain's bunk, were on, and he saw that they were almost at a complete shut down. They had made it. This was the end.

He waited for a while, as the manuals told him to do, so that the circulation would return to normal, and then pressed the automatic release button. His harness became free and he was able to climb to his feet. Ilyana was up almost immediately and Pitoyan seemed to be all right. Fawsett didn't seem too good, but he was alive and that was something. It would be up to the medicos to deal with him now.

Outside, the ground engineers were bringing up the great steps, which they only used on special occasions such as this. The steps ran on great wheels and they were powered by their own motor. The height was adjustable, today it would be raised to four hundred feet. The crew would assemble on the spacious top platform, and then they would be brought to ground level by the lift. The contraption was at last magnetically clamped to the side of the rocket and the moment that everyone had waited for had arrived.

With rapidly-beating heart Fiske pressed the button that opened the main door. He saw daylight stream in through the gap. He saw the platform in position, and motioned to Ilyana to lead the way.

The crowd outside saw the fair haired girl appear. No professional stage manager could have managed the effect better. A moment later she was joined by Fiske and then by Pitoyan. The master of the band, assembled close by below, sensed that the moment had come and gave the long-awaited signal. The strains of their National Anthem 'God Save the West' filled the clear morning air. Nobody except the grim-faced Russian officers seemed to mind that two of the three above were Russians.

From afar off Cathy sensed that something was wrong. Mike should have been up there among the returning heroes. Her heart sank with the lift as it descended to the ground. She saw the three astronauts being congratulated by the Heads of State. Then the lift went up again, this time with four members of the ground staff. The music began again. With amplification at full volume on the speakers the din was appalling. Minute followed minute until at last two men appeared with a stretcher.

'It's Mike,' she cried wildly to Conway. Then, shouting 'Mike!' she began to run towards the rocket. Conway tried to follow her but they were separated in the crowd. He knew that Cathy could never make it through the press of people. A way would be cleared for the stretcher party and Fawsett would be carried off long before Cathy could reach him.

Conway stood there for a long time and there were tears in his eyes, not so much for Cathy as for the whole human race. This seemed to be the way with all their aspirations.

Conway found a chair and sat down. There was nothing to be done until the crowd had gone. Conway calculated that it wouldn't be more than five or six hours before the place emptied. The vast herd would stream out of the arena and fill to bursting points the roads leading north. It was impossible for him to find Cathy until this happened. He knew she would be moving somewhere with the crowd, backwards and forwards with its surges, without the smallest idea of what to do. He knew she would just stand around aimlessly waiting, without the slightest semblance of a co-ordinated plan. He knew she would be still there at the end.

And so it proved to be. At last he found her, streaked and utterly weary, but not until the sun was low in the sky. Without a word he took her arm and guided her gently in the direction of the car park. It was a very long walk and the air was hot and steamy, but at last they found their mobile saloon bar.

Conway thought about getting something to eat but decided against it. It would be better to wait until Cathy became too hungry to refuse. By the time they reached their beach place she would certainly be hungry all right, it was almost a hundred miles, and at the speed that Conway estimated the traffic would be moving he reckoned on a six- or a seven-hour trip.

In the event the roads were surprisingly clear, and they made it by close on midnight. He started to take off his clothes and said, 'Better take a shower.' She began slowly to follow his example. Later he put her to bed and went off to the kitchenette. He made them each a plate of fruit salad and cheese and stiff drinks with plenty of ice and carried the tray to the bedroom.

Cathy ate for a little while and then said, 'I tried to find out where they'd taken him. But nobody would tell me. Can you find out, Hugh?'

'Not tonight.'

'Why not tonight?'

'Because everything's in confusion. Something has happened that wasn't according to plan. It's like a battle. Nobody knows what anybody else is doing.'

'He must be somewhere.'

'Of course he's somewhere, somewhere in America or in Europe. It's impossible to know where they might have taken him. Nobody I can get in touch with would know.'

'What am I going to do?'

'Wait. By tomorrow things will have begun to ease out. By the day after, or the day after that, it will be simple enough.'

He saw her looking at him with dumb disbelief.

'Can't you understand for once, Cathy? Tonight only a handful of people will know where Mike Fawsett has gone. Tomorrow a lot more people will know, and by the end of the week a whole lot of people will know. You can probably find him within three days but you cannot find him tonight.'

At last she seemed to grasp what he was driving at. He took the things back to the kitchen, made himself another drink, and went off alone to his own room.

The big show at the landing-field was of course a complete façade. The staff officers and their advisers of both sides were counting the minutes until they could get the three astronauts away. The Russians in particular wanted to get Ilyana and Pitoyan into their hands at the earliest possible moment. The first couple of hours would be critical. The party stayed as a whole until they reached a big military base about two hundred miles north of Miami. They made the distance quickly, in less than three hours, for of course the road was cleared ahead of them.

The steps were as formal and as carefully laid out as in an old-fashioned dance. First there were congratulations from all sides. The Western officers pinned decorations on the tunics of all three of them. The Russian officers did

575

exactly the same thing. There was an intense bout of hand-shaking, and at last two very powerfully built young colonels in Red Army uniform asked Pitoyan and Ilyana to follow them.

With instant perception Ilyana saw that this was the dividing point. If she once left the room with these two men it would be much harder to return than it would be to stay now. She told them in a very soft voice that she wished to stay. Again they repeated the request politely, they used colloquial Russian so that it would be difficult for the Westerners to understand them. Ilyana shook her head. They spoke in a rather louder voice. As she had expected, the request had become an order. She turned to Fiske, 'They're trying to take me away. I don't want to go.'

Fiske grinned, 'That's swell. Then you don't go.'

But now the Russians were angry. One of the colonels spoke to his General in a voice that reverberated around the room. The General did not deign to deal directly either with Ilyana or with Fiske. He addressed his Western peer, the Western General in charge. He demanded that an escort be provided to take the two Russian astronauts to the waiting cars outside. The Western General gave an order, and a young American colonel came up to her and said, 'It's better if you go, ma'am.'

The Western General knew that he was teetering on the verge of a major international incident. He rather liked the look of the trim little girl, but he wasn't risking his career for any girl. He took her by the arm and said, 'Come, my dear.' Ilyana looked wildly up into Tom's face. 'Don't let them take me,' she cried.

The vision of a grassy track came to Tom Fiske. He remembered the crushing weight of the man across his shoulder as a girl came towards him, he remembered the first time he had made love to her. 'Listen, Mac,' he said to the General, 'if you don't take your hands off her I'll bust the whole thing wide open in the papers. After what I'll do to you you'll be lucky to be retired on a five-bit pension.'

Fiske knew that in the corridors of power he was finished now, but he also knew that not even the Government, let alone the pip-squeak General, could stand up to the fury that would break loose if the girl were handed over against her will. In the past he'd managed to look after himself and he saw no reason why he shouldn't go on doing so. He'd made the grade in his own eyes, and now he'd got the girl he wanted.

The General tried to outstare him. Then he saw Fiske's hand knotted at his side, and with a muttered exclamation he swung on his heels and left the room. Fiske took all the medals off Ilyana's chest and off his own, flung them in the air, and walked out after the General with Ilyana on his arm. Nobody challenged him. The great God of Publicity was his protector.

Pitoyan saw what had happened and licked his lips nervously. He would have liked to do the same thing, not for personal or ideological reasons, but because it would have avoided a lot of awkward questions. But when they told him to go out to the cars, he fell into the trap that Ilyana had avoided. He thought it would be best to give himself time to think it over. He could always make his decision later on.

But there wasn't very much of a later-on. Once inside the car he couldn't get out, he was flanked by two big fellows, and his right arm was still not too good. They drove for two hours and then turned into an airport, a small airport. An air ferry was waiting, and it was of Russian manufacture. He was escorted to it by a party almost equally composed of Russians and Americans. It might still have been possible to have got away, but there was more than a risk that the Americans would lose if it came to a scuffle, and after what had happened to Ilyana there was no reason why they should take his side. He allowed himself to be pushed on to the plane, and within four hours, before dawn, he was in Moscow.

There was no welcoming crowd for Pitoyan at the airport, where they landed in a deserted section. A sleek powerful car was waiting. Within half an hour they were driving into Red Square. He was ushered into a room hung with pictures of the devoted leaders of the East. They were actually waiting for him, The Party was waiting, an array of strong, ruthless men.

He saw now what Ilyana had clearly seen the previous evening. He wondered where Ilyana might be at the moment. It would not have relieved the tight sickness in his stomach to have known that she was sleeping in a hotel in the Virginia mountains, her fair hair streaming over the bare shoulder of Tom Fiske.

The President began to speak, and as he did so Pitoyan gathered his wits. He knew he had to be good, and he was. The story he told had a crude sense of theatre about it.

He knew that his case would not be decided until after all possible investigations had been made. And he knew the cast of mind of the men he was dealing with. He started with the unvarnished truth. He told them of how he had calculated the way through the gravitational fields, and he told them of how the Westerners had asked him for an orbit when their transmissions to Earth became jammed. He knew that Fiske would not attempt to deny this part of the story. Fiske would not be concerned to please the Western authorities, he had seen that for himself. He told of a how a landing had been made, and of the nature of the place where they had landed. His story so far had ninety-nine per cent truth, the one per cent he omitted was the failure of Bakovsky to read the landing servo mechanism, and he made no mention of the subsequent débâcle.

So far so good, it held up. Next he told of how the Westerners had landed within a hundred miles. This was already a breach of etiquette between East and West, for he made no mention of his own distress signal. There were comments round the table. Had he any proof? Yes, he had a set of micro films in his pocket. If he could have permission to show them ... The President gave him permission.

He showed them a very beautiful photograph of Achilles

taken from orbit with the telescopic scanner. The men around him were impressed, for being ruthless does not prevent one from being impressed. He showed them the places where the two ships had landed, very close together they seemed on the slide. As for proof he could only show them pictures of the two ships on the ground. He pointed out that without flying over them, which he had not been able to do, it was impossible to show both rockets on the same picture. So he would have to show them separately. This he did, taking care that the picture of the Russian ship should be one taken from straight ahead so that it did not seem to lean. He realized that it was lucky he had not used a stereoscopic camera.

He explained how the Americans had proposed that they should explore the planet jointly, suggesting that because of the long journey both crews were really too small for the task, and that it would be better if they joined forces. Also they wished to repay the Russians for the calculation of the orbit.

There were reproving looks around the table and the President boomed, 'Beware the Greeks, even when they bring gifts.' There were approving nods at this cultured expression of the general point of view.

It was going the way Pitoyan had hoped. He told them that Bakovsky had refused the invitation because it was obvious that what the Americans really wanted was Ilyana. This was a shrewd tactic, for it must count heavily in his favour that one of the Americans had now got Ilyana. Also to quote Latin, but to himself, *post hoc – propter hoc.*

The relations between the two camps had gone from bad to worse. This nobody around the table found any difficulty in believing. It ended in a fight, a fight in which the Russian side was badly handicapped by the presence of himself and Ilyana. It was a fight of four professionals against two. In spite of the bad odds the Russians at first gave as good as they got. On the Western side the death of Crewman Reinbach compensated for that of Ivan Kratov, hero of the Soviet Union. But with the death of Kratov the odds against them became worse. It was now a case of three experienced professionals against one, against Bakovsky aided only by an inexperienced scientist and a woman. The last straw was when his own arm was broken in a bad fall, which verged delicately on the truth. Then they had retreated to their ship, as the Trojans had done behind their wall. There were nods of appreciation at this allusion to the President's remark. His imagination now alive with the history of Troy, he told them of how the Americans had approached under the cover of darkness, of how they had placed wire ropes round the ship, and of how they had finally managed to pull it off balance with the aid of a powerful winch. He showed them a photograph of the leaning rocket to prove his point.

Experts were called in at this stage to study the picture. He was asked why they had not blasted off, why they had waited there and allowed themselves to be pulled over. On the face of it it seemed as absurd as a turtle allowing itself to be turned on its back. Then he reminded them that the rocket had not been stripped down and it would have been technically unsound for them to have started back to Earth using the old worn-out motors. This figured, as the Westerners said.

The next question, of course, was why they had not stripped down the rocket. By now Pitoyan had a firm hold of the situation – because the constant sniping of the American warmongers had made work on the rocket impossible. He added that these decisions had not of course been taken by himself but by Bakovsky. This brought them back to the story, although by now they could almost fit the rest together for themselves.

With the ship off-balance it was impossible for them to do anything else but surrender. So they had come down from above and had allowed themselves to be led away prisoner to the American Camp. The Westerners took Ilyana for their own purposes. He and Bakovsky had been set to menial tasks while the Americans stripped down their ship. The great Bakovsky, also hero of the Soviet Union, had managed to conceal a grenade. Regardless of his own safety, he had thrown it right in the face of the warmongers. The proof was that their leader, Larson, was dead, and that their vice-captain, the English-American Fawsett, was now lying mutilated in an American hospital. The man Fawsett had even been paraded before the whole world immediately after the landing. But Bakovsky had been shot, shot down like a dog as he attempted to escape.

Pitoyan decided that he was embroidering the story a little too much, and he determined to keep himself more in check.

There were only two more awkward points. Why had Ilyana and himself been brought back to Earth? Crewman Fiske had taken them with him in the returning rocket for three separate and very obvious reasons. He did not wish to be entirely alone with the mutilated man during the long months of the voyage. He had clear and obvious reasons for taking Ilyana. And he had an equally obvious reason for taking Pitoyan, namely to calculate the orbit along which they must return.

Here he was at the last barrier. Why had Fiske not jettisoned them from the ship before they reached Earth? As for Ilyana, he pointed out to the Committee that the Westerners were masters of vice, and Ilyana had fallen a prey to this. Her behaviour the previous day showed just how far she had fallen. And as for himself things had been very difficult and dangerous. With his injured arm he had been no match physically for the big American. He had only been able to save himself by his wits.

Pitoyan paused for a moment, he now had the whole affair in his grasp. He told them what they must already have seen, that the American, Fiske, had known that the truth would be unpalatable, even to his own Government, so he had made up an absurd story of strange accidents on the planet. Fiske had made up stories about men being lost, of failures in their gyros, and of a curious discharge of electricity that was supposed to have killed two of them. The one hope he had of being believed, and of the true story not coming out, was for his two Russian passengers to corroborate his tale. This Pitoyan had promised to do, and Fiske, being basically a simple-minded man, had believed him. All the comrades who had met him at the landing-field would report on how he had never shown either by word or by gesture the slightest intention of asking to stay in the West. He had, in fact, come immediately home.

There was just one thing more, which Pitoyan said to himself alone. He must from now on avoid all temptation to embroider the story any more. He knew it was a good one, but thorough investigation might throw up a few loop-holes. The danger was that in attempting to plug them he would endanger the bigger and more important aspects. What he must do was to stick absolutely to his story. He must refuse the temptation to extend it at all costs. If need be he must simply claim ignorance, he must claim that there had been times when he had been completely out of action through the accident to his arm.

It is not known whether the experts who sifted Pitoyan's yarn had more than passing suspicions. History simply records that a week later Pitoyan was given a hero's welcome. A reduced parade was held in Red Square and Pitoyan was accorded the honour of addressing it. They gave him beauti-ful medals and, more important, made him a professor at his old university. With his characteristic ingenuity he soon discovered that the original short list of girls drawn up for the expedition were all almost exactly like Ilyana. About a quarter of them had married during the past year or so, but this left him with opportunities that were more than ample for his simple tastes.

It may well be imagined how steeply the tension now rose between the East and the West. The Russian Government was conditioned by a century and a half of its own propa-ganda to believe just such a story as Pitoyan had produced for them. The President called a meeting of the Supreme

Soviet and addressed them angrily for five hours. In the Western capitals, officials warned their Governments that the Russians were genuinely angry. They had every reason to be. They had lost their ship, their men, and even their chit of a girl. Much worse, they had lost their face, both cheeks; and that they would never forgive.

Urgent advice was given for the West to call a summit meeting forthwith, and for them to make every possible attempt to placate the Russians.

It was also noted that steps had instantly been taken against those mathematicians who had advised the inclusion of Ilyana in the party. The three academicians who had refereed Popkin's paper were immediately declared minus five, which meant they were exiled from the five main cities of Russia, while Popkin himself was branded minus fifty, which meant that he would never be allowed to return even to his native Rostov.

Chapter Thirteen

Cathy

The day after the landing Conway tried to find the whereabouts of Mike Fawsett but, as he had expected, none of his
contacts knew. He tried the next morning, too, and was on
the point of packing it in when a siren sounded in the lane
outside. The County Sheriff, resplendent in uniform,
stumped up the path to the bungalow. He made a strenuous
root-a-toot on the door with his fist and, when Conway
answered, said, 'Are you Conway?'

Conway said he was, and that he'd already bought tickets
for the Policemen's Bazaar.

'O.K., O.K.,' grunted the big fellow, sunlight glinting re-
splendently on his polished badge, as he heaved himself
over the threshold.

'Don't think I'm being personal, but could you tell me
your wife's name?'

Cathy appeared and took in the scene in a vague sort of
way.

'Have we done something wrong?'

'Nothing that I know of, ma'am. I'd be kinda obliged if
you could tell me your name.'

'It's Cathy Conway, isn't it?'

This was the sort of thing that drove Conway up the wall
and half-way across the ceiling.

'That's sorta what we hoped. We need you urgently up in
Washington, ma'am.'

Then he crammed on his big hat and added, 'I'd be
obliged if we could be on our way. At your convenience,
naturally.'

'Naturally,' nodded Conway.

In the car he gradually pieced together that Fawsett was in a military hospital up in Washington. The man was apparently delirious and kept crying out for 'Cathy'.

Within a couple of hours they'd been put through on the ferry to Washington. Two officers, a captain and a lieutenant, were waiting for them.

'We'd like to take the lady along right away,' said the captain.

Conway saw no point in demurring. The sooner Cathy went out to the hospital the better.

'We can fix you up for the night,' added the captain.

'Not unless you've got something near the centre of the city. I'd prefer to hunt around for myself.'

'Better you than us, sir,' grinned the lieutenant.

Conway allowed them to take Cathy away, after making a note of the whereabouts of the hospital. Then he burnt up the telephone wires chasing one acquaintance after another. He concentrated mainly on the bachelors because they were the most likely to be out of town. At last he got what he wanted, the loan of the apartment of a fellow who was away in South America for a couple of weeks. Next he hired a car, spent ten minutes with a map, then nosed out on to the road on his way to the hospital. Either Fawsett must be pooped, poor devil, or maybe he had some odd form of delirium. Some sort of loss of memory. Perhaps they wanted Cathy to try to wake his memory.

It was now about six o'clock, the peak of the evening pressure. He calculated they would certainly be back in the city by eight o'clock, in fact they might be able to chase up the apartment before then, if the medicos were through with their business. That would give nice time for him and Cathy to step out for dinner. She was bound to be upset but almost nothing on earth could put Cathy off her food for very long.

He made several mistakes at the complex junctions. The place had obviously been laid out by topologists. But at last he made it. When he gave them his name at the desk, a girl with a zebra hair-do put through a call and an usherette showed him the way. They walked along seemingly endless corridors and wound up in a plushly furnished office. An elderly grey-haired man with the resigned look of a large bloodhound shook his hand.

'I'm sorry to have to tell you, Professor Conway, your wife's had rather a bad shock. We knew that Colonel Fawsett was a very sick man, otherwise we wouldn't have asked you both to come here today at such short notice.'

'You mean he's dead?'

The man nodded. 'There seemed to be nothing we could do for him. We've not run across anything quite like it before. But of course we'll go on with the investigation.'

Conway didn't hear him. He was thinking about the night almost two years ago when Cathy had asked him to do what he could to get Fawsett into the act. He remembered the way he'd overridden his own scruples. He still couldn't decide whether he had been right or wrong. He'd known there would be danger on the expedition, but he'd never thought it would end this way.

'You mean you've absolutely no idea what the trouble was?'

'No, we know it was a disease in the fever area, that's all. Even on this planet it's a pretty wide area, and maybe it isn't surprising . . .'

'How did it happen? I mean how did the end come?'

It still seemed incredible to him that Fawsett was dead.

'It didn't take long, that's all I can tell you. Your wife sat with him for maybe twenty minutes and he didn't seem to notice her. Suddenly he seemed to recognize her and became quite violent. He'd had one or two similar crises before, but he's a strong young man and he'd managed to pull through. This time he just didn't make it. It was a very nasty experience for your wife, I'm afraid. We gave her a sedative and she's been resting. Would you like to come along and see her?'

Conway said that he would and followed the man along more corridors, not quite so interminable as before. They turned into what Conway supposed was a small private ward. Cathy was there, sitting strangely still, her head drooped, looking down at her hands. Apparently she had heard them, for she looked up for a moment.

'Would you like me to make arrangements for her to be looked after, tonight, or for as long as it might seem ...?'

Conway shook his head.

'No, I think I would like to take her back with me. You see she probably associates this place with what happened. It will be better to get her into a different environment. I can call a doctor when we get back into the city.'

'Would you like us to see to it?'

'No, I think I'd like to contact a friend. But I'll be in touch if there's any difficulty.'

Conway told Cathy to come with him. Quite silently she walked at his side, as a girl took them back to the hospital entrance. He offered her his arm on the way to the car but she refused it. They drove silently back along the highway. Conway didn't know why he'd done it, why he'd brought her with him, without saying a word to the man at the hospital. But in the first brief moment when she'd looked up at him he'd known – he'd known that this was not Cathy.

He found a space in one of the gigantic parking blocks and led the way into the main thoroughfare. The woman – or the thing – that looked like Cathy followed him, still without a word. The Mayflower Restaurant was close by. He took her in and miraculously found a table for two. She made no attempt to look at the menu so he ordered for both of them. He ordered lobster thermidor for her, which Cathy loved. He made no attempt to talk and they were through the joyless meal in no time at all. Back at the parking block he paid for the car and set about the awkward navigational problem of finding the apartment. It was almost half past nine by the time they reached it. He made a brief tour of the place; it had a kitchenette, a large room, two bedrooms and the usual plumbing. Whoever the guy in South America was he was doing all right for himself.

So far his mind had been numb with shock. He had driven the car, parked it, ordered dinner, and found the apartment more or less like an automaton. Now he began to thaw out. He wanted to know where Cathy was. He looked at the woman and said, 'Who the hell are you?'

Still there was not a word from her. My God, he thought, is she dumb? In an angry voice he repeated the question, 'Who the hell are you?'

Then her mouth opened, 'That is a difficult question, and I must have time to think before I can answer it.'

'To hell with that. What I want to know is where is my wife?'

He was beginning to tremble and was fast losing control of himself. He took the woman roughly by her arm and shouted:

'Where is my wife?'

Before she could answer the lights seemed to dim and somewhere a band was playing 'Undecided'. The floor heaved. There was noise, confusion, faces. One moment he was lying dazed on the floor being kicked savagely on the thigh.

The next moment he was on his feet and back in the apartment. And the woman who looked like Cathy was standing there shaking her head. The men were gone, and so was the pain in his leg. But he had had a bang on the head, he could feel it very definitely. He started to rub it and the woman said, 'Please do not do that again.'

It was as though the shake he'd given her had somehow contrived to waken her attention. With quick strides she explored the apartment. Satisfied, she said, 'I shall sleep in here, and you will sleep in the other room. I am very weary and do not wish to talk now. You will understand very clearly that you are not to leave this apartment. I would be glad if you would put my things in my room.'

Conway unpacked, thinking that whoever or whatever

the woman was, it was at least a relief that she seemed to be rational. He supposed he was frightened although it wasn't a feeling that he was used to experiencing very much. But he suddenly remembered the pump-handle and the fight he'd had about two years before in a dockland pub. Conway knew for a certainty that what he had just seen was not real, he had seen one of his memories.

The woman went into her room and he could hear her preparing for bed. He wondered if she creamed her face exactly the same way as Cathy had done. Had done? What had happened to Cathy? Where was she? The voice was certainly exactly Cathy's voice, but the precision of the thoughts was very definitely not. Conway lay down on the bed in his clothes and tried to think. The shock was getting him now. He must try to keep right on thinking as clearly as he could. It was obvious that Fawsett had picked up something much more serious than pneumonia. It wasn't anything as simple as a virus or a bacterium that had attacked him on Achilles. But in some way, like a more or less ordinary disease, he'd managed to infect Cathy. He didn't understand it at all, how it was possible scientifically, but he knew that there had to be some cold crystal-clear explanation. That was his link with sanity.

Suddenly it was borne in on Conway how very simply the inhabitants of Achilles, whoever they were, had managed to deal with the Earth. The human species had put a large fraction of its total activities into hopping around from place to place, in making the expedition to Achilles. And as a result it had seen – well, Conway didn't exactly know yet what the members of the expedition had seen, but he already had a shrewd suspicion that it wouldn't amount to very much. The Achilleans in return had hardly bothered to trouble themselves at all. They hadn't spent hundreds of thousands of millions in building space-ships, they had simply waited. They had simply waited for humans to carry them back to Earth. It was both simple and elegant. And now this thing, sleeping there in the next room, in the guise of his beautiful wife, could do just what she wanted to do, she could make the young men see visions and the old men tell tales. Conway rubbed his head. The visions need not always be pleasant ones.

The idea gnawing at the base of his brain was that he ought to do something about it. It could be a completely effective form of take-over. The thought of contacting the military nauseated him. Really when he came right down to it he hated the whole social structure, he knew he had hated it since his first thinking moments. They had said he was abnormal, and now he saw with an extreme clarity of perception that they were right, and he was heartily and completely glad of it. But this thing in the other room was another matter. So far it had done nothing but ride in a car and eat lobster thermidor, and make him see a vision of a scar-faced thug, but he guessed it was going to develop. He knew what he must do. He must go and tell the police and let them deal with it.

He got off the bed and tiptoed to the door. A moment later he was out in the passage-way, listening intently outside the door where the thing was sleeping – surely it was sleeping. It had Cathy's face and body, her voice even to all the little inflections, so surely it had her other bodily habits, including that of sleep.

The corridor was a rather long one, running the whole length of the apartment. It ended in the outer door. He heard a click and, looking up, saw that someone had just come into the apartment. The figure was still in the shade by the door. He moved a few yards towards it, and the figure also stepped forward into the light. He stared at it for a moment and then shuddered with panic, for it was himself who had come in through the door, none other than himself. The figure was advancing on him now, slowly and threateningly; he could see the fist knotted and he knew what would happen if he stood his ground. With a shriek he turned back into the apartment. The woman was standing in the open door of her room. She looked at him coolly and said, 'I am sorry to have frightened you. But it is my will that you shall not leave this apartment. I have need for you, so you will return to your room and stay there. So long as you do so no harm will come to you.'

He glanced back down the passage-way and the figure had gone. He looked at the woman and she stared back at him unwinkingly. At last he turned and went back into the bedroom. He was sweating furiously and longed to take a shower but he was too weak. He collapsed on to the bed and lay trembling and thinking feverishly fast. Of course there had been no figure, there couldn't be, it was in his own mind, it was there that he had perceived the vision. But knowing this didn't help, in a way it made it worse. Childishly he switched off the light to stop himself from seeing things although he realized that this was quite useless, for there was also light and dark in his own mind. It was all there ready to be released, like a record that could be played at any moment if only you knew how to play it; and this creature in the room close by knew exactly that.

The door opened with a click. He willed himself now not to see anything, but it was a voice that he heard, the voice of his wife, saying, 'It may be better if we leave the two doors open. Then you will know that I am here. Try to remember that I do not want to frighten you.'

After this the trembling got a bit less, and he kept listening, he kept trying to hear the woman breathing. He thought he could just do so. Then his thoughts seemed to disintegrate like a distant sound blown away by a puff of wind.

It was quite late when Conway woke the following morning. Even before his brain woke up he felt wonderfully refreshed, it was the way he used to sleep when he was a kid. He'd gone to bed at night, then, click – and it was morning. That's the way he felt now. Then the memories of the previous evening flooded in on him. He jumped to the window, opened the curtain, and when the sunlight flooded in the bad dreams seemed to fade. It was absurd of course, one could see things in broad daylight just as much as at night, but somehow he felt a lot better in the light. He went out into the passage and heard the woman moving about. He wondered if they had both woken at the same moment.

He took a shower, and while he was doing so the woman came and stood outside. When he had finished she slipped off her dressing-gown, completely without concern, and took her turn in the shower. Conway couldn't help wondering whether she had inherited Cathy's sexual proclivities as well as her voice and her other physical characteristics. He dressed quickly and set about making a light breakfast. His friend six places removed had an unusual assortment of food stuffs in the ice-box, so it was an unusual combination of stuff that appeared on the table. Still, it was an unusual morning. He wondered for a long moment how it came about that he was taking the whole matter so lightly. He tried to recall the horror of the previous night, but in some odd way the sharpness had been lost, as if the memories had slipped back into their proper place.

He noticed that there was a general air of incompetence in the way the woman moved around the kitchen, exactly as there had been with Cathy. This again helped him to feel a bit easier in his mind.

'Got anything to say this morning? You keep telling me you don't want me to go, but if you want me to stay there's quite a bit of explaining you ought to do,' he began.

She smiled. It was rather like one of Cathy's smiles, but not so vague, not addressed at the world in general.

'I'd like to explain if I could. But I haven't got all this organized yet.'

She tapped her head as she said this.

'It's all very confused. And I just don't know how much you could understand. I'll find out if you give me time.'

'You came over in the ship?'

'Yes of course. But it was not a pleasant trip. The creature I came in was very hysterical.'

'Fawsett?'

'That was his name. He was a man like you.'

'Why did you kill him?'

'I had no wish to kill him. It was his refusal to accept a compromise that killed him. It was he who killed another of us.'

'Another of you?'

'Yes, another of us was travelling in the body of one of the other men. Fawsett killed him. It is not nice to be trapped inside the body of a murderer.'

Conway found it difficult to understand this piece of universal ethics, delivered to him in exactly the pitch and overtones of his wife's voice.

'But why did you come?'

'To find out what this planet is like. For the same reason that you came to our planet.'

'It was a bit hard on Fawsett, wasn't it?'

'I would have left him at the end. Even if it had been necessary to kill myself I would have left him.'

'I don't understand how you can go into and how you can leave another person.'

'I keep saying that it is too early for me to make you understand. I may never be able to, but I will try later on.'

'And what about my wife?'

'Well, is this not your wife?'

The creature held out her hand and turned it backwards and forwards. 'It is a funny thing, isn't it? A hand. Isn't it your wife's hand?'

'Yes, but what about her?'

'You keep always coming back to the same point, and I tell you that I do not know how to answer. If you can tell me exactly what you mean by the words me, you, him, her, then I will answer your question.'

Conway thought for a moment.

'You mean,' he said slowly, 'that we only have a vague, instinctive idea of what we ourselves are. And that when we talk about somebody else – when I talk about my wife – I have a vague idea about something like me?'

'The point is that you are vague. You must be able to talk

593

about these things in a precise way, in the same sort of precise way you talk about gravitation and about electricity, if we are to do any better than speak in generalities.'

Conway felt the hair on the back of his neck begin to crinkle. He realized that if at breakfast the previous day he had been given one single wish it would, ironically, have been that Cathy would be able to think with the same rationality as this creature was thinking.

'As for your wife,' the creature went on, 'nothing has gone, nothing has been dissipated. If it was not so, then all this around me' – she indicated the breakfast things and the kitchen in general – 'would drive me mad, just as what you saw last night frightened you. It is only because of her that I can keep sane in this world.'

'But it isn't she who is talking now.'

'Because it is I who have control of the thinking processes. One thing I would like to know, did your wife ever think?'

Conway paused for a moment and then shook his head sadly.

'No, Cathy didn't really think, she was almost pure animal.'

'And you who do think a great deal had a very great liking for her?'

'Yes, I had a very great liking for her if you wish to put it that way.'

'That is why I was determined that you should not leave last night.'

The woman looked up at him with a smile, and it was Cathy's smile.

'I want you to take me away from here. I want you to take me back home.'

'That won't be very difficult. But why?'

'Because for a very long time I have been in unpleasant places. There is something I am hungry for.'

Conway also found himself smiling.

'What?' he asked.

'Grass.'

The idea of saying anything to anybody, even if he could have got away with it, now left Conway's mind. He booked a couple of seats on the transatlantic ferry, rang his friend and thanked him for the apartment, rang the hospital and told them that his wife seemed to be all right, but that she had expressed a wish to go home, and slammed the receiver back in its bed, thinking that this seemed to be his fate — master telephonist, first class.

They arrived at the airport with three-quarters of an hour to wait. As they walked up and down the vast concourse, Conway idly noticed some lout of a fellow eyeing his companion in a speculative manner. A moment later the woman noticed it. What followed was spectacular and terrifying. The man let out a loud high-pitched moan, fell to the ground, rolled over and over, his hands and feet thrashing the air, as if he were engaged in mortal combat. Then he lay on his back, looked up at the ceiling and screamed long and piercingly. In numbed shock Conway looked down at the woman. Her lips were parted and the corners of her mouth quivered in the way that Cathy's always did when she felt that she had paid someone out, and he remembered that Cathy had always detested people staring at her. He grabbed the woman by the arm and steered her away from the scene.

'For God's sake stop it. If they once realize you're doing it there'll be hell to pay.'

The screaming stopped and several policemen rushed towards the man. They got him to his feet and led him away.

'Don't you think I can look after myself?'

'Look, if once they know about you, if they suspected you'd done it, people would get scared. Those men with guns would start shooting. They mightn't know what they were shooting at, they mightn't even be able to see you, but an odd bullet fired at random might hit you.'

'You do love your wife, don't you? Well perhaps that is only fair, for that was your wife directing me now. You wondered where she was.'

Nobody seemed to suspect that they'd had anything to

do with the incident, and of course it would have been astonishing if there had been suspicions.

Cocktails were served once they were airborne. He noticed that the woman chose Cathy's favourite drink – a pink slayer – and did what she always did on any air trip that lasted for more than an hour, she fell asleep. Within five minutes her head had come to rest on Conway's shoulder, and her hair was beginning to tickle his face. It was from that moment that he began to think of her as his wife again.

He wondered what the other passengers would do if they were aware of the true situation. He wondered about his neighbour across the aisle, a man entirely anonymous in all his outward characteristics except that he carried a very large brief-case out of which he had taken a thick wad of papers, what would he think? What would the three men playing cards, talking about women, think? What would they do if they knew that Cathy could walk into the crew's quarters and, within seconds, make them send the plane in a screaming dive at 1,500 miles per hour down into the waters of the Atlantic. He knew there would be complete panic throughout the whole length of the plane, and the thought rather amused him.

They hired a car at London Airport and reached Alderbourne by the early afternoon. When they left the city streets Cathy began to grow excited. At the sight of the first green fields she gripped his arm tightly. This was the first inclination she'd shown to touch him. His house was built at an extreme end of the village, looking out over the Downs. She ran to the end of the garden, and when he came up to her she said, 'Can we walk out on that?'

He got out of the car and drove to a high point from which they could walk for miles. They started off, and every now and then Cathy would drop to her knees and begin examining the soft grass on which they were walking. He realized that it was the sort of thing that the old Cathy would have done if it had ever occurred to her. But it was quite certainly the new Cathy to whom it had occurred.

'Why do you do that?'

'Because we love grass. There is a great deal of it on our planet. We look after it very carefully'

The wind blew in her hair as they walked on, and she held on to his arm.

'How much of your planet did our men see?'

'They saw the great grasslands and the seas of course. We could not stop them seeing that. But almost everything else we hid.'

'How? How did you hide them?'

'By making them not see. There were two of them that did get near something, so instead of allowing them to go on we just sent them round and round in little circles.'

She chuckled at the thought and there were little red patches in her cheeks.

'Once, by a mistake, we did allow them to see a little. But only once, for they behaved like beasts. Their only thought was to destroy what they could not understand.'

She stopped and sat down and motioned him to come down beside her.

'It is funny that you are not at all like that. That is the thing that makes me most curious of all. Why are you so different?'

'I suppose because our means of communication one to another aren't too good. You've already found out that talking isn't a very good way. We start out by being pretty similar at birth, but then we seem to separate, and the gap between one person and another gets wider and wider.'

'It must be something like that,' she nodded.

'It is strange the difference between the wild frightened man that I came to the Earth inside and the girl who came to see him.'

'You mean Cathy,' he said quickly.

'Yes, the girl who is the other part of me. She was completely placid, as if it made no difference at all to her.'

'You mean she made no resistance?'

597

'None at all. It was almost as if it was a relief to her to have somebody to do the thinking for her.'

Conway laughed, and there was genuine mirth in it, for that was exactly what he himself had been doing for the last eleven years. Except that now something was doing it much more efficiently than he'd been able to do. The new Cathy looked round the landscape, she pointed at the trees.

'Those are very funny things. They're rather nice.'

Without realizing what he was doing Conway ruffled her hair. She looked at him curiously.

'That also is strange. We would never touch each other. But here with you I am happy.'

He kissed her and the warmth of her response convinced him that nothing which the original Cathy valued had indeed been lost. She moved a little away from him and he saw that her eyes were dancing.

'Very happy.'

She began to undo the buttons of his shirt, so he drew a deep breath and decided to stop thinking about the problem.

On the way back she linked her arm with his and began to sing. This was new, for although the original Cathy had a pleasant voice she had never used it, except when she thought she was alone. The songs were familiar ones, but in some way the new Cathy managed to give them an unusual twist. He couldn't say exactly how it was done but there it was.

In the evening they made drinks, at least he did, while she watched and asked questions about it. They had dinner delivered at the door – the invaluable telephone again – which saved a lot of time and effort.

Afterwards Cathy said, 'Now show me what is going on. You must remember that I am here to learn.'

'How can I show you what's going on?'

'Don't be stupid. You spend all your time sending pictures around.'

He realized that she meant the television. They switched

it on and were instantly swept into a shatteringly different world. Gone was the innocent contemplation of the grass, the trees, and of his shirt buttons, and they were watching earnest commentators talking about the world situation.

Conway was shocked to find out how far the situation had worsened during the past two days. Since the landing he hadn't seen a paper or heard a news transmission, and he hadn't realized how strongly the tension had risen, like putting the bulb of a mercury thermometer into a bunsen flame. Much of it he had of course seen many times before, but there were ominous undercurrents that were new.

Cathy seemed to grasp the issues very quickly. She watched, fascinated, as the news bulletins came in from the major capitals of the world. Conway was amazed to find her smiling at the translation of a thunderous speech which Kaluga had delivered to the Supreme Soviet. She wasn't laughing audibly but Conway had the feeling that laughter was welling deep inside her. He tried to analyse it. It was just what the original Cathy would have done if she'd understood what was going on. And the new Cathy seemed to find it just as amusing – damn it, both of them were hugging their sides. At length she motioned for him to switch off the hellish device. She was sitting on cushions on the floor, her back propped against a chair. She leant her head back, ran her hands backwards and forwards through her hair, massaging her scalp.

'Tomorrow you will take me to London. Then I will show you something that will surprise you very greatly. And it will teach these foolish people the lesson of their lives.'

She stretched herself very lazily and added, 'And now I think we will go to bed.'

Chapter Fourteen

War

While Conway and his new-found wife thus disported themselves, the world went about its serious business. Long
important messages flashed importantly backwards and
forwards from continent to continent, lines were kept clear
for them. But at a lower level, at the level of a million or
more business enterprises, the traffic in communication was
choked far beyond the overflowing point. It was obvious to
everybody that in the last few hours they had moved significantly closer to war. And everybody wanted to know just
how they would stand if the worst was to come to the worst.
The real answer of course was that they wouldn't stand at
all, but everybody behaved as if they were faced by a serious
but manageable crisis.

The actual situation was that officials in Washington and
in Paris were pretty sure there wouldn't be a war. It was true
that the psychologists had predicted that if ever it were to
happen, this was the way it would start. It wouldn't be a
slowly developing tension building up over many months.
That gave both sides plenty of time to decide in their own
minds that there wouldn't be a war. The danger was a sudden psychological feed-back that developed to the instability point, as this looked as if it might do.

Even so officials were confident. Their only problem was
to allow the tension to develop a little more but still within
controllable limits. The point of course was that the Russians were mad, and perhaps justifiably mad, so that some
very big concessions would have to be made. Probably the
Russians would have to be given parity in South America.
And for this their own public had to be prepared. They

would swallow it once they were convinced that only by making crucial concessions could war be avoided. This all added up to the obvious point that the crisis must be allowed to develop a little further. And so it went on throughout the night.

Conway awoke. Cathy's hair was tickling his face unbearably. Her voice whispered, 'Time to be moving. We're due in London today. Remember?'

It was a new development for Cathy to want to be abroad early in the morning. He climbed out of bed feeling that this was one of the days when he would have liked to go on sleeping for ever. Sunshine was streaming in at the window. Obviously it was going to be a marvellous day.

They made breakfast together. Cathy seemed to relax into her old self.

'Were you worried the other night?'

'I should bloody well think I was,' Conway spluttered. Then, catching her eye, he smiled, 'Now that things are straightening themselves out, couldn't you try and explain what happened?'

Cathy buttered another piece of toast.

'Mm. I never told you how funny you looked, did I?'

'It didn't feel funny.'

She smiled, and he had a feeling that the original Cathy was feeling very pleased with herself.

'What did it look like?'

'Well, you looked up at the door in a very startled way. Then you made a huge leap backwards and banged your head against the wall and fell down on the ground.'

'And you don't know what it was that I saw?'

'How should I?'

This at least made a bit of rational sense, how should she?

'I saw the bastard who kicked me in a fight once.'

'Of course, it had to be something that really happened, but I had no means of knowing about it. All I did was to make you frightened.'

'And it was the same with the man at the airport?'

'Yes. I tried to guess what it was that he was seeing, but I couldn't. Did you have any idea?'

'It looked as if he was fighting with an anaconda.'

'What's that?'

He realized that the original Cathy certainly wouldn't know what an anaconda was. 'It's a sort of big snake. It squeezes you instead of poisoning you. It kills you by suffocating you. Squeezes the breath out of your body.'

'Well, he seemed to have plenty of breath in his body, didn't he? I don't think that can be right.'

The course of the conversation convinced Conway of what he knew already, that some new and formidable power – which he hoped he would soon begin to understand – had allied itself with the original Cathy. The alliance apparently suited them both. The new creature, whatever it was, had acquired the full logical control, but the original Cathy was dictating all the emotional responses. He could understand that this would suit the original Cathy down to the ground, but he couldn't understand why the new creature was so ready to fall in with Cathy's old happy-go-lucky ways.

'Do you intend to go sleeping around with other men?'

'Why ever should I? You seem entirely satisfactory. Remember I have some idea of what a lot of men are like. I came here inside one of them, didn't I?'

The absurdity of the final inconsequential question, Cathy's old habit, disarmed him again. 'You used to, my wife used to . . .' His voice trailed away as he saw that she understood what he meant.

'Oh, it is obvious, isn't it? She couldn't stay with you, otherwise you would soon have come to despise her for her stupidity. It was the only way she could hold you, by constantly going around with other men and making you jealous.'

Then she looked at him with a broad smile and added, 'But I am not stupid. Besides, I could stop you going away even if you wanted to go.'

She looked very demure, and he knew that this was the old Cathy showing through. Instead of being appalled he began to laugh. It was as if Cathy had suddenly become a consummate actress, as if she were playing a new role, determined not to reveal by the slightest aside that she had ever been anything different. 'Look, let's put our cards on the table. I know it's you, Cathy, an awful lot of this – not everything but a lot – so why not admit it?'

It was her turn to laugh. 'Why do you go on tormenting yourself? Why don't you start from those things that you know for sure? You know that there can't have been a single atom changed in here.'

She pointed at her head and went on, 'Nothing that has happened can violate what you know about physics. I am as your wife. I'm a single physical whole, more or less exactly the same as I was a week ago. I'm not two bodies pushed together.'

'But there must be something else?'

'Yes, of course there is something else. There is always something else. There is something else inside you, although you don't realize it. When I have got the right words to say I will tell you about it.'

'You mean you can put it into rational terms?'

'You're talking like an idiot. Everything can be put in rational terms. But we ought to be making a move. I want to get into London by the middle morning.'

'Am I allowed to ask why? I always seem to be asking why.'

'Oh, yes. Just because I want to be back again by the afternoon. It looks as though it's going to be a beautiful day.'

Cathy was ready to leave in about a third of the time she usually took. Instead of drifting about rather vaguely from room to room she seemed to know just what she was doing. Conway got out the car and soon they were on the road, rolling along the Downs, to which he kept until they reached Reading.

He managed to park in the region of Knightsbridge, and they took a taxi towards the centre. He asked Cathy where she wanted to be. 'Oh, anywhere near Trafalgar Square.'

Conway told the driver to set them down just outside its exit into the Mall. He started to ask Cathy what they were to do next, but his voice was drowned out by the thunder of the loudspeaker system. It was mounted high up all around the Square, and the volume was prodigious, it had to be in order to drown the noise of the traffic. It had the sort of volume associated with the peal of church bells when you were standing close by, except that instead of sending out a joyous carillon they were announcing the latest news bulletin. The latest news carried by the international ticker-tape was not good.

Eventually the uproar died down. He saw the crowds looking upwards for a while to the point where the speakers had hurled down their message. Although he'd seen it thousands of times before it struck him how silly they all looked. Suddenly they seeemed to jerk themselves back to their own thoughts and went about their business.

'Wow,' he said to Cathy, 'this is it. What shall we do?'

'I want to go off by myself now,' she replied. 'Let's meet here at twelve. I'll have done what I want to do by then, and you can walk about and tell me how it goes.'

To his question of what was she going to do she made no answer. With a wave of her hand she crossed Whitehall and made off towards the direction of the Strand.

Conway saw that he had only three-quarters of an hour to kill. He wondered what Cathy was up to. He'd had an idea that she was going to go and talk to the Government, but apparently not, for that would have taken them down to Westminster. Maybe she was going to persuade some newspaper editor in Fleet Street to make an announcement of some sort. But that didn't seem right either. It was much too feeble. He thought he would go and look at the pictures in the National Gallery, but then decided to stroll in the direction of Seven Dials. You could still see a little of the London of the twentieth century here. He stood for a moment on the edge of the pavement, looking reflectively at a recently changed skyline. It was curious the way they took away one building and put another in its place, and yet still kept to the same pattern of streets. His thoughts flicked back to the recent changes in his own life. It was rather like the way the atoms changed in your body. Their identity was never quite the same two minutes running, and over the years they changed completely. But it didn't make any difference to the structure, it didn't make any difference to you. Why should it? After all, one atom of oxygen was exactly the same as another. It didn't matter in the least swopping them round as long as you didn't change the pattern. It was of course the pattern that really counted, and this must be what had hapened to Cathy. Part of the pattern, only a part, had been changed. And now both parts, the new and the old, were growing in confidence. For the first few hours, he realized, the changes must have produced a pretty numb state of affairs. Now he had the feeling that Cathy's brain had reshuffled itself and that all the parts were working together in complete harmony.

He heard a growing murmur from Trafalgar Square. Something seemed to be happening, probably a new bulletin had come through. Bloody nonsense of course, but he might as well find out what was going on. He began to stroll slowly back, his mind still occupied with his new train of thought. The noise ahead of him was increasing. A vehicle came tearing down the street at a breakneck pace. Bloody fool, thought Conway, they'll roast him for that. People began to pass him, heading out of the Square. They were hurrying, some of them running. He asked one elderly man, who was limping more slowly along, what it was all about.

'It's War. They've started.'

Conway stood still. It couldn't be true. It just couldn't be true. He knew they were fools but not such fools. It had to be a big last-minute scare, just to frighten the wits out of the people, so the Governments could give themselves manoeuvring room. The scene around him had all the aspects of a major panic, but this would be what the Governments wanted.

A woman carrying a young child ran past him, her face streaming with tears. It took quite a while before he could make his way against the human current that came against him, but at last he reached the Square. People were erupting out of the buildings, so that in spite of those who had managed to get away, some towards the river, others in the direction of Piccadilly, and others along the way he had come, the Square was still as full as ever. It was like an ants' nest, except that ants move in orderly columns. He wondered if there was any chance that he could get control of the speaker system and tell them that it was all a lot of bull. Two days earlier the thought wouldn't have occurred to him, but with Cathy to stand behind him he wouldn't need to worry much about the reprisals of bureaucracy.

It was odd that the thought of Cathy hadn't occurred to him before. Instead of being worried sick about her, as he had been in the big arena at the time of the landing, he felt now that she was perfectly capable of looking after herself. It would be as much as he could do himself to fight his way across the Square and to get back to their agreed spot by twelve o'clock.

The speakers boomed out again. A list of cities now under evacuation was being read out – Washington, Moscow, Paris, and all the rest of them. Another piece of civil defence thought Conway. Then came the announcement that the first bomb had fallen on New York, and for the first time Conway knew that this was really it. They'd played around for a century, they'd played around with tensions and counter-tensions, and now at last it had got out of control. Pandora's box was wide open.

There was a blinding chaos in the streets of New York. The southern tip of Manhattan had been wiped clean.

From Twentieth Street south it was a mass of rubble and twisted hot metal. An area on the west side from about Ninetieth Street as far up as the George Washington Bridge had also been bitten out of the city as if a giant thumb had suddenly pressed down on it. Almost a million had been killed by the blast, the very suddenness had caught them unawares. Bodies were strewn around in outrageous postures, like sawdust dolls, from north to south and from east to west. Otherwise the human form was absent from the streets. There was life still in New York, there were ten million lives, but they were not to be found in the streets. They were in the prepared fall-out shelters, wondering, desperately wondering, what had happened.

Why hadn't the warning come sooner? Why hadn't the complexed interlocking warning system given them more than a couple of minutes' grace? For the reason that it had had to be checked and cross-checked before anybody had dared to announce that this was the real thing. A warning system cannot possibly be expected to work if it is only called on to operate once. Especially if it is constantly being abused by false warnings.

Why hadn't the wonderfully delicate, computer-controlled system of antimissile missiles worked properly? The answer was that it had worked. It had intercepted almost seventy per cent of the attacking rockets, which was more than anybody in informed circles had expected.

New York was not the only city where these things were happening. Mushroom-shaped clouds were already rising to monstrous heights above Chicago and Washington. Tons of radioactive material had already been injected into the stagnant pool of air that overlay Los Angeles. All passes across the mountains were blocked by columns of vehicles. Soon the grisly toll would be exacted from cities of lower and lower rank.

The American reply had been delayed because the President's final O.K. had been delayed. The information had reached his office on the special communication circuit it is true, but the President had just not happened to be in his office at that particular moment. The planners, deep in their prepared shelters, now realized that it had been a big mistake not to fit all relaxing rooms with the latest of communication devices.

But now the Western reply had been made, it was moving at upwards of twenty thousand miles per hour through the air, the very thin air high above the Earth. A few moments later it would reach its targets, the nerve centres of the Soviet Union. Watchers far down the long avenue leading out of Red Square would see the Lenin Mausoleum, and the Kremlin itself, disappear inside a towering column of flame.

The chief launching areas of either side were hit and hit again. The operational personnel was halved, halved again, and yet again, but still the missiles continued to rise from the ground. They were no longer under human control. The master computer, buried deep inside the Earth, out of reach of all attack, continued to direct activities. Doors opened, rockets were assembled by mechanical and electrical controls, supplied with their fuels by automatic means, and transported by a moving platform to the inclined launching ramp, from which they rose into the air with a deafening roar. This was the ultimate deterrent, a deterrent that, once activated, could never be stopped, except through the exhaustion of the whole complete stockpile. There were hundreds of such sites both in the West and in the East. Unmoved by events, by death and by suffering, they all continued, like the obedient servants they were, to project their grisly human-designed pencils of destruction in an unbroken stream across the sky.

Conway saw the first bomb explode, about three miles away, he judged, in the direction of the City. He could hardly have missed seeing it, for the air was filled with a vast white flash, a vast whiteness that blinded him for the moment. Then the blast knocked him to the ground. He heard stones and blocks of concrete falling around him.

Miraculously he was not severely hit. Then came the suction. His only link with life now was the oxygen that he happened to have in his lungs. He could last for about three minutes, but by that time it might be over. The thudding became dull in his ears, and lights formed themselves before his eyes. Then it eased and he found himself able to breathe again.

Very slowly and wearily, his chest heaving, he managed to get to his feet. Wrecked vehicles and wrecked bodies were strewn around the Square. He noticed that there were far more bodies away on the left than there were over by the Strand. He realized that this must have been due to the blast, which had lifted many of its victims far through the air. He rested for a moment against a doorway, keeping a little inside lest he be hit from above. He tested his arms and legs, incredibly they seemed all right.

Then the stark horror of his position hit him. So far from being all right he was already a dead man. In the moment of the flash he must have been drenched with gamma rays. Everything was all right for the moment, but in a few hours the cells would begin to disintegrate. His hair would fall out and the skin would open up all over his body. After a few days of intense agony he would die.

Then he knew that it wouldn't happen that way. He had a few hours, plenty of time, to find a bottle of sleeping tablets. A big overdose, and he would be dead before the disintegration started. He wondered if it might be possible to get out of London, perhaps even to get home. It would be best if he could fall asleep back there high on the Downs. With a sharp pang he realized that he would never see Cathy again. He could hardly expect that she would be able to find her way back here now. There must be thousands of millions like him who would never see their husbands, wives, sweethearts, and children again.

Then the second bomb struck. It was much closer this time, and Conway was thrown high in the air by the blast. He hit the ground with a sickening thud. The suction passed again and he was vaguely aware of being still alive. His eyes had been almost burnt out by the big flash and now he could only see rather vaguely those things that were quite close by. Looking around very slowly he found himself staring into the face of the woman who had run past him on the street. The woman who had been clutching the young child. She was still clutching it and they were both dead. He could tell that by the grotesque pile into which they had been pitched by the blast.

It was then that the first suspicions came to him. How could the woman have got to where he now saw her? It had to be, it just had to be, that he was seeing things again. It explained the woman, for she was the only person he had looked at at all carefully since Cathy left him. This of course was what Cathy had come to do. He realized that it was useless to worry about his aches and pains, the best thing was just to lie there and wait.

The scene began to clear and he could focus again right across to the far side of the Square. For a moment he didn't realize that the vision was gone, that this was return to reality. It was the lack of debris that gave it away. The ghastly qualities of the scene had gone, but what the scene had lost in horror it had gained in grotesqueness. He saw vehicles piled here, there and everywhere, in an incredible tangle. It was lucky that traffic was always forced to crawl through the Square these days, for otherwise many people would have been badly hurt. Thousands of them were lying on the ground, some twitching, some moaning, some just lying supine. Every now and then someone would get up, take a run, and then deliberately crash down on the ground. He rubbed his shoulder and supposed that that was just what he himself had done.

Articles of every description were scattered as far as his eyes could see, down Whitehall, right to Parliament Square, up towards St James's Street, and down the Strand. Everywhere traffic was stopped, everywhere people were still in the grip of the vision. He picked his way carefully among the sprawling, writhing figures. A couple of smartly-dressed women, straight from a beauty salon, but now with their sculptured hair covered in dust, were staring up at the sky. Saliva was dribbling out of their mouths and they were making faint moaning sounds.

He worked his way round the body of a man dressed in immaculate City clothes. The fellow was clutching his own throat and making sounds like water gurgling down a pipe. His rolled umbrella and bowler hat were lying not far away, his brief-case burst open to disgorge a neat packet of sandwiches, at which pigeons were placidly pecking.

He reached the place where he had agreed to meet Cathy. He wondered how the devil she'd been able to do it. It was all very well to make you see something that was already in your own head. It was only a matter of disturbing the memory storage areas, but he didn't see how she'd been able to do the same thing to everybody. But perhaps they weren't all seeing the same thing. Perhaps each person had his own private vision. That was the way it must be. Then he saw her coming towards him, a grim little smile on her face.

'I'm glad you're on time,' she said.

'Where have you been?'

'Down into the City. I went into the narrow streets where the crowd was densest. That was the best place to get it started. But I had to walk back because there is nothing running.'

'I should think not. It's complete chaos. My God, you've started something now.'

'You see why I said it would be best to get back home by mid-afternoon.'

'It looks as though we shall have to walk unless I can get one of these cars started.'

He found a taxi with its engine still running. It had careered off the road into a traffic direction signal. The front was horribly buckled – a triple-century job as the garage men would say. He bundled Cathy into it and drove up towards St James's Street. There wasn't a vehicle moving anywhere so he had it all to himself. He took the shortest way back, ignoring all traffic lights and one-way-street signs. The time had gone for small things. They got back to the car and within a couple of minutes were running down Kensington High Street.

'At this rate we're going to break the record for the shortest time home.'

After that they didn't say much to each other and Conway had a feeling that Cathy was almost as overwhelmed as he was himself. They were half-way to Reading before she said, 'I knew that everybody was strongly charged up. In a way I'm sorry, but they had only themselves to blame, hadn't they?'

Conway realized that it was indeed true, they were to blame, all of them, for entertaining such outrageous notions. He looked across at Cathy and nodded. She hadn't put ideas into anybody's head. She'd simply made them see what was there already. He saw that everybody was really guilty, not only for having such ideas, but even for permitting the constant discussion of them – by the sort of commentators they had seen on the television the previous night. He saw now what Cathy had meant by saying she would teach them a lesson. He hadn't enjoyed the lesson himself but he knew it had been deserved. 'Did you actually see anything yourself? I don't mean the real thing, but the visions.'

'I couldn't avoid it. There was some of it inside me already, and in any case the discharge was so intense that some of it came into me from outside.'

Conway didn't really understand this, but he felt that in a general way he got the drift of what she was saying. 'How far do you think the effect spread out?'

She looked at him with a faint smile, there seemed to be an implied compliment behind it.

About ten miles east of Reading they ran into the outward-moving traffic jam. Quickly he worked out a route in his mind along the side roads. There was a turning that would do it about five miles farther along. It was a tiny road

612

to the left, which he did not think many of the drivers ahead would know about.

'Looks as if the effect has spread as far as this.'

'Yes, these are the people living on the outskirts of the city who have been planning to get away into the country if anything happened. They think it has.'

'Pity you had to do all this here you know. Really you should have done it in Paris, and in New York, and in Moscow.'

'There's more than a chance that it's happened there already.'

Conway could begin to see it all now. It was a psychological chain reaction, it only needed a small nucleus of people to really believe that it had happened and the whole thing would spread out like a tidal wave until it engulfed the world. He leaned out of the window of the car and shouted at the occupants of the off-side front seat in the car on his immediate right, 'What goes on?' The man looked at him in some surprise, 'You've got a big surprise coming, Charlie. It's started, the big show's started.' Conway wished that the man could have been with him in Tragalfar Square. It was a bit uncharitable, but he felt that he would have liked to see the man bashing his head against the nearest stone wall. This was the sort of bloody fool that made it all possible.

An hour later they reached the turn-off point. Conway was immediately able to accelerate the car along the small twisting road. They didn't talk much, probably both of them were wondering what the news bulletins would say. Another hour and he was pulling up the car outside their own house.

All the local radio and television channels were blank. He tried the Continental channels and they too were blank. There was nothing on the short-wave radio. It added up to only one thing, the chain reaction had swept entirely round the globe. The meaning of it all Conway didn't understand yet, but granted the starting point, that they had been made to see their own thoughts and their own memories, then the rest followed pretty easily. After all they'd lived with those thoughts and those visions for a whole lifetime, literally from their first thinking moments. Everybody had done so since the middle of the twentieth century.

They didn't say much to each other. Conway had never seen Cathy in a serious mood before. It wasn't as if many people would come to real harm. But driving out devils was a serious business. Devils might be absurd and monstrous in themselves, but their effect was very real. The very strength of his own reaction – he still remembered the blindness, the sickening crash on his shoulder, and the gamma rays – the very strength of his reaction showed just how far he himself had been indoctrinated, rebel that he was.

He tried the radio again and there was still nothing, so he went off to make tea. In a sense it was absurd, but why not make tea?

Chapter Fifteen

The Aftermath

Conway hadn't realized how remarkably quick his own recovery had been. It took the rest of the world more than three hours to make the same recovery. The people rose up from the pavement, they came out of the fall-out shelters, they came out of their graves, and they found that the sun was still shining and that their children were still alive. For the most part they broke down and wept as they had not done since they were young themselves, waking to security from the worst nightmare. They didn't know how it had happened but they knew that in some way a hellish disaster had been avoided. Yesterday their rulers had brandished their fists and shouted in loud voices at each other, and all the commentators and leader-writers had told them that the situation was very serious. And because they were very simple people they had believed it all, just as they had believed what they had been told all their lives. But today all this bluster, all this raving, this psychological calculation had suddenly been made to seem what it really was – the currency of the mad-house.

The people were much too numb yet to be angry. But soon they would come to realize the enormity of the things that had been done to them. Five hundred years earlier they had endured physical subjection. But now they would come to see that what had been done to their minds in the last hundred years by stick-at-nothing politicians, by the ambitious military and by the lickspittle psychologists – was appallingly and vastly worse. Soon with sure instinct they would know all this and the outcry would begin.

There was not a government anywhere that had shuffled

its pieces on the chessboard of power that did not appraise the situation with complete accuracy. It was known both in the East and the West, in Britain even, that not only the days of governments but of the whole anonymous social structure that had grown up over the past two centuries were numbered. The days were numbered unless a culprit could be found and a new scare generated. The semi-paralysis that had overtaken even the highest administrative officials may be judged from the fact that it took almost six hours before the testimony of Tom Fiske was remembered.

It had of course been inevitable that the authorities would catch up with Tom. They did so in fact on the very same day that Cathy had gone to the hospital in Washington. And it was also to Washington that Tom was taken. He and Ilyana were put into the grill box. Not together, which would have been easier, but separately. Their testimonies were taken by different groups of inquisitors in different buildings.

They both knew their stories must check and since they had not talked very seriously in their night together they could only stick to the truth. Both Fiske and Ilyana told the whole story, exactly as they knew it. So their completely sceptical questioners, keen fellows from Intelligence, learned about the abortive circular trips in the vast grasslands of Achilles, about the strange translucent sheets and of how the four men had really died.

They were of course put under what was effectively house arrest. Nobody had any doubts at first that the authorities were being given a vatful of the purest eyewash. They knew that Fiske and Ilyana would come clean in the end.

As the Governments began to recover from the horror of the great vision, as the pulses of administration slowly began to beat again, the statements of Fiske and Ilyana were re-membered. They were doubted, pulled to pieces, put to-gether again, argued about at the highest level of secrecy, and finally accepted as a tentative working hypothesis. Gradually the hypothesis that someone or something could make you see what you didn't want to see gained ground. It was the only way in which the vision could be explained. And it needed little deductive power to see that this ghastly thing had come from Achilles. It must be some sort of bug that attacked the nervous system in a manner as yet unknown to science.

Four people had returned alive from Achilles. Three of them, Fiske, Ilyana, and Pitoyan in the East, were essentially under lock and key. They could be looked into in detail and at leisure, the tops of their heads sliced off if need be.

The highest-level teams were instantly put on to the job. The stress induced by the medico-psychiatric treatment had little or no effect on either Fiske or Ilyana. It was minor league stuff compared with what they had experienced on Achilles. But Pitoyan cracked badly under the strain, and was obliged thereafter to spend several years recovering in a mental institution.

The authorities in Washington remembered that there had been a fourth traveller on the returning ship – Fawsett. They remembered the strange illness he had suffered from, and they began to wonder. Perhaps Fiske and Ilyana were really giving them the gen after all.

The real inspiration came from a balding thirty-nine-year-old executive, described in the ancient Time-Life circuit as a rising star among Washington's topmen. He was one of those going-places-fast young men who work thirteen hours a day at his desk, and give their wives hell after it. His job was in the Department of Inconsequential Facts. He remembered, while dallying with his secretary, the odd story of the man at Washington airport. A quick research by two of his assistants refreshed his mind with the facts of the case. The statements of witnesses had similarities with what he himself had seen during the vision. Plainly the story rated investigation in depth.

The next thirteen hours at the desk were well spent. One line of investigation lay with the ferry flight-lists. There had been almost a hundred flights around the time of the incident and it was quite some job to round up the dossiers of all the passengers. But at last several boxes of punched cards were assembled on the desk of the young executive. A quick programme was run up by the department's computer experts, and soon the big machine on the seventeenth floor of the building was dissecting the lives of the seven thousand odd passengers, comparing them with a collation of facts concerning the space-ship and its crew. The computer only needed to chew its cud for about three minutes and there was the name of Cathy Conway, printed out for all the world to see. Following Cathy's name, the essential facts of the case were neatly listed. She had been a 'friend' of Mike Fawsett – the machine even put the word friend in inverted commas – Fawsett had been sick with an unknown disease, Mrs Conway had visited him on the day before the airport incident, and finally Mrs Conway and her husband had checked in at the reception desk less than fifteen minutes before the reported time of the incident. The balding young man knew that he had it, both the solution to the problem that was baffling the top echelon, and also certain promotion.

The top echelon also knew he had it, both the solution and his promotion. Within an hour their agent in London was contacting the British Government. The British were characteristically slow in the uptake, and it was not until well into the day following the vision that they acted.

But when they did they acted with decision. A small, highly-trained military unit was directed by Intelligence to move in and surround the village of Alderbourne. The Head of Intelligence, Brigadier Fitzalan, put himself in charge of the operation. It was in fact a great mistake not to brief the police, for as it turned out the ordinary London bobby might have been more use to the Government than the highly-trained unit deployed by Intelligence.

It was about six o'clock in the evening when Conway opened his door to find Brigadier Fitzalan and a young major standing on his threshold. Conway and Cathy had pretty well recovered from the previous day, but Conway was in no mood for visitors.

'Professor Conway?' inquired Fitzalan.

'Indeed,' answered Conway.

'I wonder if you would mind me putting a few questions to your wife, Mrs Catherine Conway.'

'Put questions to Cathy? What on earth for?'

Conway knew perfectly well what for, he knew that they must have connected yesterday's events with the space-ship from Achilles. He knew they must be investigating every conceivable line. Every stone would be upturned and every little insect under it would be examined to see that it had showered properly and brushed its teeth. Cathy was obviously one of those lines. Or rather one of those stones, and he himself was one of the insects. He motioned the Brigadier and the fresh-faced Major into the house.

'I think I would like to see Mrs Conway alone, if you don't mind?' said the Brigadier. 'Major Stanley will wait. He only accompanied me for the walk.'

It was here that Conway made a big mistake. He had of course no knowledge of the story that Fiske and Ilyana told to the authorities. So he had no reason to think that this was anything more than a routine check-up. He had foreseen of course that there would be such a check-up. But Fitzalan had been shrewd enough not to arouse his suspicion by a show of force, although motorized units had already surrounded the village.

'Oh, certainly,' he said, 'you'll find my wife through there in the drawing-room.'

When the Brigadier had gone the young Major said, 'You've got a very fine garden here, sir.'

Conway decided that it would be stupid of him to seem in any way concerned, and in any case Cathy could more than look after herself. She seemed to need his help just as much as before in a lot of small things, but on the big things she knew perfectly well what she was doing.

619

'Would you like to take a stroll around?' he asked.

The young Major said he would and they went outside into the late afternoon sunshine. They'd made two tours around the garden before they heard the shouting. Conway was astonished to see the young Major draw a pistol and begin moving towards the house at a trot. Conway thought fast now. Either Cathy had lost patience or this was more serious than it looked on the face of it. If they really were on to her then things were going to be very awkward, not only for Cathy and himself but for everybody in general. The Major's gun showed that they were going to shoot first and ask questions afterwards, so he shouted, 'The bastard's attacking her.'

This ambiguous, but in a sense correct, statement caused the Major to waver for a moment. In an instant Conway threw himself in front of the man in an American-style football block. The boy came down heavily and the pistol slipped away from him. Conway got to it first.

'Come on, baby boy, march!'

They found the Brigadier lying back in a deep chair. He was breathing in big shuddering gasps and his face was a rich purple.

'I loosened his collar. That's the right thing to do, isn't it?' said Cathy.

'Jesus,' muttered Conway, and that was all he could think of to say. It was clear it would be many a long day before the Brigadier would again step up in sprightly fashion to a professor's door at six o'clock on a fine autumn evening. It was very abundantly clear.

'You'd better get him out of here,' he said to the Major. 'I don't know how many men you've got, but please understand that there's just nothing you can do. The more you try the harder you'll get hurt.'

'Can I go down and fetch a vehicle?'

'No, get out.'

The Major left, supporting the Brigadier as best he could. The retreat from Moscow, thought Conway as he watched them stagger down the pathway to the road. Very quickly he threw the bare necessities of existence, a razor, toothbrushes, a few clothes, and what he could see of Cathy's things into a bag.

'Why are you doing that?' she asked.

'Because this is a serious business. Now that they know that you did it they'll hunt us down.'

'But I can fix them all as easily as I fixed the General.'

'Brigadier. Brigadier Fitzalan. You can fix them if they come to the door and walk politely in here and sit themselves down by your side. Then you can fix them all right. But how if they lob half a dozen mortar bombs on the house? What happens then?'

'You think they might do that?'

'If they couldn't get you any other way they'd do just that. The army would start shooting. Even if they couldn't see you they'd shoot at random, just on the chance of hitting you, even if it meant killing hundreds of innocent people. And if our army didn't do it every military force in the world would close in on these islands. It is the only way they can save themselves. The whole of this society is run on an idea. If you remain loose that idea collapses. They've simply got to get you.'

Cathy became more serious now. 'Then we shouldn't have let those two men go.'

'No, we should have killed them, but that's not the sort of thing I like to do. It's better to get out.'

They drove out on to the main road and made off to the village. They got a couple of hundred yards beyond the outskirts, turned a corner and saw the first roadblock. Conway backed up the car until he could turn it. Then he drove off down a lane in the opposite direction. There was of course another roadblock. The place was surrounded. He had been badly mistaken to let the Brigadier go. Then Conway saw that the fresh-faced Major was in charge and on an impulse drove up to the barrier.

'Look, this sort of thing isn't any good. You can't hope to

deal with what happened yesterday by playing toy soldiers. You're not in the right league.'

'What are you threatening us with, sir?'

'You saw perfectly well what happened to Fitzalan. There isn't any problem in dealing with the whole lot of you in the same sort of way.'

Conway wasn't quite sure if this was true or not but it seemed a fair presumption. The boy in front of him went pale and said, 'You won't get away with it, sir. We'll get you in the end.'

They opened up the barrier. Conway accelerated towards it, and was within about ten yards of the opening when a shot came from his left. He heard Cathy cry out and at the same instant realized that it was the young Major who had fired. Instinctively he braked the car to a standstill. As he heard his wife moan there was a deep rage in his heart. Something larger than himself seemed to be expanding his mind, and he knew now why he had stopped the car. He couldn't describe what he did, but it was like loosing a bolt. He saw the Major collapse. The man didn't even cry out as he fell. Conway never knew exactly how it had happened. The other guards scattered pell-mell, with all the devils of hell on their tails as far as Conway could see. He didn't know what he'd done but it was enough. He had the car moving again now. Soon they were clear of the village, and as the road opened before them a strange influence seemed to go out of him. Cathy's eyes were open, and she murmured, 'My shoulder hurts.'

He got the car on to the side roads and looked for somewhere to stop where he could examine Cathy's wounds. He carefully tore away her blouse and saw a dark patch on her right shoulder. 'It won't kill you,' he said.

But it was going to be painful and it had carried them a long way downhill. Cathy would have to have immediate treatment. It would be difficult to get this without their whereabouts becoming known to the authorities. And Cathy herself wouldn't be in the right sort of shape to deal very effectively with their pursuers. He cursed himself for being fool enough to be taken in by Fitzalan and by that young jackass.

'I'm going to get you into London to see a friend just as soon as I can. I daren't risk the main highway, so I'm going to take the side route as far as the outskirts and it may take quite a while. They may put up barriers and you'll have to get them to open up. Do you think you can hold on for a couple of hours?'

'I think I can.' Her voice was weak but it sounded firm. He drove out from behind the hedge and started on their journey.

He couldn't be certain that the main highway would be clear. If they threw a barrier across it the sheer volume of the traffic would be an unsurmountable block. But if they merely put something across the road in one of the country villages, then Cathy would still be able to deal with that without too much trouble.

He knew that in the brief moment when she had been hit something had passed between them. It had been prepared to leave just in case the shot had killed her. Conway himself would have been the new home. Whatever it was, it wasn't going to give up easily. He shivered and he couldn't help wondering what it would have been like if the thing had stayed with him. Would he still have known who he was? He supposed he probably would.

They got three-quarters of the way to London without any trouble; then they came to a makeshift barrier set up by a village policeman and two civilian helpers. They simply stood without noticing him as he moved the obstacle. They just weren't seeing either it or him. Probably they weren't even seeing the village High Street at all. They had satisfied smiles on their faces and their arms appeared to be clutching something which Conway took to be imaginary females.

Soon he began to come into the surburban traffic. They wouldn't have much chance of finding them now. The next big danger would be his medical friend. Friend was a word of wide connotation, and in this case he could hardly expect it to mean that the man he knew in Wimpole Street would not be suspicious and would not insist on some sort of investigation being made. But that was a risk that had to be taken when he came to it.

He went wrong in a one-way system and had to drive round twice before he found the right place. He had to double park so that Cathy wouldn't have to walk more than the distance from the road to the old-fashioned house that now faced him. Before getting her out he rang the bell. A uniformed maid, or nurse, he couldn't tell which, answered the door. He gave his name and asked to see Dr Gwyn Jones. The girl told him the doctor was out but would be back shortly. So there was nothing for it but for him to take the girl into his confidence.

'There's been an accident, a shooting accident,' he said in a nervous sort of way. 'My wife has been shot. I know it sounds ridiculous, it always sounds ridiculous. I never thought it would happen to me, but it did when I was cleaning my gun.' The girl looked alarmed and suspicious.

'Oh, it's not what you think. She's not very badly hurt. I wouldn't have shot her in the shoulder if I wanted . . .'

'Hadn't we better get her inside the house?' said the girl.

'Oh yes, could you please help me?'

They got Cathy out of the car and up the steps and along a passage and into the surgery. The girl, who evidently was a nurse after all, began to examine the wound. 'You should have taken her to hospital.'

'Well, I know Dr Jones pretty well, and I thought if he could see her straight away . . . you see I'd like her to be treated by somebody I know. She can go to hospital afterwards, can't she?'

'Yes, of course. But it would have been easier at the hospital. We don't have the same equipment here, you see. But I suppose since you're here you might as well wait.'

Jones came in not many minutes later. He took one look

at the wound and whistled slowly. 'Don't say you were cleaning a gun and shot her,' he said.

'That's exactly what I do say.'

'She should really be on the operating table.'

'Can't you fix her up here?'

'I'd sooner not.'

'Can't you do it as a favour?'

'I can. But I'll have to make a report, you know, and it will have to be full and accurate.'

'All right, but will you please hurry. It's hurting her all the time we're talking.'

Jones began to prepare to do the job. Conway realized that Cathy would have to be put out, otherwise the pain would be too much. And while she was out there was nothing that could be done if the authorities should arrive. He didn't like the thought of his car, displaying what must by now be a widely advertised number, double parked outside in a busy street.

'I'm going to leave it to you, Gwyn. My car's double parked outside,' he ended weakly.

Without bothering to see how Jones and the nurse took it he marched outside and jumped quickly into his car. By a mercy the police were not waiting for him. Probably they knew it was a doctor's house and made some allowance, and his number hadn't yet reached the constables on duty. He drove for a couple of miles, and left the car without troubling himself about correct parking. They could find it now if they wanted to. He took a taxi back to Jones's house. The manoeuvre had taken him twenty-five minutes, but he reckoned they wouldn't be finished with Cathy yet. He rang the bell and the door was answered again by the nurse. 'It isn't finished yet. You really should have taken her to hospital, you know.'

'I suppose I should, but I wanted it done by a doctor that I know. I'll ring them now and ask them to send an ambulance if you like.'

'That would be the best thing. Would you like me to do it?'

'No, I'll do it myself if I could use your phone.'

'Of course.'

'What should I tell them? I mean, what time should I ask them to come here?'

'I think Doctor will be finished in about twenty minutes' time. You could ask them to be here half an hour from now.'

She showed him to the phone and then went back to the surgery. He got the hospital, told them he was Dr Jones, said he had a serious accident case, and would they come in twenty minutes' time. Then he made another call. A woman's voice answered him, and after a brief conversation he began to think that maybe his luck had turned a bit.

The ambulance arrived before Jones had finished his operation. Conway told them to wait and that the patient would be ready in a moment. He didn't mind them being double parked, and they'd be able to make a quick getaway once the job was done. He didn't want Jones asking a lot of questions. A few minutes later Jones came out to him and said, 'I'd like to have a few words with you.' From this Conway knew that Cathy must be all right.

'I don't know whether the nurse has told you, but I've had second thoughts about the hospital. I've got an ambulance outside.'

'You ought to have done that before. There'll have to be an inquiry.'

He went to the door and nodded to the ambulance men. Within a moment they were carrying a stretcher into the house. Conway followed them into the surgery and saw Cathy being moved gently. She was still under the anaesthetic, her face was wan and drained. It made Conway mad with himself. Twice he'd made the mistake of under-estimating his opponents. The men carried her out of the surgery and he made to follow them.

'Just a moment, they can wait. I'd like you to see this.'

Gwyn was holding out the bullet to him. He took it and looked it over and said, 'What's so special about this?'

'It's a military calibre. I hope you understand, Hugh.

Just as soon as you've gone I'm going to make a report to the police. In my position I can't do otherwise.'

'I wouldn't ask you to do otherwise,' answered Conway. 'And my thanks, Gwyn, I can't tell you how much it means.' He looked Jones dead in the eye. He meant exactly what he said.

The ambulance men had got Cathy into position inside their machine and they had closed up the doors at the back of it. Conway got into the front beside the driver. The other man moved in on his left. They manoeuvred through the streets with the siren going. Conway wondered if he should try to make conversation but decided in favour of a dull silence. They swung into University College Hospital and drove to the Casualty Department. As soon as they came to a halt the driver and his mate jumped out on opposite sides and moved to the back, from which they intended to take the stretcher. Instantly Conway slipped over to the driver's seat; he pressed the ignition switch and the engine sprang to life, and a moment later he was on his way back to the main gate. There were angry shouts from behind but that was a matter of small consequence. He leant over and got hold of the left-hand door and slammed it shut. Soon he was speeding back through the streets. He resisted the impulse to switch on the siren. There was no point in gilding the lily.

His route took him into the City and across London Bridge. Soon he quitted the main road and began to explore the side streets. It took quite a while to find what he wanted. It was a small apartment made originally out of a disused warehouse. He rang the bell and the door was opened by the slim dark girl he had spent the night with the best part of two years ago.

'You're alone?'

'Yes, I put off my other arrangements.'

Conway spoke urgently. 'It's not quite what you think, I'm afraid. It's my wife, she's been shot – oh no, not by me. There are reasons why I don't want to be found, I want her

627

to lie up for a week or two. Can we stay here? I'll make it worth your while if you'll do it.'

The girl looked at him for some time and then suddenly nodded. 'You did a lot for me,' she said quite simply.

It wasn't easy to get Cathy up into the apartment. They had to climb a flight of stairs which luckily wasn't too steep. But it was as much as the dark girl could manage. At last they had Cathy off the stretcher on to the bed.

He went back to the ambulance and collected all the considerable medical supplies that were carried inside it. He'd need them to dress Cathy's shoulder. When he had taken them upstairs he said to the girl, 'She'll be waking up quite soon. Tell her that I'll be away for a little while, but that she's quite safe with you. I want to get rid of the ambulance so that they can't trace us. Besides, they'll have need of it.'

He drove back into the City. It was the last risk, but even if they got him now they wouldn't get Cathy. It would take some doing to trace her to Emling's flat. He supposed that it could be done but it would take quite some time. As he came up to it he decided on impulse to park outside the Bank of England. It seemed the right sort of thing to do.

He couldn't risk a taxi of course. So he walked back the way he had come. It took over an hour, but he was well satisfied as he mounted the old warehouse steps. The girl answered his ring. 'She's awake now, and she's been asking for you. She's very beautiful.'

As the days went by Cathy improved slowly. With the antibiotics he had got from the ambulance he was able to dress the wound. It seemed to him that the chances of their being traced were practically nil. He had no intention of going out on the streets himself, so there would be no chance of his being recognized and followed, and the dark girl enjoyed the unexpected domesticity.

He had half a fear that they'd blow the whole story in the papers and that the girl, when he sent her out, would see them and might get scared. That was the one danger. In fact she was bound to get scared once she knew that it was Cathy who had caused the vision. But they'd be taking big risks to publish the story and he couldn't really see them doing it. The whole population would fly into even worse hysterics than they were in now, if they knew that Cathy had done it and that she was on the loose amongst them.

In the event he was right. The girl came back with newspapers in which his picture and that of Cathy were prominently displayed, under enormous headlines announcing:

DISTINGUISHED PROFESSOR MISSING
UNDER MYSTERIOUS CIRCUMSTANCES

The story was written up as if to suggest that the mysterious circumstances were of a decidedly sexual nature. The girl grinned up at him, 'They certainly let themselves go! Wonder what they'd say if they knew you were here.' She winked at him.

Conway watched her for a moment as she moved around the apartment. Had it occurred to her that the papers would pay as much as she earned in a year to know the whereabouts of himself and Cathy? He had a feeling that even if it did occur to her she wouldn't do anything about it. She seemed to be looking on them as the same sort of outcast from society as she was herself. It wasn't like Gwyn Jones, nice fellow that he was. It was just that the pressures were different. He wondered how the girl had managed to stay on in the place for so long. After all, Emling must have been back in the meantime. He had a feeling that Emling probably found the situation to his advantage.

It had been a good idea of the papers to publish a scandal story about them. Nobody would disbelieve it, hardly even his friends, and it would keep people watching out for him. He reckoned that if Cathy's arm could be given two or three weeks rest they'd pretty well have made up most of the lost ground. In fact they might be a bit ahead of the field, for the authorities had declared their hand now. They'd lost the advantages of surprise. It was probably true what the young Major had said, that they would get them in the end, but they'd have to fight hard for it.

During the days that followed, as Cathy grew stronger, they had time to talk. Their discussions ranged far and wide as they explored the limits of each other's minds and understanding. The dark girl shopped, did the cooking, and nursed Cathy. She saw that Conway did his share and, as she grew to know him better, teased him about his increasing abstraction while doing them. There was no doubt that his mind was fully occupied; his talks with Cathy led him into new fields of thought. His mind raced and the new ideas were so big that the thoughts themselves seemed to be outside himself and towering high above him. He felt the indescribable thrill that comes from seeing just a little farther into the structure of the world than anybody has done before. It was a wholly new and vast territory which spread before him. It was like looking into an enormous underground cavern with the dimmest of cave-explorers' lamps, seeing no detail, only gaining an overwelming impression of size and space.

He began to understand the relationship between mind and matter and their expression in terms of mathematical physics. His brain so teemed with the new ideas that he had not time to start expressing them in equation form. It was sufficient for the moment to note the salient trends of his thoughts so that he could work on them later, that is if he had much future left for such things.

He was delighted when he realized that the nature of the animating force of life was an irregularity in a wave surface, like a flash of radiation. As it travels in respect of time, so our lives are propelled through the electrical circuits in our brain. And it is the firing of impulses in the brain that controls the chemistry of our bodies.

The wave surface over a short period of time would appear like a standing wave in the four dimensional structure of the body, totally contained by the body. But once outside the body the standing waves would dissipate themselves and become lost. In this way in death the irregularity of the wave surface would become diffused, but in the event of sudden death there was no reason why a radiation should not be emitted and interact with matter again. He began to see the answers to some of the things that had puzzled him.

He said to Cathy one day, 'When you were shot you came right across to me for a moment, didn't you?'

'Yes, it was very risky but I had to chance it.'

'Risky because you had to get the direction right and all that sort of thing?'

'Of course, luckily you were very close, I had to be very close to Fawsett.'

He pondered on this for a time and then said, quietly, 'It's an odd thing that we always feel it is better to die quickly. Now I see why. It makes no difference of course if there is nothing to pick you up, but, if there is, it is better to come out all in one piece as it were.'

'That is how we always do it. Nobody ever really dies because we always arrange it so that they are always picked up by some material structure. We have discovered how to hold these fields, rather like one of your blood banks.'

'A bank of life, of personality?'

'Yes, we can take the stuff out, we can develop it and we can put it back again just as we please. When your expedition was on our planet a mistake was made and a group of them managed to get into one of our banks of life.'

'What happened?'

'They destroyed it. We were angry and killed two of them.'

Conway had known nothing about the transparent sheets and the great central transparent box with its vibrant, shimmering flashes.

Cathy said, 'They didn't understand it so they simply destroyed it.'

Conway could believe this only too well. For the first

time he was glad that some reparation had been made on his own species, not so much by the two deaths but during the agony of the vision.

Another thought struck him. 'When you influence people you obviously have the ability to spread the local form of your wave surface. We can't do that, perhaps our wave field is too closely confined within ourselves. Your field can be made to interact with others. How can you affect so many people at once?'

'I can only do it to people close to me as I only generate a small field transmission myself. I have got to depend on the receivers amplifying what I send them and then transmitting it to somebody else. They can only transmit an amplification of my signal if they naturally possess an amplification of course – just as I can't make you see anything that isn't inside you or make you understand something that you could not work out for yourself.'

'I see, a strongly developed static pattern is already there. You can use this and it is retransmitted as a sort of chain reaction. Everybody was in the right condition for it because people had been sucking up propaganda throughout their lives. As the transmission spreads the strength increases because more people become transmitters.' He grinned, 'We used to think panic was spread by a creature with a set of reed pipes.'

The papers were full of news of governments. No mention had been made of Vladimir Kaluga in the Russian Press for some time. He was no doubt on his way to Outer Mongolia to supervise irrigation projects. The American Press was blazing furiously as the political parties fought openly for control. In Britain the Prime Minister spoke in moderate terms of standing firm, glorious tradition, and his trusted team. Plainly the hatchets were out. It was clear that governments were falling, but would there be any change? Could there be a basic change without genetic modification of the species? Would he and Cathy survive?

'You took a big risk coming here, didn't you?' he said.

'Yes, it was bigger than I expected.'

'How did you intend to get back to Achilles?'

'I could have left Fawsett at any moment until the rocket quitted my planet. After that, of course, it was far too dangerous. It was also a risk to leave Fawsett and come inside me.' She grinned.

'But you want to go back, it wouldn't be natural if you didn't.'

'I knew from Fawsett, right at the beginning, that a reserve rocket had been made. There is one, isn't there? It's up in orbit moving around the Earth now, isn't it?' She looked up at the sky as she spoke.

'Yes, there is one in orbit, they haven't decided what to do with it.'

She looked at him and said, gently, 'You don't like the thought of me taking your wife, do you?'

He looked down quickly. 'No,' he said simply.

'There is no other way, you know. Even if I took the risk of trying to leave in some other way your wife would be hunted down. Even if she was not she would still grow old and come to nothing at all. She will not be thrown away when I get home.'

'How can I be sure that she's willing to go?'

'Because if she were not the whole of this body would be very sick. You see she knows that we would value her animal qualities, perhaps we don't have enough of them ourselves. Here she is just a beautiful, silly woman who will soon be old and stupid and no longer beautiful. You must see how unhappy that would make her.'

Conway sat for a long time. There were tears in his eyes. He saw that this was the best way and he took Cathy's hand and said, 'You will look after her?'

It may have been absurd but that didn't occur to Conway. There were tears in Cathy's eyes and that didn't seem absurd either.

He tried to be practical. 'If you can get out to the ship it won't be so bad. There'll be fairly complete manuals about

633

the engineering and you'll be able to find your way through the gravitational fields better than we could. There's enough of a computer in the ship I'm sure. All the controls are really very simple. They're mostly servo systems so you don't really need to do anything much yourself. They always make it out to be more complicated than it is, space-men's mystique and all that sort of stuff.'

He looked at her again, they hadn't much longer together. Helios was already past its point of nearest approach and was receding.

'How do you think you'll reach the ship?'

'I had no particular plan. I thought I might force people to put me on it.'

'I don't think the authorities could make a deal; they've taken a hell of a beating. They'll stop at nothing to be able to display your hide.'

Cathy looked at her shoulder and winced.

'I think you're right. I can manage a few people near me, but the only thing I can do to a lot of people is the sort of thing I did the other day. I'm sure it wouldn't be as easy a second time. They discharged themselves well and truly and there hasn't been time to build it up again.'

'They'll do their best after you've gone,' said Conway. 'I think if we could get into parking orbit we could force the crew of the orbit transfer vehicle to take us to the ship. I could show you the controls and that would be it.' He turned away quickly and looked out of the window, unhappy and uncertain.

They started to make their plans. Cathy's arm was healing well and she could travel now. The dark girl hired a large car for them, big enough for Cathy to sleep in at a pinch and also to carry a fair stock of food. Conway had plans, he was feeling less uncertain. The following day they left the little apartment and the girl who had done so much for them so willingly.

'What did you think of her?' Conway said as they drove away.

634

'She was kind. Did you sleep with her while I was ill?'

'No. I did spend a night with her, if you must know, about two years ago. Dig around in your memory storage and you'll find you were having an affair with a man called Fawsett. It was while you were staying in London with him. I got drunk and had a fight in a pub, and she got me out of it, luckily.'

'Don't get confused, you know it wasn't me who was with Fawsett.'

Conway grinned as he drove along, the two Cathys were in agreement on that one. The first Cathy had got herself a marvellous alibi.

Beyond Regent's Park they hit the main motorway north. It was now just after 10 a.m., and he estimated that they would reach Scotland comfortably by lunch-time. The road curved away ahead of them into the distance. Now he could let out the engine and begin to eat up the miles. Only in the unlikely event of the car packing up would they run into trouble on this early part of the journey. Petrol he could always get at the automatic pumps, so there was no reason why anybody should see them. Without coming entirely into the open the authorities couldn't be making widespread checks throughout the country. The police were obviously alerted, and millions were on the look-out for him, but they couldn't be subjecting the whole population to a series of major stoppages on the road. And Cathy could easily deal with an odd patrol car or two.

As it turned out it took them longer to get their first fill of petrol that Conway had expected, so they ate their lunch at about half past one on the moors above Rothbury in Northumberland. By four o'clock they were in the Highlands, north of Callander. He hoped the midges wouldn't be too bad if he had to sleep out of doors.

Their destination was the small launching-field in eastern Sutherland, just to the north of Kinbrace. Launchings were few and far between, perhaps once every ten days, for a few passengers on international business when that business should happen to take them up to the orbital transit vehicles. It seemed much better to wait quietly and unseen until a rocket was primed and ready in this remote place, rather than risk the major troubles they'd be sure to run into at the big continental sites. The devil was that they'd have to wait. They might have to wait a week or more. It was probable that Cathy could force them into a launching, timed to their own convenience, but only at the expense of declaring their hand at an early stage in the game. There was no point at all in standing around waiting for the blow to fall while a rocket was being serviced. Best to let them get it all nicely ready and then just step in at the end. In that way they might get two or three hours' start.

Conway made no attempt to drive as far as the rocket base. He pulled off the road about thirty miles south. It was about three hours after dark, so they did not prepare any food, but were content with sandwiches and a hot drink which they had brought with them. Conway fixed Cathy up for the night. He set up a cot for himself outside and slept inside a sleeping-bag with a strong waterproof outer cover. He was glad of this during the night when the rain started. It lasted until about an hour after dawn, with the mist rolling over the hills ahead of them, and it seemed an inauspicious start to the whole business.

When Cathy was awake they set about moving to a better spot. They were able to drive down a short incline which took them just out of sight of the road. The plan was a very simple one. They would simply watch the road. This was safer than actually watching the launching base itself, and it was just as good for their purposes, for there would be plenty of added traffic going by in the hours before any launching should take place. An unruly stream brawled past them less than thirty yards away. After a bad start the weather became progressively more fine, and Cathy spent more and more of her time outside, happy in more natural surroundings. About twice a day other vehicles stopped quite close by. The first time a couple of men walked towards the stream Conway felt himself begin to tremble, but the men passed on, seeing nothing.

It was eight days before there was the beginning of the activity they were looking for. Conway watched the lorries pass by, wondering why they didn't keep all their supplies on the base. God, he thought, what a dump! Now he was watching the road through all the hours of daylight. Eventually they came, the cars bringing the rocket personnel. He could see at a glance that it was an American-sponsored take-off. He began to count in his mind which of the orbital transit vehicles the shuttle would go out to. Still, what did it matter, he didn't know where the real ship was at this particular moment. And he wouldn't be able to find out until they got themselves sky-borne. He went back to Cathy, 'It's time we were moving. It can't be long now.'

They waited until another lorry came past and pulled out behind it. There would of course be a barrier check-up, and on this occasion he wouldn't be equipped with the right papers, in fact he wouldn't be equipped at all. He'd have to leave that to Cathy.

What they did was very simple. They waited until the guards had finished with the lorry, and had waved it on, then they simply drove through the barrier in the wake of the vehicle ahead. It was as easy as that. They just weren't noticed. Conway kept his eye on the mirror. The one danger was that another lorry might come up behind and give them the most god-almighty crunch.

They parked. 'You realize what it means? If we can get away without pulling this place inside out they won't start sending military rockets after us for maybe a couple of hours after take-off. We'll need all that time if we're to find out where the ship is orbiting at the moment. And we'll need time to get transferred over to it.'

'How shall we go about it?'

'Well, the less fuss the better. They'd let us go up if we had a brief-case full of the right official passes. If only you could make them see a whole cartload full of passes, then we'd be fine. But I don't suppose you know what they look like.'

'It isn't necessary. All that is necessary is to unlock their own memories of what the passes look like.'

Conway picked out a good-sized bag that had once contained dehydrated lobster thermidor. That was the best he'd been able to do for Cathy. 'Now remember, when they see this they've got to see a brief-case. Got it?' Then he started to collect up all the bits of paper, the instructions, the manufacturers' own appraisal of their own products; one of them read YUM-YUM IT'S HALIBUT'S DEHYDRATED KIPPERS. That evidently came straight from the joke department.

'O.K., we're set,' he said.

Conway remembered being up there once before. He had a general idea of where the take-off squad would be housed. He got within a couple of hundred yards of it, then asked one of the ground staff, and was directed towards a waiting-room, from which a large noise in general was emerging. With Cathy on his arm he pushed open the door. The place was quite well furnished. It was equipped with a bar at which three junior officers were drinking. A space had been cleared for dancing, and a couple were treading slowly backwards and forwards across it. The man was also an officer, and his companion was a girl with very blonde hair indeed. At first he thought it was a Juke Box playing, but incredibly it was a hi-fi from which the treble had been completely tuned out. He ordered a couple of Scotches, and he and Cathy took them to a table as far away from the source of the noise as they could find. It had one big advantage, nobody could talk to them very easily. He noticed that the men at the bar were shouting at each other.

They drank four more Scotches in as many hours and then there was some incomprehensible mumbling on the speaker system. The men looked around at each other, and Conway heard one of them say, 'Well, this is it.'

It was more than two hours since the couple had quit the

room. Now the man returned without the girl. Apparently he had made his fond farewell. Conway was only too keenly aware that he and Cathy would be making their farewell very soon now. They followed behind the four men as they walked first across a compound, then through a series of sheds, and at last along a corridor to a moderate-sized room laid out like a lecture room. This was clearly where crews had their final briefing. The four now looked very curiously at them. Conway selected a couple of seats about four rows back from the front. 'Don't do anything yet,' he whispered. The men started chattering away to themselves, the conversation being more or less a cover for their curiosity.

'You in on this trip, sir?'

'That's right.'

'And the lady too?'

'That's right, it's getting popular now.'

Another of the men turned and nodded appreciatively at Cathy. 'You're a welcome recruit, lady.'

A few minutes later a major and a colonel came in. They halted peremptorily as soon as they saw Cathy. 'What does this mean?' asked the Colonel.

'It means we're on this trip, of course. It's a special assignment. Here are our papers.'

Conway had never in his life done anything more ridiculous, and in some ways more difficult, than he did now. Thinking that Cathy had better be awfully good, he took up the lobster thermidor bag. Like a salesman he handed the Colonel a fistful of leaflets – PORKY'S SAUSAGES SWELL TWENTY-FIVE TIMES THEIR STARTING SIZE. To his astonishment the Colonel turned not a hair. He examined each leaflet with the utmost care, then stamped them, adding three to a wad of papers that he was already carrying, a wad fastened together by a huge spring-clip. The rest he handed back to Conway, who quite solemnly returned them to the lobster thermidor bag. The Colonel and the Major murmured for a moment, and then the Colonel said, 'You really should have had a special pass for the lady, an Outer

Echelon Pass from the Special Activities Commandant.

Without a trace of a smile Conway replied, 'Oh, I thought I'd given you it.' He knew what had happened was that the man had simply forgotten to think about it until after he'd handed back the papers. He'd think about it now, Cathy would see to that. Conway dug back again into his bag and came up with a paper relating to HALIBUT'S DEHYDRATED KIPPERS. Feeling that he was going to burst, he handed it to the man, who looked it over very gravely, returned it, and said, very gravely, 'You sure go high, friend.'

Conway exploded and became very red in the face. It needed a good deal of patting on his back by the Major before he could recover his breath. When they had gone Cathy whispered, 'You're hopeless.'

The rocket took off shortly after dawn. Luckily it was a fairly low acceleration job, and although he didn't like the way he felt it wasn't too bad. He looked anxiously at Cathy's shoulder for he had been worried that the wound might open up again. If it had it wasn't bleeding seriously. This was Conway's first trip into space, and he vowed to himself that it would be his last. He thought about the lobster thermidor bag and didn't feel too good. It seemed to take an unconscionable time manoeuvring this way and that with the small jets before they were alongside one of the main transit vehicles. The clamps were put into operation. The seals were tested. And then a narrow window connecting their vehicle with the transit vehicle was opened up. Each of them scrambled in turn through it into the larger space of the bigger ship. As Cathy came through the gap the score or so of men who operated the transit ship stared at her in blank amazement.

The first stage was now complete. From here onwards their tactics would have to change. They would have to tell the Captain of the transit to pick up the big Achilles ship in his radar scanners, and to manoeuvre them alongside. They'd have to make no bones about it. It was one thing to make a man see a piece of paper that he was expecting to see, the Colonel had had memories of the correct passes stored away in his brain, and all that Cathy had done was to pull them out of storage for him, but the crew here had no special ideas about the Achilles ship, they would have to be ordered and the gloves would have to come off. But Cathy had reckoned on this and it was up to her. He'd used his wits to postpone the crisis as long as possible. Now the fat would be in the fire. And it wouldn't be long before they'd be sending up reconnaissance rockets, and armed rockets, to see what was going on. Sooner or later the Colonel was going to discover just what papers Conway had given to him, and the ad. for PORKY'S SAUSAGES wasn't going to please him.

Cathy wasted no time. 'You'd better tell them what to do,' she began.

He told them in quick measured terms what they had to do, and he told them to get on with it.

'Now what is this, a stick-up?' said the captain with a grin. The others began to laugh, but the laughs were frozen. It was a case of the man at the airport again. The captain's face went blank, then he was clawing at the main outlet hatch, trying desperately to burst the whole ship open. One of his crew stopped him at last with a blow under the jaw. Conway turned to a young lieutenant whom he took to be the second in command. 'It's your turn now. Don't think it can't happen to you because it can.'

Two of the men tried to close in on him, but before they reached him they seemed to trip and fall. When he looked down at them he saw they were unconscious. After that the lieutenant began to do what Conway demanded of him. There were tables showing the whereabouts of the Achilles ship. They were unfortunately not in the right orbit, and it would take a while before they could get across to the proper position for making contact. Conway spent several minutes at the radio receiver. There was an attempt to collar him from behind, but the men ended on the ground with their throats constricted, gasping for breath. It was only then that the half who were unharmed realized that the danger came from Cathy. This seemed to knock the heart out of them altogether, but Conway now knew the situation to be desperate for there was ample evidence from the radio that their escape had been discovered and that preparations were being made to send up a reconnaissance force. His only hope was that it might still take some time. He'd no doubt of what would happen if they were discovered, quite a small missile would be sufficient to burst their vehicle open and scatter them helter-skelter into space. It would be hard to imagine any place more vulnerable than the transit in which they were now entombed.

At last they made it. At last they were alongside and clamped. The seals were made and a way opened into the ship. It was efficiently done, and so it should have been, for this was precisely the job of a transit. Cathy went first and Conway followed. He got to the current control before the men in the transit could unhook themselves. As soon as the strong current began to flow in the sheath of the rocket the transit was held prisoner, a tiny barnacle on its flank. He was overwhelmed by the need to hurry. He saw there were manuals and that there was a tolerable computer. He began to make the settings, the settings that would take the ship inexorably away from the Earth. Cathy could reset them once she had calculated a preliminary orbit.

Now at last time was played out. This was the moment of parting, the moment that would take them apart for ever, from now on they would separate endlessly at five million miles a day. Cathy was looking at him with eyes that were dark and strained. 'I have much to thank you for. I would like to give you a few final moments with your wife.'

Conway knew what this would mean. For a few moments he would be back with the Cathy he had rowed with over the last eleven years, and suddenly he knew he couldn't take it. With tears in his eyes he shook his head violently and began to grope his way back to the hatch. At last he reached it and ducked down, preparing to open up the door and to squeeze outwards through the narrow opening. He looked back far down the ship to where Cathy was standing, still watching him. He stood for a moment and then with a muttered exclamation he began to move towards her again. He stopped for a few seconds to put his arm around her waist and to draw her to him, then he went over to the big control panel. Quickly he released the transit, and only then pressed the switches that started the big motors. A very faint trembling seemed to fill the ship, and at last he reached down and pressed the main control lever. In an instant he could feel the drive beginning, he could feel the pressure in his legs. The great rocket began to swing outwards from the Earth, it began the journey for which it had been made, the journey to the planet of the whispering grass.

BRINGING NEWS
FROM OUR WORLDS
TO YOURS . . .

Want your news daily?
The Gollancz blog has instant updates
on the hottest SF and Fantasy books.

Prefer your updates monthly?

Sign up for our
in-depth newsletter.

www.gollancz.co.uk

Follow us 🐦 @gollancz
Find us 📘 facebook.com/GollanczPublishing

Classic SF as you've never read it before.
Visit the SF Gateway to find out more!
www.sfgateway.com